The Brothers K

By the author of
The River Why

DAVID JAMES DUNCAN

The

Brothers

K

DOUBLEDAY

New York   London   Toronto   Sydney   Auckland

PUBLISHED BY DOUBLEDAY
a division of Bantam Doubleday Dell Publishing Group, Inc.
666 Fifth Avenue, New York, New York 10103

DOUBLEDAY and the portrayal of an anchor
with a dolphin are trademarks of Doubleday,
a division of Bantam Doubleday Dell
Publishing Group, Inc.

Excerpt from "Thrall" from *Mermaids in the Basement: Poems for Women*, copyright ©
Carolyn Kizer, 1984. Reprinted with permission of Copper Canyon Press, P.O. Box 271, Port
Townsend, WA 98368.

Excerpts from *Voices* by Antonio Porchia, translation and introduction by W. S. Merwin,
copyright © Antonio Porchia and W. S. Merwin, 1988. Reprinted with permission of Random
House, Inc., 201 East 50th Street, New York, NY 10022.

Lyrics from "The Gambler," words and music by Don Schlitz, copyright © 1977 Cross Keys
Publishing Co., Inc. All rights administered by Sony Music Publishing, 8 Music Square West,
Nashville, TN 37203. Used by permission.

Library of Congress Cataloging-in-Publication Data

Duncan, David James.
The brothers K / by David James Duncan.
    p.   cm.
I. Title.
PS3554.U4634B7   1992
813'.54—dc20   91-27058
CIP

ISBN 0-385-24003-1

ACKNOWLEDGMENTS

I wish to thank my wife, Adrian Arleo, my son, Thomas Faredoon, and my mother, Donna, for their faith and great patience throughout the writing of this book, and my daughter, Cecilia, for providing us a happy ending. For getting the show on the road I thank my ex-editor, Nick Bakalar, and my agent, Michael Snell. For the kind of indispensable, hands-on, up-to-her-elbows editorial advising and debating and tinkering and championing that I thought no longer existed, I thank Ms. Casey Fuetsch. For an excellent critical reading of the first half of the novel, I thank Dr. Kevin Oderman. For their equally encouraging inability to slow down and read the same pages critically, I thank Melissa Madenski, Tom Crawford, and Casey Bailey. For saving my sanity and possibly this manuscript during my run-in with floppy disks, I thank David Ousele. For that frigging disk-drive (which I now use as a chipper to clean up tree-trimmings in my yard), I thank Apple.

In 1990 I heard a comedian named Steve Smith speak, on television, virtually the same sentence that Papa speaks about God and money. I wish to acknowledge the coincidence. Less coincidentally, my sub-chapter, "Everett Routs the Ottoman Empire," was inspired by an urge to pit my own revolutionary against the most eloquent anti-revolutionary I've ever encountered—a man named Gürtzner-Gontard in Heimito von Doderer's novel *The Demons*. By the time I'd finished Americanizing Gontard's ideas and audience I'd altered his ideas so thoroughly that I'm not sure Herr Doderer would appreciate my acknowledgment, but I *am* indebted. For his excellent proofreading of the baseball details, I thank Steve Colton. For the same kind of proofing of the Indian linguistic details, thanks to Carl and Judith Ernst. For his portraits of prison work camps and draft resisters, thanks to Robert Wollheim. For their help with the Vietnam scenes, I thank Dick Morgan and Doug Haga. For centrifuging flickers, I thank the Boyden brothers. For help with the limericks, I thank Gale Ousele. For infecting me with their love for baseball, I thank my father, E. Dean Duncan, and my late brother, Nicklaus John.

CONTENTS

BOOK ONE

Joy to the Wordl!

CHAPTER ONE

Chevalier

Thank you! Thank you!
—last words of D. T. Suzuki

Camas, Washington / September / 1956

Papa is in his easy chair, reading the Sunday sports page. I am lying across his lap. Later he will rise to his feet and the lap will divide into parts—plaid shirt, brown leather belt, baggy tan trousers—but for now the lap is one thing: a ground, a region, an earth. My head rests on one wide, cushioned arm of the chair, my feet on the other. The rest of me rests on Papa. The newspaper blocks his face from view, but the vast pages vibrate in time to his pulse, and the ballplayer in the photo looks serious. I ask no questions. I stay quiet. I feel his slow, even breathing. I smell his smoke.

On the opposite chair arm, beside my argyle shins, is a small ashtray—an upholstered sandbag with five brass grooves arching over a green glass dish. Papa's cigarette smolders in the center groove. It has no filter. It's called a Lucky Strike. Past its slow blue smoke is the diningroom window. Past the window, yellowing maples and a low gray sky. Past the maples and under the sky, a neighbor man with a pitchfork, burning an immense pile of black limbs and old brown leaves.

Papa's hand appears. It hangs above the ashtray. It is blue-veined, black-haired, brown-skinned, scarred and powerful. It takes up the cigarette and disappears behind the paper. The neighbor man throws an enormous forkful of leaves onto the burn pile, smothering the flames. Papa takes a deep breath. The hand returns the cigarette to the same brass groove, a quarter-inch orange coal on the end of it now, the smoke rising up much faster than before. A dense cloud of white billows up through the smoldering leaves. Papa breathes out. The leaves ignite. Even through the window I hear them bursting into flame. Papa turns a page, the paper makes the same crackling, burning sound, and I glimpse his eyes before the paper reopens: they are serious, like the ballplayer's.

Idly Papa's long fingers twist the ashtray in a circle. Slowly the man with the pitchfork circles his burning brush. The hand picks up the cigarette. The man forks more leaves onto the fire. The hand returns the cigarette, folds it against the green glass, crushes the hot coal with the tip of a bare finger. The man stares for a moment into the fire, then sticks his fork in the ground and walks away.

The newspaper shudders, closes, then drops, and there is his face: the sun-browned skin and high cheekbones; the slightly hooked, almost Bedouin nose; the strong jaw still shiny from a late-morning shave, a few missed whiskers at the base of each nostril; the gray eyes—clear, kind, already crowfooted, and always just a little sad around the edges.

There he is. Papa. There is my father.

The screen door slams. I lurch, open my eyes—newspaper falls from my body. I am lying alone in my father's chair. He has vanished right out from under me, leaving a blanket of sports page when he left. I look outside: the sky is still low and gray, yellow leaves still waving, but the burn pile is ashes and the man and pitchfork are gone. I look at the chair arm: the ashtray is still there, but the green glass is clean, the ashes and Lucky butt gone.

I can tell by the heaviness of step that it's my brother Irwin back in the kitchen. When I hear the icebox open, I know that neither Mama nor Papa is in the house. I hear him gulping milk straight out of the bottle. *Germs . . .* I hear the careful folding and refolding of wax paper round a plate of leftovers. *Thou shalt not steal . . .* I hear a shout somewhere outside, and Irwin darts into the diningroom, his mouth stuffed full of something, his eyes bulging, then, seeing no one, relieved.

"Where's Papa?" I ask.

He jumps, bolts the food, chokes a little, laughs. "Where are *you?*"

I sit up in the chair.

He laughs again, starts back toward the kitchen, then calls back to me, "Battle Ground. Playin' ball."

The screen door slams.

I am alone on the floor of mine and Irwin's room now, picturing Battle Ground. I've been there, Mama says. It's got the big park with the pool where I waded with my boats when it was too hot to be in the bleachers, she says. I can't remember the bleachers, I can't remember the ballfield, but I remember the pool. And now I think I remember the tall men with caps and gloves running over the grass, splashing in and out of the water, throwing and hitting baseballs and singing *Aaaaaa! Aaaaaa!* and *Hum Babe!* and *Hey, Batter!* My oldest brother, Everett, showed me how they sing. He said that *Hum Babes* are special, because Papa is the pitcher and it's his pitches that hum. I said, They call Papa a *babe?* No, Everett said, they just sing *Hum Babe* to the pitches, but some players call him Smoke because of his Lucky Strikes and fastball, and some call him Hook because of his curveballs and nose. I said I thought they were just plain baseballs. He said they were, but that curveballs and fastballs are kinds of pitches, and pitches are special throws nobody but the pitcher knows how to make, and Papa has seven different kinds, not counting his different deliveries. He didn't say what a delivery was, but he said Papa had a kind that went *ffffffffwirp!* called a sinker, and a kind that went *ffffffffweet!* called a slider and a kind that went *ffffffffwow!* called a forkball and a kind that went *bleeeeeeeeeurp!* called a change-up and a secret kind too, called a knuckler, which he only used when he was red-hot since it might go *rrow!rrow!rrow!* or might do nothing at all, and I felt almost like crying by then, I was so confused and wanted so much not to be. Everett noticed, and shoved me in a gruff, friendly sort of way. Don't worry, he said. Next summer I'd be old enough to go watch him pitch, and soon as I watched him I'd understand everything fine . . .

But I don't want to understand next summer. I want to understand *now.* So I have the sports page here beside me on the floor, open to the ballplayer with the serious face. And this is not an orange crayon in my mouth. It's a Lucky Strike. *"Ffffffffweeet!"* I tell it. This isn't the lid of a mayonnaise jar in my hand, either. It's an ashtray. *"Bleeeeeeeeeurp!"* And

Bobby, my bear, is the neighbor man and this salad fork is his pitchfork and these piled blankets are the pile of burning brush. Because I am not me. I am Smoke! I am my father! and the harder I suck the Lucky the hotter burns the brush! *Aaaaaaaaaaa!* the fire hums, babe, the flames *ffffffffwirp* and *ffffffffwow!* And when I spin my ashtray the neighbor man is helpless: I spin, spin, spin it, he whirls round and round and round. Then I throw, I forkball, I pitchfork my Lucky clear up to the sky and *rrow!rrow!rrow!* flaming leaves and limbs and papers knuckle every which way and the trees and batters and people and houses burn! burn! burn!

I saw.

I saw what Papa was doing.

And next year I'll go with my brother to watch *all* the ballplayers splash and throw and sing.

Camas / February / 1957

My parents are sitting on the old purple sofa. Mama is peeling oranges on a dish towel spread across her lap, but she's so hugely pregnant that the peels are collecting clear out between her knees. Papa says that she grew Everett, Peter, Irwin and me inside her one by one, but that she's gotten so good at it she's decided to grow two at once this time, to save money, time and trouble. "Now wait just a minute!" Mama always says to this. "Who's the greedy farmer that planted two seeds at once?" Then they laugh. I don't get it. They say this and laugh every time anybody stops by these days. If they don't say it the people look sort of sick, Mama's stomach is so big, so sometimes they even say it to the same person twice. I still don't get it. Anyhow she's huge, and the new two inside her are called The Twins, and once they're born I won't be the youngest anymore, and they might be sisters, which might be fun, and Mama will supposedly shrink back to her same old size and act more her same old way. So I guess it's a good thing.

It's Peter's turn for Papa's chair, and he's lolling in it like a cat on the hood of a warm car, trying to make Everett and Irwin jealous. They don't even notice. They're belly-down on the floor with their chins in their hands, watching some baby ducks on TV waddle through a dish of Purina Puppy Chow. "What does *that* prove?" Everett asks the TV.

"Yeah," says Irwin. "What does that prove?"

"Ducks'll eat *slugs*," Everett says. "That don't prove a thing about Purina."

"Yeah," says Irwin. "That don't prove a *thing*."

Everett turns to Irwin and glares. Peter watches them and laughs. Irwin's bigger than Everett, but two years younger, and whatever Everett says or does lately, Irwin says and does the same. Peter thinks it's funny. Everett thinks it's idiotic. Irwin doesn't care if it's funny or idiotic, he just keeps doing it.

The ducks waddle off. Ed Sullivan waddles on.

"Ed Cellophane," says Everett for the thousandth time this year.

For the thousandth time this year, Irwin laughs.

Ed Sullivan introduces Perry Como. Everybody on TV claps.

Perry Como climbs up on a stool, smiles sort of wistfully, and sings a song about catching shooting stars, sticking them in buckets, then pulling them out again in dreary weather to cheer yourself up with. "I'm *sure*," Everett snorts.

"We're *sure*," says Irwin.

Perry Como snaps his fingers to the beat. *"Never let it fade away,"* he sings, *"never let it fade away . . ."*

Then his voice fades away.

Everybody claps. Ed Sullivan comes out, clapping too. Perry Como chuckles and says something into Ed's ear, and Everett chuckles and says, "You sure are ugly!" into Irwin's ear at the same instant. Then Ed Sullivan pooches his lips out and Perry Como saunters away, so that it really does seem like what Everett said is what Ed Sullivan heard. Irwin laughs.

Ed Sullivan talks for a while now, nodding his head as if to show how much he agrees with everything he's saying. Then he holds out one hand and asks if we won't please give a very warm welcome to a big Russian word I can't pronounce. The audience applauds. The curtains open. And suddenly the stage is dark and shadowy, no one in sight, and a hidden choir of men with deep Russian voices begins doing some kind of chant with crazy little owl-hoots mixed in where you least expect them. Then, out of the darkness, a V-shaped wedge of shrouded humans comes sailing like geese into a pond, doing something impossible so effortlessly that we watch for some time before Mama whispers, "Lord! Will you *look* at that!"

There must be twenty-five or thirty of them, all in black hooded robes that reach to the floor and hide their feet, faces and shapes completely. And what's impossible is that they're gliding as quietly and smoothly as skaters on ice—and there *is* no ice. Heads bowed, bodies hidden, the

Russians slide through the shadows and over the floor as if they weigh nothing or there's no one in the robes, the spiraling lines and leaning rows of them passing each other so closely you'd think they'd crash, yet they never touch, and the thick dark cloth doesn't even quiver.

"They're so *ghostly!*" Mama shivers.

"They don't have any feet!" Irwin yells.

"They have feet all right," Papa says, "but they're taking such smooth, tiny steps in under those robes it almost looks like they're flyin'."

"But they *really* don't have any hands!" yells Irwin.

"They have hands all right," says Papa, "but they've got 'em stuck up their opposite sleeves. I wouldn't be surprised, though, if they yanked 'em out and flashed 'em at us any second now."

"Isn't that just like a Russian," Mama says, "hiding his hands up the wrong sleeves?"

Papa laughs at this—so Irwin laughs too, though I doubt he has any idea whether it's just like a Russian or not. But Papa's right about their hands: when the stage suddenly fills with light the monkish chanting flares into loud, full-throated singing, away fly the robes, out dart the hands, up pop the heads, and there they are: the Russians! And now they're wearing black boots and pants, puffy white shirts, and fur hats the same size and shape as their beards as they laugh and fly and flip over and under each other, and Everett's and Irwin's mouths are hanging open, and Mama and Pete are bug-eyed with wonder, and even Papa makes a stunned little bark when they huddle like football players then somehow send one dancer flying most of the way up to the ceiling, doing four or five flips before he sails back down. We're all so sorry when the dancing ends and Ed Sullivan shambles back out that this time it's Mama, of all people, who says, "You know what? He *is* ugly."

A commercial comes on, showing a cross section of the inside of a woman's head complete with the hammer, carpenter's saw and lightning bolts that are giving her such a terrible headache. "Those," Papa says, "were some pretty fair country dancers."

"Poor lady!" Irwin gasps, gaping at the woman's head.

"They sure were," Everett says to Papa.

Then the woman swallows an Anacin, the hammer, saw and lightning bolts vanish, and her face reappears, grinning with relief.

"Great stuff!" Irwin says, marveling at the Anacin.

"Why are we supposed to hate Russia?" Peter asks.

Nobody answers him. Maybe nobody knows. Peter scowls at the si-

lence, then answers himself in a way—by sliding his hands up the opposite sleeves of his sweatshirt.

Hearing Mama stir, I turn just in time to see her set her dish towel full
of orange peels in Papa's lap. He snorts and says thanks-a-lot as if he
means the opposite. But she says, "Open it," so he does. And instead of
the mess we expected there are two peeled oranges inside, divided neatly
into sections. He says thanks again, this time as if he means it. But this
time he doesn't sound so good—and suddenly he and Mama and all the
rest of us are staring at the brace and bandage on his left hand, realizing
why she peeled the oranges for him, living all over again the night last
month when the graveyard-shift foreman called, long past midnight,
from the Crown Zellerbach mill . . .

He said Papa had been hurt by the rollers at the mill, named a hospital,
and Mama was so stunned that she hung up before he could say another
word. Her shouts woke us and brought us running to the kitchen, but
before we had time to think she curdled our brains with a scream—
because a man, Papa's friend Roy, was standing in the dark outside the
window. When we recognized him and let him in, Roy sat down and told
us what happened—told how Papa had rested his hand, for an instant, on
a pair of big metal paper-rollers, how someone somewhere had picked
that same instant to flip a switch, how in the next instant his left thumb
had spun into the rollers and come out again, flat as newspaper, how the
mill sounds like stormsurf when it's running full-bore, yet at his lathe
three hundred feet away Roy had heard Papa's scream. "Let me drive
you," he said, when a full minute passed and none of us had moved or
spoken, because none of us could begin to imagine Papa screaming, no
matter what. Then came the rush to the hospital, the interminable wait,
and finally the coldness of the surgeon as he called us into his office,
angry at himself, angry at us, angriest at the thumb maybe, for being so
utterly crushed and ruined that instead of playing the hero in a Miracle
of Modern Science he was stuck in a room with four miserable boys and a
prodigiously pregnant woman, listening to himself snap that "the man,
er, worker, your father— No, son! What's your name? . . . Well dammit, Everett, shuttup and listen! I'm trying to tell you *no*. Not with that
thumb. Your father will never pitch, or play any kind of baseball,
again . . ."

Yet as we watch him now, our own faces falling, Papa is somehow able to
maintain his poker face. And then his off hand, the good one, starts

flickering faster than my eye can follow and orange slices go flying like Russian dancers. Everett, Irwin and Peter all catch their slices, and Pete has to whip his hands out of his sleeves to do it; my slice bounces right off my open mouth, but Papa's everywhere hand somehow darts out, catches it, stuffs it back in; Mama just cringes, hunches, and hides behind her hands, yet when Papa's hand is through flickering there are three slices in her lap, one for her and two for the twins. So just like that we're all chewing and laughing instead of staring at braces and bandages. And just about the time we've all swallowed and begun wondering just how much consolation a few orange slices can be, Papa, still poker-faced, sends seven more of them flying through the air.

Now a white-haired man in a suit like a minister's comes on Ed Sullivan and the crowd claps hysterically though he hasn't yet done a thing. "I just *love* Maurice Chevalier!" Mama sighs.

"Me too!" Irwin cries.

"I can't *stand* him," Everett mutters.

Mama glances at Everett, and scowls. Papa eyes him too, but I notice he's smiling out the side of his face that Mama can't see. I turn to Chevalier and try to decide for myself. He is nothing like a minister, despite the suit. He's dancing a little now, and singing with a foreign accent, and sometimes in a completely foreign language. Mama says it's French, and adds, "Isn't it pretty?"

"Nope," Everett grunts.

But again I try to decide for myself. It hadn't occurred to me that a language could be pretty, but I guess this one kind of is. It's got lots of "zwahs" and "lays" and "ooohs" in it, like baby talk, which can be soothing. Chevalier's singing isn't much, though. And his dancing is a joke— especially compared to the men in the robes. Chevalier moves very slowly, smiling ceaselessly and a little foolishly, as if to remind us that he's really too old for this sort of thing. And I don't mind him being slow or old or even foolish, but as the song drags on it hardly seems fair that he gets so much stage time when the robe dancers got so little. When the song finally peters out, though, the audience goes so bananas you'd think Chevalier just homered in the ninth. We must prefer Frenchmen to Russians no matter what. They cheer and cheer, he waves and waves, then the noise finally dies enough for him to cry, *"Thank you! Thank you!,"* and the whole crowd jumps up on its hind legs and starts cheering all over again.

"At least he's finished," Everett mutters.

Then Ed Sullivan walks out and hands Chevalier a white straw hat and a cane.

"Oh *good!*" Mama and Irwin gush.

"Oh *no!*" Everett groans, flopping face-down on the floor.

Papa laughs quietly. Peter does too, but with his eyes closed and his hands up his sleeves: I think he's asleep.

Chevalier puts on the hat and starts another song. Holding the cane in both hands, he begins swaying from side to side, just like we have to do at Sabbath School when Mrs. Babcock leads us in Jesus Wants Me for a Sunbeam.

"Phony old frog," Everett grumbles.

But when Chevalier reaches the chorus and the audience starts to sing along, I see his smile freeze to his face exactly the way mine does when I have to sprout my fingers out round my head, making them into Jesus' sunbeams. And seeing this—seeing him trapped in a skit that makes him look so old and sad and tired even as it forces him to cock his hat at a jaunty angle and talk and dance with his stupid cane—I realize that, phony or not, I've begun to like him.

Mama's trying to hum a harmony now, but like her hymning at church it's pretty off-key. Peter's sound asleep, his eyelids dancing, his hands still hidden up his Russian sleeves. Irwin is swaying from side to side in time to the music, bumping Everett's shoulder with every sway. Everett's lip is curled—but one of his feet has accidentally begun to keep time to Irwin's bumping. And the song is so long and Chevalier looks so sad that I find myself wanting to help him somehow. So I start swaying too. He comes round once again to the chorus. In a rusty echo, deep down below him, Papa starts to sing along.

Attic Document,
circa February 1958

A letter, from one Gale Q. Durham, manager of the Kincaid, Oklahoma, Cornshuckers (a Double A farm club of the Washington Senators farm system), to the eleven-year-old Everett Chance:

Dear Everett,

Sorry I didn't write quicker. Just got back from watching a 20 yr. old shortstop our trusty scouts called a Sure Thing kick ground balls all over Venezuela. Funny thing about our scouts: they <u>are</u> trusty. They <u>always</u> send me off to a team with a real ballplayer on it. They just make my job interesting by telling me the wrong guy. The right guy this time was a 34 yr. old 5'8" 154 lb. black-skinned-Mickey-Mantle-with-good-knees-&-brains I found playing center field right there on young Bigfoot's team. You watch them 2-A box scores & weather reports this summer, son, & if one Aurelio Lorenzo isn't hitting .300 for us by the time Tulsa's in the 90s I'll eat my fungo. Always was partial to the name Aurelio. Only word I know with all 5 consonants. But I'm beating round the bush as usual, aren't I.

Getting down to this damned thumb business, I'm proud you'd think of me at a time like this, and sorry your daddy's hurting. You, me & your papa are 3 of the tiny percentage of souls on this miserable earth who've figured out that playing ball is the highest purpose God ever invented the human male body for. The rub is, once you've known & done it what you go through when you lose it is a death, pure & simple. I've seen it 1000 times & died the death myself, & about all them 1001 deaths have taught me is <u>Dammit</u>! <u>Dying hurts</u>! If I was there to crack a beer with your daddy (or 6 or 12, let's be honest here) I'd probably wait till he was all lubed up then say, "Listen. Let it hurt when it hurts, damn it Hubert!" You know what I mean. The Papa Chance I remember tended to get a tad heroic at times. Not that I don't admire a hero. But watching some poor bounder limp around with a smile nailed to his face while his insides bleed from one end clear out the other is a thing I can't much stand. To that mother of yours I might add something like Dangit, Laura, I know you're baptized in the name of the This and the That, but when you got the kind of man who holds everything in you got to let it bust <u>out</u> once in awhile. Then of course I'd run like hell. Don't get me wrong here. I hold nothing but the highest kind of respect against your mother. I just happen to be a man who believes if God wanted us to always keep our upper lip stiff as a dang billy goat's weener He'd of made us all a bunch of Englishmen for godsake.

That's about it for the Summer Lecture Series. The main thing is the enclosed: 40 bucks towards some sort of present. And whatever he gets, make damn sure your pop spends my money on <u>himself</u>. I'm gonna be steamed if I hear he used it to pay the goddamned dentist bill for one of you brats. You tell him it's happened to all of us, the best & the worst. Tell him I hope ol' Smoke & The Hook both rest in peace. Tell him I'll never forget either one.

Yrs. as ever,

G. Q. Durham

CHAPTER TWO

Moose, Indian

Moose . . . Indian . . .
—last words of Henry David Thoreau

Camas / July / 1960

Mama is a Seventh Day Adventist. She doesn't make Papa go to church because she can't figure out how to, and she doesn't make Irwin go because he loves church and would go no matter what. But Everett, Peter, the twins and me she makes go every Sabbath unless we're sick. And today is Sabbath. And I'm not sick. And the sun is already so hot outside that everything's all bleached and wobbly-looking, as if the whole world was just an overexposed home movie God was showing Jesus up on Their livingroom wall. And whenever it's really hot Elder Babcock's sermon—even if it starts out being about some nice quiet thing like the poor or meek or weak—will sooner or later twist like a snake with its head run over to the unquiet subject of heaven and hell, and who all is going to which, and how long you'll have to stay, and what all will happen to

you when you get there, and he goes on so loud and long and the air gets
so used up and awful that bit by bit you lose track of any difference
between his heaven and his hell and would gladly pick either over church.
Then the sermon ends, and the long prayer after it, and it comes time to
belt out the big hosannah that means it's almost time to go home. Except that last hymn always has about fourteen verses. And when you
stand up to sing it you discover your blood has got stuck down in your
feet. And all through the sermon every grownup in the place has had
their mouth clamped shut trying not to yawn, so when the glad voices get
suddenly upraised this tidal wave of pent-up halitosis comes swashing out
of them and up your nose and all through the parts of your head where
the blood that's in your feet should have been, till your brain feels like it's
going to barf. That's when one of us (usually Peter) usually faints dead
away . . .

All of which is why I think this might be the luckiest day of my life, so
far. Because right this minute Elder Babcock is unloosing the twisted
snakes and the congregation is readying up the tidal wave, but Papa, as
usual, is just sitting home smoking Luckies—and for once it's Papa's
smokes I smell! Better yet, Mama doesn't let anybody watch TV on the
Sabbath, but Mama's not here and Papa hasn't got a Sabbath, so there's
the ballgame blaring, there's Pee Wee Reese and Dizzy Dean doing the
play-by-play, and it's Cleveland 3, Yankees 1 in the eighth! And better
still, the minute this game is over we're going to hop in the Fortyford and
head out for a river called the Wind, which I've dreamed about but never
seen, and go steelhead fishing, which I've heard about but never done.
Yes, it'll be hot out, Papa says, but we'll wet-wade it, so we'll stay cool.
Yep, our heads'll bake a bit and our legs'll freeze some, but our rest-of-
us'll be just right so don't worry. Pipe down now, he says. Jumping up and
down on the back of his chair is not piping down, he says. Quit fretting,
he says. Fishing is like watching baseball, he says, in that it takes such
total concentration that you shouldn't even be noticing little details like
your arms and legs and head and mind and the miles-long strings of
questions inside it. "How come?" I ask. And he laughs, for some reason.

"Watch the game," he says.

There's Dizzy and Pee Wee up in the booth, both wearing headphones,
white shirts and neckties pulled loose at the knot. Dizzy's humming
Home on the Range. Pee Wee's making a face, due to the humming. Yogi
Berra's at bat, all bow-legged from too much catching.

"Hey, Papa. I don't see how I can catch fish at all if I'm not even
noticing my arms and hands and brains, because—"

He grabs my wrist. He doesn't let go. "Kincaid," he says. "Questions don't make you a fisherman. *Concentration* makes you a fisherman. So practice. Practice fishing *now*—by concentrating on this *ballgame*."

Okay. The ballgame:

There's Casey Stengel on the dugout steps. There's Bobby Richardson taking a big lead off first. Richardson just singled with one out, and Pee Wee thinks he might try to steal, but Dizzy says it's doubtful. Diz says the Yankees don't steal much, because the rich don't need to. There's Stengel again. He's sticking his middle finger then his little finger in his right ear, then sniffing the wax on each finger—and the Indians are all watching him, trying to figure out whether earwax-sniffing is the sign for Berra and Richardson to work the hit-and-run, and if so, which finger, and on which pitch? There's Mickey Mantle on deck. There's Mudcat Grant sweating blood on the mound. And there's Kuenn, Francona and Piersall in right, left and center, who Dizzy called "the second-best out-field in all of downtown Cleveland today," which made Papa laugh for some reason.

Berra bunts—a little short one—and the Indian catcher easily throws him out. But Bobby Richardson's safe at second, and here comes Mantle. Pee Wee Reese is getting agitated. Dizzy's singing, *"Home run on the range, Where the ball flies so far that it's strange . . ."* The Mick's hitting .301, and has nineteen round-trippers already this season. Papa's sitting quiet, thinking how Mudcat Grant should pitch him. And it's true, what he said: I feel like a better fisherman already!

Richardson takes a healthy lead. Mantle digs in. Mudcat tries to stare him down, but Mantle stares right back. Stengel watches them both, his middle finger *still* sticking in his ear. I once heard Everett tell Irwin that that finger means fuck you, but I don't believe it. They'd never show Casey Stengel doing a thing like that to his own ear, right on TV.

When I consider the odds against me watching baseball on Sabbath (100 to 1?), going fishing on Sabbath (1,000 to 1?), and doing both alone with Papa because Everett, Peter, Irwin, Mama and the twins have all vanished at just the right moment to make it all possible (1,000,000 to 1?), I feel as if my life has left the world of odds-making and entered the world of Miracles. Everett thinks Miracles only happen in the Bible and that Science explains them even there. But Peter disagrees. Pete claims that Miracles happen all the time, but in such sneaky or complicated or underhanded ways that most people are too thick or busy to notice them. And the more I think about it, the more I believe me sitting here watching baseball on Sabbath has got to be one of those complicated, underhanded Miracles.

If it *is*, it all started last week at a Babe Ruth game, when Everett tried to steal home on a suicide squeeze. What happened was that the batter whiffed the bunt, the catcher caught the ball, Everett tried to give the catcher a diving forearm shiver to knock the ball loose, the catcher sidestepped, tagged him out on the skull, Everett landed forearm-first on the plate, and it was his arm that shivered. Of course there's nothing Miraculous about a busted arm. But when his team lost the game by a run and fell out of contention for the play-offs, Everett got so glum and crabby that Mama gave him permission to go to the Seventh Day Adventist Summer Camp down at Wolverton Lake in Oregon, then said if they wanted to keep him company, Peter and Irwin could go too. This was the first big hint of Miraculousness: Mama letting all three of them go even though it's raspberry season and berry-picking is the way we earn our school clothes money. I think she was hoping to prove that a place could be fun even if it had to do with Adventists. And I think she's wrong. But anyhow they left, which cleared the way for the part of the Miracle that came next.

What came next—just yesterday at breakfast—was such a nasty fight between Mama and Papa over money, then religion, then a beer a neighbor man gave Papa the night before which he drank out in the yard where I could be tempted by it, that Mama loaded Bet and Freddy (that's the twins, Beatrice and Winifred) into the Dodge and took off for Uncle Marv and Aunt Mary Jane's up in Spokane.

While she was cramming stuff in the car, Mama told Papa that she might be back when the boys came home from camp, or she might just send for them and give them a decent Christian upbringing someplace else. Papa told her she must mean a Tea Totaler upbringing. Mama shouted, "I mean *Christian!*"

Papa said, "Jesus made wine and shared it with people. What was He, a Hopi Indian?"

Mama snapped, "Jesus was Jesus, Hugh Chance. *You* won't even go to church with your own *children!*"

"Neither would Jesus," Papa said.

"He never *had* children!" Mama yelled. Then Papa smiled his nicest smile, and she saw he was pulling her leg and broke out in a grin, and I thought the fight was over. But then—I don't know how or why she did it —Mama just *amputated* her grin, and looked at Papa like she hated him. And his smile fell from his face like ice cream off a little kid's cone. It made me sick. I wanted to pick his smile up, clean it off, and hand it back somehow. But it was too late: he was mad as she was, now. Real quietly, he said, "He never liked churches, though."

"Who?"

"Jesus."

"How do you figure *that?*"

Papa pulled out his Luckies, letting her wait for his answer, and I noticed his eyes had gotten slitty and sleepy-looking, which is how they used to get on the mound, Everett says, when he really bore down on a hitter. I didn't like it. I didn't like him bearing down on Mama. He threw a curve first: knowing she's never smoked and never will, he offered her a cigarette. She ignored it. "How do you figure?" she repeated.

Papa stuck the Lucky in his mouth, lit it, and sent smoke streaming like a brush-off pitch, just past the side of her face. "As a kid, all He did at church was argue with the rabbis," he said. "And as a grown man He went to church twice, if I remember right. Once to kick out the salesmen and ticket-scalpers, and once to cure that poor bastard with rabies."

"Well you *don't* remember right!" Mama shouted. "Christ founded a *new* church! You'd know that if you ever opened a Bible! And that new church—"

"And that *new* church," Papa cut in, his face suddenly savage, "is two thousand years old now, and every bit as senile and mean-spirited as the one that killed Him!"

"How *dare* you!" Mama hissed. "How dare you say such a thing in front of these children!"

"How dare *you* throw a fit in the name of *God* over one damned beer!"

"I've seen the hell one beer can lead to!" Mama cried.

"And *I've* seen the hell your friendly preacher calls salvation!" Papa roared. " 'Come unto me all ye Tea Totalin' prudes, bores and Bible-thumpers, bring your wallets and purses, and if your husband watches baseball or sips a beer with a neighbor on *my* Sabbath pay day then damn him to hell and whip his kids off to Spokane!' "

"*Satan!*" Mama gasped, grabbing my arm and nearly throwing me into the car. But while she circled round and got in herself, I jumped back out and slammed the door. "Get *back* here!" she shrieked. But I wouldn't. And her voice was so terrible that Bet and Freddy started crying, which made her so mad that she just tore out the driveway without even asking Papa if it was all right if I stayed.

He told me it was okay, though. He said not to worry, Mama would be back. He said they were just two knuckleheads blowing off steam, and he was sorry I'd had to listen. I told him I sort of liked listening, but he said no, it wasn't right. He said they wouldn't be fighting at all if he hadn't crushed his damned thumb two winters ago. I asked how he could know that. "Simple," he answered. "I wouldn't be here. I'd be on the road somewhere, playing ball."

As always, the thought of baseball turned him silent, and sent him groping for another Lucky. He fired it up and sighed out smoke, saying, "Oh well. You and I were due for some time alone together." I told him we'd never in our lives had time alone together—not a whole day or night anyway. "That's what I mean," he said. "We're due."

So yesterday he left me at Grandawma's on his way to the mill, then picked me up late after working overtime. Grandawma asked us to stay for dinner, but Papa told her no thanks: when he and Mama have been fighting he doesn't like to sit around listening to his own mom's big theories on why. Grandawma seemed disappointed. She'd spent half the day getting ready for him by lecturing to me. She'd told me that Mama was naturally religious, and that having four sons and a ballplaying husband merely kept her that way. But having two daughters and a millwork- ing, chain-smoking, non-Sabbath-keeping, ex-ballplayer husband had made her more than religious: it had turned her into a "hyperprotective paranoid fanatic." Grandawma is English, and has two college degrees. Everett says that's why she can't make sense to kids like me. Her hero is somebody named Charles Darwin. He was just a scientist, Everett says, but she keeps this huge picture of him on her livingroom wall, as if he was Jesus, to her. I asked Papa once what the big deal about Charles Darwin was. All he said was that he preferred Charles Dillon. That's Casey Stengel's first two names. Anyhow, "Just you wait!" Grandawma kept telling me. "Just you wait till those two girls get older! Your mother's going to make your *actual* lives hell trying to keep her daughters out of that *paper* hell in the Bible!"

"Just *you* wait!" I wanted to yell back. But I was chicken. I didn't know what she meant by "paper hell" anyway, unless it was the place where Papa works. Of course papermills aren't in the Bible, but Grandawma never reads Bibles so she might not realize. I was glad when Papa came to get me, and glad we didn't eat there. Mama may well be a hypo-para- thinga-madoodle, but she doesn't say crummy things about Grandawma behind her back.

Getting back to the Underhanded Miracle: we had to run from Grandawma's house to the car, and Papa drove to the bank as much like a maniac as his dead thumb and 1940 Ford would let him. We made it inside the doors at ten seconds to six, just as the bank manager was locking up, and while Papa cashed his paycheck he told me we came within ten seconds of having ourselves one heck of a boring weekend. But I told him no we didn't, because he was forgetting about Babe Ruth, and he said, "Oops. You're right." He forgot I have this piggy bank that's a clear-glass statue of the Babe, and it's full to the nose, and none of it's pennies. Irwin had one too, only his was Lou Gehrig. But one time at church this missionary guy came and showed us films of himself baptizing big long rows of brown people called Laotians in an even browner river out in the Mission Fields of wherever Laotians live, and Irwin got so inspired he took a hammer, smashed Lou Gehrig's head in, and gave it to the missionary. The money, that is. It was over twenty dollars. Mama cried when he did it, she was so proud. Everett about puked. Peter laughed. Papa just shrugged. Everybody's different about money. Supposedly it takes all kinds.

After the bank we got burgers to go at Zack's In & Out—one for me and three for Papa—and on the way home we stopped by Six Corners Market, where Papa bought himself a whole case of a kind of beer called Lucky, and a whole carton of Lucky Strikes. When the grocer kidded him about buying Lucky this and Lucky that, Papa scowled and said, "I need all the luck I can get. Even the kinds I got to pay for."

"Ain't that the truth?" the grocer said—only it came out "Ain dat duh troof" because he's from New York or Philly or somewhere. Papa says they all say "dat" and "troof" back there.

Papa called the grocer "Soap" and Soap called Papa "Smoke," so I guess they knew each other, or used to. Soap had a walrus mustache, puffy eyes, a mashed nose which he used instead of his mouth to talk through, and ears like big wads of old gray chewing gum. Papa told me Soap used to box professionally, and to *get* boxed professionally too, which is why he looked that way. Soap laughed and nodded. Then Papa said Soap got the nickname because he was slippery in the clinch and liked to sting guys in the eyes. Soap shook his head at this, and said that really the name came from everybody bouncing their fists off his face so often it kept their hands nice and clean. "So you be smaht, son," he said. "Listen to Soap. You stig wid baseball like Smoke here, huh? Huh? Wuz duh boy's name, Smoke?"

"Kincaid, Soap Mahoney. And don't listen to that clean-hands crap, Kade. Soap murdered more'n his share."

The old man smiled as we shook hands, and I started to smile back.

But when I felt his hand it scared me: it was cold, and as thick and scuffed as one of those old-time webless baseball gloves.

"So how 'bout dat thumb?" Soap said to Papa. "Gettin' some feelin' in it? Doin' some throwin'? Is duh comeback in duh works?"

Not even trying to hide his instant irritation, Papa said, "You've been asking the same dumb questions for two years, Soap. The answers are still no, no and no."

"So I'm still waitin' for yep, yep an' yep!" he said cheerfully.

"Be a hell of a wait," Papa muttered, and he spun and stalked off toward the door.

I was embarrassed by his rudeness, but Soap just smiled benignly at his back, then beamed down at me as if he and I both knew, even if Papa didn't, that any day now ol' Smoke'd be magically healed and right back out on the mound where he belonged. I knew no such thing, so I just blurted "Bye!" and hurried to catch Papa. But halfway to the door I heard Soap holler, turned, and saw a five-cent roll of Bazooka bubble gum about to hit me in the face. My hand flew up. To my amazement, I caught it.

Soap gave me another ravaged, all-knowing smile. "Wud I tell ya?" he said. "Runs in duh family, huh?"

It was easily the best catch of my life, but I nodded like I knew what he was talking about. Then Soap looked hard at Papa, and didn't smile at all as he said, "Dat gum is lucky, Smoke. An' *nobody's* gotta pay for it."

Papa still looked irritated, but he nodded and thanked him. I put the lucky Bazooka in my pocket.

Back in the car, I asked Papa if he'd ever boxed. He didn't answer. I asked if he'd ever seen Soap box. No answer again. I asked if he liked Soap Mahoney. No response. I said, "Mama never shops at Soap's. How come you do?"

Nothing. He just drove.

I said, "Mama says Safeway's lots cheaper."

"She's right!" Papa snapped suddenly. "They ever give you free lucky gum at the goddamned Safeway?"

I decided I'd better change the subject. I said, "Soap likes you a lot, doesn't he?"

The car rolled up to a stop sign. "We're just a lot alike," Papa muttered.

I laughed a little, thinking he was joking. "How?" I asked. "How are you and that old geezer alike?"

Papa dug a bottle opener out from under the butts in the ashtray, popped open a beer, and started drinking. A pickup truck pulled up behind us, and after a while started honking. Papa just kept pouring it down. The truck finally revved its engine, slammed into reverse, and squealed around us, the driver laying on the horn as he passed. Papa ignored him. He drank till the bottle was empty, slid it back in the case, pulled out another, opened it, and stuck it between his legs. Then he looked at me. "We're both washed up," he said. "Both athletic wrecks. That's how me and that old geezer are alike."

It wasn't true. Papa was nothing like Soap Mahoney. He still played first base and hit over .500 for Crown Z's fast-pitch softball team. And even with the dead thumb, even at thirty-one, he was the best athlete my brothers or I had ever seen. But when he let out a long belch and the air filled with beer fumes, I rolled down my window and kept my mouth shut. Papa drove, and drank his beer.

Except for the beer in the yard that made Mama so mad, I'd never seen Papa drink. I'd never seen anybody drink except the bums down in Portland. But once you saw the bums you never forgot. They had eyes like mustard, mayonnaise and ketchup all stirred together; the skin of their faces was like Soap Mahoney's hands; their teeth were bashed in or caramel-colored, if they had any, and their mouths dribbled tobacco or blood at the corners; they wore pieces of dead people's old suits, wore greasy overcoats that flapped like mangled wings, wore sores instead of socks on their ankles; and after they'd drink a while they'd just sit or lie down right on the sidewalk, letting real people walk over them while they argued with people who weren't even there.

Once, while we were walking over some, Peter said to Everett that the bums had to listen to a whole sermon just to get a bowl of free soup at the Harbor Light Mission. Everett spat and said no wonder they stayed drunk. Then Mama scared the hell out of us, and out of some bums too, by hauling off and slapping Everett so hard he almost fell down on a fat old Indian passed out against the wall there. Yet it was Everett who instantly said, "I'm sorry." Because he knew, we all knew, that she didn't hit him for any weird religious reason, or for spitting on sidewalks, or even out of nervousness at having to step around bums. She hit him because her father was a drunk. A mean one too. Died before any of us ever met him, but Mama still has dreams about him. And even dead he was the reason why drinking terrified her.

He was also the reason why—when we got home and Papa lined his whole case of Luckies up in the icebox like he planned on drinking them all that night—I went straight to the bathroom, locked the door, and got down on my knees to pray. I'd had mixed luck with prayer lately, and wasn't all that high on it. But this time I gave it my very best shot. Keeping my eyes squeezed shut, calling Jesus "Thee" instead of "You," sticking "-eths" on the end of words like "beggeth" and "beseecheth" just like the Elders did at church, I explained the whole situation. I told how Papa and Mama had had a bad fight, how He and a beer had been the cause of it, and how now Papa was out there drowning himself, with nobody home to save him but me. I reminded Him how Mama's awful old man used to beat up his sons when they hid his whiskey, how Papa might do the same to me if I hid the beer, and how I knew He loved little children such as myself and wanted us to seek His help whenever we were in trouble. "And this is trouble," I told Him. "So if You would disappeareth the rest of Papa's beers for me, Lord, I sure would appreciate it. I thank Thee. Amen."

I felt pretty good afterward, just like the Elders say you should feel. I'd taken a big fat crisis off my own shoulders and loaded it all on Jesus, which seemed unfair in a way, but was exactly what the Bible recommended. It got boring in the bathroom then, but I stayed five minutes to allow things to happen, knowing that in working with a guy like Christ you had to be willing to make sacrifices. Then I went to the kitchen to check the results. I found all nineteen of the undrunk Luckies still standing in the icebox, and the twentieth out by the TV, sliding down Papa's throat.

I admit I wasn't surprised by this result, but I *was* annoyed by it. In fact I fired off another prayer (leaving out the "-eths" and "Thees" this time) to let Jesus know that only a wise guy would think I was asking for the beers to disappear down *Papa*. But then He started answering me in my head the way He does sometimes. He made me remember, for instance, that He knew *everything*. Knew, for example, that I had Soap Mahoney's lucky Bazooka right there in my pocket and could easily have made a wish to disappear the beer on that. Feeling selfish, I admitted I was kind of hoping to save the lucky gum.

But God helps those who help themselves, right? He said.

"Where in the Bible does it say that?" I asked.

The Bible doesn't say that. You *say that.*

"All I know," I argued, "is that I asked for Your help in a crisis, and as usual I didn't get it!"

It's your father, kid, and your lucky Bazooka. Think about it.

"What a friend I have in Jesus!" I snapped right back.

But He just laughed. He could see right through me. We both knew I was just being greedy with the lucky gum. I stomped back into the living-room and refused to give up even a corner of a piece while Papa downed a fifth beer, a sixth, a seventh, even an eighth. I grew so sure that he was going to pass out or puke or smash windows or beat me any second that it took me a long time to notice that he'd stayed fairly normal, except that he belched more, and ducked out to pee a lot. But he was better than normal in other ways. For instance he talked back to all the people on TV, imitating their silly voices and faces, making smart-aleck jokes at the idiotic stories, and arguing with everything the commercials tried to sell us, just like Everett likes to do. And when I asked if I could sit in his lap even though I'm too big for that sort of thing, he let me do it. We watched TV till 11:30, three hours past my normal bedtime, and after a while I felt so peaceful watching him guzzle beer and make wisecracks I halfway wished he'd get bombed every night. Last thing I remember he was carrying me up to bed, and I weigh a ton, but eight beers and all, he never once staggered. So after he slid me in under the covers and kissed me goodnight I shot off another sleepy prayer, just to forgive Jesus for not answering the prayer I'd prayed earlier. I suppose He knew all along how much beer Papa could hold. And who knows, maybe Papa had prayed himself. Maybe he'd asked Jesus to let him drink his fill in his own house in peace for once, and begged Him to ignore anybody who sent up mes-sages to the contrary. Prayer is mysterious, and God is even worse. I don't completely understand it yet.

Later—when I got frightened in bed and I guess cried a little because Papa's eyes were like mustard and ketchup and his teeth were all rotten and screwed up and then I woke up and Irwin's bed was empty and I could hear the darkness breathing so I called and called and for the longest time nobody answered—Papa finally came plodding up the stairs three-fourths asleep, and laid down beside me, which he hadn't done in so long I could barely remember. He didn't get in my bed. Mumbling something about wiggleworms, he pushed Irwin's bed against mine, flopped down on top of it, folded his arms behind his head, shut his eyes, and said, "Don't you worry, Kade. I called Uncle Marv and Aunt Mary Jane's. And Mama's fine. She's just gonna spend a little time up there."

I nodded, but felt confused. I hadn't been worried about Mama. I'd forgotten all about her. So was *he* worried? "What you and I need," he said, "is a song."

Before I could even agree he started singing a cowboy tune called Cool Clear Water in a voice so low and soothing that before it ended I was digging my thumbnail into my forehead—which is a trick Peter taught me to keep from falling asleep in church—because I was afraid if I dozed off, Papa would stop singing and leave. But Papa's is a voice, once it's warmed up, that carries you with it whether you want to go or not, and by the time Cool Water ended and The Old Man Is A-Waitin' For to Carry You to Freedom began, my forehead, thumbnail, brain and thoughts were all smooshed together down into the pillow.

Follow! Follow, follow, he sang, *Follow the Drinkin' Gourd . . .*

It was a song the slaves had sung to the Big Dipper, Papa once told me, back when they were lost in the woods trying to run away North. They called it the Drinkin' Gourd, he said, because they used gourds for dippers, because the poor don't buy what they can grow. But the mystery of the song to me was who this "Old Man" was who was waiting for to carry them to freedom. When I'd asked around, Irwin thought it was Abe Lincoln, Peter guessed it might be Jesus, and Everett and Mama figured it was God since they called him "Old Man." But Papa told me that really no Old Man carried the slaves to freedom. He said they'd walked the whole way themselves, and carried each other, and that most of their offspring were having to walk and carry each other still. I'm not sure what he meant by all that. But I do know that once, just last winter, after a strike shut down the mill and Papa got into serious trouble with his union for not picketing, because he was out moonlighting for a carpenter, because we were out of money and almost out of food, a guy named Theodore Bikel came on the car radio and sang this very song, and Papa got serious and sad as I've ever seen him, and said the song was about us now too. A *white mill nigger,* he called himself, and Mama didn't even shush him. "Except," he said, "there's no North for us to run to."

But now he sang it like last winter never happened, and as his voice dipped low for another *Follow, follow* the people in the song appeared to me—a whole band of them, dressed all ragtag, carrying babies and bundles, hunched low in the starlight as they moved across a field of corn stubble toward a black wall of trees. Knowing they were dream-people and that I'd fall asleep if I kept watching, I tried to make them enter the trees and disappear. But they were still in the open when I heard Papa singing *How can there be a cherry that has no stone?*, which was a whole 'nother song. And even in the wrong song the ragtag people kept moving north through the corn stubble, and when they did reach the wall of trees, instead of vanishing they signaled me to come on in with them. So

I did. I stepped right into the trees. And even in the dark we saw that the very first tree we'd come to was just loaded with cherries, though it was corn-stubble season, so I was sure, now, that I was asleep. But I sat down with them anyhow, watching as the ones who could climb began dropping sweet black cherries down to the old ones and little ones who couldn't. And when I caught a cherry finally, and slipped it in my mouth, its taste and my body and Papa's voice and the people and tree all began to make that whole and perfect sense which nothing ever seems to make by day. *How can there be a cherry that has no stone?* the music asked, and at once I saw the mama silhouette picking pits from the cherries. *How can there be a baby with no crying?* it asked as she passed the pitted fruit to her infant, who made no cry as it sucked the sweet juice. *How can there be a story that has no end?* it asked as we all leaned back against rocks and tree trunks and let the cherry juice and song go humming all round and through us. Then I remembered it must be Papa still making the music, it must be his voice we still heard, alone and outside our world somewhere—and I looked around at my friends, the silhouettes, afraid that, should he grow tired and end the song, our whole sweet world would end too.

But then I felt his real hand on my real head, felt his gray eyes watching me, though my eyes were closed. And he sang every last verse again.

And then again.

And unless I dreamed it, yet again.

When I woke it was hot, his bed was empty, it was Sabbath, and downstairs I could hear the Yankees and Indians already going at it. So all of that, more or less, is how I came to be sitting here in the situation I'm calling an Underhanded Miracle. Maybe most people won't think a Miracle should include bad or wrong things like Papa and Mama's fight or Papa's dead thumb or his eight beers in it. But take a close look at Jonah's whale or Balaam's ass or Peter's cock crowing three times and you'll see that every one of those Miracles happened when Jonah, Balaam and Peter were doing a wrong or bad thing. So maybe this Underhanded Miracle of my family scattering every which way, leaving me to watch baseball and fish with Papa on Sabbath, is kind of our whale, and maybe it'll spit us out and put us back together even better than before.

Or maybe it won't. How would I know? Either way it's Cleveland 3, Yankees 1, and soon as this game's over we're heading up the Wind! So *concentrate!*

·   ·   ·   ·

Stengel has finally stopped smelling his fingers and faking signs. With two out and one on in the eighth, it's no big secret that Mantle will be trying to bust fences. The Mick takes a ball, then takes another, and when Mudcat Grant stops to yell at the ump, Papa says he doesn't blame him. He says both pitches were sliders thrown so close to the outside corner that Mantle couldn't hit them and the ump couldn't tell what they were. But inside every ump, Papa says, is a baseball fan, and for some reason baseball fans all love Mickey Mantle, so the fan in the ump called them balls.

Mudcat fires a high fastball next, for a called strike. Then he throws a low fastball—and in a split second you can see why everybody loves Mantle. One instant he's just standing there like any other yokel, but the next instant his body coils and explodes, and even through the TV you can hear the sweetest kind of bat-crack as the ball gets golfed to Kingdom Come. While it's sailing toward the bleachers, though, and Pee Wee is going apeshit about how hard it's hit, Papa just mutters, "Strike two." And I notice Dizzy huffing and puffing like the wolf that blew the little pigs' houses down, because he knows it's foul too, and is trying to blow it fair.

"FOUL BALL!" hollers Pee Wee about two years after we realized it.

"Jammed him," Papa says.

"Jammed him," says Diz.

Papa grins.

I like Dizzy Dean a lot. I suspected I would even before I was ever sick enough to get to stay home from church and watch him, because Everett told me he got in trouble once for saying "Call us Diz and Pee for short" right on national TV. Pee Wee Reese seems nice enough, and I guess he was one heck of a ballplayer, but as an announcer Pee isn't a bad name for him, since he just sort of pees out what's happened after it's happened even though you saw it better yourself. Right now, for instance, he is saying that Mantle just struck out ("Change-up," says Papa), and that it's a crying shame his homer drifted foul because foul homers don't count, and if it had counted the score would be a lot different than it is right now. Dizzy is more the way Everett is at a ballgame. He tells you things you hadn't noticed, and things that have nothing to do with what's happening, and he gets mad at umps, makes fun of bad plays and players, calls errors "eras" and basemen "sackers," tells lies, brags, invents fake statistics to win arguments, and generally grates on Pee Wee's nerves till you feel you're really living through a flesh-and-blood ballgame instead of sitting in your house staring at a box. Right now, for instance,

Diz is saying that a foul ball should be considered fair, provided a pitcher hits it. A foul that pops backward over the backstop and into the fans should count as a homer for a pitcher, he says. And when Pee Wee says he's not so sure about that, Dizzy roars, "You were a *shortstop!* What do *you* know?"

"I'll tell you what I know," Pee Wee says. "I know all you folks out there are gonna be real pleased with these fine products!" And onto the screen pops a couple of housewives who start having a poop fit when they see how clean their new dish soap got the dinner plates.

Papa is different than anybody I ever saw watch baseball. We get to watch the World Series with him when the games don't fall on Sabbath, and we watch live minor league ball together most Sundays (usually the Triple A Tugs down in Portland, who Papa used to massacre almost single-handed, and who he might be pitching for today if it weren't for his thumb). Papa's ball-watching style is to just sit there like a hawk on a fencepost, not saying a word unless something really good or really strange happens, but when the game's a tight one he looks almost crazy, his eyes get so big and black. He looks crazy right now, in fact, and he's only staring at the dish soap.

He's just fired up another Lucky. I used to like to watch him smoke, but his hands didn't shake then, and he didn't smoke even half as many. I guess he quit once, when I was little, but after the thumb thing happened and the twins were born and Mama had an operation called a hysterectomy and afterward almost died and was so weak and weepy for a year that Grandawma and her bulldog Gomorrah had to give up their house in Pullman and come live with us to help out with the twins, he took it up again with a vengeance.

Papa's friend Roy told Everett recently that Papa would be a foreman at the mill if it wasn't for his thumb. If that's true, it doesn't make much sense, since as a foreman Papa wouldn't need his crushed thumb at all. Maybe Roy means he's not a foreman because of the lawsuit . . .

Papa's lawsuit started last March, when Mama read in the paper about some surgeon down in Portland who removed a big toe off a guy and built him a new thumb out of it. Papa wasn't any too excited by this, but Mama made an appointment anyway, and they drove on down to see what the surgeon would say. The guy's name was Dr. Boyd Franken, and he was a frank 'un all right: I guess when he saw Papa's scars and X rays he started cussing so bad that Papa had to ask him to quit. He apologized, but said that the creature who'd tried to rebuild Papa's thumb must have been a Mallard or Pintail or Quacky Campbell maybe. Papa told Dr. Franken the guy had seemed human enough. "He better never lose a button off his shirt, then," Franken said, "because he'd kill himself trying to sew it back on—not that you or I would miss him." Holding Papa's hand open, he showed both my parents how the duck-doctor should have saved the bone he'd replaced with plastic, and how the screws were unnecessary, and how he'd made such a hash of the tendons and nerves and skin grafts that Papa had been scarred and crippled up a lot worse than he should have been, not to mention the agony he must have gone through before it all went dead. Mama said that Papa turned gray when he heard all this, but that he only said, "What's done's done." But Papa said that Mama turned purple when she heard it, and she went after his old surgeon the next day, even though Papa didn't want her to. But the guy was already dead.

Dr. Franken filled out a bunch of papers and sent them to the mill, saying that Papa had been a victim of "malpractice" and that the damage was "irreversible," but that by having the dead part of his thumb cut off, his big toe transplanted onto his hand, and a fake toe called a prosthylactic or some such thing sewed onto where the real toe used to be, Papa would most likely end up with a thumb that had feeling in it and could do a thing or two. So the mill sent Franken's papers to their insurance company, who sent them on to their own doctors, who hemmed and hawed for four whole months then told the insurance company that the whole idea was expensive and risky and "completely unwarranted." So that's what the mill told Papa. "I guess that's that," he'd said, lighting up a Lucky. But Mama said, "The *hell* it is!" And she got on the horn to Dr. Franken, told him what had happened, and he had another swearing fit worse than his first, but Mama was so mad at the insurance company that even though he used words like "flaming assholes" she didn't realize till later that he was cussing: she said she thought he was quoting the Psalms.

We couldn't afford a lawyer, but after a long struggle Mama and Doc Franken finally talked Papa into taking his case to his union. Then Papa's union talked to more doctors yet, and to their own lawyers, and decided to take the mill's insurance company to court. The courts are so slow that we won't know what's happening till sometime this fall, but if Papa's union's lawyers whip the mill's insurance company's lawyers, then the mill, or the insurance company, or anyhow somebody besides us is going to pay Dr. Franken to build Papa a new thumb. That's the best I can understand it, anyhow. Papa says it's one heck of a kerfuffle. Mama says it's all in God's Hands. I think that means they don't quite understand it either.

Everett is sure that Papa will win the suit, have the surgery, and make a sensational pro baseball comeback. Peter's not so sure. He says that Papa's toe is going to make an awfully big, awfully weird thumb. Everett says its weirdness could give Papa's pitches extra stuff, but Pete says he isn't sure Papa wants stuff. He thinks Papa might settle for things like being able to work a pair of scissors or pliers left-handed again. Papa is completely boring on the subject. All he ever says is: "We'll see."

The Indians are up now, top of the ninth. I was having trouble concentrating, so I'm standing behind Papa's chair, letting *his* concentration leak into mine, which is another trick Peter taught me. Peter claims that a person's mind is much larger than their brain. He claims your mind actually hovers out around your head in a pulsing, invisible ball of varying size and color. Peter claims lots of things. He reads an awful lot.

Vic Power, the Indians' Negro first baseman, is the hitter. It's weird to see a big black man like Power getting called an "Indian." Come to think of it, it's pretty strange to see a bunch of white guys running around calling themselves "Indians" too. How are *real* Indians supposed to feel about this? I mean, what if there was a team of white guys, with an Indian first baseman, called "the Cleveland Negroes"? It'd make exactly as much sense. Better yet, what if there was a team of Negroes and Indians called "the Cleveland White Guys"? I think a lot of pale-faced folks wouldn't be all that thrilled. That's one big advantage the Yankees have: black, red, brown or white, they look like Yanks, and act like Yanks, and *are* Yanks. None of this cutesy Oriole or Cub or White-Indian crap for them.

But my concentration is really shot. Whitey Ford struck Power out on three straight pitches, and I didn't even know it till I heard Dizzy saying that the way Whitey handles pressure brings to mind another fine young pitcher of his acquaintanceship, namely himself. Pee Wee didn't laugh at this, but Papa did. Jimmy Piersall is the hitter now.

It doesn't seem fair, though, Papa laughing. He never laughs when *we* brag. He won't even let us brag about *him*. Everett once tried to defend some bragging he was doing about Papa by saying that the Diz once said, "It ain't braggin' if you done it." Papa said, "That was Dizzy talking about Dizzy. You're Everett talking about me." Everett said he didn't see the difference. Papa said, "Well, there is one." Everett said he still didn't see it. "If you think I'm worth bragging about," Papa told him, "you'll take my word for it." Everett said, "What is this? *Father Knows Best?*" But he hasn't bragged about Papa since.

Mama still brags about him, though. She and Everett both know what Papa's done as a ballplayer better than Papa himself. Everett can recite all Papa's statistics and reel off lists of all the big league sluggers he's fooled, but Mama watched Papa play for years when Everett was just an ignorant little blob in her lap, so she has more stories. The trouble with Mama's stories is that after she tells a good one she'll sometimes put on her Pious Face, sigh, and say, "Sometimes I'm afraid I know baseball better than I know my own Bible." Last time she said it, though, Everett told her that God didn't even *own* a Bible, so chances were He knew baseball better too. Mama looked sort of squirmy, but she laughed.

The person who never brags or laughs about baseball or Papa is Grandawma. I don't know if it's her Englishness or college or Darwin or what, but when she was living with us last year she once told Everett and me that baseball had turned Papa into a complete nobody. Of course Everett hit the ceiling. "If Papa's a nobody," he yelled, "who's paying for Gomorrah's stinking dog food?" Grandawma told him the dog's name was Isadora. "Picky about names, huh?" Everett said. "Okay. Name me three big league ballplayers."

Grandawma was just irritated enough to give it a try. "Babe Ruth!" she snapped. "Lou Gehrig! And, um, Oscar Unitas!"

When we burst out laughing she asked what was so damned funny. Everett told her, "You only know Ruth and Gehrig because of Irwin and Kade's piggy banks. So how can you say what baseball has turned Papa into? You don't know what it's turned *anybody* into. You don't know what baseball *is*."

Everett's the only kid I know who refuses to back down from grownups in arguments. Most times I even think he wins, though the grownups never admit it. The trouble with Grandawma, though, is that she makes you spitting mad, so you fight her, but then her head starts to palsy so bad you feel like you're beating up on old ladies, so you stop. Then, despite the wobble, she turns around and says something that makes you even madder. That's exactly what she did this time. "I don't *want* to know what baseball is," she told Everett. "I refuse to squander mental energy pondering the technicalities of anything so patently inane."

"*All* ballplayers are nobodies to you," Everett retorted. "Even the greatest, and kindest, and most heroic. So Papa couldn't please you to save his life. So you might as well be quiet and leave him alone."

"A long time ago," she said, wobbling so bad it seemed her head might roll clean off her shoulders, "your father showed signs of keen intelligence. Then he made this boy's game his entire life. Thanks to this boy's game he barely finished high school. Thanks to this boy's game one small injury has ended his career. Thanks to this boy's game he is a man with six children, no money, no employable knowledge or skills, and he stands an excellent chance of being trapped in that miserable mill for the rest of his life. So no, I *don't* understand baseball. But I see what it's done to my son. He's a beautiful young man with the jaded, hopeless eyes of some pathetic old derelict. And you wonder why, when I see you and Peter hell-bent on following in his footsteps, I am not enthusiastic!"

What she said about his eyes scared me. But all it did to Everett was make him madder. "Papa could make *you* sound stupid too!" he roared. "He could make *your* life sound wasted and *your* eyes sound ugly too! But he doesn't, does he? So how come he learned better manners playing ball than you learned in college? And while we're at it, how come *you're* not happy? How come you like fossils and dead scientists better than living people?"

"Don't you *dare* take that tone with me!" she cried, her voice quavering like someone dying.

"I apologize!" Everett shouted. "I apologize for loving my nobody of a father. I'll try to learn to *despise* him, like you!"

With a quickness that stunned me she snatched Everett's wrist and gripped it. "We're *all* nobodies," she said, and her calm was awful, her head nearly still. "We're nothing, and less than nothing. You're a *child*, Everett Chance. A callow, arrogant little mill-town child. *Oh, if you could see some of the things these old eyes have seen!*"

Her dry, red-rimmed eyes turned suddenly, fixing on mine, and I looked away in terror. But there was no escaping her voice: "You know, *I* had brothers once. Three fine brothers, and a father I dearly loved. And they died, every one of them, in the Great War. I must tell you, sometime, what they thought they were fighting for. And I must tell you exactly how and why they died."

Everett was quiet, and scared now too. She'd been part of a family as real and nearly as big as ours. They'd had everything we had, and money too. And it was gone, every bit of it. This grim, palsying old woman was all that was left.

"But enough of this," she sniffed suddenly, her face and voice so changed, so eerily pleasant that the bitterness still scalding us seemed like something we'd dreamed. "I notice you didn't mention Oscar Unitas.

What's the matter, Everett? Have I shocked you by passing my little quiz?"

I thought Everett might laugh at her again, but he didn't. He just nodded, and said quietly, "You pass, Gran. You pass."

Given her opinion of baseball, I don't know how this could please her. But it obviously did.

Much as she dislikes baseball, Grandawma likes the Bible even less. This is because her hero, Charles Darwin, discovered evolution before God even mentioned it, proved scientifically that men are just apes at heart, and got the Christians all worked up because none of this was in the Bible. That's what Everett and Peter say anyway. Late one night when we were sitting around yapping, Peter said to Everett that if the Christians had any horse sense they'd just sit down and write themselves a new Bible, sticking some evolution in there this time. He said the biblical creation story was a dud anyhow, especially if you were a girl, since God made everything in the Universe, claimed He saw it was good, and then when the First Lady went out naked for a walk to enjoy all this so-called goodness, a completely evil Devil in snake's clothing came down out of a tree, lied his head off to her, got her thrown out of Paradise and cursed into having it hurt like hell to have babies, and she was *still* such a nice person that she didn't go back with a stick and kill that damned snake. Whose fault *was* all this? Peter wanted to know. Who claimed it was "good" in spite of the snake, then tried to cover Their tracks with a lot of cockamamie hoodoo about Forbidden Fruit and Trees of Knowledge and Eve's wicked curiosity? And what harm could a little Darwinian evolution possibly do to a mess of a story like that?

But Everett told Peter it'd be a snowy day in hell before the Christians wrote themselves a new Bible. Too many bugs in the plan, he said. In the first place, who do you ask to do the writing? An Adventist? A Catholic? A Baptist? If you picked just one, he said, the others would kill you. And if you picked one of each they'd kill each other. In the second place, he said, most Christians would refuse to rewrite the Bible anyway, because they'd want God to do it for them, because most of them think it was God who sat down and wrote the one they've got.

"Well, wasn't it?" Irwin butted in, looking pretty shocked.

"See what I mean?" Everett said to Peter.

"Oh that's right!" said Irwin, smacking himself in the forehead. "It was Jesus!"

Peter and Everett looked at each other, then slowly shook their heads.

"Okay! I give!" Irwin cried, laughing like a loonbat. "Who *did?* Who *did* write the Bible?"

"King James," said Peter.

"Oscar Unitas," said Everett.

Irwin went loonbats again.

"Anyhow," Everett said to Peter, "you can bet any amount, any odds, the Christians will stick with the Bible they've got, sure as the Chicago Cubs'll stick with Wrigley Field—even though it's got no lights."

Peter nodded. "Nightfall is to the Cubs," he said, "exactly what Charles Darwin is to the Christians."

"Quit jumping around!" Papa hollers.

Oops. I guess I was sort of hanging on his chair by one leg and one arm, and maybe kicking and swinging around some. It's Darwin's fault, though. He's who got me thinking about apes. When I drop to the floor I hear Pee Wee Reese start yelling and see Roger Maris running, but thanks to my dud concentration I missed the pitch that whoever it was—Jimmy Piersall, I guess—hit. Maris leaps, grabbing a drive bashed clear to the warning track. But when Papa hollers, "Great catch! Great catch!" my brain changes channels again, coughing up a picture of me in the Wind, catching fish.

Papa says we could get trout today, no trouble, but we're not going to because we'll be after summer steelhead, which are like trout, except huge. He caught one two weeks ago that almost broke his pole, and it was the most beautiful thing I've ever seen dead, and one of the most beautiful things, period. It took all eight of us two days to eat it, and the smoke from Papa's cigarettes and the blue-gray ballplayers on the screen are the exact same color as the steelhead's back, and its sides were as silver as a brand-new—

"KADE!"

"Oops. Sorry, Papa." I guess I was banging my head on the back of his chair. The thing was that if I squatted down and lined my eye up just right, I could make it look like the blue-gray batter was using Papa's Lucky for a bat, so I was conking my head on the chair when they were supposed to swing.

"If you can't sit still and watch," Papa says, "go get the mail. I think I just heard it come."

I want to watch, but I want to bang around and jump and roar and wonder about the Wind and Darwin and steelhead and not being in church too, and look! A commercial. *Run! Catch the mail! Great catch!*

The screen door slams behind me. I sprint like Roger Maris after Pier-sall's long drive. But the day is so bright I can't see where I'm going, the air's so hot my lungs burn, and who wants to be Roger Maris anyhow? I slow to a walk.

It's more interesting, walking. I can see, and try to think if I want, though I doubt I'll want to. There's a mirage lake in the street that almost looks worth fishing. The mailman's jeep is in it up to the hubs. Everywhere I turn the air is watery, wiggling upwards. The whole world looks warped. I hope steelhead like weather like this. The local animals and people sure don't. The whole neighborhood has disappeared except for one small bunch of starlings, who are running through a sprinkler like a bunch of ugly little kids might. They act just like kids, the starlings do, till one of them stops to eat a bug. But come to think of it, some kids will even do that. There's this kid at school, Meredith Starr, who'll eat flies for a penny apiece till he's had three, then with the three cents he buys an extra milk to wash down his lunch. It looks so awful when he snorfs them that you can't help laughing, but it's actually kind of sad, I guess. Meredith is one of these kids who smells but can't help it. He was born without a dad and his mom's too crazy to cook, so he eats about a ton at school. I give him everything from my lunches I hate, which is called Charity, which is something the Babcocks tell us at Sabbath School al-ways to give to wretches like Meredith Starr. I'd do it anyway, though, since he really seems to want it, and when it's pukey stuff like eggplant or mashed cabbage it's fun to watch. He can gulp it down almost as fast as Gomorrah.

The mailman is feeding a row of boxes two blocks down the street, up to his hood now in another fake lake. Even the shade is hot and bright: I think the sunlight must be bashing the top side of everything so hard that some dark-colored version of light is starting to leak clear through. It would scare me to hook a steelhead. I've never caught a fish, except minnows by hand, so I hope I just catch a trout. Everett caught a steel-head once and wasn't a bit scared, but he's not scared of anything except Grandawma's dead family, and maybe Mama's dead dad. I might not be scared either, except last summer Irwin brought a catfish home from the Columbia for a pet, and the first time I tried to pick it up it spiked me so bad my hand got infected and hurt for three weeks. I was glad when the chlorine in our water finally killed it, though it made me sort of wonder why it doesn't kill us. We buried the catfish by the trash burner, and Irwin made a wood cross for it, and a sign that said: HERE LIES TYRUS

COBB JUNIOR. That's what Everett said to name it, since Tyrus Cobb
Senior liked to spike people too.

I open the mailbox. A letter from Everett, addressed to me! Postcards
from Irwin and Pete! The commercial! It must be over! *Run!*

The screen door slams behind me. I try to dial a wider opening into my
eyes, but the TV's so dim compared to outside that the ballplayers look
like ghosts. I tell Papa we got mail from the Three Stooges. He says,
"Great!" but just goes on watching the game. When my eyes finally
adjust, though, I see why:

Roger Maris is up, no outs, top of the ninth. Maris homered in the
third with nobody aboard. That's the only mistake Mudcat Grant has
made all day, Papa says. And even Maris's homer was just a routine fly, he
says, except for a hard wind gusting into right. I can't wait to see the
other Wind, I tell him. The river, I mean. No, it won't be too windy
there, he says when I ask him, it's just called that. Yes, it's sheltered, he
says, it's in a deep canyon. Yes, there are trees in the canyon, and yes,
there will be steelhead, but that doesn't mean we'll catch one. Spikes?
Like who? No, they won't have spikes like Ty Cobb. No, not even the
bucks. No, no antlers either. Yes, it'll be great, he says. QUIET! he says.
He says he'll only answer baseball questions from now till the game is
over.

The score has gone:

NEW YORK: 001 000 00 . . .
CLEVELAND: 100 010 10 . . .

Roger Maris takes a ball, then a strike. His hair's so short the sides of
his head look like wads of skinned chicken meat, and there's dark bags
under his eyes, and he's incredibly sweaty and nervous-looking. I usually
like watching home runs, but there is something about Roger Maris that
makes even his homers boring. I don't hate the Yankees like most people,
so it's not that. I just don't care to watch Roger Maris. Everett feels the
same way, only worse. Everett says he's from Mars, which is why he's
named Maris, so maybe it's a racial thing. Whatever it is, it worries me a
little, because one of the things Jesus used to say was to love everybody
the same whether they're geeks, Yanks, Wops, Micks, Meredith Starrs or
what have you, and when I look at Roger Maris I'm not sure I'll ever be
able to pull it off.

Peter says there was once this Italian saint called San Francisco (the
same guy they eventually named the Giants after) who loved Jesus a ton

and was a truly wonderful person, except for one small thing. He couldn't stand lepers. And I guess they were coming out of the woodwork, there in Italy in his day. But one night in a dream, Pete says, who should come walking up to San Francisco but Jesus Himself, and what does Christ do but order poor San to go out and kiss the first leper he sees! Pete says San Francisco woke up quaking in his boots or sandals or whatever. And of course, no sooner does he step out the door than the skankiest-looking leper ever invented comes dribbling right toward him down the road! For a minute there, Pete says, poor San can't figure out whether to shit or eat a doughnut. But he loves Jesus so much that he somehow staggers up to the leper, puckers his lips, shuts his eyes, and manages to get the job done. Except (here's the great part, Pete says) right while they're smooching San peeks and sees that this walking oozeball was actually Jesus all along! This was the big breakthrough the saint needed, apparently, since afterwards, Peter says, he went out and converted all the Italians and fish and wolves and sparrows to Catholicism, and eventually got himself crucified on a Miraculous Cross up in the mountains that wasn't even there really. Anyhow, Peter says, the thing is, everybody on earth must eventually face up to their own personal leper. In other words, he says, someday Everett and me will have to get past our feelings about Roger Maris. We may even have to kiss him if we don't watch it, he says. Of course Everett told Pete straight off that it'd be a snowy day in hell before he kissed Roger Maris. But Peter just laughed and said what if Jesus *forced* him to? What if He forced him to walk right up and lick Roger Maris's crewcut? Everett about barfed.

I think I might do it, though. That is, I think I might do it if I knew that licking it would turn Roger Maris into Jesus. But then again, what if the Jesus I turned Roger Maris into just went on playing right field for the Yankees? They'd be even more unbeatable! Everett would *murder* me. And all the Catholics would be running around with a little ballplayer on a cross around their necks, and the ballparks'd fill with holy water and priests instead of ice-cream and peanut vendors. It'd be chaos, most likely. So I don't know. Hopefully the chance to lick it will never arise.

Peter reads lots of religious books, like the one about San Francisco. That's where he gets most of his weirder stories and ideas. He has this oddball teacher at school, Stefan Delaney, who thinks Pete's a genius and started giving him stacks of special books to read. But not long ago Mama flipped her lid over one called the Bog of Vod Geeta, which she felt was filling Pete's head full of heathen ideas and turning him away from God.

How could it do that, Mr. Delaney wanted to know, since God was exactly Who the whole book was aimed at? And I wouldn't know, since I've never read the thing. But I do remember the day Mama flipped her lid, and I didn't blame her a bit. . . .

We were all in the car coming home from Spokane, and Mama was reading an adventure book about Tibet that Uncle Marv had loaned her. Being a good Adventist, Mama was against books about things such as Tibet unless a missionary wrote them. But she's the opposite of practically everybody on earth in that she has to read in a car to keep from getting carsick, and the Tibet book was the only one her skunk of a brother would loan her. So anyhow, at some point in the book the author-adventurer got himself invited into this smoky little Tibetan house, sat down to dinner with the whole Tibetan family, and started eating stuff with names like *Zahpahhayabrugmancharya* and drinking stuff with names like *Padmaywhang*. And as she was reading about this, Mama started squirming all over the front seat, giggling and muttering to herself and acting all delighted, till every last one of us was gaping at her. And when Papa finally asked what on earth was going on, Mama just turned to him with this wonderful, dazed smile on her face, smacked her lips, and said, *"Yum! Yak butter!"* And we almost died laughing—literally—since Papa gawked at her so long he nearly drove off the road.

But Peter—who is so soft-spoken most of the time—didn't laugh at all. Instead he got red in the face and shrill in the voice and started drilling Mama with pointed questions, trying to get her to cross her heart and hope to die admitting she remembered a past life as a Tibetan. It was strange. I mean, there he was trying to prove some mysterious point about Buddhism or rebirth or some damn thing, but all he reminded me of was ol' Mrs. Babcock at Sabbath School bullyragging us about how we must praise Jesus and hate sin all the time, whether we feel like praising and hating or not. I don't know yet, between Pete and Mama, whose beliefs are better or truer. All I know is that by the time he finished grilling her, nobody felt like laughing about her yak butter anymore.

When she got over being stunned, Mama got good and mad and started firing pointed questions back. That's when she found out about the Bog of Vod Geeta, and about Peter believing in past lives and Hindu Christs and the world being a kind of gigantic delusion and everybody really being a Drip of God and I don't remember what all. Then Pete started this big stupid fight with her, arguing about how Krishna and Buddha and several other guys were actually Jesus in different human disguises, and vice versa, which any fool could see was a wacko thing to fight about even if they were, since they also obviously weren't. By the time it was over Mama had strictly forbidden him to read any more of Mr. Delaney's heathen religious books. So of course now he reads *tons*, every night, under the covers by flashlight. Mr. Delaney even gives him batteries. And Mama was right: Peter's head *is* getting filled with heathen beliefs and stories—and they're really great! Pete's just a kid, but already he has more interesting ideas and tells better tales than anybody I know, even Everett, though Everett makes better pissed-off speeches and tells funnier jokes. I think I might even agree with Mr. Delaney about Pete being a genius, though it's an odd thing to think about your own brother. And in his feisty way sometimes I think maybe Everett's one too. Irwin, though, is practically a dunce from a schoolteacherly point of view, yet sometimes just watching him laugh and eat his dinner and grow new muscles and tickle Bet and Freddy and misunderstand Pete and Everett's discussions and stories and punchlines is more fun than the discussions and stories themselves.

When you get right down to it, it's a great family I got. But then it's easy to love everybody the same amount when they're your family. It's not nearly so easy when they're weird Yankees like Roger Maris or total bideeps like Meredith Starr. At times it seems to me like it might have been more practical of God to make everybody in the world blood relatives with the same last name. Everett says that if God had done that, though, brothers would have had to marry their sisters and the kids would've turned out to be mutants. So maybe it's for the best the way things are. Then again, it might be all right being some sort of mutant, lolloping down the street doffing your hat at all the other lolloping mutants, all of whom you knew loved you like a brother or sister, and all of whom you loved. Then again, it might not be so great. I don't know. Some things you can't figure out until you do them.

Roger Maris takes a ball, then a strike, then poles one of his typical boring high fly balls out into right. Harvey Kuenn gathers it in. One out.

I open Everett's letter:

Dear Everybody but Gomorrah,

My counsellor is making us write to say we're fine and dandy and learning oodles of wholesome Adventist propaganda, but the fact of the matter is a terrible thing has occurred to us. Our beloved Irwin was killed and eaten this morning by a cougar this morning, and is with Jesus now, unless he is in "Heck." Oh well. No big loss, except sizewise. But we're all pretty concerned about the cougar.

Wolverton Lake is pretty. Pretty lousy fishing, that is. I would of took canoeing but can't paddle with this stupid arm which by the way itches like a dirty bottom (ask the twins if you can't understand what I'm saying here, guys), so I took Trekking. So did Pete. We're learning to read maps and compasses today, and how to follow the ol' Drinkin' Gourd if our compass busts (provided it's night and not raining and we're stupid enough to hike in the dark, which our counsellor definitely is). We've found two secret lakes already though, and will be climbing a mountain 9,383' high (big deal).

The food is the usual vegetarian dog-doodoo, especially the "meat," which is fake of course. But the loss of Irwin more than makes up for a few inconveniences.

That's it for now. Until next week, I remain your lovely son (or brother where applicable),

Everett

Mama isn't going to like Everett's letter. She believes Jesus and "Heck" are not joking matters. I pass it to Papa, but he just sticks it in his shirt pocket. "In a minute," he says. "One out, nobody on. The Yanks have just about had it . . ."

For some reason, I blurt, "No they haven't."

Papa looks at me. "Huh?"

I feel almost embarrassed about it, but all of a sudden I have this odd feeling. "The Yankees will win," I say calmly.

Papa smiles. I've never predicted anything before and he knows it. But I've never felt like this before, either. It's weird. I'll bet Mama felt just like this the day she said *Yum!* about the yak butter. "Is that so?" Papa says.

"It's so," I say—and my yak butter feeling agrees. "It's in the bag."

Then I glance at the TV, see Tony Kubek coming to bat, and start having doubts right on top of my certainty. The TV says he's 0 for 3, and hitting .258. If in doubt, Everett says, act tough. "Wanna bet on it?" I snarl at Papa.

"You're so sure," he says, "I'd just be throwing away good money."

"Darn tootin'," I tell him.

Kubek takes a slider. The ump calls it a strike. Papa says it's the exact same pitch Mudcat threw Mantle earlier, but Kubek's not Mantle so now it's a strike. I shrug, acting tough.

Peter's postcard is of a mountain called Three-fingered Jack, though I only see one finger. All the card says is, "HIYA. LOVE, P.A.C.E." P.A.C.E. stands for Peter Arthur Chance Esquire. Pete likes to put on the dog a little sometimes.

Kubek takes a fastball high and inside. One and one. Everett calls him The Kube. He says The Kube is from outer space, same as Roger the Martian. Everett's odd that way. Anybody he doesn't like, he says they're from outer space and makes up a planet that explains them. The Kube's from a planet where everybody's head is made out of a block of wood, he says. He says if Kubek ever gets beaned he'll probably get a base hit out of it. He's got planets for all the more famous Yankees except Mickey Mantle, who he can't help but like, and Yogi Bear, who he says is from earth but of course isn't human. Stengel he calls Spacey Tangle. He says that Tangle's planet is just a big briar patch, and so is his brain, and that every time Spacey opens his mouth he proves it. Papa says Stengel's got a great baseball mind, though, and Papa's usually right about people. Everett's just more fun to listen to.

Of course Irwin adores the Yankees. But whereas most Yankee fans only adore them so they can yell *I won! I won!* Irwin adores them because of Everett—because what Irwin really adores are science fiction movies, and watching the Yankees dismantle somebody on TV with Everett in the room is like watching the earth being invaded and destroyed by a gang of inhuman bozos. It's a pretty great show.

The Kube hacks at a sinker that almost bounces off home plate. Strike two. Some Yankees start yelling at the ump about a greaseball, but Papa says it wasn't, and he's right apparently: the ump checks the ball and finds nothing.

I ask Papa if he ever doctored pitches. He says no. Then he says, "Well . . ." Then he says he may have taken advantage of a drop of sweat or a nick now and again, but that sweat and nicks are okay because they're part of nature. "I was a nature-type pitcher," Papa says, more than a little lamely.

"So spit's part of nature too?" I ask.

"Just watch the game," he says.

Mudcat is fooling with his mitt and belt and armpits and back pocket and shirt and hat now, trying to make Kubek worry about grease. Papa calls this Psychiatric Work. Kubek tries stepping out of the batter's box and fooling with a resin bag, but compared to Mudcat's mitt, belt, pits, pocket, shirt and hat, The Kube's little resin bag is just pathetic. He looks doomed. Mudcat throws another sinker, and Kubek knows he can't hit it after getting psychiatrized like that, so he just watches it. Low. Barely. Ball two.

Pee Wee wonders aloud whether baseballs really get doctored much. Dizzy snorts and says the question is whether they ever don't. Pee Wee acts shocked. Then Dizzy calms him down by admitting he was exaggerating. The true immortals, he says—himself for instance—don't need nicks and grease and spit. "So you never doctored the ball?" Pee Wee asks. No sir I did not, says Dizzy. But once, he says, when he was playing for the Cards, he did pitch a game with a godawful cold, ran out of poop in the fourth inning, started getting shelled, and pretty soon got so upset by the whole experience that his nose started running like a faucet . . .

The Kube fouls off a curve.

Well, sir, Dizzy says, he was wearing short sleeves that day, so he had nothing to wipe the nose with but his mitt, and he had to catch the ball, didn't he? So even though he is a man of principle and had no such intention, he started throwing snotballs by accident . . .

Papa rolls his eyes. Pee Wee says, "Uh-huh." I start laughing. The Kube fouls off a fastball.

For a couple innings, Dizzy says, he just mowed 'em down. But the ump got suspicious when he threw a slow snot curve that completely reversed direction three times . . .

Pee Wee says, "Uh-*huh*." Papa grins. Kubek fouls off a junk pitch. For a man who's doomed, he's hanging tough.

The ump finally canned him, Diz says, when he noticed the ball had turned green. Dizzy argued that it was grass stain, but the ump wouldn't listen because his mitt was green too, and *slimy*. Okay okay, Dizzy told the ump, I'll level with you. There's thousands of tiny snails in the St. Louis outfield here, and they leave these gooey little trails of green slime. Ump claimed the ball hadn't been in the outfield. They're in the infield too, said Dizzy. *Get out!* said the ump. Hold your horses and the boys and me'll catch you some, Dizzy said. OUT! screamed the ump. They're good eatin', Dizzy told him. Ump looked tempted, but still gave him the boot. "Anyhow we won," says Diz.

"Uh-huh," says Pee Wee. Papa smiles.

Then Kubek sees another perfect fake-grease sinker coming at him, and he feels so helpless that he just gives up the ghost—but his ghost does something brilliant: it bunts. It's not a very good bunt, way too short, but with two strikes against him he caught the Indians flat-footed, and for a wooden-headed fellow The Kube is not slow. Romana, the catcher, has to fire a snap throw. It arrives in time. It also arrives an inch or so over the top of Vic Power's big first baseman's glove, and sails way out into right field.

Papa roars and starts pounding my back. Kubek pounds for second. Harvey Kuenn runs the ball down in right, but there's no play at second. Kubek stands beaming like Pinocchio on the bag. "That could hurt 'em!" Pee Wee says. "That error was a mistake! Mistakes at this stage could hurt these Indians bad!"

Papa is looking at me like I'm some kind of terrifyingly tricky guy. "You're not Riverboat Sloan the gambler, are you?"

"Nope."

"Starvation Whitey, the famous pool hustler and all-round man of chance?"

"Nope."

"How 'bout a prophet, then? The next Ellen G. White maybe?"

I can tell by his face that he thinks this is funny, but I don't get it. All I know about Ellen G. White is that she was this super-religious 1800s lady who resembled our bulldog Gomorrah and wrote a book called The Gift of Prophecy, and the Adventists liked her book so much they hang her picture all over their churches, making it look like it's always Halloween. All I know about Ellen G. White is she isn't funny. Peter read her book once, and discovered she was the culprit who talked Adventists into banning meat-eating and makeup and jewelry and such. He said she also laid down the law about not going out on the town on Friday nights, but Everett argued that, judging by her face, it'd be a snowy Friday night in hell before anybody ever asked her. Everett said Sister White wasted her life as a prophetess, because she could've struck it rich as a bookie. But Peter told Everett no way. All Ellen G. White knew, Pete said, was how to hornswoggle religious people—who are the most hornswogglable people on earth—whereas a good bookie knows how to hornswoggle *gamblers*, who are nothing but a bunch of hornswogglers themselves. Find yourself a prophet with the gifts of a good bookie, Pete says, like Krishna in the Bog of Vod Geeta, and maybe you got something. Otherwise, he says, forget it.

But Papa's still looking at me, waiting for an answer . . .

"I'd rather be a bookie than a prophet," I tell him.

He frowns at me a second, then laughs so hard you'd think I was Bob Hope.

I still don't get it. "Concentrate!" I tell him. "Concentrate on the ballgame!"

· · · · ·

Cletis Boyer should be up next. Everett calls him Foetus Boyer, but luckily I forget why. Papa says Boyer usually bats about last, but he was red-hot last week so Stengel juggled his whole lineup to move him up to sixth—and today he has popped out, hit into a double play, and gawked at a called third strike. Stengel jerks him and sends in Elston Howard.

Elston Howard is the Yanks' normal catcher now that Yogi's getting old, but I guess he needed rest, or else the Bear was feeling frisky today. Howard's planet is exactly like ours, Everett says, except the first and last names are all reversed: Howard Elston, his name should be.

The fans are giving Mudcat Grant a standing ovation. They just figured out that except for Maris's solo homer he's been pitching a two-hit shutout against the best team in baseball—because the public address announcer just told them so. They go on cheering so long that Howard Elston has plenty of time to loosen up, while Mudcat just stands there getting tight and nervous. I take a look at Irwin's postcard. It's a picture of a cougar. It says:

Dear All, Here's the cat that ate me. Nice of it to mail this cute pix of us, huh? I'm the one on the inside. I'm healthy as ever, just a bit dead and chewed up is all. Miss you guys, specially the babies.
    XOOX, Winnie

Mudcat tips his hat a few times to try and shut the fans up, which makes them scream all the louder. "Patience, folks," Dizzy mutters. "There's not much else to cheer about in lovely downtown Cleveland."

Mudcat gets so fidgety he finally steps onto the rubber despite the noise, winds up, throws as hard as he can—and almost takes Howard Elston's head off. The fans cheer even louder, thinking it was a knockdown, but Papa says the pitch got away from him. The TV screen flashes from Mudcat looking jittery to Howard Elston getting up, his face furious, his big white pinstriped butt all filthy.

"Nice camera work," says Dizzy.

"Takes you right on down there," says Pee Wee.

Then Howard Elston grabs his crotch in his hand and pulls on it like he's trying to yank it clear off. The camera veers wildly up into the fans. "No stoppin' them Yanks," says Dizzy in a perfect deadpan.

The screen flashes to Pee Wee, who's covering his eyes with one hand, struggling not to laugh. "This is some kinda ballgame we got goin' here in sunny Ohio," he says, I think by accident.

Howard Elston takes a big blooping change-up for a strike. Mudcat calms down and throws the wicked slider next, for strike two. Then he shakes off his catcher's signal, shakes him off again, throws a fastball, and Howard takes one of those big angry swings that look like the ball somehow goes right through the bat. All it hits is mitt, though. Strike three. Out number two.

"Nobody left," says Pee Wee, "but Mr. William Skowron."

And here he comes. Moose Skowron. Hefting four bats, then three, then two, then one, overworking the poor fat batboy traipsing along behind him. Kubek hops up and down on second base, looking like he's got to piss bad. The fans start giving Mudcat another endless ovation. *"Home, home on the range,"* Dizzy croons, *"where the Mooses and the Indians play . . ."*

Pee Wee groans.

"Where seldom is heard an encouragin' word, but them Yanks just won't give up no way."

"Very nice," sighs Pee Wee.

"In-prom-two," drawls the Diz. "In-prom-two's my four-tay."

"That and French," Pee Wee says.

Moose Skowron looks nothing like a Moose. He's just big, like Irwin. He's also a lefty like Irwin, and Irwin's usually lucky, so maybe Moose will be too. Then again, Papa is a lefty . . . I decide to beef up my prediction. I reach in my pocket, pull out the roll of lucky Bazooka, nip off a chaw—and *yum!* I can taste it clear down in my toes: *yak butter!*

"It's the Moose!" I tell Papa. "He's gonna tie it up, right *now!*"

Papa scowls. "Home run?"

"Nope! No, it won't be a homer!" And for an instant I can see it: a cloud of dust, a swarm of sprawled bodies . . . No, it can't be. I'm going nuts. Let's go fishing.

Mudcat throws Skowron the same low slider Papa keeps calling a strike. Once again the ump agrees. Kubek takes a gigantic lead off second, but the Indian shortstop and second baseman ignore him and stay deep, figuring to make Moose the final out.

Mudcat throws the slider again, Moose takes it again, the ump calls it a strike again, and Stengel charges out of the dugout, showing the ump in jerky, violent sign language that the pitch didn't reach Moose's knees, which is true. But the ump pays no attention, and the fans all scream at Stengel. He scrinches up his face, sticks his middle finger in his ear, starts cleaning things furiously, and strolls back to his burrow. The count stands at 0 and 2. Skowron's face is grim. But I *still* taste the yak butter—

and the next pitch (Papa says it was that same good slider) Moose smashes so low and hard you can't even see the ball till it's in right field and Kubek is clear to third base. The ball skims the grass once. Kuenn fields it cleanly and wings it home. It was hit so hard that the play should be close. Romana, the catcher, is blocking the plate. The throw is a bull's-eye. But Kubek fakes right, hook-slides left, and Romana doesn't get a mitt on him till his feet have already swept the plate. "SAFE!" Pee Wee yells, beating the ump to the punch for once. "And it's a one-run ball-game!"

"But what's got into that Moose?" says Dizzy.

Papa leans forward, and slams his chair arms. All the stupid TV is showing us is Kubek dusting dirt off his rear. "Come *on!*" Papa hollers. The screen finally flashes.

"Uh-oh," says Pee Wee.

And there is Moose Skowron, galumphing along in the no-man's-land between second and third. He must have expected The Kube to knock Romana down rather than slide around him, so he kept right on running. But when Romana fires the ball down to Phillips at third they've got Moose by twenty-five feet. "Hot-box!" says Papa. So much for me and my yak butter.

But wait. Phillips is crouched, the ball in his bare hand, ready for the cat-and-mouse feints and tosses of the hot-box. But Skowron is not a mouse by a long shot. Phillips wastes a full second figuring out that the Moose's only plan in life is to keep on charging, then wastes another half second looking amazed by what he's figured out. He still has a half second to sidestep, like a bullfighter, but instead he uses it to brace himself like a skunk with a pair of headlights streaking toward it on a night highway. He gets the exact same results: *"Eeeeeeeugh!"* goes Dizzy as the bodies collide. About eight feet later Phillips lands mostly on his head. Skowron lands on his belly, which lands on third base. And the ball bounds into shallow left and dribbles off toward the fans.

WHAM! Papa's right hand slams the middle of my back, and he hoots and cackles as if my yak butter and me are all that's causing these ridiculous things to happen. Meanwhile Skowron sees that Phillips, his senses, and the baseball have gone three different directions and that Francona, the left fielder, and Held, the shortstop, are a long way from the loose ball. So he jumps up and heads for home. Mudcat Grant and Vic Power do the same, I guess to back up Romana, but they look more like a posse out to get Skowron for splattering Skunk Phillips all over the road. *OOOF!* Papa whams my back and howls again.

Francona reaches the baseball first, cocks his body like a gun, and fires a blur that crosses the entire TV in a slow blink of an eye. The ball hits

Moose square in the back at the same instant Moose hits Romana: *"Eeeeeeeugh!"* goes Dizzy again.

And there they are: my sprawled bodies! my cloud of dust! Romana like a beetle on his back, wiggling but unable to get up; Skowron, like a corpse on its face, near home but not on it; Mudcat, Vic Power, the ump, and Hector Lopez, the on-deck Yankee, all gaping down at them, the ump making no sign because there's no sign to make: Moose's hand is just inches from the plate, but not a finger of it's twitching. And something's missing.

"Somethin' ain't right," says Dizzy.

"The baseball!" Pee Wee hollers. "Where's the golldurn *ball?*"

As if they heard him, Mudcat and Power start scrambling over bodies, looking for it. Lopez drops to his knees and screams in Moose's ear. Power finds the ball under Romana's limp shoulder. Lopez screams louder. Moose's head twitches a little, his half-dead mind going, *Hmm. Them fingers by the plate. Mine maybe? Hmmm. Better touch home with 'em 'fore Casey gets mad . . .* And as the fingers start moving Power dives for the nearest piece of Moose-meat—

and the ball in his hand crashes/*Moose's finger brushes*/onto Moose's foot/*against home plate*/too close to tell!/*tie goes to the runner?*/"SAFE!" thunders Dizzy. SAFE! signs the ump. And this ballgame is tied!

"He's SAFE!" roars Pee Wee. "This ballgame is all tied up!"

"And for dessert today," drawls Diz, "how'd ya'll like a piece of our famous rhubarb pie?"

For a second I don't know what he's talking about. Then, sure enough, the Indians pour out of their dugout and in from the field ready to scalp Skowron for squashing their teammates, and Yankees roar up out of their barracks ready to defend Moose's dead body to the death. Some fans jump down out of the bleachers. Some cops light out after them. Dizzy starts yodeling the Lone Ranger theme song. And Pee Wee explains everything at a full yell: *"But interference terburnippa furniture!"* he explains. *"Either or other buhnerka-buhnerka automaticker Moose debimfus!"* he explains.

ROWRRRRRRRRRRRRRRRRRR! explain the fans.

Papa keeps hooting and whamming my back like there's no higher compliment in all of baseball than back-whams. Stengel and the Indians' chief shout at all three umps while the umps shout back. A big gob of Yanks circle Moose, a bigger gob of Indians circle the Yanks, both gobs shrieking and woo-woo-wooing like retarded braves and bluecoats in some dumb Hollywood rerun. But Moose never moves, and you just can't kill a guy who's already dead, because what's the point?

The woo-woo-wooing starts to lose momentum. Romana somehow staggers to his feet. "God, catchers are tough!" Papa says. The cops nab the runaway fans. Phillips is helped from the field by a player and a trainer. A stretcher floats through the circling mobs, lands at Skowron's side, and two men in white coats carefully load him, hoist him, and start to bear him away.

Then Moose's eyes open. He sits up, and looks around.

"That man was playin' *possum!*" Pee Wee shouts.

"Like fun he was," says Dizzy.

"I don't think so either," Papa says. "He was out cold."

The Yankees surround Skowron, jumping up and down, lamming his head and shoulders. "He *figured them Indians'd scalp him!*" Pee Wee screams. "So *he played possum till his calvary arrived!*"

"Then his own dang calvary whomped the livin' kidneys out of him," says Diz.

The Yankees really *are* pounding on him. Moose doesn't look very happy, or very healthy either. "That man has got *smarts!*" shouts Pee Wee.

"When he's coldcocked," says Diz.

"Professor William Skowron!" hollers Pee Wee.

"Professor P. W. Reese," mutters Dizzy.

"Kade the Bookie Prophet," says Papa.

"I'm not either!" I laugh, remembering Krishna.

"What a ballgame!" shouts Pee Wee.

"Extra innings, looks like," Papa says, still beaming at me.

"I love baseball!" I tell him. "Let's go fishing!"

He laughs once more, then wipes his face and forehead with his sleeve in that careful way pitchers do, so as not to be accused of throwing spit. He nods. "We can catch the rest on the car radio."

"What I wanna know," Dizzy wonders, "is how they're gonna score that mess."

"Darn good question," says Pee Wee. "And we'll be back with the answer, right after these very fine messages."

CHAPTER THREE
Excepting Christ

Bear ye one another's burdens, and so fulfill the law of Christ . . .
    —Galatians 6
For every man shall bear his own burden . . .
    —Galatians 6
Honor thy father and thy mother . . .
    —Mark 7
And call no man your father upon the earth . . .
    —Matthew 11
Love thy neighbor as thyself . . .
    —Matthew 5
Let the dead bury their dead . . .
    —Matthew 8
Peace I leave with you, my peace I give unto you . . .
    —John 14
Think not that I am come to send peace . . .
    —Matthew 10
Lord, I believe . . .
    —Mark 9
Help thou my unbelief . . .
    —Mark 9

Camas / October / 1960

Mama is standing on the front porch holding a huge piece of square-pan pie out in front of her like a hymnal. Bet and Freddy are flanking her, each clinging to one of her knees. Irwin is clumping up the sidewalk in the Indian Summer sun, just getting home from school. "It's a secret!" Bet yells at him.

"Guess who!" hollers Freddy.

"They mean guess what," Mama says.

Irwin frowns, till he notices the pie: blackberry, a mountain of it, still hot from the oven, with an ice-cream snowcap sending vanilla creeks trickling down steep purple sides. Like a sleepwalker, he gropes two-handedly toward it. Mama whips it away. "You've got to guess the secret," she says.

His face crumbles. "No fair!" he yells, pointing at me. I'm sitting on the steps enjoying the show—and devouring an equally majestic mountain, snow first.

"Kade already figured it out," Mama says.

I grin as smugly as possible. Mama sits on the steps beside me, knowing we may be here a while. Irwin's first guess is typical: "UNCLE MARV IS HERE!" he roars, as if extra volume will make stupidity smarter.

Mama rolls her eyes. "You think I'd bake pie in honor of a thing like my brother Marvin?"

Irwin looks disappointed. He's gaga about the guy, because when Marv isn't running the Butee Bar (that's his and Mary Jane's hair parlor up in Spokane) he's a part-time farmer, which is what Irwin wants to be full-time someday. I take a noisy bite to get his mind back on business. He starts to salivate. "It's the pie itself!" he shouts.

Mama shakes her head.

"It's a new car!"

Mama winces.

"A new house, then!"

She rolls her eyes again.

"A wedding? No! A funeral, yeah! No! Wait! I got it! It's that, that, that, THAT READER'S DIGEST DREAM CRUISE TO HAWAII!"

His shouts are so loud the twins take cover under Mama's apron. They're laughing in there, though. "Shoot!" he says. "I give! I'm stark rarvin' starvin'!"

"The saying is *stark ravin' stravin'*," I tell him.

"It's rarvin' starvin'!" he blusters. "It's *my* stomach! I ought to know!"

"You've got to guess anyhow," says Mama.

He groans so pitifully that the twins come out from under the apron, thinking he's actually in pain. Noticing their concern, he smiles his biggest, cuddliest smile at them—which I have to admit is damned big and cuddly. They smile two cuddly little smiles back. "My li'l buddies," he croons, setting Bet on one knee and Freddy on the other. "My two bestest little friends!" They beam up at him. Unbelievable suckers. "Hey!" he says in an incredibly loud whisper. "How would my buddies like a neat special treat?" Their eyes get big. They nod their heads. "All right!" he says. "Listen. Just tell your big pal Winnie what this silly secret of Mama's is, and he'll give you each a nice big juicy bite o' pie!"

Freddy covers her mouth and scrambles down off his leg. Bet scowls and sticks out her tongue. Irwin looks flummoxed—till he notices Bet's tongue. It's bright purple. "They ate already!" he moans.

"They don't know the secret anyway," Mama says.

The pie is great. The secret's better. Irwin's misery makes both better yet. I lean toward him, stuff in another bite, and tell him, "Yo ife cweam iv melling away to nuffing." And when he sees it's true Irwin's face starts to melt too.

Then something in him snaps—you can almost hear it. He is suddenly serious. He looks almost intelligent. "Uh-oh," Mama says. "You pushed him too far, Kade."

She's right. Irwin likes to avoid thinking, but when he's forced he's not half bad at it. "All right, dangit!" he mutters. "It's got nothing to do with us four, 'cause we're all too boring to have secrets."

"Hey now!" Mama protests, but Irwin goes on thinking aloud.

"It can't be Everett 'cause he's at school and nothing good happens to Everett at school. Pete? No. When Pete has a secret nobody *ever* finds out. So it's got to be Papa . . . except it can't be, 'cause he's at the mill. Grandawma? Naw, she's too— Hey wait! *Papa.* I know! That *thumb* business! That Perry Mason deal! You know, his court suit! his law case! his whatever you call that weird *surgery* deal!"

Mama shakes her head but hands him his pie. "Your father goes to court next Thursday," she says, unable to hide a smile. "Of course anything could happen, but his lawyer says he's got a darn good chance of—"

"HOORAW!" Irwin thunders. "*Papa's gonna win his thumb back!*" He starts whooping like an idiot, stops to stuff in a huge bite of pie, then goes right on whooping out these awful purple *wahoos* that look like his mouth is full of guts. Bet and Freddy watch, full of admiration.

"Let's not count our chickens," Mama says nervously. "He hasn't won a penny yet. He's going to need our prayers."

"It'f not Furvday yet!" Irwin blurts through the pie. "Fenk *povitive*, Mama!" And he goes back to his gory wahooing as he demolishes the entire berry mountain in the time it takes me to eat about three bites.

"We helped," Freddy brags, swinging on his knee.

"Yeah!" hollers Bet, who takes after Irwin in shouting almost everything she says. "We helped a lot! Mama said!"

"*You* helped?" Irwin snarls in a big mean voice. (They love big mean voices.) "How could *you* help? Are you lawyers or what?"

They don't know what he's talking about, but grin at him anyway. Then he grabs them by the backs of their homemade overalls and hoists them, one in each hand, clear up in front of his face. "How did *you* help?" he repeats. "I wanna know!"

"They helped with the pie!" Mama says. "Now put them down."

Irwin pretends to start to drop them, gets a gasp out of Mama, then jerks them back up in his face. "Do you little hemorrhoids expect me to believe you had anything to do with that delicious pie?" he growls. "Ha! Do you hear me? *HA!*"

Dangling high over the lethal concrete, the twins cover their mouths with fat purple fingers, then emit polite little tea-parlor titters.

"So tell me what *really* happened!" Irwin says. "You just got in her way all day, didn't you! You just went bummo in your pants and whined '*Mommy-I-Wanna-This! Mommy-I-Wanna-That!*' all day, didn't you! DIDN'T YOU!"

"We pin-rolled the dough!" squeaks Freddy.

"And now we wanna airplane!" bellows Bet.

"There will be no airplaning!" Mama says. But the twins look great, hanging just alike in the sun there, arms out like wings, brown hair and skinny legs dangling.

"Contack!" shouts Freddy.

"*No* contact!" Mama shouts.

"But, Mama honey!" Irwin says in a thick Southern drawl. "They pin-rolled the dough! You *know* what the Good Book says."

"None of your darned Bible games now!"

"*Games?*" Irwin lowers the girls, letting them hang at his knees like a couple of buckets. He looks incredulous. He looks perfectly serious. "And you call yourself a *believer!* Do I have to spell it out? Have you backslid that far? Very well then. Deuteronomy three, sixteen: '*And they who pin-roll the dough shall be airplaned. Verily, unto illness shall they be flown about the yard. Unto airsickness, yea, and unto every other type of disaster shall they be propellered. And their poor mama shall watch though it cleaveth her heart in twain to do so!*' "

Irwin's getting awfully good at fake Bible quotes. He's picked it up from Everett, who rattles them off so smoothly you'd swear he was giving you the straight Moses till you stop to think about what he said. Mama's face is a wrestling match, Scowl versus Smile. But the twins are still dangling, and mothers do hate danger. Scowl wins. "That's enough of your nonsense!" she snaps.

"It's not *my* nonsense!" Irwin says solemnly. "It's the *Lord's!*"

The girls make the sounds of twin engines starting. He swings them up to shoulder height again. Mama gets truly mad. "You think you're so cute! But what if one of those coverall buttons snaps off?"

"*This!*" I holler, and I flop back on the steps, writhe like my spine is crushed, roll my eyes up under the open lids, and send a big purple pie-glob sliding out the side of my mouth. Irwin howls. Mama about barfs. The twins barely notice: they eat this way all the time.

"They pin-rolled the dough, Mama!" Irwin yells over their engine noises. "It's God's Law! It's, it's *out of my HANDS!*"—and he lets out a gasp as the twins seem to leave his grip and plunge toward the concrete. Bet shrieks, Freddy whoops, Mama's hands fly to the top of her head, and I choke, though only from laughing: if there are any two things I trust in this family it's Mama's button-sewing and Irwin's muscles.

"Ready aim FIRE!" Bet hollers when her skull doesn't quite smash against the steps, and Irwin zwoops them up and takes off sprinting. Mama watches, her hands flat on her head like a prisoner of war's, her bare toes writhing in her red rubber thongs, and weird, doglike whimpers rising in her throat. But as Irwin roars round the yard and the twins scream and squeal, as he yo-yos and loop-the-loops them, almost but never quite splintering their sweet little noggins against everything hard, sharp and dangerous in the world, the whimpers move from Mama's throat down to her belly, change into laughter, and gain volume and power till she's howling and helpless, her face young and wild and pretty as the delinquent teenaged daughter of the woman she looked like seconds ago. Irwin pretend-trips on the water faucet. He pretend-crushes the girls when he falls. He pretend-screams and flails the twisted arm and leg he's pretend-fractured. And the three of them, the two of Mama, the entire five or six of us laugh like there's nothing funnier in this world than crushed toddlers and fractured limbs.

That was the kind of mood Papa's upcoming court case put us in. And all week long we *did* "fenk povitive," and *did* pray for him to win the settlement and the odd but usable new thumb he deserved. Our cause was just, our aim unselfish, our prayers heartfelt and devout.

And on Thursday, Papa lost.

Attic Document,
circa 1963

School: John McLoughlin High
Class: Mr. Hergert's Freshman English
Assignment: The Long (Long Long) Essay

THE HISTORY OF MY DAD FROM HIS BIRTH
UP TO KINCAIDS'S
BY IRWIN DAVID CHANCE

Chapter 1. The Parents

My father Hugh Chance was born in 1929 in Chicago Illinnois on
May 5 1929. He was no relation to Frank Chance the famous first
baseman, Dean Chance the famous young pitcher, or Fat Chance the
famous expression (ha ha). But his father Everett Chance, named after
my brother (you remember Everett!) was a mathamatics professor at
the Univercity of Chicago (Illionois) who really wished he was a Pro
Ballplayer, and almost was once, for the Cubs right there in Chicago,
who weren't so bad at times in those days, and Wriggly Field has
always had one of the finest parks in all of Pro Ball inspite of its got
no lights. The father's wife (Hugh's mom) Marion Becker Chance
however never liked baseball, for Marion was an Englishwoman and
could not for the life of her understand it. The game of crickit on the
otherhand is practicly nothing but English baseball, which most
Englishmen live and breath for, yet Marion never liked it either. So
maybe she just wasn't cut out for sports.
Marion did very much like Charles Darwin the famous scientist so

hated by such Christians as our pastor at church Elder Babcock due to Evolution however. Marion Becker Chance has always been an extremely serious type woman, who for instants loves to go down to OMSI more than anyplace else on Earth as they call the Oregon Museum of Science and Industry for short, and lovely spots such as the beach find her buried in rocks at feet of cliffs with her back to the beautiful blue ocean, digging around for fossils and such.

Besides a Scientist Marion is also a Pacifist and an Atheist. This means she is basically against most things, such as War, Sports, and God. Don't get me wrong here. She is a fine woman in her way. Just a bit too serious and sinnical, we feel. My brothers Everett and Peter (you remember Pete!) think this wierd outlook of Marions must of started up because her two brothers or maybe three were either all three or both killed during W.W.1, which Marion calls The Great War, inspite of W.W.2 being Greater. It also probably never helped when both her parents died shortly thereafter of a combination of broken hearts and the Spanish Inflewenza. Anyhow The Great War destroyed England forever, Marion claims, inspite of it still being there as I like to kid her, although kidding Marion is about like feeding the pearls before the swine in most cases, since pearls, swine and Marion all laugh about the same amount. Anyhow this destroyed condition of England was why Marion Becker Chance migrated to America, along with sorrow being the other chief reason. But then she turned around and never became a U.S. Citizen either, which later had very serious aftereffects for both her and my dad both, by whom I mean of course our hero, her son, Hugh. In 1928 however, Marion cleaned up her glum act long enough to snag a big southpaw math teacher at the Univercity there in Chicago, named Professor Everett Chance as mentioned. But we call him Everett Senior to fend off confusing him with our own Everett, who we call plain old Everett, for short.

Getting on with our story then, Everett Senior according to reports was about as All American of a guy and as great of a guy as a guy could get apparently, thereby proving what they say about opposites attract so far as him and long-faced English Marion was concerned. Unfortunately Everett Senior is also now dead at present, almost as if everything Marion touched turned into a corpse at some fairly quick point in time. In my heart I feel that this bad luck of hers is a big fat HINT, and that things would go much better for her if she would only except Christ as her personnel Lord and Savoir. But as our Everett says, it'll be a snowy day in H-E-Blank-Blank before Marion Becker

Chance does a thing like that. Meanwhile she continues to love Charles Darwin, hate God, Sports and War, and be known to us as Grandawma since that was how Everett said her name when he was a tyke and it stuck, and to this day her apartment resides less than a mile from our house here in town, unfortunately allowing no pets so that her skanky bulldog Gomorrah stinks it up here with us. But I like her. Grandawma I mean. Gomorrah too, as far as possible, I suppose.

Getting back to the son my father Hugh. After six years of life in Illinoiss he can't remember all that well due to his smallness during this period of time, Hugh moved to Pullman Washington where he grew up due to his dad Everett Senior took a job there at the State College of Washington (GO COUGS!!) to teach mathamatics as usual, but also to coach Varsity Baseball as well. He didn't tell Marion about the baseball part till after they were in Washington however, which turned out to have loud and violent aftereffects.

Getting back to the parents here a minute, Everett Senior felt it wasn't any of his wife's dang business, him deciding to coach baseball. Whether or not the man should wear the pants in the family, he should at least be allowed to wear his own pants, was how he felt about it. Marion however felt that the whole family was more or less jammed into one big pair of pants so that everything anybody else did could be bichbichbiched about by anybody else. Of course this goes against everything the Bible has to teach us about mankind, womankind, and the pants. But Marion hated the Bible, so what could you do? "NOBODY IS TELLING YOU TO COACH BASEBALL!" Hugh reports Everett Senior spouting at his firey wife when she kept having duck fits. Hugh gets quite the bang out of chucklingly recalling his folks's loud and colorful debates of this period, both about baseball and other matters such as

ARE WOMEN TRULY SMARTER?
ARE ATHELETES ALL A BUNCH OF WAR-MONGERERS?
WHOSE TURN TO DO DISHES? and of course
GOD? since Everett Senior was a good Episcopalian as a kid and always believed on Him no matter what, right up until he died in Germany, same as me, except of course I'm Adventist not Episcopalian and have not died, as of yet.

But getting back to the southpawed Hugh here, it is interesting to notice how inspite of her hate of sports Marion
Number 1, was lefthanded and
Number 2, loved to throw things!

Glasses, plates, and even objects, such as large lamps, got regularly smashed to smithereens in hers and her husband's loud and colorful debates, Hugh reports. Gladly, neither opponent came to much harm, except how words will sometimes cut deep, between throws. There were close ones though. The most famous close one for instants was this fork Marion hurled clear across the kitchen only to stick deep in the oak table between two of Everett Senior's helpless fingers. To Marion's shocked dismay however this only overjoyed the stalwart husband, by proving that both sides of the family had tremendous arms, so surely young Hugh would have one also!

Getting off the subject here a minute, this same oak table resides in our kitchen to this day, causing my brothers and me while eating dinner, breakfast, lunch, between-meal-snacks or whatever to break out pondering those four deep forkholes. She is so skinny! we ponder. And only four foot eleven! we ponder. How the heck did she do it! So one day Pete and Everett decided to experiment, throwing forks at a similar type piece of wood at a similar type distance and angle till totally exhausted, and listen to this! THEY NEVER STUCK A ONE! This finding began to make what Marion did seem like a total Miracle, or as young Kincaid says, like a total waist of a Miracle. But at the Miracle Point here it is interesting to notice how the experiment hit each of us four brothers different, depending on the type of person we were. Everett for instance, a Doubting Thomas Type, decided Marion must be lying and actually just stabbed the fork into the table trying for Everett Senior's hand. Peter on the otherhand, a Religious Type though a bit weird from such Christian standpoints as my own, felt that anger is so powerful of a force that a really powerful anger could convince a thrown fork to stick superhumanly even if we can't stick one ourselves under more regular types of conditions. Meanwhile myself, a Faithful Adventist Type, agreed with Pete, as did young Kincaid, a Fairly Normal Type who by the way will be in your class the year after next and is one smart cookie Mr. Hergert! Anyhow, Papa finally got so sick of us pondering those four deep fork-holes that he filled them with puddy and painted the whole table dark green.

Getting back off the sidetracks then, Everett Senior instead of becoming a famous math genius or fossil expert such as Marion hoped in his spare time became Varsity Baseball Coach at Washington State College from 1936 up to 1942, which is a pretty famous thing to be itself if you ask me. You can still see his picture and read about him in old Cougar yearbooks, and you'll find his name proudly listed under

COACH on the trophy in that glass case at the football stadium there, for winning the League Crown once, in 1939. HOW MANY MATH AND FOSSIL EXPERTS'S NAMES DO YOU SEE LISTED ON THAT TROPHY? is what I sometimes want to ask Marion. I don't do it however, as she is quite old and rickety enough as is.

Kincaid:
Sabbath School / Washougal, Washington / February / 1963

Brother Beal has stuck me in The Corner again. What happens in The Corner is you sit facing the wall with a Bible in your lap till you've memorized this week's Memory Verse. What Brother Beal hasn't yet figured out is that I don't learn my Memory Verses on purpose. I like it in The Corner.

There are six of us here this morning, which is about average unless it's some verse such as *Shew me a penny* or *Jesus wept*. Beal's helper, Sister Durrel, had to scour the whole basement to come up with enough Bibles for us. Then, when she was passing them out, she smiled and gave the only illustrated one to me. I about died! Sister Durrel is so beautiful compared to everything else at Sabbath School it's like my eyeballs turn into compass needles, and she's North. One time up in church I stared at her so long that Everett got embarrassed and gouged me in the ribs, telling me to knock it off, but I gouged him right back and said, "Why should I?" He gouged me again and whispered, "Because Sister Durrel is at least eight years older than you, and engaged to Brother Beal, and if she was your age she wouldn't have breasts and her thick brown hair would be in scraggly pigtails and she'd be as knobbly-kneed and snot-nosed as every other girl you know!" I'll admit I hadn't thought of some of that. But I gouged him right back again and said that if she was my age I'd ask her to marry me anyhow: I'd just set the wedding date for the age she is now.

It was by accident that I discovered how much nicer it is getting sent to The Corner than it is sticking with the Sabbath School class. The main trouble with the class isn't Brother Beal's lectures, which are only boring. It's these cockeyed study groups they break us up into. After a hard week of *real* school, the last thing a person needs first thing Saturday morning is some goody-goody mom or dad grilling them on this Sabbath's lesson in *Pathfinder Magazine* or *My Little Friend*. The Corner is supposedly a punishment: you sit with your back to the class, and you can't talk. But what good is freedom of speech if all you can use it for is answering goody-goody study group questions? To me it makes more sense to get thrown in The Corner, where the freedom of not-speaking allows you to sit back and rest. Resting is what Sabbath is all about anyway. It's what God Himself does with His Saturdays. It's right there in the Bible, Everett says: "Six days shalt thou labor and do all thy work, but on the Seventh Day God rested, so human beings should do the same. And getting all gussied up and going to church is *not* resting." All Mama ever says to that, though, is, "Pipe down and get your tie on."

Everett and Peter are in an older class that hasn't got a Corner, and the twins are in a kiddie class that's actually just a bunch of brats fidgeting and crying. But Irwin is in my class, and I've tried to share the good news: I've told him how nice it is here in The Corner. But he refuses to take advantage of it due to this Memory Verse Streak he's got going . . .

For 160-some Sabbaths in a row now Irwin has nailed his Memory Verse dead—and the way Brother Beal treats him, you'd think it was DiMaggio's hitting streak. "Iron Man Irwin" he calls him. It's kind of embarrassing. Still it's a nice thing for Winnie, since he's a bit of a dodo at real school. He feels he's keeping the streak going for Jesus. He even told his study group how his memory didn't work worth a hoot till he asked the Lord to come into his life and make some repairs on it. Of course Beal and the other Sabbath School teachers could eat that kind of crap for breakfast, lunch and dinner, but I think Irwin really meant it. He seems genuinely fond of Jesus. Peter does too, come to think of it, though he gives his Sabbath School teachers ulcers of the brain by being just as fond of Buddha and Krishna and Finn MacCool and Odin One-Eye and King Rama and I don't remember who all, thanks to his ongoing adventures with heathen reading material. Everett on the other hand thinks of Jesus as just one more of these out-of-this-world Nice Guys who, as Leo Durocher predicted, finished dead last. It's right there in the Bible, Everett says: "Christ admits it Himself. 'I am the Alpha and the Omega. The First—and the Last.'"

It's strange the way everybody has their own pet notion about Jesus, and nobody's pet notion seems to agree with anybody else's. Grandawma, for instance, says He's "just a defunct social reformer." Then there's Papa, who once said He's God's Son all right, and that He survived the crucifixion just fine, but that the two-thousand-year-old funeral service His cockeyed followers call Christianity probably made Him sorry He did. Meanwhile there's Freddy, who's six now, and who told me she saw Christ hiding under her bed one night, but that all He'd say to her was

"*Pssst! Shhh! Pharisees!*" And Bet, who spent a whole day making a Christmas card for Uncle Marv and Aunt Mary Jane last year, then got so proud of the card that she refused to mail it to anybody but herself. "That's the Christmas spirit!" Everett told her. Then we looked to see what she was so proud of, and it turned out to be this whole army of crayon angels, in these gold sort of football helmets, charging into Bethlehem while in the sky above them huge red and green letters copied from a Christmas carol book Bet couldn't yet read proclaimed:

JOY TO THE WORDL!
THE SAVIOR RESIGNS!

Personally I'm not sure just who or what Christ is. I still pray to Him in a pinch, but I talk to myself in a pinch too—and I'm getting less and less sure there's a difference. I used to wish somebody would just *tell* me what to think about Him. Then along came Elder Babcock, telling and telling, acting like Christ was running for President of the World, and he was His campaign manager, and whoever didn't get out and vote for the Lord at the polls we call churches by casting the votes we call tithes and offerings into the ballot boxes we call offering plates was a wretched turd of a sinner voting for Satan by default. Mama tries to clear up all the confusion by saying that Christ is exactly what the Bible says He is. But what *does* the Bible say He is? On one page He's a Word, on the next a bridegroom, then He's a boy, then a scapegoat, then a thief in the night; read on and He's the messiah, then oops, He's a rabbi, and then a fraction—a third of a Trinity—then a fisherman, then a broken loaf of bread. I guess even God, when He's human, has trouble deciding just what He is.

The class has split into study groups now. This is the part that makes The Corner truly worth being in. In Sister Durrel's group they've started reading about the furnace Shadrach and his brothers got thrown into, but at least they've got Sister Durrel to stare at. Over in Brother Beal's group they're listening to a story out of *Pathfinder Magazine* called "Why Bobby Degan Told Satan No," and all there is to look at is Beal himself and a clump of dead milkweed growing in a concrete window well behind him. In Brother Benke's group, just behind me, this weird religious kid named Stanley Stubenfelker is telling how he wrote a special prayer for his grandparents' fiftieth wedding anniversary that made his whole dang family cry, so can he please recite it to the group? Brother Benke says,

"Why, certainly, Stanley." But on about word three of the prayer my best friend, Augie Mosk, starts crying his eyes out, and Irwin laughs so hard that Benke gets mad and sends Augie to the other Corner, where he's resting now, like God and me. Way over in Sister Harg's circle, which is all girls, they're also trying to study the Fiery Furnace, but they've got the giggles. I thought they were giggling at Augie at first, but now I see that the problem is their stage props. They've got a big feltboard leaning on a chair, with a felt oven on it, and a felt Shadrach, Meshach and Abednego cooking in the oven. Jocie Best covered the brothers with red felt flames, and that was fine. Then Zulie Dawson added three big blond-haired Guardian Angels to protect them, and that worked too. But when Dollie Edgerton tried to stick the golden halos on the Angels the felt on the halo-backs was so worn out that they kept falling on the floor, and without halos the whole scene somehow lost its religious feeling and started looking like three Swedes and three beatniks in bathrobes committing suicide together in a sauna, so *tee hee hee hee hee!*

I take the Bible Sister Durrel gave me, flip it open at random, and look to see what God's Good Book has to say to me today. My first flip is typical: "*And Doeg the Edomite turned, and he fell upon the priests, and slew on that day fourscore and five persons . . . And Nob, the city of the priests, smote he with the edge of the sword, both men and women, children and sucklings, and oxen, and asses . . .*"

Ugh. I try again: "*And they made an end of all the men that had taken strange wives by the first day of the first month . . .*"

Okay. That's enough words. Time for illustrations. I hunt down every color plate in my Bible one by one, bending each at the corner so I can find it again. Then I decide to conduct an award ceremony among them . . .

First category? How about Stupidest Picture?

Ah. Our first nominee is one of Jesus trying to drive a pack of money-lenders out of the temple with a whip about the size of a spaghetti noodle. And here's another candidate: an idiotic-looking Peter staggering across the water, his mouth wide open, his arms splayed out like a toddler's, while Christ just watches, grinning like a mean big brother, rowing backwards in the boat. But hey! The surprise winner, I see, has just got to be Noah's Ark. It seems like the typical illustration at first—just a big wooden barge perched on a mountaintop, with the rainbow arching over it and a puddle-pocked landscape looking soggy but fairly inviting down below. But soon as I look more closely it hits me: when Noah and the animals get around to stepping out the Ark door, they're all going to fall about four thousand feet straight down this humongous cliff and land splat in a pile of big sharp rocks.

Next category: Sexiest Picture. But in Bibles, this one's always tough. My first nominee is Salome, standing in front of King Herod flashing a nice pair of dancer's legs—but the head of John the Baptist bleeding all over the TV tray in her hands cancels the legs out fast. Here's one of a Delilah, happily hacking Samson's hair off, with a face a little like Sophia Loren's—but it's Samson who's got by far the showier legs and breasts in the picture. That leaves just one other illustration with any amount of skin showing: the old standby, Eve and Adam in The Garden. They're stark naked, which you'd think would help, but their backs are to the camera, and Adam's lumpy body makes it darned easy to believe that God made him just the other morning out of a big wad of clay. On close inspection there does seem to be a sexy area on Eve at first—a nice little place where her naked waist curves in, then out again, as it works its way downward. But right where the crack in her bottom should start the trusty bushes rush up and wreck the view. It's not the bushes that totally luke the thing for me, though. It's Eve's hair. Not only is it egg-yolk yellow, it's all teased and ratted up, as if Uncle Marv had just been working her over at the Butee Bar up in Spokane . . .

I'm not sure what the word *sexy* even means sometimes. I don't even *care* what it means, normally. It's the kind of thing you think about at church, though, because there's nothing else to do. In the end I pretend I'm a girl just long enough to give the award to Samson.

Best Picture? Now this one's easy. It's one of David, all the way. Not the king, just the kid. All he's doing is walking along by a stream, a stick in one hand, a sheep across his shoulders, the slingshot he'll eventually nail Goliath with dangling from his belt. I suppose the big meadow he's crossing could be the green pasture he gets made to lie down in before he heads on over to the Valley of the Shadow of Death, but the illustration doesn't make you think of that. It doesn't make you think of anything. That's what I like about it. There's nothing biblical going on—nobody getting burned or sacrificed or swallowed, no one getting driven out of or cast down from or dashed against anything. It's just a normal piece of world for once: some nice running water, some strewn rocks, a wide empty grassland. The yellow flowers by the creek could be buttercups. The stream could be packed with trout. The only flaw is the sheep—but it isn't the illustrator's or David's fault that the sheep bugs me. It's Micah Barnes's fault. Micah is the new assistant pastor's kid. He's the one who told me a year or so ago that some people fuck sheep.

Of course I called him a filthy liar. But he just laughed, popped open his Bible, and actually *proved* what he'd said! Somewhere in Leviticus, it was. There were no actual scenes describing guys and sheep humping away, but there were detailed instructions on how you had to kill them if they did. The whole idea about made me puke. I mean, why would Moses even *mention* such a thing? I would certainly never have thought of it on my own! He even went on to list several other types of animals you had to kill guys for screwing.

I feel sorry for Micah Barnes, though. He's the kind of mixed-up little church rat you meet pretty often in Adventist basements (which is where they always seem to stick the kids). His dad's an up-and-coming preacher, so Micah spends his whole life stuck in church camps, church schools, church basements. And since all he hears there is how good and holy the Church is and how cruel and filthy the Outside World is, and since he hates his good and holy basement life, he assumes he'd rather be in the Outside World, and so tries to prove how much he knows about it —by acting cruel and talking filthy.

The first time we met, Micah walked up to me, pointed like I was something in a cage, and screamed, "God *damn*, kid! You got ears just like a monkey! *Hahahaha! Monkey Ears!*"

Next to the mud pies Everett slings around, this little dirt clod didn't even wing me. I just gave Micah the cold hard stare and turned to walk away. But then this girl, Vera Klinger, had to stick her oar in. And to complicate matters, Vera has a harelip. You can't really see the thing, but you sure can hear it. "Nat's nod nice!" she snapped at Micah. "Nyou soodn't snay sengs nike nat!"

Micah was stunned for a second. Then he went apeshit: "*HAHAHAHA!*" he shrieked. "*Nough snitty, nittle nirl! Nup nyours! Nup nyours!*" So, right there in the basement of God's House, I had to punch the new assistant pastor's kid smack in the mouth.

It wasn't much of a punch. I figured that with a lip like hers Vera must be used to insults, and I could see already that the new kid had strange problems, so I took the kind of contact swing a batter does when the hit-and-run is on. But Micah went down like my fist was a shot put, curled up like a salted slug, screamed like a baby with a diaper pin sticking in it —and then had the gall to tell me later that he was "turning the other cheek," like Jesus says to do! Of course Brother Beal ran over and tried to find out what had happened, but Vera started nuttering and nurring at him so frantically that he gave up, sent Micah to the bathroom, then ordered me for the first time in my life to go sit in The Corner with the

Memory Verse dunces. I was mad for a while. But I ended up enjoying The Corner so much I haven't learned a Memory Verse since.

Irwin's <u>HISTORY OF MY DAD</u> continued

Chapter 2. A Year Of Great Confusion

Everett Seniors's new Cougar coaching job was during the Great Depression, and to prove it Hugh reports actual Washington State Varsity Ballplayers practicing ball in corked logging boots and some guys barefoot even, just to show you how unable they were to afford cleats. Imagine if you will some corked logging booted guy's logging boot landing on some barefooted guy's bare foot. YOUCH! to say the least. Imagine also how some prospects had no gloves and injured their hands quite seriously trying to catch the stupid ball at times. These were the hazards of The Grand Old Game in those days, so that we can thank our lucky stars to live now instead!

It soon became visible at quite a young age that Hugh Chance was already a better ballplayer than most of Everett Seniors's actual college players, especially his left arm. This became most visible of all when he was twelve and started pitching BP as batting practice was known as, at which he enjoyed striking out Cougar sluggers one after the next with his fastball until his dad had to start yelling at him. "EASE OFF!" he had to start yelling. "I WANT MY TEAM TO PRACTICE HITTING, NOT STRIKING OUT!" he also yelled. So Hugh eased off, though secretly the whole thing gave him one heck of a kick in the pants.

To jump backwards in time for a more sad instants of his fine arm, Hugh killed a meadowlark right out of the air with an apple at a distance of approximately third base to first when he was ten years of age, causing his father to say it was nothing to brag about and disgusting Marion into sending him to bed without supper. <u>Be darn careful what you aim at even when certain you won't hit it!</u> is the lesson Hugh claims it taught him.

Not so sad but more illegal was another arm story that happened when he was thirteen and bet several Cougar ballplayers that he could bust the back window out of the Twin Falls Flyer caboose with a baseball in one throw, and I mean the <u>back</u> window here, not just some side window such as any moron or juvenile delinquent could bust. This means the Flyer is flying sixty miles per hour straight away from you so that you've got to throw the ball faster enough than sixty to bust glass plus accurate enough to even hit it, the caboose window being quite small. The whole bet however turned into a humble lesson in overcockiness for young Hugh, who bet three guys a buck each then made such a perfect throw that he hit that little cross of wood dividing the older type wooden cabooses's windows into four pains dead center, and never busted a thing. Cutting cordwood with a bucksaw at a dollar per cord was how Hugh payed off his debts. Such was a youngsters's future when it came to gambling! is the lesson Hugh claims he learned this time out as he sawed and sawed and sawed and sawed and sawed and sawed and sawed and sawed and sawed and sawed and sawed and sawed and sawed. Imagine if you can the blisters! While you're at it imagine a whole cord of wood costing but one dollar! How the world changes is beyond me!

But getting down to baseball here, what young Hugh had going for him in his gifted southern paw was a big strong body for a boy his age plus a fastball that hopped "like a dang jack rabbit!" as Mel Franks, one of the Cougars always striking out on it, used to say. This blazing hopping fastball was also extremely accurate as you can see from the caboose. Which was lucky. Because the odd thing was how every time Hugh went to throw a curveball Everett Senior turned purple and screamed at him. "SAVE THAT ARM!" he screamed. "YOU'LL BE NEEDING ALL THOSE LIGAMENTS AND TENDONS CURVEBALLS TEAR OUT OF YOU AT SUCH A GROWING AGE WHEN YOU ARE A THIRTYSOME YEAR OLD VETERAN STILL PLAYING PRO BALL!" he screamed. This had been Everett Seniors's own mistake as a youngster, Hugh reports, and being the type of young man who hung himself upon his dad's every word Hugh never learned a curveball worth a hang due to this screaming, which later had serious aftereffects. But there are payoffs to be had hanging from a dad's words too, such as getting so sharp at math, science and other subjects that they skipped him a grade, I think maybe the fourth. And even without a curveball as an eighth grader a year too young for his age, Hugh pitched two no-hitters, went 8 and 0, got straight A's and hit over .500 if you can believe those numbers!

In high school, however, Life was soon to take a far more serious bent for Hugh and his family, especially Everett Senior if you can call getting killed a bent in Life. First off the Depression had ended. Secondly W.W.2 had started up. The third thing: Everett Senior was

too old to join the military unless he wanted to. But all along as I
have not yet mentioned he had an expired pilot's license left over from
his youthful talents as a barnstorming pilot of small airplanes. So when
America started losing the War a little, such as at Pearl Harbor and
such, Everett Senior decided we could use a good man who flew and
signed up for the Air Force wing of the United States Army.

In Everett Seniors's (now known as Master Sergeant Everett
Chance's) last letter home to Hugh and Marion, he told how he had
started flying a little Piper Cub recognisance plane around France,
Switzerland, Beljum and such. "I have finally made it up to the
Cubs," was how he put it, "even if it is only the Piper and not the
Chicago!" Young Hugh cracked up heartily over this. Old Marion
however never grinned a lick, for as a Pacifist she hated Piper Cubs,
Churchill and Hitler, ovens and bombs, Eisenhower, Italy, and all else
to do with the World Situation at such a tough point in History.

Hugh on the other hand decided he should try even harder to do all
the things which he decided to try and do, and to prove it he made
the varsity baseball team his freshman year and went 6 and 2, then as
a sophomore went 9 and 1 and hit .420, including his first no-hitter.
But smack into the middle of this great ballplaying dropped the
bombshell him and Marion had hoped all along not to be waiting for.
Everett Seniors's Piper Cub had either broke down or run out of gas
deep behind enemy territory. The lousy Germans had him captured!!

For many months the terrorized pair of Hugh and Marion went
about their business in a daze of sad suspense, hearing not a word of
what was happening to their nearest and dearest prisoner in all the
world at a time when it was crawling with them. As a junior on the
ballfield Hugh played his worried-sick heart out, going 12 and 0 with
two one-hitters, one two-hitter, three three-hitters and no no-hitters,
all of them shut-outs, as his high school Marcus Whitman High
(named after the famous missionary and his wife who told the Indians
Jesus would help them and when He didn't massacred them) won the
State Championship. To top it off Hugh got Straight A's, made first-
team All-State, and was elected Scholar Athelete Of The Year for the
whole state of Washington for his age, thereby putting one heck of a
crimp in Marions's bichbichbiching about the study-time he wasted
playing ball.

But a lot of thanks he got! For next came the bitter pill any boy on
earth hopes never to have to swallow! In a Defense Department
envelope arriving practically minutes before the War would of ended

with everyone fine, there it was, the bitter pill: Hugh's dad had gotten shot! probably in the back! hundreds of times for all we know, knowing the stinking Germans! while escaping from prison camp.

It was official: he was now DEAD!!!!

For Hugh this came as quite a shock. Barely knowing who or what he was, he entered into an awful period of what felt like thick fog all around him during which he started smoking Lucky Strikes, his brand to this day. After this long Fog Period he reports entering more of an Angry Period where his senior year on the ballfield he spent like some strange machine or zombie mowing down team after team on almost pure fastballs, getting nicknamed SMOKE because of it, going 14 and 0 in the middle of it, setting a State Strikeout Record that will never be broken since they play a different number of games today, and winning a second straight State Crown for Marcus Whitman High practically one-handed.

On the other hand I have to report his grades that year went totally to pot. He just didn't care was the problem, he later reported. Marion was a basketcase, Hugh himself was in his Foggy then his Angry Periods, Pro Scouts were after him like flies beating down him and Marions's door trying to talk the sad-faced young man and his gereaved mom into becoming a Bonus Baby his eighteenth birthday instead of heading on to College as planned, etc. Life in general was such a total mess overall that before long Hugh could do nothing but throw fastballs, smoke Lucky Strikes, and hold on tight to one last straw. "If a scout from the Cubs comes and makes me a square offer, I will sign, in memory of DAD!" was the straw. "Otherwise it's college for me!" was the other segment of it. But no Cub scouts ever came, and later on Hugh forgot his own good advice. And no wonder, for,

"YOU ARE READY!" those clowns the Scouts kept screaming while "YOUR SCHOOLING!" screamed his destroyed mom while "SMOKE! SMOKE! SMOKE!" screamed Whitman Highs's berzerk fans while "DAD! DAD!" Hugh screamed in his own brain. For what Everett Senior would have said concerning all these mixed-up compartments in life was what the big lonely southpaw was wondering at this rugged point in time.

This was a year of great confusion for young Hugh Chance.

Kincaid:
Sabbath School

When the time comes, all you have to do to get out of The Corner is tiptoe over and whisper the Memory Verse to Sister Durrel. If you blow it she even helps you with it. Then you go take a seat in Brother Beal's crowd while he polishes off the morning with a short sermon that's like a pre-game warm-up to get you a little bit bored before the Big Bore of Elder Babcock's sermon upstairs in church.

Today's Memory Verse is in red ink in my Bible. Red means it's Jesus talking. "Whosoever shall humble himself as this little child," He's telling somebody or other, "the same is the greatest in the kingdom of heaven." I repeat the Verse to myself seven times without looking. Then I peek at Sister Durrel, and start trying to suck up courage. This is the hard part . . .

I know what'll happen first. I'll say, "I'm ready, Sister Durrel." Then she'll say, "Call me Nancy, Kincaid. You make me feel like a nun!" Then I'll feel horrible for making her feel like a nun, but I'll keep calling her Sister anyway, because I'd *die* if I ever called her Nancy. That's one thing about Brother Beal. The guy can walk right up to her and say "Nancy" as calmly as if he was saying "soup" or "cement" or "pencil." I guess if Sister Durrel had to get engaged, it might as well have been to Beal. I didn't feel that way at first because he acts like such a big weenie here at church. But last summer at Camp Meeting a thing happened that showed me there is a lot more to him than you'd ever guess from knowing him on Sabbaths only.

It was a Friday, near sundown, and we'd been playing softball all afternoon. I was pitching for both teams to make it even—just underhand bloopers—and Brother Beal was coming to bat for about the tenth time. Beal was a baseball star at Walla Walla Adventist College a couple years ago, and even went on to play semipro ball till his manager canned him for refusing to play on Sabbath. It's hard to blame the manager, though. Beal, like all Adventists, believes the Sabbath begins and ends at sunset, so he was missing both the Friday night games and the Saturday doubleheaders, which were about three-fourths of his team's schedule.

Anyhow, he was quite the slugger when he played. But there at Camp Meeting he'd just been bunting all day to tease us, since he was so damned fast we couldn't get him out anyway. Right as the sun was sinking, though, Sister Durrel showed up with a lawn chair and sat down to watch, and Beal gave her a big cocky grin, and she smiled back a smile so much more beautiful than anything he'd ever deserve that when he kept right on grinning as he stepped to the plate, then said, "This one's for *you*, Nancy," I just couldn't take it. I decided to wipe the grin right off his face.

Fast pitches are illegal in Camp Meeting softball. Overhand pitches are even more illegal. I threw one anyhow. Winding up fast to increase the surprise, I blazed a perfect strike in there—and Beal's grin *did* vanish. The problem was, so did the softball. The problem was, Beal's body coiled and uncoiled in a split second, there was an eerie *boaf!*, and that flat blob of a ball just disappeared. He obliterated it. The speed of the illegal pitch only made matters worse. I turned to the sky and started looking, finally spotting an ugly little grass-stained moon, still rising in the company of a flock of swallows, high over a meadow so far beyond anything we'd ever considered "outfield" that it was like something out of the Book of Revelation had happened. The ball flew so high and far it made our diamond and players and the entire afternoon's playing seem as if a bunch of pygmies had been shooting marbles on a rug and calling that a ballgame. But it was what happened after the ball returned to earth and bounded on into a lily pond that changed my mind about Beal for good.

About the time he reached second base, a few of us began to notice something odd about the Brother's baserunning. It wasn't hard to put a finger on, either. He wasn't running bases at all. He was *dancing* them. Our first reaction was to gawk. There stood our big pious weenie of a Sabbath School teacher on second base, eyes closed, body motatin', zonked face impossibly unembarrassed as his hands mojoed a solo on a sax no more visible than the Holy Ghost. Then he stepped off the bag, swivel-hipped his way toward third, and the second reaction set in: kids started to laugh. Their parents didn't, and I didn't, but almost everybody else did. They couldn't help it. Beal's neck was working like a chicken's; he was doing snaky, Egyptian-looking things with his arms and hands; and he was sliding his big sneakered feet sometimes forward, sometimes back, and sometimes into such quick, drunken, graceful tangles that you weren't sure whether he'd fall on his face or take off flying.

But what really won me over was his butt. What finally made it impossible for me not to like the man was how right out there on the Adventist basepaths, right in front of eighty or ninety of the kind of pious adult spectators who spent their every Sabbath if not their entire lives trying to forget the existence of things like butts, Beal's buns were trying to light a fire by friction inside his jeans; they were gyrating like a washing machine with its load off balance; they were thrashing against his pants like two big halibut against the bottom of a boat. And the wonderful thing, the amazing thing, was how once his older audience got over the shock of it, they began to look amused at, then fascinated by, and finally downright grateful toward his writhing reminder that yes, buns did exist, and yes, every one of us owned not one but two of the things, and yes, like the God who created them in His Image, they did indeed move in mysterious ways. Meanwhile the sun was sinking and the softball was floating serenely among the lilies of the pond until *kerrfloosh!* Dougy Lee Babcock dove in after it. And the Elder himself—our stern umpire—had turned so crimson watching Beal's stern that his face looked like a big fat paintbrush trying to add its frantic scarlet to the sunset to hurry on the Sabbath, since once Sabbath began, dancing would become a sin and he could order Beal to stop.

But it wasn't Sabbath—not yet it wasn't—and when Beal rounded third he danced clear off the basepath and started orbiting his halfmoons round and round the planet that was Sister Durrel, who blushed a little but managed to smile beautifully back at him—and at *all* of him, top to bottoms. At which point the sky got so red and the light so golden that I couldn't even look at her, she was so pretty, and all over the ballfield kids were collapsing from over-laughing as, far off in the pond water, Dougy Lee Babcock surfaced with a lily pad on his head, shouting tiny, jubilant shouts and looking like a chip off the old Elder as he raised the dripping ball aloft like the newly baptized pate of some saved sinner, while Beal waltzed, a whole world away, onto home plate, and kept waltzing on it throughout the waves of wild cheering and applause. Beneath the cheering I heard Elder Babcock snarl that Beal was out, for leaving the basepath, and that he ought to be ashamed for acting like he was acting in front of all us innocent children. To which Beal responded by cranking his butt a little more, grinning over at Sister Durrel, and singing out so everybody could hear him, "But I'm not *acting*, Elder. This is *exactly* how I feel!"

Ah, what a moment . . .

In the long run, though, the memory makes Beal's transformation here at church all the sadder. He looks great strolling in the door in his dark blue suit, but the instant his hand touches a hymnal or podium *poof!*, he shrivels down into his collar, wrinkles up his forehead like an organ grinder's monkey, and holds his body so stiff you'd think he believed God would strike him dead if he ever so much as flexed one bun.

Which is one more reason why I stay in The Corner.

But of course the main reason, the real reason, is Sister Durrel.

Irwin's <u>HISTORY OF MY DAD</u> continued

<u>Chapter 3. Beautiful Laura Vivien Dubois</u>

What made young Hugh's confusion even worse, but a lot better too that sad year of his dad dying, was a gorgeous young girl whose dad was also dead recently known as Laura, though with her dad it was not Germans but a smaller enemy commonly known as The Bottle which did him in slower but just as totally. This didn't stop Hugh and her from finding out they had about six tons in common however.

From Cleveland Ohio with a full name of Laura Vivien Dubois, Laura moved with her mom and brothers to Walla Walla Washington to escape the disgrace of the dad partly, and partly because her mom and her were good Seventh Day Adventists full of high hopes that the two young brothers, Truman and Marvin, might let Jesus into their lives away from the streets of Cleveland they ran so wild in and maybe go on to the Adventist College there in Walla Walla, which however they never did.

What the brothers did do though, one fine May day, was strike out five times between the two of them in a ballgame with big sister Laura watching proudly to make it worse, against a handsome young southpaw by the name of Smoke more commonly known as Hugh. They would of struck out six times, too, if Marvin hadn't decided to wreck the Perfect Game Smoke had going by stepping into an inside pitch his last time at bat and getting bashed by it, which you've got to admit if you've seen Smoke throw took a ton of guts, though not all that many brains.

Unfortunately Marv picked a high fastball, which coldcocked him so royally the doctors said it would of killed him if it hadn't been a glancing type of blow. On the more fortunate side however, the injury aroused an occasion where Hugh and Laura ended up leaning worriedly over the same blacked-out maniac named Marv in the same bed there at Walla Walla Adventist Hospital.

For a while Laura and Hugh just sweated blood, said "Oh dear Oh

dear," rung there hands and so forth. But "She sure smells good!"
Hugh couldn't help thinking after a while. And "He is so softhearted
for a guy who hurls that ball so hard!" Laura started thinking. Then,
leaning closer and closer over the fallen young warrior, they began
falling so far into Love At First Sight that by the time Marv opened
one eye and said "Who am I?" they had more or less forgot, for who
the heck cares who Uncle Marv is in such situations? (Really he's a
great guy! I'm only teasing for when he reads this!)

At this point Hugh had one of the many brainstorms that sprinkle
his fertile mind from time to time. Pretending to feel horrid over how
Marv had bashed his own brains out, Hugh invited him to let bygones
be bygones the coming Saturday and go watch a Walla Walla VS
Lewiston Bush League Pro Game with him, compliments of Hugh.

"Hay! Great!" Marvin replied.

"But hay!" Hugh added. "Better bring along this sister of yours too,
since she's had quite a serious shock due to that pitch that got away
from me and needs a brief vacation as much as the both of us!"

"Fair enough," said Marvo.

To Hugh's surprise, though, Laura's face here took on a more serious
bent. "Much as I'd love to, we can't, dangit!" she observed, "for
Saturday is our Sabbath."

"Hay! Not mine!" grinning Marvin chuckled back.

"It is so!" Laura yelled in no uncertain terms, worried sick over
which eternal place starting with 'H' Marv might end up spending
Forever in if he didn't shape up.

"No way!" rowdy Marvin informed her.

"Hay! No fights now," Hugh clucked. "What are you guys anyways?
Jews?"

"We are of the Seventh Day Adventist persuasion," Laura reported
proudly.

"You mean YOU are!" butted in Marv.

Laura said nothing, but her beautiful eyes stabbed holes in Marvin's
face like two big daggers.

"Hay now!" Hugh stated soothingly. "Whoever is what, do not fuss,
for I've just had another one of the brainstorms that have sprinkled
my mind like fertile rain from time to time my entire history! On
Sunday afternoon Tucson plays the Indians up in Spokane. A Double
Header no less! It's a long drive, but I don't mind. What say I take
the both of you on up to that?"

"THE INDIANS ARE COMING TO SPOKANE?" Marvin screamed, nearly coldcocking his sore head again with his own loud noises.

"We originated from Cleveland," Laura explained after Marv had fainted back onto the pillows.

"Well," Hugh remarked with a sneaky sparkle in one eye, "Spokane is called the Indians, too, because they are Cleveland's Triple A Farm Club."

"CLEVELAND'S FARM CLUB IS IN SPOKANE? WAHOO! OKAY! OH OW! MY HEAD! HURRAY!" responded the hospitalized voice from the pillows.

Here I must butt in to report that this Cleveland-Farm-Club stuff was a small but harmless load of crap Hugh was feeding them in hopes of making Laura more interested, for he knew all along that Sacramento was really Cleveland's Triple A Farm Club, and Spokane was only Baltimores's. The important thing here was this: Hughs's load of crap worked like a charm!

"Sounds fun!" Laura agreed with Marvin in a gentle whisper, looking at Hugh and visa versa with red hot looks on their faces!

So that settled that! The very next Sunday the whole threesome of them tore on up to Spokane on a trip now known amongst our family history as The Three Hundred Mile Date!

Kincaid:
Sabbath School

With one finger she beckons me toward her. My face is instantly burning—but this always happens. I clear my throat and force myself to speak. "I'm ready, Sister Durrel," I say. But it is Mickey Mouse's voice, or even Minnie's, that comes piping up out of me. This always happens too.

"Call me Nancy, Kincaid," she whispers. "You make me feel like a nun!"

She smiles up at me, and I try to smile back, but my cheeks and mouth seize up as if I just got back from a dentist, so I gape at her, novocaine-faced, instead. She takes the same finger she beckoned me with, hooks it deep in her thick, brown, freshly cut hair, pulls the hair back behind her ear, and tilts the ear up toward me. I gulp. This has never happened! There's always been plenty of hair between my mouth and her ear! And now I'm supposed to talk into it! She looks at me. I look at her ear. "Well?" she says.

I lean a little closer. *Violets.* She smells like violets! And I see tiny violet veins pulsing in her neck, and her ear is like a blossom, and the skin of her cheek looks so warm and soft that as I lean down to recite the verse I wonder, for just an instant, what would happen if I kissed her: I picture her slapping me, picture her kissing me back, picture her saying she's always loved me in secret, picture Brother Beal's fist boafing my face the way his bat did that softball.

Then I try to picture the Memory Verse . . .

It's gone. Vanished. This has never happened either! I try to breathe, but can't; try to remember, but can't; try to swallow, but can't. She tries priming the pump. *"Whosoever therefore shall humble,"* she whispers—but my brain is melted wax. *"Himself as this little child,"* she says—but my eyes and mind are both stuck to my shoes now, glued like dogshit to the scuffed little Buster Browns I thought were so neat when Mama bought them for me, and which now hurt my feet and resemble the whole half-grown, shabby, stupid rest of me so much I'd like to puke all over them. *"The same is greatest in the kingdom of heaven,"* she whispers. But I say nothing.

She aims both big green eyes at my fat red face. "What's the matter today?"

"I just can't," peeps Minnie Mouse.

"Try," she says, and her breath smells beautiful, like Dentyne.

"No!" I squeak, my cheeks burning like a butt that just got a hard spanking.

"Do it for *me,* Kincaid," she pleads, and her voice sounds encouraging. But now I can see that she's biting her lip to keep from laughing, and that though the teeth doing the biting and the lip being bitten and the green eyes watching me are all beautiful, they *know* that they're beautiful, *know* that's why I'm like this, and even *like* me to be like this—because me being like this is proof that she's beautiful. So that's what I am. Her proof. I am the butt-cheeked Buster Brown-shoed mirror she holds in front of her face to study her beauty in. And I would rather be the floor, or a chair, or a smear of grease on the wall.

She is still smiling as she unhooks the beautiful hair from behind the beautiful ear. The hair bounces once, beautifully, then lies beautifully still. "What's the matter?" she whispers. "I won't bite you." But her teeth look sharp.

"I'm sorry!" squeaks Minnie.

She laughs, and looks at herself in my face some more. "Okay," she says.

I nod my head enthusiastically, but haven't the slightest idea what she wants.

"We're finished," she says, smiling. "We're done. For today, anyway."

I nod some more, but stand frozen.

"You can *go* now!" she laughs.

"Oh!" I squeak. "Oops! Okay! Thanks! Goodbye!" Quick as I can I turn, take half a step, and crack my leg against a chair. It crashes over. I stand it back up, but hear the inevitable swiveling of suits and dresses as sixty-some faces spin around to gawk. My own face bursts into flame. I move fast down a long row of kids, heading for the furthest empty seat, but somebody, Micah Barnes, sticks his foot out: I trip, fall to my knees, my right hand flies out, my fingers catch in some girl's hair, the girl shrieks, Micah hoots, everybody looks, the girl shrieks louder. "Sorry!" I croak, staggering away.

"Knock it off, Barnes!" Brother Beal shouts. "Kincaid! Sit *down!*"

I plop down in the first empty space I come to. Luckily there's a chair in it. My face is scalding me. I can't focus my brain or eyes. I loosen my tie to keep from strangling. I hear Micah snickering, because he tripped me I think at first: then I glance sideways and realize I'm sitting right beside Vera Klinger—and she's blushing and beaming like she thinks I'm here all because of her! Micah pants and squirms in his chair. Half the kids in the room are smirking at me. I notice Brother Beal wrinkling up his forehead: time for the closing sermon. My brain is a furnace inside my skull. I consider bolting for the door, but if I tripped again or Beal yelled at me I'd flat out die, so I try something even more desperate: I decide that, come hell or high water, I am going to listen, for once, to every last word that Brother Beal has to say . . .

But it's even harder than I'd expected: "*GrownupsareGod'schildrenjust askidsarethechildrenofgrownups,*" he wheedles in a voice so inflectionless and stale it seems to brown the very air. "*ButinourMemoryVersetodayJesus isnotsayingthatgrownupsshouldactlikechildren,ohno,it'snogoodforanybodyto actchildishnono,whatOurLordJesusissayingtoeachandeveryoneofushereto- dayisthatGodistheUltimateGrownupandJesusHimselfistheUltimateChild andwhatthistrulymeanstousherebelowisthatweshouldallstriveourveryvery hardesttobuh-blah,buh-blah,buh-blubble . . .*"

Vera is staring at my pant leg!

I cross my legs, and cover the top one with both hands.

She stares at my hands!

I stick them in my pockets.

She stares at my pockets!

No escape! I strain to focus on Beal again, but the heat in my brain makes his body wriggle like a phone pole miles off down some desert highway. "*Andlistennowyouyoungpeople,*" he drones. "*Payveryveryveryclose attentiontomenow,becausethis,accordingtoHolyScripture,isthekeythatun-locksthegatetothekingdomofheaven. Areyouallwithme? . . Good,because buh-bleah,buh-blah,bluh-bloobly . . .*"

There's some faint promise here, though—something in the words *kingdom of heaven* that I swim for, in my ocean of misery, as if toward a life raft . . .

Oh yeah. The dream. I had a dream about the kingdom of heaven, just a few nights ago. A very real sort of dream, it was too. So real that when I woke up and saw Irwin awake too, I told him all about it. But all he said was, "You're lulu, Kincaid." So I went in to Everett and Peter's room, woke Peter, and whispered my dream to him. And *he* said it didn't sound like a dream at all, but like a vision. He said it sounded as though my soul had left my body, and had actually flown off to the kingdom. "You're lulu, Pete," I told him. But as Vera keeps staring at my legs and Micah keeps sniggering and Beal keeps bluh-blobbling I begin to wonder: *was* Peter lulu? Or is it possible? Could I, without killing myself, get my soul to fly right on out of this godforsaken room while my body just sits here and waits for things to end? I have no idea, but I decide to try. I begin by remembering, as carefully as I can, every last detail of my dream of the kingdom . . .

Irwin's HISTORY OF MY DAD continued

Chapter 4. The Three Hundred Mile Date!

The Three Hundred Mile Date started out on late May the Something 1947 at seven o'clock on a Sunday morning, with young Hugh at the wheel of his late dad's 1940 Ford screaming down the highway like a bat out of a certain Hot Place we've heard plenty about but hope never to visit. Hugh made it to Walla Walla around eight, picked up sleepy Marv and thrilled Laura, and the hungry threesome of them shot north like bad news, hitting Spokane by ten thirty, a town Marvin would have died at the time if you'd told him he'd one day set up his fine ladies' hair parlour The Butee Bar in it.

Their huge breakfasts that morning Laura remembers as having hot chocolate with whipcream and Eggs Benedict among other treats in it, all compliments of Hugh, who spared no expenses since he knew his time with Laura was numbered, what with her living so far away and school almost out and all. Unfortunately Marvo had a stomach on him about the size of a lake and nearly cleaned poor Hugh's wallet out of house and home that day. With Laura to look at though, Hugh pretty much neverminded.

At eleven directly afterward, among the finest box seats in Spokane Stadium, the happy young daters settled down to some serious baseball watching, with Hugh showering corndogs, Nutty Buddies, Cokes and such on Marvin all day, since every time Marv went to fetch them him and Laura got a minute to chat amongst themselves for a change. These chats were where the young couple first encountered the six or seven tons they had in common. For instants it came out during the first few innings that Laura knew baseball almost as insideout as Hugh did, and that both their dads were dead recently (though most likely headed opposite directions in the Here After), and that they both liked Fords better than Chevies, burgers better than hotdogs, dead dogs better than corndogs, and root beers better than Cokes. In case this wasn't enough already, the last straw to break their backs was when Laura's birthday turned out to be May 4, 1929, just one day more than Hughs's! Watch out for those Older Women, Big Fella!

The one thing they found out they didn't have in common was when Hugh signalled a peanut-vendor to toss Laura a box of Crackerjacks, only to discover to his horror her sticking both hands on top of her head while the corner of the Crackerjacks box drilled her helplessly in the face, nearly jabbing out one lovely blue and green eye. "I can't catch Hugh!" Laura cried when it was all over.

"Hay! No kidding!" Hugh remarked, handing over his handkerchief for a permanent gift to wipe up all future blood from not catching things with. And seriously Mr. Hergert, to this day my brothers, dad, sisters, uncles, cousins and such have to remember not to toss Laura a thing, because she still can't catch the broad side of a barn!

The entire Double Header whipped before the young couples's eyes in about two minutes, as Time is so famous for doing when you're having fun. Uncle Marv remembers the Indians sweeping Tucson both games. Laura and Hugh however remember the opposite. Marvin also remembers them being the Cleveland Indians instead of just Spokane though, inspite of this is impossible according to the ticket stub Laura kept along with the bloody handkerchief for a souvenir. So I'd have to go with Hugh and Laura on who won.

After the games they headed back toward Walla Walla, with Laura sliding closer and closer across the carseat towards Hugh till in the dark somewhere down around Steptoe, when bloated Marvin fell to sleep, the young pair pulled quietly off the road to enjoy their first kiss, smack dab in the middle of which "AH HA!" Marvin yelled, jumping up at them, causing Laura to whack him a good one forgetting his injured head so that poor Marvo had to jump out of the car and vomit up all his corndogs and Nutty Buddies, after which they had a good chuckle and drove on, once it quit hurting so bad.

When they got back to Walla Walla around midnight Marv never moved or made a sound, so that the young lovers had to lean down and make sure he wasn't dead before walking hand in hand into Laura's clean but somewhat dumpy home, since they were totally poor, and met the mom, Beryl Dubois, a fine looking older woman with serious heart trouble who was not all that well mentally either, thanks to too many years with her late drunk of a husband. The brother Hugh struck out three times, Truman, was inside the abode there as well, and made a dumb first impression on Hugh by holding out his hand to shake hands, then trying to crush Hugh's hand while shaking hands with it. "Pleased to meet you, Mam!" Hugh told Beryl, ignoring Truman's feeble monkeyshines on his big right paw.

Then all were saddened and Truman knocked it off when Beryl observed, "Pleased to meet *you*, Wilver!" and went on calling Hugh Wilver the whole night, who was apparently some guy nobody ever heard of who Hugh closely resembled to Beryl's harmless but somewhat demented mind, which several heart attacks and a hard life had worn to the nub of its rope.

Seeing how things stood, Hugh realized that whatever went on between him and Laura was going to be just between him and Laura, so to speak. This was both a big fat relief and a very sad thing, he reports feeling at the time. "I'd best be shuffling on home," he pronounced after an awkward period of all of them sitting around grinning and staring at each other had very very slowly crept past.

"Goodnight then, Wilver!" Beryl called out in her good-hearted but not so accurate way.

"Goodnight to you, Mrs. Dubois!" Hugh rejoindered understandingly.

Then him and Laura walked deep in thought to the car, booted out the slumbering Marvo, and looked far into each others's eyes there under the late stars of night. "So! Goodbye then!" Hugh remarked in a joyful whisper. "But hay! Not for long!" he tacked on, placing a gentle peck on Laura's forehead, which was the best he felt he could do what with strange brothers and moms practically crawling out of the woodwork around there.

"I hope not!" Laura claimed, all smiles as well.

And with that smile in his brain like a huge iron magnet Hugh shot on home to Pullman like a house afire, arriving home at 2 a.m. with 299 miles on the faithful Fortyford for the day, so that he decided to wheel her on around the block a couple times to make it the even Three Hundred their famous first date is now named after. Dog-tired but dead happy, the young man next staggered happily on in to bed!

Kincaid:
Sabbath School

At first glance the kingdom of heaven looked a lot like a golf course. I'm not interested in golf, so this was a complete surprise to me. Another odd thing is that when people talk about heaven they usually refer to it as being "up," but I had no feeling of upness. The place felt right around sea level to me. The temperature was cool, maybe 55, 60 degrees. The sky was partially cloudy, with maybe a ten percent chance of rain. There was no wind, but the air was so fresh I felt we must be near an ocean, and the kingdom stretched on and on in such a rolling, barren way that the land itself seemed like a sea.

There were no trees in sight—another surprise. There were also no heavenly mansions, no pearly gates, no gold harps, gaudy thrones, winged cherubs, or any of the heavenly claptrap you worry about thanks to churches. The truth is, I'd never been in a place less like a church, and can hardly say what a relief this was. There was no God in sight either, which was a little disappointing, since I've always wondered what He looks like. The only living beings in sight weren't heavenly at all, actually. They were the other people in the tour group I was part of. But that might give some idea just how beautiful the place was: even being part of a *tour* group was fairly easy to take!

To describe it in words makes the kingdom sound stark and empty, like the scrub desert of eastern Washington or something. But this is only because words can't paint the feeling that everything had. The fewness of things only made you notice this feeling more. The air, for instance, smelled something like sea air, but whereas sea air makes you hungry, kingdom air made you full, and it wasn't a fullness like when you're stuffed from overeating: it was more like that foodless fullness you get at the end of a really good movie. Like when the Captured Girl is about to be killed because she won't tell The Secret, and she takes a last look at the hills with tears in her huge brown eyes, and there comes The Hero you thought was dead, riding down out of nowhere with his sword flashing or gun blazing, making hamburger out of Evil while the music surges through you and the goose bumps shoot up and down you. That sort of fullness. Like I said, I can't explain it.

The swells of land rolled away far as the eye could see, every swell covered with a grass softer and prettier than any golf course grass on Earth. But maybe the nicest touch of all was in the dips between grassy swells, where there were hundreds of little pools, like tide pools (though there was no ocean to fill them). Just looking at the way the grass crept so carefully down to the edge of these pools, and at the way the moss- and lichen-covered rocks ringed them in, I felt they must be the key to the whole place, so naturally enough, I started strolling down toward one. And that was when the conductor first turned, scowled, and motioned me to stay with the group. (I didn't mention that we came on a train, or that it had a conductor. It was just a grimy old diesel engine and a couple of beat-up boxcars, really. It seems flagrantly sinister, looking back on it. Why would people go to heaven in *boxcars?* I didn't worry about it at the time, though, since we'd already climbed out of the cars when the dream began.)

I tried to describe the special feel of the air. I should mention the feel of the colors. Take anything, take the grass for example. You would have to say that it was a combination of green and yellow. But it was not, by a long shot, any sort of earth green or earth yellow. It was a Kingdom-Only Green and Yellow—unbelievably beautiful at first, then beautifully believable—that looked as though rays of sunlight were trapped and glowing inside each blade. The glass-blue and star-blue and sky-pink wildflowers had that same glowing-on-the-inside look. So did the purple mosses and scarlet lichens round the pools. And so (though this sounds impossible) did the quiet colors, like the tans, browns and grays of the stones.

Except for the tour group and the train I could see only one flaw in the entire kingdom. You couldn't see the sun, but the sky was full of broken clouds, and there were a lot of golden sun-shafts slanting down between them. To me, these shafts seemed overdone.

I suppose the conductor was a flaw too, but I felt sure he was just some hireling from Earth, and anything from Earth has a right to seem flawed. The guy looked Catholic, actually. At least he had a little cross on a chain around his neck. Other than that he was just a regular old-fashioned train conductor, with the bored face, Captain Kangaroo suit and little Union Army cap they all seem to wear. He appeared to know what he was doing, though, since after we'd gaped at the landscape and breathed the air for a while he finally led us over to the nearest pool himself, then leaned down, plucked some bright yellow fungus off a rock, popped it in his mouth, and said in a polite but somewhat bored conductor's voice, "Everything here in the kingdom is perfectly good to eat."

Hearing this, our whole tour group started laughing and scrambling and snorfling around, grabbing gobs of wildflowers and grass, stuffing them in their mouths, chewing away. But it bugged me to see such lovely things getting mangled, so I skipped it and bent down to inspect the pool. Once again, though, the conductor eased himself in between me and the water, looked at me like a teacher does when you're not paying attention, and said, "Wouldn't you like to taste something too?"

I shrugged, but he didn't move, so I picked up the plainest thing I could find—a pebble—popped it in my mouth, started clunking it around, and grinned at him. "Give it a chew," he said. "You'll be surprised." So I did chew it—cautiously at first, then harder and harder— and was amazed to discover as I crushed it into sand, then into mush, that my teeth were like industrial diamonds and my jaws were like a vise. I felt like Paul Bunyan, hell, I felt like Superman—and just the pleasure of such godlike chewing got me so excited that when the pebble-mush began melting and turned out to taste better than the best chocolate in the world, it seemed like a waste somehow. I mean, I swallowed it anyway, but I sensed as it was going down that the special quality—the joy that had been in the taste—couldn't go down with it. It just wouldn't fit inside me. There was simply no way to squeeze a thing so vast and heavenly into a container as small and earthly as myself.

The instant I realized this I began to feel incredibly sad. Then I looked around at the tour group, and saw that they were all making the same dismal discovery: they were all standing there chewing their grasses or flowers, tasting God-knows-what wonderful flavors, yet their smiles had all faded till they looked more like cattle than people—big, drab old dairy cows working their cuds, dimly knowing that no matter how much kingdom they chewed and swallowed, the heart of it, the heavenliness of it, just couldn't be digested. They were just too big and thick and dull. And realizing this, they also couldn't help but realize that they didn't yet belong in this beautiful place, and so would have to leave it.

This seemed to be the precise moment the conductor had been waiting for. Pulling out a big gold watch, he gave it a businesslike glance, clicked it shut, and in his bland bored voice called out, "Time to climb back aboard." Every man, woman and child looked heartsick, but every one of them obediently turned and began to amble toward the boxcars in a cowlike line. I got in line, too, and dawdled along at the very end of it. But something had turned over inside me. I'd begun to feel cheated, and more than a little bit miffed. Our glimpse of the kingdom suddenly struck me as a cruel joke—like some paltry guided tour of a Bavarian castle or Beverly Hills mansion given to a group of retarded people before hauling them back to the skuzzy old asylum they'd come from. I felt helpless, but rebellious too—and it was the rebelliousness that made me think suddenly of my brother Everett. What would he do in this situation? I asked myself. And it didn't take long to figure out: he'd say *Screw this cattle-car shit!* and start looking for a loophole that'd let him stay in the kingdom as long as he pleased.

Hide, I thought first. But one quick look at the landscape nixed that idea. The place was so damned bright and pure and open that no one from Earth could possibly hide there: my drabness would stick out like a housefly on a TV screen. Unable to think of anything else, I kicked at a rock in frustration—and *FFffffinng!* it shot off over the grass like a bullet! The conductor spun round to see who'd done it, but I'd already ducked back in line and begun imitating everyone else's abject, bovine trudging. *But wait a minute,* I was thinking. *I got a kick like a rifle and teeth like diamonds. Who am I here, anyway? And what do I know about what I can do? Maybe I could outrun that stodge conductor. Maybe I can fly! What makes us so damned sure we're not ready for this place?* And with that in mind I turned—and saw the tide pool. *If the pebbles here are edible,* I thought, *maybe the water's breathable. Maybe I can just hide inside a pool till that miserable train is gone . . .*

I started sneaking back toward it, and noticed as I went that my stealth was astounding: my tiptoeing hardly bent the grass blades. When I reached the water's edge I hunched down to see if the pool would be deep enough to hide me. And even though I gasped and drew back, even as the sweet chills ran through me, I felt I'd known all along what I would see:

just under the surface the water opened up. The top of the pool was like an entrance to a cavern. A few inches down it blossomed out into a wide, shimmering underwater world. And though the water was deep and everything beneath it seemed to be in miniature, it didn't take long to recognize just what world it was. The little green ridges, the shiny spots between them—it was the kingdom itself. Or a smaller, finer version of it. Bending closer, I found the minuscule version of our earth-drab train, complete with its own line of tiny, cowlike people filing aboard. Next I located the miniature of the very pool I was squatting beside. And then the second wave of chills hit: hunched by the pool-in-the-pool was a minuscule boy. A boy who must somehow correspond to, or perhaps even *be*, me. Half terrified, half delighted, I leaned down for a closer look—and the tiny boy's face rose *up*. I hesitated, and scowled. The boy in the pool looked up, and smiled. He was like me, he was *exactly* like me. Yet he wasn't me at all. There was none of my confusion in him, none of my nervousness, nothing the least bit sad or dull or hesitant. His features were mine exactly, with a single, all-encompassing difference: they had that indescribable quality—the *kingdom* quality. He belonged to the world or worlds around him as surely as the greenness belonged to the grass, and the longer we watched each other, the more I felt like a huge, sloppy, cartoon caricature of the being who the boy in the pool really was. Everything about him was matchless, perfect. And the instant the word *perfect* popped into my head, I realized, despite his size and resemblance to me, who he could only be. The boy in the pool was Christ. Not Jesus exactly, or not just Jesus, but a Christ. *My* Christ.

And he was looking right at me.

To my amazement, I spoke first. "I *wondered* where you were hiding!" I said. Then laughed. I couldn't help it. It was so good to see him in there, yet so funny to find him so much like me, and so *tiny*. "Nice kingdom you got here," I added, laughing again. "But it didn't feel quite right without you. Or should I say, without me?"

This time he laughed too, and though there were no bubbles or sound I could feel his delight rise up through the water: which made me laugh even harder: which made him do the same. But that very instant someone shouted, "No! *No no!* What are you doing there? *Don't!*"

That damned conductor! And he was huffing right toward us. "What now?" I asked the boy.

He sent one tiny finger upward. *You're Number One?* I thought, inanely. Then I realized he wanted us to touch. "No! Don't! *No!*" the conductor bellowed as he ran. But slowly, carefully, I began lowering my enormous finger down toward the minuscule finger of the boy. "Stop! You *must stop!*" the conductor roared, and his pounding stride began to sound so close that I plunged my arm in faster, making ripples that obscured the boy's face. Yet I found his finger, and when we touched I had the sensation that he was laughing once more. His finger was strong—immovably strong—and so tiny it felt almost like a pinprick; but through that minuscule point I began to feel something like a pleasing electric shock pour into me, spreading, building, surging up my arm and through my body till the entire pool spun and boiled, drenching me, blinding me, while an overpowering suction steadily drew me down. *It doesn't hurt!* I thought. *This isn't hurting at all.* But the conductor kept screaming "No! Noooooo!" and his voice seemed so truly frightened that, even though I'd neither liked nor trusted him, I felt there must be something wrong. Then he shouted, "Your *family!*"

And I hesitated.

"You didn't tell them! Papa! Winnie! Your mother! You didn't even say goodbye! And there's *no returning! No coming back!*"

Hearing this, I resisted. I didn't cry out or struggle: I only resisted the downward pull for a heartbeat or two. But when those heartbeats ended I was lying on dry grass, spluttering like a drowning man—though only the fingers of my right hand lay in water. Then I saw that the water was shallow. It was just an empty, sandy-bottomed puddle. *Wake up, Kade,* the conductor was saying, his voice and touch surprisingly gentle now. *It's a dream, buddy,* he was saying. *It's just a dream . . .* But as I opened my eyes to Irwin, squeezing my shoulder and speaking the conductor's words, I realized that my lashes, and a tiny indentation in my pillow, were quite wet. Tears? Sweat? Pool water? I honestly didn't know. Having seen my pool turn so quickly to puddle, then pillow, I fully believed (for a few seconds anyhow) that Irwin's words meant he too knew that it was us— he and I, our junky house and room, our mill-town lives and thoughts and family—who were the dream, and that the kingdom, and the boy, were perfectly real.

"Any questions?" asks Brother Beal, looking even more church-scrunched and bleached out than usual. And my heart goes out to him, because it's so clear that there can never be questions, because his words ask no questions: his sentences, his sermons, are just so many rows of miserable tourists shambling dead away from the kingdom and back into their appropriate boxcars. "Any comments then?" he asks. And I want to shout: *Yes! Why don't you hit a ball a mile and dance like you did last summer? You're alive when you dance! We love your dancing, Brother! And I'll bet the tiny Beal in your pool does too!*

But I say nothing.

"All right then," Beal murmurs, wearing a perfect replica of the kingdom tourists' half-happy half-miserable smiles. "Would anyone care to offer a closing prayer?"

Then Vera Klinger—who I'd completely forgotten here beside me—starts waving her hand and craning her body like she'll die if she's not chosen.

As usual, Beal pretends not to see her. But as usual, no one else volunteers. Finally Beal looks at her. And they both look desperate. But as usual, Beal's desperation climbs back in its boxcar, while Vera's doesn't budge.

Brother Beal sighs, and gives her a grim nod. Sixty-some heads bow—and sixty-some bodies stiffen in their chairs, knowing all too well what's coming. Vera closes her eyes tight, and draws a breath so deep it sounds more like a sob. The torture begins:

"*Nyearest Nyeesus!*" she calls out, her voice, her whole body quivering. "*Nank nyou!, nank nyou!, for yall nyour nyimmy nyimmy nmlessings, nand for nthis nay of Nhristian Nyellowshipt!*"

At the words *nyimmy nyimmy* Micah uncorks a snicker—and there are *lots* of answering snorts today. Maybe there always are. Maybe I just hear them today because I'm stuck next to her. My stomach clenches. Most of me wants to snort with the others, but part of me, remembering the pool in the kingdom, makes me gouge my knuckles in my eye sockets and fight to hear her prayer. "*Mlease, nLord!*" Vera cries, as if she's pleading with an ax murderer. "*Mlease fornivvus our snins and nrespassenth! Nwee are nso nunworthy, nso nvery nvery nunworthy!*"

Noses blow violently; half-stifled giggles circle the room like pigeons trapped in a barn. Beal keeps his head bowed, but clears his throat and steps threateningly around his podium. "*Nopen our narts, nwee veseech nThee!*" Vera prays.

"*Narts! Narts!*" Micah moans, and the pigeons flap even more wildly.

Irwin says he heard there's an operation that can fix lips like Vera's, but that her parents feel the thing's a special cross God gave her to bear. Everett says it's the parents who deserve the cross: somebody should nail their upper lips to one, he says. Peter says her name means "Truth," and that she has nice eyes, and might be pretty when her mouth gets fixed. Whatever she might be, however she feels, she's on some kind of rampage now:

"*Nyelp us to nlove nyou nmore and nmore!*" she prays as Micah laughs outright, "*and nmore and nmore!*" she pleads as girls grab Kleenex, "*and snill nyet nmore!*" she begs as boys fizz up and overflow like jostled bottles of pop. "*Nenter our narts!*" she cries, her voice breaking, her body trembling so violently it makes my chair tremble too. "*Nenter nthem now! Nright now! Nwee are nso nlost, nso nvery nlost, nwithout nThee!*" And even as it occurs to me that this must be *real* prayer—even as I see that what is being laughed at is the sound of someone actually ramming a heartfelt message past all the crossed signals and mazes of our bodies, brains and embarrassments clear on in to her God—when I open my fists and peek at Vera I see a face so exposed, so twisted with love, grief and longing, that if she was my sister I would take off my coat, and I'd wrap her up and hold her, and I would beg her never, ever to do this naked, passionate, impossible thing again.

"*O nYeesus!*" she gasps. "*Nyearest nLord! How snorely nwee need nthy mresence!*"

"*Snorely!*" someone croaks.

"*Amen,*" growls old Sister Harg.

"*Gugh!ugh!ugh!*" goes Micah.

"*Thank* you, Vera!" Beal bellows, hoping to put an end to it.

"*Nmake us nworthy, Nlord!*" she cries, hearing nothing but her prayer. "*O mlease! Nmake us nworthy!*"

"*Amen!*" shouts Sister Harg.

"*Gugh!ugh!ugh!*"

Vera's prayer goes on forever.

Irwin's **HISTORY OF MY DAD** continued

Chapter 5. The Four Big Things

Like any kid with half a brain Hugh wanted to go to college, and he got full atheletic scholarship offers from Washington and Oregon State College, the Univercity of Oregon and Idaho, and I think maybe Montana and California too. But life was not so simple as where I'm sitting for a talented young ballplayer of not quite eighteen years of age by the name of Smoke! There was college on the one hand, sure, but on the other hand four big things came butting in to royally confuse the issue.

First off Marion got cheated out of her War Widow money by the

U.S. Goverment inspite of her husband getting murdered while escaping from Germans protecting that very Goverment! This continues to kill me to this day! There sits Uncle Sam on his fat duff, saying that because Marion was English and not a natural member of our country they weren't going to give her one red cent, and all along he's using a language known as <u>English</u> to cheat her in! Sure, Marion had refused to become a U.S. citizen, and sure, she may have imported elsewhere if her kid hadn't loved it so much here. But Everett Senior was no less dead due to that! And what about young Hugh's share of the dough? So as the result of the nerve of some people and their fat desk jobs in Washington DC, Marion Becker Chance was left in the Poor House, causing Hugh great concern.

"I DON'T WANT THEIR STINKING MONEY!" he reports Marion yelling at the time. "I'LL JUST GET A JOB!" he reports her yelling. But her only jobs in Pullman so far had been babysitting professor's wives's kids for ten cents an hour which the stupid professor's wives would then get to gabbing and forget to even pay, plus being Chairwoman of a bunch of local Atheist and Pacifist Groups who in spite of how they just drank coffee and wrote boring pamphlets to each other had got Marion pretty well blackballed there in Pullman as far as real jobs were concerned. "GO TO COLLEGE ANYWAY!" she screamed at Hugh. But Hugh Chance was not the sort of young man to sit around happily eating goldfish in raccoon coats or play ball and read Shakespeare while his own mom starved to death. "I WILL MAKE IT!" she kept screaming. But "HOW?" Hugh screamed right back. "AS A FORK-THROWER IN THE CIRCUS? AS AN ATHEIST TEA-PARTY HOSTESS? AS A TEN CENTS PER HOUR BABYSITTER?" As a result of this line of questioning Marion got so insulted that she has never quite forgiven Hugh to this day. Anyhow, her freshly widowed state and resulting money troubles was the first of the big things.

The second big thing was when Laura's mom Beryl died of the bad heart Hugh had noticed evidence of so clearly the night she ditted out and kept calling him Wilver. This left Laura, Marv and Truman orphaned on their own, which though sad to Laura was fine by Marv and True since it put the kibosh on the big plan to pack them off to an Adventist college. They had both quit high school, hit the streets, and started looking for work when some sort of church social workers found them, sent them back to school, and stuck them in Adventist Foster Homes they hated so much at first that it was a surprising shock to all concerned when they gradually grew to love them. What happened was that Truman got fostered right next door to the body shop where he learned the excellent body work he still does to this day. And Marvin struck it even luckier, getting stuck out on a big wheat ranch where he not only learned about farming but discovered that the place contained a daughter known as Mary Jane as well, a big strapping girl with a laugh like all outdoors who thought Marvo was a total joke from Cleveland at first, but later on flipflopped and married the guy!

Meanwhile Laura was having no such fun. She was too old for Foster Homes, knew no one to live with in Walla Walla, wanted to go to college wherever Hugh went to if she could only get excepted, but was a whole year behind him thanks to Hugh once skipping a grade, plus her report cards weren't such hot stuff either. As the oldest kid she had also inherited the unpayed rent and funeral bills and was too proud to take and chuck them in the trash where they belonged. So while living in a dive of a boardinghouse trying to finish high school Laura worked swing shift at a skuzzball factory making fake meat out of soybeans there in Walla Walla to pay for the dive of a boarding house, meanwhile smiling at Hugh on their dates all the while, saying stuff like "I'm doing fine, Hun!" Fortunately Hugh saw this as just one more load of the same type of crap Marion kept feeding him when she'd scream, "I WILL MAKE IT!" These were two lying damsels in distress if ever there was one, was Hugh's thinking. So Laura's tough situation was the second big thing.

The third big thing was that right at this point who should come tromping up to Hugh's doorstep like a somewhat overweight cigar-chomping Angel from Heaven but the famous Chicago White Sox scout Bucky Koter! And what should Bucky do but offer Hugh a $3,000 bonus plus a guaranteed $2,500 per year salary for two years to sign! And the whole time Koter is doing this, what should Marion be doing but brewing him up a cup of coffee made out of half soy sauce, half almond extract, half stale Postum and half used MJB grounds boiled up in a filthy soup not fit for rats! And what would a great scout like Koter do but calmly drink it! This is an absolute true story, ratty coffee included! This was also one of the biggest bonuses and first two year contracts in Baseball History offered to a Schoolboy Wonder up to that point in time, which was not only a great honor but 8,000 Big Ones, more money than any young man Hugh's age ever dreamed of! And in a way the even greater honor going on while Hugh read the fine print of the contract was when Marion asked Bucky if he'd like a second cup of rat-puke coffee, and Bucky calmly rejoindered, "Almost certainly, Mam! How delicious!" and drank Hughs's health to the bitter dregs! Obviously, Smoke Chance was one hot prospect! So Bucky Koter and the 8,000 Big Ones were the third big thing.

The fourth big thing was just a little thing really, just a little thought that started weighing Hugh's mind as he was pouring over Koter's offer while his mom was pouring out the ratlike coffee. Hugh's thought was simply that even if they weren't the Cubs, the White Sox were still Chicago. And the instant Hugh thought this he remembered how his own dad's famous last words to him were written in the exact same type of screwed-up logic! Remember? He'd wrote, Although my Piper is not a Chicago it is still a Cub! So, WHAT A COINCIDENCE! was Hugh's next thought, if it was even his own thoughts thinking by now and not the ghost of his dead dads's brain doing the job for him! CHICAGO! MY BABYHOOD TOWN! the Mystery Brain continued, AS WELL AS THE TOWN MY OWN FAVORITE DAD ONCE CHERISHED FOND DREAMS OF ALMOST PLAYING PRO BALL IN! Okay then. These strange and ghostly reflections were the fourth big things!

So there he was with four big things on the one hand and the one huge thing of A COLLEGE EDUCATION on the otherhand. What a decision for a young man to make of such an age!

Yet in the end Love, and also Money, won out totally as they so often do! Hugh signed with the ChiSox! Then him and Laura were happily married in a small ceremony made slightly smaller when furious Marion Becker Chance refused to come. Marvin was Best Man, and an Adventist gal from the fake meat factory, Dotty, served as Best Woman. But whereas Marvo is now my favorite old hair-ratting dirt-farming uncle, nobody knows what became of Dotty, which is just about par for the course isn't it? The first person you meet becomes your uncle while the next just drifts off like a cobweb. Somedays it's a mystery just to be alive!

Meanwhile everything looked about perfect for young Hugh and Laura if old Marion would only cool off, which she gradually started to do, like at about three o'clock last Wednesday. (I'm only kidding!) The main catch in life for the good-looking young couple at this point was how Everett Senior's death by Germans happened before he got around to showing Hugh how to throw a decent curveball. Revealing to her husband that she had more than just another pretty face lurking between her shoulders, clear-thinking Laura pointed this no-curve problem out right off the bat. "High school ball with no curveball was one kind of ball, Hugh!" she cried. "But Pro Ball will soon be another!"

"Hay I know I know I know I know!" was Hugh's somewhat curt reaction, for he was already working his arm to the bone on the problem. Nevertheless, how right the young wife was!

Kincaid:
Camas / February / 1963

It's Sabbath afternoon. Papa and me are sitting in the papermill parking lot, waiting for his friend Roy to get off work. Roy was supposed to be through at 3 o'clock, but the mill clock says 3:14, and nobody argues with the mill clock: its hour hand alone is half the size of a telephone pole.

Back in 1960—not long after Papa lost the lawsuit that could have fixed his dead thumb—Jan Lacey, the guy who cleans the pigeon shit off the mill clock's numbers, fell backwards out of the 0 in the 10 when a yellowjacket stung him. It was lunch hour, I guess, because a bunch of people saw it happen. They said he did a slow, sloppy backflip but landed right side up on the asphalt, neat as you please, right between two parked cars. He broke his pelvis, as I remember, and several bones in his legs and feet, but was healthy enough to be on the TV news later the same evening, so we all gathered round to watch. They showed the huge, high clock first, then panned slowly down the concrete wall to the place where Lacey landed. Next they took you right up to his hospital room, where he lay grinning at the bright lights and camera despite the casts and pulleys and cables holding all his broken parts in place. The TV news lady came up with a pretty good question, for a change. "What were your exact thoughts, Mr. Lacey," she said, "what flashed through your mind as you plummeted down toward what must have seemed like certain death?"

While the camera slid in for a close-up, Jan screwed his face up and thought hard about it. He thought for several seconds—which seemed like an awful lot of thinking for somebody on TV. Then he said, "Oopseedaisy."

The news lady cocked her head, obviously not understanding. "Yep," Lacey said, all solemn and nodding. "Oopseedaisy. Those was my very words."

We all found this funny, and laughed pretty hard. But when Papa heard it he almost died. I mean he writhed and howled in his chair till the tears streamed and his face and stomach cramped and he started coughing and choking. Then he caught his breath and started in all over again. All that evening, clear to bedtime, all any of us had to do was whisper "Oopseedaisy" and he would lose it again. I remember his whooping, his writhing, his wet, helpless face. I remember it all perfectly. I remember it because he hasn't laughed once since.

When I was little and Papa first started working the mill, I once heard him say that he'd become "a time-clock puncher"—and immediately I imagined him somehow climbing that huge concrete wall and literally punching the mill clock to a standstill. I thought he could do it if he wanted. I thought he could do anything, I really did. I'd never seen him play baseball, but from what I saw of him at home and gleaned from Everett's and Mama's stories, I believed Papa was Bob Feller, Solomon and Pecos Bill rolled into one. In one of my earliest memories, Papa is still in uniform, and so sweat-drenched it seems he's been swimming, after an incomprehensible but apparently glorious feat called "Afore-hid Shudout." Leaping from the back of some ballplayer's old pickup, he dashes to the front porch, plucks me out of Mama's arms, kisses my nose, then throws me so high in the air that at the summit of my flight I look down and glimpse an exquisite little forest of baby maple trees growing in our old wooden gutters. I dreamt of that forest for *years* afterward; beautiful dreams they were too—because in them Papa would throw me up again, and I'd just stay there, floating and looking for as long as I pleased. And there would be animals in the forest! Ant-sized coyotes, perfect little elk, mothlike owls, all grazing or gliding through the minuscule maples. I dreamt this so often that the wall between dream and memory finally gave way, and when I'd conjure the one time Papa really tossed me over the gutter, I could swear I really did see buff rumps and antler-flashes as the tiny elk dashed away through the trees. And though I mentioned it to no one for fear they'd think me selfish (or worse, think me adorable), when I was six and Papa crushed his thumb and had to quit baseball, I never cried or felt any real pity for him till I realized there could be no more Afore-hid Shudouts, and that he'd never throw me up over the tiny owl and elk forest again.

And now. Now he's sitting here beside me, gray-eyed, gray-templed, gray-faced, smoking a Lucky. Now he is *always* smoking a Lucky. It seems there's nothing else in the world he really wants to do.

It's foggy out, and getting dark already; I can barely make out the 10 that Jan Lacey fell from. It's also cold. I don't mention this, though, because the Fortyford's antique heater is so full of exhaust leaks that Peter pukes and the rest of us get headaches if we ride any distance with it on, and neither Papa nor Roy nor even Uncle Truman can fix it, and there's no point in griping about things nobody can fix.

We're giving Roy a ride home because his Travelall is in the body shop. He spun out on an icy bridge on the upper Washougal last weekend and raked one side of it along the guardrail. He caught two nice steelhead that day, though, and said the scrape was almost worth it. Even Papa hooked a fish that day, but he didn't stick it hard enough and lost it on the third jump. He got skunked again this morning while we were at church. He almost always gets skunked. Roy has better luck, or maybe more skill. He loves fishing like Papa loved baseball, and has pounded the Washougal ever since he was a kid. He says the salmon and steelhead runs this year are the worst he's ever seen, and that the shit the papermill keeps dumping in the river is the reason. Then Monday through Friday he works at the mill. He feels bad about it, but says that nothing else pays so well. Fishing sure as hell doesn't.

Papa's window wing is open to let smoke out, but it seems to me it's just letting cold in while the smoke gathers in a cloud all round his head. I stay slumped so it floats above me, but Papa's hair and clothes, his breath and hands, everything about him reeks of Lucky smoke. Outside, though, the cold has spread mill smoke over Camas thick as a frosting over a cake, and even Luckies smell better than mill frosting. So I guess Papa's window wing doesn't matter.

Tired of cold, stink and silence, I ask Papa what makes a papermill smell the way it does. He shrugs. He hates talking about the mill. Or I assume he hates it, since he never does it. But I hate being ignorant too, so I say, "I mean like scientifically. I mean, what chemicals or whatever make that awful yeast and sewer smell?"

He just shrugs again, but now I feel like talking, even if it's just to myself, so I do: "Remember those Adventists that came from Ohio last fall for a visit?"

He doesn't even shrug this time, but I go on with the story: "The World Series was on, but Mama made us go out and greet 'em anyhow. And it was a nice clear day, with a nice strong breeze. We couldn't smell the mill at all. But the first thing the Ohio people did when they climbed out of their car was go, 'Eeeeeeuuu! What's that smell?' Mama started apologizing, as if it was our fault, saying it always smelled like that around here. But before she could explain why, Everett cut in and told 'em, 'Yep. Don't you folks worry. It's just a little medical problem. Poor Winnie here. It's his crack.' "

Remembering their faces, and Irwin's face, and Mama's, I burst out laughing. Papa just sits, staring off into the fog. "That wasn't even the *best* part!" I gasp. "The great thing was how, even after Mama explained it was really the mill, for the rest of their visit every time Irwin walked past one of them, they'd start copping nervous peeks at his rear!"

I laugh so hard it warms me right up. Papa doesn't even smile. "Remember?" I ask, and he tilts his head toward his left shoulder, then straightens it again. But I can't tell if that means yes, or that his neck is stiff. So I give up. I stare into the fog too.

There's nothing in sight but the mill clock, but you can actually watch time pass on this clock, so that's what I do: I watch the tip of the phone-pole-sized aluminum minute hand glide across the concrete face of the building. I remember Irwin once saying that he liked the mill clock because it made a person stop and think. And I remember Everett replying that it made you think all right: it made you think it might not be a bad idea to go buy yourself a big ol' horse pistol and blow your brains out. I don't feel quite like blowing my brains out, but when I try for a while to move my hand as slowly and steadily as the mill clock's hand is moving, it's sure not fun. The human mind and body just aren't built for anything so slow and boring. If Father Time has a brain, I'll bet it's about the size of a BB.

I guess what the mill clock makes me stop and think about is the Aesop fable of the tortoise and the hare. The clock seems like the victorious tortoise, and the men filing in and out of the mill seem like the stupid speedy hares. I've always hated Aesop's stories. Especially the little punchlines at the end where he plays preacher and tells you what everything supposedly means. If Aesop was alive today I'll bet he'd be writing yarns for *Pathfinder Magazine,* calling them things like "Why Tommy Tortoise Told Satan No." I'll bet Aesop's brain wasn't much bigger than Father Time's. I wish there really was such a thing as a Time-Clock Puncher, though. I wish some gigantic, surly, stone-fisted, Soap Mahoney-type guy went wandering around the world smashing every clock in sight till there weren't any more and people got so confused about when to go to the mill or school or church that they gave up and did something interesting instead.

Papa snaps on the radio, twists knobs, punches buttons, and gets several kinds of static before he remembers the thing went dead last summer. He sighs in Lucky smoke, then sighs it out again. I wish he'd say something. Maybe he's tired of me always joking. Maybe he'd like me to be serious for a change. "What's it really like," I ask, "I mean, what do you actually *do* inside the mill?"

"Nothin' much," he mumbles.

"Do you ever do anything you *like* doing in there?"

He sucks his Lucky right down to his fingertips. "Don't matter," he says. "I'd still have to do it."

"What does Roy do?"

" 'Bout the same."

"But what really goes on?" I ask. "After all these years I don't even know."

"Nothin' much," he mutters again.

I look at the mill: the night lights have all come on—whole constellations of them—spotlights and floodlights and huge square-bulbed power lights, suspended and shining from walls and wires, lighting the fog from here to the middle of the Columbia; the mill's got its own railway system, with full-sized boxcars rolling in and out of buildings; it's got its own fleet of tugs, dragging football-field-sized log rafts, one after the other, in off the river; it's got wings as big as whole office buildings, with snarls of exposed vents and flumes and overhead or underground pipes feeding them a steady river's worth of water, some of the pipes and flumes big enough to drive semis through; I can count fourteen lighthouse-sized smokestacks just from where we're sitting, with steam pouring so thick out of nine of them that they look like the source of every cloud on earth; I can feel the fog vibrating from the machinery in the building behind the giant clock. I look back at Papa. "Sure doesn't *look* like nothin' much."

He rubs his temples. "Look," he says irritably. "This mill is a bunch of machines making paper out of trees. Me and Roy and a thousand other yo-yos work the machines. That's all it is, Kincaid. You seen one mill, you seen 'em all."

"But I've never seen even one! Not on the inside."

"Then you're lucky," he says. As if that's that.

But why should it be? It's not as if him sitting there sucking down cigarettes till they stain his fingers orange is more important than talking to me. No longer trying to keep the defiance out of my voice, I ask, "How *exactly* do they make paper out of trees?"

Sliding another cigarette up out of his shirt, Papa mutters, "Where's that Roy?"

"How do they make paper out of trees?" I repeat. "I want to know."

"It's complicated," he says.

"I'm smart," I tell him.

"If you were smart," he growls, "you'd know that how mills make paper out of trees isn't worth talkin' about."

"What if I own a mill someday?"

"If you were smart," he says, "you'd know you won't be owning any mills."

"If I was smart," I snap right back, "maybe I could figure out a way to get my own *dad* to talk to me now and then."

He turns on me. His eyes are slits. "You're runnin' off at the mouth and thinkin' it's clever," he says. "And I've had enough."

"You'd call *any* talking runnin' off at the mouth!" I tell him.

"*One more word*," he says, his mouth a slit now too. "You want to know about the mill, look out the goddamned window."

I look out the goddamned window. It's too goddamned foggy and dark to see. "If the place where you spend every day of your life isn't worth talkin' about," I ask, "what is?"

"*You're* the smart one," he says, and the words are literally muffled by his mouthful of smoke. "You tell me," he says, inhaling it.

I try to think of something great—something truly *fascinating* —just to show him. And to my surprise, I do. "There's a harelip at church!"

This seems to get his attention, but it's not exactly how I meant to begin. "She, uh, she's just my age. And she looks normal, and seems nice enough for a hare—er, she *is* nice. Except when she goes to talk, the lip makes everything sound like it starts with *n*. Like baseball would be *nasenall*, or Jesus *Nyeesus*."

He smokes his Lucky.

"The thing is, there's an operation that'd fix her right up, but her parents won't let her have it. They claim the lip's a cross, see. Like Christ's cross. And some people think the parents are nuts, and some think they're right. So what I wondered was, what do you think?"

"Take a vote," he sighs.

I feel myself getting mad. It makes me talk even faster. "Her name's Vera, and she's a good person, you'd like her I'll bet. Except there's one thing about her, besides the lip I mean, which isn't exactly normal, and I don't know if you'd like this thing or not."

Smoke runs like water up his nostrils. He stares straight ahead at nothing. I can tell he doesn't give a shit what the thing about Vera even is. Which makes me all the more determined to describe it.

"She likes to pray, see. And I don't mean like Irwin or even Mama like it. I mean she makes up these prayers—great big long suckers—and says 'em right in front of everybody. It's not like showing off. It's like they just *pour* out of her, like she'd die or something if she held them in. Except every time Vera opens her mouth every kid in the place starts snickerin' and snortin', and the grownups get mad, and nobody listens, and the whole place goes nuts. Yet every week, when Brother Beal asks for the closing prayer, Vera, knowing what'll happen, *still* raises her hand, *wanting* to say it!"

Papa doesn't react.

"Seems weird, doesn't it? But brave too. Don't you think?"

No answer.

"She said one today, and they laughed so bad Beal started hollering '*Thank you, Vera*,' just hoping to end the noise. But it was like she couldn't hear, like the noise never mattered, because she really *was* praying, see, not just pretending, so no one counted to her, except maybe— you know. *God*, or something."

Papa's face is so empty I shut my eyes to keep from having to see it. I want to shut my mouth too, but I feel a little like Vera must have felt; this thing has me in its grip; I've *got* to speak. "We talked about it, driving home—about Vera's parents calling the lip her cross and all. And Mama said we shouldn't take sides. She said, 'Judge not lest ye be judged.' Then Irwin said that when we see somebody with a cross we should help them carry it, like the guy did for Jesus in the Bible. But then Everett hauled off and said, 'Great, Winnie! Carry Vera's cross! Yeah! Except what does *that* mean? Does it mean beat up the sixty twerps who laugh at her? Does it mean we wink and flirt with her as if the lip isn't ugly as sin and her parents aren't batty as hell for leaving it that way? Does it mean we should mangle our own lips *nand nall snart snalking nike niss?* Or is it just a piece of pious crap you're belchin' up to keep from having to do anything *real* to help her?'

"And man oh man! Mama got so mad I thought she was going to get us in a wreck . . . But then Peter broke in in that calm way of his that grabs your attention even better than Mama or Everett getting mad. There were some crucial things Vera's parents were forgetting about crosses, was what Peter said. One was that Jesus was nailed to His by *enemies*, not by Mary and Joseph. And another, he said, was that it killed Him. Christ's cross killed Him. We've got to remember what crosses are, Peter said. They're not just decorations on steeples. They're murder weapons, he said, the same as guns, or gas chambers, or electric chairs.

Only much, much slower. So Vera's parents, he said, were one of two things. They were either fools without the slightest idea what Christianity or crosses are. Or they were unbelievably evil.

"And not even Mama could argue with that. But then Everett spoke up again, saying that if any of us *really* wanted to help Vera, we would march straight up to her parents next Sabbath, and tell them exactly what Pete had just told us. And you should've seen Irwin! He got all excited and started nodding his head like he not only agreed but planned on doing it. But when Mama saw him in the rearview mirror, she said, '*Don't you dare!*' But I wouldn't be surprised if he *does* dare, Papa! I really think Winnie might! So what do *you* think? I mean, *should* he? Do you think Irwin should tell them?"

"Tell who what?" he murmurs, rubbing his eyes—

and suddenly something in me hurts more than I can stand. "Weren't you *listening?* Didn't you *hear?*"

He takes a drag so long and deep it can't leave his lungs by the time he needs to breathe again, so he inhales the same smoke twice. "I don't know what all goes on at your church," he says. "That's your mother's department."

I want to control myself, I want to calm down, but I also want to slug Papa so hard I knock the smoke right out of his head. Because it's a *lie.* It's a bald-faced, idiotic lie for him to sit there with his wrecked thumb and dead eyes telling me that Vera and her lip and his own sons and crosses are all "Mama's department." "Quit fidgeting," he tells me. And I can barely keep from blurting that he'd fidget too if his father was a liar. "What's *with* you today?" he grumbles. "You're squirmin' like a two-year-old."

I can't breathe, I can't see, I can't sit still.

"Get those muddy boots down off that glove box!" he snaps.

And out it comes: "Then *you* quit smoking!" I shout. "And quit *lying!* And quit sitting there like a goddamned *corpse* out of some damned—"

I see the fury come into his eyes, but I don't see the fist that smashes the left side of my face. My head snaps hard into the seat and bounces so quickly back to where it had been that for a moment I think, *Nothing happened.* Then my skull feels like it's caving in. My mouth fills with blood. I cover my head and fall sideways. "Kade!" Papa cries, grabbing my shoulder. I shove his hand away, and crawl over against the door. "Oh, Jesus! Kade! I'm *sorry!*"

I feel a stabbing in my eye, and a roar like the mill's in my ear. I feel

Papa's hands on me, hear wild apologies tangled in the roaring. The blood keeps welling, keeps pooling in my mouth, so I pull myself up to spit it all over his fucking car. But when I glance at him first, to be sure he's looking, I see he's white-faced, staring at his left hand—and the hand is trembling harder than I've ever seen anything human tremble. I swallow the blood, and turn back to the window.

"Oh *God* I'm sorry!" Papa moans through the roaring. "Kade, I'm *sorry!* But what *is* it with you? What do you *expect* from me?"

I don't answer, don't move or make a sound, except to swallow more blood.

"You know, millwork isn't *baseball*," he says, and his voice too is trembling. "You—Everett—Peter—do any of you understand that? It's not a game, not an art, it's not even a goddamned skill. It's just a dead thing I do for money so we can eat. I'm a millworker, Kade. And millworkers are the people who can't be who they wanted. Do you understand that?"

I don't answer. Let *him* see how it feels to pour your heart out to a statue.

"Listen!" he begs, sounding broken. "Please! I *never* should have hit you! I never will again. I'm terribly sorry, and want to show it. So tell me *please*, right now if you possibly can, what it is you want from me. Tell me what you and your brothers think I should be doing different, and if it's in my power, if it's possible at all, I *swear* I'll try to do it."

For a moment I say nothing, fearing I'll sob, or choke on blood, if I speak. But then words well right up with the blood, I'm helpless to stop them: "I *know* you hate the mill," I tell him, and tears come the instant I speak. "I *know* you love baseball, and aren't doing what you want. But at least Vera *fights*. She says her dopey prayers no matter what!" I lean against the door, gasping for air and strength to finish. "All I want is for *you* to fight, Papa. To fight to stay alive inside! No matter *what*."

For a moment it seems he's turned to stone again. Then I hear him moving toward me, till he's just inches away. I don't look or turn, but I feel it now—not just his hand or voice but his entire body, right up against mine. And it's quaking like a cold wet dog's. Or like Vera's when she prayed. *He's just like me!* I think, amazed despite the pain. *He's just a grownup boy, stuck in a body, stuck in a life. And his life isn't working. It's not working at all. And he's got no father, his mother can't understand, he's got no one to help him fix it.*

Feeling this, knowing it, I turn and try to hold my father, as he's so often held me. He makes a small rasping sound when my arms slide round him, then wraps me up, very gently, and holds me back. He says nothing more, but I feel his broken breath, his broken love, his fear and heartbeat.

We're still sitting this way, and still trembling, when Roy's faded red plaid jacket appears in the window.

BOOK TWO

Dogmatomachy

CHAPTER ONE

The Shed

Unable to function as plants, we must serve as manure.
—Edward Conze

Camas / Spring / 1963

On Sunday morning, the day after he punched me, Papa donned his old Schenectady White Sox training sweats and a pair of six-dollar running shoes, hopped in the Fortyford, drove up the hill to the McLoughlin High School track, and did sixteen quarter-mile laps as fast as he could run, walk, or stagger them. When he got back home he was blotchy-faced, gray-skinned, and smelled so close to dead that Peter involuntarily retched as he walked past. I about retched too, when the first thing he did upon limping into the kitchen was grab his Lucky Strikes down off the top of the refrigerator. Instead of lighting one, though, he grabbed the carton in a stranglehold, hissed, "You did this to me!," ripped open every pack, shredded and pulped every last cigarette, then swept up the whole mess and flushed it down the toilet. From that day forward he ran four miles every day after work, and didn't smoke another cigarette.

On Sabbath morning a week after he hit me, Papa drove down to an abandoned commercial dairy beside the new Reynolds aluminum plant on Vancouver Lake and spent the day salvaging beat-up studs and cedar siding from one of five barns that were about to be razed and burned. The dairy—Jazzy Jersey Farms it was called; everybody in Camas used to drink their milk—had gone out of business shortly after the aluminum plant came on-line, for the most basic reason imaginable: the cows had all died. The bovine mass death was front-page news for several days running, and for a week or two a lot of people seemed to want to shut the plant down. But when Reynolds Metals bought the dairy for about three times its worth and started grazing beef cattle in its supposedly lethal pastures, the public outcry died as quickly as had the dairy cows. The only person who stayed worked up about it was Everett, who happened to meet a girl at church who swore on three Bibles that her dad worked at Reynolds Metals, and that his job was to patrol the pastures in a tractor every morning before daylight, and to drag away and bury any beef cattle that had dropped dead in the night. Everett called *The Vancouver Guardian* and *The Oregonian* with the story, but nobody would believe him, so he borrowed a friend's flash camera, got up at three o'clock one morning, and started off on his bike for the Reynolds plant in hopes of documenting the cover-up himself. Unfortunately a state cop stopped him two miles from our house, asked what he was doing bicycling in the dark without a head- or taillight, and when Everett told the truth, three Bibles and all, it inspired the cop to escort him all the way back home, wake our whole neighborhood with a siren blast, and tell Mama and Papa that their son was going to end up behind bars if he didn't quit telling smart-aleck lies to officers of the law.

Be that as it may, in March 1963, when Reynolds Metals announced a plan to raze and burn all the old dairy buildings, Papa borrowed Roy's pickup and trailer, got to the barns before the bulldozers did, salvaged a huge heap of cow-kicked, weather-beaten lumber, and hauled his mysterious booty into our backyard. He spent all day Sunday sorting and stacking it, and after dinner went out again, to make eight knee-deep holes in the lawn with a posthole digger. When my brothers and I asked what he was up to, he mumbled, "Buildin' project." When we asked what kind of project, he grunted, "Shed." When we asked what kind of shed, he muttered, "Wooden." Obviously, he didn't feel like talking about it. But this shed was the first thing he'd tried to build since clear back before he crushed his thumb. And in the following weeks, every night after running, he worked on it till he was ready to drop, pulling rusty nails out of boards, cementing eight pressure-treated fifteen-foot four-by-fours into the postholes, framing in three walls, nailing up the old cedar siding. So naturally we were curious. And naturally our fourfold questioning got pretty obnoxious. The interesting thing, though, was that the longer Papa slaved at his mystery shed, the more cheerful he grew, and the more uncharacteristically skilled at treating our badgering as a kind of mental Ping-Pong game, poinking back silly answers as fast as we could fire off questions:

"Come on! What's this shed *for?*" Everett asked (for the fifth or sixth time) the night we helped him nail on the roof.

"It's an Indian burial lodge," Papa answered, "for Cleveland's whole team."

"Not really!" Irwin cackled.

"No, not really," he said, driving a nail home. "Really it's a walk-in closet to hide my cross in, so the neighbors won't have to watch me out here dyin' on it."

"Don't tell them pests and yo-yos," I said. "*I'm* the one who's been helping the most. So tell me. And tell the *truth.*"

"Oooooh," went Papa, the tenpenny nails dangling like galvanized fangs from his mouth. "The *troof!* Ofay. Here id is. Dis sed, Kade, is a healf fpa, a houf of worfhip, an inftitufun of higher learning, an' a cuftom-fented guefthouf for Irwin'f buddy, Uncle Marf."

While Irwin howled, Peter said, "I don't want to bother you, Papa, so I won't ask what it is. I'd like to know. But only when you feel like telling us."

"That's so thoughtful," Papa said, "that I'll tell you right now. This structure, Peter, is going to be an extremely bush little baseball stadium. Unless you ask me again while pretending not to. Then it's gonna be your inheritance."

Papa's shed, when it was finished, was twenty feet long, sixteen feet wide and twelve feet tall. It had north, south and west walls—all of them windowless and doorless—and on the east end there was not only no window or door, there was no wall. The "floor" was the dying grass and granite-hard, kid-packed dirt of the backyard, with a few dog-maimed plastic soldiers, lost marbles, Barbie doll limbs and chunks of totaled Tonka trucks inadvertently thrown in for texture. There were no shelves inside his shed, no benches, no furniture, not even a nail to hang a coat on. There was a view: out the open east end you could see the blistered backside of our garage and, above that, a row of eight identical frosted bathroom windows on the second floor of the Fir Haven Apartments (a yardless, treeless, chicken-cooplike structure named, I guess, for the old-growth Douglas firs they'd cut down in order to build it). And there was light: a pair of naked 100-watt bulbs dangled from opposite corners of the ceiling, casting the kind of garish light that made you want to confess to crimes you hadn't even committed. There was fragrance too: despite the missing wall, the smell of antique cow crap was so intense inside that it was a relief to step out and smell unadulterated Crown Z papermill stench instead.

To sum up, Papa's shed, when it was finished, was three-quarters of a large, malodorous wooden box without heat, without paint, without charm, and without ostensible purpose. Which was why I felt forced, the first time I stood in it alone after dark, to conclude that what I'd taken to be Papa's new lease on life might in fact have been a quiet but complete loss of sanity. The odd thing was, this notion didn't much bother me. Having spent half my life studying the things that schoolteachers, church preachers and papermill and aluminum plant owners considered "sane," I figured Papa's sanity couldn't do us any more harm than everyone else's sanity was already doing.

Irwin's <u>HISTORY OF MY DAD</u> continued

<u>Chapter 6. Early Times In The Minors</u>

Laura Chance got pregnant quick as could be, "IF NOT QUICKER!" as her brother Uncle Marv liked to joke, the infant in question turning out to be my oldest brother Everett Marshall Chance, named after his granddad of the same name born January 21, 1948. So as the Good Book promised, the Lord took one Everett away, but soon gained Himself another. Meanwhile the proud young dad had turned Pro!

Still known as Smoke, Smoke alias Hugh Chance started out with Medford in the Single A California League, which was weird since Medford was in Oregon not California. But at least somebody down there finally coached him how to throw a slider, which once he got the hang of he had a fine season with inspite of him being the youngest man on the team. Going 11 and 6 with a 3.46 ERA, winning five straight games at the end of the season, young Smoke also hit .298 with six home runs as a combination pitcher/pinch-hitter that year. Which brings up the touchy subject of: <u>Why</u> on <u>Earth</u> didn't <u>his</u> <u>lunkhead</u> <u>coaches</u> <u>switch</u> <u>the</u> <u>Big</u> <u>Fella</u> <u>to</u> <u>the</u> <u>outfield</u> <u>to</u> <u>keep</u> <u>that</u> <u>booming</u> <u>bat</u> <u>in</u> <u>the</u> <u>line-up?,</u> the answer to which remains a mystery depending on who you ask. Why leave a .298 power hitter playing pitcher where he bats one game out of five is one side of the coin, for sure. But how do you tell a kid with great speed and control who just went 11 and 6 and won five straight to quit pitching is the other side. HOME-RUNS WIN BALLGAMES! says one train of thought. BUT HAY! PITCHERS WIN PENNANTS! says the other train.

My brother Everett tries to whitewash the situation into black and white by having fits to this day over what a great outfielder Papa would of been if he'd of been an outfielder. But to me this seems like one of these Why Should The Chicken Cross The Road? kind of deals. Look at Everett himself for example. Here sits a five-foot-six-inch-a-hundred-thirty-pounder who goes on trying to play CATCHER for gosh sakes instead of something realistic like second base for his size, all because of his childhood dream of growing up to catch Papa in a Pro Game! And he calls himself smart and logical! "I'M STILL GROWING!" he screams at me all the time. "AND ANYHOW YOUR HERO YOGI BERRA IS ONLY FIVE FOOT SEVEN!" he screams, as if he too is some sensational freak of nature. But why am I even saying this, Mr. Hergert? You had Everett. You know what he's like. Everybody's a big baseball genius except where it comes to themselves is concerned. So Papa stuck with pitching.

In 1948 the White Sox moved Hugh, Laura and tiny Everett clear across country to Stenecktadee New York in the Triple A International League, which Papa says sounds real nifty like they played ball over in Europe and Japan and what not. But what the old International League really was, he says, was a lot of twelve hour bus rides through the moose-infested swamps of New Hampsure, Maine, Quebeck Canada and I don't remember where all where you ended up pitching in blizzards and black-fly attacks while thirty or forty bored hockey fans swore and threw beer cans at you in French. You hurled your guts out up there though, Hugh says, since you knew if you got sent to the showers you'd either catch Athelete's Foot or the hot water would be busted or both.

Meanwhile back in Skenechtudee the young baseball-widow of a wife was going even crazier than our hero, what with boredom, fussy little Everett, not knowing anybody in those parts, and missing Hugh all ganging up on her. About the time she figured she was losing her marbles however she found out she was only pregnant again, this time with young Peter Arthur Chance causing the stomach problems, whose birth in Pullman Washington the following Off-season came six weeks premature November 31, 1948.

Pete was healthy enough for a four-pounder and has since grown into the best ballplayer in the family except maybe Papa as well as the brainiest of the bunch. But the premature delivery business was quite a strain on the young parents at the time. "THIS TWO SONS IN ONE YEAR STUFF HAS GOT TO STOP!" the pooped-out Laura told her tall husband afterwards in a statement quite typical of how well known she was becoming both to Hugh and other ballplayers for her dry sense of humor. No sooner had she said it though, then she got pregnant AGAIN! So maybe God's sense of humor was even dryer!

Backstepping to the baseball side of things, Skenechtadie was a cellar club Hugh's freshman season there, and at 9 and 13 with a 4.85 ERA the young prospect more or less just horror-showed his way through the worst year of his baseball history while the last year of money of his guaranteed salary petered out his fingers like so much water under the bridge. Meanwhile the teams's coaches and players tore at each others's throats, two managers got fired, and Hugh got beaned twice, once by his own roommate in batting practice, during which he broke his wedding finger because of the ring in one of several fistfights, thereby reeking havoc with his pitching and hitting both. His won-lost record and ERA were second-best on his club that year, but what a club! So in 1949 Hugh got browbeaten by the Brass into a stinking one year contract with no raise.

1949, though, turned out to be the sunshine on the other side of the coin there in Stenecktedy, thanks mostly to a new scout in the Sox organization known as Mr. Luigi. A native of Brazil or some such place, Mr. Luigi was an odd little man of strange ways and habits who knew foreign ballplayers like the map of his hand, and Hughs's whole life cheered up for the better when the little oddball sent up eight new players with names like Manual, Cheechee, Oriolio and Jesus pronounced Hay-soose which he'd dug out of such unherd of places as Cuba, Hadey, The Dominion's Republic and either Porto or Costo Rico, I always forget which. Of course there English was terrible if it even existed, but they were sensational ballplayers compared to all the big slow white guys and Canadians who stank it up for Skenachtudie so bad the year before. "Who needs English when you're winning your first AAA league title?" was what Hugh wanted to know. "Besides which our Spanish wasn't so hot either!" as the fair-minded Laura points out.

Several of Luigi's Brown Legions as they came to be known as went on to become Big League Stars, including Rodrigo Something-or-other the great shortstop for The Cubs, I believe, and the catcher Benito Lhosa would of too, Hugh says, if he hadn't of had only one eye. As for Smoke himself, he claims he still had no change-up, no knuckler, no sinker, no forkball nor any of the tremendous junk he later developed except the slider, and he pitched no better than he did the horrid 9 and 13 year before. Yet on nothing more than sheer guts, willpower, control, brains, talent, youth, grit, determination, plus much better coaching and a whole different ballclub, the fireballing youngster's Won-Loss Record skied to 14 and 2 by late July, with a 1.99 ERA that led that hitter's league by about seventeen miles!

Then it came. The Call from the Big Time! Come on Upstairs and start your first Major League Game in September, Big Fella! cried the Chicago White Sox Braintrust over the phone to Hugh one unforgettable summery evening, I don't recall the exact date. So wouldn't you know the Korean War would crank itself up into something serious, and right at that moment young Hugh would get himself drafted!

Of course old Marion Becker Pacifist Chance had an unholy cow when this news ripped home to Pullman. WHERE IS JOHN WILKES BOOTH WHEN WE REALLY NEED HIM? she kept shouting somewhat nastily. She also carried around a big sign on her bicycle bumper (she couldn't drive a car and still can't as of yet) that cried U.S. OUT OF NORTH AMERICA! till somebody slashed her tires all up. Meanwhile Hugh was mailed off to Boot Camp, and Laura, little Everett and teenytiny Pete had to move back to Pullman and live with Marion, what with money shortages and Laura being royally pregnant again.

But poor Laura! Not only did the return to Pullman mean sitting around slaving over a hot stove, two babies, vacuums, ironing and such while pregnant all day, she also had to listen to every last one of Marions's cows! "FIRST THEY SLAUGHTER MY HUSBAND! THEN THEY CHEAT US OUT OF OUR PENSION! THEN THEY BUTCHER MY SON!" Marion would shriek in Laura's ripely pregnant direction as if Koreans were already dancing up and down in young

Smoke's dead brains. Even in an English accent, this sort of talk was not the ticket for a happy healthy pregnancy, so it was during this period that Laura got in the habit of drownding out Marions's cows by praying rather loudly to herself right there in front of everybody, asking God, Jesus and so forth for strength to ignore her mother-in-law's cows and save Hugh and her babies from danger, death and the like, which she still does to this day. It was also during this period that Laura started never missing church religiously, which is interesting to notice since it was yours truly inside her, since out of us four brothers I'm the only one who can stand church so far.

The good news, though, was that before Hugh even finished Boot Camp Laura's fervied prayers for his safety were answered! All Uncle Sam wanted him for, it turned out, was to play ball on an Army baseball team! Strange and wonderful are the ways of prayers and Armies!

Kincaid:
Camas / Spring / 1963

One day along about the time the big league teams were moving out of Florida and Arizona and up into the cold with the rest of us, Papa and Roy drove home from the mill an hour early, and out of Roy's pickup unloaded the first really good clue as to the nature of Papa's building project: a load of clean topsoil, which they heaped right in the center of the shed's floorless floor. I knew at that moment that Papa was building a pitcher's mound in there. And I took some joy in this discovery. My joy was guarded, however, by a dozen or so unanswerable questions which the mound raised, like welts, in my mind. For instance:

"What possible good will a pitcher's mound in a manurey backyard hutch do him with the rest of the ballpark, not to mention the team, completely missing?"

And "What good will any sort of mound anywhere do him with his pitching thumb still dead as a doornail and his life still chained to a daily stint at the mill?"

Still, once I knew that the shed had to do with baseball—once I realized that he was focusing (however fuzzily) on pitching, and that this new focus had him looking darned near as happy as he looked insane—I kept my questions to myself. While the trapeze artist is in mid-flip, while the tamer's head is halfway down the lion, while the magician's saw is passing through the lady in the box, even the thickest kid in the audience knows it's no time for questions.

Papa eventually made his pitcher's mound perfect. He spent four or five hours, two nights in a row, painstakingly shaping, reshaping and tamping down the dirt with shovels and feet and a big iron bar before he was satisfied enough to plant a pitcher's rubber smack-dab on the summit. Then—one balmy, half-mooned mid-April evening when my brothers were all off at their various ball practices and Mama and the twins were inside the house—I suddenly had Papa, his shed, and his happy insanity all to myself . . .

The first thing Papa did that night was drag the old wood extension ladder out from under the house and lean it against the back wall of the garage. Next he stuck an electric drill and a few other tools in his carpenter's belt, climbed the ladder, and began wiring two lights in up under the garage eave—spotlights this time, great big powerful ones. When he got them both working he aimed their brilliant beams in a V straight down the wall, then tried—and failed—to sound casual as he told me to grab a tape and check the distance from the pitcher's rubber to the spot where the beams struck the ground. "It's a clue, Kade," he said. "A good one."

But I needed no clues. I'd finally pieced it together. This was no harebrained fraction of an imaginary ballpark. It was something perfectly practical—assuming that its builder was a pitcher. Papa's backyard shed was an all-weather bullpen, and the garage wall was simply its backstop. He'd just built himself a warm, dry place in which to practice pitching year-round. Trying to play it cool, and failing just like Papa, I said, "I don't need a tape. I can eyeball it. It's sixty feet six inches—exactly."

He didn't laugh when I said this. He barely even smiled. He just said, "A regular Sherlock," meaning Holmes, I guess, and tossed down his keys like I was sixteen and had asked to borrow the car. "Bring back anything odd you might find in the trunk of the Fortyford," he said.

I ran round the house and down to the car at the curb, yanked open the trunk, and was not at all surprised to find a battered old home plate lying there. What did surprise me was that the instant I picked it up, wham! *yak butter* . . . Papa's whole project ceased to feel arcane or mysterious and began instead to make a boy's kind of sense. Common sense. *Baseball* sense. Had it been a new plate I don't know what I'd have felt, but something about this beat-up matter-of-fact one made everything Papa was doing seem just as matter-of-fact. Some sort of genuine athletic comeback was in the making here. I just knew it. I could taste it. But only on the inside of me. Outside of me the whole project still seemed so crazy and vulnerable that in order to protect it I carried that indestructible house-shaped old slab of rubber back around the garage as if it were blown glass or precious china. "It won't break," Papa laughed when he saw me coming. "You can pound it in yourself," he added, "soon as you've done the preliminary honors."

I asked what honors those were. He pointed at the garden hoe and rake leaning against the toolshed. "How about weeding me out a batter's box?"

I set to work like a pirate who's just found the X on the map. Meanwhile Papa went back in the garage, and returned with a used twin mattress. When he'd spotted this pee-stained relic at a Goodwill drop-box a few weeks back, he'd cried, "Perfect!" and tied it to the roof of the car— causing my brothers and me to wonder yet again about his mental health. But when he got it home he'd calmly covered it with two sheets of black plastic and a third layer of rainproof Army surplus canvas, and now its purpose was obvious: padding and soundproofing for his garage-wall backstop. Nailing two stout metal bookshelf brackets to the wall, he hung the mattress from them by its handles.

He disappeared into the garage again, and this time was gone long enough for me to de-sod the "batter's box," pick out every last rock and weed, and work the dirt smooth as the top of a fresh pumpkin pie by dragging the back of the rake over it again and again. While I worked the day turned dusky without my noticing. But what I did notice, under the spotlights, was the odd, half-canceled dual shadows that I was casting. They looked uncannily familiar. I straightened up, tried to place them, couldn't, and had just started raking again when it hit me: they were almost exactly the sorts of shadows that ballplayers cast at a night ballgame. Like a painter trying to get perspective, I backed away from my efforts then, and was delighted to see that, at least in this light, my hokey handmade batter's box had truly begun to resemble a few square feet of bona fide bush league ball diamond. *And if a homemade batter's box can get this real this fast*, I thought, *there's no reason why Papa can't make it out of this yard, out of the mill, clear on out of this town and back into pro ball . . .*

At which point I heard the school bus bringing my brothers home, my brain kicked in, our yard turned back into a yard, and I mumbled aloud, "Naw. No way. Don't be ridiculous."

"What's ridiculous?" Papa asked—and I jumped. I hadn't heard him slip up behind me.

"Nothing!" I snapped. "Nothing's ridiculous!" But he looked a little hurt, so I added, "You weren't supposed to hear is all. I was thinking out loud."

"About what?"

I shrugged. "You and baseball."

"Oh," he said. "Well. Me and baseball. That *is* ridiculous."

We both began to laugh then, and for a moment that yak butter belief in a comeback filled me a second time. But right at the height of it Papa stopped laughing, looked around the yard, waved a careless hand at everything we'd done, and said, "You know, Kade. This whole thing, this shed business, it really *is* ridiculous." Then he smiled—and sadly, almost shyly added, "But Vera says her stupid prayers no matter what. Right?"

This remark washed over me in slow, silent waves: the shredding of the cigarettes, the tortured four-mile runs, the scavenged lumber and laborious building project—it was some kind of elaborate apology, some sort of self-imposed penance for having hit me. It was a gesture, a wonderful gesture. But a gesture nonetheless. "Look, Kade," he said, reaching down and squeezing my sagging shoulders. "My situation, baseball-wise, is hopeless."

My throat began to close. I looked away to hide the welling in my eyes.

"The thing is," he said, "I don't want you getting worked up over nothing when I start spending time out here. I built this shed because throwing baseballs keeps my head on straight. I did *not* build it to inaugurate some sort of fairytale comeback. Do you understand that?"

I stared at the little piece of diamond we'd just made.

"No matter how well I may eventually seem to be throwing, and no matter what your all-knowing brother Everett may say, all I'm ever gonna do out here is toss the pitcher's equivalent of harelip prayers. Okay?"

My tongue felt thick and dry now—not a hint of yak butter anywhere.

"Don't think of it as baseball, Kade. Call it my hobby, or some weird kind of worship maybe. Call it psalmball, or shedball, or thumbball if you like. But remember it's not baseball. It's not a comeback. You've got to promise me that."

A lump of sandstone lay in my throat. I couldn't speak. But he waited. He waited till our eyes met, then bent my will like an arm wrestler bends a wrist: I had to nod to keep from breaking. "Okay," he said, handing me his hammer. "Let's pound in that plate."

We did so. But I took no pleasure in it now. And when Papa stepped back and sighed, "That's it, such as it is . . ." he just looked like a worn-out millworker.

Mama banged on the kitchen window, signaling that dinner was ready. Papa waved and nodded. But he didn't move. Tired as he was, he too seemed reluctant to leave the summery air and ballpark lighting. We walked up to the shed to turn off the lights in there, but I stepped onto the mound first, toed the rubber, and looked down the pipe at the batter's box. It seemed a long way off. If it were me throwing I wasn't sure I'd even hit the mattress. Papa eyed me, shook his head, and said, "Go stand in the box down there and make like a batter. I'll show you a stance."

I ran down to the wall, picked up the garden hoe, gripped it like a bat, and stepped into the box. But when I looked back at Papa, I was shocked: the distance between us had somehow shrunk to almost nothing. And with those naked bulbs blazing behind him he was unrecognizable—an ominous, mountainous shape blocking out the light. I took my best batter's stance and gripped the hoe hard, but my father's body was so unfamiliar, so confident and so *large* that I felt ludicrous. I watched him work his neck and shoulders loose, his left arm dangling all the while, limp as a hangman's noose. I watched him peer at a catcher hidden in the wall at my back, shake off a sign, nod grimly at a second. I watched his lungs and hangman's arm suddenly fill with air and energy, watched him swirl into a slow, full windup. But when he suddenly, violently hurled his right leg and left arm and whole shadowy being toward me, I shut my eyes, fell back out of the box, and landed flat on my backside—though I knew, or thought I knew, that his hand held no ball.

Papa snorted. He thought my fall was an act. I dusted my rear, forced a grin, and tried to pretend the same. "Shedball," he said again, shutting off the lights. "Just harelip prayers, Kade. Don't forget."

I didn't. But I didn't forget, either, that some prayers just maybe, just might, receive answers.

Irwin's HISTORY OF MY DAD continued

Chapter 7. The Goon Squad

What the U.S. Army figured, Hugh reports himself figuring at the time, was that a Pro Ballplayer was worth more against Koreans as morale boosters than as a common foot soldier. This became extra

true after hardly any Big League ballplayers got drafted in the Korean
War due to how the owners of Big League Ballclubs were a bunch of
regular Einsteins when it came to finding loopholes to keep their star
players out of the military with. So the few stars the Army nabbed,
they decided to show off, Hugh says. And the best way to do this, they
figured, was to make a Morale Boosting Club out of them.

Sounds fun, doesn't it, cheering up all the scared young recruits by
playing exhibition ball for them instead of marching off to War with
them? But think again sucker! Because the Team Of Stars was only
one team, and to really boost morale they needed somebody to play
against. And even though he'd been 14 and 2 for Triple A Skenechtudy
and was on his way Upstairs, Hugh Chance was just Mister No-Face
No-Name as far as your typical Army fan or officer was concerned.
Such was how one of America's finest young prospects came down
with a splat on Baseball's saddest excuse of a ballclub ever!

Known amongst themselves as The Goon Squad, they were mostly a
bunch of scruddy Big League bench-warmers, bush leaguers, and as
many as possible Oriental fellas to remind the cheering U.S. troops of
the Korean enemy as the Star Squad knocked the snot out of them
every night at Fort This or Fort That. What about OUR morale? the
Goon Squad sometimes wondered. But to the Army's way of thinking,
morale boosting was pretty much a Punch and Judy type show
intended to teach our lads in uniform to go reef on Communists the
same rough way the Stars always reefed on the Goons.

It made for one weird brand of baseball, Hugh reports in retrospect.
Especially since the Stars had a lieutenant who just happened to be an
ex-Double A manager managing them, while meanwhile the Goons
were skippered by this deadbeat sergeant who spent most of every
game on a walkytalky taking orders from the lieutenant on exactly how
that game should be thrown. That's right folks! THROWN! The
games were totally rigged is what I'm getting at! As long as they stank
it up the Stars lieutenant let the Goons pretty much swing away so
that things would seem lifelike to the dumber fools amongst the
spectators. But if the Goons got the least little rally going, the
lieutenant would kill it in a variety of several different ways.

One of his favorites was wiping Goon runners off the basepaths by
ordering the sergeant to order his Goons to steal on the next pitch,
then signalling his own catcher and pitcher to pitch a pitch-out. In
this way the Star catcher would nail the runner by several miles, after
which the fans heckled and jeckled the poor Goon all the way back to

the bench about how slow he was. Another neat trick of the
lieutenant's was how Goon pitchers were allowed to throw hard
enough so that things didn't look like sheer BP out there, but weren't
allowed to throw full speed fastballs, change-ups, or anything inside
enough to be considered a brush-off, nor fast curves nor knucklers nor
knock-downs nor any other major offensive type tool of the Hurling
Trade. One last trick: gopherballs. These were phoned in by the
lieutenant like pizzas over the walkytalky, which the Goon sergeant
(waiter) relayed to his Goon pitchers (cooks) by picking his nose with
his little finger, meaning that Hugh or whoever had to ooze over a
nice no-hop fastball (pepperoni pizza) for the Star batter (pizza-eater)
to clomp halfway to Hong Kong.

   The results of these tricks? Every last game the Goon pitchers got
royally destroyed.

   One night at Fort Sill in the heat of battle though, Hugh got carried
away and ignored several flagrant nose picks with the bases loaded,
fanning two famous sluggers in a row to retire the side. So when he
got back to the bench, there stood the lieutenant on the walkytalky,
reading him off about how missed signals in Army Morale Booster Ball
were Treachery and War Crimes and Court Martial Material. Ordering
the big southpaw onto K.P. for about the two hundredth time, the
lieutenant told Hugh if he repeated the mistake he would find himself
in a snowy trench on the Mongol Border so fast his head would melt.
And the worst part was how "Yes SIR! Very sorry SIR!" poor Hugh had
to grovel inspite of being so sick of tossing gopherballs that snowy
Mongol trenches sounded somewhat lovely and peaceful. What with
the Big Leagues awaiting him however, and what with Laura, Marion,
Everett and Peter all depending on Hugh for love, rent, groceries and
such, he decided he'd better mind his pees and cues.

   A portion of my dad's history lives on to this day when my family,
while watching ballgames, calls a hung curve or fat fastball a North
Korean or No-K for short, meaning the opposite of a K, which is a
strike-out in baseball lingo. Anyhow, it was while serving up No-Ks on
a diamond the Navy made on Guam by dumping oil on a beach then
running over it in a steamroller that Hugh got the letter from his
lovely wife telling how the Good Lord had sent along something
drastic to cheer their lives up with, namely a drastic sized baby of 12
POUNDS 10 OUNCES, born Christmas Eve no less, who the doctor
reported laughed merrily when he spanked it after it was born, though
Laura was of course too punchy due to childbirth, drugs and such to

verify the jolly sound. This laughing infant was the biggest baby ever born alive to the hospital there at Pullman, and continues to be the largest best-looking kid here at John McLoughlin High School of downtown Camas Washington to this day. He was also the third Chance's son to be born in three years, as I'm sure you've noticed Mr. Hergert, since you've gotten old and gray teaching all three of us. I'm sure I don't need to add that the young monster of which we're speaking here was none other but IRWIN DAVID CHANCE MYSELF, as Laura and Hugh named me in their next letter to each other, after two very old and dear friends of theirs whom I can't go into at this time due to being too hungry to go on writing for now. (I should take a second to add however that I'm only kidding about you being old or gray!)

Kincaid:
Camas / Spring / 1963

Papa took his new pitching sessions surprisingly seriously. He wouldn't let us come out to watch him, wouldn't let us use his shed when he wasn't in it, wouldn't even let the twins have tea parties in it when he was at work. He said everyone on earth needed a little place to call their own, "and that smelly shed out there is mine."

Of course his forbidding us to watch him throw had the same effect on Everett and me that Mama's forbidding of "heathen reading material" had once had on Peter: no sooner did he lay down the law than we began figuring out ways to break it. You could get a crummy side view of his pitches from Irwin's and my room upstairs, but if Papa saw our faces in the window he'd say, "Nothing to do?" then give us some tedious house-work or chore. So Everett and I scouted around, and eventually discovered, in a laurel hedge between our backyard and the laundromat next door, a niche that was maybe thirty feet behind the shed, and a little to one side. It wasn't exactly a box seat. All we could see of Papa's motion was the grotesque double shadow it cast on the lawn in front of the mound. But we could hear the grunts of effort he put into each pitch; we could watch the baseballs streak out into the light; and we could see the fleeting dents they made in the strike zone he'd painted on the canvas, and call them balls or strikes.

Papa wasn't kidding about "harelip prayers," though. His resurrected pitches were fast, even to Everett's educated eye, but shockingly wild. We soon grew accustomed to the resounding *thwham!* of balls denting the bare garage siding, followed by a *whump!* inside the shed (Papa's fist slamming the wall), a hissed *Chee-rist!* or *Sheee-it!*, and a palpably disgusted silence. Every time he fell into one of these funks I expected to see him stalk out of the shed and into the house to announce that he'd sworn off his new hobby forever. But instead, sooner or later, out would come another scorcher, which usually also missed the mattress and blasted the bare wall so hard I half expected the ball to stick.

It was hard, at first, not to burst out laughing at these great thwammings and whumpings of balls and fists. But after a few nights something changed inside us, and the same sounds nearly tempted us to cry. What bothered Everett were the fist-slammings and other shows of temper. Papa had always been the calmest man on the field, Everett said. As a young fastballer he'd needed the calm because his tremendous speed was so hard to control, and as an older, cannier junk pitcher he'd needed it still more, because when junk pitchers give way to adrenaline surges they lose the cockeyed perspective that gives the juju to their junk. But there in his shed, Everett said, Papa was throwing more than just adrenaline: he was throwing his frustration, his anger, his dissolved hopes, his fear, his fatigue; he was taking everything inside him and just slinging it, helter-skelter, out into the night. "It's not even pitching," Everett soon concluded. "Whatever it is, it's not pitching."

I agreed, but was not so troubled, because Papa had warned me that this would be the case. What moved and disturbed me about his pitches was that they really did resemble Vera's praying. He and Everett didn't have to listen to her every Sabbath, so they couldn't know, but his shedball throws had the same "no matter what" earnestness, the same abject helplessness, and they aroused in me the same weird blend of embarrassment and admiration as I listened to the preposterous results. His left thumb, like her lip, had the same bad-dream quality, too, in that the harder they tried, the more laughable their efforts grew. Yet with identical, terrible stubbornness, Vera kept praying and Papa kept throwing. And the more he missed the mattress, the louder he blasted the bare wall, the fiercer and deeper my love for him grew.

Irwin's <u>**HISTORY OF MY DAD**</u> concluded

<u>Chapter 8. Escape From The Goons!</u>

February 25 1951 was a day even those of my family members not yet born fondly remember. It started out in the evening with another dumb morale booster game in front of a huge crowd of green recruits at an Airbase in Hawaii with one of those crazy Hawaaian names Hugh calls Fort Oopawanapoonawahinipopo for laughs. In the third inning though, our hero smashed a tremendous home run with two aboard, giving the Goons a temporary 3 to 2 lead over the Stars, in addition to which the Stars's 2 runs were purely due to several No-Ks the fat-assed lieutenant had ordered poor Hugh to throw. So the real score was Goons 3, Stars Zip, and as Hugh trotted round third he shot the lieutenant a look that said how well the two of them both knew it. And boy did Hugh's look hit the bull's eye! By the time he reached the bench, there was the lieutenant on the walkytalky, jabbering about how the Goon Squad was getting uppity and the Stars were getting punchy so today by golly they would play for keeps! No fake errors! No gopherballs! No pitch-out-doomed Goon base-stealing nor any other form of Morale Building whatsoever! "JUST KNOCKDOWN DRAG OUT HARDBALL!" the lieutenant yelled, "WITH TRIPLE K.P. DUTY FOR THE LOSERS, AND MAY THE BEST TEAM WIN!"

In defence of what happened next Hugh said the Stars could of beat the Goons four fair games out of five normally, and that it was only due to months of half-speed fastballs and fake-hung curves that they'd forgot what real hurling looked like. But I must also point out that once Private Hugh Chance started throwing his genuine scorchers they couldn't see the old horsehide at all! After a couple innings Hugh started feeling so sorry for the Star hitters that he let them glimpse the ball again. Unfortunately the only balls he let them glimpse were the blazing snapping curveballs which started out at their terrorized faces causing them to dive for cover, then nipped down over the inside corner for the most embarrassing kind of called strikes! And with nothing to lose and their whole self-respects to win back, Hugh and his buddies just cruised! The egg-faced Stars could do nothing right. The jolly Goons could do nothing wrong. The results? One of the hideous disasters of Army Morale-Building History! After eight innings

of slaughter with the score standing at 17 to 2, no outs, and the basepaths loaded with laughing Goons, a furious Brigadeer General came storming out of the stands and ordered the game called to a halt on account of darkness even though it was still totally light!

Hugh's six innings of real stuff, in case you're interested, was a five-hit shutout, in addition to which he hit for The Cycle as it is known as, adding a sixth inning triple and eighth inning double to his third inning homer and first inning single for one each of every type of bingo known to man! Anybody who didn't think Hugh Chance was Big League Material at this point better get there head out as the saying goes! When the game got called the Goons realized they might of poured it on a bit thick, though. The poor recruits in the stands were silent as a rock, making none of the happy murmurings you hear normal fans murmur as they dribble out the exits. IS THIS WHAT THE NORTH KOREANS ARE GOING TO DO TO US? their sadly youthful faces seemed to wonder into the bleak and quiet stillness of the fragrant Hawaaian evening. Things were not exactly hunkydory in the airplane hanger the players used for a lockerroom either, since the Goons shared it with the slaughtered Stars. "There is a fight in the air if ever I smelled one!" Hugh reports smelling at the time. "Before this night is over I wouldn't be surprised if the boys and me end up in the Fort Oopawanapoonawahinipopo Brig!" he reports thinking. "But it was worth it!" he claims thinking as well.

Right at the extreme danger point though, a voice like a sonic boom came crashing through the unhappy hanger. "SO THIS IS THE ARMY'S GREAT MORALE-BUILDING BASEBALL PROGRAM?" it boomed. And there stood the smoking Brigadeer who'd called the game on account of fake darkness! Removing the Star Lieutenant to the far end of the hanger, he about chewed his rear end off as the saying goes! But that was nothing compared to what came next!

What came next was he walked straight up to poor Hugh Chance of all people and ordered him to report to his private office, where he shoved him in a chair, handed him a cold beer with plenty more where that came from, and roared, "AT EASE PRIVATE! I WANT TO CHAT IS ALL!"

Poor Hugh could only nod and gulp at his beer like so much rat urine. He'd never chatted with a guy with so much ribbons and crap decorated on his chest in his life. Knowing that when guys like Brigadeer Generals set you down for a chat they aren't just messing around, Hugh soon discovered today was no exception! "Do you enjoy playing ball for that Goon Squad?" was the first interrogation.

"Well Sir!" Hugh quivered, "frankly I would prefer to be home in the States, pitching Pro."

"What professional team are you normally affiliated on young man?" was the General's next inquiry.

"I was called up from Triple A to the White Sox just before I got drafted, Sir!" Hugh said. "But I didn't have time to report, Sir!"

"Rotten luck!" went the Brigadeer.

"NO KIDDING SIR!" Hugh practically screamed in his face, forgetting who he was talking to for a second.

"Have you got a family?" went the Brigadeer, not seeming to mind.

"YES SIR!" Hugh blasted off again. "Bu-but pa-pardon the shouting Si-Sir!" he stuttered pitifully. "It's just that we'd already had three sons in three years when my wife came up to Fort Lewis last fall, and at the Fort there we er, went on a picnic and er, well er Sir, er, one thing led to another er, and there's another family member on the way!"

"Well, Private," went the General. "Something has got to be done."

"About wha-what, Si-Si-Sir!?" Hugh jibbered.

"About YOU!" growled the decorated stranger in the opposite chair.

"Oh, that!" Hugh groveled.

"If these ballgames are supposed to be Morale-Building dramas, then you are not much of an actor!"

"I guess not, Sir!" Hugh squeaked.

"There's no guessing to it," the Brigadeer said. "I know talent when I see it, Private. Don't you see the problem? You are too unknown to pitch for the Stars, but too good to be a Goon. It's simple. How much time have you got left in the service anyway?"

"Four months Sir!" Hugh barked.

"Well, Private," said the General. "That's four months too long!"

"Yes Sir!" Hugh gagged, thinking MONGOL TRENCHES AND YOUNG DEATH HERE I COME, JUST LIKE MY DAD!

Then came the punchline! "What would you think of an immediate honorable discharge?" scowled the Brigadeer.

"Come again Sir!?" poor Hugh finally stumbled.

"How would you feel about clearing out of the Army and heading back home to the ChiSox and to your family, where you belong?"

"YOU'RE NOT SERIOUS SIR!" Hugh blasted. But how wrong he was! And though we don't know to this day how the Brigadeer pulled all the strings and cut all the red tape he pulled, we found out why he cut it! For as the two men sat drinking beers far into the night, it came out that in real life the General was Number 1, from Chicago, and Number 2, as a civilian had been known as Mr. Blank (Sorry Mr. Hergert but I'm under orders not to report his genuine name in full in case it'd get him in trouble!), and best of all, Number 3, one of Mr. Blank's acquaintances as a kid back in Chicago had been a fine young pitcher who was a math whiz as well, yet had a strange hole in his head where gambling was concerned since the only team he would bet on was the Chicago Cubs! "Does such a man sound familiar, Private?" inquired the Brigadeer with a new and tender touch leaking out into his voice.

And with tears nearly blurting from both eyes, "Yes Sir!" Hugh softly rejoindered. For he saw that the Brigadeer's long-lost friend was his own late father Everett Senior!

To make a long story short, in two week's time Hugh was right back home with Laura and his sons where he belonged, then two weeks later was kissing them a fond goodbye and scooting back out the door to where he also belonged at the White Sox spring training camp in Florida or else Arizona, I forget. The rest of course is History! Or it would of been History, except in training camp Hugh twisted the snot out of his left ankle against second base in a stupid sliding drill, then tried to come back too soon with a wrecked pitching motion so that he tore the bejeezus out of his big left shoulder causing him to lose both his famous fastball, his pinpoint control, his slider, and so forth till he ended up stinking it up so royally he got swapped in a seven player deal the Sox wangled with the Senators, who took one look at their mangled young southpaw and sent him clear down to a Double A squad in Oklahoma!

So Hugh, Laura, Everett, Pete and me moved to Kincaid Oklahoma for two whole seasons, where to our amazed surprise we ended up loving the place so much we named my little brother after it just to remember those happy days by. ("Lucky I wasn't born in Stenechkudee!" Kincaid told us once he got old enough to crack jokes of this type.)

On that note concludes THE HISTORY OF MY DAD FROM HIS BIRTH UP TO KINCAIDS'S! And what a History it was! Though to tell the truth, if I'd of dreamed any dad of mine had even a tenth this much information to him I'd of wrote my Essay about somebody who died the instant they were born instead. Like you for instants! (I'm only kidding, Mr. Hergert! Seriously!) I mean it though. Full grown adults get darn complicated when you set their life down on paper end to end. Yet it's almost worth it when you finish, just to look at ol' Hugh clomping around the house in his skanky old baseball t-shirts or whatever, knowing what you now know about him. "GOSH! WHAT A GUY!" one can't help thinking. Or Laura too, walking by this very second in her bathrobe and curlers. "WHAT A GAL!" you come to realize. Even crusty old Marion Becker Chance in her weird way. "WHAT AN OLD BIRD SHE IS AS WELL!" one can't help mentioning.

So thanks again for your attention here, and also for the excellent grade you're about to reach up and give me! (Just kidding!)

THE END!!!!!!!

CHAPTER TWO

Strike Zones

nothing is stationary
everything wiggles
   —John Gierach

the backyard

I'll never forget the time Papa taught me about strike zones. It happened the night after I'd hoed out the little batter's box for him—another one of those unseasonably warm spring evenings. Papa had again rushed home from the mill before my brothers got home from ball practice, and when I'd seen the new spotlights snap on I'd rushed outside in a tizzy, thinking I was about to see him pitch for the first time. When, instead, he came trudging out of the garage in his dirty work clothes carrying a brush, a pint of thinner, and a quart can of Dutch Boy white, I couldn't hide my disappointment. Slouching against the garage, I grumped, "What's *that* for?"

But Papa didn't seem to hear. He'd pulled a piece of white chalk from his pocket, stepped up to the canvas-covered mattress, and begun scowling at it as though he and the mattress were having an argument. When the scowl deepened, I figured the mattress must be winning. Sighing every bit as theatrically as the McLoughlin High kid who'd recently played Hamlet in the worst play anybody in Camas, even Grandawma, had ever seen, Papa commenced to draw. There wasn't much to the drawing he did, though. He just chalked up a rectangle maybe fifteen inches wide and three feet tall. Didn't even bother to get the sides straight. I understood now that he was making a target at which to aim his pitches, and that he intended to paint it Dutch Boy white when he was done. What I didn't understand was why this simple process had him looking as though it were taxing his brain to the limit. Slapping a tape measure against his chalked-in rectangle, he swore under his breath, grabbed a rag, furiously erased it, then chalked up another rectangle slightly shorter than the first. But after a few seconds he threw his tape at it, cursed, and erased this one too. Then he spun on me and snapped, "It's *nonsense* to paint a strike zone at all!"

Knowing it wasn't safe to speak, let alone sulk, I snapped out of my slouch, grabbed a screwdriver, pried open the paint, found a stick and started stirring, striving all the while to look as innocuous as the Dutch Boy on the can.

"Why?" Papa demanded. "*Why* is a fixed strike zone nonsense?"

I was perfectly honest: I shrugged.

"Think about it!" he huffed. "Say we make our rectangle about the size of the strike zone on a six-foot hitter. This leaves out shorter and taller hitters, that's an obvious defect. But the deeper defect, the *crucial* defect is, where the hell *is* the strike zone on a six-foot hitter? Where is it on *any* hitter?"

I thought about it, as commanded, but was forced to shrug again. But this time Papa cried, "*Exactly!*" and whammed me happily on the back.

Bewildering as all this was, my confusion on another point had vanished: the reason my father did not wax lyrical about warm spring nights or baseball fever was that he wasn't the poet, he was the topic. Papa didn't present the case for baseball, he *represented* it, and to stand in front of him wondering if the scent of mown grass and plum blossoms made him think of baseball was like asking a bloodstained man with a fly rod and ten dead trout on a stringer if he ever thought about fishing. "The reason no one can say where the strike zone is," he said with vehemence, "is that the *actual* strike zone has almost nothing to do with the width of the plate or the size of the hitter. The *real* strike zone is located somewhere else entirely. Isn't it, Kade? Isn't it?"

Heck if I knew. What I did know was that he'd begun to remind me of someone. But before I could think who, he was proclaiming, "Damn right it is! The strike zone that matters, the only one we've got to work with really, is the one locked up inside the skull of the plate ump. And that, m'boy, is why it's no rectangle, no well-defined shape, no sort of plate-wide knee-high armpit-low configuration at all. A strike zone is a damned *illusion* is what it is, Kade. It's a *figment*. It's a geometrical will-o'-the-wisp perched on a twig inside the ump's law-abiding little brain."

I had it: the intensity, the thought-swamped smile, the "I dare you to disagree" manner, the enlarged pupils—for the first time I could remember, Papa was behaving exactly like Everett. On one of his late-night philosophical jungle cruises, no less. I was flabbergasted. Could my calm, soft-spoken father be the genetic source of the beans my big brother was so full of? It didn't seem possible. But there was no time to speculate: he'd taken his rag, erased every line from the mattress, said "Look here!" in a way that sounded like I damn well better, and quickly chalked up a yard-high, upside-down pear. Like the mandibles of a giant ant, his gaze grabbed and held me. "Know what *that* is?" he demanded.

I was terrified to confess that I didn't. But Papa saved me the trouble. "Of *course* you don't!" he bellowed.

I shook my head, nodded, shrugged, giggled, and threw in a *Whew!* for good measure. Meanwhile Papa's face had broken out in a very Everett-like leer. "*That*," he said, "is a genuine Josh Kendall strike zone. Damned if it's not. Umped me twice at Schenectady, once in Tacoma, he's a big-shot American Leaguer now. But I watched him work two games on TV last season, and Kendall's zone is *still* a goddamn inverted pear!"

I smiled and began to contemplate the pear, but Papa was already ragging it into oblivion, and chalking up a small, thin oval in its place. "Now this little beauty," he said, "is a Wally MacCloud. Works the Nationals now, Wally does, but he still hasn't heard of the inside or outside corners. Likes a lot of action, MacCloud does. Lots of walks, hits and homers for the hitters. Early showers for the pitchers. A high-scoring game for the fans." He borrowed Everett's most derisive sneer and stabbed the little oval with it. "You hear a ton of talk about a *pitcher's* earned run average. But what about the ump's? They've got 'em too, you know, and the way they vary is a damned disgrace! Wally's ERA was up around 15.00 the year I knew him. That's 7.5 runs per team per game, Kade! I pitched six innings of what might've been shutout ball against him in Phoenix once, gave up six Wally-walks and five earned Wally-runs, and still won the game 14 to 9. Does that take the cake or what?"

I grinned and started to allow that it did, but Papa held up a palm and shouted "Wait!" as if all grins and cakes must be reserved for what he was about to show me . . . He wiped out MacCloud's oval, then chalked up a small, triangular shape, like the roof of a little pagoda, but nearly touching the ground. "I know this looks more Twilight Zone than strike zone," he said, "but I swear it's *right* where Eddy Aaberg called 'em."

He was waiting for me to do something. Oh yeah. I grinned and said, "Now *that* takes the cake!"

Papa laughed, and nodded. "Talk about a pitcher's ump! The Moundsman's Best Friend, ol' Aaberg was. For which reason he's still umping A ball down in California, calling dust-covered third strikes, throwing apoplectic hitters and managers out of games while the pitchers just stand there trying to keep a straight face. Needed art school, not ump school, Eddy did. A life-drawing class, maybe. The man just never got it through his head that kneecaps aren't ankles, waists aren't shoulders, and some hitters' shoulders are actually a bit wider than their necks."

Papa beamed at the pagoda. "Wreaked havoc with the hitters, Aaberg did. But he turned out some fine young golfers once they gave up and quit playin' ball."

First Adventist Church of Washougal

Everett was crammed—like all the other POWs (Prisoners of Worship) —into a crowded pew, cringing like a fresh-kicked dog as the sixty-member Walla Walla College Choir blored out what the church bulletin called "a rousing medley of Authentic Negro Spirituals." It must have been ninety degrees inside the church. Everett couldn't figure out how the choir was still standing. Must be their faith, he reasoned after a while, since it was primarily the brain that needed oxygen to function, and faith, as he saw it, was a kind of scripture-breathing brain-eating termite you turned loose in your head on the day you were baptized, causing your need for oxygen to steadily decrease. Loosening his tie when Mama wasn't looking, sighing three sighs to get one sigh's worth of air, Everett wished for the millionth time that he had Peter's constitution. But not (at least today) for its baseball ability. What he envied this day was its squeamishness—because when Pete had stood for the opening hymn he'd fainted on the spot, so he was now outside in the shade, basking in the oxygen-rich zephyrs. Most of the POWs looked as alert and slap-happy as the choir, though. Four-part "Authentic Negro" harmony was an unheard-of commodity in these parts. The choir was singing,

> Keep so busy praisin' my Jee-suss, keep so busy praisin'
>   my Jee-suss,
> Keep so busy praisin' my Jee-suss, ain' got time to die!

That's what you think, Everett thought.

But he saw tears of joy threading down Irwin's cheeks; saw Bet's flesh covered with goose bumps despite the heat; saw Mama's stone-stolid face lit up like neon by the glory; saw behatted POW heads and shiny-shoed feet bobbing and tapping all over the place. Even Elder Babcock had busted out one of his Antedeluvian Patriarch Grins and started tapping a big wing tip against his throne chair—out of time to the beat, of course.

> Mmmm, I praise Him in the mornin', mmmm, I praise Him
>   in the evenin',
> Mmmm, I praise Him in the mornin', ain' got time to die!

There was actually one "Authentic Negro" in the white-robed white-faced Walla Walla choir—an even greater rarity in this town than four-part harmonies. He was a short, overweight kid with a face almost as black, shiny and pocked as Babcock's wing tips. His wire-rimmed glasses gave him a scholarly look, and one front tooth, made of something silver, made Everett wish he had one every time it flashed. But the kid's face had been serious to start with, and when the choir eased into "Old Black Joe" it grew downright morose. Everett felt miserable for him. How must he feel, standing up there crooning crapped-out songs about whip-scarred plantation chattel to a big White-God-worshipping flock of crackers?

> I's a-comin', I's a comin', dough my head is bendin' low,
> I can hear dem faifful voices callin' Old Black Joe . . .

bleah. The absurdity was too great, the oxygen too scarce, the sky outside too blue: Everett's mind began to drift; he started to compose his own little medley:

> Stephen Foster wrote dis song, doo-dah, doo-dah,
> An' he was white as de day is long. Oh, doo-dah day . . .

He shut his eyes, smiled, realized no one could hear him over the choir, and started to croon it aloud:

He nevah ran no nights, he nevah ran no days,
He nevah put no money on no bobtail nag,
No doo-dah way . . .

Then Everett did Stephen Foster one better: he turned himself black: he became the sad, silver-toothed Walla Walla Negro kid. But once he became him he saw no reason not to stretch himself out, to make himself taller, thinner, stronger, better-looking, till he was no longer some Token Black Tenor surrounded by cross-licking hicks. He was the glint-toothed leader of his own scarlet-robed eighty-member all-black choir now, with a (why not?) twenty-piece blues band backing them, and a (what the heck?) dumpy Token White fat boy back in the percussion section—a dead ringer for Babcock in his youth—playing a . . . let's see, a triangle. Yeah. Everett shut his eyes, gave his audience a solemn nod, and informed them in the mellifluous, almost Elizabethan English he'd learned as a lad in Trinidad that they were about to perform a *contemporary* spiritual, with *eight-part* harmonies—a song composed, of course, by the dashing young E. M. Chance himself.

He turned to his choir. The young Camas ladies, in unison, lifted their church bulletins to fan their lust-flushed faces. He raised his baton, and—

arrrrrgh! The Walla Walla Warblers charged like rebels at Gettysburg into "When Dem Saints Go Marchin' In." Everett shuddered, scrinched his eyes and brain shut, focused on the rows of beautiful black faces in his mind, delicately raised an eyebrow, dropped it, and in a soul-stirring, hair-raising a cappella, the Big Black Plus One Cracker Choir thundered:

Dem heads are gonna roll when Jesus comes!

The POWs froze. The elders paled. The infants all smiled. The Lord God grinned.

Yes dem heads are gonna roll when Jesus comes!
Y'all gonna be sad you called us nigger
'Bout time He pulls dat heavenly trigger!
Yes dem heads are gonna roll when Jesus comes!

E. M. gave the elders a little eye juju, sent a black fist skyward, yanked it back down, and his twenty-piece blues band crashed in behind the choir:

Well you fat cats are goin' to court when Jesus comes!
Yeah you fat cats are goin' to court when Jesus comes!

> *Dere won't be no trick tax exemption,*
> *You either gonna burn or get redemption!*
> *Yeah, you fat cats are goin' to court when Jesus comes . . .*

Back in the stifling gray banality called "reality" the Walla Walla saints were marching out, and when Irwin and a few other kids started to cheer for them, Elder Babcock and all the other old war-horses who'd figured out that God hates gratitude quickly squelched it with massive scowls. But Everett didn't know it. His eyes were shut so tight his lips were drawn up like a mummy's; he was covered with goose bumps, shining with sweat. Bet nudged Freddy, Freddy nudged Irwin, and Irwin nudged Everett and whispered, "Jeez! Looks like you liked the music!" But Everett didn't hear that either: he just upped an eyebrow—raising his Blacks Plus Cracker Choir one step higher—and beamed beatifically as they roared:

> *Well we ain' goana be in yo' shoes when Jesus comes!*
> > *(when Jesus comes!)*
> *No we ain' goana be in yo' shoes when Jesus comes!*
> > *(when Jesus comes!)*
> (Take it Ella): *No I ain' goana be in yo' shoes*
> > *All o' you twisters o' God's Good News*
> (Billie Holiday): *An' I ain' goana be in your sandals,*
> > *You gossipin' biddies and lovers of scandals!*
> (Mr. Chuck Berry): *Or your shitkickin' redneck boots*
> > *When Gabriel's horn goes a rooty-toot-toot!*
> (the Walla Walla kid): *'Cause I'll be singin' an' clappin' my hands*
> > *In my cheap loafers from Thom McAn's!*
> (Ever'body!): *No we ain' goana be in your shoes when*
> *Jesus comes!*
> > *(When Jesus cuh-huh-hummmmmms!)*

"What's he *doing?*" Bet whispered.

"He's all sweaty!" said Freddy.

"An' he's getting so jumpy!" Bet added.

"Uh-oh," Irwin whispered sideways to Everett. "Mama's watchin'."

But Everett was gone. *"Last verse!"* he told his choir. "Jump it, tromp it, whomp it!"

> *Yes dem heads are gonna roll when Jesus comes!*
> *It be the Lord God's turn to bowl when Jesus comes!*
> *You smart folks better clear de aisles*
> *'Cause dere gonna be sinners heaped in piles!*

An' you may think we's whistlin' Dixie
But the King o' the Kings, He ain't no pixie!
Dere won't be no trick tax exemption,
You either gonna burn or get redemption!
AN' DEM HEADS ARE GONNA RO-HO-HOLLLLLLLLLLLLL

"Everett!"

WHEN JESUS—

"Everett!"
"Huh? Oh. Yes, Mama."
"You tighten that tie!"
"Oops. Sorry, Mama."
"Quit fidgeting!"
"Okay, Mama."
"And get that *look* off your face!"
"Sorry, Mama."

the backyard

"It's all in the mind," Papa said.
   "The mind," I repeated.
   "Strike zones live in the mind."
   "In the mind."
   "Don't forget."
   "I won't."
And with that, Papa froze. Or didn't freeze, exactly. But he grew so still, there in front of his troublesome chalk drawings, that it seemed he might remain there all night long. Then, in an instant, he scared the hell out of me by winding up and firing his piece of chalk clear up over the roof of the Fir Haven Apartments. And the very next instant, there he stood again, perfectly calm and still. A classic Peter gesture. But this didn't surprise me. I'd noticed this resemblance many times before.
   "Another variable, even with real, mental strike zones, even after you've figured out the ump," he said in his quiet new voice, "is the whole voodoo element."
   He paused to glance around the yard, checking shadows and shrubs as if he feared someone might be out to steal the truths he was about to impart. "I'm not kidding, Kade," he said. "And I'm not talking crystal

ball crap either. If a strike zone is just a shape in an ump's head, which it is, then there ought to be ways of climbing inside that head and tinkering with the shape. Which there are. Pitchers of course want to expand the zone. Hitters of course want to shrink it. Either way, this ability to reach into an ump's gray matter and distort his whole strike concept, *this* is what I'm calling voodoo."

Obeying an impulse, I casually said, "I don't believe in it." I was lying. I not only believed, I was enthralled. But listening to Peter's stories I'd often noticed that the more skeptical Everett or I pretended to be, the more powerful his stories became. So I said, "If it's real, name somebody. Name one guy who really uses it."

"Williams," Papa said without hesitation. "Unquestionably, Ted Williams. The greatest voodoo hitter of our time."

After Cobb the Demon, Gehrig the Cherub and Ruth the Dumb Deity, Williams the Curmudgeon was my favorite ballplayer. But I kept playing the skeptic. "How?" I demanded. "Tell me how he does it."

"Any big crowd-pleaser," Papa said, "any Mantle or DiMaggio or Mays can pull off a little voodoo at home games. Ump calls a strike on the corner, hometown hero turns and gives him a disgusted look, and all hell breaks loose. Strikes called on heroes aren't what the fans pay to see. And the fans are a factor, Kade. They're scary when they're roused, believe me. Where hometown voodoo backfires, though, is when the ump is stubborn. And lots of 'em are. Fans start raggin' a muley ump, he just gets pissed at Mr. Hero for showing him up and calls 'em even meaner."

I nodded, and switched hands; I'd been stirring the Dutch Boy so long I had cramps. "Ted Williams, though," Papa said, "was anything but a hometown hero. He had a coolness, a remoteness, that people mistook for arrogance when he first came into the league, and the fool Red Sox press, even the fans, managed to despise him for this. It was just small-minded nonsense. What they were booing was his concentration, after all. And Williams concentrated so well he didn't give a damn about the press or fans. But after a couple seasons he realized that the hometown dislike *was* robbing him of the ump intimidation that creates hometown voodoo. If he was ever going to enjoy the advantages of a hitting hero, he was going to have to come up with something a lot more ingenious than the Disgusted Hometown Stare, see? So now listen to what he did!"

Papa paused at this point, put his palms together in front of his nose, and rubbed them so hard and fast it looked like he was trying to generate friction and set his face on fire. It was one weird gesture. I'd no idea *where* this one came from. "First off," he went on, "Williams always understood a crucial fact. He knew that it's by working with what we're given that we get really good at a thing. Our natures, our character, the way we feel at gut level, this stuff is as unchanging as the color of our eyes or hair or the shapes of our bones, is what I think. And since slobbering crowds and fawning reporters only distracted Williams from his job, which was crushing baseballs, he went right on snubbin' 'em. Do you follow?"

I nodded.

"So where does following his nature get him? It makes him some nasty enemies in the stands and the press box, that's for sure. Those enemies cost him at least two MVP awards. But down on the field it keeps him loose, let's him live for his hitting, wins him a reputation as a player's player and a real no-nonsense guy. And—getting back to the voodoo potential—it also earns him nothing but respect from every ump in the league. Because, believe me, umpires hate fans as much as fans hate umps.

"Fine and good. Next Williams strings together a couple great years at the plate, so that the sportswriters, much as they detest him, have to start begging him for interviews, because the fans, much as they hate him, are dying to know what makes the arrogant creep tick. But Williams sticks to his guns: he slams doors at reporters, slams line drives at the clucks in the bleachers, and leaves it at that. But writers have to write *something*, don't they? That's *their* nature. So they start winging it. They start making things up, churning out legends—Williams the Recluse, Williams the Crank Scientist, Williams the Genius, Williams the Un-sung Hero—till first thing you know he's baseball's answer to Greta Garbo. And of course once this happens the writers forget all about their old dislike: they'd cross Boston on their *knees* to get an exclusive with the mysterious Splinter. And seeing all this, sensing the time is ripe, Williams finally strikes . . ."

Papa tried and again failed to ignite his nose. "One bleak Boston winter's day Mr. Theodore No-Nonsense Garbo Splinter Williams finally grants some overjoyed worm of a writer an exclusive audience. Just asks the guy over, sets him down in his comfortablest chair, lets him fire away with the questions. Of course the dolt starts off with the usual: 'What's your favorite breakfast cereal?' 'Who do you like for President next election?' 'What's the meaning of life?' 'How long's your weenie?' and so on. But Ted's a fisherman in the off-season. He knows how to be patient. He sincerely and scientifically answers every query but the last. Then out pops the question he's been waiting for: 'How the heck do you *hit* so good?'

"And it's voodoo time, folks!

"No-Nonsense leans back in his chair, looks as sincere and scientific as ever, and says, 'Well, I study the pitchers very closely. My mechanics and bat speed are good. And I've got good concentration. But listen . . .' And he suddenly swoops down and stares, like the hungry old owl he is, deep into the journalist's little mouse eyes . . ." (Papa swooped down and stared into mine.) "And he says, 'Everybody knows that there are quick wrists and slow wrists, but not many know that there are quick and slow *eyes* too. And *my* eyes . . .' (Papa did some eyebrow push-ups, to let me know that these were the voodoo words) 'are the key to my hitting, they're my secret weapon. Because my eyes are so quick that I can see any pitch, even a fastball, *all the way in to where it jumps off my bat . . .*'"

Papa stopped just long enough to squeeze back a laugh.

"Well, Kade, the writer is just hoodooed. Nobody has *ever* said anything like this! Hell, Ty Cobb hit .367 lifetime, and even *he* admitted that a good fastball was a blur and that every swing he ever took at one was just an educated guess. But not No-Nonsense. Not Theodore. He sees the *whole pitch,* clear on into and off his bat! So the writer humps it home to his typewriter, bangs out his story, flashes Williams's astounding secret to the world. And when the umps (who already admire the dust Williams spits on) pick up their morning papers, they think *Jeepers creepers, what peepers!* and buy it lock, stock and barrel."

Papa shook his head, and finally let his laugh fly. "That's all it took, Kade! When the next season rolled around, Williams found his strike zone was damned near anywhere he wanted. The inside and outside corners had vanished. Every ump in the league had become his personal Wally MacCloud. Because what ump would *dare* contradict the baby blues that saw in a fastball not a blur, but a hundred and eight scarlet stitches on four fat white cheeks? *That* was voodoo, Kade. One well-placed fib, a lot of fan-snubbing, and Ted Williams puts together maybe the last .400 season we'll ever see. If World War II hadn't eaten his next three seasons, his career average and slugging percentage would've been right up there in the Next World with Tyrannosaurus Cobb and the Sultan himself. No doubt about it, Kade. Williams's eyesight was good, but his voodoo was downright splendid!"

John McLoughlin High School

On August 6, 1945, Edward Conze—arguably the greatest Buddhist scholar of this century—was riding in a train through England when he opened his morning paper and read of Hiroshima, and of the world's first nuclear attack. He later wrote, "I have a very deep stomach, and normally cannot be sick. But on this occasion I vomited straight out the window. This was prophetic insight. For at that moment, human history had lost its meaning."

Two decades later, in the fall of his junior year of high school, Peter was forced in a class called Modern Problems to watch a film about a possible solution to the modern problem roughly known as "Russia." This film was a black-and-white documentary, produced by the Pentagon. Its subject was one of the late-Fifties' aboveground H-bomb tests in Nevada.

The military technicians who engineered the test may not have been the most artistic filmmakers of their day, but they were far from unimaginative. They recognized, for instance, that in blowing up an expanse of uninhabited desert there must be something more than miles of barren sand and sagebrush for the cameras to film and for the viewers' minds to grasp. They therefore decided (rather like the third of the Three Little Pigs) to build a little brick house, to situate it exactly one mile from Ground Zero, and to make it the poignant, underdog star of their show, first by stocking and furnishing it with an array of animate and inanimate items that might be found in any American home at the time of a Russian nuclear attack, and then, of course, by attacking it.

Surrounded as it was by miles of scrub desert, the Pentagon's house turned out to be a forlorn and lost-looking little abode. *But in my Father's house are many mansions,* Peter thought as he watched. And no one could fault the Pentagon technicians' thoroughness in stocking this one: they carted in fresh and refrigerated foods, a pantry full of canned goods, a freezer full of meats and vegetables (*I go to prepare a place for you,* Peter thought); they hung never-to-be-worn jackets and hats on an oak coat stand in the front hall, toted in a few unsuspecting house plants, plugged in a radio and TV; they displayed unexpected domestic flair, laying wall-to-wall, never-to-be-tracked-up carpet on the concrete floor, hanging never-to-be-faded dime-store prints of famous European paintings on walls, placing never-to-need-dusting knickknacks on shelves and coffee tables; they even included some live witnesses—white-footed mice, both brown and white rats, and a variety of "common household pests" such as cockroaches and ants, all in neat little cages. In short, all that was missing by the time the technicians finished was a forlorn and lost-looking little American family to match, and inhabit, the abode. And leave it to the Pentagon not only to recognize this lack, but to do something about it!

They didn't recruit a family—though with their budget and powers of propaganda they no doubt could have. But they did the next-best thing: they *built* one. When the camera zoomed in on the plate-glass window on the shielded side of the house, when it first showed them all seated in straight-backed wooden chairs round a carefully set, candlelit supper table, wearing dapper Sears clothes and fixed, uncomprehending smiles, Peter needed time to believe his eyes. But the filmmakers gave it to him. The apparition wouldn't go away. The Army really had constructed four lifelike, white-skinned, 100%-patriotic dummies—a Daddy, a Mommy, a Little Boy and a Little Girl. "The Last Supper!" one of Peter's pals cracked as the camera finally drew away. But no one laughed.

With the hushed excitement of a TV golf announcer, the narrator explained that a nearly indestructible movie camera had been mounted in a bomb shelter two miles from the house, that a huge zoom lens was aimed right at the plate-glass window, and that by using glare-resistant filters and infrared film they planned on getting accurate, slow-motion footage of everything that went on in the Dummy Family's diningroom during and after the blast. With that, the camera zoomed in on the four happy, lifeless faces, and the narrator counted down, Five, Four, Three, Two, One . . . But at Zero, nothing happened. Seconds passed. The house remained standing. The Dummies kept smiling. "Gee, Wally! That wasn't so bad!" said the boy who'd made the "Last Supper" crack, and there were a few snickers. "Better light another one," someone said, and half the class began to laugh.

Then the family simply vanished. It was not at all dramatic. The little lost house and everything in it disappeared in a flash of such pure and silent whiteness that Peter thought the film had broken. But then they began to perceive movement within the whiteness. No one, least of all the Pentagon narrator, could describe what they were seeing, but there was clearly a billowing, an erupting, a majestic swirling of heat and light pouring toward them and through them and far, far beyond them. It was mesmerizing. It was even beautiful. And it went on for a long, long time.

Finally the screen darkened, there was a stasis, and the Modern Problems students sighed, thinking the Dummy Family, though deceased, was at least at rest. But they were wrong. The billowing not only resumed, it reversed direction. The first wind, Peter realized, had been the *ex*-plosion (*I go to prepare a place for you*)—everything blown effortlessly aside as when a boulder lands in a pool and crushes the water away in all directions. But the second wind the reversed wind, was the *im*-plosion (*and if I go and prepare a place for you, I will come again, and receive you unto myself . . .*)—the melted molecules of brick and insect and appliance and desert all rushing like water back into place, after the thrown boulder has sunk. And while the explosion's swirling whitenesses had been photogenic, the implosion grew steadily darker and muddier-looking, and it went on, and on, and on, and on till even the Pentagon filmmakers grew bored with the monotony of the devastation they were seeing, and so cut to the aftermath.

But here too, a full day later, there was little to see or say. Which plume of smoke, which fleck of hot ash, which pile of raped molecules had been cockroach or coat rack or synthetic boy or girl could not even be asked, because these things hadn't just been destroyed. They'd been un-created. A piece of planet had been splashed away like liquid, but what returned was not the rubble of what had departed: it was a no-place, an un-place, a seething gray *nada* where even the phrase "*ashes to ashes, dust to dust*" had no meaning, for this dust had been removed from any cyclic process; this ash would kill you if you touched it; this was deader than death.

"Good flick!" one boy cracked as the film ended. Then the lights came on, and Peter's buddies were dumbfounded to see their cool, collected, .500-hitting compadre sitting there committing the ultimate faux pas for aspiring macho men: he was weeping. Pete, and a couple of girls. He made no sound, but the tears were just streaming down his cheeks.

He left the room without speaking, and groped his way down the empty hall. He couldn't stop crying, and had no idea where he was going. But even so, it couldn't be said that he was haunted by what he'd seen. He was not, for instance, seeing visions of his hometown billowing in the whiteness; he wasn't thinking that history, or life, or school had lost their meaning; he wasn't even thinking thoughts like *Russia is real* or *Hate is real* or *The Dummy Family is my family*. It was worse than that. He wasn't able to use his mind at all. His strong, clear thinking had simply imploded, leaving him groping down a hallway in sheer, mindless panic, like a fly trapped in a jar. And when he came to the plate-glass window at the end of the hall, when he pressed his face against it and began groping for a catch, lock or lever, his blind hands discovered that in big public high schools the windows don't open. So he had no place to vomit.

the backyard

"Of course a good catcher can play voodoo games too," Papa said. "I've seen hitters jook a foot or so of strike zone out of an ump's head, then seen my catcher steal the shrinkage right back. But voodoo's rare in a catcher. It's a mind game, voodoo is. And when it comes to brainpower, well, let's just say that when they call catchers 'backstops,' they're barely exaggerating in lots of cases."

"But Everett's a catcher!" I laughed.

"Everett *plays* catcher," Papa said, "but he's a second baseman if he's a ballplayer at all. He just catches 'cause he's stubborn. But he's too hot-headed for voodoo anyhow. And the way he argues, he'll never need it."

I laughed again.

"Now, Jack Henry up in Tacoma, he was a *real* catcher, and he could voodoo umps. Did it by following his nature too, same as Williams. Except in Jackie's case the trick was to play dumb. He was a bright guy, really. A whiz at accounting, of all things. Did his whole team's taxes in the off-season just to relax, became a CPA when his knees went to hell. But he had a rustic sort of face, so he cultivated a fresh-off-the-farm manner to go with it, and all during a game he'd keep this dumb commentary going, I mean some real numbnut drivel. But underneath it, see, he'd be slowly, strategically eating away at the ump's freedom of thought. His best trick was to grunt *Myuh!*, like that, every time a clean strike came blowing in on a batter. Except Jackie's *Myuh!*s sounded so accidental and dumb they made you feel sorry for him. But by the sixth or seventh inning those same *Myuh!* s would be sounding for pitches a hair outside or a tad low, and the ump'd be so used to 'em he'd still be yelling *Steee-rike!* without quite catching where the ball had actually gone." Papa snorted, picturing Jackie.

"What about moving the mitt after you catch the ball?" I asked. "I've seen Everett practicing that."

"Framing the pitch?" Papa shook his head. "That's not voodoo. You see it in the bigs, I know, but I say it's stupid. The trouble with framing, see, is that even though the ump's concentrating on the trajectory of the pitch, his peripheral vision sees the catcher's mitt move, so that gradually he gets this peripheral feeling that his intelligence is being insulted. And believe me, anything that insults the plate ump's intelligence is a *bad* idea. What happens pretty soon is, anytime the mitt moves, even to grab a legitimate strike on a corner, the ump thinks 'Frame!' and calls a ball. That's why when my catchers tried it I told 'em to knock it off, loud, right in front of the umps and everybody. Of course Jackie's *Myuh!*s were sort of like verbal framing. But they seemed to insult his *own* intelligence, which made it very different. Voodoo's subtle, see? It's simple mind control, really. But it seems magic at times. And it's part of most every game. The guy who first convinced me it's important was that one-eyed Haitian you've heard me yammer on about . . ."

"Which guy?" I asked, playing dumb again. I'd heard his Benito stories a dozen times each, but I loved the way he told them.

"Benito Lhosa," he said, knowing I was faking.

"Remind me," I said, knowing he would.

And he did, beginning, as always, with the same formula portrait. "You know who I'm talking about. My catcher, that last year in Schenectady."

"Oh yeah."

"Not a big guy, Lhosa. Maybe six foot and 170. Willowy for a backstop. Said he lost the eye as a kid. Fell out of a tree, stick went right through the lid. He could still open and close it, but the lid was scarred up and the eyeball was out of round, bumpy like a broken marble, and skewed off to one side. So Benito kept it shut.

"Didn't matter much, though. The man's hands hung off his arm-ends like oversized crawdad claws, his fingers were long and strong as an ape's, and with an arm like his, what does depth perception matter? I mean, you squeeze one eye shut to aim a rifle anyway. And that's what Benito's arm was. A damned rifle. Any base he threw to, *zing!* the ball just vanished and reappeared there. I told you 'bout the time we played the White Sox in exhibition and he picked their so-called speedster, Dickie Waters, off second from a squat. Of course Waters was an imbecile. Which was fortunate, with a name like that. But still, what a throw!"

He whistled, remembering it.

"Benito hit .225 the year I played with him, and that was good for him. The bat was his downfall, naturally. Takes two eyes to fine-tune a swing. But he belonged in the majors anyhow. Hell, he played Two A ball for G. Q. Durham clear into his forties, which is unheard-of for a catcher. He was thirty-seven the year he caught me, and the best field general and defensive catcher you or I will ever see. With two eyes he'd've been immortal. As is, he's a bush league legend. And who knows? Maybe with two eyes he wouldn't have had that same crazy fire . . ."

Papa went on talking, but I found myself distracted, wondering why the crushed thumb couldn't do for Papa what the eye had done for Benito, why it didn't give him "that same crazy fire." But then I glanced around, with two eyes, at his whole cockeyed backyard baseball arrangement—and it hit me: *maybe it had* . . .

"Lhosa never learned English," he was saying, "but it didn't much matter. He did his voodoo without saying a word. It was beautiful, it was so simple. He made a point all game of never so much as glancing at an ump, never protesting, never squawking at all, until they *really* missed a call. I mean missed it so bad that even the worst ump knew it himself. Then, very slowly, Benito would turn till the ump could see his face. He'd appear to just be looking off into the stands with his good eye, see. Except he knew, from years of voodoo experience, exactly what angle his bad eye skewed off to. So there he'd stand, aimed and cocked so to speak, till the ump got tired of it and said, 'Play ball!' . . . Then, ever so slowly, the lid started lifting . . . till there that mangled, milky, off-center dead thing would be, staring the poor ump right in the face while Benito just kept looking off into the stands like an innocent bystander . . . *Brrrrrrrr!*"

Papa shook his head. "That did it, believe you me! One attack from Benito's blind eye and our strike zone'd swell like wet oatmeal. I'd put nothing across the middle for the rest of the game. And *that*, my friend, was voodoo!"

What happened next was odd: after all those stories, all the careful consideration, Papa suddenly snatched the paint can and brush away from me and slopped a careless but indelible white rectangle up on the canvas. "The whole point," he muttered as he worked, "the gist of all this, Kade, is that what shape I paint here makes no damn difference. 'Cause this ol' wall has got no mind to jook."

Stepping back from the mattress, Papa held up his dead thumb the way the kind of painters who wear berets do, and squinted over it at his handiwork.

"Very nice, *oui?*" he asked.

I just shrugged, feeling sad for him suddenly. But he had himself a strike zone.

Downtown Camas

"Rain," in the bizarre but rather poetically expressed view of McLoughlin High's head football coach, Duffy Basham, "is a democrat. It falls on
both teams alike, it don't hurt when it hits you, it helps out on defense
by causin' fumbles. Face it, men. Rain, like most democrats, is your basic
wimp. An' so are *you* if you let it affect the way you play football."

For these "reasons" there had never been a rain torrential enough to
inspire Coach Basham to cancel a McLoughlin High varsity football practice, and he held a "hundred and ten percent belief" that there never
would be. But when, one week in mid-November 1964, we had six inches
of wet snow one day, followed by a warm southwester that melted every
flake of snow and brought three inches of "democrats" in a single night,
Coach Basham discovered something new about rain: when enough of it
falls, gridirons become lakes in which you can't play football no matter
what percent of you believes what.

That explains how Irwin and Scooter Basham (Duffy's son, and the
other defensive tackle on McLoughlin's third-place team) ended up in
the Basham basement shooting a few friendly games of eightball after
school. But nothing (or nothing very complimentary) can explain how
Irwin let himself get talked into playing for a dollar a game. Scooter was a
notorious eighteen-year-old hustler who'd lived beside this very table for
a decade. Irwin was a fifteen-year-old nudnink who called a cue "a pool
pole," the rack "the triangle," and didn't know stars-and-stripes from
snooker from slop. There were also psychological factors to be considered:
Irwin, though only a sophomore, was an all-league tackle and the apple of
Coach Basham's eye, whereas Scooter, a talentless senior, wouldn't have
played football at all if his virulent old man hadn't been a hundred and
ten percent determined to whip his great sulking hulk of a son into
something more than a pool-hustling democrat. There was an economic
factor to consider as well: Irwin was flat broke. But the existence of
factors to be considered was never any guarantee that Irwin would consider them. He preferred to entertain happy thoughts, like how the flat-
ness and greenness of the pool table made it look like a football field, and
how he'd get to play offense instead of defense, and how the pockets gave
him *six* places to make touchdowns instead of just one, and how he was
ten times the footballer Scooter was, so what he lacked in experience he

could make up for with hundred and ten percent effort. It'd be close, he figured. "Sure, Scooter! Let's play!"

The remarkable truth is that Scooter Basham never took a game from Irwin. He didn't get the chance: Irwin sank the eight ball five straight games (once on his second shot, once on the break!) while Scooter just stood there clutching his eventually to be legendary belly and laughing till his jaws cramped. Then Irwin got serious: reaching deep down inside to tap his Hundred and Ten Percent Power Source, he opened Game Six with a great lunging "pool pole" thrust—and ripped a ten-inch gash in the felt of Scooter's table. That took care of the laughter. It also brought on a pathetic little Basham basement catharsis: "If my old man wouldn't kill me for wrecking his defense," Scooter snarled, "I'd bust this cue right over your empty fuckin' head!"

"Good thing he'd kill you!" Irwin chuckled.

"You owe me fifty-five bucks, shit-lips," Scooter sputtered. "Five for the games, and fifty for a new surface."

"Fair enough," Irwin said. "But this is fun, Scoots! Let's keep playin'."

"Let me explain something," Scooter fumed, grabbing the cue from Irwin's hand. "This was *not* fun. I invited you here 'cause I needed some bucks and took you for a sucker. But I was the sucker. You're too *dumb* to be a sucker. You're too dumb to be a *shithead!* My old man says you're dumber'n anything on four legs, let alone two. He says that's why he likes you!"

Feeling himself beginning to get angry, Irwin conjured an image of the Lord Jesus, smiled sadly, and said, "Sorry you feel that way, Scooter Booter."

Scooter snatched Irwin's rain slicker off a chair, started to fling it in his face, then had a better idea. "I'm keepin' this for collateral," he said. "Now get out 'fore I take your shoes and pants."

"Fair enough," Irwin said. And off he set—hatless and coatless in a cold November rain, with two miles to cover on foot—thanking Jesus that he hadn't lost his temper.

The highway was flooded from shoulder to shoulder. The first passing truck soaked him so thoroughly that water filled his shoes. Some people may have found this situation conducive to resentment or regret. Others may have found it conducive to hypothermia. Irwin took a look at the impassable wetness and sopped shoes, whispered, "Perfect!," stomped straight into an ankle-deep rivulet, and at the top of his lungs began to warble, *"I'm seeeeenging in the rain! Just seeeeeenging in the rain! There's a smiiiiiiiiile on my face! I'm haaaaaaaaappy agaaaaaaaain . . ."*

As if he hadn't been terminally happy in the first place. People in passing cars began honking and waving and spraying him on purpose. He sang and kicked and tried to splash them back. By the time he reached the two-lane bridge over the Washougal River he'd totaled his penny loafers but earned several horn ovations from vehicles in both lanes. His goal, he decided, would be to coax a few millworking football fans out of the taverns downtown to do some dancing and singing with him. But as he stepped out over the river he said, "Holy *smoly!*" and froze in his tracks.

The last time he'd crossed here there'd been a thirty-foot drop to a slow green pool below. He knew both bridge and pool exceptionally well, because he and Everett had been arrested and hauled into Juvenile Court the previous summer for jumping off the former into the latter. Today, though, the thirty-foot drop was filled with twenty-eight feet of caramel-colored floodwater . . .

What struck Irwin, what froze him at first, was sheer contrast: the long fall through warm summer air, all that empty space, solid water now. But as he moved out onto the bridge what began to impress him even more was the deception. Flooded though it was, the river was not raging: it was smooth-surfaced, like muscles, and surprisingly quiet as it shot beneath his feet. Yet the entire bridge hummed and vibrated with the force of the current, and there were trees in the water—not just driftwood logs but entire Douglas firs and massive old maples—moving easily as fast as the cars and trucks that passed just over them. Irwin watched a hundred-foot fir slide toward him, saw it slip, tip-first, down under the bridge, felt the sidewalk gritch and quake as limbs and chunks of root wad were torn from the tree by the girders beneath his feet. "Holy *smoly!*" he repeated.

At the far end of the bridge, three police cars and a metallic-green state motor pool sedan pulled over and parked in a row. Five Washington State troopers climbed out of the squad cars and huddled up, looking, in their bright yellow ponchos and big Smokey hats, like something that had escaped from a toy store. Meanwhile a man in a suit got out of the sedan, opened an umbrella, stuck a clipboard under his arm, bustled out onto the bridge, and commenced leaning out over rails, peering down at footings, and studying the vibrations set up by passing trucks and underpassing trees. Realizing they might be about to close the bridge, Irwin started toward them, hoping to eavesdrop. Then he noticed Greg Hervano among the troopers—the same cop who'd nailed him and Everett for jumping off the bridge last August, but a gung ho McLoughlin High football booster. Which explains the greeting Irwin gave him. "Hey, fuzz!" he bellowed at the top of his lungs. Then he jumped into the gutter-stream and put some of his best Gene Kelly moves on. He'd just begun to wonder why he got so little response when he noticed that all five Smokey hats were now aimed upriver. Then he heard the yipping, turned upstream himself,

and saw the dog. Off-white, sopped, tiny—maybe nine inches at the shoulder. And it was looking at, yapping at, almost pleading with Irwin as it scrabbled and clawed to stay aboard the roof of a three-quarters-submerged doghouse that was drifting, fast, straight toward him.

the backyard

"Funny story about Lhosa," Papa had said as we'd cleaned the paint paraphernalia. "Because of the eye, I guess, Benito didn't like knuckleballs. Didn't handle 'em any worse than anybody else, just hated 'em worse. For which reason, after we'd worked a few games and grown fond of each other, I started unleashing a surprise knuckler at him now and then, just to piss him off." He glanced down at his paint-lined knuckles, and laughed.

"First few times I tried it, he just chewed me out in Español. When I kept it up, though, he got serious and took to firing the ball back so hard, in English, that it about burrowed through my hand. But baseball gets dull without the stuff and nonsense, so I still teased him with one once in a while. Then, late in the season, Benito came up with the perfect retaliation. What he did was start throwing knucklers back at me, right out of the crouch. Best damned floaters you ever saw. It was all I could do to knock some of 'em down. So it became a thing between us—me trying to catch him off guard with my half-ass knuckler, him making me dance around like a dolt trying to knock down his great one.

"So one time, against Freeport it was, in the ninth inning of a 3-to-2 or 4-to-3 game—can't remember which, but it was our favor—I opened the inning by striking out a guy on straight fastballs, then went and hung a curve that some big meat bounce-doubled over the left-field fence. That put the tying run on second with one out, which was bad. But it also got my adrenaline going, which in those days was good. Benito signaled two fastballs, and this poor kid who was pinch-hitting swung so late on both he came closer to hitting Lhosa's tosses back to me. So with the count at 0 and 2, Benito asked for a third straight heater, and I nodded, fine. Then I wound up and sent in a big fat floater. Damn good one too. Kid swung a half hour early this time, and that was strike three and out number two. But before I could gloat or grin or anything, Benito caught it and squeezed it and fired back the damnedest revenge-knuckler I ever saw. A butterfly on dope, this thing looked like. I mean it was *everywhere*. I put my whole body in front of it, stuck out my mitt, missed it by six inches easy, but luckily the thing dove, smacked me dead in the thigh, and landed at my feet. Unluckily, though, my funny bone was turned on full blast now. And when that big meat of a base runner feinted toward third, even though he was the tying run, he struck me funny too. I stooped to get the ball to chase him back, but I was in stitches. And I just booted it, *smack!* A regular soccer kick, right toward the plate.

"Of course the runner broke for real now. But of course so did Benito. And even though I knew I should be running in to back up the plate or some such basebally strategy, I also knew Lhosa's arm was so good and I'd booted the ball so hard that there was only one way this thing could turn out. So I just stood there, laughing myself sick, while sure enough Benito sprinted out, pounced, gunned it to third, nailed the poor meat by two yards, and that was the ballgame. But the great thing, Kade, was how the fans loved it—and they were *Freeport* fans. The great thing was, the Freeport *team* even loved it. Hell, the meat we'd gunned down at third even grinned and nodded to us as he left the field. Dumbest game-ending putout we'd all likely to live to see, and everybody seemed aware of it, united by it. They gave Benito and me a standing ovation, we gave them a bow, and for a minute or two there it felt like the Brotherhood of Man. The next day the Freeport paper said we'd obviously rehearsed the whole thing. Mama saved the piece, it's in the attic somewhere. 'The ol' Fake-Miss, Kick and Throw Play,' the writer called it. Baseball's answer to the Harlem Globetrotters, he called Benito and me."

Downtown Camas

Officer Hervano said later that it all happened incredibly fast. Irwin ran to the place where the doghouse would hit the bridge, clapped his hands to get the dog's attention, started whistling and yelling, "Come here, girl —or boy! Come *on*, boy! *Good* boy! *Jump!*" And the dog whined and wagged its tail as if it wanted to do just that. Then Hervano spotted the chain attached to its collar, realized it must be attached to the doghouse (why else would the dog have stayed on the roof as a flood washed it away?) and, knowing Irwin as he did, set off at a dead run. Just as quickly,

Irwin climbed onto the concrete rail of the bridge. The other cops began waving their arms and bellowing "*No!*" Ignoring them, Irwin hooked the heels of his feet behind the aluminum handrail, then hand-walked his upper body down the concrete face of the bridge. One of the cops, Officer Worth, began firing off his gun. Irwin ignored that too. Hervano saved his voice and put everything he had into his sprint, but at the sight of Irwin's hair and fingers dangling in that river his dash turned into the sort of lead-limbed, slow-motion running one does in nightmares. Worth fired more shots, and the whole Greek chorus of cops kept bellowing, "*NO! STOP! NO!*" Then the submerged doghouse hit the bridge and cracked like an eggshell, the dog slid with a *yipe!* into the river, Irwin sank one hand deep in its fur, and the crushed house was sucked under the bridge. Hervano was so close now that he could see the hopeless flex and strain of Irwin's entire body as the river pulled the house and chain and dog effortlessly down (*I go to prepare a place for you*). Then one heel slipped from the handrail—and still Irwin kept his grip on the fur. The river sucked the chained dog under; Irwin drew a deep breath; Hervano gasped *No!* as he lunged, got a hand on Irwin's penny loafer, got two hands on it, started to pull. *But if I go and prepare a place for you, I will come again, and receive you unto myself* . . . The foot slid from the shoe.

Greg Hervano fell back onto the sidewalk, the ruined shoe in his hand. He said he could only hear, he couldn't see, Irwin slide quietly into the river.

"The longest minutes of my life," Hervano told my family and me that night, "were the ones I spent at the downstream railing, watching that smashed-up doghouse wash away down the Washougal—with no dog. And no Irwin."

Papa shook his head, and stared at the pathetic shoe in Hervano's hand. Mama smiled through tears. "*God*, Winnie!" Everett kept saying. "Why'd you *do* it?"

"I've been a cop ten years, and have seen a lot," Hervano said. "But this one got to me. Milford and Worth blocked off the bridge, and Hymes called State Search and Rescue, but we knew it was hopeless. We knew the body had to be right under that bridge, jammed up against a girder maybe, or tangled in a pile of limbs and logs. And it was that closeness, the fact that he was *right there* under me—"

"I was right thu-there under you all ruh-right!" Irwin shivered. "Bu-but I—"

"You shuttup!" Hervano roared, bonking his head with the sole of the sopped shoe. "This is *my* version. Wait your damned turn!"

Irwin managed to keep quiet, but from that point on Hervano's story was interrupted by blasts of giggling, especially from the twins, who, by the way, were wrapped in under the bright yellow cop poncho still draped round Winnie's shaking shoulders, both of them fawning over the stinky little mutt that lay curled in the Smokey hat in Irwin's lap, wearing the same idiot grin as its savior.

"Anyhow," Hervano continued, "the boys saw I was having trouble and let me be, so I was just standing in the gloom there, thinking stuff like *Why do the nice kids get it while the scumbags live and thrive?* and *Why didn't I grab ankle instead of shoe?* and *Maybe if I stand here long enough the damn bridge will wash out and drown me too, and I won't have to go face the boy's family,* when all of a sudden I hear this hollow voice over toward the south bank, going *Eeech! Aach! Ooooh! Awch!* like somebody walking barefoot across gravel. And, honest to God, I think, *It's his spirit!*"

We drowned Hervano in laughter. *"The voice of his poor drowned spirit!"* he shouted over us. *"And it's cold, the poor thing!"* This is exactly what I think. I even notice, and feel touched, that his spirit voice sounds just as out-to-lunch as his earthly voice did. But when I look toward the end of the bridge where the spirit voice keeps ooching and eeching from, I'll be hanged if this pardon my French *dog* wasn't standing there shaking river off itself! So what did I do? What did I think? I'm telling the truth now. I thought: *His spirit has entered the dog!*"

Our laughter buried his story again, but Hervano's face stayed fierce. "You think it's *funny?*" he asked us. "You get a chuckle out of the fact that *your* tax dollars are going to pay the salary of a guy who, seeing a presumably dead dog suddenly appear on a bridge, puts his academy training, his ten years of experience, and his steel-trap mind to work and thinks, *It's Irwin! He's gone into the dog! And he's cold, poor thing!?*"

He waited out another storm, then put a finger to his lips. "Stupid, it would seem. Dumb, it would seem. But let's not forget *this!*" He held up the soggy penny loafer. "Because isn't it possible, isn't it even likely, that if you stay in contact with any part of this contagious idiot for too long" (he bonked Irwin's head with the shoe again) "you start to think just like him?"

We all dissolved, but Hervano remained ferocious. "So there I stand in the glum and dumb, haunted by dogs and loafers, when I'll be hanged if the little Spirit Dog doesn't turn around, peer back down into the bridge footings, and set its dingle-berried little *tail* to wagging. Then a big white hand pops up onto a girder. Followed by the pure-white, toeless foot of what I figure is going to be a regular ol' Casper of a friendly ghost. But lo and behold, not five minutes after dying—though even Christ himself had the good manners to stay down three days—up onto the girder swings the *ugliest* pardon my French face of the *stupidest* excuse of a hero I ever hope to see. And why I ran to help it up, why I didn't just kick it straight back in the river it keeps trying, summer and winter, to commit suicide in, is beyond me!"

As we applauded and howled and hugged and thanked him, Officer Hervano allowed himself a tiny smile at last. But Irwin didn't. In fact his face had turned red and he'd stopped shivering as he muttered, "What I did wasn't all that crazy. I knew there was a crawl space above the water main on the downstream side of the bridge, 'cause Everett and me crawled out it ten times at least, last summer, to jump. So I knew if I could just undo Sparkle's chain before we washed out from under the bridge, we could—"

"Wait wait wait wait wait!" Hervano interrupted, bonking Irwin yet again with the shoe. "*Sparkle?*"

"His name," Irwin said, reaching into his pocket. "It's on his collar."

Hervano started to check the tag, but caught a whiff of dog and decided to take Irwin's word. Mange or age or all-purpose scrofulosity had stripped most of the fur from Sparkle's back two-thirds, leaving it looking (to borrow Everett's description) "like an exposed brain with legs and acne." But the stench rising from the fur still clinging to his head and shoulders made you think it might be best if the disease denuded him completely. "You know," Hervano said through a plugged nose, "I think Irwin's spirit might've entered that mutt after all."

"*Anyhow*," Irwin blored, trying to ignore our raucous laughter, "I knew that if we could get up on that pipe we'd have it made. And that's just what happened! And here we are, safe and sound!"

"*Except*—" Hervano said, bonking him with the shoe.

"Except what?"

Bonk! "You *know*."

Irwin reddened. "Except I didn't think the river'd be so fast," he admitted. "I mean, I'd just hit the water and I was *already* to the pipe. No time to undo the collar or anything. So I just grabbed on, looped the chain round a bolt, and hoped. But if the current hadn't snapped the chain, if the house had pulled us away, I'm not sure what would've happened."

Peter and Papa shook their heads. Mama thanked God. Hervano bonked Irwin. "What else?"

Irwin sighed. "I didn't think it'd be so cold either, really. I mean, even after I got hold of the pipe and Sparkle was safe on it and I was hanging in the current there, I couldn't work my legs. Almost, I mean. I mean I couldn't get 'em onto the pipe. At first. But then I did. So, like I said, it wasn't all that crazy."

Bonk!

"Okay okay! It *was* crazy. But we made it."

Hervano patted his holster.

"Oh yeah." Irwin grinned. "But if Greg ever sees me jump off that bridge—"

Bonk!

"—off *any* bridge, or even into any moving water, ever again, I, uh, I gave him written permission to just, uh, go ahead and shoot me."

For the first time all night, Hervano was positively beaming.

"He filled out a ticket, and we both signed it," Irwin admitted. "But on the same ticket it says I get to keep his Smokey hat."

Bonk!

"Oh yeah. On one condition. He keeps my shoe."

Bonk!

"Ooooch! And gets to use it on me whenever he likes."

Bonk!

"Such a deal," said Everett.

CHAPTER THREE

Psalm Wars

If I were God
I wouldn't answer my prayers either
  —Tom Crawford

Camas / Winter / 1964

All our lives Mama had made it a point to keep supper waiting for Papa when he had to work overtime. Even if it meant dining directly before bed, then thrashing away the night in the throes of peptic nightmares, we all had to wait. The intended effect, I think, was to increase our respect both for the soothing presence of the family provider and for the bland but bountiful cuisine of the family cook. And, for years, Mama's stratagem worked as intended.

But Papa's alternating runs and pitching-shed workouts were a new twist. In the scheduling department, they were not an occasional but a nightly delay. In the culinary department, they resulted in night after night of soggy or oven-dried suppers. In the biblical department, they had nothing to do with his sacred role as provider. And in the aesthetic realm, by the time Papa finally showered and joined us he was usually such a limp, spent rendition of himself that it threw us off our feed just to have to look at him. It was therefore decided, six or eight months into his new regimen, that Mama would serve the main family dinner at six o'clock sharp, provider or no provider. "It'll be good to feel like a baseball widow again," she said to Papa the night they informed us of the new program. And I remember the wave of affection I felt as she said it; I remember thinking what a close-knit family we were.

But any gathering of eight human beings has an astounding potential for complication. Picture a toy castle made of alphabet blocks. Blocks don't touch, smell, hear, think, vie for food, philosophize, sing, punch, pray or passionately read, misread, believe and disbelieve auctors as varied as Dr. Freud and Dr. Seuss, Billy Martin and Billy Graham, Yogananda and Yogi Berra or Henry Miller and Henry Huggins, so our toy castle is a gross oversimplification. But just to illustrate one of the crucial principles of what Everett calls "suppertable psychophysics," consider how a single block down at the base of an alphabet-block castle is visually just an insignificant detail. It's removal might pass unnoticed. But stomp hard on the floor after such a block's removal and the whole edifice may well go tumbling . . .

Well, Papa's presence at the Chance family suppertable—or, more specifically, the anemic little grace he'd mutter every night before we fell upon our food—turned out to be such a block. I'd never questioned this prayer, had never thought about it, had scarcely listened to it, really, but all our lives Papa had deployed the same *Book of Common Prayer* standby, and had invariably uttered it in exactly the same way: speaking so swiftly and monotonally that he sounded more like a bashful auctioneer than a supplicant, he'd mumble *GiveusgratefulheartsourFatherandmakeusever mindfuloftheneedsofothersthroughChristourLordAmen,* and that was that. Wham, bam, thank you, ma'am. This, in all its unprepossessing glory, was the indispensable block. Of course it was only after the thing was removed and the whole fam-damn-ily exploded like a barn in a tornado that any of us realized what a paragon of spiritual diplomacy the little prayer had been. That Papa had learned it as a child from his ballplaying, war-victim father had made it acceptable both to Everett (who loathed piety but adored old baseball heroes) and to his antipode, Mama (who adored piety, the more ostentatious the better); the rapid-fire monotone was an inane but serviceable counterweight to the subtle passion of the language; the solemnity of Papa's face and manner balanced the inanity of his tongue speed; and the whole holy diphthong spilled out of him so fast that there was no time for Freddy to clown or for Bet to fuss or for Mama to genuflect or Everett to apostasize or Peter to cerebrate or Irwin to guffaw or me to lust after my dinner. Papa's prayer was a three-and-a-half-second masterpiece—a rustic but reliable footbridge that led us so blithely over the deadly crevasse of our religious differences that we scarcely realized the crevasse existed—

until the night he left us alone, and stepped out to his backyard bullpen to throw little round prayers of his own.

the hedge hideout / winter / 1964

There are, as far as I can tell, just two types of people who can bear to watch baseball without talking: total non-baseball fans and hard-core players. The hard-core player can watch in silence because his immersion is so complete that he feels no need to speak, while the *persona non baseball* can do it because his ignorance is so vast that he sees nothing worthy of comment. For the rest of us, watching any sort of baseball-like proceeding without discussing what we're seeing is about as much fun as drinking nonalcoholic beer while fishing without a hook.

That's why, if it weren't for the new freeway just a block and a half south of our house, Papa would have heard Everett and me jabbering in our hedge hideout the first night we crawled into it. As baseball aficionados and mediocre players both, it was doubly impossible for us not to converse loudly and at length about the intricacies of the one-man ballgame being played in our backyard, and thanks to the freeway's riverine roar we could do it without getting caught. It was odd to have something to thank a freeway for.

We snuck out to check on Papa's shedball progress once a week on the average, and as time passed both his pitching and Everett's hedge-bound analysis of it became far more skillful than I'd at first thought possible. Despite the dead thumb, Papa gradually developed four distinct pitches. And despite our laurel-leaf-and shed-obstructed view of the proceedings, Everett was able—by pointing out the varying spins, speeds and trajectories—to teach me how to identify all four. He dubbed them "the Heater," "the Hangman," "the Knucklebrain" and "the Kamikaze."

The Heater was a fastball, and Everett said that Papa's was more effective than ever in that it was still lightning fast, but was also so wild now that it would scare the living guano out of anybody on earth except

maybe our Uncle Marv. The Hangman was basically just a hanging curve
—the sorry remnant, Everett guessed, of the darting slider that had once
been Papa's money pitch and had earned him the nickname Hook. The
Knucklebrain was a no-spin no-dance no-account knuckler that any .250-
hitting Single A musclebrain could have kabonged into the bleachers of
his choice. But the Kamikaze was our favorite: it was a high-speed sinking
fastball that dove as violently and late as any Zero-flying pilot who ever
bought the farm for Tojo. More often than not the thing went up in
flames ten feet in front of the plate, or missed the mattress altogether
and blammed the garage siding. But when it managed to hit the strike
zone, the Kamikaze looked so actionable and unhittable that it really did
seem like something piloted, something more flown than thrown.

For all its perspicacity, Everett's shedball analysis was, for him, a melancholy business. Hunching in a damp niche in a dirty hedge watching
pitches being flung into a wall by a crapped-out millworker was, after all,
a far and farcical cry from his boyhood dream of catching Smoke Chance
in a major league, or minor league, or at least a sandlot game. Hooked as
he was on the idea that Papa's new hobby was a surreptitious comeback,
and haunted as he was by memories of Papa's glory days, Everett couldn't
help but be depressed by most of the pitches that limped out into the
light.

But to my mind, hunching in that hedge stands out as the best thing I
did that year, and one of the best things I've ever done, period. The dank
laurel, the darkness and the need for low-voiced secrecy created an atmosphere that made our talk more considered than the ebullient, hormone-
garbled yammering we were prone to elsewhere. And with an eight-piece
family crammed in a house the size of ours, it was a balm to discover a
place, however squalid, where intimacy with one of my brothers was not a
necessity but a choice. But it was that maimed little remnant of what had
once been Papa's great art form that has really stayed with me. There is a
part of me that wants to state flat out that I learned more in the hedge
about the defiance of dullness and career death, about the glory hidden
in defeat, about the amazing inner capacities of a straightforward, no-
frills man—even a man stripped of hope—than I've learned anywhere
since. But such grandiose claims and language clash with the swaddling
clothes my hedge insights came wrapped in. All I remember feeling at
first was the sad satisfaction of knowing that, whatever he was doing in
that shed, he was doing it partly for me, and that watching even his most
brain-damaged Knucklers and hungest Hangmen beat watching him
chain-smoke himself to death in front of the TV. But as the weeks passed

and he kept slamming bucketful after bucketful of baseballs against that padded wall, a wall in me began to give way: I began to sense a new realm of athletic possibility, or a different sort of scale upon which to weigh a life . . .

the suppertable / winter / 1964

At the very first six o'clock no-Papa supper we had bowed our heads and sat there for some time before we realized that Papa's chair was empty, and that no prayer, no trusty little footbridge, was forthcoming. If she'd been incredibly wise I think that Mama would have let that spontaneous, unified silence serve as our prayer. What she did instead was open her eyes, scowl at Papa's chair for a moment, then clear her throat and announce that grace-saying would, in his absence, be a duty shared by all. Like a poker player, she dealt first to her left. As a result, for three nights running Everett and Peter and I maintained the tried-and-true tradition of the pell-mell request for *gratefulheartsourFather.* Then the duty shifted to the other side of the table, where Freddy, Irwin and Bet lurked, with weird devotion in their hearts, and God-knows-what in their muzzy little brains.

Winifred's turn came first, and began most inauspiciously: wearing an involuntarily red face and a voluntarily sullen scowl, she whined, "Dear Jesus, oh, *Mama!* I don't know how!"

"Say any prayer you like, sweetheart," Mama said reassuringly.

Freddy gave it a moment's thought—or more likely a moment's no-thought—then squeezed her eyes and fists shut, reeled off a deft rendition of "Now I Lay Me Down to Sleep," and wrapped it up in a style touchingly reminiscent of Papa by chanting, in a single exhalation, *"An' blessPapaWinnieEvertKadePete MamaDawmaBet'n'GomorrahAmen"* (listing us, as always, in order of personal preference). Opening her eyes again, she turned to her idol, Irwin, hoping for a word or look of approval. When instead a delighted but thunderous peal of laughter came crashing down on her head, she burst into tears.

Mama managed to shut Irwin up and calm Freddy most of the way down, but by the time she'd done so Freddy had figured out that "Now I Sit Me Down to Eat" might have been more appropriate for the occasion, so she wanted to give it another shot. Mama sighed, and I'm sure would have told Freddy to save it for next time if Everett hadn't started grumbling about his food getting cold. Unfortunately for all of us, Mama seemed to think she was omnipotent at times, or at least refused to back away from such preternaturally difficult tasks as teaching Everett to stop grumbling. Zapping him with a pointed scowl, she gave Freddy the go-ahead.

I noticed that Freddy looked hard at Papa's empty chair before scrinching her eyes shut. And in light of what followed, I think she must have been contemplating some of the changes that had come over him the past year: how often he was still sweating and blotchy-faced with fatigue when she kissed him goodnight, for instance; or how his hair had begun to silver, as though he was exposed daily to a snow that did not fall upon the rest of us. Be that as it may, what she blurted out this time was "Dear Jesus. *Papa hurts.*"

And you could feel the words fly through the room like an archer's arrow, piercing hearts. For a moment there was silence. Then we grew aware of the wind and the pouring rain outside, and realized in slow unison that Papa was out there in it, exhausted from his day's work at the mill, yet so "hurt," so wounded by his life that he was able to take solace in a bucketful of rubber-coated baseballs. I believe, today, that the ability to find such solace is a wonderful thing. But for some reason it struck us all as pure tragedy that winter night. "*Papa hurts,*" Freddy repeated, and a second arrow pierced us. "And he doesn't look or smell right either," she added. "So *please,* dear Jesus, whatever it is that's hurting him, make it go away!"

She hesitated a moment, checked our faces, decided she'd succeeded, and mumbled, "Amen, I guess." And no one laughed or even smiled at this. In fact the person most likely to—Irwin—was on the verge of tears.

That was the first night.

the hedge

The truth is, Papa was hurting less and less. He'd been running six miles every other night for months now. His nicotine fits had faded. And though his pitching was still crazy and he still swore about it, he would just as often whistle, or joke with himself, or even sing as he pitched— and I'd noticed that there was less and less correlation between his sound effects and the accuracy of his pitches. Normal baseball results no longer seemed to matter to him. If he was throwing strikes which the dead thumb twisted into wild pitches, the hell with it, he'd whistle anyway. The truth is, as the weeks passed Papa seemed to take increasing pleasure in everything he did in the shed. Even the swearing and wall-punching eventually began to sound like something he enjoyed. He got better at them too.

This gradual change of focus made a deep impression on me. If Papa had known that Everett and I were out there spying on him, the effect wouldn't have been the same: his knowledge of our presence would have reduced his shedball into a hackneyed lesson in "Never say die!" But because he believed he was alone, his efforts were not just an athletic Aesop fable. They were a genuine, two-sided battle—like a ballgame is supposed to be. They were Papa's two-sided struggle to reconcile who he had been (the finest athlete a lot of people had ever seen) with who he had become (a millworking, shedball-playing father of six). And the key to that reconciliation grew more evident every day.

I could call it "detachment," or "purity of effort," or "a refusal to judge by results." But as I watched from the hedge I felt no need to squeeze it into a formula. I was learning not by words like these, but by the nonsensical songs and babblings and sound effects that accompanied Papa's destinationless pitches out into the night, that there are genuine alternatives to the black-and-white categories into which most of us dump our lives. I was learning not by thinking, but through a father/son osmosis, that winning and losing, success and failure, are like the chalk strike zones I'd watched Papa draw. There was no question that shedball wasn't aimed at the Bigs, or even at the bush. It was just an oddball backyard hobby built upon the shards of Papa's old baseball dreams and accomplishments. But while many ex-ballplayers hoard their shards, sucking on them and staining their lives with them the way Papa had done with his Lucky Strikes, Papa himself had finally crunched his shards underfoot, found a new and pure kind of effort to make, and commenced punching walls, swearing, joking, whistling and living his life as if the past had passed. And in the present he was surviving. Perhaps even thriving. He didn't know. It wasn't his business to know. His business was to simply keep making the effort.

the suppertable

The next Papa-less night at grace time it was Irwin's turn. And he too was moved by the emptiness of Papa's chair and by another spring rainstorm to put in a word to the Powers That Be on Papa's behalf. Unfortunately, he chose as his elocutionary model our stalwart pastor, Elder

Denzel D. Babcock. Bowing his head, flaring his nostrils, drawing a deep breath and gripping both temples in his big right hand, he squinched his eyes shut and suddenly boomed, "*LORD!*" And when Mama lurched halfway out of her chair, it was only a matter of time before Everett, Peter and I went off like champagne corks.

"Of course I believe in You to the *hilt!*" Irwin emoted. "You know that as well as I do! *Better* than I do even! You know *everything*, Lord. I'd be the dead last of Your servants to question that! . . ."

His style had a certain Jimmy Stewart-ish sincerity to it. But sincerity at triple volume is something else again. Though Bet and Freddy were gawking at him with admiration, or at least awe, the rest of his congregation was in serious trouble: there was a sound like paper tearing in the back of Everett's throat; Peter had covered his face with both hands; I was panting like a dog having puppies; and somebody's stifled hysteria (Mama's!?) was shaking the table so violently that milk was sloshing down the sides of all our glasses. Then Irwin let it all hang out:

". . . But out in the *dark*est, *black*est streets o' Camas Washington tonight, Lord, out in that godawful *cold* and *wind* and *rain*, a solitary man is runnin' his lonely *guts* out! . . ."

(The twins remained enthralled, but Everett had turned sea-anemone purple, Mama's head was bent so low her neck looked broken, I was making the noises of the puppies being born, and Peter was sliding down out of his chair like wax running down a candle holder.)

". . . And WHY?" Irwin bellowed. "Why is that man out there in the *cold* and *black* and *dark?* I'll tell You why, Lord! He won't admit it. Not to us. Maybe not even to himself. But the reason that man is out there tonight is he's tryin' to *fight* and *claw* and *scratch* his way back into *baseball*, Lord! We see it plain as the nose on our faces! And that is why I *beseech* thee Lord God Christ Almighty! That is why I am on my knees . . ." (He flung his chair back and plunked down on his knees.) "That is why I am saying that it'd be *great* thing, just a *dandy, dandy* thing, if You and Your Father decided to help that *lonely! wet! running!* man win his long dark fight. *Thank* You Lord! Amen!"

Bet and Freddy burst out in wild applause. Peter vanished under the table. Everett choked, reached for his milk, accidentally knocked it over, then let his face plop down into the puddle. Mama jumped up and ran to the kitchen closet—I thought for a mop—but instead she just shut herself inside, and an eerie rasping, sobbing laughter began leaking out through the door. My newborn puppies and I threw back our heads and howled. Irwin just sat there grinning, perfectly pleased with all of our reactions.

the hedge

One cold damp evening in early March, Peter slipped out of the house and joined us in the hedge. He looked embarrassed as we made room for him: espionage went against his noble nature. He'd been as interested as us in Papa's new hobby from the start, but being a private person himself, he had more respect for Papa's privacy.

To my surprise, Everett didn't tease him. Maybe he was as curious as I was to hear what Peter would say. We watched fifteen or twenty pitches without saying a word. Unlike Everett and me, Pete was a hard-core ballplayer, and so felt no need to speak. After a while, though, I saw him cock his head, scowl, and turn toward the laundromat parking lot—where what sounded like a horse was clomping across the asphalt toward us. "Hey!" it called out way too loudly. "Where *are* you guys?"

Peter stuck a hand out. In crawled Irwin.

It was Winnie's first visit too. His reason for refusing to spy had been that the Bible says "Honor thy father." But Everett had finally convinced him that spying on Papa's secrets *was* doing him a kind of honor. "Cozy little spot you got here!" he said, wiping some greenish hedge gunk off the side of his face.

"*Whisper!*" Everett told him.

"Who's watching the twins?" I asked.

"Mama's got 'em in the bath."

"Was that a fastball or curve?" Peter asked.

"That was the slider," Everett said.

"Too straight for the slider," Peter argued.

"Too slow for a fastball," I said.

"We call it the Hangman," Everett explained, "because it hangs. It's the best he can do, Pete."

"I see," said Peter.

"*I* don't!" Irwin blurted. "How can he play ball without the trusty ol' slider?"

"He's *not* playing ball!" Everett snapped. "Can't you see? He's farting around in a manurey old shed. And keep your voice down."

"He's not farting around," I said defensively. "He's staying in shape.

He's doing something besides smoking. He's keeping his head on straight."

"Which is more'n I can say for *us!*" Irwin said. "Ha! We're fuckin' *nuts*, hunkerin' out here in a filthy ol' hedge!"

Irwin's cussing always sounded forced to me. He hated cussing, normally, but he loved Everett and Everett cussed, so around his oldest brother Irwin did what he hated out of love. "Go back inside if you don't like it," Everett told him.

kerBlamm! A pitch got away from Papa and slammed the bare garage wall.

"Mmnffmunffle!" went Irwin the same instant: it would have been a full shout, but Everett had lunged over and covered his mouth just in time.

"The Heater!" I whispered, feeling as proud as if I'd thrown it.

"But watch," Everett told them. "He usually tries the Kamikaze next."

Peter and Irwin shifted around for a better view, and sure enough, out into the light flew what looked like another Heater—till it snapped, like a yo-yo on a string, down into the dirt in front of the plate. Peter let out a soft whistle.

"Like a Whiffleball in a head wind!" Irwin said, when Everett let his mouth out.

"Does he ever control it?" Pete asked.

"One in six is a strike," Everett told him. "Three in six are WPs."

"What are WPs?" Irwin asked.

"Wombat Poops," said Peter.

"Winnie Peckers," Everett said.

"Wild Pitches," I told him, but by then he just snorted and refused to believe me.

"How do you s'pose he throws it?" Peter wondered.

"We think it's some sort of two-fingered fastball," Everett said.

"Could be a scuffball," Peter said. "Or even a spitter, the way it moves."

Throughout our long spying careers, Everett and I hadn't even considered these nefarious possibilities—but Everett immediately began nodding his head sagely, so that Peter would think we had.

"Looked like a fuckin' *bean*ball to me!" Irwin blurted.

"You're too *noisy*," I whispered.

"And too full of 'fuckin's,' " Everett said. "You don't hear your older wiser brothers talking that trash. What kind of Christian are you?"

"Sorry!" said Winnie, looking surprised and abashed.

"Fuckin' *forget* it!" Everett snapped.

Irwin laughed, but remembered to keep it quiet.

We spread out a little, got as comfortable as we could, and for twenty or so pitches nobody but Everett said a word, and all he did was whisper the title of each pitch. I could barely see Irwin's and Peter's faces, but I could tell by their body language and sudden intakes or expulsions of breath that they got the picture right away. The Heaters, when they were accurate, would make you think *Comeback!* Then the Hangmen and Knucklebrains would float like turds down a toilet and you'd think *Damn! Poor Papa!* But then a Kamikaze would do its hissing nosedive from night into light and you wouldn't know what to think: you'd just hope he threw another one soon. "He's got more left than I thought," Peter said after a while.

"Wish we could see him," Irwin whispered.

"You can see a double shadow of him," Pete said.

"Yeah," Irwin shivered. "And it's givin' me the creeps!"

"Watch it closely, though," Peter pointed out, "and you can tell whether he's using the full windup or the stretch."

Again Everett nodded like we'd known this all along. And again we hadn't. Ten minutes in the hedge and Pete had discovered two nuances we hadn't noticed in months. And I'll bet he'd seen others he hadn't bothered to mention. That was a big difference between Everett and Peter. They both had good minds, and were both perceptive. But when Peter saw or thought of something interesting, he just took it in stride and moved on to the next thing, whereas when Everett saw or thought of something, he couldn't *wait* to tell you all about it—and he'd try to kill you with laughter or shock or wonder when he did.

Watching the eerie dual shadow, I could see that Papa was throwing out of the stretch now, tossing the three-quarter-speed straight balls that Everett called "free throws." It was a worthless pitch from a professional standpoint, a batting practice pitch; but after a batch of Heaters and Kamikazes he apparently felt the need for something he could control. He was amazingly accurate with them tonight: alternating between the low inside and low outside corners, he never missed the intersecting lines of his painted strike zone by more than a hand's breadth. It made me nervous after a while: made me think he might suspect he had an audience.

"He's got more control left than I thought too," Peter said.

"Which only makes it worse," Everett muttered.

Peter just shrugged. "In the *Mahabharata*," he said, apropos of nothing that I was aware of, "there are five brothers, and—"

"In the *what?*" Irwin interrupted.

"The *Mahabharata*," Peter said. "A Hindu scripture. Just think of it as the world's second-best Bible, okay?"

Irwin nodded obediently. But Everett snorted, and asked, "What's the best?"

"*Ours* of course!" Irwin gushed.

"The *Ramayana*," said Peter.

"So there were five brothers," I said, hoping for a story. "What about 'em?"

"It's too long a story to tell here," Peter said. "I'm heading inside."

But just as he stood, a Kamikaze snapped down out of the blackness and whumped the strike zone dead center. Peter sat back down. "I've *never* seen a pitch move like that!" he whispered.

"Wonder how he throws it," Irwin said, as if we hadn't just discussed this.

"Spitter, probably," said Everett, as if he'd thought of this possibility first.

"What I wonder," I put in, "is what those five brothers did."

"*The Macabre Rotters*," said Everett.

"World's second-worst Bible!" Irwin blurted. "Tell us a story, Pete!"

Peter still looked antsy, but he wanted to see another Kamikaze, so he decided what-the-heck. "They were called the Pandavas," he said, keeping his voice low and his eyes on Papa's shadows. "They were heirs to the throne of the greatest kingdom in India. And one day when they were about our ages, this priest—a Brahman named Drona—came to teach them the arts of weaponry and warfare."

"A priest who teaches *warfare!*" Everett snorted. "Nice."

"The Pandavas were Kshatriya caste warriors," Peter said. "In that culture, it was a Kshatriya's duty to protect his kingdom. If he didn't, the warriors from some neighboring kingdom would come squash 'em like flies and plunder their wealth and women."

"Nice!" Everett repeated.

"A weird setup, maybe," Peter said with a shrug. "But the Pandavas didn't make the world. They were just born in it, like us. And Drona was a military genius. So he was hired to teach them what they had to know."

"A *mercenary* priest!" Everett interrupted. "*Nice.*"

"Drona was a professional, Everett. Like Papa used to be, and he—"

"Papa played *base*ball, Petey. Warriors *kill* people."

"I'm just trying to tell the story the way it goes, okay? In the Pandavas' day, the athletes didn't play ball. They played war. With your permission, Everett, the world was different then."

"The preachers were the same," Everett retorted. "Bunch o' damned hypocrites."

"Drona wasn't a preacher and he wasn't a hypocrite," Peter said in the slow, patient tone of one who has lost all patience. "You don't know what you're talking about."

"Enlighten me," Everett whined through his most insufferable smirk.

"Enlighten yourself!" Peter snapped. "Which would *you* choose? A world where the warrior-athletes fight small battles and kill no one but each other? Or a world where the warrior-athletes are free to play baseball, but where, sooner or later, one or two warriors are probably going to set off an atomic barrage that will exterminate *everybody*—ballplayers, women, old people, children, animals, birds, trees, flo—?"

"Don't get *huffy!*" Everett huffed. "Let's hear the story."

Peter turned to check on the pitching, but Papa had stepped out of the shed and gone to the wall with his buckets to pick up his baseballs. Peter turned back to Everett, thought for a moment, then went on in a whisper. "Drona was a poor man, but by choice. Even after he married and his wife bore a son, they remained poor as sannyasins—Indian monks. They were so poor that their little boy, Aswatthaman, had never tasted milk. But Drona and his wife knew how to make their simple life interesting, so the kid didn't care. Then one day some older boys came to Drona's yard, supposedly to play with his son. But when they thought no one was watching they stirred a bunch of powdered white chalk into a bowl of water, gave it to Aswatthaman, and the little boy downed it all and started dancing around like a baby goat, thinking he'd finally had some milk . . ."

"Those bastards!" Irwin broke in.

"When the older kids started to laugh at him, Aswatthaman stopped dancing, and realized he felt sick."

"I never liked powdered milk either," Everett said, still trying to resist the story. But Irwin looked ready to either burst into tears or tear somebody apart.

"On that day," Peter said, "watching those older boys laugh while his son threw up, Drona decided to become a teacher. And he eventually won a kingdom through his skills. But even then he continued to live like a penniless monk. Which, if you ask me, Everett, is not the way a preacher or a hypocrite lives."

"Okay okay!" Everett said. "Drona's sweet and wise and a hell of a provider, and cute and sexy and lethal, but nice! So can we hear the flipping story?"

the suppertable

The next night at grace time Beatrice tried her level best, in her plaintive soprano, to follow in the footsteps of the mighty Irwin. And she too brought down the house: "Lord JAYSUS!" she hollered, sounding like an ambitious baby quail trying to ape Elder Babcock. "Come ON! He's still *out* there! And the thumb's still *wrecked!* So fix it NOW, Jesus! *Tonight!* We *know* You can do it!"

The facial spasms brought on by our impending hysteria distracted Bet for a moment. But, remembering Winnie's tenacity, she sucked in air and piped, "Really, Jesus! We *mean* it! Don't worry, Lord! You can *do* it! You just gotta *try!*"

With that, we exploded. And when Bet started crying, like Freddy had done, even Mama only laughed harder. So Bet gave up and decided she might as well laugh too.

Order was restored, and the mood was euphoric—that night. But a dangerous religious precedent had been set. Thanks to Papa's abdication of his suppertime throne our graces had degenerated—in just one trip round the table—from the redundant but reliable supplications of the late Middle Ages to the wildly subjective salvos of the modern-day Bible Belt.

the hedge

"When it came time for Drona to teach the Pandavas the art of archery," Peter said, "he led them all down to the edge of the forest, then told the eldest brother—the crown prince, Yudishthira—to follow him into the trees. I'd better explain that the brothers all had different sorts of godlike or miraculous fathers, sort of like some American Indians have different totem animals. Yudishthira's father was Dharma, the God of Justice."

"Naturally," said Everett, polishing his fingernails in the gloom.

"Anyhow," Peter continued, "Drona led the crown prince to a clearing in the woods. Then he pointed up into a tree, and Yudishthira looked, and saw a target there—a little bird made of straw and cloth.

" 'Take your bow,' Drona told him, 'and aim an arrow as if to cut off the bird's head. But don't release the arrow.'

"The crown prince did as he was told.

" 'Now,' said Drona. 'Tell me *exactly* what you see.'

" 'I see the tree,' said Yudishthira, 'and the bird, and my arm and bow and arrow. And you.' "

"Great peripheral vision!" Everett said approvingly.

" 'Stand aside,' Drona told the prince."

"You mean he didn't even get to *shoot?*" Everett protested.

Peter shook his head, and turned to Irwin. "Next Drona called Bhima, the strongest of the brothers."

Irwin's teeth shone like moons in the dark. Peter turned to check on Papa. He was throwing "free-throws" again—low and inside, low and outside—as if keeping a kind of time to the story . . .

"Bhima was the Son of the Wind, and he had his father's strength, and his windy disposition. Bhima also loved his brothers more than his life, which was great for them, but could get sort of dangerous for other people. When, for instance, Bhima entered the clearing and saw the bow in Yudishthira's hand and the target bird up in the tree, he guessed his brother had shot at it, and missed, and might be feeling bad about it. So he forgot all about his own bow and Drona and everything else, and told Yudishthira if he wanted that dumb bird, he'd fetch it for him right then and there by yanking the tree clean out by the roots . . ."

Everett got a hand over Winnie's mouth a split second before he let out a delighted roar. Peter waited a moment to see if Papa had heard, then carried on as though nothing had happened: " 'Just take aim at the bird,' Drona said to Bhima, 'and shoot when I tell you.'

"The Son of the Wind heard his teacher, but he didn't move till Yudishthira had nodded to him. 'Now,' Drona said. 'Keep aiming, but tell us exactly what you see.'

" 'I see that bird,' said Bhima, 'and the green leaves, and Drona's shining white hair. I see my own brown muscles, and my arrow and bow, and more muscles, and my big brother, and more muscles yet, and—' "

"I can't help it!" Irwin laughed, slouching down in a hopeless attempt to hide his epic physique.

" 'Stand aside,' Drona told him. And next he called the twins, Nakula and Sahadeva."

Irwin was thunderstruck. "Bhima and Yudawhoozits had twins too?"

"Well," Peter said. "Their parents did."

"Jeezle *peezle*, Pete! It's like they're *us*! It's like this story is about Everett and me and Freddy and . . ."

"Just let him *tell* it," Everett growled.

"Sorry."

"Nakula and Sahadeva strung their arrows and took aim. Then Drona asked them the same question: what, exactly, do you see? And their answers were the same as their brothers', except that they also saw each other.

" 'Stand aside,' Drona told the twins. And last of all, he called for Arjuna . . ."

At that very moment a wild pitch, maybe a Kamikaze, slammed the bare wood wall, but I don't think that's what made the chill shoot through me: I think it was the last Pandava's name. Because right as the chill was peaking, Everett too said, "*Arjuna* . . ." then smacked his lips as though yak butter were melting on his tongue. "Why do I feel as though I've heard of him?"

"Me too!" Irwin cried. "And I never heard of nothin', usually."

" 'String your bow,' Drona told Arjuna, 'and take aim as if to sever the bird's head from its body. But shoot only when I tell you.'

"Arjuna nodded, just once. He planted his feet firmly. He took a deep breath, and began to draw his heavy bow. The Son of the Wind was standing right next to Arjuna, watching and smiling. But when the bow grew so taut that it made a perfect half circle, Bhima's left eye started to twitch, and he laughed and stepped back a little. 'What do you see?' Drona asked Arjuna.

" 'A bird,' he answered.

" 'Describe it.'

" 'I cannot,' Arjuna said.

" 'Why?' his teacher asked.

" 'I see only the neck.'

" 'Release the arrow!' Drona said, and when the bowstring sang the arrow flew so fast that the brothers couldn't follow it. All they saw was the target bird's head, drifting like a leaf to earth."

Irwin and Everett and I heaved identical sighs. Papa threw another Kamikaze, this time for a strike. Peter knew how to tell a story.

"Drona faced Arjuna, and gripped his shoulders in his hands. 'I will make you the greatest archer the world has ever seen,' he said, 'if you will make me one promise in return.'

"Arjuna said, 'It is made.' "

My brothers and I waited. But Peter said nothing more. He looked distracted. Distracted and sad. "So?" Irwin asked. "What was it?"

Papa threw another blazing strike. And when Peter continued, his voice was reluctant, perhaps even frightened.

" 'What have I promised?' Arjuna asked.

" 'Only this,' Drona said. 'That if ever I come against you in battle, whether alone or with an army, you must fight to win.'

"The Pandavas had all been smiling. They were no longer. 'You're our teacher,' Arjuna said. 'You're our friend. You're like a father to us.'

" 'And you have given your word,' said Drona.

"Arjuna bowed his head and said, 'I am bound.' "

Our smiles had gone the way of the Pandavas'. A fastball hit the canvas. Again the dent was in the center of the strike zone. "Did they?" Everett asked.

Peter said nothing.

"Did who?" Irwin asked. "Did who what?"

"Peter knows what I'm asking," Everett said.

Maybe he did, but he didn't answer.

"What I don't get," Irwin said, "is if Everett's the crown prince, an' I'm the Son of the Wind, an' the twins are the twins, who the heck's Arjuna? Is it you, Pete? Or Kade? And by the way, who's Drona?"

"This story is about the Pandavas," Peter said quietly. "Not the Chances."

Another pitch hit the target dead center. Irwin grinned and said, "Yeah. Sure."

Then Everett scowled and said, "They did."

"Huh?" went Irwin.

"They did meet in battle," Everett repeated. "For Arjuna to become the greatest archer, he had to kill Drona, didn't he? Didn't he, Peter?"

Peter said nothing, but Irwin burst out, "Aw come on! *Arjuna* wouldn't do that!"

Everett snorted. "I guess you know all about it, Mahatma Irwin."

I expected Irwin to laugh at himself, or to back off in some way. But he was vehement. "The Son of the Wind knows!" he insisted. "Arjuna wouldn't! Right, Pete? Because how could you be the world's greatest anything and kill your friend and teacher?"

For once, Irwin had silenced Everett. Another fastball hit the target, right in the dent left by the one before it. Papa was on a roll.

Peter said, "Drona died at the Battle of Kurekshetra. They say it was the greatest battle ever fought. Meaning it was filled with the greatest heroics and strategies and performances, I suppose, but also the greatest treachery, the most blood, the most death. And grandsons fought their grandfathers, cousins their cousins, friends fought friends, and pupils fought their teachers. And yes, the Pandavas and Drona *did* turn out to be on opposite sides. But Arjuna didn't kill him."

"I *told* you!" Irwin gloated.

"Who did?" Everett asked, violently shoving away the elbow Irwin kept gouging into his shoulder.

"The brothers all knew," Peter said, "that Drona could never be defeated as long as he held a weapon in his hand. He would have killed them all. But remember the little boy who drank the fake milk? Drona's son, Aswatthaman? He became a great warrior too, and fought with Drona against the Pandavas. And Bhima knew that Aswatthaman meant everything to his father. The Son of the Wind understood this perfectly, because his own brothers were dearer than life, or honor, or women, or anything else, to him."

Irwin began to look distressed.

"So during one of the battles," Peter went on, "when a king allied to the Pandavas was about to attack Drona, Bhima had a terrible idea. This king wasn't much of a warrior. Drona would have made short work of him. But Bhima waited till the king launched his doomed attack. Then he disguised his voice, and threw it, as only the Son of the Wind could do, so that from his own camp Drona suddenly heard one of his own generals shout, '*Aswatthaman is dead!*' And Drona's weapons just fell out of his hands. His heart broke. He just sat down in his chariot on a little grass prayer mat, and the king, Bhima's ally, rode up and cut off his head. So it was no one, really. Or it was grief—grief and the Son of the Wind's lie—that killed Drona."

A Kamikaze snapped down into the strike zone. "Well!" Irwin said, clearing his throat loudly, "anyhow, it's not about us!"

Everett started to laugh.

"The world was *weird* back then!" Irwin said, making a weird face to emphasize it. Everett laughed harder. "India was an oddball spot in those days," Irwin blustered. "So don't let it worry us! Let not the olden days get you down today, huh, guys?"

Everett's eyes were streaming, Pete and I were laughing too, and the fact that Irwin was genuinely distressed made his rampant backpedaling all the funnier. "But really!" he said. "If one of us *was* a Pandava, we just plain wouldn't fight in that situation! Turn the other cheek, right? That's all there is to it, right? We'd just flat out refuse!"

Peter stopped laughing. "What if you'd promised, Irwin?" he asked. "What if you'd given your word, like Arjuna?"

"I'm never fightin' nobody!" Irwin insisted. "Ever!"

Peter just smiled at this. But Everett, imitating Irwin's voice and bluster to cruel perfection, added, "Not even if some maniac comes after Mama with a knife! Not even if some goon with a Presto-log dick decides to rape my girlfriend! I'm just gonna *run*, like Jesus says!"

Papa threw another Kamikaze. Again it snapped down into the dent left by the previous pitch. Irwin's face reddened and his mouth opened and closed several times before he managed to mutter, "That's not what Jesus says."

Meanwhile Peter closed his eyes, and in a soft voice began to recite: "*Arjuna placed the deep blue gem on Drona's brow. The severed head was beautiful as a dark hill covered in new fallen snow . . .*"

There was a quiet, during which I found myself picturing, very much against my will, Papa's head, with its new snow at the temples. Then Irwin cleared his throat. "No offense," he said, "but I'm headin' in. I don't like weirdness. And if you ask me, you guys are gettin' weird."

He left us.

Peter and Everett and I didn't move.

Papa threw three straight fastballs right into the dent.

The bird's severed head kept falling.

the suppertable

At the next no-Papa grace time it was Everett's turn to pray again—and Mama still blames him for all the hell that broke loose. But I don't. I feel there's no blame to place. Everett was sixteen years old at the time, chock-full of hormones, chock-full of doubts about the Sabbath cult he'd been born into, and chock-full of pride in the intelligence it took to entertain and articulate such doubts. If his siblings were going to start indulging in a bunch of cornball hillbilly graces, all right, he figured. But his turn was *his* turn. And he was having nothing to do with the buckle, band or notches of any sort of Bible Belt. So . . .

Bowing his head over his macaroni, and speaking in a voice gone suddenly creaky with nerves, he said, "Dear God, if there is One . . ."

And the walls came tumbling.

"*Not one more word!*" Mama hissed.

"Dear God, if You exist," he repeated.

"Silence!" Mama shouted.

"Dear God," he said again, "or whatever we mean by that word—"

"*Shuttup!*" she shrieked. And Everett's attempts to pray and Mama's efforts to stop him fell so close upon each other that they formed an insane litany:

"Dear God, if there is any such Being—"

"*Shame* on you! Get up to your room this instant!"

"Dear *Jesus*, then, if there really was a resurrection—"

"Shut your mouth this *instant!* I've been expecting something like this from you, and I'll not have it! Not in my house!"

"Dear God, if You exist!"

"You don't know anything about *anything!* And you will leave this table this *instant!*"

"If You're still kicking, Lord, if there's any life the preachers haven't beaten out of You, I'd sure appreciate it if You'd make Mama here pipe down, because—"

"*Satan, get behind me!* Beatrice, Winifred! Cover your ears! No! Go to your rooms! Everybody out! I will not have this in my—"

"*Dear God If You Exist!*"

"*The Lord is the Shepherd I shall not want! He maketh me lie down in still waters! He restoreth my—*"

"Dear Pops, Spook and Junior! Please help Mama see that I'm not trying to lead her lambies astray. I'm only trying to be *honest*, dammit, and—"

"*Yea though I walk through the shadow of the valley of death . . .*"

"I'm *sick* of reciting pious Betty Crocker recipes! I don't know Who You are or even *if* You are, and instead of speaking David's or Luke's or Matthew's minds I want to speak my *own* for once—"

"*And your mind is a sewer that Christ alone can cleanse!*"

"Speak for yourself, Mama! DEAR GOD IF YOU EXIST—"

Mama jumped to her feet, swung from the heels, and slapped Everett so hard he fell clear over against Peter. But when he lifted his face again he looked her in the eye, then slowly, arrogantly, but also biblically turned the other cheek. "Dear God, if there is One," he whispered.

Mama let him have it again, this time with her fist.

"Dear Christ, if there was One," he murmured.

And she slammed him a third time. His eyes glazed, his mouth started bleeding, Bet started screaming, Freddy and Peter were in tears. "Dear Holy Ghostie, Dear Post Toastie," he blithered, "Dear Tricycle, Dear Triceratops, Dear Larry, Moe and Curly . . ."

She'd literally knocked him silly. And she was ready to hit him again. But Irwin jumped up, and stood between them.

"Leave him alone, okay, Mama?" he said. And he was smiling, nearly laughing as he said it. But it wasn't a request: it was an order.

Mama said nothing. She just blasted Irwin's face as hard as she could. And at that moment—at the sight of her little white fist bouncing off Irwin's big smile—I completely lost contact with my body. My mind remained conscious, I kept listening and watching, but I'd entered a state of such complete thralldom to the situation that I honestly don't think I'd have moved or acted even if Mama had picked up a steak knife.

"Please, Mama," Irwin said, and his smile, instead of fading, had intensified. "Let's all calm down now. Everett too."

She hit him again. He hardly flinched. "You'll hurt your hand," he said.

Mama picked up her plate. Bet screamed. Then Peter, moving so quickly I could hardly follow, lunged and grabbed Mama's wrist from behind. She struggled briefly, perhaps kicked him once or twice, then Irwin had the other wrist. For a moment she fought them both. Then she froze. And then she began to let out a series of horrible, convulsive gasps which, even in my wooden state, I recognized as the death rattle of my brothers' and my childhood.

"It's just *us*, Mama," Peter said, awkwardly trying to pat her shoulder with one hand as he gripped her wrist with the other. "We're not your crazy father. We're just your boys. It's just Everett, Mama. And Irwin and me."

His voice was soothing, at least to me, and though there were tears in his eyes his composure was amazing. "We know Everett and all his big theories, Mama. We've heard them plenty, and I don't think one of us agrees. But they're his honest feelings, Mama. And he's not going to corrupt or ruin us just by saying, at grace time, what we've all heard him say at other times. Remember the verse *Work out your own salvation with fear and trembling?* I think that's all he was trying to do, Mama. Till he lost his temper, anyway."

You could tell she was listening. You could tell Peter's words soothed some part of her, tempted her to calm down. But being tempted, even by forbearance, is still being tempted. And a lifetime of sermons had left no doubt in her mind about who the Master of Temptation was. Abruptly stiffening, she turned and shrieked in Peter's face, "*Get thee behind me, Satan!*"

"I'm not Satan," he said as calmly as he could. But she'd stunned him, you could tell; she'd sickened and weakened him. Then with a sudden mad lurch she pulled both her wrists free, leapt away from Peter and Irwin, and with her hair in her face spun round till she was half crouched, right in front of Everett, like an animal about to spring. It was the worst thing I'd ever seen. The language of her body, the hatred in her eyes, these were things that none of us, the seven-year-olds especially, should ever have had to see. Not in our mother. Not aimed at one of us.

Not knowing what else to do, Irwin and Peter placed themselves in front of Everett. But she looked between them and spoke her hate: she screamed—a horrid, insane shriek of rage. And when it was over she grabbed Bet and Freddy and dragged them, howling and hitting and fighting her all the way, back to their bedroom, where she slammed the door so hard the entire house rattled like the cheap, hollow box we usually managed to forget it was.

Irwin sat down, still wearing the dregs of a smile. Then he hung his head in his hands, and silently started to cry. Everett's mouth was still bleeding; his face was a mottled red and pale gray. "Are you happy?" Peter asked, plunking down in the chair beside Irwin. "Are you proud of yourself?"

"She *hates* me," he said, sounding stunned now, and frightened, and maybe even a little sorry. "She *despises* me! She really does!"

Over the sniffling of the twins back in the bedroom, we heard Mama sob, *"Examine me, O Lord! Try my reins and my heart, for thy loving kindness is before mine eyes, and I have walked in thy truth . . ."*

Peter's forehead dropped onto Winnie's shoulder. "The Psalms," he groaned.

"Betty Crocker!" Everett shouted down the hall.

"Shuttup, Everett!" Irwin and Peter cried in unison.

But Mama had heard him. *"I have not sat with vain persons!"* she hollered through the door. *"Neither will I go in with dissemblers. I have hated the congregation of evildoers, and will not sit with the wicked . . ."*

"Or with the honest!" Everett shouted.

"Please, Everett!" Irwin begged.

"Deliver me not over unto the will of mine enemies!" Mama cried. But in the meantime Everett had darted into the livingroom and returned with Mama's enormous old family Bible.

"I can recite recipes too!" he bellowed, flinging the thing open and slapping pages around till he'd hit on the Psalms. "I can roast and fry and poach *you* too, Mama! Just listen! *When mine enemies and mine foes came upon me, they stumbled and fell! Though an host shall encamp against me, my heart shall not fear . . ."*

Mama couldn't compete in volume, but there was a maddening self-righteousness that gave her screech terrific piercing-power: *"For false witnesses are risen against me, and such as breathe out cruelty! I had fainted, unless I had believed to see the goodness of the Lord in the land of the living . . ."*

"Draw me not away with the WICKED!" Everett thundered, easily drowning her out, *"nor with the Workers of INIQUITY, which speak Peace to their DAUGHTERS, but snivel MISCHIEF unto their SONS!"*

"You're making that up!" Peter said, grinning in spite of himself. It shamed me, but I'd begun to smile a wooden smile too. Everett had a marvelous voice and accent. He sounded like some power-crazed English king in his huge stone castle, reveling in the sheer rock-and-roll power of his lung-blasts.

"Thou hast lifted me up!" Mama quavered, sounding forlorn, in comparison, as a violin bowed by a chimpanzee, *"and hast not made my foes to rejoice over me!"*

"Plead my cause O Lord if there is One!" Everett roared gloriously. *"Plead my cause with her that strives against me! Fight against her that fights me!"*

And now even Irwin and the twins began laughing. There is a trigger in even the most mannerly children that is pulled when one of their peers refuses to back down from the ruling adult—and Everett had found that trigger in all of us, and was squeezing it again and again. Our laughter meant little. It was helpless, not cruel. Yet by the sound of her voice we knew that Mama was mistaking it for a mass revolt—a veritable six-headed outburst of the satanic. And her misapprehension, her desperation, somehow only made us laugh harder.

"But in my adversity they rejoiced," she half shrieked, half groaned. *"The abjects gathered themselves against me, and I knew it not! They did tear me, and ceased not! Hypocritical mockers, they gnashed upon me with their teeth!"*

"Nice!" Everett called out. "Very nice! But listen to this!" And trilling his r 's, swinging his arms operatically, bastardizing verses as he went, he boomed, *"Deliver me, O Lord if there is One, from the woman who imagines mischiefs in her heart! Continually is she primed for war! She has sharpened her tongue like a serpent! Adders poison her lips! So SHEBANG! Let the mischief of her own lips cover her! And KABLAM! Let burning coals fall upon them! And A-HEY-BABA-LUBA-AND-A-BIM-BAM-BOOM! Let her lips be cast into fire, into deep pits, that they rise not up and—"*

There was a report, like a gunshot, and pages were suddenly every-where, floating like the feathers of a shotgunned grouse as what was left of the family Bible flew through the kitchen, slammed the far wall, then slid to the floor, a dead thing. There stood Papa, his clothes and hair drenched with rain and sweat, his face black with fury. *"Lord, how long wilt thou look on?"* came Mama's stricken wail. *"Rescue my soul from their destructions, my darling from the lions . . ."*

"He just did," Peter whispered. But Papa spun round and, with a sin-gle, lethal glance, silenced not just Peter, but all of us.

Towering over Everett, he pointed at the Bible body crumpled on the floor. "Next time," he said, speaking *very* softly, trilling no *r*'s, moving nothing but his lips, "that's *you.*"

Everett turned white as a newborn baseball, took one cautious, back-ward step, nodded his head, and collapsed in a chair.

Papa turned, and stalked off down the hallway.

"Where is now the heathen's God?" Mama screeched.

Then Papa flung the bedroom door open so hard she must have gone flying, because his first words were, "Oops. 'Scuse me, Laura. But for God's sake stop that squawking and tell me what the hell's happened here?"

Set free by his arrival, Bet and Freddy came scampering into the kitchen, grinning like imps as they inspected the remains of the Bible. The bedroom door closed quietly. "Good action!" Bet giggled, parroting a phrase she'd stolen from Irwin. When she and Freddy began to babble, though, Peter pulled them both into his lap and kept them quiet. We waited a solid ten minutes, the twins squirming afresh every twenty sec-onds or so. But Peter wouldn't release them. He sensed, we brothers all sensed, that the impassioned mumbles and cries and sobs behind the bedroom door would very likely determine just how much love would be left in our family from this day forward . . .

It did not bode well that Papa, when he finally emerged, looked every bit as angry as when he'd gone in. Nor that Mama didn't follow. Slowly, meticulously, Papa washed his hands and face at the kitchen sink. When he'd finished, he dished himself a huge plate of macaroni and salad, sat down with the rest of us, and muttered, "There's been enough praying for one night. What say we try to eat without choking ourselves to death?"

We did as he said.

Mama didn't come out.

Psalm War
Addendum

It may be different for other people, but we in our green youth have to settle the eternal questions first.
   —Ivan to Alyosha Karamazov

upstairs / Psalm War night / 1964

It was nearly midnight and there was school in the morning, but my brothers and I weren't even close to being sleepy as we lay side by side by side by side on Everett's and Peter's beds. It didn't help, I'm sure, that our faces and flesh were a lurid red and the room was wracked by the nerve-wringing buzz of a scarlet neon **OLY** sign that Everett had scavenged from a Dumpster bin a few days before, or that Mama and Papa were still arguing, often savagely, downstairs in their bedroom.

We'd been talking about everything under the sun but the blowup with Mama. But after a long, **OLY**-raped silence Everett finally broached the subject with his usual light touch: "I got us all in deep shit," he grunted.

Irwin and I just looked at him, but Peter nodded.

"I think Mama's nuts on this religion crap," he said, "but I got you guys in hot water with me, and I'm sorry about that."

"Heck, we don't mind," Irwin said, smiling beatifically. "It'll work out."

"*I* mind," Everett said flatly. "And it *won't* work out. Not between me and her."

"Sure it will," Irwin said blithely. "Everything always works out."

"The *hell* it does," Everett growled. And, hearing his tone, I wanted to warn Irwin to concede the point.

But he just let out a yawn and said, "Sooner or later everything comes out in the wash, just like the good Lord intended. That's what I believe."

"Then explain concentration camps to me, Mr. Sunshine!" Everett snarled. "Explain six million dead Jews, or even Grandawma's dead family. Explain that woman up in the Tri-Cities last week who didn't like the sound of her baby crying so she threw it down on the kitchen floor and stomped it to death! How did *that* come out in the *wash*, Winnie the Pooh? And if you say the baby went to heaven, buddy, I'll bust you! Because what about the mother? What sort of 'wash' is *that* crazy bitch going to come out in? And if you say 'hell' I'll hit you again, because how did she get so fucked up in the first place? What sort of life, what sort of a world, turned her into a monster in the first place? Huh?"

Irwin looked ashen, even in the red light. It's dangerous to wax mindlessly sunny around a dark cloud like Everett. No one spoke for a good while, and in the silence I realized that my splitting headache, though partly due to what had gone on with Mama, was mostly due to Everett's neon **OLY**. It was obvious to all of us that the thing had been chucked because its buzzing drove people stark barking mad. But on the day Everett brought it home, Mama had ordered him to trash it, and in the battle that ensued he'd sacrificed his fifty-cent weekly allowance, and now he was so proud of what the thing had cost him that we no longer had the courage to ask him to shut it off.

"What would you have said," Peter suddenly asked, "if Mama had let you finish your prayer?"

Everett made a face. "It was silly. Forget it."

"Now wait," Peter reminded him. "Like you just said, we're in hot water with you. I for one would like to know why."

"Me too," I put in. Irwin said nothing, though; in fact his eyes were closed, his face was still pale, his lips were moving, and I'd have bet ten thousand dollars that he was praying about or for that woman up in the Tri-Cities who'd stomped her baby. He was like that with his praying: he liked to take on the big jobs.

"Well," Everett began, "I warned you it's stupid. But the other night, after Freddy's little prayer, I got to thinking about how easy my life is compared to Papa's. Then I started thinking what a strange notion it is that Jesus supposedly got strung up on a cross to save zillions of other people—as if his one life, in exchange for zillions, was some kind of even trade." (Irwin visibly slammed the brakes on his prayer, and turned to listen.) "It didn't make much sense to me, really," Everett said, "but what I thought was: What the hell. If that's how things actually work, why not propose a similar swap—on a much smaller scale, of course—to help Papa out. Why not ask God, if He exists, to let me do for Papa what Jesus supposedly did for everybody on earth. Why not ask to trade some of my good luck for some of Papa's bad, just to get his life back on track. That was the general idea."

"That's not stupid at all," Peter said.

"I don't think so either," I agreed.

"Me neither," Irwin said. "Except . . . I don't quite get it. Yet."

Everett stood up and started pacing. "What I was feeling, Winnie," he said, "was that maybe the reason prayers never get answered is that everybody prays the wrong way, and for the wrong things. People ask God for *good* things all the time, and never offer anything in return. But if God exists, if He really made the world and is all-powerful and all-wise and all that, then I figure He made *all* of the world, *including the bad stuff.* So if He 'saw that it was good,' He meant just that. From *His* point of view, bad stuff must somehow be 'good,' or at least must serve some sort of divine purpose. I was trying to give God the benefit of the doubt, see? And look where it got me!"

"But Satan!" Irwin blurted. "You're leavin' the devil out."

"If God exists," Everett said, "He made Satan too."

"Sure He did," Irwin nodded. "But then Satan got proud and mean and was cast down out of heaven, and that's why the world has evil in it! That's why things like concentration camps and that lady in the Tri-Cities and—"

"*Stow* it, 'Iron Man'!" Everett said. "I've been to Sabbath School too. I've read the bloody material. And none of it changes the fact that if God knows *everything,* He sure as hell knew what His little dark angel would do after he was invented. If God is God, Irwin, there's just no way some devil could be a match for Him. Just look in your Bible. Look for even one line that shows *God* worrying about Satan. It's not God who worries about him, it's *religious* people. And the reason *they* worry about him is because preachers tell them to. Preachers make big fat incomes by shoving Satan down people's throats, so of *course* they dress him up in fangs and pull him like a rabid bat from their hats every week. But if you ask me, people sin because they *want* to, not because Satan makes them."

Irwin looked like he'd bit into a lemon, and Peter looked like chocolate was melting in his mouth. But Everett just looked like he was saying exactly what he believed—and I half wished Mama was there to hear it. "Anyhow," he said, "the way I see it, God either made everything there is, Satan included, or He didn't make anything, because He isn't there. He either knows everything, or He's nothing. He's in charge of *all* of it, or *none* of it. So what I was thinking about prayer—especially *ours* lately— was that when people turn it into begging, when they use it to try to blackmail God into giving them nothing but miracles and money and new cars and babies and marriages and all that, what they're really asking Him is to remake, or even unmake, what He's already made. They're asking Him to eat His words, His inventions, His art, His creation, all of it. If God is God, the only sort of prayer that seems to make any sense to me might go something like:

" 'Hello there, God. I know Thy Will is being done today, as usual, and I think that's terrific as usual. Of course to *me* Your Will looks like a crazy mess that's getting the rich richer and the poor poorer and the innocent killed and babies stomped and starved and the whole world in danger of being blown up any minute by atom bombs and all. But You know all about me thinking that, since You made me. So, uh, sorry. And please, go right ahead and do Your Will no matter what I think, even if it kills us. Talk to You tomorrow, Lord! Love, Everett.' "

Peter and Irwin were both grinning, but Everett looked dead serious from beginning to end. "That," he said, "is why, at supper, I was gonna propose to God, if there is one, not that He change His will, not that He remake or unmake the life he gave Papa, but just that He hand *me* enough of the rotten part of Papa's life, and Papa enough of the good part of mine, to get him back out on the ballfield. You see? But now"—he sat down, sighed, and shook his head—"now I see that I was just being stupid."

"Why?" asked Peter.

"Why what?"

"Why do you say your prayer was stupid? I like it! I like this transference-of-luck idea."

"It's not the prayer that was stupid," Everett muttered. "It's praying to someone who isn't there that's stupid."

"But He *is* there!" Irwin bellowed.

"Whisper, you moron!"

"But He *is*."

"Then *you* do it," Everett said. "It's not too late. You're the big believer, Irwin. Why don't *you* ask God to put Papa's bad luck on you and your good luck on him. Go ahead! Do it up good! And we'll see how much it changes anything."

"*I'll* do it," I said.

"Me too!" Irwin cried.

"Then let's everybody do it," Peter said, laughing at the look of disgust on Everett's face. "That way, if it works, we'll spread the rotten luck over a wider area."

Everett shook his head. "I should be a damned preacher," he muttered.

"You *are* a damned preacher!" Irwin laughed.

Then somebody knocked, hard, on the door. We all sat up straight, expecting Mama, and expecting trouble. But it was Papa. In his pajamas. Looking half asleep. And more than half dead. "Lights out and into bed," he mumbled. "Now."

"We wanna do somethin' real quick first!" Irwin pleaded.

"Now," he repeated.

"It's *important*, Papa!"

"NOW!"

Irwin started out of the room, but when he got behind Papa's back he pointed at him, waved and nodded to us, and on his lips we read the words: *Do it . . .*

Peter and I nodded back. Everett smirked and shrugged. I started to follow Irwin down the hall, but as I ducked under Papa he grabbed my shoulder. "Wait," he said. "Kade'll be there in a minute," he called to Irwin. "Go to bed."

"Okay!" Winnie hollered back. Then he laughed the loon-laugh, and added, "Good luck, Papa, if you know what I mean, guys!"

Papa cocked his head for a second, but was too tired to stay curious. Closing the door behind him, he staggered in, plopped down on the part of the bed Irwin had just vacated, rubbed his forehead and brows and eye sockets as if he couldn't figure out what had gone wrong with them, then squinted miserably up at the **OLY** sign.

Everett quickly leaned over and pulled the chain.

Looking from Everett's face to Peter's to mine, Papa sighed heavily, and said, "You three are getting older."

We nodded, and waited for more, but the silence went on so long that his statement began to seem like one of those moronically undeniable assertions that certain thick-skulled adults make just to force kids to agree with them. Fortunately, Papa wasn't that sort of adult. "Irwin has grown bigger," he finally said, "but in a way he hasn't grown older. That's why he's not in here with us."

I felt my face and ears go red. We all knew Winnie was a bit childish for his age, but I never expected to hear Papa just say it outright. "Your minds have grown older, is what I mean," he said. "And more independent. You've all figured out, for instance, that there are serious problems with churches, and serious problems with your mother's brand of religion."

My brothers and I tried to control our feelings, but the thrill and relief of hearing a grownup we respected admit to a fact we'd been bandying about for years was too much: we broke out in three big grins.

"I talked a long time to your mother about this," Papa went on, "and she finally agreed—or at least quit disagreeing—with the idea that there's no point in forcing you boys to go to church with her anymore. So from now on the churchgoing—for you three and for Irwin—is strictly on a volunteer basis."

Our jaws went slack. Then Everett whooped aloud, or started to—but Papa backhanded his knee and snapped *"Shuttup!"* so fast that the whoop came out sounding like he'd been punched in the gut. "I'm not finished," Papa said, his face as hard as it ever got.

Everett put a lid on it.

"I don't expect this new arrangement to change Irwin's opinion of churchgoing one bit. And I won't tolerate you teasing him about that, Everett and Kincaid. Or trying to educate him into sharing your beliefs, Everett and Peter. You boys are four very different animals, and the older you get, the more unalike you'll get. So I want you to start respecting your differences here and now."

"I won't say a word," Peter said solemnly.

"Me neither," said Everett, trying his best to sound sincere, though the effect was somewhat marred by the shit-eating grin smeared across his face.

"Another thing," Papa said, "and this is just as important. Baseball—and I mean *professional* baseball—has got damned near every problem that churches and religion have got. Don't you think it doesn't."

Peter, to my utter surprise, was thoughtfully nodding at this bizarre statement. But when Everett and I glanced at each other, we both knew we were thinking exactly what we'd been told not to think. Papa saw it too. "You don't have to believe me," he said. "Learn it the hard way if you like. But I'm telling you the truth, as I see it. I've got beliefs too, you know. I don't want my sons bowing down to boneheads and flags and false idols any more than Mama or Babcock or Moses and them do."

Seeing he'd lost me, Papa circled back round again. "I went to church as a boy too, Kade. Episcopal churches, most of these were, but they weren't all that different from Mama's. And I've been going to ballparks ever since. So based on experience, I'm telling you guys: baseball and churches have got the same boredom factor, the same hypocrisy, the same Pie in a Big League Sky, the same bone-hard benches, the same loudmouthed yo-yos mixed in among the decent fans in the pews, the same power-loving preacher/managers delivering the same damned 'Do what I say or you're doomed' sermons. Hell, they've even got the same stinking organ music."

He was nodding his head the way Ed Sullivan did—as if he was two people, one agreeing with the other. But I couldn't buy it. "Maybe I'm wrong," I said, "but I like 'Take Me Out to the Ballgame' *way* better'n 'Stand Up for Jesus' or whatever."

He gave me a wan smile. "Sure you do," he said. "Now. But wait'll you've heard it *five thousand times*. You're gonna find out it's the same damned song."

Hmm. I'd never thought of that. Papa knew things I couldn't possibly know. He was in his thirties. He was old.

"One more thing," he said, "and this is the most important of all. Just because you think church is boring and awful, and just because Mama made you go to church, doesn't mean that *Mama* is boring and awful."

"I've never thought that and never will," Peter said.

"Good," Papa said. But he wasn't looking at Peter: he was looking at Everett—who was staring at the floor. "She's giving you this new freedom willingly, Everett," he said. "Not without a hell of a fight, of course, and not without fear. But this is one hell of a concession for a woman like her. Do you hear me?"

Everett seemed to have turned to wood.

"You've got to remember something," Papa said. "You've got completely different backgrounds, you three and Mama. You come from different worlds. And your world may not be heaven, but believe me, for a good long while your mother's world was a living hell. Are you listening, Everett?"

He sighed, but nodded.

"Look at me, then."

Everett looked.

"If you knew your mother's father," Papa said, slowly, ominously, "if you boys knew the things that man put Laura's mother through, and her brothers, and Laura herself, you'd not only understand why she is *exactly* the way she is, you'd respect her for it." He paused, trying hard to control his anger, but more words leaked out: "If that man had lived, if I'd met up with him one more time—"

"You'd of kicked his butt from here to Cleveland!" Irwin roared through the closet wall.

"You shuttup and get to sleep!" Papa told him.

We heard a muffled laugh, and a "So sorry!"

"I don't know," Papa said, rubbing his temples. "I don't know what I'd have done." He took a long slow breath. "This may not come out right, but I'll say it anyhow. Your mother's girlhood was so terrible that when she finally discovered the Adventist Church, it seemed like absolute *heaven* in comparison."

He waited for our reactions. But we couldn't react. None of us could begin to imagine anything that terrible.

"That's the real reason she went nuts tonight, by the way," he said. "She wants to share her heaven with her kids. Do you understand? She wants the best for you, but gets it mixed up at times with what was once best for her. So it's hard for her to stand back. Hard to let go. Hard to let you each seek your own sorts of heavens. Understand?"

We nodded that we did. We may even have thought we did. But I know now that I for one certainly did not.

Papa told us goodnight then, and we all went straight to bed. But because of our excitement over being free of church, Peter, Everett and I forgot something: we didn't give a thought to the swap we'd talked about making—our good luck for Papa's bad. Only Irwin (who was snoring like an Evinrude outboard when I slipped into our room) had remembered it, and prayed for it. And I'm not going to say his prayer ever made a difference. I'm not going to say it affected his life, or Papa's, or that there's a God or no God, or that we can or can't share one another's burdens. I'm only saying what happened that night. But in light of what later became of Papa, and what became of Irwin, it makes me very sorry —whether it made a difference or not—to have failed to ask for my share of the load.

BOOK THREE

Rebels
& Scientists

A poem, by the seven-year-old Winifred. Or rather, a poem by Basho, translated into English, printed in a 1951 *National Geographic* article called "What Now, Japan?," discovered by Freddy years later in our attic, slightly but significantly revised by her, and entered in a Clark County School District Creative Writing Contest, where it received no award, mention or comprehension whatsoever. Nevertheless, a poem:

Camas, Washington.

Ah, Camas Washington . . .

Camas Washington!

CHAPTER ONE

Gunshots

Every consistently played fantasy sooner or later explodes into life.
—Heimito von Doderer

Gather an athletic millworker, a patriarchal matriarch, four testosterone-ous teenaged boys and a tautology of first-grade girls under the roof of one rickety, four-bedroomed, one-and-a-half-bathroomed house and what you'd get, if that house were ruled by an ordinary mortal, would be abject chaos. Fortunately for us, our home had always been governed by our mother, and Mama's greatest gift, in fact her life's vocation, was her ability to comprehend, integrate and orchestrate the 2,920 days (365 × 8) of the Collective Chance Family Year into a manageable series of events. With the possible exception of the ever-popular "Shuttup!" the piece of advice most frequently and profitably slung round our house had always been "Ask Mama!" She was a maestro at conducting her family. The kitchen was her podium, an immense wall calendar her score, and a piercing I-will-brook-no-nonsense voice the combination baton/scepter/ cattle prod with which she set the tempo and integrated our multitudinous entrances and exits. Only she could tell you at all times which of her seven charges was where, doing what, returning home when, at which time she'd soon have them accomplishing such and such a task or keeping such and such an appointment. More importantly, only she could comprehend and wield the bewildering hierarchy of domestic values that made quick decisions possible and quashed most interfamilial conflicts before they could fester into feuds. What—to cite a historic example of these values—is the more important promise for a seventeen-year-old boy to keep: the one to take his seven-year-old sisters on their first-ever ice-skating excursion or the conflicting one to chauffeur his transportationless grandmother clear across town and back for the year-end bash of the West Vancouver Women's "Great Decisions" group? Don't ask me. Ask Mama.

The one Chance family member whose comings and goings she did not try to control was Papa—and the reason for this reluctance was not the force of his personality or the nobility of his character: it was Mama's own Bible. The Holy Bible, according to Laura Chance, stated that the duty of the Christian Wife was to "cleave unto her Husband." She never told us quite what this cleaving consisted of, and they did discuss Papa's use of his time (often vehemently, and at unbelievable length), but Mama never commanded or threatened him when they disagreed, and if he was willing to pay the hell it took to outlast her in an argument, his decision was final. For these reasons the Cleaving Principle struck my brothers and me as one of the few promising concepts in an otherwise fairly emasculating scripture. In fact, Everett and I used to pore over our Bibles during Elder Babcock's interminable sermons, hoping to stumble upon some long-forgotten verse in Habakkuk, Haggai or Hosea advising the Biblical Mother to cleave unto her sons as well. What we found instead was terrifying: Mama had somehow got it backwards! What the Bible recommended, in both the Old and New Testaments, was that the husband cleave unto his wife! Needless to say, we kept this grisly discovery to ourselves.

At any rate Mama's cleaving—canonical or not—was an ongoing act of good faith that inspired an analogous good faith in Papa, and so carried their marriage over some very rocky terrain. And her conducting—irritating or not—was the indispensable key to our daily struggle against the forces of entropy and chaos . . .

So when—the morning after the Psalm War—Mama abruptly stopped conducting Everett, Peter and me and instead began to wage a kind of Cold War against us, it was not just a passing disaster: it was the instantaneous unraveling of our family as we knew it. For what she called "Christian reasons," Mama stopped advising, stopped solving domestic koans, stopped helping the three of us in any way. And when Papa saw it happening and tried to reason her out of it, she went from intractable to irrational to hysterical to abusive, and finally just set her Bible in her lap and turned to stone.

I remember seeing a TV news clip, one night that year, of the famous UN Assembly during which Nikita Khrushchev fell silent, slipped off his shoe, and proceeded to bang it steadily against a microphoned table throughout the testimonies of every delegate whose opinion on the Cuban Missile Crisis differed from his own. It was an unforgettable performance. World War III was the thinly veiled topic, the fate of all humanity was at stake—and there sat the Russian Premier, for hours on end, banging away with his shoe. In terms of diplomatic skills, in terms of a willingness or ability to alter his course or sidestep a crisis, Khrushchev's mind and his foot had become perfect equals: if his brain had been in his sock and his foot on his shoulders, no opportunity for meaningful negotiation would have been lost.

And so it was, beginning the day after the Psalm War, with my mother. Except in her case the mind-substitute was not her shoe, but her Bible. Beginning the morning after the blowup, she no longer spoke her mind to Everett, Peter or me at all: she just flipped herself open now and then and rattled off a few blazing Letters of the Law. She had become as infallible as scripture. And as predictable. And as inflexible, deaf and blind. She had carried Christian literalism to its logical extreme: she'd become a holy inanimate object.

Camas / June / 1964

I was staring out at the street through the open diningroom window, so stupefied by the first real heat of the year that for some time my notion of entertainment had been to squash my nose against the window screen to feel the tiny waffles the meshed wire made in my nose-tip, when an immaculate royal-blue Mercedes-Benz convertible suddenly shrieked to a stop right in front of our house, slammed into reverse, burnt two strips of backwards rubber, and squawked to a second stop just inches in front of Papa's rustbucket '40 Ford. The driver left his brown leather seat and charged our house as if it was a lake and his pants were on fire. Meanwhile Papa went to the front door, and Mama and the rest of us (the others assumed there'd been a wreck) all came running so fast that we were bottlenecked, like Keystone Kops, in the diningroom door as Papa swung the front screen open. So when the stranger's first words—or first *roar*, actually—turned out to be,

"Jesus *shit*, Chance! How the hell are *you* doing?"

I could not for the life of me figure out why the big cramp of joy on Mama's stone-pious face not only failed to disappear, but intensified. Bursting through the bottleneck, she rushed the stranger, glommed on to his proffered paw, and cried, "My *goodness!* What a wonderful surprise!"

Pumping her hand as if to test how well her teeth were anchored, the stranger bellowed, "*Wonderful?* You think so, Laura? Better wait'll I'm through corncobbin' the feces right outta poor Hugh here 'fore you decide how goddamn *wonderful* it is!"

My rapidly fading sense of reality notified me that for the second time in two utterances our guest had used filthy language. I looked at Papa for corroboration: he was in happy hysterics. I looked at Mama: she was grinning from ear to ear. Elbowing Everett, I whispered, "Who *is* this clown?" Then I saw that the disease had infected him too: his normally solemn features were contorted by a smile so huge and joyous that he nearly resembled Irwin.

"*Shush!*" he hissed. "This is great! You won't believe this!"

I already didn't.

"Kids," Papa called in, seeing us all still jammed in the doorway, "this is Dr. Boyd Franken, our old surgeon friend. But it's time for you all to wash up for supper."

Though we were the ones who should have been disappointed, the surgeon, upon hearing Papa's last sentence, suddenly clutched his left eye socket as if an icepick had been driven into it. "*Ohhhhhhhhh!* Gawd *noooooooooo!*" he moaned. "You're eating *dinner! Christ*, Laura! Look at me! Big dumb shit barging up here like this! I'm *sorry!* I'll come back later! Hideous horrible! Damn! I'll be back!"

Never had I witnessed such vehement, foulmouthed, idiosyncratic remorse over so slight a transgression. But the wonders, this muggy night, were unceasing: not only did Mama fail to attack his mouth with a bar of soap, she went right on beaming as she cried, "Oh *no*, Dr. Franken! It's no intrusion at all! In fact, why don't you *join* us. There's plenty!"

For some reason, this suggestion only icepicked his other eye: "*Ohhhhhhhhhhh! Gawd noooooooooooo*, Laura! I mean, I'll bet it's great and all. But shit. I just ate. So I'll just head outside here till you're all—"

"We wouldn't *hear* of it!" Mama gushed.

"Come on in," said Papa, who all this time had been holding the screen door open. "Or I'll step out. I'm not eating anyhow."

"Not *eating!*" the surgeon bellowed. "Whaddya mean, not eating? None of this *polite* crapola now! Go eat your godforsaken supper, man! I can wait."

"No, really," Papa assured him. "I was about to take a run."

There was just no telling what sort of innocuous information might suddenly rear up like a rogue two-by-four and smite our new acquaintance over the head. Gaping at Papa for several disbelieving seconds, the doctor finally blored, "WHAW! A RUN? Like on your FEET? With all that BREATHING and SWEAT and shit?"

Papa laughed and nodded.

"Oh. Well. Hell then," he said. "That's different! I don't mind stoppin' a man from *running!* God *damn!* I *hate* running. Screw it then. All right! Look out, Laura! I'm comin' in."

I can't fully explain the effect this man was having on us, but I can say this: most of us entertain in our minds a steady stream of notions concerning what is real, a second stream of notions concerning what is not, and together these two streams give us the single sense of perspective, just as our two eyes give us the single sense of sight. But when the stream of reality and the stream of unreality abruptly collide or crisscross, our sense of perspective goes exactly as bonkers as does our vision when we cross our eyes. And Dr. Boyd Franken—being a walkin' talkin' rootin' tootin' constantly short-circuiting collision of the real and appropriate and the unreal and inappropriate—had a magical ability to bonker not just my perspective, but the perspectives of my entire family. A striking example: Mama's sudden tolerance of toilet language. *Everybody's* tolerance of it, for that matter. We'd just been invaded by a self-described "big dumb shit" come to "corncob the feces" out of our beloved father, yet there we all sat, grinning so hugely that the only one of us who looked the least bit normal was Irwin. This man obviously contained some sort of catalytic converter that rendered the filth of his language as natural and inoffensive as dirt in a garden. A second example: Doc Franken stood perhaps 5′9″, and was quite thin. Yet when our 6′2″ 200-pound father opened the front screen to let the doctor in, he nearly reefed it off its hinges then kicked a chair back against the wall, as if making way for a hippopotamus—and then Mama took over the same delusion, lock, stock and hippo. Seizing the doctor by the elbow, she steered him over to the couch, physically turned him around, then shoved him down into place so firmly that it was obvious she thought he might storm up over the couch back and out through the plate-glass window if left to his own devices. And the weird thing was that her behavior seemed absolutely necessary: I feared the very same thing!

Papa sat in his easy chair while Mama pulled up her rocker, both of them still grinning, and both parking their buns on the front edge of their chairs as if they just couldn't wait to hear the next stream of un-deleted expletives. The good doctor didn't disappoint them either: "I feel like a damn douche bag droppin' down out of the sky like this, but Jesus *shit*, you two! It's great to see ya!"

Papa smiled and nodded, but at this second reference to the Lord's by-products I thought Mama's face finally began to register some disgust. I was right about what it registered, but dead wrong about the cause: in the kind of voice you might expect to hear from someone who's just finished backing the car over three or four of your kids out in the drive-way, Mama gasped, *"Doctor!* I forgot to offer you *coffee!"*

Leveling his jolly psychopath's glare upon her, Franken roared, "So you did, woman! Get your butt in gear!"

While Mama giggled and wriggled and ran to fetch this madman cof-fee, Papa did her one better: he fetched him his kids. "Come say hello," he said, seeing we hadn't budged from our doorway. "But move it. Doc Franken's a busy man."

"Judas Priest!" the Busy Man gasped as we filed into the livingroom. "How many o' these you *got* back there anyhow? Hahaha! *Jesus,* Chance! No wonder you're flat fuckin' broke all the time!"

Papa beamed with pleasure as the six of us who'd flat fuckin' broke him found various perches from which to gape at our guest. "So where's my good buddy and colleague in crime?" the doctor said. "Where's ol' Emmet?"

Everett strode forward, his face nearly split and bleeding from its three-sizes-too-big grin. "Well, Bud?" Franken said. "You wanna tell 'em, or should I?"

Blushing like a rookie trombone soloist at church, "Emmet" piped, "You better!"

"You two know each other?" Mama said, looking delighted as she bus-tled in with an entire coffee-and-tea-making factory balanced on her best silver tray.

"I uh, we um, I phu—" Everett sputtered.

"We met on the street!" Franken broke in, smiling, nodding, and obvi-ously lying. "Yessir, I was over here in Camas on business last week when

I spotted this young fella struttin' along down by the, uh . . . Where the hell was that, Em?"

"Oh, right up by the high school, Doctor," Everett squeaked.

"Right! And soon as I saw him I says, why, if I'm any kind of physiognomist at all, that young stallion's the spittin' image of lovely Laura Chance! I hollered over and ast him, and sure enough he was, so we got to talkin' about Hugh here and how we met and so on. And the upshot of that talk, as I said, was this proposition we hatched. Which is a goddamned outrage, I may as well admit. But that dudn't mean we won't try to browbeat poor Hugh into doing it up anyhow, huh, Em?"

"*Ee-heehee-ee-ee-hee-ee!*" piped the ditty little dork who used to be Everett.

"The thing is, Hugh and Laura," Franken continued, "I'm opening a new clinic down in Portland. Or I'll open it once it's built. But my problem right now is the lot I'm building on. It was bulldozed a year ago, so it's nice and level and all. But the goddamned Himalayan briars have completely overgrown it since then. And it just so happens I'd had four estimates done on what it'd cost to clear and landscape it the day before I bumped into Em here . . ."

He paused for a moment, and sipped from his china cup with such serenity and delicacy that I was momentarily able to recall an astounding fact: in real life this walking car wreck of a man was actually some sort of skilled surgeon! When the cup clinked back in its saucer, though, unreal life intervened: "You really ought to *see* these landscape clucks! Peas in a pod, every one of 'em. *Huuuge* filthy pickup truck, five empty beer cases in the back, rifle in the gun rack, sawed-off bazooka in the glove box, and so many Playboy Bunny girl pictures spraddled round the cab it looks like a goddamned gynecology textbook in there! Then there's the one big bumpersticker saying **NIXON IN '60!** and the other one sayin' they'll give up their guns the day we pry 'em from their cold dead rectums. Christ Almighty! And then to find out what it costs to *hire* these jackoffs! *Over my dead member!* I told 'em. You got to speak to these buck-suckers in their own lingo, eh, Laura?"

Mama clucked sympathetically—though the same Nixon bumpersticker was pasted on the back of her Dodge wagon. Meanwhile Franken reached for his cup, took another serene, surgical sip, returned cup to saucer, and the instant it clinked into place, the ongoing car-wreck continued: "So I'm still steamin' from these encounters when I see young Emmet sauntering down the street there, and *bingo!* Brainstorm. Say! I says. Does that luckless butt-hook you call a father still have that quack-dinged thumb? Oh be sure! he says. How many brothers you got anyhow, Emmet? Three, says he. How many of you know how to put in a day's work? Three, he says. Which one's the dud? The bookworm, he says. But there's a muscle-brained maniac, he says, who'll more'n make up for the worm."

"So what's this leading up to?" Papa asked. "You want these boys to clear away your briars? Is this a job offer? Because if it is, you can cart 'em away right now."

My brothers and I chuckled politely at Papa's joke—if it was a joke. But Franken snorted, "The boys? Come off it, Chance! What good are these half-pint incendiaries without a Cap'n Bly to crack some whip? It's *your* big strong body I'm after, man!"

Papa seemed surprised at this twist. "Listen, Hugh," the doctor said. "I need that lot *landscaped,* not just cleared. And I'll roast in hell or even pick my heinie in heaven 'fore I'll hire the job out to a bunch of rednecked Nixonite extortionists. But I don't want a covey of underaged nitwits out there maimin' shrubs and bustin' handles off shovels either. So what I'm hoping for is an economic compromise. I'd start the boys at minimum wage, work 'em up the scale soon as I saw honest blisters (or boot 'em if I didn't), and you could make 'em bank their take for college, paternity suits, or whatever hoaxes, snares and delusions they'd be needin' it for later. But the lads are worthless to me without you, Chance. And *you* are worthless to me with that fossilized turd you call a thumb still hangin' off your hand there . . ."

Papa's face reddened, but Franken barged on: "So what I'm proposing is this: I'll take off your toe and try to build the thumb we talked about, way back before that union lawyer blew your court case. If the surgery's a failure, you're out a toe and owe me nothing. But if the transplant lives and thrives, you run my landscapin' crew, do my clinic up right and proper, and I don't pay you a red cent in return."

My brothers and sisters and I had burst out whooping and cheering before he could even finish. But Papa neither smiled nor moved. Our cheering died. "What is it, Papa?" Everett asked.

"We'd work hard!" Irwin shouted. "We promise! You wouldn't have to lift a—"

"Now cork it right there!" the doctor cut in. "Pop's got a head on his shoulders. He sees this whole deal for the potential screw job it is. So let me add a few extras. I'll provide the anesthesiologist, the prosthetic toe, the hospitalization and any plastic surgeries you'd need in the months following. All you'd have to wangle is the time off work. And as for

Operation Landscape, I'll supply the pickup, materials and tools. But after seeing Winnie here, I'll tell you this: you supply your *own* damned lunches!"

We all exploded again—except for Papa, who just looked blank. "I'm no saint as a boss, either," Franken said. "You and your band of illegal child laborers are gonna have to whip a briar patch like the one that Disney bitch planted round poor Sleepin' Beauty and turn it into a land-scaped park fit to appease the troubled souls and malpractice-happy minds of countless clucks and cluckesses upon whose loved ones I'll be inside carving. So that's the deal. What do you say, Chance?"

Papa said nothing. He just glanced at the doctor, looked down at his knees a while, then abruptly stood—and left the room.

Doc Franken turned to Mama, his bluster and cheer suddenly spent and gone. "Christ, Laura! Have I offended him or what?"

"I don't know what's the matter," she said. "Excuse me." And she left too.

The rest of us stayed put, watching the doctor, but he looked so preoc-cupied and nervous now that we were afraid to speak. After a while Freddy got up off the floor and, with a heart-melting smile, climbed right into his lap. But even this got almost no reaction. Then Mama reap-peared in the doorway.

"He says he doesn't know yet," she began, her lower lip trembling. "I mean, he doesn't know whether he can accept, or what to say, except . . . except that this is the kindest, most generous offer that *anybody, ever*, has—"

"Aw horseshit!" Franken bellowed, turning red as a geranium and nearly tossing Freddy on the floor as he stood and bolted for the door. My brothers and I jumped up and tried to follow, but he was already down the porch steps when he turned and hollered back over his shoulder, "You tell that sap to wait'll he sees those briars 'fore he decides I'm bloody *Santa* Claus! And tell him I need to know *tomorrow*, Laura, because I needed this job done yesterday!"

By the end of that sentence goodbyes and thank-yous were out of the question, because he was already in his Mercedes, spewing high decibels and diesel and radial smoke out the driveway, all down the street, and over the crest of the Clark Street hill.

"What a guy!" Irwin managed to gasp when the smoke had finally cleared.

"I'd do his landscaping just to listen to him talk!" I sighed.

"Where did he *come* from?" Irwin marveled.

"And why'd he come *now?*" Peter wanted to know.

Then we noticed the way Everett had leaned himself up against the mailbox and started smirking at his nails, smug as a cat with a mouthful of feathers.

"All right," Peter said. "What went on the day you two met anyhow?"

"That's just it," Everett said. "We *didn't* meet."

"Aw come on!" Irwin blurted.

"I swear. I never set eyes on him till today."

"Then why'd he come?" I asked.

Everett obviously wanted to loiter there a while, savoring the spectacle of our rabid curiosity. The trouble was, only Irwin and I could be depended upon to remain rabid. We all knew from experience that Peter, if teased an instant too long, would just walk away and never show any curiosity about the subject again. The odd thing was, his ability to take it or leave it made every one of us want to tell him every secret we had, whether he was interested or not.

"All right," Everett said. "Okay. Listen. Here's what happened. I figure there are basically two ways of seeking unseen help in this world. One's called prayer. The other's called the telephone. So when I got good and sick of the one that doesn't work, I walked downtown to a phone booth and tried the one that does. The Bible says it best, guys. *By their fruits ye shall know them . . ."*

The way this glib little speech poured out, I wouldn't have been surprised to find that Everett had composed, memorized, and rehearsed it— perhaps even in front of a mirror. And judging by the triumphant look on his face, I think he expected us to draw drastic religious—or antireligious —conclusions from it. So when, instead, Irwin darted forward, threw both arms around him, picked him high up off the ground, and started twirling him round and round in circles, cooing, "The *sneaky* guy! The *wise* guy! Thank you, Jesus, for my sneakiest brudder!" the sight of Everett's face plummeting from glory to horror was, for Peter and me, pure joy.

"You macaroni!" he fumed, both arms writhing but pinned by Irwin's hug to his sides. "You pinworm, you maggot!" he sputtered, both legs kicking backward at his captor's shins. "Did *Jesus* phone Doc Franken?"

"No sirree bob!" Winnie laughed, flailing him round like a rag doll to keep the kicks from landing. "He phoned *you,* Big Bubba! Heart to heart! Then *you* phoned the Doc and the Doc saved the day, thank you, Jesus!"

Hearing this exegesis, Everett quit kicking and just hung there, looking like he'd swallowed a quart of rancid mayonnaise, while Irwin jounced and flounced him around God's blue sky any old way he chose. "Jesus' angry li'l buddy!" Irwin chortled. "God's sneaky li'l switchboard operator! What a beaut he is, Lord! *Thank! You!* for *this! guy! Jesus!*"

Camas / August / 1964

Papa's vacation time was gone, his sick leave was gone, our savings were gone, and it would be another month before he could go back to work at the mill. But on the day Grandawma came palsying into the livingroom to inspect Doc Franken's handiwork, Papa was able to slip off a brace, lift a pale left hand, give her a crooked little grin, and barely but perceptibly wriggle a discolored, disfigured, but decidedly thumblike appendage at her. "Hiya, Mombo," he said.

Grandawma darted forward, gave his cheek a quick, dry peck, pulled away before he could kiss back, dragged her bifocals out to the tip of her nose, leaned down, and gave things a thorough inspection. "It's grotesque," she concluded at last.

"It's a wee bit top-heavy," Papa admitted. "It was a good-sized toe."

"It looks like a *mushroom* cloud," she said disgustedly.

"Irwin said a hydroplane, Laura a toadstool, Freddy a toilet seat. At least your description lets me feel dangerous. But look here. What do you think of this?" He pointed at the cast on his left foot, and wiggled his new prosthetic half-of-a-toe.

"He's certainly not *shy!*" she sniffed.

"Hear that, Leona?" Papa said to his toe. "She thinks you're a he!"

"I was not addressing your toe, dear boy. I was talking about this *miracle* worker, this medical *genius*, this Dr. Frankenstein of yours. The man has gleefully crippled you at both ends, to what purpose I can't possibly imagine."

"Imagine this," Papa said curtly. "Two inches of dead thumb, or two and a half of dead toe. Which would *you* prefer?"

But Grandawma was ignoring him—and pulling something out of her handbag. "I've brought you a kind of . . . oh, 'get-well present,' I suppose you'd call it. Though you're hardly ill, and why you would volunteer to be a surgeon's guinea pig is beyond—"

"A stale scone?" Papa interrupted in a falsetto, deliberately offensive English accent. "Or a tin of salmon paste? A kidney pie, perchance, or a moldy crumpet? I daresay you're too kind, Mother."

"Your opinion of the British," she sniffed, "is about as trite and de-meaning as—"

"—your opinion of ballplayers," Papa cut in.

She nearly smiled. "Perhaps. At any rate, I've brought you this." And without further ado, she handed him a cashier's check for two thousand dollars.

Old habits are hard to break, and Marion and Hugh's habit of conceal-ing every honest emotion they aroused in each other was a lifelong one. This time, though, she'd stunned him so deeply that all he could do was puff his surprise up into a parody of itself. "What the hail's *this?*" he drawled, gawking like a hayseed.

"What does it look like?"

"Like you rolled a tycoon," he said. "Like you struck oil under the rec-room floor. Like you sold Irwin to science. Like—"

"That will do," she sniffed.

"It'll do all right. It's where it *came* from that worries me."

Drawing in a slow breath, and speaking with even greater precision than usual, Marion Becker Chance replied, "It's just a little something I put away . . ." (sniff!) ". . . during my illustrious career up in Pull-man . . ." (sniff sniff!) ". . . as a Pacifist and Atheist *tea*-party hostess."

This time Papa couldn't mask his feelings at all. "You've been waiting *fifteen years* for this touché!" he marveled.

"Seventeen," she replied without a trace of a smile. And at that, they burst out laughing at the same time, for the same reason, for perhaps the first time in their adult lives. Of course Grandawma, as usual, snapped her pleasure off as if it were a light switch, leaving Papa to wind down alone. Waste not, want not. But since it had apparently been this same obsessive frugality that had made her lavish gift possible, he was in no position to resent it. In fact it gave his laughter a second wind.

"Are you even going to thank me?" she finally asked.

"I want to apologize *and* thank you," he said. "I'm sorry I offended you all those years ago—and even sorrier you took the trouble to *remember* it all this time! But listen. This is really too much. I mean, I just can't accept this."

Instantly angry, Grandawma snapped, "Then it's not *yours* to accept! I'd intended to give it to Laura in the first place."

Papa said, "I seem to see my name here under *Pay to the Order of* . . ."

"Only because I wasn't sure that Laura would be home," she replied, getting madder by the second, "whereas *you*, after being maimed by that grotesque surgical personage, could be depended upon to be *potted* like a *poinsettia* in this *vile* chair." (Papa was laughing hard now, but it didn't distract her.) "Keep it or don't. It makes no difference to me. Laura can divide it among your children if his *nibs* is feeling com*punc*tious today. But *that* money is for *this* family while those . . ." (sniff!) ". . . those *ridiculous* . . ." (sniff sniff!) ". . . while those *digits* of yours heal."

When she fell silent, Papa quit laughing, and at last let his real concern show: "What about you, Mother?"

"What *about* me?" she huffed.

"Where did this come from? What is it, your life's savings?"

"What use is a life's savings to an old crone with so little life left?"

For the second time in moments, she'd surprised and worried him. "I thought you were a stoic. Is this self-pity I'm hearing?"

"It's third-grade arithmetic, you nitwit!" she snapped. "I've got one dependent: me. You've got *eight* counting your maimed self. And my dependent, saints be praised, has very few years left, whereas yours, if they live to be my age, have a cumulative four or five centuries! Self-pity indeed! It's *you* I pity! I'll be well out of it when the likes of *Everett* hits his prime! That boy needs college *badly*, Hugh. So let's be honest. Who needs this money more?"

He still resisted. "Things change, needs change. You know how broke we always are. So seriously, Mother. What about *your* needs? What if you decided you'd like to go back to England for a visit? What if you lost your mobility, or needed some kind of surgery yourself? What if you wanted to buy a—"

"What if, what if, what if!" she fumed. "Don't argue contingencies with me! My travels are traveled, and in any medical emergency it would be my very great pleasure to burden the United States Government for every penny I could filch. Now take the money and be still!"

"But what about the—"

"Take it!"

"I really think we ought to be considering what—"

"Take it!"

"But—"

"Take it."

Camas / autumn / 1964

By the time we'd finished landscaping Doc Franken's clinic—a story in itself, characterized by such wonders as an unasked-for goldfish pond, a flock of pink plastic flamingos, a herd of larger-than-life plywood dairy cows compliments of the old Jazzy Jersey connection, and also by a water-balloon war between Irwin and the good doctor, which grew so ruthless in its final stages that Irwin sneak-attacked and drenched his adversary just seconds before he was to deliver a keynote lecture to two hundred physicians at a surgeons' convention, thus inspiring Franken's first and last visit to the First Adventist Church of Washougal, where, disguised by a mouse-colored fedora, dark glasses, slicked-back hair and a huge briefcase labeled **HOLY BIBLES,** he slipped up behind Irwin, Mama and the twins as the faithful were pouring into the church, opened the briefcase, whipped out a latex prophylactic swollen beyond recognition (thank goodness) by an easy half gallon of jet-black disappearing ink, and exploded the thing squarely on top of Irwin's head—by the time this enjoyable but decidedly digressive episode was over, then, Papa had healed enough to return, toe in hand, so to speak, to his backyard pitching.

Once again he insisted that no one watch. Not Mama. Not Roy. Not even his deus ex machina, Doc Franken. He'd gotten fussy about his shedball accoutrements too: we were no longer allowed to borrow his mitt, his resin bags, his plain or rubber-coated baseballs, or any of the rest of it. Worse yet, while pruning the laurel hedge one day shortly before the surgery, Papa noticed a sizable hole in it, fetched some twine to tie the hole shut, poked his head in, and found himself staring at an inch-deep layer of gum wrappers and sunflower-seed husks, and two apple-crate bleachers worn smooth by boy-sized bottoms. To my surprise, he didn't get angry. He didn't even bother to ask whose hideout it was. He just gathered all four of us brothers together and said that anyone caught in the hedge while he was pitching would move everything they owned directly out into the laurel, and proceed to live there, rain or shine, world without end, amen.

Everett still believed he had come up with a way of keeping tabs on Papa's post-surgery pitching progress. Papa's shedball garb had invariably consisted of a gray cotton sweatsuit, a baseball cap, a pair of black leather cleats, an outdated Rawlings infielder's glove, and if the weather was chill, an exhausted-looking but meticulously mended 1920s-vintage Chicago Cubs warm-up jacket inherited from his father, Everett Senior—who must have bought or begged it, since he never came that close to becoming a Cub himself. But one variation to this outfit, Everett noticed, was the cap: Papa owned sixteen in all—one from each team he'd ever played for, from high school on—and during our hedge hideout days Everett said he had noticed a definite correlation between Papa's choice of cap and the quality of his pitching. When he'd first started out, for example, he usually wore the antique yellow-and-green doofus cap with the tiny bill and anemic little Whitman High W on it, whereas by the time he'd mastered the Kamikaze he was consistently wearing the blue cap with the orange pinstripes and the bold Medford **M**, from his Single A California League days.

It was a neat little notion, so when Papa began throwing again, Everett anxiously began checking his headgear for progress. The theory went belly-up at once, though, when night after night Papa kept donning the meaningless, khaki-and-gold **USGS** cap his "United States Goon Squad" teammate, Cap Ackerman, once mailed him as an April Fools' gift.

That left us, finally, with just one feeble clue: sound effects. Each evening, during the uneasy silences on either side of our accursed suppertime graces, we'd listen to a few of Papa's pitches whump against the mattress on the garage wall. But as the weeks rolled by, these whumps never changed: they always sounded as if Mama was out back by the clothesline, halfheartedly beating dust from a rug with a broom. There were no more thwams of balls against bare wood—which implied improved control. But there was no more power either. And Everett and I both found this so disheartening that before long we quit paying any attention at all.

One night around Halloween, though, I noticed Mama, of all people, smiling faintly at what I took to be some private musing—till I heard a mattress whump, saw her smile grow infinitesimally less faint, and realized that the volume had crept way up. The sound was insistent now, more as if thugs were throwing body punches into some poor bastard out behind the garage. And still no thwams, still the good control.

Then—one cool wet night in late November—the thugs got tired of fooling with punches, and started using a muffled gun.

Days passed. Snow fell. We moved into December.

The gunshots came closer.

It was a beautiful sound.

CHAPTER TWO

Rebels
& Scientists

The muskrat will gnaw its third leg off to be free.
  —Henry David Thoreau

1. The Rebels

I think that Everett and Peter, like me, expected the weeks following Papa's declaration of our religious independence to be wondrous ones—a time for healing, and maybe for a heady redefining of the nature and purpose of our existences; a time of noticeable freedom, spiced with lots of free-form, late-night cosmological and philosophical joyrides.

But my brothers and I had *always* indulged in a lot of late-night conversational jungle-cruising—and in the early days of our post-Adventist period we were stunned to discover the extent to which Elder Babcock's weekly hellfire harangue had given our free and easy wanderings their delicious barbecued flavor. The truth is that religious freedom as a stimulus to zesty conversation, to inner awareness, or to any sort of spiritual redefinition was a bland disappointment. What we'd gained from the

Psalm War explosion was three hours of idle time on Saturday mornings. The price of those three hours had been our relationship with our mother. It was not what I'd call a bargain.

The bargain got worse, though, when Mama granted us a second, un-looked-for independence. "You boys are now free to worship as you please," she told us one evening shortly after her Cold War against us commenced, "so I think it's time I gave you the freedom to do more than that. I think it's time you did *everything* as you please. What do you think of that?"

We had to admit it sounded promising. "I would still ask you to obey the law," she said, "and to be decent to your brother and sisters, and to attend high school till you graduate. And I'd prefer that you not smoke in the house, since it would drive your father crazy. But other than that, I think it's about time you three began making all your own decisions. Don't you agree?"

None of us smoked at all, let alone in the house, so I just laughed, feeling sure that she was joking. But when Everett grinned and said, "Well, gosh, if you insist," and Peter murmured, "Sounds okay by me," Mama pounced like Benito Lhosa on a bad bunt. "Done!" she said—as if that was that.

And sure enough, that *was* that: beginning the very next morning the three great religious revolutionaries found themselves "free" to spend not just their Seventh Days but every day of the week doing things like preparing their own breakfasts and lunches (or starving), laundering their own clothes (or stinking), and earning their own "expense accounts"—in my case via a 5 A.M. bicycle paper route—to cover the costs of barbers (Mama had cut our hair), or shoe repairmen (she'd seen to this too), or J. C. Penney's bargain basement clothes (our nonexistent skills as seam-stresses rendered hand-me-downs useless). Meanwhile Irwin the Jolly Jesus Man went right on living his well-fed, well-groomed, prayerful Life of Riley, chortling things like "There but for the grace of God goes me!" and laughing himself sick every time one of us heretics jammed a sewing needle in a thumb, pulled on a kneeless pair of jeans, or trudged morosely off to school in underpants dyed pink from a washing with a new red sweatshirt.

Of course we deserved both the laughter and the underpants. We'd had no idea how much Mama had done for us. We'd been ingrates—and in a way it was a relief to discover it, because it made the inexcusable treatment Mama had been giving us seem almost excusable. We there-fore set out to make some serious amends. A couple of days into our

Domestic Independence period we collected every penny we had and went on a shopping spree: Peter bought Mama a dozen red roses, I got her a two-pound box of Van Dyne's candy, and Everett completely outdid himself, buying her a beautiful new family Bible (though he stamped the gift with his indelible touch by including a horrid little Hallmark card with three pigtailed Chinamen on it, bowing beneath the words **"BY GOLLY WE SOLLY!"**). We also wrote her a joint letter, making it clear that we'd been pigs and knew it, that the gifts were not intended to be bribes, and that it was only her friendship we wanted back, not her services. We even offered to cook *her* meals and do *her* yardwork and ironing and cleaning and shopping and laundry—if she'd only teach us how.

Her response? She told Peter, "Give the roses to the sick"; told me, "Give the candy to the gullible"; told Everett, *"You're* the one in need of that Bible. And it's your Heavenly Father you should be mailing that silly card to." She added that she would do her own housework and cooking and shopping, "as God intended Christian wives and mothers to do," and that she didn't really need our friendship, thank you, she had the Lord Jesus Christ's.

We were stunned. For the time being, we managed to hold our tongues. But we could all plainly see that, like the banging of Khrushchev's shoe, this sort of shit could get old fast.

2. The Scientists

Shortly after the Psalm War, Bet and Freddy invented a game called "Famous Scientists." It was not a coincidence. The new game had nothing whatever to do with church, sports, prayers, pitching or any of the other family obsessions. In fact it was not so much a game as an all-out surrender to a way of life the rest of us were too religious, too athletic, too complicated or just too busy to comprehend—and that was the way they wanted it.

Famous Scientists, in Bet and Freddy's eight-year-old view, were an elite handful of absentminded, charmingly disheveled, Margaret Mead or Louis Leakey-like personages who at some point in their earthly careers had simply said "Forget it!" to pedestrian jobs, lives and ways of thinking, and began to spend long, scintillating days working one ingenious experiment after another. It was a naïve definition, certainly. But the beauty of it—and the marked advantage over more sophisticated definitions—was that it obliterated the usual gap between theory and action. Famous Science had nothing to do with things like knowing the difference between lepidopterology and otorhinolaryngology or Andy Celsius and Gabe Fahrenheit. All Famous Science had to do with was saying "Let's be Famous Scientists!" to someone who could be depended upon to say "Okay!," and then to behave and experiment accordingly.

During Mama's most Bible-headed periods the twins sometimes remained in Famous Science Mode for days at a time, and as the years passed it became crucial for my brothers and me to recognize this mode, because our Scientists were increasingly attracted to the field of experimental psychology, and their "lab rats" of choice were their ever-credulous brothers. It can be more than a minor annoyance to find that the innocuous chat you've just had with a seemingly air-headed, bubble-gum-smacking, preadolescent girl was in fact a prefabricated, carefully calculated quiz designed to lay bare the most inane foible of your personality. It can also be troubling to find that every cross-grained, self-damning sentence you just blabbed without thinking has been immortalized in one of Famous Science's increasingly nefarious lab notebooks.

But the psychological dismemberment of male siblings was a later twist. Most of the early Famous Science research tended to be either in no recognizable field of science or else in three or four fields intrepidly bulldozed together. Take, for example, a little experiment known to its progenitors as "Centrifuging Flickers":

A red-shafted flicker is a lovely mottled woodpecker with war-painted cheeks, auburn pinions and, when fleeing, a rump as startlingly white as any Caucasian skinny-dipper's. They were so common in Camas that, during hard winter rains, six or eight of them would frequently come to roost in the warmth and dryness of our second-story eaves—and hearing, just inches from our heads as we lay in bed, the talons of a sleeping woodpecker tightening their grip on the siding was a stirring experience. Unfortunately, the flicker's sole method of expressing gratitude for a warm night's sleep was even more stirring: it came smack at the rosy crack of dawn, and consisted of a beak-on-siding applause that sounded, from the sleeper's side of the siding, about like machine-gun fire sounds from the point-blank side of the machine gun. Mill-town people cherish their sleep. After all, come morning it's time to go work at the mill. For this reason a lot of starling-brained Camas residents used to deal with their red-shafted machine-gun problems by leaning out their windows and blasting away with retaliatory BB, pellet or even shotgun fire. I'm proud to say that the Chance family resorted to more enlightened measures: we just unleashed our Famous Scientists on them.

"Centrifuging" was a concept the twins had gleaned from Famous Science's most formidable new ally and supporter, Marion Becker Chance. While buttering a homemade scone for each of them in her apartment one morning, this fanatical pacifist and devoted birdwatcher unwittingly mentioned that a centrifuge was any rapidly rotating apparatus that used centrifugal force to separate substances of different densities—for instance butterfat from milk. That her increasingly scientific hence increasingly adorable granddaughters would take this innocuous bit of information, add a flashlight, a stepladder and a smelt-dipper's net with a twelve-foot handle to it, and proceed to apply it to one of her favorite woodpeckers was unthinkable. But, as anyone who's ever seen a mushroom cloud, a cooling tower or an aerosol can of cheese spread can tell you, the unthinkable is often the very thing the Famous Scientist comes up with.

Centrifuging flickers was a straightforward process: waiting till well after sunset, when the roosting flickers had gone into their rainy-night torpor, our two Scientists donned raincoats (the birds only came during downpours), snuck out under the eaves, flashlighted a prospective victim, set up and climbed the ladder, and caught a stupefied flicker in the smelt net. After "tagging" the bird's ankle with a piece of adhesive-tape labeled "CENTRIFUGED 2-25-'65" (or whatever the date), they would fold it gently but tightly back into the smelt net, turn on Papa's shedball spotlights, start giggling with anticipation, march out into the middle of the backyard, grab the very end of the net's twelve-foot handle in their four little hands, and proceed to centrifuge their captive's brains out by twirling round and round, fast as they could go, while the experiment's greatest fan (guess who?) sat howling and loon-laughing his appreciation from an upstairs window.

We're not sure whether the Scientists ever actually separated, say, a flicker's blood from its lymphatic fluids or its gizzard juice from its stones, but we *are* sure that not one of the tagged-and-processed birds that wobbled off into the night ever showed its Caucasoid rump in our eaves again. One good centrifuging lasted a lifetime.

3. Divergence of Rebels

When in the Course of Human Events it became necessary for three of four Brothers to dissolve the Theological Bands which had connected them with their Mother, and to assume among the Powers of the Earth the separate and equal Station to which the Laws of Nature and of Nature's God entitled them, they discovered, to their utter amazement, that nothing much changed: they spent a couple hours each Saturday listening to the Elders Reese and Dean (as in Dizzy and Pee Wee) instead of Babcock and Barnes, and that was about it. But when, as Free and Independent Sons, they were granted (or saddled with) the Power to do their own Cooking, Cleaning, Mending, Shopping, Personal Maintenance and Grooming, Laundry, Ironing and all other Domestic Acts and Things which Independent Sons must of right do, they discovered, to their everlasting astonishment, that *everything* changed . . .

I, for starters, was transformed within weeks into a feminist. The term hadn't made it anywhere near Camas yet, so I didn't know that was what I'd become. But I can think of no better word to describe a thirteen-year-old American male suddenly forced to discover that no working citizen of this bizarre country can hope to maintain a tenable existence without possessing (1) a car and (2) an unpaid, unthanked, faceless, sexless drudge—i.e., "Traditional Housewife." Being too poor, young, ugly and honest to woo, purchase or steal either, I pedaled around town on a rattletrap Huffy bike that was as close as I could get to the car, and became the even more rattletrap drudge myself. It was a spectacularly rude awakening. To have ironing boards folding up on your fingers while the school bus is honking outside the window; to walk into department stores with eight or ten hard-earned bucks in your pocket and a two-hundred-dollar void in your wardrobe and be expected to consider this humiliation a self-indulgent "shopping adventure"; to have—before an arduous school day has even begun—to make a bed, prepare a breakfast, ride a crappy bike eleven miles to deliver 103 papers, take a shower, prepare a lunch, wash your dishes, and *then* be expected to know what to do with that disgusting wad of guck that's left in the drain strainer after the water goes down . . . Suffice it to say that these were not the sort of experiences I expected Freedom to be paved with.

As might be expected, Everett underwent an even more radical transformation. He was so desperate to prove that he hadn't been dependent on Mama in any meaningful way that he refused to do anything for himself or his clothes or his room which he hadn't been doing before. As a result, my most dapper and fastidious brother was transformed within weeks into an ersatz bohemian skuzzball who smelled like moldering gym socks and lived in half a bedroom that looked like a Winter of '76 campsite at Valley Forge. To add inanity to injury, he also began struggling— when friends and schoolmates sniffed out telltale odors of rebellion upon his person—to pass off his increasingly subfuscous wardrobe and squalorous digs as a matter of style by affecting the same beatnik lingo and mannerisms that had previously been the object of his most withering scorn. The transparency of this ploy set even Irwin to smirking. But Everett is nothing if not stubborn: he entrenched himself in this counterfeit beatnik personae for so long that even he eventually had no choice but to call it "real." Fortunately for his social and sex lives (though not for his grip on honesty), he was soon able to feign having had a prophetic finger on the pulse of the nation all along—for our generation was about to spawn that peace-preaching sartorial and hygienic disaster, the American Hippie.

Peter attacked his domestic and economic difficulties in an equally extreme but far more honest way: he became, so far as I know, Camas, Washington's first self-made Buddhist monk. Paring away possession after possession, he soon owned nothing in this world but three shirts, two pairs of pants, two pairs of black Converse high-tops, a perennially empty wallet, three or four hundred paperback books and a top-of-the-line Wilson outfielder's mitt, which, in a pinch, could double as a begging bowl.

It was not that big a change for Peter (he still owned the same *sorts* of things, just fewer of them), but combined with Everett's transmogrification it had a disturbing effect on their room. What had always been a fairly standard, all-American boys' bedroom—and for Irwin and me the most educational, or at least stimulating, room on earth—suddenly split in half. To the right of the window an anarchistic ragpicker seemed to be trying to start a revolution, or at least acquire squatter's rights, while to the left an athletic bhikku sought a bookish enlightenment.

Far more troubling than this visual tension was the unseen tension between the inhabitants. Everett's basic feeling was that we three were suffering an outrageous and punitive suspension of our rights as sons, and that some sort of equally punitive counterattack should be launched as soon as possible. But Peter wasn't interested. In fact, Peter seemed, except for the friction with Everett, even more serene and satisfied in his ascetic circumstances than he'd been before. Knowing that his thinking infuriated Everett, but wanting to explain his position to me, he began to give me the occasional surreptitious "dharma talk." I remember one in which he told me that our family had never been far from poverty. But while there was abject poverty, he said, "the usual kind," there was also something that contemplatives and monks talked about, called "voluntary poverty." He said that both meant few possessions, simple food and clothes, maybe no car, and so on. But whereas abject poverty was like being thrown overboard in a storm, like Jonah, voluntary poverty was like diving into a calm, clear sea because you saw the beauty of it and wanted to take a swim. I still remember the intensity of his voice and the flash of his eyes as he added, "We've arrived at the ocean's edge, Kade. So why fight it? Why not dive?" And I remember how hard I tried to appear moved by his pearls of wisdom.

But the truth was, I wasn't ready to go swimming in any damned river, pool or sea whether I dove or got thrown in or was washed out of bed in my sleep. The truth was, both sides of Everett and Peter's room looked alien and comfortless to me now, and it wasn't the choice between rebellion and renunciation that generated that comfortlessness: it was an unnameable sadness that filled both halves—a loss of unity, or solidarity, or brotherhood. Something precious was being taken from us, or squandered by us. And neither Everett the Revolutionary nor Peter the Monk was taking even a moment to look back and mourn for it. But to me . . . To me it felt as though two old and intimate friends, after sixteen years spent hiking shoulder to shoulder, had come to a fork in the trail, and without even noticing had taken different paths. When they first looked up and saw what had happened, they were not at all far apart: they could still speak quietly to each other, could still see each other perfectly well. But they just kept going! All those years spent side by side, yet they didn't hesitate, didn't wave goodbye, didn't even acknowledge that they'd parted! Somehow this chilled me to the heart. It seemed that only I understood that, blithe as their divergence had been, it was permanent. So as my big brothers hiked intrepidly on, I—the slow, over-round, over-adoring brother who'd spent his whole life traipsing happily along behind both of them—just stood back at the fork, watching them veer farther and farther apart, and grieving for us all.

4. Convergence of Rebel and Scientists

"The Hump of Energy" was a Famous Science experiment as tedious to outside observers as "Centrifuging Flickers" was interesting, but it remained a great favorite on sultry summer afternoons. To work this meager wonder the two Scientists would simply take time out from running through the sprinkler, disconnect the garden hose, stretch it straight out across the lawn, then give one end of it a violent, four-handed snap. The Ω-shaped hump that proceeded to fly from their hands down the length of the hose gave the experiment its name. They would do this six or eight times, scrutinizing the Ω with a look of far greater interest than they possibly could have felt. Then they'd reconnect the sprinkler, sprawl belly-down in the grass beneath the spray, and while the sun baked them hot and the sprinkler bathed them cool they would proceed to speculate —at unbelievable length—upon the possible "meanings" of the hump.

The charm of the experiment completely eluded my brothers and me. All that talk about a wiggle in a hose seemed more like an affliction, an attack of logorrhea maybe, than a scientific experiment. What we didn't know was that Grandawma, in a little lab journal she'd begun to help the twins keep, had written a description of the experiment that made quite a bit of sense. In a few flamingly uncharacteristic sentences she even attempted to gear her language down to the level of eight-year-olds. Here's what she wrote:

The "Hump of Energy" is only superficially an experiment in physics. The undulation in the hose is of course a mild curiosity, but the more profound challenge here is to your imaginations—for which reason the very dullness of the hose becomes its chief value. Your aim should be to let the "Hump"—the little undulation—pass cleanly into your minds, and then to follow your thoughts wherever the undulation leads them. Don't work too hard at this. Don't judge or censor yourself, or each other. Just spin and bounce and juggle your ideas the way a circus seal juggles the ball on its nose; then, when you feel ready, start tossing your ideas back and forth, like two seals. Silly as it may seem at first (it sounds rather like <u>baseball,</u> doesn't it!), this is very like what scientists do when developing an idea. To maintain a spirit of playful cooperation, to keep the thinking lively while showing your partner's daftest notions no disrespect—these are the aims of the experiment, and the only valid measures of its "success."

When Grandawma had first taken up with our two Scientists I'd feared that one more feisty faction had just shouldered its way into the family ideological wars, and that some rabid new form of brainwashing had begun. It was a pleasure to discover how wrong I was. In a completely noncombative way, the grumpy old so-called Atheist was attempting to sew together some of the rips being torn in our family in the names of "Christ" and "salvation." It's amazing, sometimes, how far away the name of a thing lands from the thing itself.

One scorching-hot day during Famous Science's inaugural summer— long before my brothers and I learned of Grandawma's congenial definition—the "Hump of Energy" caught no less a thinker than Peter by surprise. Having just mowed a humongous lawn a few blocks up the street, he'd returned home dripping with sweat. And since, in those days, Peter's feelings about having sweat on his body were akin to most people's feelings about having feces on theirs, when he saw the sprinkler whirring and my sisters lolling beneath it, he took a short sprint, did his patented headfirst base-thieving slide across the soft, sopped grass, and came to a tidy halt right between them just in time to hear Beatrice say, "If a hose could reach from here clear to Spokane, do you think there could be a man strong enough to jerk it hard enough to make the Hump travel all the way?"

The twins were fortunate: if Everett had been the one to overhear this sentence, he'd have taken the words "hump," "hard," "hose," "jerk" and "all the way" and more or less robbed the twins' ears of their virginity. But Peter was a gentleman: all he did was groan. And when the twins ignored him, this pleased him. He liked it that the Scientists, while engaged in speculation, paid no heed to the banal protestations of the laity.

"I don't know about Spokane," Freddy hesitantly replied. "I mean, I don't know how far a hump of energy could travel down a hose, because if some muscleman or machine or something jerked it *really* hard, I guess the hose might just break."

"I never thought of that," said Bet.

I didn't either, Peter thought.

"But I do think," Freddy continued, "there might be all sorts of humps of all sorts of energy that go traveling all sorts of directions people can't see. For instance when a person gets mad at somebody . . ." (Her words came quicker now, and her breathing had become audible.) "Like when you get *really* mad and maybe slap somebody or jerk their arm or something, like Mama does to us sometimes, I think an invisible hump of energy might go flying all the way up their arm and right into their skeleton or insides or whatever—a hump of mean, witchy energy—and I think it might fly round and round in there like a witch on a broomstick flies round the sky, and go right on hurting invisible parts of the person you don't even know you're hurting, because you can't see all the ways their insides are connected to the mean thing you did to their outside. And from then on, maybe that hump of mean energy sits inside the hurt person like a coiled-up hose or a rattlesnake, just *waiting* in there. And someday, when that person touches somebody else, maybe even *way* in the future, that rattlesnake energy might come humping up out of them by accident and hurt that next person too, even though they didn't mean to, and even though the person didn't deserve it." She paused for a moment. Then, with feeling, concluded, "I think it happens. I really think it does."

"I think it does too," Peter said.

He felt Bet's scowl, knew that he was trespassing on Scientific turf, but finished his thought anyway. "I think what you said can happen, *does* happen. But every witch who ever lived was once just a person like you or me, that's what I think anyway, till somewhere, sometime, they got hit by a big, mean hump of nasty energy themselves, and it shot inside them just like Freddy said, and crashed and smashed around, wrecking things in there, so that a witch was created. The thing is, though, I don't think that first big jolt is ever the poor witch's fault."

Bet thought about this, and finally nodded cautiously. Freddy said nothing. The sprinkler hissed like a Halloween cat. "Another thing," Peter said, "is that *everybody* gets jolted. You, me, before we die we'll *all* get nailed, lots of times. But that doesn't mean we'll all get turned into witches. You can't avoid getting zapped, but you *can* avoid passing the mean energy on. That's the interesting thing about witches, the challenge of them—learning not to hit back, or hit somebody else, when they zap you. You can just bury the zap, for instance, like the gods buried the Titans in the center of the earth.Or you can be like a river when a forest fire hits it—*phshhhhhhhhhhhhhh!* Just drown it, drown all the heat and let it wash away . . ."

Bet was scowling again, but Freddy just lay still, watching his face. "And the great thing," he said, "the reason you can lay a river in the path of any sort of wildfire is that there's not just rivers inside us, there's a *world* in there." Seeing Bet's scowl deepening, he added, "Not because I say so. Christ says so. And Krishna. But I feel it sometimes too. I've felt how there's a world, and rivers, and high mountains, whole *ranges* of mountains, in there. And there are lakes in those mountains—beautiful, pure, deep blue lakes. *Thousands* of them. Enough to wash away all the dirt and trouble and witchiness on earth."

Bet's scowl was gone now, because her mind had eased down into a place where hiss of sprinkler, splash of drops and babbling of brother were all just soothing sensations. But Freddy was still watching Peter's face, and still listening when he said, "But to believe in them! To believe enough to *remember* them. *That's* where we blow it! Mountain lakes? In *me?* Naw! Jesus we believe in, long as He stays out of sight. But the things He said, things like *The kingdom of heaven is within you,* we believe only by dreaming up a heaven as stupid and boring as our churches. Something truly heavenly, something with mountains higher than St. Helens or Hood and lakes purer and deeper than any on earth—we never look for such things inside us. So when the humps of witchiness come at us, we've got nowhere to go, and just get hurt, or get mad, or pass them on and hurt somebody else. But if you want to stop the witchiness, if you want to put out the fires, you *can* do it. You can do it if you just remember to crawl, *right while you're burning,* to drag yourself if that's what it takes, clear up into those mountains inside you, and on down into those cool, pure lakes."

Bet was half asleep by now, and Peter was gazing at the spray as if into a blaze, when, quite suddenly and quite loudly, Freddy burst into tears. "*What!*" Bet shouted, jumping clear to her feet. "Is it a bee-sting? What *is* it?"

"I'm sorry," Freddy sobbed, hiding her face. "I'm sorry. But . . . but I'm just so *glad!*"

"*Glad?*" Bet was flummoxed. "About a bee-sting? About *what?*"

"The mountains!" Freddy whispered, eyes closed, tears streaming. "The lakes."

5. Science Meets Prophecy

For a believer in the empirical method and an acerbic critic of religious hocus-pocus of all kinds, Marion Becker Chance was surprisingly fond of making prophetic statements. Her prophecies were invariably dire. She made them only in the privacy of her apartment. Her "chosen people" were invariably her grandchildren. Her purpose, however, was far more pragmatic than that of the usual doom prophet: all Grandawma really wanted out of a prophesy was to scare our pants off. Having personally experienced, as an inmate in an ancient British parochial school, how much quieter and better behaved a quailing, apprehensive child is than a happy one, she would do her prophetic best, whenever our boisterousness threatened her china or fragile furniture, to create an atmosphere conducive to the dread of untold evil and impending disaster.

Unfortunately for her possessions, we were on to her. Though she used her irony-armored voice, hawklike face, red-rimmed eyes, innate pessimism, disastrous past and palsying to considerable effect, we knew all along that she was no prophet. She was just an overgrown Famous Scientist in disguise.

Her favorite doom prophecy was a surprisingly anemic specimen. It went something like this: "The one thing, perhaps the *only* thing you can all be certain of, is that your lives are going to be very different, and probably very much darker, than you'll ever dream or expect as children."

"That's great news, Gran!" was Everett's famous reply to this. "I was expecting I'd turn out exactly like you!"

Poor Grandawma. Another common doom, this one foretold for the twins as soon as they grew old enough to act the least bit giddy around little boys, went like this: "You think you'll grow up to marry a handsome prince, don't you? Well, let me tell you something, young lady. You shall, you shall. And *that's* when you'll find out that the fairy tale has it backwards. A few kisses, a few years—that's all it takes to turn the handsomest prince on earth into a big, ugly frog."

Freddy's best response to this came when she was seven—and already a discerning student of her big brothers' vernacular. She said, "You mean like Charles de Gaulle?" Bet's most interesting reply to the same prophecy had come a year or two earlier. It went, "I'll *never* kiss a boy! Not even a prince. But if I do, I hope he turns into a cute little doggy." We were difficult kids to scare.

In 1965, however—in the midst of a religious Cold War that *had* begun to scare us—Grandawma finally made a prophecy that had the desired effect. It was that same anemic one she'd made a dozen times at least to my brothers and me—about our lives being doomed to turn out differently than we expected. This time, though, she found a way of giving it some real oomph: not sixty seconds after she said it, she died.

•   •   •   •

It was a bright, sunny spring morning. The twins had spent the night on the hide-a-bed couch in Grandawma's livingroom. Their joint plan for the day was a bus trip down to Portland to visit the city zoo and the Oregon Museum of Science and Industry—the Famous Scientists' Medina and Mecca. Grandawma's health had been fine. In fact she'd been on a roll, bustling on foot around the school basements, libraries and junk stores of Camas, begging or buying old microscopes and chemistry sets, butterfly nets and lab notebooks, fossils, gyroscopes, geodes, atomic charts, Indian artifacts and anything else she could think of to enhance and prolong the twins' science phase. The three of them were seated together at her little oak breakfast table, eating oatmeal and drinking orange juice and tea, when it happened. Freddy had just idly recited the Quaker Oats motto aloud: *"Nothing Is Better for Thee Than Me."* But Bet —whose mouth had been full of the same tepid bite of the stuff for two or three minutes—took vehement exception: "That's a lie!" she blurted, dribbling milk down her chin. *"Tons* of things are better for thee than *oat*meal!"

"It's an exaggeration, certainly," Grandawma said. "But you'll not leave this table till you finish what's in your bowl. And if you speak again with your mouth full, I'll double your helping."

"It's the Right Thing to Do," Freddy read from the box.

Bet sighed, rolled her eyes, and started lapping milk from the bowl with her tongue.

"Stop that at once!" Grandawma snapped.

"I'm a kitty cat," Bet said gloomily.

"Perhaps you were. But now you're human."

"Whooo saaaaays?" she meowed.

"Your sister and I, and this nice Quaker gentleman on the box," Grandawma replied patiently. "We are going on a scientific expedition today, and cats are infamously inept scientists. Just look at the way they dissect mice and frogs."

"I like *playing* Famous Scientist," Bet said, unscientifically slapping her spoon against the gluey mush in her bowl, "but I don't want to *be* a scientist. Not when I grow up."

Grandawma scowled, both at the statement and at the slapping. Bet looked to be in a state of rapid devolution. If the trend continued, she might lapse clear back into one of her *Irwin* moods! It would be the ruin of the day. Marion Becker Chance narrowed her eyes and sniffed loudly. The time had definitely come to brew up a little behavior-altering apprehension: "You may well grow up to become a gargoyle, or a harridan, or a

guttersnipe!" she snapped. "We can't possibly know—and thank goodness not! What most of us become as adults would *terrify* us as children."

It was working better than usual: Bet had already stopped slapping her
spoon, sat up straight, and was betraying no feline qualities whatever as
she peeped, "Why?"

But Grandawma decided she'd best rub it all the way in. "I don't quite
know," she said, unleashing the palsy now, and glowering far off into a
hideous future. Then out she came with it: "I only know that the one
thing, perhaps the *only* thing we can always be certain of, is that our lives
will turn out very differently, and very much more darkly, than most of us
ever dream as children."

It may have been a bit cruel, but it was also an unusually effective
piece of behavioral engineering: the two girls stopped eating and reading
and stared morosely down into their bowls, their hands neatly folded,
their rambunctious little mouths closed, their comportment perfect. The
room was silent, but for the tidy ~~~~~~~~~~~ing of the electric wall
clock. Marion took a grimly satisfied sip of tea, placed her cup in its
saucer with a dainty clink, and was about to broach the subject of the
Natural Science Exhibit they'd be studying at OMSI that day when, for
the first and last time in her life, her behavior modification technique
backfired and became a genuine act of prophecy:

First she looked up at the ceiling and said, *"Oh!"*

It was her last word. She said it softly, but with such hushed enthusiasm, perhaps even delight, that the twins' immediately looked up at the
ceiling too. But there was nothing there but plaster.

Next Grandawma closed her eyes, opened her mouth, and slowly began
to bow her head—another thing they'd never seen her do. Bet later said,
with a somewhat wooden air of piousness, that it looked as though she'd
been bowing her head to pray. But Freddy said not. Freddy said she
bowed so slowly that it was more like an OMSI exhibit they'd once seen
on the laws of kinetics. To me this seems the likelier explanation, since
when the center of gravity passed the meridian the bowing head became
a falling head that didn't slow or alter course till Grandawma's brow
smacked the front rim of her cereal bowl, the milk and oatmeal splashed
up onto her neat gray bun, and the bowl stayed balanced, like a little cap,
right there on top of her head. The twins gaped at her, saying nothing.
Grandawma gaped down at the floor, also saying nothing. Her arms were
folded neatly in her lap; her rambunctious old mouth was closed; except
for the food on the floor and the bowl on her head, her comportment was

perfect. The room was silent, but for the tidy ∿∿∿∿∿∿∿∿ing of the clock. She'd even stopped palsying.

Then—quite suddenly—she bounced, as if she'd had a single violent hiccup.

It was her final movement. Peter later theorized that this bounce had been caused by the soul's departure from her body. Everett, however, ruthlessly maintained that it was only the soul *attempting* to leave her body, and that since she'd never believed in it the poor thing was so weak and malnourished that rather than fly away it could only "hop, then croak—like one of those prince-cum-frogs in that backasswards fairy tale she was always trying to scare the twins with."

Either way, when our grandmother, or the top half of her body, came down from the bounce, the forehead missed the bowl, hit the edge of the table, slid on past the table when the neck bent back, and flopped neatly down between her knees; meanwhile her arms slid out of her lap, her hands swished down her sides, and her free-falling knuckles hit the hardwood floor with a rattlingly eerie clunk which both girls recognized at once as the sound of utter finality.

From opposite ends of the table, they leaned down and peered at her. She didn't move. She didn't make a peep. Nor did she breathe. "Are you all right, Gran?" asked Beatrice.

"She might be all right," Freddy said. "But she sure is dead."

"She just fainted," Bet said doubtfully. "Huh, Gran."

"She never faints. Anyhow, it's not stuffy."

Bet began thinking this over. Meanwhile Freddy slid out of her chair, seated herself, cross-legged, on the floor beneath the table, and took advantage of this unique opportunity to study her first nonliving human without motherly or brotherly interference. "Don't leave me up here!" Bet cried. And grabbing her little black lab notebook, she too moved down to the floor.

"It *does* look like fainting," Freddy admitted, studying Grandawma's head-between-knees posture. "I mean, that's just how Peter used to sit so he wouldn't faint in church, back before he started *not* sitting that way, so he *would* faint, so he'd get to leave."

Bet nodded.

"Maybe dying *feels* like fainting," Freddy theorized.

"I hope so," Bet murmured. But she was not up to the usual scientific banter.

"Didn't look like it hurt much."

"No," Bet said—and for a moment it looked as though she might manage to jot some of these observations down. But then she half gasped, hugged her notebook to her chest, turned to Freddy, and said, "They turn *cold* . . . don't they?"

Winifred nodded.

"How long do you suppose it takes?"

Freddy thought about it. "Maybe about as long," she said finally, "as for a hot bowl of oatmeal to cool down."

It was the wrong metaphor: Bet put on an extremely grave expression, turned to her sister, and said, "You mean as long as it takes to cool down on the table? Or on your head?" Then she burst into hysterics.

"Don't!" Freddy said.

Which made Bet laugh harder.

"It's not funny."

But Beatrice was beside herself. "Did you see the mush go flying?" she howled. "Did you see the bowl on her *bun?* Ha ha ha! Dove right in and tried for that last bite! Hahahahahaha! You can get down now, Gran, that's a good girl! *Nothing was better for thee than he!"*

Freddy never smiled or said a word, but Bet was still trying, through a hemorrhoidal kind of squeezing, to glean a little more escapist hilarity out of the idea—when they both suddenly heard the dripping, turned, and saw the urine, raining down through the wicker chair seat, pooling on the floor beneath. Bet let out a last staccato bark. Then, in a small, very surprised voice, she said, "Gran? Are *you* doing that?"

The body didn't move. The urine kept dripping. Bet began to quiver.

"I think," Freddy whispered, "I think they—bodies, I mean—they just do that."

Bet turned away, and for a long time they were silent. Then, in the same surprised, minuscule voice, Bet said, "I *loved* her, Freddy. I loved her a lot." And though she never sniffled, never sobbed, just held her head rigid and sat there shivering, tears began streaming down her cheeks.

For a long time Freddy couldn't speak. She just watched the spilled milk swirl along the borders of the other pool. Finally, though, she said, "I loved her too, Bet. And . . . and if we really loved her, I . . . we . . . I think we've got to love her still."

Bet drew her knees up and clenched them hard to try and slow the shivering. "What do you mean?" she asked.

"I mean"—Freddy shook her head—"I mean she wouldn't want this. I mean we, I . . . I think I've got to clean her up before we let an ambulance or anybody find her."

Hearing this, Bet just hid her face between her knees and curled up like a foetus. But she heard Freddy sigh after a bit, then crawl out from under the table, cross the kitchen, and unbutton the never-before-used pink terry-cloth hand towels from the oven handle; heard her fetch sponges and soap from beneath or beside the sink, fill a saucepan with water, return to the table; heard her wipe the surface clean, draw a breath that sounded as trembly as her own, move to the floor, hesitate, then slowly continue cleaning.

When Freddy returned to the sink Bet finally peeked, saw the floor was spotless, saw a pile of clean rags lying beneath the wicker. She heard Freddy dump and rinse the saucepan, run fresh water, wring her towels and sponges, and they were soothing, these sounds: it could have been 'Dawma or Mama just cleaning as usual. But when Freddy recrossed the kitchen, took a stand by the chair, and Bet realized what must come next, she hid her face and curled up even more tightly than before. Then all but the one sound stopped: ∿∿∿∿∿∿∿∿∿∿∿∿∿∿∿∿∿∿∿∿∿∿∿∿∿∿∿∿∿∿

This stasis went on so long and Bet had curled so tightly and deeply down into herself that when she finally heard a loud sniff she believed, for an instant, that it had come from Grandawma, and that she was about to get scolded for being under the table. But when the sniff was followed by a sob, then by the broken breathing that accompanies silent weeping, Bet knew it was her sister, knew that her strength had finally come to an end, and knew that no one was going to help them, that no one was coming to soothe them, that the situation was not going to change unless she herself somehow managed to change it.

She tried the easy route first: scrinching up into an even tighter ball, she whimpered, "Dear Jesus. *Help!*"

The result was instantaneous: Freddy's sobs became uncontrollable, half the water in her saucepan spilled onto the floor, and she gasped, "*Bet!*"

"Phooey!" Bet said with a sudden strength born, I guess, of exasperation with her fear and helplessness. But even the crudest of prayers has a way of making things difficult to interpret. Take this odd (given the context) utterance, "Phooey!" It appears that Bet either said it to Christ because she felt He wasn't helping her, or to no one because she was frustrated. But who's to say her prayer hadn't invoked Him so fast that both the exasperation and the phooey came from the Christ in Bet as He moved the frightened child in her gently aside, in order to help?

I don't know. I suspect only fools understand prayer. All I know is that after uttering hers, Bet said "Phooey!" then unfolded herself, crawled almost angrily out from under the table, stood up across the chair from her undone twin, tried to picture Peter's inner mountains and lakes, failed utterly, tried to smile at Freddy, failed utterly, but finally reached, nevertheless, for the towel in the saucepan. All I know is that, after wringing it out with weak, trembling hands, she began, ever so gently, to cleanse the bowed head, the withered neck, the steel-gray hair. All I know is that this somehow enabled Freddy to start helping too, and that when the ambulance and Mama arrived a half hour or so later, our grandmother was lying on the floor neatly wrapped in a blanket, dignified, dry and spotless.

CHAPTER THREE

Kinds
of Salvation

"Quit yo' foolishness," she said, *"before I knock the living Jesus out of you."*
  —Flannery O'Connor

For we are saved by hope.
  —St. Paul

1. Salvation of Teachers, via Graduation

One thing you inherit when you've got three older brothers are a lot of threadbare, holey-elbowed, pill-collared, hand-me-down shirts. Another thing you inherit are teachers. All my teachers at McLoughlin High had taught at least one of my brothers; some had taught all three; most of the latter, by the time I got to them, were in about the same sort of shape as the shirts.

When it came to sheer aptitude, Everett was an excellent student, and in a better world than this one might have earned straight A's. This being the world it is, though, Everett kept spotting all these enormous improvements that people ought to be making on it—and it is a rare high school teacher who enjoys seeing their world being enormously improved upon by youths.

There are natural leaders and unnatural leaders; most public school teachers fall with a thankless thud into the latter category. Everett, on another hand entirely, was a natural *ring*leader. Add to that his short temper, tall IQ, fearlessness, good looks, great gifts as a mimic, and addiction to regaling all comers with kamikaze comedy routines, and what you get is a kid with power. Everett drew a certain kind of giddy teen following the way dog-doo draws flies. And when a mere kid is endowed with both power and followers, the very least of the problems likely to result is a checkered academic career.

Everett's, for example, had only two B's in it. All the way through high school he nailed down either A's (for Aptitude) or C's and D's (for Contentiousness and Dissidence). Then there were his suspensions: as a freshman he earned his first for getting into three fistfights in two weeks (all three times with towering seniors, who merely wanted to initiate him with the traditional red lipstick, but to their amazement kept finding their own lips or noses dripping red instead); as a sophomore he nabbed a second for crawling up under a stage at a football game and standing a chocolate milk shake on the throne of the Homecoming Queen an instant before she sat back down; as a junior he managed two, the first for talking three-quarters of his class into walking out on a right-wing American History teacher's lecture in praise of George Armstrong Custer, the second for borrowing a friend's compound bow and four genuine obsidian-tipped arrows (courtesy of the collection of Marion Becker Chance) and doing a Little Bighorn number on the same teacher's tires after he awarded Everett's "Crazy Horse Was a Greater American than Lincoln" essay an F.

"You're doing just great, son!" Papa told Everett somewhere along in there. "Just pick the college of your choice—and kiss it goodbye! I hope you like working at Crown Z better than Roy and me do."

He got the message: as a senior he moved to the top of the honor role despite his Valley Forge wardrobe by simply avoiding those teachers whose politics he couldn't stand. He then put his natural ringleadership, fiery eyes and eloquence together to achieve one of those bizarre triple coups conceivable only in public high schools when he was: (1) elected president of the student body, (2) appointed editor-in-chief of the school paper, and (3) voted "Prettiest Eyes" in the Senior Class Hall of Fame.

His two-fisted tenure as president and editor-in-chief was a yearlong nightmare for the McLoughlin High faculty, but for the college-bound students it may have proven a useful primer for the last three years—the blitzkrieg years—of the Sixties. Though the great causes of Camas's Class of '66 were usually what Everett called "measurement issues" (such as what length of hair, length of skirt or length of kiss should be allowed on school property), he imported terms like "petition," "student rights," "boycott," "free speech" and "solidarity" all the way up from exotic Berkeley, California, and managed to forge a place for them in a student lexicon hitherto dominated by such American Gothic terms as "rumble," "rack," "boss," "cheater," "skeezer," "PG" and "knockers." His presidency and editorship also helped bring him an unlooked-for economic and karmic windfall when, coupled with his prodigious SAT scores and a couple of passionate letters by teachers impressed with his turnaround, they offset his mangled GPA and suspensions just enough to win him a modest but feasible work/study scholarship to the University of Washington.

"One down!" Papa shouted the day the whole family saw Everett off at the Vancouver Greyhound station.

"Five to go," Mama groaned.

Peter posed an entirely different sort of problem for the McLoughlin High faculty. Known to some of his friends as "Stanley Einstein" (a combination of Musial the Hitter and Albert the Thinker, though something along the lines of "Ramakrishna Clemente" might have been more to his liking), Pete was, at first glance, the Perfect Scholar. He never missed an assignment, aced every test, never rioted, seldom made wisecracks, raised his hand before speaking, and so on. But in his scholarly way he could be a source of teacherly stress surpassing even the Natural Ringleader. The problem, in his case, was sheer voracity of intellect. The public school teacher's modest but worthy goal has always been to drum a modest but measurable quantity of knowledge into the largest possible number of student heads, and to twice a month receive a modest but measurable paycheck for doing so. But my immodestly bright number two brother had no interest in any such process. Peter didn't want to change the world: he wanted to fully comprehend it. He wanted to know everything there was to know about everything, and in this quest an instructor's head was just a grapefruit to be sliced in half and squeezed remorselessly dry. Since very few students could even begin to understand him, there was no danger of Peter attracting anarchistic followers. For days, even weeks, he'd just sit there in his studious mode, sponging up the disheveled lectures while knocking off homework for two or three other classes, or reading a novel or philosophical tome in German or French. But should his curiosity be fully piqued by something a teacher said, should some scientific quandary or epistemological conundrum galvanize his normally dispersed powers of thought, Peter's cheeks would flush, his pupils dilate, his voice rise, and the questions would leap from his mouth like hounds from the back of a pickup, crashing through the fences of the topic at hand, smashing aside the course description, dragging everyone off on a panting, plunging intellectual coon hunt that almost invariably ended with the poor instructor treed, or at bay. Perhaps one pedant in ten respected him for this. Perhaps one in twenty could gracefully deal with it. The rest dreaded or loathed him for it.

With the Iconoclast Chance and Genius Chance out of the way but four Unknown-Quantity Chances yet to be endured, some teachers had fled to other school districts, others had shed hair or teeth or broken out in eczema, and still others had fortified themselves with their bottle of choice, be it booze or Maalox, when into their rooms galumphed the Inculpable Chance—the blue-eyed, incessantly beaming, intrepidly affectionate Irwin. Toting a First Day Bouquet for his lady instructors, or a four-bit cigar for the gents, he would sometimes launch his year with a disclaimer than ran something like "Don't worry, Teach. I'm nothin' like my big brothers. I listen hard, be nice, try my best, and end up with C's anyways . . ." But I doubt that disclaimers were needed: teachers are just people, and most people fall in love with Irwin at first sight, and stay fallen. For this very reason, though, Winnie too tore a chunk from his teachers. In his case it happened all at once, in early June, on the day he packed his dimpled cheeks, Grecian musculature, guileless baby-blues and puppy's heart up with his books and pencils, gave ol' Teach a last hug, promised he'd be back to visit, and strolled off down the hall forever, blissfully unaware of the piece of their hearts dragging along the linoleum behind him.

2. Salvation of Grammarians, via Basalt

A single, formidable exception to the hand-me-down-shirt syndrome was our grim, grammar-dispensing ninth-grade English instructor, Delmar Hergert. Everett's pet theory was that the man was simply half inorganic —the offspring, possibly, of some horny hiker who'd had a wet dream while napping atop Beacon Rock. Be that as it mayn't, Del Hergert looked like a walking talking gray-haired chunk of Columbia River basalt when Everett sauntered into his class in September 1961, and he hadn't weathered a whit when Bet and Freddy fled the same class in June of '72.

Not only did Del Hergert refuse to age, he refused to laugh, frown or in any way color his face with emotion, refused to modify his words with humor, anger, affection, irony or even volume, in fact refused to do anything at all except pass or fail, with basaltic unbias, those students who had succeeded or failed to master the basic laws of English grammar by the year's end, and to have demonstrated that mastery in a lengthy test and even lengthier "original essay." All my siblings and I had to concoct monstrous essays for Hergert. Irwin's heroic "History of My Dad from His Birth Up to Kincaids's" was only the longest. Mine, the following year, garnered the distinction of being the most brownnosingly boring: my strategy had been to tailor my topic to the man it was intended for, so I'd nearly died of ennui writing about—you guessed it—Columbia River basalt formations. Peter's essay (on the Great Religions of the East), Bet's (on the Space Program) and Freddy's (on the Oregon Trail) all made me feel better by being only slightly less anemic than my own. Only Everett had been sufficiently uncowed by Hergert's basaltic visage and personality to take full advantage of the word "original" in the assignment description, and that's why he penned the only essay besides Irwin's that is still tolerable to read.

It was called "Junk Genius," and though it was written two years before Irwin's "History of My Dad," it picked Papa's baseball biography up where Irwin had more or less left it—with Papa dramatically saved by the mysterious "Fort Oopawanapoonawahinipopo" Brigadier General from "Goon Squad" and "Mongol trenches," only to end up broke, bum-winged, and sold by the White Shlocks to that most inept and aptly dubbed of ballclubs, the Washington Senators, who in turn took one peek at Papa and zipped him off—with his three sons, wife and the embryonic edition of me—to a Baseball Erewhon called Kincaid, Oklahoma, and to a Double A team called, believe it or not, the Cornshuckers.

"Junk Genius" earned Everett a number of peculiar honors. The first was a red-inked U (meaning Unacceptable) from Mr. Hergert, due to "extensive use of profanity." The second, third and fourth honors—all compliments of a now defunct periodical called *Sporting Digest*—were a free year's subscription, a wall plaque, and (oh joy!) a baseball bat *exactly* like the one Everett's antihero, Roger Maris, used to club his sixty-first home run! Having no idea that they were gainsaying a redoubtable old grammarian, *Sporting Digest* selected "Junk Genius" as second runner-up in their "1962 Sports Story Open," thereby swelling Everett's already sizable head to the bursting point. Fortunately for those of us who lived with him, they immediately shrank it back down again by publishing a version so drastically condensed and dehydrated (good old-fashioned "#$%&*!"'s where the "extensive profanity" should have been, for example) that reading it was rather like trying to consume instant coffee without first adding water. But the last and most peculiar honor the paper received came in the form of a letter of bombast and protestation addressed "to the McLoughlin High School Tinkling Brass" by one G. Q. Durham—the Junk Genius of the title.

Faithfully preserved in Mama's attic archives, Durham's letter is too confounding to quote in full. But his closing remarks should serve to demonstrate the inimitable G.Q. style:

. . . So if the straight poop is still worth a good goddam in this horse-crap Hypocrite's Hey-Day & Age, young Everett there should have an A plus coming for his picture-perfect protrayals [sic] of my private & unique methods of instructing the science of junk pitching, commanding a ballclub & employing the King's & various lesser types of English. So please convey to the scholarly Mr. Yogurt [sic] that if anybody's got an F coming it's The Bull, not the boy, & he can mail it here any time he likes & be overjoyed to know that my mean ol' mom'll whale the living tar out of me. But please convey to him also that if he insists on bullyragging helpless youngsters by shelling out Fs to the wrong person, Bull Durham looks forward to dealing in kind with Mr. Yogurt personally the next time my duties carries him out that way. This is no threat. Just a sweet & mild promise. Hugh Chance's boy has done both yours & my organizations proud & ought to be commendated [sic] in kind.

Yours in baseball,
G. Q. "Bull" Durham,
Ex-Head-Scout Washington Senators,
Ex-Pitcher (5 teams American & National),
Ex-Manager Kincaid Cornshuckers,
Current Free-lance Scout & Junk Authority Extrordinnair [sic]

The Bull's real name was Gale Q. Durham. What the Q. stood for was anybody's guess, but what the Bull stood for was definitely not the man's size, strength or brand of tobacco, but his manner of "employing the King's & various lesser types of English." His ominous letter on Everett's behalf was typical: at the time he penned it, the mighty Bull was a bald-headed, tub-gutted, hypoglycemic stroke victim who stood all of 5'9" (though antique baseball cards listed him at 6'1"), weighed a doughy 199, grew winded when forced to rise from a chair or box seat, and needed bifocals if not binoculars to read the labels on his beer bottles, let alone to size up any sort of baseball prospect. The Bull sported one kidney, two small but patriotic eyes (red, white and blue), anywhere from two to five chins depending on whether he was watching grounders or pop-ups, and a pair of indelible mouth-corner tobacco stains that made him look like a puppet with its jaws hung on hinges. A baseball uniform—particularly a Washington Senators uniform—didn't add one iota of grandeur to the overall picture. In other words, what made the Bull the Bull was not what he was, but what he was full of.

The big leagues do have an aura of power, though. And a tobacco-stained threat-letter scrawled on official (if obsolete) Senators stationery by a fellow named Bull could strike more than a little fear in the average pedagogue's heart. For a grammar-dispensing chunk of Columbia River basalt, however, there was only one way to deal with such mail: Delmar Hergert calmly corrected its grammar and spelling, gave it a bright red F, mailed a copy straight back to Bull, and handed the original—with red-inked corrections—over to Everett, accompanied by a handwritten note that read:

While my stand on profanity remains unaltered, this drivel has inadvertently demonstrated your exceptional memory of and ear for this pitiable bombast's vernacular. That you apparently cherish both the memories and the dialect is a subjective judgment the wisdom of which I shall not here question. In recognition of your gift, however, I offer this compromise: recopy the entire essay in <u>legible</u> longhand, substituting blanks (i.e.____) for obscenities, and I will change your grade from U to B+, thereby enabling us to be permanently rid of one another.
"Yours in baseball,"
D. M. Hergert

Everett did exactly what the basalt chunk suggested, but couldn't resist adding a note of his own:

While my stand on verisimilitude, and to that end profanity, remains as unaltered as yours, I've learned something valuable through all this: G. Q. Durham is a great pitching coach and bull____er, but D. M. Hergert is an equally great grammar teacher.

Yours in English,

Everett M. Chance

3. Salvation of Nothing, via Espionage

While I became a pre-Feminist, Everett a pre-Hippie, Peter a pre-Bhikku, Bet and Freddy Famous Scientists, Grandawma a surprisingly fond memory and Papa one hell of a skilled backyard-mattress basher, Mama had also undergone a major change: she'd become a Fanatic.

Not a raving Fanatic. At least not audibly raving. That might have been healthier, actually, because Mama's raving went on almost solely in her head, where there was no way to hear it, hence no means of challenging it, hence no means of preventing her from believing every bit of it. Fully believing herself to be at war with Satan, fully believing Irwin's, Bet's and Freddy's salvations to be at stake, her love for the rest of us— even her love for Papa—simply sank out of sight. The submerging of this love immediately began to kill a very large part of her. But it also freed the fanatic to begin conducting a covert holy war against us.

Her first act of war was to try to balance the odds by secretly enlisting the mightiest ally she could think of: Elder Babcock. Her second act of war, at the urging of this ally, was to completely disgrace herself: at Babcock's suggestion Mama became a kind of religious McCarthyite, Everett, Peter and I became the "witches," and she became our hunter. That we happened to be her offspring didn't matter (Matthew 10:36). That she was attempting to chop her family in half like a big chunk of stove wood also didn't matter (Matthew 10:35, 37 & 38). That she set out to do this "chopping" by surreptitiously plundering our rooms, notebooks, closets, wastebaskets, and any other place she thought might contain evidence of our moral or religious corruption eventually did matter to some of us (Exodus 20:15). But witch-hunters don't think about niggling little rules like the Ten Commandments. Witch-hunters think they're right, they think you're wrong, and they think that as long as they can prove it, how they prove it doesn't matter.

The exact purpose of Mama's pilfered evidence, as far as we were ever able to understand, was to show it to Irwin and the twins at a sort of

Inquisition/Surprise Party to be organized and supervised by (who else?) the Elder. The purpose of this gathering, in turn, was to convince our orthodox siblings to give us rebels the same *Agree with me or I'll damn you forever!* ultimatum that Babcock and Mama had already given us. Like many a Christian before them, Mama and the Elder justified their machinations with Christ's famous sentence: "I came not to send peace, but a sword." And like many a Christian before them, they completely forgot that the only sword-shaped weapon Jesus ever actually used was the one He died on.

Still it was an interesting plan. At least it was bold, dramatic and, from Bet's and Freddy's perspectives, rather flattering: not every eight-year-old girl on the block got invited to sit in judgment over older brothers charged with heresy, Satanism and the like. Of course the plan was also ridiculous, and doomed to bring nothing but pain, confusion and embarrassment to everyone concerned. But this is the Fanatic's great disputative advantage over other people: "What's a little confusion or pain," they ask, "compared to eternal salvation?" And of course this question can't be argued: who wouldn't gladly be robbed of all they own today if they were certain that the thief would "come again" and hand them a billion-dollar compensation payment tomorrow? But this question doesn't address the real problem. In a head-on collision with Fanatics, the real problem is always the same: how can we possibly behave decently toward people so arrogantly ignorant that they believe, first, that they possess Christ's power to bestow salvation, second, that forcing us to memorize and regurgitate a few of their favorite Bible phrases and attend their church *is* that salvation, and third, that any discomfort, frustration, anger or disagreement we express in the face of their moronic barrages is due not to *their* astounding effrontery but to *our* sinfulness?

The Austrian writer Robert Musil summed up the Fanatic's great rhetorical advantage in just ten words: "There is no truth which stupidity can't make use of."

Another Austrian, novelist Heimito von Doderer, put it this way:

"Even the most impossible persons who do the most unforgivable things possess substantial reality; from their points of view they are always right—for let them only doubt that and they are no longer such impossible persons. And we must pay close heed to those who play such ungrateful roles, for these roles are indispensable. It is no small thing to be a monster or a spiteful idiot, and in the first case to think oneself beautiful, in the second a highly intelligent person. Such characters must be represented. Someone has to do it."

. . . .

I've often wondered what Mama and Babcock could possibly have found to say to each other the first time they huddled over a heap of her espionage findings. What did they make, for example, of a confiscated poem I wrote called "Why Apple Pie"? The inspiration for this ditty was that Everett had been making remarks about the corresponding sizes of my body and appetite, and Irwin had been finding these remarks so amusing that he'd committed some to memory and taken to trotting them out at night when I was trying to get to sleep. For this reason, when I was given a parody-writing assignment in Honors English, I decided to prove to the two svelte louts that my sense of humor was as big as the rest of me—even when the rest of me was the topic. It went like this:

WHY APPLE PIE
by Lewis Carroll

Sometimes when people ask me why
    I am so fond of apple pie
I make myself stand up and grin
    (depending on the mood I'm in).

I stand and grin from ear to ear
    then do a thing that's rather queer:
I stand there grinning like a ghoul,
    then down my chin I drip some drool!

I DRIP SOME DROOL!
    I START TO DANCE!
I STICK MY FINGERS
    IN MY PANTS!

But seldom are my friends so nice
As to ask why I like pie twice.

Among its intended audience the reactions were predictable: Everett (who loved even bad parody and undoubtedly envied my poem) yawned to hide his smile and said it didn't sound like Carroll at all. Peter (who hated parody and, I'm sure, disliked the poem) smiled politely and said, "Quite the little parody there, Kade." And Irwin (who loved every silly thing his brothers ever did) spoke not a word: he just made the whole effort utterly worthwhile by falling off his bed laughing, and later insisted on tacking it to his wall—

where Mama found it, recognized my handwriting, and pounced like a crow on a road kill.

So what did J. Edgar Babcock and Agent Double O Mama make of it? My guess is, the very worst they possibly could. With her straight and narrow knowledge of literature, I wouldn't be surprised but what Mama paid my parody the supreme compliment by assuming that I had, out of sheer perversity, simply copied down some obscene drivel by an idiot named Carroll in order to pollute poor Irwin's Jesus-loving mind. The Elder, however, expert as he was in the ways of Satan, had apparently formed a more colorful opinion: "Drool." *Hmmm.* "Fingers in pants." *Hmmmmmm* . . . I have no way of proving that he actually told Mama to start checking our rooms for evidence of pornography use, group masturbation parties or Babcock-knows-what other defilements. But I did come home from school an hour early one day to find Mama—months after she'd quit cleaning or even visiting our rooms—buried to the waist in under Everett's mattress. When she finally backed out (empty-handed) and saw me standing in the doorway, she turned crimson as the **OLY** sign next to her head and began furiously stripping the bed, muttering, *"Filthy!* Just *filthy!"*

She was right: what she and Babcock were up to *was* filthy. And in the end, it bore filthy results.

4. Salvation of a Shoulder, via "Gettin' the Picture"

When he worked for the Senators in the Forties and Fifties, G. Q. Durham had a corner on a market which nobody else in professional baseball seemed interested in at the time. The Bull's field of operation was the athletic wreck, the broken-down talent, the potential salvage operation. Here's how Durham himself put it in a little "automobiographical [sic] confidence" he shared, late in life, with our family:

. . . If there is one thing besides money on God's green earth this U.S. of A. has got more than anybody else of it is every type of used junk on earth. Including junk ballplayers. Yet the hirers and firers of today ain't interested. Among the baseball thinking of today the tired old password is New! New! New!, so off they trot out both ends of the word through every damned dictatorship in every South and Central and Mexican America on earth trying to locate that short brown foxy Newness, totally ignoring the faithful black and white dogs right under

their lamebrained noses, right here at home on the range. That was
why I built me a little operation that tapped into what we had the
most of. I'm talking used cars and appliances here. I'm talking thrown
rods and fried circuits, singles punchers who lost the punch, flame-
throwers who lost the fire, sluggers who lost the meanness, wife or
balls. I was a regular Statue of Liberty down there in Oklahoma. Give
me your pooped and your poor was my motto, and I'd give 'em a sniff
in return. Because if there was baseball in the blood, I'd smell it at a
glance. I'd whiff it right through the street clothes, right through the
injuries, right through the drink and divorces and gambling debts and
every other type of crap. It's been my one lifelong talent, this nose in
the middle of this face here. And on the day I met Hugh Chance, let
me tell you, he <u>reeked</u>. Lame arm, diaper-stench, bad attitude and all,
the man reeked so bad of baseball I didn't see how he could walk
down a street on two legs. Seemed to me he ought to <u>roll</u> . . .

On the day Papa showed up lame-armed, bad-attituded and reeking of
kid piss and baseball on Durham's porch in Kincaid, Oklahoma (pop.
1010), in 1951, the Bull had started slinging around his nicknamesake the
instant he opened the door. "Hugh Chance!" he burst out.

Papa nodded grimly, unable to hide the despair he felt at first sight of
this pig-eyed, sweat-covered, beery-looking old Okie.

"Any kin to Tinkers to Evers to Frank Chance the first baseman?"

"No, sir."

"How 'bout to Fat?"

"No," Papa sighed.

"How 'bout to Last, then? Or our ol' friend No?"

"Maybe Last," Papa said. "But not No. Not yet."

"You look a little down, Chance. What's the trouble?"

"Double A *is* down," Papa answered. "I'm just looking how I am."

G.Q. shook his head. "Like an outfielder, Chance. That's how you're
lookin'. It's clear as beer."

"What's an outfielder supposed to look like?"

"A natural athlete," Durham answered.

"Then what's a pitcher look like?"

G.Q. fluffed up his paunch like a big feather pillow. "Me," he snorted.
"Too often anyhow. It's the evil 'at comes o' the two-day workweek."

With that he turned inside his big, shambling farmhouse, headed
down the hall, and, when they reached the livingroom, raised a red dust
cloud as he flopped down in an overstuffed chair. Housekeeping wasn't

his strong suit. Furniture repair wasn't either: Papa tried a wire-braced rocker close by the chair, but as the thing took his weight it gave off such a tremendous report that he flung himself out to one side. As he gathered himself up off the floor, though, he noticed the Bull smiling at him so serenely that he got the feeling Durham might seat all his prospects in the same chair on purpose, as some kind of crackpot reflex test. He tried the couch next, because it was biggest. It held. But so did the fat man's interest in outfielders:

"Scoutin' report says you hit .290 in Single A, .278 in Three A, with power in both."

Papa nodded guardedly.

"So you hit like an outfielder too."

"I've heard about you, Mr. Durham," Papa sighed. "I mean about you being quite the salvage artist and all. But I'm a pitcher. It's my calling. I'm going to heal up, then pitch again. Okay?"

"You got one choice, son," the Bull said amicably. "You either bat a whole lot worse, or you don't mind folks sayin' you bat like an outfielder."

"One choice is no choice," Papa said. "I learned that much in the Army."

G.Q. shook his head. "How you look at a thing, Chance, how you feel about a thing, there's *always* choice in that."

Papa eyed his new manager more carefully. No doubt about it, the man looked like a pig. But pigs, he remembered, could be very intelligent animals.

"That shoulder hurt your hitting any?" Durham asked.

"No," Papa admitted. "It only hurts when I throw. Curves are worst, but speed's bad too."

"Ever play first base?"

"Never."

"Can you catch the goddamn ball?"

"Yes."

"Then hot damn!" the Bull cried, bursting up out of his chair and wheeling off toward one of his two beer-crammed refrigerators. "That seals it! This is great! This is good! Let's celebrate!"

"Celebrate what?" Papa asked.

"My new first sacker, Hubert."

"I told you, Mr. Durham," Papa said coolly. "I'm a pitcher."

G.Q. froze in front of his Number Two refrigerator, then turned and trudged, slow and beerless, all the way back to Papa's couch. Once there he sat down right beside him (causing Papa to blush), looked at him sadly, and then, with surprising quickness, lightly punched his left shoulder. Papa was on his feet, fists cocked, before he knew what he was doing. The only thing that kept him from decking his new manager was that Durham didn't stand up. "Case dismissed," was all he said. "Pitcher's got an arm in that spot, son, not a gob o' raw nerve ends."

Half miserable, half furious, Papa began to pace. G.Q. stood, and headed back toward the kitchen. "I'm not disputin' your vocation, son," he said. "I'm just practicin' mine. I manage ballplayers. You play ball. An' I'm sayin' that, if you play for me, all of you but your left arm is the new first sacker for the Kincaid Cornshuckers. I'm sayin' that's all the baseball gods wrote for you this year. I'm sayin' if you don't like it, go play for one of them teams hirin' players who can't even goddamn *throw*."

Fully awake now to the absurdity of his position, Papa paced faster, but kept his mouth shut. "As for healin', Chance," Durham added, "and as for the future, let the left arm and pitcher in you think on this: you make *one* hard throw, you get excited an' fire that ball just *once*, all season, an' I'll ship you somewhere so bush you'll need a goddamned machete just to find the mound. You got that?"

"No I don't got that!" Papa fired back. "What if a runner's going? What if I *have* to make a throw?"

"Whip off your glove an' fling 'er right-handed!" Durham roared.

"I can't *throw* right-handed!" Papa roared back.

"I like *ballplayers*, Chance, not worriers! An' I like you, so you must be a ballplayer, so stop the goddang worryin', will ya?"

Papa didn't stop worrying, but he did pause to admire Durham's logic.

"Shit, son!" snorted the Bull. "It's Two A ball down here. *Throwin'* don't matter."

"It don't? I mean, it doesn't?"

"Hell *no* it don't! It's pure Yahooism in these leagues. Buncha numbnuts is what we basically got here, standin' around waitin' for talent to rain down like pigeon crap. Buncha anti-intellectuals pissin' their lives away, waitin' for God to up an' turn 'em into Mickey Mantle."

"Well, uh, I'm not worrying now, sir" (Papa tried to phrase it politely this time), "but what if, say, for instance, some runner was going to score from third, and I was holding the ball over at first?"

"*Keeerist*, son! What do *you* think? Just flip 'er to the nearest guy and let *him* fling it!" And with that Durham doddered off once more to his refrigerators, yammering, "My first sacker! Hot *damn*! This is good! This is fine! We gonna have an outfield, gonna have an infield, gonna play some offense, gonna play some defense. Hot *damn*, Hubert! We gonna have us a year!" Meanwhile Papa thought about it: he imagined himself actually flipping the ball to his nearest teammate while enemy runners were streaking round the bases—and when he heard a soft snort, turned, and noticed Durham's beady-bright pig eyes peering in over the icebox door, he realized that what he'd been imagining had been making him grin. "Now you're gettin' the picture!" G.Q. cackled.

Papa gave up completely, and started to laugh.

So in the summer of '51—the summer I was born, though by then the birth of a baby boy was something my parents scarcely noticed, let alone mentioned to friends—Papa spent an anomaly season as a power-hitting but virtually nonthrowing first baseman (and G.Q. was right: no one took advantage of it), thereby rehabilitating not only his shoulder but his blithe love for the game. Meanwhile he and Mama found a surprisingly decent, dirt-cheap two-story frame farmhouse, planted the first garden they'd ever stayed put long enough to harvest, and Mama made some friends and located some child-care that enabled her to deal with four sub-school-age sons with a semblance of sanity, if not quite grace. So, come late September, even before G.Q. suggested it, they decided to winter over in Kincaid rather than return home to Grandawma's cramped place in Pullman. Mama, in addition to tending the four of us, managed to harvest her garden and put up preserves, canned fruit and vegetables for the first time since marrying. And Papa took a full-time graveyard-shift job as night watchman at a Shell oil refinery, skipped sleep every Sabbath to babysit us boys while Mama went to church, then rushed off, still sleepless, to a square- and swing-dancers' honky-tonk, where he held down an incredibly self-defeating Saturday night job as a combination bartender/janitor who the first half of the night poured booze down his patrons till they barfed, and the second half had to clean it up. Yet he and Mama both insist (from the safety of retrospection, anyway) that they've never loved a house or town or two-year chunk of family or base-ball life more. The irony—as so often seems to happen—is that their unwilling departure was forced by Papa's attainment of the very goal that had brought them to Oklahoma in the first place: his complete rejuvenation as a pitcher.

Three afternoons a week, all winter long, he and G. Q. Durham played an hour or so of indoor catch inside the local Moose Lodge. And one night in early winter, during one of these catch games, G.Q. announced, point-blank, that the straight fastball pitcher led "the sorriest damned baseball existence alive." Papa had responded by firing in a fast one, and saying (as Durham cursed and shook his stinging hand), "I'd've thought it was the *catcher* of the straight fastball pitcher."

"Catcher's got the second sorriest," G.Q. winced. "But the pitcher's got it worse. Predictability's the killer. Game after game o' standing out there, a complete surprise to nobody, nine o' them versus the one o' him, playin' power versus power till his arm falls out its hole. I say that's no way to live, Hubert. I say that's—"

"Walter Johnson seemed to like it all right," Papa interrupted.

"*I'll* come up with the big league examples round here!" Durham roared. "You know damn well that for every Johnson there's ten thousand Randy Crudenskis."

"Who's Randy Crudenski?" Papa asked.

"*Now* you're gettin' the picture," G.Q. answered. "An' Crudenski was faster than you and Johnson both."

Papa smiled, and tossed an apologetically slow curve.

"What slays me in your case, Hubert, is the waste. A fastballer with brains like you an' junk like me could be deadly for decades. But some-thin' in even the smart fastballer hates his own brains. Somethin' in him just *pines* for that four- or five-year career endin' with the ripped-out shoulder or shredded elbow."

"I don't long for that, Gale," Papa said.

"Then shall we do somethin' about it?"

"How do we start?"

"Maybe with a big league example besides Johnson, huh? Were you aware before we met, for instance, that I myself was once a highly suc-cessful hurler?"

Honest to a fault, Papa shook his head no.

"Well now, I take that as a compliment," Durham lied. "Everybody knows G.Q. the Junkman, but almost nobody remembers Gale Durham the pitcher. And do you know why?"

Papa didn't.

"Because the same spirit that infused my pitches infused a total lack of memory of those pitches. What's that grin? You think I'm joking? Hey! Listen here. You ever hear of two fellas name of Foxx an' DiMaggio?"

"You mean Trot and Dom?" Papa teased. But when the Bull was lectur-ing he was oblivious even to his own wit, let alone someone else's.

"I mean Joltin' Joe an' Jimmy," he said reverently. "The two one-man demolition squads o' their day. Because I faced 'em fifty times each, easy, an' they roughed me up some, sure. But listen. The only one of 'em ever homered off me was Foxx, an' he hit a grand total o' *one!*"

Durham left such a gravid pause here that Papa finally said "You're kidding!" just to be polite.

"Nine thousand an' some-odd home runs between 'em, those two. But as God is my witness, they never dinged Gale Durham but the once. An' do you know why?"

Again, Papa didn't.

"Because a DiMaggio or Foxx don't sit around waitin' for your hung curve. He steps right up an' makes gopherballs outta the best heat an' hooks on this planet. So your good curve an' fast one is exactly what you never throw 'em. You don't get no DiMaggio an' Foxx excited. You don't challenge the class genius to a spellin' bee. You just stand out there lookin' as lost an' ignorant an' hopeless as possible. And then you lull an' disgust 'em with mediocrity an' garbage. You throw 'em gooseshit, see? An' dead slugs. An' waffleballs. You sling 'em right on in where they'll get hit too. You *want* 'em hit, see? 'Cause a man can hit gooseshit an' dead slugs till his bat wears out, but he's never gonna hit 'em very far now, is he?"

Papa guessed not.

"In eleven seasons," Durham gloated, "I won 89 ballgames for three American an' two National League teams. An' I'd of won 100 easy if it weren't for the war, an' maybe 120 if it weren't for *that*." He jerked his thumb at a stack of empty beer cases over by the wall.

"Some sacrifices have to be made," Papa said.

"An' some don't," averred the Bull. "Me, I made one each o' both."

Papa was still trying to work this last statement out when Durham said, "Now come here, Hubert. The time has come for me to show you some-thin'. Used to call it the road apple. It's like a sinker only different. Dumber. Weirder. *Slooooower* . . ."

Two months later Papa pitched the Cornshuckers' opener. Charged with adrenaline, he shook off his catcher with impunity, had a one-hitter go-ing through four and a third innings, and had struck out five of the first fourteen batters he'd faced, all on fastballs, when G. Q. Durham called time, trudged morosely out to the mound, and confused every ump, fan and player in sight by kicking dirt all over the socks of his unhittable pitcher. "You throw three fast ones to any one man for the rest of the day," he said, "and you're on the next bus to the C Stands for Clap League in West Texas!"

Papa nodded, privately chalked the game up for lost, and proceeded to rely on varying speeds and deception instead of power for the first time in his life. It was a frighteningly odd experience: almost every batter he faced, even the pitcher, got wood on his dead slugs and road apples. But they seldom seemed to get much on them. Papa scattered six hits over the last four and two-thirds innings, walked one, struck out one, gave up two earned runs, knocked in two himself, won the game 6 to 3, and felt so fresh and relaxed by the time it was over that he wished it was a doubleheader so they could all go right on having fun. "That there," Durham said afterward, "was called nine against nine. Whole different proposition, ain't it?"

Papa agreed so thoroughly that by the middle of June he was a different pitcher: oddity had become his norm. He varied speeds and directions like a drunk driver, developed a whole new set of mound quirks and spasms and deliveries and mannerisms devised almost solely to encourage batter bewilderment, and he was 10 and 3, with an ERA of 2.54. "Shit, son," G.Q. told him one day. "You could of botched a few for my sake." "What do you mean?" Papa asked. And Gale showed him the letter: the Senators were moving him up to Tacoma, in the Pacific Coast League. "Success" is the common name for it. But our whole family—including Papa and our adopted pig of an uncle—was in tears the day we piled into a U-Haul and left our half-grown garden and home in Kincaid, Oklahoma, for good.

5. The Bland Inquisitor

In the year of God-knows-whose Lord 1965, on an evening in late January, twenty-five or so pieces of writing, scribbling, doggerel-versifying, drawing or doodling stolen (or, as the Elder preferred, "confiscated") from the personal effects and wastebaskets of Everett, Peter and Kincaid Chance over the period of half a year were placed inside Babcock's briefcase and plunked ominously down in the center of our diningroom table. Seated, without the least sense of impropriety, in Papa's chair was the Elder himself. To his right were his co-Inquisitors, Mama and Elder Wade Barnes (father of our old friend Micah *"Nup nyours! Nup nyours!"* Barnes). At the opposite end of the table was the innocuous softball hero and Sabbath School teacher, Brother Randy Beal. And to Babcock's left was the innocent audience for whose spiritual benefit all the ponderous monkeyshines were about to be performed: Winifred, Beatrice and Irwin.

The time of the gathering had been carefully chosen: the resident anarchist, Everett, was unanarchistically bagging groceries for $1.00 an hour at Pullasky's One Stop Market; the pundit, Peter, was doing homework at his egghead Catholic girlfriend Julie's house; the sane parent, Papa, was maintaining his sanity by humiliating the competition in a one-night-a-week basketball league at the Vancouver YMCA; meanwhile the paper boy/drudge, yours truly, was upstairs trying to squeeze six or eight hours' worth of homework into the single after-dinner hour available before my nightly lapse into stupefaction.

Elder Barnes opened the festivities by asking everyone present to bow their heads, and they prayed—or rather he prayed for them—asking the Lord for guidance, wisdom, patience and a number of other things He hasn't seen fit to bestow upon either Elder to this day. Babcock then cranked out an introduction too long for Irwin or the twins to later remember, though they did recall him saying that they were "three fine Christian children," that "your brothers have unfortunately chosen a very different path," and that, little as he or Mama wished to shock or frighten them, they felt compelled for the sake of "your three precious souls" to reveal startling evidence of their brothers'' "obscene" and "sacrilegious" tendencies.

Needless to say, he had their completely confused attention as he flipped his briefcase open. Unfortunately, he started things off with the "Why Apple Pie" poem. *"There* it is!" Irwin cried the instant he saw it. (He'd been afraid I'd thrown it away.) He then let out a loon-laugh, started reciting the thing from memory, and soon had the twins and Beal writhing in a suppressed-giggle fit so virulent that even the stereo grimaces of the Elders couldn't quell it.

When Mama had finally managed to shut everybody but Beal up, Elder Babcock tried a fake book jacket—a homemade sixteenth-birthday present from Everett to Peter, sporting a meticulous pen-and-ink illustration of a cowpoke, decked out in ten-gallon hat, spurs, chaps and six-guns, leaping high in the air in order to give himself a vicious kick in the mouth with the toe of one of his own boots. Beneath that, in a painstaking calligraphy that looked like rope, was the book's supposed title:

KICKIN' THE JAW OFF'N YER OWN FACE: A STUDY
OF COWBOY ZEN
By Peter Arthur Chance

After reading this aloud, Babcock pulled every stop in his theater-organ voice and roared, "Zen, I will have you know, is the name of the most *Satanic* branch of the Atheistic (!) Japanese (!!) cult (!!!) of *Boooooodism!"*

This temporarily knocked the giggles out of Beal. But living as they did with Everett, the twins were not so easily impressed by theatrical baritone lung-blasts. "Grandawma was an Atheist," Freddy casually remarked to her sister.

"A Famous Scientist too," Bet said, while the Inquisitionists gaped.

"She was fun!" Freddy sighed.

"We sure *loved* her!" Bet gushed.

"And we sure love Pete too," Irwin put in before the Elders could regroup, "and you know, he's kind of a Buddhist."

Then even Brother Beal got into the act: "Nancy and I met a Buddhist family over on Maui last winter. They visited the Adventist church there in Lahaina the day I did the guest sermon, and invited us to see their pagoda later that week. Beautiful place. And *awfully* nice people!"

Nothing like a little twentieth-century chitchat to ruin a late-Gothic mood. Refusing to depart from what he saw as an utterly damning point, Babcock tried describing Peter as "a rampant collector of Satanic paraphernalia" and "a devout worshipper of false Christs." He then plundered his briefcase for items intended to prove this thesis—all of them stolen by Mama, that very evening, from the walls and shelf in the back of Peter and Everett's closet, where Pete had been teaching himself to meditate. There were *National Geographic* pictures of Russian icons and Tibetan Buddhist tankas, handwritten sayings from various sutras and scriptures, a tiny plaster Buddha, a brass incense burner, a little three-inch gong. And Babcock and Mama were happy to note that Irwin and the twins finally *had* begun to look shocked. What they failed to guess—until Bet expressed it directly—was why: "Boy oh *boy!*" she gasped. "Is Pete ever gonna be *mad* when he finds out you guys took that stuff out of his closet!"

Irwin and Freddy both nodded passionately. And again it was the Inquisition, not their audience, that was nonplussed. What they just couldn't grasp was that we kids loved and kept track of each other. The Famous Scientists had long ago joined Pete in the closet, and noted in their lab book that his pulse was slightly slower after meditation than before. As for Irwin, he'd once snuck into the same closet just to slip an ice cube down Peter's back, but was so impressed when Pete hardly flinched and went right on meditating that he twice tried meditating himself (though he fell instantly to sleep both times). The problem was simply that our siblings knew us well and were, unlike Mama, unwilling to pretend that they didn't. The accusations of "Satanism" and "sacrilege" therefore came off sounding like a game of make-believe, and though the twins and Irwin liked games, they found this one a little too ridiculous and mean-spirited to want to play.

Still hell-bent on making some sort of diabolical impression, Babcock tried reading the untranslated Persian half of an ancient Zoroastrian prayer called "The 101 Names of God" (also stolen from Pete) in the most sinister voice he could muster: *"Mino-Satihgar!"* he groaned. *"A-minogar!"* he grimaced. *"Gat-gar . . . Garo-gar . . . Gar-a-gar . . . Gar-a-gar-gar . . . A-gar-agar . . . A-gar-a-gar-gar . . ."*

The audience response? Desperation; a riot of constipated mirth; even Elder Barnes lost it long enough to let out a tiny, Micah-like snigger.

Baffled by the unmanageability of his tiny congregation, Babcock tried a few quotes from various sages which Peter had copied out in a little spiral notebook. From the Zen patriarch Dogen, he read, "If we seek the Buddha outside the heart, the Buddha becomes a devil." Then he bellowed, "But the Buddha already *is* a devil!"

The response? Snorts; belly cramps; face cramps; ripping sounds in sinuses . . .

From the Prophet Muhammad, he read, "Let a man answer to me for what waggeth between his jaws, and what between his legs, and I will answer to him for Paradise . . ." Then he huffed, "Is that any way for a prophet of *God* to talk?"

The response? Quaking bodies; bulging neck veins; flecks of pressurized snot shooting out noses . . .

If Babcock were smart, he'd have surrendered right there. Needless to say, he did no such thing. Losing his temper completely, he shuffled wildly through the briefcase, but was unable to find what he was after for so long that when he finally succeeded, he cried out, *"Ah-ha!"* He then triumphantly revealed to all eyes a wrinkled-up, wastebasket-salvaged color-pencil study of a nude woman next to whom even Mae West would appear anorexic—bulging pink thighs, humongous breasts, belabored brown nipples, ruby-red lips. Boldly labeled "EVERETT'S DREAM WOMAN," the sketch had been devised and deployed to tease Irwin, who had taken to speculating long and rather tediously upon the "Girl of My Dreams" of late. What Babcock expected it to arouse were indignant gasps and embarrassed blushes. What it did instead—thanks to his own happy *"Ah-ha!"*—was bring down the house: *"Wah-haw-haw-haw! Whoo-hoo-hoohoo!* We're sorry, Edler! I mean ELDER! *Whaw whaw whaw!* We just can't help it!"

That pretty well nailed the lid on the Inquisitorial coffin. Elder Barnes tried to quell the hysteria by threatening the very threesome they'd come to save with eternal hellfire. When that didn't work Mama tried cutting Irwin's allowance and threatening the twins with spankings. When that too failed, the eternally clueless Babcock—with a coal-black "That does it!" scowl—reached deep into the entrails of his briefcase and dragged out the greatest proof of iniquity in his possession: shaking a half dozen mildewy *Playboy* magazines in the three "precious souls'" faces, he roared so loud that I heard him upstairs, "Which of you will *dare* tell me *these* are funny?"

But Irwin did far worse than that. First he began to loon-laugh so uncontrollably that he knocked his chair over, lost his allowance forever, and got himself grounded clear up into his mid-forties or so. Then he managed to wheeze that normally he hated tattling, but that since this gathering was just a big old tattletale session anyhow, what the heck, it was too funny not to tell: the *Playboys* had been a going-away present to Everett, when he quit church, from his young friend and lifelong admirer, Dougy Lee Babcock.

While Elder Babcock turned to stone and Mama turned a number of interesting pastel colors, Elder Barnes heaved a sigh of relief: he'd felt sure that Irwin was about to finger Micah. Meanwhile Brother Beal scratched his nose, checked his watch, stared at his lap, but was finally reduced—by his herculean struggle not to explode with laughter—to the public twiddling of his thumbs. The twins might still have joined in Irwin's mirth, but they'd never seen *Playboys* before, felt confused by the mixed reaction to them, and were pooped out anyhow from all the fun they'd been having. So for quite a while—maybe fifteen or twenty seconds—there was no sound in the room but Irwin's loonlike glee. And though Babcock was too angry and ashamed to look at him, let alone stop him, he never forgot that sound. And he never forgave it.

When it finally dawned on Irwin that the Elder was genuinely humiliated, he cut his laughter off and apologized for it. A long silence ensued. But no length of silence could hide the fact that Mama and Babcock had just been doused in the very dunking chair they'd hoped to use on Everett, Peter and me. All they felt now was confusion. And all they now wanted from their tribunal was a dignified escape route. Lucky for both of them, Babcock was just the fellow to provide it.

Throwing everything back into his briefcase and slamming it shut, the Elder stormed off into the one kind of prefabricated activity he knew could never be sullied by contact with anything so unpredictable as tolerance or intelligence or laughter: the nonstop, slag-slinging sermon. Yet the entire gathering—Irwin and the twins included—was nothing but grateful for the molten verbiage he proceeded to pour over them, because yes, it was hot, but it was a steady, predictable heat; and yes, the words threatened, insulted, and condemned them again and again, but the sound of the words, the physical experience of them, only warmed and lulled them. Like sitting in a sauna, like watching TV, like listening to loud rock or getting pleasantly drunk, Babcock's brimstoning allowed each listener a total cessation of energy and thought, severed each from his neighbors, and preserved for each the dignity of his or her privacy until the embarrassment of their botched togetherness could end.

CHAPTER FOUR

Epiphany
of a Toe

Boys, this game may be your only chance to be good . . . You might screw up everything else in your life and poison the ones who love you, create misery, create such pain and devastation it will be repeated by generations of descendants. Boys, there's plenty of room for tragedy in this life . . . Don't have it said that you never did anything right. Win this game.
—Garrison Keillor, "The Babe"

–I–

When Papa found out about the "Washougal Inquisition," he got into a two-hour shouting match with Mama, slept on the couch that night, came home from work with a thrift-store set of twin beds the next day, dragged his and Mama's old double mattress out back, and converted it into a new target pad for his shedball pitches. "Is that a metaphor or a simile?" Everett asked Peter as they stood watching out the kitchen window. I remember this remark clearly, because I didn't understand it, and didn't like it when Peter laughed.

Next Papa, for the first time ever, walked down the block to the crappy little 7-Eleven that had replaced the Walsh family's old corner grocery, bought himself a short case of Miller beer, and toted it home on his shoulder, sort of like a bazooka. Sliding all but one into the refrigerator just as the rest of us were sliding into our chairs for supper, he poured his one bottle into a white plastic Huckleberry Hound glass, carried it over to our forever-alcoholless suppertable, sat casually down in the heat of Mama's blowtorch stare, and rattled off his trusty old *Giveus-gratefulhearts* grace. He then said, "I live here."

This statement got no argument. But it didn't turn down the blow-torch either.

"I'm the father here," he added. "And I pay the bills here. That gives me the right to make some decisions. Not all the decisions. But some. So here's three."

Mama still just sat and stared.

"Decision One. From now on I keep beer in the refrigerator. It's for nobody but me—Everett, Kade, Irwin, you got that? For Laura's sake I put this condition on me: if I ever drink more than two in a night, I lose my right to keep it here. But otherwise, get used to it. This world can be a pain, and beer can't change that. But it's a slight relief at times. And this teetotally religious crap is getting this family nowhere. Everett, wipe that idiotic smirk off your face. Bet, please stop wiggling."

Everett wiped. Bet stopped. Mama didn't move or speak.

"Decision Two. Eight people live here, and the God I believe in put us here to love and respect each other despite our differences. I used to think this was so obvious it didn't need saying. But after last night I see that some of us don't believe in love or respect anymore, so those of us who do are going to have to fight back. I started fighting back at lunch hour today, when I phoned that Babcock character and told him he's no longer welcome in our house."

Everett flew up out of his chair with the beginnings of a great *"Hallelu-jah!"* in his lungs, but Papa's fist slammed down on the table and Everett dropped back into his chair so fast that it seemed as if Papa had punched him on the top of the head. "What I need from you," Papa said, "is silence."

Everett got the message. Papa turned back to the rest of us. "Phoning Laura's preacher that way was high-handed, I know. But not near as high-handed as it was for that jackass to sit down in my chair and try to teach my children to fear each other. Bet, please! Don't kick the table. Everett, a smirk isn't silence, and that's your last warning. Irwin, listen. If you're still fond of Babcock's sermons and like his church, by all means, keep going. I'm not trying to change the way anybody worships. It's only in this house he's not welcome. And I hope you see why."

Irwin grinned hugely, and said, "It's fair." But Mama slid her chair back, and not as if ready to fight: she looked ready to flee. It surprised me.

"Decision Three," Papa said. "According to the God I believe in, the six kids who live here are equal. So I see no reason why, for months now, the three who go to church have been cared for in ways that the other three haven't. To me, that's the opposite of Christianity. To me that smacks of Babcock. And like I said, he's no longer welcome here."

Papa glanced at Mama, but she just sat there, pondering some nothingness in the center of the table. "Your mother has to do what she thinks is right," he told us. "But so do I. And I've kept quiet too long. I want you kids to know we disagree. I think it should be six school lunches or no school lunches, six mended shirts or no mended shirts, six goodnight kisses or no goodnight kisses. So my third decision is, well . . . just a warning, really. I don't want to make trouble, but I just don't like the way we're living. So, what I'm saying is, if things don't change, I may move out . . . at least for a while."

I was still struggling to take this in when Irwin roared, "Okay! Okay then, Papa! Things *will* change!"

"Don't do it, Papa!" "Stay!" "Please don't!" "Things'll change!" the rest of us chimed in.

"From now on I make my *own* lunches!" Irwin bellowed at Mama. "And everybody else's if they want! And I'll do the laundry too—the whole house's I mean. Even nasty ol' *Everett's!* Even his Atheistic ol' *socks!* Starting *now!* I mean it!" And with that he plugged his nose, held his breath, and dropped like a deep-sea diver down under the table, where he started wrestling the rancid high-top tennis shoes and unmentionable socks from Everett's ankles and feet. But while Everett blushed and kicked at him and the rest of us broke out laughing, Mama stood, turned, and started down the hallway—and I saw that she was weaving like a drunk: twice she had to grab the wall to keep from falling.

"And Freddy and *me*," Bet's voice nearly shattered the windows with shrill goodwill, "we can keep scientific track of Mama! Like if she doesn't kiss Kade goodnight, we won't let her kiss us. Or if she makes a face at Peter, we'll make her make faces at us. Or if Everett's room's a mess, she'll have to leave ours messy too!"

"Your hearts," Papa said, wincing down the hallway, "are in just the right place. But listen." His voice dropped to a whisper. "I feel like we're starting to gang up on Mama, like we're leaving her out of the fun, see. So what say, before we do anything drastic, we try ganging up in a better way? What say we all go back there, right now, and try to tell her how much we love her? That way, maybe she'll feel so much a part of us she'll want to treat us all equal on her own."

This was the sort of idea that hippies (including me) would pretty well beat to death in a few years. But it seemed fresh and wild at the time, so that was what we did. Piling out of our chairs, we traipsed down the hall, burst into her bedroom, and found her crying hard and closing a chaotically packed suitcase. But we encircled and glommed on to her with our fourteen arms and hands anyhow, and told her in three octaves and seven voices how much we loved her. It was embarrassing, at first, at least to us "rebels." But as the thing took hold, as we saw, for instance, how Papa had shut his eyes and was cooing his very softest and kindest no matter how dumb it sounded, we began to feel how ridiculously sweet and true this expression of love was, till there stood Everett, patting Mama's shoulders and hair the way one pats a kitty, shiny-eyed with regret for making her so mad all the time; and Peter, holding her hand, telling her how much he missed talking with her, having her tease him, hearing her laugh; and me, touching whatever I could reach in there between Irwin and Freddy, unable to speak, but moved to tears by the overwhelming, mountain-moving force I felt our united love to be . . .

Yet the instant we'd touched her, Mama's tears had stopped and she'd put on a stiff smile. And the longer we encircled her, the more pained and terrible that smile became. Then, the instant we released her, she dropped the smile, lifted her suitcase so that it formed a barrier between her and Papa, and said, "I love you all too. And I'm your mother. Which gives *me* the right to make some decisions. Here's just one."

Knowing more or less what was coming, it stabbed me to see Irwin still beaming at her with stupid hope. "I'm leaving," she said—and still Irwin's smile didn't fade. "You seem to need your father more than me, and to respect him more than me. So I'm going to go stay with my brother and Mary Jane. It's getting to be a habit, I know. But it's hard for me here. I spend my whole day here, every day, feeling so mad I could spit. I'm so ashamed and afraid of the terrible things some of my children have chosen to believe that I, I just don't know what to do. I keep hoping it'll get better, I keep hoping you'll see the light. But it never does. You never do. So I'm leaving."

Love really does generate tremendous power. But what the truisms about it fail to add is that the results of that power are almost impossible for human beings to predict or control. All our sevenfold love did to Mama at that moment was give her the strength to lift her heavy suitcase as if it were made of balsa wood, and to float away after it without once looking back.

"Don't go!" Irwin pleaded as she vanished down the hallway. And he, at least, meant what he said. But when the rest of us chimed in—as we'd done when Papa spoke of leaving—the hollowness of our pleas echoed far longer and louder than the pleas themselves.

–II–

"I just don't know what to tell you," Papa said when we finally sat down to supper without her. "We tried. It didn't work. I don't know what to say."

Most of us were nodding, or shrugging, or feeling confused. But then a surprising thing happened: Peter turned to Papa, and in an accusing, almost angry tone, said, "I think you *do* know what to tell us."

The rest of us gaped at him. But Papa, for a moment, seemed stunned, maybe even a little frightened—and Peter saw this. "I think there's something about Mama," he said, "something *important*, that explains why she gets this way. And, whatever it is, I think it's time you told us."

Papa pulled enough of himself together to snap, "What are you *talking* about?"

But Peter was undeterred. "I can't say exactly. I just know that Mama used to love us too much to act this way. So there's got to be a reason. And you know her best. So you must know the reason."

The twins and Irwin were still gawking at Peter, but Everett was eyeing Papa now, and looking more than a little troubled as Papa said, "Listen, Peter. If I knew any such secret, yours or hers or anybody's, I'd just have to keep it. That's what secrets are."

"So there *is* one."

"I didn't say that. I only said I wouldn't give a secret away. If you think Mama has one you should know about, ask her yourself."

"But she won't *tell* me!" Peter cried. "You know that, Papa! She thinks I worship Satan! She acts like she *hates* me! And by not telling us why, you leave us no choice but to think she's mean and unfair and crazy."

Papa said nothing to this, and his face had gone so dead that I had no idea whether it was fury or confession that he was close to. But he was close to something, because when he picked up his beer he drank, without pleasure or pause, till it was gone.

"What if," Peter said, "not knowing this thing, we just can't love her anymore? It's getting hard. It's even hard for you, and you *know*."

"Not one more word," Papa whispered.

"I only want not to hate her back!" Peter said—and when his voice broke we realized how hard it was for him to defy Papa like this. "I only want not to treat her the way she treats me."

Papa wouldn't look at him. He just toyed with his white plastic cup. But there was obvious sorrow, and maybe sympathy too, in the way he was staring at Huckleberry Hound.

–III–

I wish I'd had the love, the wisdom, the empathy or even just the raw curiosity to try and find out, back in the mid-sixties, why Mama would storm off the way she did. She always went to stay with her brother and his wife, outside Spokane. She always left in such terrible hurt and anger that it seemed she would never return. And she always came back, calmer but basically unchanged, after three or four days. I've learned enough, in the years since, to know that she was leading a life as intricate and dramatic, as painful, and as worthy of respect as my father's. But this paragraph is revisionist. Mama's absences were a relief to me, her returns a mild disappointment, and unlike Peter, I had no great curiosity about the motivations of either. I felt at times that she loved me. I also felt, almost constantly, that she disliked me. And I was satisfied to reciprocate. It damaged us. But that's the way it was.

–IV–

Papa's star-crossed pitching career, in my opinion, did more to shape Everett than all the books he ever read and classes he attended put together. Papa's bum baseball luck had some effect on all of us: for instance, it gave us all a soft spot for snakebit heroes, and made all of us but Irwin quick to smirk at any successful person who thought they got to where they got by simply being gifted. But Papa's baseball history did so much to shape Everett's darkish outlook on life that it may be impossible to understand Everett without a complete knowledge of that history. So here is the rest:

After his Oklahoma conversion from straight power-pitching to power-and-junk, Papa went 10 and 13 for the Tacoma Timbers in 1954 and 9 and 15 in 1955. Before even mentioning the won-loss record, Everett would have put the numbers in perspective by pointing out that Tacoma was a cellar club both seasons, and the worst hitting team in the league in '55. Papa had the most victories (and most losses), most complete games, second-best earned run average (2.95), second-best winning percentage, and also the best pitcher's batting average on the team over the two-year span. So when both the Timbers' parent teams (the Senators in '54, the Giants in '55) never called him up for a look, and then, for the '56 season, the Timbers offered him a one-year contract with no raise, Papa decided he'd seen enough of Tacoma. Shredding the contract, he walked out of the Timbers' office, telephoned the Portland Tugs (against whom he had a career record of 5 and 0 and an ERA of 1.19), arranged a tryout, and enjoyed a camp that included five scoreless innings and an RBI double in exhibition against Tacoma, and three no-hit innings against the Tugs' parent team, the Pittsburgh Pirates. Yet when contract time came, the Tugs cited his age, his old injuries and the twenty-eight Tacoma losses instead of the fact that they'd never once beaten him, then offered so little money that Papa asked for an hour or two to think it over. Strolling over to the nearest cafe, he was stirring sugar into a bitter cup of coffee and thinking about cashing in his baseball chips when a guy in a Panama hat and dark glasses walked up, removed both, revealed the face of a stranger who nevertheless grinned like a long-lost friend, and said, "Hugh Chance? The name's Jinx Dodds. And I'm a *real* pirate, not a Pittsburgh phony. I steal ballplayers from fools who can't appreciate 'em. And I'd like to steal you."

"Real pirate" was a slightly poeticized description. But Jinx Dodds really was a part-time real estate broker, developer, slumlord and gambler, and he really did own an unaffiliated Class B team in Washington State, the Battle Ground Bulldogs. He also possessed the piratical clout, cleverness and cash necessary to match the Tugs' monetary offer, *and* to pitch Papa in a way that would allow him to hold a full-time job on the side.

So that's what Papa did. After finding—with the ubiquitous Dodds's help—both a rental house in Camas and a full-time job at the Crown Z mill, Papa celebrated turning twenty-seven years old by winning twenty-seven games for the Cascade League Champion 'Dogs, including six shutouts, three two-hitters, eight home runs and a .364 batting average that would have led not just pitchers but the entire league if he'd had a few dozen more at-bats—

and all summer long a diminutive, lippy, worshipful batboy named Everett handed him his antique Rawlings and his holy Adirondacks and became so hopelessly enamored of the idea that this rare summer of glory was the way the world was meant to be that almost everything that would happen to his father or himself for the next decade or more would strike him as a cheat, a stroke of hideous luck, or an intolerable bore.

Papa's was an almost unheard-of sort of minor league season, in that anybody who plays that well for even a month at that level is usually sent up to a higher league. But the players who get sent up are usually twenty-one or younger and consider any higher league "up," whereas Papa had played so much Triple A ball for so little money that he was no longer interested in any definition of "up" but the highest. He actually turned down two modest but honest Pacific Coast League offers late that summer, simply because his two-paycheck Bulldog/Crown Z arrangement was too lucrative to give up. He even promised Jinx Dodds to come do it again next year if no major league offers came his way.

By September, though, news of his spectacular season had wended its way to the top, and by October so many teams had hinted at so many offers of such wildly varying concreteness that he was shopping around for a sports lawyer to help him sort things out. In November, though, when he learned that Mama was pregnant yet again, he suffered a fit of caution and career doubt that ended in a down payment on our Clark Street house instead of the lawyer. And that was when and where it all ended. Handling his own negotiations, Papa was leaning toward Cincinnati (who was offering him more money to play two months of winter ball in the Dominican League than he could make in four months at the mill) when Mama began to hemorrhage, found out she was carrying twins, and was told to stay in bed if she wanted to keep them. So Papa had given his regrets to the Reds and stayed home to help her, but was still talking tryout with St. Louis, Baltimore and Cleveland when he crushed his thumb at the mill.

But eight years later, in January 1965, that perennially dissatisfied, never-say-die ex-Bulldog batboy, Everett, undertook a second dial-a-prayer project on his ill-fated father's behalf. Trying the same lucky downtown phone booth he'd used to contact the miracle-producing Doc Franken, he piled in his hard-earned bag-boy quarters, dialed Oklahoma, and, *mirabile dictu*, conjured up the white cracker drawl of the infamous G. Q.

Durham as easily as Abraham used to conjure down the ineffable drawl of God.

Unlike Abraham, Everett didn't just listen when he got G.Q. on the line. He'd written out a veritable soliloquy beforehand, rehearsed it in front of Irwin, Pete and me, and even allowed us to critique and embellish it. And in finished form, as delivered by Everett, the spiel was a tailor-made purple-prosed phone-filibustering masterpiece. It began with the triple admission that (1) Papa was too old for the minors, (2) he had too many kids to leave the Crown Z money, and (3) he'd apparently lost all desire to throw a baseball outside his backyard. But from there it went on to say that although Durham was unquestionably *the* Junk Genius— the greatest wrecked-ballplayer-rebuilder who ever lived—it was our very own Papa who, right here in downtown Camas, had brought Durham's philosophy to new and epiphanic heights by taking a thumb made of half his own damned *toe* for chrissake, and twisting it into a tool that had perfected the Kamikaze—the most devastating diving fastball that four visiting baseball experts had ever seen. (He neglected to mention that these "visiting experts" were us four brothers.) True, Papa threw his killer pitch only at night, and only as a kind of contemplative exercise. But since it was G.Q.'s peculiar genius that had inspired this paragon, Everett felt we owed him an invitation to come see it for himself. Not to arrange any sort of tryout or comeback, mind you, but just to drop by the next time his scouting duties brought him out our way, quaff a few ice-cold tubes of the amber liquid, and partake of the purely artistic joy of watching the crowning achievement of his own career fly, like an epileptic beam of light, through the soulful squalor of a mill-town backyard night . . .

–V–

Irwin's first memory is as complicated as Irwin himself is simple. It's of a hot dry evening in what he later learned was Kincaid, Oklahoma, of a sinking red sun hanging over an endless green expanse he later learned was a minor league outfield, of being set down, wearing nothing but diapers, at the edge of that expanse, and of crawling as fast as he could, way out into it. Lying down on his side in order to better study the infinitude and chlorophyllitude of it all, he heard Mama's dry, distant, incomprehensible voice drift over him (*yeah, out in left field as usual*), snorted happily as he turned to crawl still further off, but found his path barred by two big black shoes and a pair of tree-sized, blue-stockinged legs. Thinking he'd discovered his daddy, he snorted again, grabbed the stockings, used them to pull himself up to a standing position, peered up the legs—and sure enough, there was his father's gray-and-blue uniform. But it had somehow been bloated (the heat? the round red sun?) into something so moon-shaped and -sized that he couldn't see past the belly, couldn't find the face, so he leaned back still further to peer still higher— and fell flat on his head and back. It didn't hurt much, thanks to the grass, but by the time he'd regained an up-down orientation and turned to relocate the shoes, the stockings and legs and entire beach-ball body had blopped down onto the grass beside him. Goo-sound-that-precedes-the-word *"Papa!"* Irwin cried, crawling right up onto the belly. But as he salamander-walked up over the summit and caught sight of the face, he froze: it wasn't Papa! It was the most tiny-eyed, multi-chinned, lobster-red, bloated human visage he'd ever seen. Even before the lips zipped open and the mouthful of brown teeth flanged out, Irwin's infant mind knew that he was in serious trouble. When a horrid, henlike cackling began to quake the belly beneath him and a stream of swampy fluid phoooted sideways out the snaggled teeth, he realized this trouble might prove fatal. He therefore did the only sensible thing: diving face-first onto the grass, he gathered his hands and knees together and started sprint-crawling off into the infinite greenness for all he was worth . . .

It was while tearing along, listening to the plaintive cries of his mother *(Don't worry, he won't hurtcha!),* the hooting of distant ballplayers, and the cack-'n'-hack of the blubberman blollopping along after his diapered behind that Irwin felt the pure instant of despair that nailed the episode to his memory for life. As this despair decreed, the creature soon caught him in its fat red claws, reared up on its hind legs, let out another cackle, and—*bye-bye, Mama! bye-bye, red sun and green world!*— lifted his tender infant abdomen up to the putrid-toothed mouth. But when, instead of ripping him open, the monster only gave his belly a wet, snorffling kiss that stained him brown and sent a blissfully cool shiver shooting from pate to toes, Irwin's despair was transmuted on the spot into the infant version of one of the world's most ruthlessly optimistic philosophies.

Flopping onto his back, the moonman grabbed Irwin's tiny fat hands in his huge, even fatter ones, stood him up on the lunar belly, hollered *Play ball!,* and Irwin began stomping round and round the bounding surface, gaping joyously down into a bobbling chaos of brown and red teeth and chins, soaking cackle-vibrations in through the soles of his bare feet, and roaring with a delight so loud and contagious that soon the fat man and spectators and an entire Two A ball team were infected with it too. *All right that's enough!* came his mother's tiny and for some reason stricken wail as Irwin flopped down on his pet monster's gut, squeal-begged for more, and down or up the kisses rained, onto his ears, his neck, his arms, legs, belly *(Stop them, Hugh! Please! Stop him!)*—rough, wet, wildly aimed dog, bear and walrus kisses tattooing him with stains that would later be scrubbed away mercilessly as sins *(You've got to stop them!)*, but which now covered him, after a squirmy eternity of heat (which eternity, he later learned, was only the length of an afternoon's ballgame), with wave after wave of cool, ecstatic shivers . . .

And on Groundhog Day 1965, we had just gathered for our third consecutive Mama-less supper when someone rang the front doorbell, and Everett gasped "Elder *Babcock!*" so convincingly that Papa had clenched his fists and reddened before he caught Everett's expression, and laughed. Then Irwin ran to the front door, swung it wide open, and there stood a shabby, tavern-odored, red-eyed, corpulent old stranger he figured must be some lost wino or panhandler. But when the old guy let out the kind of wheezy tenor cackle that by then reminded us TV-news-watching Northerners of nothing so much as the KKK, and when that cackle sent a cool, ecstatic, embarrassingly nonsequacious shiver shooting up Irwin's legs and back, his body instantly knew who he was seeing, though his mind and tongue were still groping for a name. "G. Q. Durham!" he finally gasped.

"Hot *damn!*" the old man cried. "This is great! This is good! Look at the size o' *this* son of a Hubert!"

–VI–

Hiding in the old toolshed, unable to see a thing, but so close to the pitching shed that we could hear even grunts and head-scratching, Everett and I heard Durham say, "You're gonna have trouble fieldin' bunts on that retread foot there, Hubert."

"The hell I am," Papa told him. "All that mattress ever does is bunt, and I never field a one." And with that he fired his twentieth or so Kamikaze, which must have taken another wicked down-snap, since for the twentieth or so time G.Q. spat, then whispered, "Sheeee-it."

"How long," Durham asked, "in terms of innings, an' how often in terms of days, do you think you could do what I've been watchin' you do here?"

"I throw fifty to seventy hard pitches every other night," Papa said. "But it's got nothing to do with innings. There's no hitters, Gale."

"So we're talkin' relief," Durham mused, ignoring him. "We're talkin' stopper. I like that, Hubert. It suits your serene, stubborn goddamned nature."

"We're talkin' backyard hobby, is all we're talking," Papa said. But after the hiss and thud of another pitch and another appreciative "Hot *damn!*" Papa laughed like a happy kid. Hobby or not, he liked throwing in front of a fan.

"Know what's gonna happen when they see the action on that thing?"

"When who sees it, Gale?"

"The folks upstairs. Enemy coaches, mean-minded hitters, malicious ol' umps. Know what they're gonna think?"

"I'm through facing hitters," Papa said. "We've been over this, what, ninety times now? But go ahead. If I *was* upstairs, what would they think?"

"That you've overcome your number one flaw."

There was a silence. Then, in a lowered voice, Papa said, "Laura?"

If the Bull hadn't let out one of his harebrained cackles, Everett's snort would have given us away for sure. "Hubert!" the old man chided. "*Shame!* I meant *spit*, you nimnam!"

"Spit?" Papa sounded confused. "I never threw spit, Gale. You know that."

G.Q. phooted out a weighty-sounding hocker. "Whaddya think I meant by 'flaw'?"

While Everett struggled not to snort again, Papa said, "So you think the other team'd suspect me?"

"Action like that, they'd be fools not to."

"Good thing I'm retired, then."

"Why's that, Hubert?"

"I *am* usin' spit."

There was a several-second lull, during which Durham must have been gathering all the outrage and energy he had in him, because at the end of it he gasped, "You *wouldn't!* You're *not!* You *can't!*"

"I would, I can, and I am," Papa answered.

"My *Lord*, Hubert! Where's your moral fiber and all that type o' crapola?"

"What's immoral about a backyard spitter, Gale? Who's gonna complain? The mattress? The garage wall? The neighbors?"

"Them ain't the fibers I mean!" Durham retorted. "The gall of a man, the shiftlessness of a man, the two-facedness of a man who'd let one o' the all-time additives experts stand here thinkin' he was seein' sheer, bare-balled genius—*that's* the lack that wounds and troubles me."

"Oh," Papa said. "Well. For that I do apologize. The genius you've been watching, like my thumb and foot, has been ever so slightly doctored."

"Hot *damn!*" Durham roared, and a chill shot through me. Nobody could hot-damn as blissfully as G.Q. "This is *good!* This is *fine!* I'd of sworn on my life them balls was as dry as my own, if ya don't mind stoopin' to catch a sad ol' man's meaning."

Papa's gleeful snort showed he'd no qualms about making the stoop.

"Where the hell're you gettin' it, dammit? An' what're you usin', Hubert? How're ya workin' it in?"

"Trade secrets," Papa said—and I could just picture his demure smile.

"Well I'm damned!" Durham said.

"That we've always suspected."

"The so-called master bows to his student," said the Bull. And from the grunt and groan that followed, Everett and I deduced that, so far as his gut would allow it, that was exactly what Durham proceeded to do.

When they came inside for a beer afterwards (or in Gale's case, for four beers afterwards) and all six of us kids surrounded them, demanding the old man's expert opinion, I think his response surprised even Papa. "Soon as Hubert gives me the word," he said, "I'll be on the horn, seein' but what I can't arrange a little tryout with the Twins."

Standing right beside Durham's ear, Irwin roared, "You mean the *Minnesota* Twins?"

"No!" Gale said with a wince. "I mean your little sisters."

While Irwin and the twins cracked up, Papa grabbed Durham's shoulder and squeezed it hard. "Damn!" the old man shouted, trying to wrest his hand away. "A whole family o' bullies! Pick on somebody your own size!"

"Then you do the same," Papa said, trying to nod, subtly, toward Irwin and the twins.

But G.Q. didn't get it. "What the hell are you ravin' about?" he asked.

Papa let go of his shoulder, sighed, and spelled it out. "No more comeback talk, Gale. You'll get the kids all excited."

"Then it's even Steven," G.Q. retorted, " 'cause whaddya think your pitchin' just did to *me?*"

"Cut it out!" Papa snapped.

"Ah ha!" Durham cried. "*Now* I see the true problem. He dudn't like the Twins. Okay. All right. I admit they aren't much to write home about these days. So how 'bout this. It'll have to be a secret, 'cause it's one o' these Benedict Arnold-type deals, but Smokey Alston an' me go a good ways back. So what say I get you a shot with the Dodgers?"

"Forget it, Gale," Papa said—as Everett's disbelieving ears nearly popped off the sides of his head (and later that summer Alston's Dodgers and Durham's ex-Senator Twins won their respective pennants).

"Okay," Durham replied. "I hear ya. No Twins. No Dodgers. Fine. How about a go (sorry there, Everett) with the despicable damned Yankees down in St. Petersburg for chrissake?"

"You're worse than all my kids put together, Gale."

"Well," Durham said, still playing dumb. "It's true the Yanks, thank God, ain't what they was since they fired ol' Casey. But hey! How *about* Stengel? Would a tryout with the mangled young Mets be grim and lowly enough to make our humble Hubert happy?"

"A tryout," Papa answered, "as you very well know, just isn't the point."

"Refresh my brains, then," G.Q. said. "What *is* the godforsaken point?"

"That not even the Mets are interested in a thirty-five-year-old gimp with a plastic toe on his foot and a real toe on his pitching hand."

"Now *you* listen to *me!*" Durham barked. "The Twins, Dodgers, Yanks, Mets an' anyone else in their right baseball minds is interested in any man, woman, chicken, fish or Space Man who pitches the way you're pitchin'."

"The way I'm pitching," Papa said, "is completely illegal."

But G.Q. only looked disgusted. "What is a man? Eighty, ninety percent water? An' when does he play ball? In summertime—Sweat Capital of the Year! So how is an ump ever gonna monitor what's runnin' nonstop out every pore o' everybody in the place? The truth is, you couldn't throw a bone-dry legal pitch if you wanted to, Hubert."

This argument completely convinced six-sevenths of Durham's audience. But Papa didn't even appear to hear it. G.Q. tried again:

"I checked them balls an' found nuthin'. I watched you an' *saw* nuthin'. An' if the likes of me can't see it, Hubert, the likes of *umpires* sure as hell won't. The spit that's gone 'fore it reaches an ump is what we in the trade call incidental percipitation. An' I say, if it's incidental, it's *legal*."

I felt like applauding, this time. But Papa just sighed.

"Oh, all right," G.Q. growled. "Think small, then, dammit. With the majors, mind you, age is no problem. In the minors it gets sticky. But if I explain that gettin' you is gettin' both the best minor league reliever an' the second-best pitching coach in the land, two for the shape o'one, some PCL team ought to go for it. So pick your climate, Hubert! Albuquerque? Hawaii? Salt Lake?"

But Papa kept droning no, no no. He said Gale had gotten all carried away by a damned spitball. He said it'd been nine years since he'd faced a real hitter, he'd just been made a foreman at the mill, he had seven people depending on his paycheck, and he was too old to go knocking around with a bunch of ass- and dream-chasing teenagers anyhow. He'd learned that much from living with his own. One good year, the Bull countered, even in the minors, and a quality baseball man like Papa could "crawl out of that shithole mill" and into a job as a pitching coach or scout that'd brighten the rest of his days.

"I appreciate the thought, the praise, your time and trouble, and all the rest of it," Papa said. "But there are other things too. My kids, for instance. The scholarships the older ones are fighting for now are worth more than a year's minor league salary. So they can't move. But I can't leave 'em alone here either. We've got troubles here, to tell the truth, Gale. Laura and me aren't doing that great lately, and if I . . . well, it's too thick for explaining. But I'm *needed* here."

"Then it's clear as beer," said the Bull. "You try out with Portland. Won't have to move an inch if it's the Tugs."

"Tell you what," Papa said. "Promise me they'll match my Crown Z pay and keep me till I'm sixty-five, and okay, fine. I'll try the Tugs."

"Keeeeerist!" Durham exploded. "Where's your sense of *adventure?*"

"This family," Papa said, "is all the adventure I can stand right now."

"Then stand 'em less for chrissake! Where's your sense of *baseball* adventure?"

"You just saw it," Papa said calmly, "out in that shed."

"But why, why, *why?* Why jail it up out there?"

"Because I'm baseball ancient, Gale. I've *had* my adventures. And if I don't pay some bills the next few years I'm gonna screw up the adventures of my kids."

"So you admit it," the old man said bitterly.

"Admit what?"

"You've betrayed the game," Durham said. "You've sold out."

Papa's face blackened. "To that mill? Me? You're dead wrong there, Gale!"

"Then what *is* a sellout?" G.Q. fired back. "Explain this love for your paycheck and retirement benefits some other way. And explain the whole damned rest o' this ensemble while you're at it. What is this St. Hubert Savior of Kids crap? What's this mill foreman, middle American, PTA an' NRA an' Three A *Car* Club member shit? Dwight D. Christ! Votin' the straight Republican ticket now, are we, Hubert? Ain't drank none neither, I s'pose, sance we jined the charch?"

"Are we gonna part enemies, Gale," Papa said, "or are you gonna shut your mouth?"

"What I'm gonna do, my onetime ballplayin' friend," Durham said softly, "is die lovin' the game of baseball. An' what you're gonna do, if you betray that same love, is die confused."

That did it. The old man had finally loosed an arrow that flew straight to Papa's heart: we felt it hit; we saw Papa start to bleed. "Look at *me*," G.Q. said. And for a terrible moment he let all the passion and animation fall out of his face, so that it just hung there, gray and slack and listless. "*This* is baseball ancient," he said. "An' now look at you."

We looked. And saw a beautiful, vital, miserably confused man.

Durham said, "Just tell your kids and me the truth here, is all I'm askin' o' St. Hubert the Confused. Don't, number one, throw fifty pitches better'n the best fifty o' my big league life, then tell us you ain't got the stuff. An' don't, number two, argue spitball morality with me. The Good Book itself says a man should earn his livin' by the sweat of his brow. Now the situation with Laura I know nothin' about. But don't, number three, Hubert, try tellin' me it's good for these kids to see their old man stay a factory hand, an' hate it, for a buck. Don't tell me that not bein' true to the work you've always loved most an' did best is a help to your kids. Just repeat after me, if it's the truth: 'I give up on baseball, Gale. I just don't love the game no more.'"

Somehow the silence that followed, in my ears, had a stadium roar. And Papa found nothing to say to quiet it.

"You got one choice, son," Durham said finally. "These kids here think you're a ballplayer. You an' Laura used to think so too. An' I'm here to tell the world you sure as hell still *pitch* like a ballplayer. But an honest player let's the *game* decide when he's finished. There's no other honorable escape. So you got one tryout left, Hubert. Show the game what you got, an' let *it* decide."

–VII–
Tempe, Arizona / February / 1965

"Oh, now *there!*" The Tugs' pitching coach, Buddy Sears, was sprawled in a box seat behind home plate, sipping a Coke, basking in pale winter sunlight, and grinning as he pointed Papa out in the crowd of walk-ons and no-hopes that had survived the first two cuts. "There's a *real* prospect!"

But Johnny Hultz, the Tugs' manager, just nodded and said, "Good eye, Buddy."

"No no!" Sears laughed, and pointed more emphatically. "I mean that tall *gray* drink o' water, in the *khaki* cap. The guy with the limp. And the road-killed mitt. And all them nice, coachlike wrinkles."

Again Hultz just nodded matter-of-factly. "Name's Chance," he said. "Pitched for Tacoma when I played for Portland. Never could hit the son of a bitch."

"Bullroar!" Sears chuckled.

"No bull," the manager insisted. "He's got a plastic toe on one foot, a real toe for a thumb, and he throws a pitch his kids call the Kamikaze."

"Oh, right!" Sears was in stitches now.

"Best sinking fastball we may ever live to see."

"Says who?" Buddy wheezed.

"That's another story," Johnny told him. "G.Q. The Junkman Burman or Furman, he called himself. Woke Beth and me with a midnight phone call two weeks ago to say sorry, he never could figure out the time zone thing, but that hey, an all-around baseball genius and old nemesis of mine was comin' to grace our camp, so don't by God let the gray hair and plastic leg and freak hand and ten-year layoff fool me. 'That I won't, Junkface,' I tell the guy. 'But now, if you don't mind, I'm gonna hang Alexander Graham the Phoneman Bell's contraption the fuck up here and get me a little shut-eye.' Click."

Sears chuckled politely, but he'd grown bored with all of Hultz's details. "So that's ol' Junkface out there, is it?" he said.

"Pay attention, Buddy. Junkface was the phone guy."

"Whatever you say, Johnny."

The following afternoon, when an assistant coach gave Papa an opportunity to show his stuff, Johnny Hultz—despite his opinion of G.Q.'s phone call—slipped away from the infield drill he'd been running, stepped into the shade of a dugout, and soon saw that the sinking fastball really was incredible. Six batters, four grounders and two K's later, Buddy Sears joined him in the dugout, flashed an incredulous grin, and said, "You weren't makin' any o' that shit up yesterday, were you?"

Hultz shook his head.

"Way to go, Junkman!" Sears roared as Papa stepped off the mound to give the next prospect a turn.

"Name's Chance," said Hultz.

"Whatever," Buddy said, and laughed.

And with that word, "whatever," Hultz fell from elation to depression —because on the basis of pitching alone he knew already that Hugh Chance deserved to make his team. But Buddy's "whatever" underlined the inarguable fact that his pitching, like his name, didn't make any difference: minor league baseball just isn't a gray-hair's game.

Five days and two player cuts later there was still no one in camp who could hit the Kamikaze. And everyone knew Papa Chance by name. And everybody who wasn't a meathead admired him in so many different ways that, like some esteemed old pro dropped down from the bigs, he was usually accompanied by an entourage of young players. Some just studied him in silence, some joined him at meals to badger him for stories about the old days, and some showed up at his door at night in search of a little discreet, pressure-free advice on a hitting or pitching or personal problem. As for John Hultz, he couldn't take his eyes off Papa Chance when he took to a mound either—but the entourage business was really starting to burn him up. Not only could the gimp still pitch, he was the People's Choice as manager! And any day now Hultz himself—the Organization's Choice—was going to have to alienate his players and betray his own baseball instincts when he told this knowledgeable, courageous, deserving old duffer to pack his bags and head back off into whatever oblivion he'd come from. For a while he considered letting Sears do his dirty work. But Buddy, for all his knowledge of pitching, was such a tactless old blob at times. Chance deserved better. "Especially," Hultz thought, "from a guy who never could hit him."

So late that afternoon, when he found his doomed prospect deftly slapping fungoes out into a prancing, dancing band of hormoneous young outfielders, he puffed himself up into something he hoped would appear dispassionate and managerial, then barked, far louder than he'd intended, "Chance!"

Papa turned and scowled.

Embarrassed by his own bark, Hultz let the air out of himself, scratched his aching head, and muttered, "What the hell are you doing here, anyhow?"

"Hittin' fungoes," Papa said, turning to slap out another one.

"That's not what I mean," Hultz sighed. "Come on. Come talk to me." And with that he marched miserably off toward the one unused diamond of the camp's five. Papa handed his fungo bat to a kid not much older than Everett, shrugged, and jogged to catch up.

"Okay," Hultz said as he paced furiously back and forth in front of a waist-high wall of motor-oil ads. "Let's hear it. What, in your own words, did you come here for?"

Noting the man's obvious frustration, Papa opted for the barest kind of truth. "To play some ball," he said.

Hultz shook his head. " 'Hittin' fungoes.' 'Play some ball.' That's cowboy talk, Chance. Let's try sentences."

Papa looked Hultz in the eye, and in a perfect deadpan said, "Sorry—pardner."

Both men laughed, and for a moment Hultz relaxed. Then he noticed the crow's-feet the laughter brought out around Papa's eyes. "Damn!" he blurted. "How old *are* you, anyway?"

"Thirty-five," Papa said. "But I turn thirty-six May fifth."

When Hultz just gaped at the thoroughness of his reply, Papa smiled and added. "It's too old not to be honest."

"That's not honesty," Hultz muttered. "That's attempted suicide."

Papa grinned. Hultz didn't. In fact, he said, "Chance. You make me mad."

Papa tried to read his face, couldn't, and so asked the obvious: "Why?"

"Because you're a gentleman and a baseball scholar, the players all love you, your geek-show pitching is the talk of the camp, and if this place was run like the *Queen for a Day* show you'd bust the applause meter and tote home the new Frigidaire. But that's not how things work here."

"I understand," Papa said.

"Then you must understand that your age just flat puts me in an impossible situation."

Papa shrugged, but he didn't nod. He wasn't *that* suicidal.

"You're just about my age, Chance, so it should be easy to put yourself in my shoes. Could *you* tell the Pirate brass you wanted to bump some young kid they've been scouting since high school to make room for a hot thirty-six-year-old prospect with a fake toe and weird thumb who hitched here and is broke too and has twelve kids by the way, so they'd better pay him a bonus and an extra-big salary?"

Papa smiled at the description, but said, "For the right prospect, I might."

"Christ!" Hultz protested. "You said you were too old not to be honest!"

Papa shrugged. "Guess I'm not as old as you thought."

The two men eyed each other. The two men liked each other. It didn't solve the problem. "Just what did you want out of this camp?" Hultz asked, pacing furiously again. "You know this is a kiddies' league. You know the key word here is 'potential.' Why did you come? What can I possibly do for you? Tell me your thinking, Chance. And try to *impress* me this time, dammit."

But Papa just shrugged again, and murmured, "Everybody likes doing what they do best."

"No way!" Hultz shook his head. "That's not *near* good enough."

"Maybe not," Papa said. "But try my cleats on here a minute, Mr. Hultz."

"John to you."

"Okay, John. This is a baseball camp, and I'm here playing ball. There's guys trying to hit here, and I've been gettin' 'em out. There's guys trying to pitch here, and I've been pitching better. But they're teammates too. So when they come to me for help, I tell 'em what I know. As I always understood it, these things are the object of the game. And if that doesn't explain me being here, if being the right age is the object now, then I don't see how some fancy speech is gonna help."

After a silence, Hultz nodded and said, "Better. Very good, in fact. But slip my shoes on again and you'll see I *need* that fancy speech. Because I like you. But if I tell my bosses I'm making room for your bones on my bench, it'll take magic words just to keep 'em from slappin' a straitjacket on me. So come on. Help me think."

Papa tried. He groped through his mind for some sort of argument, saw the hopelessness, felt panic, started to speak anyway, but then realized he couldn't, or didn't want to. All he really wanted was to remain where he was—to go on smelling the scent of the desert and grass of the five green diamonds; to go on listening to the varied pops and cracks of leather and bad wits, fungo bats and bubble-gum wads. And not for a week or two. He wanted measureless amounts, days and days. He had promised himself and us, before leaving Camas, that he'd enjoy what was enjoyable here and head home when it was over. But he'd forgotten something: this too was a home. It was a world he'd loved all his life, had never left willingly, had always feared leaving. And here it was: that same old fear, strong and sick-making as the first time it hit, half a life ago, when he'd torn up his shoulder at a Sox camp. Feeling it again, knowing how it would scourge him if he let it grow, or poison him if he shoved it down and took it home to his family, Papa realized he had no choice but to try, right in front of John Hultz, to call up the one tool that might help him.

So that's what he did. Turning a little to one side, he shut his eyes, relaxed his shoulders as if before a pitch, took a slow, deep breath, and began conjuring the ten thousand harelip throws he'd made in his back-yard shed. With that one long breath—O *Nyeesus!*—he summoned the rain, the muggy heat, the fatigue and despair, called up the thwams on siding, silly thuds in the dirt, helpless punching of walls, then reached deep for the fruit (*How snorely we need nthee!*) of that two-year effort, which was simply the ability not to judge a pitch—not the worst or best of them—but just to sling out what was in him, come what may . . .

He'd been gone maybe ten seconds when he turned back to John Hultz. But when he returned, he was calm. "I figured it might come to this," he said. "And I've got no magic words for your bosses, John. I'm just here because I work in a papermill, which doesn't come natural to me. Whereas playing ball, that does come natural. From the day I could hold a ball I've played this game. And when I've had to quit—from injuries or whatever—my insides have kind of quit on me too. So soon as I could I'd be back at it, even gimpy, even if it was just in my own backyard. I've never used up the ballplayer in me, John. I doubt I ever will. And since you're about to boot me outta here—no offense taken, and none intended—I'd rather go hit a few more fungoes to the boys there than stand here jawing with you."

With that, Papa smiled and offered his hand. And Hultz shook it. But he couldn't smile back.

The leap from Papa Chance to a beefy red close-up of Buddy Sears was a major comedown for Manager Hultz—and he'd already been down. It didn't help matters when Buddy's first words turned out to be: "So what'd you tell the old fuck?"

"The truth!" Hultz barked.

"Which one?" Sears cackled, oblivious to Hultz's mood, as usual. "Goodbye? So long? Or adios, Gramps?"

"What I told him," Hultz said, staring in dismay at an incredibly cloudy, viscous-looking bead of sweat dangling from the tip of Buddy's nose, "is that there is no justice in this world."

"Well," Buddy said, "leastways the old fuck won't have to wait long for the next."

Hultz took a hard look at Sears as he began howling at his own wit, glanced back out at the "old fuck" hitting fungoes, looked back at Buddy —and had a sudden idea that made him smile so hugely that Sears, thinking his joke had finally been appreciated, started howling all over again . . .

The next morning Hultz made an early phone call to Pittsburgh. By lunchtime he'd made a dozen more—some to other camps in Arizona and Florida, some up to Saskatchewan, one back to Pitt, one to Kincaid, Oklahoma. The very next morning he received a call from Pittsburgh which he savored so much that he let it marinate in his mind all day. Then, after dinner, he phoned Papa Chance. "Meet me at my office!" he barked. "I've got one last question for you."

Papa was carrying his suitcase and wearing his Goin' Home clothes— plaid shirt, brown leather belt, baggy tan trousers—when he walked into Hultz's office. "One question, before you go," the manager repeated.

"Fire away," Papa said.

"I don't know what's got into our front office, but they've taken it into their cantankerous heads to shunt poor Buddy Sears up—or down, depending on how you look at it—to our Two A club in Saskatoon, Saskatchewan. So what I was wondering, my one question was, would you care to take his job as our pitching coach?"

Papa was completely stunned by this. So stunned, in fact, that he had to shut his eyes a while, in order to conjure another pure shedball response. When he was through, though, he'd come up with a regular Kamikaze. "I'd like it a *lot*," he said, "on one condition."

Hultz was immediately suspicious. "Name it," he said.

"Make me your stupid-situation reliever," Papa told him.

"My what?"

"Can I explain?"

"You damn well better."

"Baseball's a nice game, John, but we both know that the summers get muggy, the season gets long, there's the bus and plane rides, the extra innings and packed schedules, the loneliness, the drinking, and all the rest of it. What I'm saying is that sooner or later there comes some nights when the players' brains and bodies turn to Jell-O and the games get kind of strange. The result is what I call the 'stupid situation.'"

With no sign of comprehension, Hultz repeated, "Stupid situation."

"Like the butt end of a July doubleheader, say, where the other team scores fourteen runs in two innings, and you run through six or eight pitchers, and the fans all leave and the bullpen's empty, but you've still got three more outs to play. Or all those late-season games, after the team's been stripped by the big leagues and is out of the standings, where you're still on the road and there's a—"

"What the hell are you driving at?" Hultz snapped, waving his hand like his face was full of flies.

"Okay. All right. Listen, John. I'm *very* grateful for this offer, I'd *love* to be your pitching coach, and I'd throw body and soul into the job. But what I'm driving at is, I also want to play some ball—even if it's only as your stupid-situation reliever, and that—"

"God *damn* it, Chance! This is the opportunity of a *lifetime* and you're about to waste it! You're a baseball nonentity! You're a *zero*, fella! And I stuck my neck *way* out to get you this shot!"

"I may be a gimp and a zero and all sorts of other low-down things, John. But as your potential pitching coach it's my duty to tell you that, for three or so innings every other day, I'm also the best pitcher you've got."

"Arrogance will get you nowhere!"

"Honesty isn't arrogance, John."

"Okay, okay. So you can throw. I admit that. But you're not thinking like a coach here, Chance. Say you just worked your boys hard, for weeks, on some crucial technique, then strolled out on the mound, used it yourself, and got shelled. See what happened? You just lost all your credibility. You just painted the ugly picture that erased your thousand wise words."

"That's why I say 'stupid situation,' " Papa argued. "If, in the kind of noodle-bodied, no-brain baseball farces I'm thinking of, I went out and practiced what I preached, my students would be nothing but grateful no matter what happened. If I won they'd get baseball relief. If I got shelled they'd get comic relief. Either way they'd get a rest, which was what they really needed."

"I can't *believe* this!" Hultz huffed. "You shouldn't be asking me for *shit!*"

"But shit," Papa said, "is all I *am* asking for, John. I want to be the janitor who cleans up garbage games. And if you're worried about professional jealousy, I thought of that too. We can make an announcement. We can tell my pitchers I'm not competing for the Pirate jobs. I need to keep my family anchored in Camas the next couple years anyway, John. A pure, no-hope Tug is all I want to be."

Hultz had resumed gaping. So Papa took advantage of it: "Remember that road trip last July where you played nineteen games in eleven days? Remember that young outfielder, Jimmy Krentz, who had the nervous breakdown when it was over? Or the young reliever, Kleiner I think it was, who worked five times in a week and tore his rotator cuff? Or the August home stand with four straight doubleheaders, where you pitched your utility man, Pat Snell, wasn't it, and your left fielder too? And how 'bout that play-off game at Tucson with the basketball score, where you worked eight pitchers, including *all* your starters, and two of them had to—"

"All right!" Hultz barked. "Quit showin' off. I see you study your goddamned sports page."

"Listen, John," Papa said, with passion now. "I not only study it. I make the goddamned paper it's printed on. And I would take the lowest salary you give a player/coach to *stop* making it. So please don't think I'm picky. I want to help every way I can. I want to coach—*and* to pitch stupid relief."

"Chance," Hultz said. "You're a pain in the ass."

"John," Papa said. "I *love* playing baseball. And I'm still damned good at it."

"Christ," muttered Hultz.

–VIII–

Two days later we received this letter back home in Camas:

Dear Family,

Not sure if this is good news or bad, but I've been offered a couple odd jobs with the Tugs, and I'm going to accept. Immediate warning to all: not much money in it. $185 a month *less* than I was making at the mill! Second warning to Everett and other dreamers: no real ballplaying future in it either. But there's some chance of a steady coaching future. And, getting back to the economic part, let me say something blunt. Though I still dearly love you, Laura, I don't feel you're up to much that's good around the house these days. So what I'm thinking is, maybe you could get a job?

I'll be in Portland, and home if it's still standing, in two weeks. I know that's longer than I said, but I didn't expect to become the Tugs' new peanut vendor, let alone the jack-of-two-trades I'll explain about when I get home. I hope you'll all forgive me the selfish side of this. If it doesn't work out I'll quit and become something lucrative, like a bank robber. But this is so unexpected I just had to give it a try.

Love,

Papa

As usual, G. Q. Durham said it worst. In a letter of congratulations in which he tried, after God knows how many beers, to make Papa's feat relevant and even inspirational to Mama, he wrote:

. . . What's a big toe weigh, Laura? Three ounces? Because if so I believe our own dear Hubert is about three-ounces Christ. Get my meaning? I'm saying the man's toe died on the cross so a fallen thumb could bust up out its grave & live again? I'm saying we got nothing left now but to stand clear & see how high the blame thing rises!

The "blame thing" didn't rise at all really. But starting in 1965, at the preposterous age of thirty-five, Papa proceeded to enjoy five and a third seasons as a coach and left-handed pitcher of "stupid relief" for the Triple A Portland Tugs. Which was resurrection enough for us.

BOOK FOUR

The Left Stuff

EVERETT

Roger Maris,
Radical of the Sixties

*Who isn't suffering from aberration nowadays? You, I, all of us are in a
state of aberration. There are ever so many examples of it: a man sits
singing a song, suddenly something annoys him, he takes a pistol and
shoots the first person he comes across . . .*
—Madame Hohlakov, *The Brothers Karamazov*

Numbers, for all their vaunted accuracy, can be amazingly inaccurate
little doodads. The era we think of as "the Sixties" is an example of this.
According to arithmetic this improbable decade began on January 1,
1960, but those of us who snoozed through the years '60 through '62 for
the most part agree that they took place during the so-called Fifties. The
Sixties, as we know and love and hate them, didn't begin in earnest till a
subterranean nullity named Lee Harvey Oswald took it into his head to
go hunting in downtown Dallas in the autumn of '63. And they didn't
completely end till the year we call '73, when another nullity, this one a
penitent, secretly met with a journalist in a Washington, D.C., parking

lot and effectively did for Richard Outhaus Nixon what Oswald had done for J.F.K.

One of the great charms of professional baseball used to be that it provided us statistics-lovers with a kind of Mathematical Wildlife Refuge —a nationwide network of painstakingly calibrated and manicured playing fields wherein statistics could frolic about unmolested, appearing to those of us who admired them to possess accurate, consistent and at times even mythic meanings. True, the game had been marred off and on by absurdities and injustices, but like the nation that first invented then worshipped it, our National Pastime seemed to possess an ability to cough up new rules, definitions or heroes before a crisis ever quite stripped it of all credibility and appeal. Against its early lowbrow amateurism it pitted the two-league system and the "World" Series; against the tyranny of greed-crazed owners it hurled the Players Association; against the dull superiority of pitchers it threw the live ball and the shrunken strike zone; against discrimination it pitted Jackie Robinson, Hank Aaron, Roberto Clemente, Willie Mays.

But in the mythoclastic climate of the Sixties it was the statistics themselves, the very scriptures of baseball, that were finally called into question. And once our faith in the stat was undermined—once the same irresolvable complexities that muddied our knowledge of the outside world invaded the pristine arithmetic of the Refuge—the game we'd once seen as the heroic enactment of a living American mythology seemed to devolve overnight into that branch of the Entertainment Industry catering to those unable to outgrow their grammar school fascinations with hitting, spitting and throwing.

Many factors contributed to the Sixties' dissolution of statistical precision—platooning, relief pitching, night games, a longer schedule, artificial turf, indoor stadiums, designated hitters, divisional play-offs and rampant league expansion, to name a few. But without doubt, the most infamous contributions to baseball's apocryphal new arithmetic were the sixty-one 299-foot pop-ups which a crewcutted New York outfielder managed to boink, in the year 1961, over Yankee Stadium's 296-foot right-field fence. I am referring, of course, to Roger Maris's breaking of the single-season home run record of the Homeric Babe Ruth.

In a peculiar attempt to stem the tide of numerical unmeaning, then Major League Baseball Commissioner Ford Frick conducted a one-man witch-trial against Maris that culminated in the public tattooing of an asterisk to the new record—a punctuation mark intended, I assume, to serve the same general purpose as Hester Prynne's scarlet A. But this method of restoring credibility to the stats deserves an asterisk or two of its own. Think about it. In Frick we had a man who apparently believed that at the sight of a little black snowflake, a mere *, the myriad fans of the future would never cease to remind themselves that Maris's sixty-one-homer season had been eight games longer than Ruth's sixty-homer year. Never mind that due to league expansion and owner greed *everybody's* '61 season was eight games longer, and *all* post-Fifties' baseball accomplishments have deserved the same asterisk; never mind that Maris not only played his home games in the same stadium as Ruth, but faced significantly better pitching due to the higher mound and the advent of relief specialists; never mind that he endured far greater media pressure, overcame the disadvantage of night games and artificial lighting, and, thanks to injuries and illness, had to doink his sixty-one dingers in three fewer at-bats than St. Babe needed to blast his sixty. Ford Frick was a man of faith in the power of the *.

The perfect justice of a Hereafter is seldom obtainable in the here, but in the Otherworldly world of baseball lore the Commissioner's asterisk has in fact received an unusually just reward: question a crowd of baseball buffs today and you'll find that Frick, if he is remembered at all, is remembered solely as the guy who branded Maris's sixty-one homers with the*.

Whereas *everybody* remembers Roger Maris.

But what exactly is it that we remember? Is it the home-run-hitting, the skinhead haircut, the greatness of his team, or even the flawed record? I don't think so. I think it was a stranger sort of mark that Maris made on the minds of those who watched him closely that season. It was hard to articulate the disturbing aspect of his performance as it was occurring. But by season's end there was a growing suspicion that his new record might be more a tragedy than a victory, and that the key to this tragedy might be the unsettling transformation of the record-breaker himself . . .

Because Roger Maris was, by natural gift and inclination, not a fence-basher at all. He was a stupendous all-around athlete. Blessed with good foot speed, great bat speed and a slingshot arm, he was more a high-average hitter in the Roberto Clemente/Stan Musial tradition than a slugger in the Jimmy Foxx/Harmon Killebrew mold. He won a Golden Glove and the American League MVP award in 1960, and was clearly the best all-around player on the Yankees' pennant-winning team. But in 1961 a finger of fate seemed to reach down and diddle poor Number 9.

The proof of the fateful diddle was in his game: without knowing why he did it, Maris began to play ball like a different person. An obsessive person. A person who'd accidentally discovered and applied to baseball what the practitioners of countless modern military, industrial, economic and scientific disciplines had already learned: namely, that by jettisoning one's diverse abilities in order to condense and intensify the will like a magnifying glass intensifies sunlight, by forgetting all about being a complete person and throwing one's whole being into a single obsession, one stands a very good chance of achieving some narrow excellence. Such as an almost preternatural ability to boink 299-foot fly balls.

This brings us to a surprising definition. Insofar as the word "radical" implies a drastic departure from accepted thinking and practices, it is only accurate to say that this crewcutted all-American Midwest farm boy was in fact the first famous radical of the Sixties. Who but a radical would sacrifice all-around excellence to focus on a single, iconoclastic facet of his existence? Who but a radical could earn so much antipathy from the meat-and-potatoes populace for so little reason, but still go on choosing public misery for the sake of his cause? As this increasingly two-dimensional, nerve-powered, lifetime .260 hitter mounted his anxiety-ridden assault on the most famous feat of the three-dimensional, muscle-powered .342-hitting bon vivant whose bat built Yankee Stadium, even the most rabid New York fans began to feel that something odd was going on. Mickey Mantle also hit a lot of home runs in 1961—fifty-four of them, in fact. But the contrast between his and Maris's homers was vast. The Mick was just a canonical hero on a roll—a contemporary legend in chivalrous competition with legends of the past. Maris was a new kind of creature altogether. If Ruth was the Sultan of Swat, Maris was the Technician of Boink. For the sake of these boinks he had virtually given up the game of baseball, or at least given up the all-around game he'd played better than anyone just a year before. And the trouble that resulted was, in a sense, the same trouble into which the entire industrial world has fallen: *obsession works*. Not beautifully, and not without tremendous costs. But for Roger E. Maris it worked sixty-one times.

Numbers, for all their vaunted accuracy, can be amazingly inaccurate little doodads. When Ruth's record finally teetered and fell, Maris found that in the opinion of many he hadn't scaled a height or conquered a legend at all: he'd become an object of dislike. Many people felt, and even behaved (*), as if he were more the assassin of a legend than a conquering hero. When the Holy Relic Manufacturers trotted out their **"61 IN '61"** trinkets, the stuff wouldn't sell; when the kids took to the sandlots the following spring, they went right on pretending they were Mantle and Berra and Mays; when Maris himself began his '62 season in a slump, the fans booed his game and emotions into a complete collapse; and when the Yankees traded him away to St. Louis, instead of retiring his number, they casually handed it to Graig Nettles a few years later.

Maris was hardly the first technician to attain staggering fame through obsessive effort, only to later regret the cost. In his *Autobiography*—published a full century prior to Maris's feat—Charles Darwin made a confession that reads like a manifesto of the One-Pointed Specialist's inner condition:

> Up to the age of thirty, or beyond it, poetry of many kinds . . . gave me great pleasure, and even as a schoolboy I took intense delight in Shakespeare, especially in the historical plays. I have also said that formerly pictures [paintings] gave me considerable, and music very great, delight. But now for many years I cannot endure to read a line of poetry: I have tried lately to read Shakespeare, and found it so intolerably dull that it nauseated me. I have also lost almost any taste for pictures or music. . . . My mind seems to have become a kind of machine for grinding general laws out of large collections of fact, but why this should have caused the atrophy of that part of the brain on which the higher tastes depend, I cannot conceive . . . The loss of these tastes is a loss of happiness, and may possibly be injurious to the intellect.

That an all-consuming focus on a single object of desire could achieve a quantitatively spectacular result was no surprise to any thinking person in the early Sixties: the mushroom cloud that accompanied J. Robert Oppenheimer's dissection of the atom was an unforgettable demonstration of the general principle. But that the same intensity of focus which made any great quantitative achievement possible might also render it qualitatively bankrupt—that a Golden Glove MVP could accomplish a fabulous feat and end up looking, feeling and playing, the following year, like a battle-jagged vet just back from some interior front line—this was the "un-American" surprise and the bitter public lesson of Roger Maris's life.

Technical obsession is like an unlit, ever-narrowing mine shaft leading straight down through the human mind. The deeper down one plunges, the more fabulous, and often the more remunerative, the gems or ore. But the deeper down one plunges, the more confined and conditioned one's thoughts and movements become, and the greater the danger of permanently losing one's way back to the surface of the planet. There also seems to be an overpowering, malignant magic that reigns deep down in these shafts. And those who journey too far or stay down too long become its minions without knowing it—become not so much human beings as human tools wielded by whatever ideology, industry, force or idea happens to rule that particular mine. Another danger: because these mines are primarily mental, not physical, they do not necessarily mar or even mark the faces of those who have become utterly lost in them. A man or woman miles down, thrall to the magic, far beyond caring about anything still occurring on the planet's surface, can sit down beside you on a park bench or bleacher seat, greet you in the street, shake your hand, look you in the eye, smile genially, say "How are you?" or "Merry Christmas!" or "How about those Yankees?" And you will never suspect that you are in the presence not of a kindred spirit, but of a subterranean force.

In 1961 the best all-around player in baseball became a kind of machine for grinding out long fly balls. As he neared Ruth's record the man in Maris recognized the Technician of Boink for the inhuman force it was, and began to grapple with it, sensing that his balance—that is, his life— was at stake. He began to lose sleep, and to have trouble eating. His hair began to fall out in clumps. Near the end of the season he would break down during post-game interviews, sometimes ranting, sometimes weeping in front of reporters. Like Darwin and Oppenheimer, Maris found after attaining his end that he had little left with which to re-prove his humanity but his confusion and regret. He would say for the rest of his life that he wished he'd never heard of Ruth's record, let alone broken it. But he did break it—and radically altered our conception of baseball heroics in doing so. Millions of traditionalists never quite forgave him for this. And one such traditionalist may have been Roger Maris himself. That may explain why the Technician of '61 so soon became the Strike-out King of the mid-Sixties, the introverted beer distributor of the Seventies, and the cancer victim of 1985.

CHAPTER ONE

Our Brilliant Careers

Once you're where you think you want to be you're not there anymore.
  —Tony Gwynn, outfielder, San Diego Padres

–I–

If there were such a thing as an unadulterated baseball story, and if Papa's life had been one, I guess I would now describe his first few relief appearances, strain to make drama out of the year the Tugs won the PCL's Northern Division pennant (1968), carefully neglect to mention that their "world series" with the Southern Division champ was canceled on account of rain, and call it quits. But this is the story of an eight-way tangle of human beings, only one-eighth of which was a pro ballplayer. Ballplaying was Papa's art, but his family was his plight. Even his new nickname, "Papa Toe," implied that his baseball story couldn't be extricated from us. And on the day an eighth of us signed a contract to help coach and pitch "stupid relief" for the Tugs, it brought surprisingly little resolution or relief to our eight-way family tangle.

We were all very happy for him—Mama too, I'm glad to say. And when the season began we piled into the car—rebels and Adventists alike—and began making the pilgrimage down to Tug Stadium, where we lolled in our choice new all-season seats, watched Papa walk around in his Tug uniform, and waved like idiots whenever he happened to grin at us. But as the weeks passed and he continued to do nothing but stand in the dugout talking strategy with John Hultz, or coach first base, or at best stroll out to the mound to steady a rocky young pitcher, we began to find it necessary to tell each other how great it was to be a baseball family again. And then Mama and Bet began to stay home; and Peter and Freddy began to read books; and Everett and Irwin began to spend their time ogling the players' wives (who'd suddenly become shockingly close to us in age), and coddling their leaking, squalling infants in order to facilitate the ogling; and even I began to wonder whether my box seat was in any way preferable to my old outpost in the laurel hedge.

The basic baseball problem was that the season was too young and the team too full of energy and hope for "stupid relief" situations to arise. Hence the glory of Papa's resurrected baseball career consisted solely of seeing him in uniform—or, back home, of hardly seeing him at all. Both glories wore off fast. Thus did my siblings and I learn one of the hard lessons of life: the best way to strip the allure and dreaminess from a lifelong dream is, very often, simply to have it come true.

But the flip side of the same principle has enabled my brothers and me to maintain a great deal of dreaminess about our own little baseball careers . . .

–II–

Everett was the only one of us who really burned with the desire to play ball. But then any desire Everett ever had, he burned with it. What finally quelled this particular conflagration was the number of times he had to listen to high school coaches damn him with faint praise like "He makes up in desire what he lacks in ability," or "He's a real scrapper out there," or "Whatever else you have to say about him, that li'l Everett always gives it his best shot."

As a freshman at McLoughlin High, li'l Everett stood 5'5", weighed 130 pounds, played a sure-handed but feeble-armed catcher, hit .315 in the leadoff spot, and led his team in walks and on-base percentage. As a sophomore he played the same position for the JV B-team, but only hit

.270. As a junior, still stuck at5'5", if not 5'4" (I think that tension may have literally shrunk him an inch that year), he barely made varsity, was stolen blind as a second-string catcher, and hit .214 as one of those diminutive, coach-emasculated pinch hitters sent in against wild pitchers with orders to squat down low in hopes of a cheap walk. It was a year of total baseball humiliation. In fact it drove the family agnostic to search the soul he didn't even believe he had to decide whether or not to continue playing ball.

After several weeks of agonizing, Everett decided that his problem was not the fastballs being hurled past him by boys six or eight inches taller and a half hundred pounds heavier, but his eyesight. (What can you expect from a soul you don't believe you have?) He therefore began a kind of antiheroic quest, journeying first to an optometrist, who told him, "You've got eyes like an eagle!," then to an ophthalmologist, who said, "You're 20/20, son," then to a second optometrist, and a third, and so on, till finally he found some sort of eye quack who never did say, in writing, whether he was nearsighted or far, but who at least agreed to sell him a natty-looking pair of glasses.

The odd thing was, the things worked. Whether it was luck, or placebo, or whether he simply needed a homeopathic dose of window between himself and those big pitchers, Everett went out for second base as a tortoise-shelled senior, fought his way into the starting lineup, and even became something of a standout. Though he looked (in the words of one of Irwin's girlfriends) "cute as a button" in his big specs, his style of play was far from buttonlike: he fought with umps, fought with opposing players, made only three errors all season, hit .281, "did some real scrapping out there," "made up in desire what he lacked in ability," "gave it his best shot," helped his and Peter's team finish second in the district, and scored the winning run in the play-off game that sent McLoughlin High to its first state tournament in two decades. He even began to talk (while Peter reddened and Papa tried not to smile) about college ball, future minor league tryouts, and a Chance family dynasty.

He then struck out four times in a 15 to 2 loss to North Wenatchee in the play-off opener, handed his new infielder's mitt to the first kid he passed on the street afterward, stomped his superfluous glasses into the sidewalk, and commenced to grow head and facial hair and study politics and poetry.

–III–

To reach the crappy little ballfield where we JV B-teamers went about the blooper-riddled chaos which we, with the crazed optimism of young Zen students, also called "practice," you had first to traverse the football field and the quarter-mile cinder oval where the track team worked out, then skirt the varsity baseball team's posh diamond. So every day, if I dawdled along slowly enough, I got to sneak a look both at Irwin—the new Washington State prep record-holder in the javelin—and at Peter—the two-time All-State center fielder—before slinking off to my Sorry-State career as a B-grade first baseman.

Like all earthly pleasures, though, dawdling had its price: those wide-open, grassy expanses were, for me at least, a psychological minefield. The "mines" were a number of adult American males, all of whom happily barked in reply to the name "Coach." The "explosions" were caused by the coaches' unending readiness to ignore the "Comparisons Are Odious" adage. It was my being one of the famous Chance brothers that brought on the comparisons. And it was my athletic abilities that made them odious.

That I wasn't ashamed of my baseball prowesslessness is, I think, eloquent testimony to the noble character of my family. I was close to spastic on a ballfield, and they all knew it, but with Papa's eternal minor-leaguing setting the cautionary example, my family had become as athletically tolerant as Babcock was religiously intolerant. Perhaps part of the tolerance stemmed from an unspoken suspicion that the cause of my spasticity was poor vision in the eye Papa had long ago punched. But I'd noticed no Before & After contrast. I think I simply inherited Mama's contradictory love of ballplayers and inability to deal with having things thrown at her. At any rate, my diamond exploits, though less lauded than Papa's or Peter's, were considered no less interesting or enjoyable around our suppertable, for my family had an unfaltering willingness to make oral literature (be it history, farce or myth) of any sort of baseball escapade. The game in which I made three errors and watched three called third strikes in five innings, for instance, was viewed as a game in which I had taken part in six interesting and enjoyable baseball feats. It was a mere quibble, to the Chance clan, that all the enjoyment happened to have been had by the opposing team.

But at the lofty level of high school, the athletic system of values is not

defined or governed by one eccentric family. It is the Royal & Ancient
Brotherhood of Coaches that calls the shots there. And it is, in my experience, a rare high school coach who cherishes the athlete whose chief
virtue is the enjoyment he gives to the opposing team . . .

"Who's that sorry little tortoise?" the varsity track coach, Bobby Edson,
bawled into the face of the JV A-team baseball coach on April 20, 1966—
a date I remember perfectly because (1) it was Hitler's birthday and (2) it
was the day I hung up my mitt, cap and cleats forever. Bobby Edson, like
most coaches, was a kind of mystic: he believed the cosmos was endowed
with an ineffable muffling system that rendered all the racist, sexist,
tasteless and denigrating remarks made by coaches inaudible to the students about whom they bellowed them.

"That there, believe it or not," bawled the JV skipper (another muffler
mystic), "is the youngest Chance brother."

"Naw!" Edson blored. "I mean that *fat* kid, with the goggles. The one
gapin' at my Winnie tossin' his javelin out there."

"Yup. That's Toe's youngest. Katie, they call 'im. Appropriate too, I
hear."

"Think he might firm up any?" Edson wondered. "Wasn't Winnie kind
of a chunk at that age?"

I felt their eyes on my back now, probing my bike tires, X-raying my
infrastructure, analyzing my aura for signs of "Late Bloomer" potential.
"Nope," the JV CAT-scanner finally sighed. "Winnie's a rock. Always has
been. Damn nice kid's the rap on Katie there. But no speed, no suds, no
arm, no nuthin'."

I kept my back turned to hide the slow incineration of my face. Meanwhile the varsity baseball coach, Donny Bunnel, joined them from somewhere, and turned their attentions back to the two family prodigies by
bellowing, "Can you feature what my team'd be doing with Irwin battin'
cleanup behind Pete instead o' chuckin' spears around out there like a
goddamned Jaboom?"

"Shit, Coach," Edson retorted. "Can you picture what *we'd* be doing
with Pete winnin' sprints and quarters and anchorin' relays instead of
doodlin' around your pissant ballfield?"

"Ought to breed 'em," said the JV geneticist.

"There you go," said Edson.

"Get old Toe to sow a wild oat or two, an' us harvest the crop," said
the JV agriculturalist.

"There you go."

"Any more of'm comin' up at all, Donny?" the JV genealogist wondered.

"Twin girls is it, I hear," said Bunnel.

"Too bad."

"Yep. Too damn bad."

"What's become of the oldest?" Edson asked Bunnel. "Kinda colorful character, ol' Herbert, wudn't he?"

"Everett," the JV pundit corrected.

"Oh, he was colorful all right," Bunnel snorted. "He was a fuckin' handful!"

"So what's he up to now, Coach?"

"Ain't heard boo. Shall we ask Katie?"

"There you go."

"Hey, Chance!" Bunnel bellowed. "Come on over here, li'l buddy!"

I turned around, faked a "Who? Me?" look, then trotted over, trying my li'l buddy best to outgrin them. "Coach, Coach, Coach," I said, giving a democratic nod to each. "What can I do you for?"

"We were just wonderin'," Edson said, "what's become of that brassy brother Herbert of yours."

"You mean Everett?" I asked.

"What I tell you?" the JV wazir crowed.

"Now why do I want to call him Herbert?" Edson muttered.

"So what's he up to now, Katie?" Bunnel asked.

"My name," I said, as politely as possible, "is Kincaid."

"Picky picky picky," smirked Bunnel.

But I'd just had a minor brainstorm. "It's not me that cares, Coach," I said in a stage whisper. "It's my big brother Pete. He gets *wild* about teasing! Why, he just flat *quit* his summer camp softball team when the coach kept calling this boy named Pat 'Patricia.' "

Bunnel turned pale for a second, then grinned and clapped me on the shoulder. "So then, *Kincaid!*" he cried. "What did you say ol' *Everett* was doin' these days?"

"He's up at Washington," I said. "Got a pretty decent scholarship."

The grin vanished. All three coaches gaped at me in disbelief. I didn't get it for a second. Then, reading their one-track, one-diamond minds, I added, "An *academic* scholarship. He aced his SATs is all."

"Ohhhhhhhhh!" went the coaches, relaxing completely. "A Husky now, is he?" "Up at U Dub, is he?" "Damn!" "That's great." "Good for him!"

"A good student, Everett," opined the JV emir, "when he kept his trap shut."

"But good as he was," Bunnel gloated, "he wasn't near the student my Peter is."

"I hear your peter's quite the little student all right," Edson sniggered. "I heard all about you and the new Español teacher!"

Unison: *Hawr hawr hawr hawr!*

"Hey now!" Bunnel huffed. "Clamp it, Bobby!"

"Yes, Bobby!" Edson moaned. "Please! Clamp it harder—*she* said!"

Repeat chorus: *Hawr hawr hawr hawr!*

"Uh, er, you're a pretty fair student yourself, I hear, Kincaid," Bunnel sputtered.

"Not ol' Kincaid!" wheezed Edson. "He hasn't *touched* that Spanish teacher!"

Hit it: *Whaw whaw whaw whaw!*

McLoughlin's coaches were not complicated men.

"So what's Everett studying up at U Dub?" the JV wazoo asked.

"Typing, I bet," Bunnel cut in. "Like types o' taverns, types o' beer, types o' hell-raisin', types o' hangovers . . ." But he was a temporary outcaste now: nobody deigned to *hawr-hawr* with him.

"How 'bout types o' coeds, Donny?" Edson cracked. "Types o' positions, types o' lubrications, types o' hot water to get into with the wife, types o'—"

"Stow it, Bobby!"

"Oh yes, Bobby! Please! Stow it harder—*she* said!"

Whawr whawr whawr whawr!

"What's Everett really studying, though, Katie?" Bunnel asked.

"Kincaid," I said.

"Oh, damn!" Bunnel looked genuinely panic-stricken. "I'm sorry, Kincaid! I didn't mean it."

"He meant it!" Edson hollered. "He meant every filthy word! *Katie* he called you! So tell Pete to quit the sumbitch's ball team pronto, and come on out for track!"

Whaw whaw whaw whaw!

Red-faced and outnumbered, Bunnel lamely repeated, "So what did you say Everett was studying up at U Dub?"

Without even thinking, and while the other two coaches were still chuckling, I answered, "He seems to be focusing on modern poetry at the moment."

Then a wonderful thing happened: for maybe five full seconds the coaches went dead, like three big TVs the word "poetry" had somehow unplugged—

and the day grew not perfect, nor still, but still enough to hear perfectly the singing of a thousand red-winged blackbirds in the swamp
beyond our diamonds—a choir, tremendous, convening there daily, their
ecstasy reduced to white noise by our first catch or throw—till this moment: the coaches' decommissioning: a word . . . "poetry". . . and
their song came raining out of the cottonwoods, innocent, joyous, pouring over anyone willing to listen. The rush of understanding was too
quick and condensed and physical to call a "thought": I simply knew, via
song, sunlight, redwings and cottonwoods, that there was a world I was
born to live in, that the men I was standing beside lived in another, and
that as long as I remembered this their words would never hurt me again.
I knew—the redwings were all telling me—that there was ancient ground
here, and ancient songs, and that if I laid my mitt, cleats and uniform
aside I could stand on that ground, and maybe learn to sing on it
too . . .

"Modern poetry," Coach Bunnel repeated, looking as though Everett
had somehow betrayed him. And I was suddenly hard put not to laugh—
or to start singing.

"He was always a little different, was ol' Herbert," Edson murmured.

"Ol' Everett," the JV savant corrected. But it no longer mattered. I
suddenly liked the way Edson got the name wrong. I felt free to like all
three of these men now, because I'd realized I didn't have to *become*
them. I was standing right next to a world in which Everett was Herbert,
blacks were Jabooms, Pete and Irwin were heroes, and I was a no speed,
no suds, no arm nuthin'. But I was not standing *in* it. Some simple shift
inside me had turned their words into the harmless white noise, and the
blackbirds' singing into the heart of my day.

Ospreys eat fish. Deer eat foliage. Switch their diets and they'll die.

I gave my first unguardedly friendly nod ever to each coach, told them
I had to go, walked back to the locker room, took off my baseball uniform, put on my street clothes, and set out unencumbered into the
singing, the cottonwoods, the entire spring day.

–IV–

*H*ey, Kincaid. How's it hangin', buddy?
Little limp to suit me, Donny.
Sing it: *Hawr hawr hawr hawr.*

But hey! What about you? How's that affair with the Spanish teacher going?

Oh! Hot damn! Just great, Kade! Thickish legs, but what a pair o' yum-yums! My wife's flatter'n plywood, y'know. Say, though. Has Everett sent you any more o' them rapturous letters 'bout Whitman or Pound or Yeats or any o' them bruisers?

Not lately, Donny.

Well, when he does, swing on by the office so us coaches can give 'er a read. We're pretty excited, y'know. We're thinkin', the way that brother o' yours used to scrap out there at second base, he's gonna make one hell of a fine poet!

Hey! Okay, Donny. I'll do it. And give those yum-yums your best shot for me.

Hey! Will do, Kade. Wake up! Hey, Kincaid! Wake up! Your brother's up."

"Oh! Hey. Thanks Mr. Ledbetter."

I was lolling on the sun-drenched bleachers, by the varsity diamond, with old Spaz Ledbetter, a retired janitor, a baseball fanatic, and the only other village idiot besides me who came most days just to watch the varsity team practice. Peter was in the batter's cage. Lance Clay was pitching—and smiling like a two-hundred-pound gray-haired princess on a parade float as he threw.

Mr. Clay taught math, but he'd played minor league ball ages ago, and had by far the best baseball mind and body on the McLoughlin High faculty. Since he wasn't the sort of jackass who could bray at kids all day, he let Donny Bunnel coach the team and grab the "glory." But most of the real coaching that got done, Mr. Clay did. He was also the perfect BP pitcher. He was left-handed, like Papa, had pinpoint control, so the players didn't have to worry about getting beaned, and since he was in his upper forties the only pitches he had left were a crisp but predictable curve, a no-hop fastball and a change-up he betrayed with a sniff. ("Allergic to deception," Peter said when he noticed it.) Clay was still too much for most varsity players, but Pete lined every pitch he threw; never popped one, never chopped one, never put anything on the ball but the meat of the bat. And Mr. Clay, as usual, lost all track of time and the rest of his team, and just poured them down the pipe like water. *Zzzooop!* went his pitches. *Fwack!* answered Peter's bat. *Zzzooop, fwack! Zzzooop, fwack!* The two of them were a show.

Then Coach Donny Bunnel, fresh from his daily gabfest over at the football field, strutted into the dugout, clapped his hands, and hollered, "Hit-and-run!"

Pete nodded, and punched his next three drives over into right field.

"Sacrifice!" yelled Bunnel.

Peter bunted four or five tricklers down the first- and third-base lines.

"Okay!" he hollered. "Now try for a tater!"

Lance Clay's parade-float smile vanished, but he dutifully grooved a fastball. Peter bunted it straight back on a line. Clay caught it, and the smile was back. But Bunnel wouldn't have it. "Come on. Smack it, Pete. I wanna see some loft."

"I don't hit taters, Coach," Peter said.

"Your turncoat spear-chuckin' brother sure as hell does," Bunnel said.

"Irwin's no turncoat," Peter said. "He never was a ballplayer. He was just a freak of nature with a bat."

"Is that any way to talk about your brother?" Bunnel asked.

"I'm *quoting* my brother," Pete said. "He's a lot smarter than most people think. Why do you think he went out for track?"

"Tell you what, hotshot," said Coach Bunnel. "Just shuttup and show me how far you can hit the ball."

To my surprise, Peter did. He hit a fly to deep center, a pop-up to shallow left, fanned two pitches completely, then hit two more to center. The flies all traveled maybe 300 feet, and were easily caught. They looked like line drives that got too big for their britches. Pete was leading the league in hitting and the state in stolen bases; he led his team in walks, slugging, RBIs, on-base percentage and almost every other stat that was good. But Irwin, as a sophomore, had hit six home runs in half a season, and in practice had once crushed a Clay fastball 460-some feet. So, like a big bratty kid, Bunnel wanted the brother he couldn't have. "Put some soul into it!" he goaded.

"He's gettin' blisters," Mr. Clay said. "Next batter."

Later the same day, Lance Clay had pulled Peter aside and told him never to screw with his swing for a meathead like Bunnel again. "Just keep hitting line drives," he said, "and pretend you can't help it."

Pete said he would. Clay then told him that Papa, in his Tacoma days, had been one of the best minor league ballplayers he'd ever seen.

"I think he's one of the best still," Peter said.

"So what do you think," Clay asked, "about your skills, compared to his?"

Peter reddened a little. "No offense," he said, "but that's the kind of question I'd expect Coach Bunnel to ask."

"Well," Mr. Clay said, "I asked it. And for a reason."

"I think I'm eighteen and Papa's thirty-seven," Peter said. "I think I play high school outfield and he pitches Three A relief. So it's apples and oranges."

"I hear you hit his pitching," Clay said. "Does that imply anything about your apples and oranges?"

Peter shook his head. "It's just BP. He never knocks me down, never brushes me back. It's not for blood. You know how huge the difference is."

"What I know," Clay said, "I doubt you'd want to hear."

Peter said nothing for a second. Then he smiled and said, "That's a good way of making somebody want to hear something."

Clay nodded, and turned serious. "I think you're scared," he said. "Your father's been your teacher, he's been like a god to you boys. And I think you're afraid to outshine him. I think that's why your hitting fell apart at the end of last season."

"I was off," Peter admitted. "But I didn't exactly fall apart. I hit .280 in the play-offs."

"Which, given your average at the time, was the equivalent of a .300 hitter batting .065."

"Spoken like a true math teacher," Peter mumbled.

"I'm not trying to insult you," Mr. Clay said. "I just think it's time you *did* outshine your father . . . because you've got more to be afraid of than that."

"Like what?" Peter asked.

"You worry about being as good as your dad. But listen to an old baseball man who's studied you both. That ship has sailed and gone, Peter. You are *much, much better.*"

After a soliloquy like that, Mr. Clay must at least have expected some show of surprise. But Pete just stood there the way he does, weighing the words without expression. Then he shook his head. "No," he said. "That's not it, Mr. Clay. That's not what I'm afraid of at all."

And now it was Clay whose face showed the surprise.

"What I'm afraid of, concerning baseball," Peter said, "is that I'm going to hurt my father. It might happen soon, too."

Thinking Peter lacked confidence, thinking he was only afraid of disappointing Papa, Mr. Clay smiled his parade-float smile again, and said,

"How? How do you think you're going to give your dad this big baseball hurt?"

But Peter had another surprise for Mr. Clay. "I know I'm good," he said softly. "Maybe as good as Papa, in a different way. What I don't know is whether, after this season, I'm going to play any more baseball at all."

Lance Clay knew at once that Peter was telling the truth, but it was completely unforeseen, and it hit him like a beanball. His face drained of color, his crow's-feet lost their ingrained look of kindness, and his eyes filled with confusion, then hurt, then anger. "Well," he said. "You're right. If that's what you decide, you *will* hurt your father. And other people too, if that matters to you. Me, for instance."

With that, Mr. Clay turned, and walked away. And though Pete played out the season—and never played better—he never saw the parade-float smile again.

–V–

John Hultz didn't use Papa even once in May or June of the '65 season, but Papa didn't gripe. What he did do was keep flaunting his stuff every chance he got. For instance he raised Hultz's ire (and duplicated a stunt he'd pulled against his dad's WSU teams as a twelve-year-old) by striking out Tug hitters when he was supposed to be throwing BP. And whenever he was out in the bullpen warming up his young relievers, he fired curves, knucklers and G.Q. garbage-balls back at them to keep his hand in. In July, though, the Pirates (then in fourth place in the National League) made a huge raid on the Tugs, calling up their two best starting pitchers and their shortstop, then dealing away two outfielders and a reliever. It pretty well gutted the team. And that was when Johnny Hultz, figuring their pennant hopes were shot, started using Papa once a week or so in "stupid relief."

At first Hultz claimed he was just indulging an old man who'd become a friend. But in August the Tugs went on an unexpected tear, and something happened to Hultz's claim: he was "indulging" the old man two and three times a week now, for three, six, even nine outs per outing, and not just in lopsided games. He didn't discuss this heavy new reliance with anyone, least of all Papa, but it wasn't hard to figure out. When Papa entered even a ridiculous game, even a slugfest or a late-night extra-inning War of Zombies, there were three increasingly predictable results.

The first was that the other team found it very difficult to score runs—which was of course good, but not good enough to justify Papa's nonprospective presence in a prospects' league. But the second result was more mysterious, and even more valuable, so I'll try to describe it at some length.

With Papa on the mound, the young Tugs for some reason seemed to get a whole new lease on their ballplaying lives. Instead of a potentially glorious, in point of fact underpaid, nerve-wracking, tenuous career, baseball began to seem like a decent way to simply pass a summer's evening. *Look at that sinkerball!* they'd say. *Look at that fastball for chrissake. You can be old and busted down as the Toe-man and still play this damned game. And look at him grin back at his bullpen. Look how much fun the old fart's having! That's the way you do it!* Watching Papa have his fun, many of the young players began to have trouble recalling just where their anxieties and personal crises had been located. Their body language would change. They'd begin to make wisecracks and dumb cracks and old-fashioned novocaine-brained baseball chatter. Then, as far as Hultz or anyone else could tell, they'd stop thinking entirely and just play ball for the pleasure of it—and it is a well-known fact that when entire teams stop thinking and start playing for fun, wonderful things happen.

It's hard to overemphasize the importance of this kind of thought-stopping influence, so let's consider it from another angle. A pitcher throws a baseball eighty or ninety miles per hour at a hitter standing just twenty yards away. This means the hitter has about the same amount of time to decide what to do with a pitch as a chestnut-backed chickadee needs to take a crap. As any good birder will tell you, this is *very* little time. Nevertheless, ballplayers spend it in a wide variety of ways. One of the common options, and possibly the worst, is to spend it thinking. In the time it takes a pitch to reach the plate, a really quick-minded hitter can get in as many as five syllables' worth of baseball thoughts. Here are three typical examples:

1. "Inside . . . *ooops!* . . . strike."
2. "Change-up . . . *shit!* . . . fastball."
3. "Fastball . . . *oh damn!* . . . change-up."

The obvious moral here is that once a pitch is released, there are very few baseball thoughts worth thinking. This is why the preferred option of most good hitters is to spend pitch-to-plate time not thinking at all. "No-Think" is the name Peter gave to his mental state while awaiting a pitch —because a harrowing complication in this option is that even the thought "Don't think!" is a thought. No-Think means: the ball comes:

react. No decision-making, no reasoning. A pure, carefully trained, hope-fully inspired reflex is all that's wanted. And the difficulty of achieving No-Think—the paradoxically effortless effort required to gain access to this realm of pure reflex—is *the* explanation of virtually all the quirkiest quirks of ballplayers the world over. It's what leads them to chew the unseemly substances, scratch the unseemly body parts, chant the gibber-ish, browbeat the Lord, sleep with their bats, pop mystery pills, worship everything from Shiva's lingam to dead chicken parts, and so on . . .

So the Tugs' inexplicable transformation, with Papa on the mound, from a bevy of uptight young ballthinkers into a loose team of No-Think ballplayers was no small thing. On the contrary, it was the kind of inexpli-cable blessing that smart managers will hire, fire, lie, cheat, pray, beg and steal for—because more often than not it leads to a third predictable result: wins.

John Hultz never did learn to like the idea of a pitching coach who outshone his students, and he never quit grumbling about it. But if a triweekly demonstration of tranquillity-under-adversity by old Papa Toe was what his boys needed to get Result #3, Hultz decided he could live with that. By early September he'd even developed a special sign for it: back in the days before dugout-to-bullpen phones, a skipper simply raised his right arm for his right-handed reliever or his left for the lefty. But when Johnny wanted Papa, he would raise neither. Instead he'd start wandering around the dugout, grumbling in disgust. Then he'd shake his head, heave a cranky sigh, glare out at his bullpen, lift his left leg like a dog at a hydrant—and point at his big toe.

–VI–

Irwin (when he didn't strike out) was indeed a "tater" hitter, and he had an absolutely astounding arm. But we knew all along that his heart had never been smitten by the Chance family game—and his head was out of the question. He led every team he ever played on in the kind of errors born not of inability but of gross space-cadetism. He was the kind of outfielder who would rifle a perfect throw from deep left to home—when the runner was on his way to second. He once made a brilliant diving catch for out number three, did a somersault, bounced to his feet, stuck ball and glove in his armpit, tipped his cap in response to the fans' and teammates' frantic screaming, jogged clear on in to the dugout—and found that there'd only been two outs, and that while he was jogging along in glory, two runs had scored. So it was no great disappointment to anyone but the tater-loving Bunnel when Irwin's baseball career came to an abrupt end.

The end came—as with me—on the way to practice during his sophomore year. What happened was that he spotted an abandoned javelin jabbed into the grass beside the cinder track, wondered how the thing might look sailing through the blue spring sky, grabbed it, stepped over to the empty football field, and found out. In his own words he "just took a little run an' gave 'er the ol' heave-ho."

"Looks neat, dudn't it?" he remarked to Coach Bobby Edson, who'd come running over in hysterics while it was still in the air . . .

"Whaddya call those things again?" he asked, while it was still in the air . . .

Edson just sank to his knees, while it was still in the air . . .

Irwin felt confused, but sank to his knees too once it landed: he thought Coach Bobby wanted to share a spontaneous moment's worship. He wasn't far wrong either. What Edson wanted to do was mark the rip Irwin's baseball cleats made in the turf when he released the javelin, go get his tape, measure the throw, and worship that—because Edson knew at a glance that without loosening up, without knowing a thing about technique, without even setting down his damned baseball glove, Irwin had just broken the school whaddya-call-it record by an easy five yards.

If Irwin had attempted, at that point, to continue on over to the ballfield, I think Edson would have suffered a nervous breakdown. The Coachly Talk of Inspiration he proceeded to give Irwin may even have been a kind of nervous breakdown—which I suppose only made it a paragon of its kind. What it depicted was the absolute certainty of javelin-throwing putting Irwin on a fast track to glory: league and state records would come first; then the free four-year ticket to the major university, not to mention the coed or coeds *(hawr hawr hawr!)* of his choice or choices; after that were the record-shattering performance at the '72 Olympics, the front of the Wheaties boxes, and "for a guy with your looks" probably Hollywood. Possibly due to the LA smog the future grew slightly hazier here, but Congress, if not the White House, and later the throne on God's immediate right were likelihoods.

But Coach Bobby's sermon, like most, was a waste of breath: Irwin had been sold on the javelin the instant he'd let fly. As he put it at dinner that night, "Why slouch around in an outfield-type situation waiting to get to throw things to certain bases when I can go out for track and throw those whaddya-call-its as far and often as I want?"

–VII–

Another brilliant career that developed in our family during these years was unrelated to athletics, but so closely related to our athletes that it produced positive athletic results. It was Mama's business career. When Papa, in '65, had written from the Tugs' spring camp suggesting that she stop fighting home holy wars and get herself a job, Mama never argued, never sulked, never said a word. She just took him up on it—with a vengeance.

Having spent our childhoods thinking of Mama as the ultimate Beatrix Potter Meets Mary & Martha Hausfrau, I think we all half expected her initial ventures into the rough-and-tumble world of commerce to go about as smoothly as, say, Peter Rabbit's first tour of Mr. MacGregor's garden. At the very least I hoped she'd have no more fun than I was having on my 5 A.M. paper route. But I was in for a disappointment so complete that it soon gave way to admiration and pride: using the same ferocious energy and organizational skills with which she formerly ran our family, Mama built up a housecleaning service that within a year employed seven people, including Bet, Freddy and—surprise!—me. (She didn't even try to make me eat crow: she just offered me a chance to triple my income and to sleep till 7:30 again.)

I was good at math, slow at cleaning, and have a pleasant voice if I do say somyself, so when the housecleaning service grew huge Mama made me her secretary, and she became our full-time quality-control inspector and CEO. But as with any good tycoon, one successful venture did not begin to satisfy her: when she saw a window of opportunity, she dove through it. The housecleaning service set up connections that dropped a fairly lucrative gardening and lawn-mowing business right into Irwin's lap. And conversations with a housecleaning client who happened also to be a chef turned into a home dessert-making operation that within two years catered to several of Portland's best restaurants, and helped Bet and Freddy start salting away bucks for college.

Put it all together, even subtracting the good spending money that Irwin, the twins and me were all making, and Mama's average income was soon a cool four hundred a month more than Papa Toe was making. And all through this rocky period of their marriage she would have me total her earnings each Friday before sunset, write out a whopping check for ten percent of that total, write this tithe amount on the outside and stick the check on the inside of an envelope with the First SDA Church of Washougal's address stenciled on it, and prop it against the Canada geese salt and pepper shakers on the kitchen table till morning—where Papa and all the rest of us would be sure to notice it as often as possible. "You see!" was the unspoken message she was sending to every infidel in the house: "If you gave the Lord His due share, *you* could be making this kind of money too!"

She was still proselytizing. But at least she was learning to be subtle about it. And—ironic as it may have felt to Papa—her business successes had turned his little baseball miracle into something he could afford to relax and enjoy.

–VIII–

In late August 1965, an *Oregonian* sportswriter named Deke Gant interviewed Papa by telephone, rapped out a well-intended but embarrassingly "poignant" story about him, and called the thing "A Baseball Lazarus." Fearing some gruesome new nickname could be at hand, Papa did his best to dodge the phone calls and ignore the teasing that followed. But he needn't have worried. The nickname Papa Toe had caught on with the Tug radio broadcasters by then, and they soon had it tattooed on the minds of the fans for good. The only effect the "Lazarus" story ended up having on Papa was one I think he enjoyed (though he would never admit it): it helped win him his first genuine hometown fan club.

To introduce them properly I must begin by explaining that Portland, Oregon, has always been a notoriously bad baseball town. Tug games, even on 25¢-beer nights, are seldom attended by more than four or five thousand. On free-admission nights the stadium will fill to its 18,000 capacity, but it's an aficionadoless mob of Little Leaguers, Brownies, harried den mothers and wretchedly beerless dads who cheer more loudly for the mascot idiot crashing into walls in a plastic Tugboat suit than for anything that occurs on the ballfield. The genuine Portland baseball night is what other sports towns call an off-night; it is attended by a bemused, weather-beaten, decidedly blue-collar clump of about a thousand people—the true, diehard Tug junkies; and though his face and form had already been familiar to them, these were the people to whom Papa was formally introduced by the "Baseball Lazarus" yarn. And it was love at second sight.

Tug junkies are not your average baseball fans. They are baseball moths who come to the stadium because it's got the brightest lights and the most highly skilled game within a two-hundred-mile radius; they come to nurse damp smokes and warming beers, to frustrate the peanut and ice-cream vendors by eating their own brown-bag snacks, to watch a light-whitened ball zoom around for fifty-four outs, and to cheer or boo the exceptionally good or bad bits of zooming. But they don't come to root. That's one of the things I like best about them. Tug junkies are tried-and-true, case-hardened *minor* league baseball fans. They know their players will be whisked off to the Bigs the moment they get the least bit heroic. They know the entire team will be sold to a different major league franchise every few seasons. They know Portland is a shit baseball town and that these ephemeral bands of young hopefuls and sinking old pros are the only show they're ever going to see. So why get all loyal and excited about it? Let the rooters move to New York or LA and add their feeble squawking to the Yanks' and Dodgers' legions. For a Tug junkie, a fix is a fix and to hell with who wins. And what these people loved about Papa, I'm sure, is that he was one of them. He had the kids, the graying temples, the mill-town past, the industrial injury. He was a fellow moth, making less money than he'd made at the mill because he too loved the lights and the skilled bits of zooming. And his modest resurrection from Crown Z to Tugville was a lot more comprehensible to them than the usual hotshot twenty-year-old's quick tour of duty en route to the bigs.

But with their attention upon him now, the Tug moths couldn't help but notice what Johnny Hultz had also discovered: Papa Toe's insertion into a mid-inning crisis often made good things happen to the entire team. The moths' reaction to this perception was nothing like Hultz's, however. What they began to do—to the dismay of a Tug pitching coach whose last name happened to be Chance—was boo the ears off of any young Tug starter who got himself into the least bit of a jam. And if Hultz didn't act upon their booing, if he only sent Papa to the mound to try and steady the poor lad rather than replace him, all thousand of them set their beers and smokes aside and at the top of their nicotine-tanned lungs started chanting, so that you could hear it on the streets four or five blocks away: *Papa Toe! Papa Toe! Papa Toe! Papa Toe!*

It may have been silly, I may be a sap, but the first time I heard them do this I leaned down over my program and wept till Irwin and Everett finally took off their jackets and draped them over my back to hide me.

After that it was just plain fun, though. "Did you hear those damn morons in the stands again?" Papa would grouse after the games. "Papa Toe my ass!"

"Yeah." "Shoot!" "Damn!" "What a buncha jerks!" we'd all reply—in hoarse, scratchy voices.

–IX–

In May 1966, Peter chose a full academic scholarship to Harvard over baseball scholarships to three different Pac Ten schools and pronounced his athletic aspirations dead. He then tortured a handful of college scouts by hitting .667 in the district play-offs, and going three for four as Mc-Loughlin lost a heartbreaker to South Pasco in the first round of the state tournament. His contradictory retirement and great hitting weren't the final confusion Pete had to offer his alma mater either: when the team voted him Player of the Year for the second straight season, he brought his baseball career to an unsettling close by refusing, at the post-season banquet, to accept the award.

Irwin and Mama were at some sort of church extravaganza that night, and Everett was in Seattle. But the rest of us attended the banquet, and were equally flabbergasted when Peter stepped to the podium amidst a round of wild applause, glanced at his little trophy, set it on the floor by his feet, turned crimson, and said, "Direct democracy doesn't exist in the United States anymore."

It was a jarring non sequitur. A few hopeful giggles anticipated a punchline. But it never came. Peter said, "People who vote for candidates bought by private business interests are not politically free in any real sense. That's why I feel that voting has become a farce. And an award like this one, though I know it's well meant, feeds us right into this farcical system. I don't want my life to be a farce. So I'm sorry, but I can't accept this. I'm quitting baseball anyway, so the award should go to somebody who'd really appreciate it."

The clammy silence that followed was bad enough. But then Peter spoke up again, saying that, in parting, he wanted to quote a man he'd once thought was a fool but had lately come to respect very much. " 'This world in arms,' " he read from a sweaty scrap of paper he held in both shaking hands, " 'is not spending money alone. It is spending the sweat of its laborers, the genius of its scientists, the hopes of its children . . . . This is not a way of life at all in any true sense. Under the cloud of threatening war, it is humanity hanging from an iron cross. It—"

"Which famous Communist are you recitin' for us there, Pete?" the freshman baseball coach, Nord Curtis, bellowed. And it was a popular sentiment: there were nods, murmurs of approval, a smattering of applause. But it couldn't have worked out worse for old Nord.

"I hate to tell you this," Peter murmured, "but I was quoting Dwight D. Eisenhower."

There was one brief chuckle—from Lance Clay, I think. But the rest of the auditorium fell into a sullen confused silence. And as Peter began to drone passionately on about the Cold War and atom bombs, about Hiroshima and hate, about the emptiness of victory and the fullness of emptiness and Russia and Buddha and the hidden purpose of life, even I, who loved him, wanted to drop down on the floor and crawl out the back door on my belly. It seemed he might go on forever when Coach Donny Bunnel stood up in disgust, physically shouldered him away from the microphone, grinned out at the audience, and said, "Off to Siberia with *that* one!"

He got a laugh so huge and relieved that even the twins couldn't help joining in. Peter walked quickly off the stage and headed straight out a side exit. Then Papa—with no readable expression, no visible embarrassment, nothing but the businesslike scowl of a relief pitcher with a little fire to put out—stood up, crossed the auditorium in front of everyone, and headed after him.

"And now," Donny Bunnel said, picking up the abandoned trophy, "how about a big round of applause for this year's *real* most valuable player, our All-League first baseman and cleanup slugger, *Artie Kawaso!*"

It was several seconds before the crowd, or the bewildered Kawaso, realized that Coach Bunnel was serious. But when they did, and Artie headed for the podium, the roar was deafening. *"Jeez!"* he crooned into the mike as Bunnel handed him the trophy. "What a weird— I mean, *jeez!* Man oh man! What a surprise! *Really!"*

"Now *that's* a speech!" shouted Nord Curtis.

And now I too joined in the storm of relieved laughter.

"I mean, *jeez!*" Artie said. "But hey! Listen! Coach! Mom and Dad! Guys! Pete too, I guess! You're great! Thanks a *bundle!*"

Papa caught Peter partway across the parking lot, but said nothing to him. He just fell in step, and let Peter walk wherever he chose. Of all places, Peter picked the varsity baseball diamond.

Once there he walked into the dugout, plunked down on the concrete bench, and braced himself for more hostility. But it never came. Nothing came at all. Papa just stared out at the darkened diamond, and Peter waited and waited, till he sounded hostile himself as he blurted, "So was what I did in there just crazy?"

Papa sat down beside him, thought about it, then shrugged. "You were talking about things I know so little about that, even if I did think it was crazy, you should probably just ignore me."

Peter let out a sigh of relief.

"If I were you, though," Papa added, "I'd have let everybody ignore *me* too."

"What do you mean?"

"I understand you're quitting baseball for a reason. A religious feeling, some important kind of searching. But Nord and Donny, your team-mates, their folks, they don't see that at all. To them you look more like some crazy farmer burning down his barn and his big herd of cows, then bragging about how little he owns."

"That *their* barns are burning!" Peter cried. *"That's* what I was trying to say! Because when Gautama, before he became Buddha, saw old age and sickness and death, he said the world and everything in it looked like it was going up in flames. And that's what *I* feel too, Papa! For *years* I've felt it. So I tried to explain, to say why I didn't want their stupid trophy. I tried to be *honest,* Papa. What more could I do?"

"Less," Papa said.

Peter scowled. "I don't understand."

"You said the trophy's stupid, so you gave it back. But you also say Buddha is compassionate, and that you want to be like him. Doesn't add up, Pete. If the trophy really was stupid and they gave it to Buddha, wouldn't he keep it so nobody else would get saddled with a stupid thing?"

Peter had grown very quiet.

Papa said, "Those coaches in there think *you're* stupid too, you know. But they still had the honesty to give their Best Player trinket to their best player. And you insulted that honesty by giving the trinket back."

By now Peter looked crushed.

"I don't know," Papa said. "You woke 'em up anyhow. But this con- crete's killing me. Mind if we walk?"

They turned away from the ballfield and started slowly back toward the parking lot. But the silence was heavy, and as they moved in under the streetlights and glanced at each other, Peter stopped cold, and said, "What's with us, Papa?"

"It's our barn, I think," Papa murmured.

"Huh?" As usual, the preacher hadn't taken in his own sermon.

"Buddha's right," Papa said. "It's burning."

Peter still didn't seem to get it.

"As long as you played ball," Papa said, "I could know what you were going through, and even help you now and then. Which was a kind of greed, I admit. But it was also a kind of love. And toward a Buddhist son, see, I can't be greedy *or* loving. I can't be anything. All I can do is say goodbye."

For a while they stood there, shoulder to shoulder, watching bugs bat against a blue streetlight. Then Peter's face began to cloud. "Hey," Papa said, grabbing his arm and striding off energetically. "I'm not trying to make you feel *bad*. I'm trying to keep *up* with you! If things are burnin' they're burnin'. If we can't be ballplayers together, maybe I can start bein' a Buddhist."

Papa was literally marching them now, but Peter dragged along in his grip like a big sulky child. "Come on!" Papa laughed.

Then Peter stopped in his tracks and covered his face. "I'm gonna miss you so much!" he sobbed. "I love you!"

And the two Camas Buddhists were suddenly hugging each other. They got an awkward grip, maybe from being so close to the same size. But they didn't let go. They kept on trying.

–X–

The same week, on Friday, Everett snuck down from U Dub (despite a load of term-papers-in-progress) to watch Irwin compete in the district track meet. To no one's surprise, Winnie joined Mama and the twins at church the next morning to praise Jesus for his first state javelin record. Meanwhile Everett joined Peter and me in front of the TV, where the Cubs and Cards were having at it, and I was happy as a clam—for a few minutes.

But my brothers were behaving very oddly that morning. They seemed distracted, vaguely excited (though the game was a dull one), they spoke scarcely a word to each other or to me, and every few minutes one of them would jump up, even when runners were in scoring position, and dash upstairs. I finally decided they must be preparing some prank for Irwin, and felt glad enough to see them doing something together that I let them have their fun (though I was a little sad they'd left me out of it). But before the game was even close to over, Everett abruptly packed his things and left for Seattle. And when Irwin got home, no joke or prank occurred.

Everett was waiting tables in Seattle and Peter was counseling at a summer camp in Vermont before I solved the riddle: a kind of farewell conversation—or debate, actually—had been taking place throughout the ballgame's early innings. The reason I hadn't known was that it had been silent: the debate was written on the back of their bedroom door.

Peter and Everett had a several-year tradition (borrowed from the Glass brothers in the Salinger novel *Franny and Zooey*) of writing down choice lines from whatever they happened to be reading, then tacking these scraps of paper to the ravaged inside of their bedroom door. Peter's lines—like the Glass brothers'—tended toward the mythical or metaphysical, while Everett's, as might be expected, were all over the road, swerving from the eschatological to the deliberately puerile to the erotic to the onomatopoeic, with an occasional foray into the profound (perhaps just for surprise). The ritual had ended when Everett went off to college. But—maybe after his debacle at the baseball banquet—Peter had tacked the following scrap to the door, expecting no one to see it:

My father will perhaps say that it was too early for me to leave for the forest. But there is no such thing as a wrong season for Dharma, our hold on life being so tenuous. This very day I begin to strive for the highest good: that is my resolve!
   —the bodhisattva prince, The Legend of the Buddha Shakyamuni

But after Everett's arrival, this line had mysteriously appeared beneath it:

On the whole, I'd rather be in Philadelphia.
   —W. C. Fields

So it began. As far as I know, my brothers never acknowledged or spoke of the debate that followed. But here it is, as written, starting with Peter's response to W. C. Fields:

If this triad of old age, illness and death did not exist, then carefree pleasures and jests with others in the same position as myself would surely give me pleasure . . . But when I consider the impermanence of everything in the world, I can find no delight in it . . .
   —same prince, same legend

If you can't copy him, don't imitate him.
   —Yogi Berra

You must make your mind up and plunge yourself into the bottomless abyss.
   —Butsugen

That the abyss is bottomless is the bad news. The good news is, it must also be topless!
   —Louisa May Alcott, Little Buddhas

How strong and powerful must be your mind, that you can cling to sense-objects even as you watch all creation on its way to death. By contrast, I become frightened; I find neither peace nor contentment, and enjoyment is quite out of the question, for the world looks to me as if ablaze with an all-consuming fire. I want to depart from here today, and win the deathless state for all.
   —same prince, same legend

He who strives to be of use in this world soon burdens the people with his own insufficiency.
   —Lao Tzu

Cease to feel affection for me, and hear my unshakable resolve: either I will extinguish old age and death, and you shall see me again; or I will go to perdition, because my strength failed me, and I could not achieve my purpose.
   —same prince, same legend

My devotees dwell within Me always: I also show forth and am seen within them. Though a man be soiled with the dirt of a thousand battles (or ballgames), let him but love Me and that man is holy. O son of Kunti, of this be certain: the man that loves me, he shall not perish.
   —Krishna, to Arjuna, Bhagavad Gita

This being so, you had better go away now, and cease, my friend, from grieving.
   —same prince, same legend

–XI–

Irwin's track career was meteoric. He set an official school javelin record in his first meet as a sophomore, a new league record by the end of the year, and became the third All-State prep athlete in the family (after Papa and Peter) when, as a junior, he broke the Washington record by nearly four feet. As a senior—after notching a league discus record and breaking his own state javelin record twice—he was scouted in person by the infamous (in these parts anyhow) Bill Bowerman of the University of Oregon, and was awarded a full scholarship to sell out Everett Senior's WSU Cougars and our own Everett's UW Huskies and become what the latter called "a University of Zero Duck."

But at this point the fast track to the Wheaties box turned to mud: during his very first term at the university in Eugene, Irwin leapt for a touchdown pass in a frat-house flag-football game, landed against a parked bicycle in the makeshift end zone, but remained determined—as Coaches Basham, Bunnel & Co had taught—to hang on to the ball at all cost. In this case hanging on required a 360-degree handspring that used his right arm alone, since his left was cradling the football. He pulled it off too—and the six or eight fans went wild. But the cost was about half of the ligaments and tendons in his prodigious right shoulder.

He had surgery, twice, at the University of Zero Medical School in Portland. And the damage did not prove at all detrimental to his overall health, or to his outlook on life. ("The Good Lord has dinged me for a reason!" he told the beaming members of the SDA Church of Eugene one fine Sabbath in the spring of '68.) But it had finished him forever as a track star.

EVERETT

Renunciation

Everyone suspected that whatever America wanted, America got.
Why not Nirvana?
  —Gita Mehta, *Karma Cola*

When I was thirteen and Peter twelve, Mama and Papa took it into their heads to celebrate a new AAA membership (the car club, not the bush league) by setting forth into the bowels of one of those pre-posthumous purgatories we euphemism-loving Americans call "a family vacation." Vowing to explore what the free (with membership) AAA Travel Guide called "the Breathtakingly Beautiful Oregon Coast," they jammed the lot of us into the Dodge Dart wagon, bent over their free (with membership) AAA road maps, and began toodling down mile after merciless mile of serpentine highway, hoping to break down in the middle of nowhere and test out the free (with membership) AAA towing service. Meanwhile we six youths hunched—four in the back seat, two in the way back—watching the wiper blades and defroster slap and huff impotently at opposite sides of the doubly humidified windshield as Irwin joyously pointed out such scenic wonders as the endless skeins of manure-filled barnyards, the quarter-million-acre slashburns and the overloaded log trucks threatening to blast us away to the real Purgatorio while the reputedly "Breathtaking" coastline lurked in omnipresent fog a few hundred feet west of us, invisible as God for the duration of the drive.

The point of this digression—and the most unforgettable moment of the entire thirteen-day ordeal—occurred in a dismal-looking little sawmill-and-dairy town the sign called "Cloverdale, Oregon's Best-Kept Secret," where I happened to glimpse a market upon which were painted the words:

OUR STEAKS ARE SO TENDER WE DON'T KNOW HOW
THE COWS EVER WALKED!

My reaction, upon spotting this bizarre gloat, was to read it aloud. I thought it funny, and believed the whole claustrophobic family could use a good guffaw. My belief was seven-eighths correct. All but one of us did laugh. What I'd failed to take into account was the depth of imagination and shallowness of stomach of our oddball eighth, Peter, who closed his eyes and commenced—with the eerie competence of some snow-eating yogi—to conjure a Tantric Mind Cow so horrifically overfattened and smooshy-fleshed that it was literally unable to rise from the cesspool of its body and walk. It took him perhaps thirty seconds to smear this mooing snot wad across the canvas of his mind. He then gently tapped my shoulder and said, "*Mmmmb*Roll your *mmmmb*window down! *Mmmmb*-Fast!" As it was cold and damp outside, as I've never responded well to point-blank commands, and as his *Mmmmb*ian dialect was new to me (I thought he was trying to be funny by talking "tender," like the steaks on the sign), I failed to process his request with anything like the speed the situation required. As a result, Peter's stomachful of half-digested breakfast shot straight into the closed window, splattered down my neck and chest, and found its final resting place all over my legs and lap.

Looking past this illustrative lap-load, I find myself unable to ignore a troubling question about the whole spiritual thrust of Peter's earthly sojourn. To wit: what is the correlation between his burning desire to attain union with God and his utter inability to slog through a little everyday Americana without either fainting or blowing lunch?

Think about it. If you were the sort of red-blooded, Chicago Bear-lovin', ass-chasin', shit-kickin', four-wheel-drivin' honcho who could, without question or indigestion, daily swash down three or four Styrofoam-swaddled units of Booger King cuisine with a quart or two of the

wee-wee that made Milwaukee famous—if you were, in other words, con-
stitutionally and psychologically willing and able to enjoy "Life" just the
way Uncle Sam, Aunt Fate and your Sony TV serve it up—chances are
you wouldn't be in any all-fired hurry to renounce the world, shrivel your
innards, hone your mind, mortify your pecker, snuff your ego and polish
off your cycle of births and deaths in one swell foop. But if, on the other
hand, you were the sort of thin-skinned, hyperimaginative orchid-on-legs
who fainted splat on the floor every time you got stuck in an elevator full
of beefy-breathed businessmen, or who upchucked your daily bread at
the mere thought of a mucus-muscled Moo Cow, you may well find this
world a vale of queasy tears and be ready to trade it in on the first
alternative world you heard of. You might even be willing to attempt
trading it in on something downright iffy—like, say, severing the Chain
of Causation, attaining Enlightenment, and emanating as a faceless,
stomachless, never-again-to-be-nauseous bolt of bodhihood up into the
fathomless bosom of the One True Oneness . . .

I know that I possess your basic rationalistic, earthbound, Conscious-
ness-1 sort of mind; I know that my lifelong love of baseball renders me
wildly biased; I know that my descriptions of the Absolute range from
parody to travesty. But taking all this into consideration, I still feel that
the distinction just made between two types of Americans raises serious
questions about any individual act of renunciation. Is renunciation just
plain renunciation? Or does it vary according to the personality and circumstances of the renunciate? Can one person's painful purification be
another person's piece of cake? I think it can.

To get specific: if some omnivorous lover of every sort of meat, drink
and pleasure known to man—Irwin, for instance—were to renounce the
world and commence to live the renunciate's life, he would really be
making stupendous sacrifices. But what about Pete? What worldly riches,
what heartfelt loves, what deep pleasures, chronic addictions and hopeless cravings was this vegetarian bookworm truly sacrificing on the day he
announced—before leaving for bloody *Harvard* for godsake!—that he was
"renouncing" his past and setting out to attain "Gnosis"?

I'll tell you what *I* think he was sacrificing: fainting and barfing.

When Peter renounced the world he grew up in and the people he
grew up with, I believe it was an act exactly as heroic as that of a person
who, finding himself prone to violent seasickness, renounces yachting.

Hell, Pete was hardly "in the world" in the first place. That was just the
problem. He knew more about thirteenth-century Sufi Orders and the
Ptolemaic Universe than the rivers and hills and sewers and mills of

southwestern Washington. The guy made me nervous. Take away his voracious reading and Oriental trappings and what was left was damned near a Puritan. And even the great exception to his puritanical predilections—his brilliant ballplaying—was no exception if you sort of squeezed your sphincter into a knot and thought about the game for a minute that way. After all (squeeze hard now), didn't baseball take place on a playing field so precisely devised that it was known, like the Buddha's definitive Sutra, as "the diamond"? Didn't it impose upon its participants (keep squeezing) a monklike uniformity of appearance and a code of conduct backed by a plethora of stringent, dogmatic rules? Didn't baseball in fact (squeeze really hard now!) bear far greater resemblance to a Monastic-Order-with-Fans than to one of those noisy, colorful, paradoxical, unpredictable, two-sexed, alternately lovely and deadly clanjamfreys we call a "world"?

Okay. Relax it now. It doesn't matter anyhow, since in the end Pete even renounced baseball.

It is said in *The Legend of the Buddha Shakyamuni* that when the bodhisattva set out to seek enlightenment, his charioteer took him to the edge of the forest, left him alone there, and he proceeded to "emaciate his body for six years, and carry out a number of strict fasts very hard for men to endure." When Peter set out to seek enlightenment, it was in a jet headed for Boston, then a cab headed for Cambridge, where his first stop was the financial-aid office, his second the college bookstore. It is said in *The Legend of the Buddha Shakyamuni* that at the moment the young prince sat himself down under the Bo Tree, "no one anywhere was angry, ill, or sad; no one did evil, none was proud; the world became quiet, as though it had attained perfection . . . and all living creatures sensed that all would be well." When Peter sat himself down in his dorm room, Malcom X, Robert Kennedy and Martin Luther King were about to die, a hundred American cities and campuses were about to disintegrate, and a military offensive named for the Buddha's birthday was about to reduce Vietnam to ashes.

None of which was Peter's fault. But when it comes to renunciation, "no pain, no gain" is what I've slowly, reluctantly, inexorably come to believe. And when Pete opted for scholarly monkhood, I think he was just trying to outsmart his pain. The Peter who left for Harvard was not looking to integrate or balance his inner and outer selves: he was looking to trick his outer self into nirvana. He'd chosen a diet, not a leap into an abyss. He'd calculated that by considering the physical world "illusory"

and burying his nose in metaphysical texts he could go on doing something comfortable while his ignorance and sufferings and hometown and
troublesome family just fell away like so much ugly excess poundage.

Obviously, I question his calculations: to slough off half a self in hopes
of finding a whole one is not my idea of good math.

CHAPTER TWO

The Left Stuff

1. Hats

My dear fellow, intelligence isn't the only thing. I have a kind and happy heart. I also write vaudeville skits of all sorts . . .
  —the Devil, *The Brothers Karamazov*

In 1945, when Edward Conze read of the atom bomb dropped on Hiroshima, he vomited out a train window and declared history meaningless. In 1964, when Peter saw his first atomic blast in a Pentagon documentary, he staggered down an empty hallway, vomited into a closed window, and decided he'd better become a bodhisattva as fast as possible—if not faster. In 1968, when the White House, Pentagon and Congress were debating whether or not to drop nuclear bombs on North Vietnam, Everett didn't declare or decide or vomit into or out of anything. But he did write a play. It was called *Hats*.

During his sojourn as an English major at Washington, Everett fell temporarily but heavily under the influence of Ken "I Took the Pill Without Asking Any Questions" Kesey and several other writers who were

trying to work with, or in spite of, psychedelic drugs. Fascinated in particular by the altered-consciousness portions of the novel *Sometimes a Great
Notion*, Everett once used his uncanny ability to make even idiotic impulses sound like indispensable qualifications for humanity's emergence
into a Bold New Age, and talked three of his friends into joining him on a
quasi-Keseyian literary experiment of their own. The result of this experiment—or so Everett argued at the time—was his first and (so far) last
play, *Hats.*

The friends' names were nothing like Dale, Didi and Phil, but to protect their innocence, should any still exist, that's what I'll call them. The
experiment (through no fault of Kesey's, by the way) involved driving up
to a reservoir near the foot of Mount Rainier, locating a small unpopu-
lated beach, taking two "hits" of organic mescaline apiece, placing Phil's
Underwood manual typewriter on top of a driftwood log, arguing vehemently about whether it shouldn't be *under* the log since it was an Underwood, resolving the argument by placing a small piece of wood on top
of the typewriter, removing their clothes because Didi said that William
Blake had now and then done the same, then taking turns clacking away
at some free-form verbiage which they hoped would later read as
strangely as they'd all begun to feel.

The original plan had been to limit each contestant to an hour at the
typewriter, but the mescaline proved so good (or bad, depending on how
you look at these things) that in no time, so to speak, none of the writers
could tell time. A second problem arose when Dale and Didi elected to
type simultaneously, lost interest in the keyboard after its letters became
an indistinguishable paisley tapestry, and began trying to force the Underwood to take dictation by bellowing ontological questions at it instead. "Hey, Everett!" they'd roar down into the bewildered machinery.
"Who the hell is Phil?" Or "Hey, Phil! Who are Everett?" Or "Hey,
Everett and Phil! Who the hell be you guys?" Or "Hey, Dale and Didi!
Who we am?"

When, at Everett's suggestion, they abandoned the typewriter in order
to stick their heads underwater and shout down into the far more respon-
sive lake, Phil, or whoever he was by then, took his shot at the Underwood, and for a long while typed at a furious pace. But when, after an
amount of time I fear we can call only "an amount of time," Everett
strolled over to check out Phil's prodigious output, he found perhaps
twenty pages' worth of the numbers 2 through 8 typed out in a single-
spaced column, thus:

2345678
2345678
2345678
2345678
2345678
2345678
2345678 . . .

Everett was not impressed. He picked up a stick, slipped it around the oblivious typist's back, and shoved down the left shift key, causing the poor fellow's perfect column of 2345678s to be marred by a sudden @#$%¢&*. "Damn!" Everett said, pointing at it. "Too bad, Phil! You're disqualified!"

When Phil began to weep, Everett threw an arm round his shoulder and led him down to help Didi and Dale find out who the hell be the lake. He then rushed back to the log, cracked his knuckles over the keyboard, and let his altered consciousness stream onto the page as planned. The result, as far as even Everett could later tell, was several pages of self-indulgent gobbledygook. But while he was clacking away he happened to overhear Dale, Phil and Didi "playing tricks" on the apparently gullible lake by pretending they were really Einstein, Yogi Bear and Queen Elizabeth. Pathetic as this was, it struck the altered-Everett funny, and he managed (barely) to type out a little of their dialogue. Then a thundershower hit, the drugs began to wear off, and they drove back to Seattle, only to realize, first, that everything they'd written was drivel, and second, that they'd left Phil's Underwood up at the lake.

This left Everett with what he felt was a clear choice: one option was to admit to his disgruntled friends that the mescaline experiment was a ridiculous and dangerous outing that had cost a perfectly good Underwood its life; the other was to convince them that the day had in fact been a smashing literary success, that their Einstein/Yogi Bear/Queen Elizabeth skit was brilliant, and that if they only developed it a little it could lead to great things. Obviously the latter option was as harebrained as Congress. But faith is amazing stuff. Even faith in nonsense. And Everett, at the time, really did have faith in what he called "the Keseyian Antitradition of Literary Inspiration via Psychedelics." The result of that faith—though written primarily under the influence of caffeine—was his first and last play.

•   •   •   •   •

Hats was an ambitious work in that people of all nationalities, ages and walks of life appeared in it. It was also a provincial work, in that it was riddled with local and national political references, TV puns, sight gags and private jokes thunk up by Everett and his cronies while heavily under the influence of 1968ism. By the time he'd whipped it into final form, though, Everett had incorporated a few clever theatrical devices (for instance, a play within the play) and come up with a cast so incongruous that they would probably have gotten some laughs without even speaking. And after harassing local playhouse producers and directors for weeks as only he could harass, Everett got *Hats* staged at the Boathouse Theater on Lake Washington. So one fine summer's Saturday, Irwin and I (after he'd joined Mama for church) drove up in his nifty little Nash Rambler and caught the opening-night performance.

The obvious eccentricity of *Hats* turned out to be its chief dramatic purpose as well: everybody in it, no matter their age, race or activity, was at all times wearing some sort of hat or cap, and attached to each one, by dangling springs, were two enormous revolvers. One revolver was painted red, with a yellow hammer and scythe on its handle. The other was star-spangled red, white and blue. Both—even when bobbing dangerously about on the end of their springs—were constantly cocked, and aimed straight at the hat-wearer's brains.

The only set was a kind of forest made of trees, bushes, telephone poles and TV antennas. In honor of the play's supposed inspiration, Yogi Bear wandered out into this forest first, wearing his usual green necktie and putzy hat—plus the revolvers. "Hey hey hey! Am I starvin' today!" he said. Then he started looking around for pickanick baskets.

Hoss Cartwright from *Bonanza* came out next. And in addition to the revolvers attached to his ten-gallon he had a big horse pistol which he was aiming at Yogi, obviously intending to pot him. As he was about to squeeze the trigger though, Tarzan (wearing a blue baseball cap with a hot-pink T on it, plus the two guns) came swinging out on a telephone wire making his famous jungle cry—which scared Hoss into swinging the big horse pistol around on him instead. Tarzan scowled at him. Hoss scowled back. "You Injun?" he finally asked.

"Ungawa!" answered Tarzan.

"Well gosh!" Hoss chuckled. "Sorry, fella! You had me a-goin' there for a second!"

"Ungawa!" laughed Tarzan.

"Say," Hoss asked. "You haven't seen Pa anywheres, have ya?"

Tarzan shook his head, then asked Hoss in grunts and gestures whether he'd seen Jane or Cheetah.

"Well," Hoss answered. "Now you mention it, I *did* see one fine-lookin' woman, dressed a lot like you are, headin' off into the shrubs with that rascal Little Joe. I reckoned she was Injun. She any kin to you?"

"Ungawa!" screamed Tarzan, and off he ran with his head-pistols springing.

Eddie Haskel of *Leave It to Beaver* was the play's narrator. He strolled among the various characters like a sneering Beatrice through an Inferno, exchanging gibes or just rolling his eyes at some, giving bad advice or deliberate misdirections to others. For instance, noticing the entwined legs and cowboy boots of what was obviously a pair of writhing lovers sticking out of the bushes, he said, "Hey, Tarzan! Check it out!" And Tarzan ran over, yelled "Ungawa!" and dove right in on top. But while the curses and clothes and leaves came flying up out of the shrubs, Eddie turned with a smirk to the audience and said, "Heh-heh-heh! The Apeman just jumped Roy Rogers and Dale Evans."

Before going any further I should mention Irwin's reaction to it all. He had let out his first roar of laughter with Yogi's first "Hey hey hey," roared again each time a new character so much as appeared onstage, and in no time had everyone around him roaring too. In fact, having never seen the play without him, I have no idea whether the sidesplitting and curtain calls and surprisingly merciful reviews in the *Times* and *Post-Intelligencer* the next morning were due to the drama itself or to the deadly infectiousness of Irwin's laugh.

I can't remember exactly what came next—and it hardly matters. Mr. Ranger showed up to keep an eye on Yogi; Sergeant Friday and Captain Kangaroo were there; Queen Elizabeth was for some reason helping Wilma Flintstone look for Fred; then Albert Einstein appeared, formed a terrible crush on Wilma, and started following her around, espousing increasingly complicated theories to try to impress her. The subplots had multiplied to the verge of chaos, the serious theatergoers had long since walked out in disgust, and Irwin had pretty well howled himself to exhaustion when the stage suddenly darkened, a spotlight fell on Eddie Haskel, and he turned to the audience and came out with a kind of soliloquy: "What we're all basically doin' in these woods is searchin', right? We're all lookin' for somethin'. For the Apeman here, it's Jane and Little Joe. For the Yog it's a pickanick basket. For Hoss it's Pa. For Roy and Dale (heh-heh-heh!), it's their own private bush. But meanwhile, check out these hats we're all wearin'."

For the first time, the characters all took notice of their preposterous headgear. "Can you believe it?" Eddie asked, boinging his revolvers around a little. "Can you believe us all dorkin' around up here in these little doom-units? What a buncha fuckin' jerks."

"Say there, young fella!" Roy Rogers interrupted. "That's no way to talk. I *like* my hat!"

"Me too," said Hoss.

"I think they're *sexy*," cooed Dale Evans.

"Gosh!" said Hoss.

But then a man in the audience started hollering and fussing around—and we saw that he too had a two-gunned hat stuck on his head. A woman up in the balcony stood up and screamed: same problem. Then it was a little boy down front—a kid no more than five, cute as a guinea pig and a born ham actor. "Get it offa me! *Please!*" he pleaded. "It's not funny anymore!" And somehow he managed to burst into such pathetic, convincing tears that Irwin's eyes filled with tears too. Then a couple stood up in the middle of the audience—a man and woman I'd wondered about, since they'd been necking a little, and it was not the sort of drama to inspire that. Anyhow, they started trying to wrestle the hats off each other's heads out of love for each other. But *their* hats were invisible. They were damned good invisible-hat-wrestlers too. (Everett later said they were mimes.) They made the problem so dire and real that before long fifty or sixty people, none of them planted actors now, were wrestling with sinister nothings welded to the air above their skulls. And when the theater-wide struggle was at its height the spotlight hit Eddie Haskel again, and he smirked his famous smirk and said, "Now you get the picture. Now I can say it and maybe not offend you. We're *all* a hopeless buncha jerks. These Kremlin/Pentagon party hats are stuck to our heads to stay."

"Hey hey hey! What a shitty toupé!" quoth Yogi Bear.

"No cussing, Yogi," carped Mr. Ranger.

"Please! Get it off!" the kid in the front row whimpered.

"I like mine!" Roy Rogers insisted.

"Happy Trails," said Eddie Haskel.

That was the gist of Act I, and perhaps the emotional climax of the play. But it was not the end of the entertainment. The second act dealt with the incompatibility of antiwar activism and romance, and was, if anything, even sillier than the first. Einstein was a central character. He kept tediously expounding upon things like radiation, megatonnage and so on, trying to talk people into Banning the Hat. But every time he came close to inciting a few characters to protest, the French cartoon skunk Pepé Le Pew would come bounding in and start poeticizing about springtime and love and beautiful women—and Queen Elizabeth would form a royal crush on Captain Kangaroo, or Liberace would tear off after the beefcake Tarzan, or Roy Rogers and Dale Evans would continue their search for a private bush, and the antinuke movement would fall to pieces. Even Einstein, under Pepé's cupidean influence, would eye Wilma Flintstone suggestively, and his theories, against his will, would grow longer and longer. He finally "climaxed" by telling her that an American dollar bill was six inches long, that a mile was five thousand two hundred and eighty feet, that ten thousand five hundred and sixty dollar bills laid end to end would cover a mile, that it was ninety-three million miles to the sun, that nine hundred eighty-two billion eighty million dollars laid end to end would therefore create a bridge of dollars from our planet to the sun, that any child realized that the construction of such a bridge would not be wise since the sun's heat would ignite the money and burn the entire bridge, but that, since the year 1950, the United States Pentagon had burned the equivalent of not one but *two* such earth-to-sun dollar-bridges, and to what end? Why, to purchase the deadly hats everybody was wearing! Before the audience could begin to contemplate these dire calculations, though, Queen Elizabeth commenced bragging to Captain Kangaroo about how a pound note was considerably longer than a dollar, inspiring Liberace to nudge Wilma Flintstone and lisp, "So is Fred!," which caused Wilma to retort, "How would *you* know?," to which Liberace replied, "That's exactly what I hope to show Tarzan!," upon which the dismayed Apeman hollered "Ungawa!" and vanished into the woods. And when Eddie Haskel hollered, "Hey, Lib!" and pointed out a wriggling thicket, the pianist tiptoed over, dove right in—

and landed on top of Roy Rogers and Dale Evans.

*H*ats ran all summer at the Boathouse, was produced in two other in-state college towns, and Everett not only became a campus celebrity but was known for a few months in wider circles as "the young guerrilla-theater playwright," "the head who hatched the hilarious *Hats*" and so on. In trying to capitalize on such labels, though, his original theory of composition failed him: no matter what chemicals he used to inspire or lash himself, all subsequent attempts at plays were stillborn.

Everett liked to claim at the time that it was the antiwar movement which forced him to sacrifice his budding career as a playwright. But there were less specious reasons for his flash-in-the-pan. *Hats*, after all, had not been the work of a would-be dramatist who sat down with a sense of literary calling: it had been the one-night outburst of a cornered Kesey fanatic hell-bent on proving to his buddies that the hapless Phil's typewriter had died for a noble cause. This, even for Everett, was unusually silly subject matter, but the motivating force was typical: at his silliest as at his best, Everett's oratorical and literary styles have always been contrapositive; he needs an action against which to react, a thesis against which to pose an antithesis, an offense by which to be offended. He has always been a kind of verbal and literary boxer—a compulsive counterpuncher, really. And the confrontations and causes of 1968 had just turned his world into a counterpuncher's paradise. He did begin to write and fight against the war, militarism, racism and so on, but he sacrificed very little that he valued, least of all a career as a playwright, in order to do so. Activism suited his contrary nature to perfection. The only inconsistency, the only serious discrepancy I saw between Everett's personality and his new political passion was that he had supposedly begun fighting for the very stuff he had always found hardest to deal with:

peace.

2. The Thing

Did you hear about the baby just born that was both sexes?
It had a penis and a brain.
—overheard at the University of Oregon Medical School

All intentions to the contrary, Irwin was unable to remain a virgin past his third year of high school. I mention this in introducing Everett's sex life because the order in which siblings or close friends attain sexual experience frequently inflicts profound psychological repercussions upon those who bring up the rear.

Every time Irwin answered an Altar Call at church, it was for the same time-honored reason: he had once again fondled some young maiden overfondly. Perhaps I should explain that the Altar Call, at least by preacherly intention, is a demand for a once-in-a-lifetime act of total repentance and religious rebirth on the part of a "sinner." So when Elder Babcock would cry out for that last lost soul still skulking out in the pews, when he'd demand that this wretch—he or she knew who they were!— immediately swallow their pride, step forward, and let the Holy Spirit pour like Sani-Flush into their toilet bowl of a heart, it did not please him at all to see no one but the redundantly saved Irwin jump yet again to his feet, stride up to the altar with a big grin on his face, chunk down on his knees, and re-re-reconsecrate his life to Jesus. Another irony was that every time Irwin made this trek, a number of ex-fondled and unfondled girls in the congregation were staring overfondly at his backside, hatching schemes and battle plans which pretty well guaranteed he'd soon be back at the altar again.

All intentions to the contrary, Everett remained a virgin until he went away to college. But he knew a little about Irwin's escapades—and he did not handle this knowledge well. Irwin tried to be discreet about his amorous exploits, but when he'd come home from dates with his underpants lost and his shirts on inside out or crawl in our window in the wee hours with a maddeningly fuggy hum rising off him, it wasn't hard to draw conclusions. And our conclusions, vague as they were, drove us to gang up and grill Irwin so long and mercilessly that he could sometimes be forced to speak . . .

"They have this thing!" I remember him announcing to three brimming vats of testosterone disguised as his brothers one night when he was only fifteen, but fresh back from a tryst (in what they later learned was poison oak) with a lovely, full-breasted, lithe-bodied seventeen-year-old Adventist girl whom Everett had been ineffectually chasing since kindergarten. "This wonderful little funny little thing down there! Kind of a toggle-switch deal! And when you work it for 'em, when you barely even toggle it, man oh man! They just go *nuts*. I mean, you wouldn't, they just sort of, they start to, man oh man! and then they kind of, it gets all sort of, I don't know! until it, oooooh! and they sort of, waaaaaaaah, and you can kinda . . . aw *shoot*, you guys! I can't explain it! All I can say is *watch out for that thing!*"

Needless to say, we did. Constantly. And everywhere. On the ground, in the sky, in the fine print on sides of cereal boxes, in our lockers at school, in roadside gutters on the way home. The thing was now seared on our brains; it was the star of our semiconscious lives; it was the ineffably cute swimmer who sent the white shark of lust knifing through the sea of our blood, giving us the obvious Attacking Shark Shape in the obvious place during every dull sermon, every school class, every sultry night or lull in the day. But before long it grew painfully obvious to Everett and me—particularly in the vicinity of mirrors—that, lacking Irwin's godlike body, godlike joie de vivre, godlike luck and other key godlike equipment, possessing in fact no parts like any part of Irwin save the wildly pulsating hormones, we looked very much like a couple of charmlessly horny doofuses from Camas, Washington, and very little like the sorts of Romeos whom beautiful girls jump out and ask to work their things for them.

To deepen our Doofuscosity, the deceptively monkish Peter, when he was sixteen, tried to describe to us (after Everett had refused to let him sleep for four or five hours) what transpired when he and an equally intellectual girlfriend had come to some sort of agreement, met in some intelligently selected trysting place, and indulged in some sort of technically sexual behavior. But it was nearly as hard for me to imagine what sort of antics would produce an account like Peter's as it was to imagine a genuine "thing." He told us: "Well, yeah, it was fun, I guess. But the trouble, see, was that we knew we didn't love each other. So even though we got excited and all, it came down to a matter of, I don't know, not mauling each other exactly, but just sort of *operating* each other. Like a couple of cars or something. Yeah, that's about right. It was like we'd each invented this car, see. But there was no way of seeing how well our two cars ran without her getting into me and me getting into her and each of us test-driving each other. So that's what we did. We test-drove our cars. And we *were* our cars. Which was very exciting, and confusing, and made us feel all this gratitude and shame and wonder and embarrassment toward each other. But when it was over, we felt way too much the way you'd feel after test-driving a regular old Ford or Chevy or something. You know. It was like, okay, everything runs great, yeah you're welcome, thank you too. And that was it. Which just isn't right. The driving itself was just too wonderful to end up feeling like that. So I won't do it again. I mean, not in that way. I want a form of wonder that doesn't turn me into a car. I want a wonder that *lasts*."

"Well, I want a wonder with *breasts!*" Everett roared.

But no such wonder offered itself. Everett had girlfriends in high school, but there was no joint "test-driving." And even after he arrived among the sixteen thousand coeds at Washington and found himself devastatingly attracted to a new subspecies known as the "hippie chick," he had to undergo a transformation so complete that it resembled a left-wing parody of a successful right-wing business career before he was able to attract them in return. For starters he established social credit, and the equally crucial social discredit, by becoming one of the first truly longhaired males anybody had ever seen. He then upgraded his living situa-

tion by trading his dork-ridden dorm-cubicle in on a room in a romanti-
cally deciduous off-campus hippie house. Next he began developing his
product (himself) by playing every remotely romantic role he could find
time for, becoming a classroom wit, a street-corner flower-seller, an ac-
tivist in whatever causes were most active, a waiter at the hippest U
district coffeehouse, an aspiring poet, a soapbox orator, the chief humor-
ist and honky-baiter for an underground paper. He then insured these
investments by going to work for the university's bona fide bluestock
newspaper, but concealed this unsightly hint of career conservatism by
becoming its most incendiary columnist with his weekly offering, "Give
Chance a Peace."

At that point Everett finally arrived at his long-sought solution to the
puzzle of The Thing. But the name, face or nature of the girl he found it
with hardly matter since a whole string of less long-sought solutions soon
followed. In fact, after *Hats* and "Give Chance a Peace" brought him
name, fame and a little gold earring that Gay Liberation would one day
force him to rue, Everett attained so many short-sought solutions to the
Thing Puzzle that it lost its mysteriousness altogether and became a
requirement, like PE. He no longer wanted a woman. He wanted *Woman*.
He wanted to show the godlike Irwin what it was to be *really* desirable.
He wanted what Lao Tzu and Chuang Tzu did not mean at all by "the
Ten Thousand Things."

In other words, he no longer knew what the fuck he wanted. But Irwin
and I saw him seldom enough, and he was still charming and funny
enough, that we figured he was thriving and pretty much admired him to
the skies. The only one of us who felt differently about Everett at this
time was Peter. But Pete lived three thousand miles away, and his rare
letters—which were mostly to Freddy—talked about religion and meta-
physics, not about his big brother.

3. Everett Routs the Ottoman Empire

*It is not impossible that it should fall to the lot of this work, in its poverty
and in the darkness of this time, to bring light into one brain or another—
but, of course, it is not likely.*
  —Ludwig Wittgenstein

"Like most of you, I oppose the American military mission in Vietnam.
Unlike some of you, I don't consider that opposition 'revolutionary.' Per-

haps it's your country's unusually bloodless beginnings that give the word 'revolution' its mythic ring to students in this country. But having studied many revolutions, and having survived two of them myself, I have become familiar enough with some of their hidden costs to want to share them."

The speaker was one Dr. Edward Gurtzner—an antiquated, cigar-chewing Austrian history professor who'd witnessed the tenth anniversary celebration of the Russian Revolution in Leningrad as a child and the Nazification of his homeland as a student. In a recent letter Everett had called him the best lecturer on campus, and added that his European Intellectual History class took place in a hall full of three hundred students, so that if I wanted to attend I could do so and remain faceless. Everett would make suggestions like this casually, but stuck as I was in a Stone Age called "high school," I did not receive them casually. University life had become magical to me, and I slipped away to visit Everett every chance I got. To me the University of Washington seemed like the center of an embryonic world that was about to burst forth and revivify, if not replace, the stale old world at large. And in this embryonic world my brother had become some kind of combination firebrand, stand-up comic, knight-errant playboy superstar. I read his crazy columns, heard him quoted in coffeehouses, found him clowning for a different young woman every time I visited, joined him on a march or two, and felt he'd become a hero of our time. He was, of course, full of crap, and always had been. But he was also full of goodness, and I never doubted that the goodness would eventually KO the crap. Anyhow, when his letter mentioned Gurtzner, I called that very night to find out the professor's schedule, skipped school and hitched to Seattle the very next day, and made my way into a back-row seat maybe ten minutes into a lecture. And though I didn't know what I'd missed, the little I'd heard had me feeling already that I'd arrived, once again, at the center of things.

"In order to become a true revolutionary," Dr. Gurtzner continued, "you must first of all jettison your ability to recall or honor the complexities of a nuanced historic or personal past. More details explain things more, but less details confuse things less, and a leader out to galvanize thousands of zealous followers must consistently shun complexity, even at the cost of lucidity and truth.

"For this same reason, friendships with those who fail to become co-revolutionaries must be eliminated. The revolutionary ideology, once installed in the mind, must be the sole regulator of all human relationships. Those who refuse to undergo the same 'installation,' however much you may love them, are no longer to be trusted. Jefferson himself complained of this loss. There were excellent people among the Tories. There are *always* excellent people on both sides. And to adopt an ideology is to take to one side only. This is why even the most justifiable revolution is certain to destroy friendships, families, cross-cultural exchanges and every other nuanced type of human connection. Believe me, this is an inevitable cost."

The size of the lecture hall, the wild garb and serious faces of the students, the gravity and formality of Gurtzner's manner, all of it thrilled me. Everett hadn't spotted me yet, but I'd no trouble spotting him, sitting way down in front, wearing blue jeans with little U.S. flags on the knees—and I was even thrilled by the knee emblems. But I'd begun to feel just a little confused by what I was hearing. In fact I tried to catch Everett's eye, to assure him with a wink or grin that I didn't think Dr. Gurtzner was talking about any loss of nuance or growing distances between him and our family, or at least between him and me. But he was too far away, or too intent, to spot me.

"Because he has eliminated both his past and his friendships," the old man continued, "the revolutionary soon finds himself disenfranchised, impoverished and surrounded by compatriots whose beliefs he has already memorized, whose utterances he can therefore predict and whose company he often begins to abhor. This is what we might call the Valley Forge stage of the revolt. And it takes a great cause indeed to carry the rebel forces past it. Rebel comrades are, after all, not natural friends, not community, not family, but merely unchosen, inescapable company. And since it is frequently those persons who can't tolerate their own personalities who are the first to pawn their inner selves in for an ideology, rebel leaders have a tendency to be what we might justifiably call 'intolerable people'—people whose early abdication of their lives has given them seniority and authority over those who are often their betters."

Hearing the way Everett cleared his throat (and the laughter it created around him), I was certain that he intended to say or do something to "set the record straight" soon. A lot of students were glancing at him, so I guess everyone who knew him felt the same way. It made Dr. Gurtzner's lecture nerve-wracking, but also terribly exhilarating: "Out on the streets, and in the society at large, what the increasingly disgruntled rebel forces soon long to see is not peace but panic and upheaval, not understanding or tolerance but solidarity, not the weaponless fight to instill life in ancient traditions but a vandalistic smashing of all tradition. Once the struggle moves from the text and tongue out into the world, *all* cultural icons and social modi operandi are to be obliterated, for chaos adds fuel to the revolutionary fires. As for the increasingly frequent injustices, the abdicated responsibilities, the injuries of the innocent, the expatriations and deaths caused by the rebel forces themselves, these are to be written off as minor compared to the oppression inflicted upon humanity by the power to be toppled. 'Regrettable but necessary side effects' is a favorite phrase . . ."

"Bullshit," said Everett. Loudly. And I felt the blood rush to my face.

"Pardon me?" said Professor Gurtzner.

"I said bullshit. Because what are we talking about here? *Which* revolution? You started out on Vietnam, so you must mean the student revolt in this country. Right? So what about it? What are we students upset about? 'Nam. Racism in the South. The Cold War and the arms race. Because *that's* the violence. Yet that's what this university's rationalistic conscience finds acceptable. That's what it supports with grants and research that sooner or later boil down to more violence. So what's this crap about violent *revolutionaries?* It's the *non*revolutionaries, it's the fucking status quo, who are killing people! So, with all due respect, I say bullshit."

A lot of students were murmuring approval, and a few were shouting "Right on!" But the old man remained perfectly calm. "The next time you wish to express an opinion, Mr. Chance," he began, "a raised hand will do." He then turned to the class and said, "I was not discussing the student protest in this country, actually. I was making some general statements about the revolutionary character, based on the revolutions with which I am familiar. As I recall, I was about to say that these 'regrettable side effects' inflicted by the rebel forces usually bring about one of two results. The most common is a totalitarian backlash, some form of police state. The less common is outright social chaos, to give 'revolution' a less romantic name. And in the iconoclastic smog of such an all-out upheaval, several new species of what we might call 'secondary leaders' appear as if out of thin air. The first to be heard from are usually leather-lunged, brash, clever young men who can think on their feet and coin memorable phrases. 'Steal This Book!' 'Ho Ho Ho Chi Minh' . . ."

Almost everyone laughed at this. But Everett didn't.

"These clowns and wits are often courageous, and can be excellent entertainment. They enflame crowds, make lightning-quick rationalizations of indefensible actions, and truly believe, in their paucity of belief, that 'anything is possible,' 'everything can be improved,' so why not smash it all and rebuild from the ground up? Far less amusing are the social architects and manipulators who follow in the wake of the revolution proper. The twist Alexander Hamilton so soon gave to the ideals of Jefferson is, perhaps, too subtle an example to make my point. What Stalin did in the name of Lenin and Marx may be more familiar to you. In any case, what this second wave of ideologists inevitably ignores, or what their indoctrinated minds perhaps cannot perceive, is the aimless complexity, the lushness, the infinite variety of life. This is why their programs, their social solutions, are always so rationalistic in conception and inflexible in implementation. It's also why they so soon resort to violence. And since these people have very limited senses of humor, this violence often lands first upon the very wits and defiant heroes who had won the people's hearts in the first place. At this point—which is usually reached with dismaying swiftness—the revolution and the people it was meant to help have already gone their separate ways."

Everett raised his hand. The doctor continued: "I would like to emphasize that this separation of the leaders from the people is inevitable in *every* case. Almost any people will rebel against terrible oppression, but no people can remain revolutionary for long. I don't claim to know the reason for this. I cherish the mystery. For no reason, or mysterious reasons, it is the natural tendency, if not the essence, of a people to create and cultivate endless variety. Whereas the aim of all ideologues—including revolutionaries—is to create sameness."

Everett raised his other hand now, and raised a chorus of mirth as he sat there like a man held at gunpoint. But the doctor was unflappable. "What no social, political or religious program will ever manage to take into account is the people's inevitable love and reverence for what mankind really does hold in common. The earth and the hearth fire. The rivers and sky. The richness and complexity of human relationships, and of the changing seasons. The divinity they believe infuses it all. This is why revolutions begin with justifiable unrest, and may rise to open rebellion, but also why, after turning to violence, they rapidly begin to subside."

Now Everett stood up, his hands still held high, and cried, "See where hand-raising gets us? Will all those women and children in Vietnamese rice paddies who wish not to be napalmed please raise their hands when the next squadron of Phantom jets fly over?"

There was laughter, and murmurs of approval and disapproval. He said, "Will all those innocent Hanoi bystanders who wish not to be obliterated please step outside and raise their hands during the next midnight American B-52 barrage?"

There was outright applause. He shouted, "Will Martin Luther King, Jr., please raise his hand so that J. Edgar Hoover's hirelings will know which of you look-alike black dudes he's supposed to waste?"

Another big cheer. And some angry scowls too. Judging by the faces, I'd say the students were divided just about in half. But Everett's half were making all the noise right now.

"Our Mr. Chance," Dr. Gurtzner said calmly, "has selected me as his enemy today. Yet, like him, I oppose the war. And like him, I deplore the death of Dr. King. Unlike him, I feel there is a difference between a lecture hall and a street corner. I refuse to forget, for example, that Dr. King was a scholar, and that the facts he discovered in libraries and lecture halls helped reveal to him how best to conduct his life outside them. If Dr. King had marched in his classrooms, or name-called in them, or massacred the truth in hopes of inciting his classmates to riot, he would not have been the—"

"I *spoke* the truth, buddy!" Everett interrupted. "It's human beings who are being massacred, by powers well represented at this school! And the hidden message of your soft-spoken tirade against every revolutionary from Jefferson to the Chicago Seven was: Shuttup, sit down, and accept it! You're just students."

Dr. Gurtzner sighed, shook his head, and slowly lit the cigar he'd only mouthed all day. Turning to his class, he said, "Anyone too undisciplined, too self-righteous or too self-centered to live in the world as it is has a tendency to 'idealize' a world which ought to be. But no matter what political or religious direction such 'idealists' choose, their visions always share one telling characteristic: in their utopias, heavens or brave new worlds, their greatest personal weakness suddenly appears to be a strength. In a 'religiously pure' community, for example, any puritanical blockhead who was unable to love his neighbor or turn the other cheek can suddenly sweep the entire world into the category of 'Damned' and pass himself off as 'Saved.' Similarly, in Mr. Chance's revolutionary army, the rudeness and petulance of a mere spoiled brat can suddenly pass itself off as passionate concern for Vietnamese peasants or the black Southern poor. I hope the rest of you are not too impassioned to note, however, that neither these people nor their oppressors are present in this room, and that the enemy he seems bent on exposing is just an old professor who detests the same war."

Dr. Gurtzner got a lot of applause for this reply—including mine. But before it was over, Everett boomed, "I hope you're also not too self-complacent to notice that there's a valid disagreement here nonetheless.

There's an ROTC building on this campus, nuclear vessels in our harbor, manufacturers of weapons components all over the city and military research being done in and by this university. This school, this town, this whole state is rolling in Pentagon money—*peasant*-killer money. And pardon my brattiness, but I don't see anything *polite* about ignoring these things. What I've been hearing all day is basically this: since our government doesn't happen to be murdering anybody in this very room, since it's only inferior American males who aren't rich or bright or lucky enough to be students here who have to nail the Vietnamese people to the crosses that this school helps build, let's forget the whole problem!"

Everett got an ovation for this blast too, but the volume was not quite what it had been. People were using their brains now, so they were more interested in hearing Gurtzner's reply than in making a public show of the correct political sentiments. Puffing away at his cigar, and pacing round and round his lectern, the old man said, "Undetected and unpunished murderers stroll the streets of this and every city on any given day, Mr. Chance. We know this for certain. But if all people refused to fulfill their obligations and duties until all such criminals were caught and punished, we'd soon die. Because a Skagit Valley poultry farmer ignored global oppression and injustice long enough to harvest the eggs in our omelets this morning, you and I have the energy to stand here talking. It is now my duty to ignore the same problems long enough to give what I have to offer to this class. If you have no such duties, Mr. Chance, then you are free to leave us for the streets, and to shout and curse and hand out leaflets to your heart's content. But this is a scholarly gathering. Our chief difference of opinion is with regard to vocation, Mr. Chance. Perhaps because I have one, and you don't."

"What *is* your vocation?" Everett asked.

"If you chose to be a student," Gurtzner replied, "I think I could demonstrate some proficiency as a professor."

"Of what?" Everett fired back. "Advanced cigar smoking 308? Undermining Just Causes with Eloquence 404? You're an exterminator, not a professor! You're trying to exterminate the Counterculture."

Dr. Gurtzner sighed, turned to the class, and said, "I hope the majority of you are not too excited by these epithets to observe that Mr. Chance, for all his superficial spontaneity, is now speaking solely from the text of his ideology. He now considers himself 'Counter' and me 'Culture.' He is the 'Saved' and I the 'Damned.' When this stage is reached, rational dialogue is of course impossible, and the fellow in my position has no choice but to accept Mr. Chance's personal jesus as his lord and savior, so to speak, or to call in the National Guard, or perhaps to shoot himself in despair. Today, however, let me close by answering his accusation as best I can.

"What I would wish for the so-called Counterculture is that it be more than a disenfranchised tribe whose sole rite of initiation is disillusionment with the existing culture, as symbolized by one's parents, the Pentagon and the Ku Klux Klan. I would wish that its members accept neither my tweed coat nor Mr. Chance's knee patches as a sign of authority, but judge us both by the cogency of our thoughts. I would wish that rather than fancy itself 'counter' to the culture, its compassionate ideas would take root in the land and people, and begin to transform them both. But if Mr. Chance does in fact speak for his 'culture,' I fear this breath of fresh air, this grass-roots movement in which even old men like myself have placed such hope, will soon become an empty excuse for youthful effrontery, a faddish cloak for self-indulgence and drug dealers, and a primary cause of a fascistic political and cultural backlash."

With that, the old expatriated Austrian gathered his notes, gave us a last little bow, and strolled away from the smoke-shrouded lectern and out the side exit to a wild round of applause . . .

But then Everett—who to my mind had just been thoroughly dismantled—was surrounded by a crush of admirers! "Far fucking *out!*" shouted his housemate, Stoner Steve, pounding him on the back.

"Down goes the Ottoman Empire!" cried a red-haired woman who apparently couldn't quite recall where Austria was.

"You routed him, man!" chortled a guy with hair sproinging out to his shoulders.

"Bodacious words!" drooled a stoned-looking fellow who was suckling an empty pipe.

"Thanks, man" "Hey, thanks" "Thanks a lot," crooned my brother.

"I'm Melanie," gushed a fawning young lady in some sort of gunnysack dress. "And I just *had* to thank you for letting the old fossil have it between the eyes. I mean, when he'd let you talk at all, you were incredible!"

Everett shrugged. When he should have retched. I didn't get it.

Then a brunette in a black leotard top that blew half my circuits and a pair of timeworn jeans that blew the other half moved to the front of the circle, smiled a smile I'd have seriously considered dying for, and I thought, *Good God! No wonder he acts like this!* But then, to my astonishment and delight, she gushed, "I just *had* to thank you for letting the old fossil give it to you between the eyes! I mean, when you weren't pathetic, you were almost totally full of shit. And it was brave of you. You're a hell of a straight man. It takes courage to sacrifice yourself like that."

Everett's jaw dropped—soundlessly for once—while the girl spun away in a cadenza of black and blue that left my brother's heart and brain the same colors. We all stared helplessly. "Who was *that?*" somebody finally asked.

"*Natasha,*" smirked Melanie.

"Natasha who?" croaked Everett.

"How would *I* know?" Melanie huffed. "Natasha the Russian-lit freak. Natasha from Arizona. Natasha the fascist bitch who thinks Chekhov, Goldwater and Tolstoy are God."

"Far fucking out," remarked the adaptable Stoner Steve.

4. Tariki

If a man wishes to be sure of the road he walks on, he must close his eyes and walk in the dark.
—St. John of the Cross

To trip over a bike and damage a shoulder was no great setback for a faith-filled phenom like Irwin. The shoulder, for anything short of javelin-throwing, was still perfectly serviceable, and Irwin had always been able to give up gifts and glory as blithely as he attained them. The only problem with this injury was the timing: it was sustained at the height of the Vietnam draft. The loss of his athletic scholarship therefore meant that he had to carry a full academic load, to make decent grades in order to maintain his student deferment, and to take out student loans as well as get a full-time work-study job as a campus grounds-keeper in order to continue with school. This sudden change from doing what came naturally (throwing javelins) to what came effortfully (working sixteen-hour days as a scholar/drudge) was the toughest transition he'd ever been called on to make. But it wasn't the quantity of work that made it so. Irwin loved manual labor, was the extreme opposite of lazy, and was a decent student too. It was his character, his nature, that made his situation so difficult.

Proponents of Zen say that there are two ways of attaining self-knowledge. One is called *jiriki*, which translates "self power"; the other is *tariki*, which translates "Other Power." The medieval Scholastics used the terms "will" and "grace" to describe the same two principles. And

Irwin's great strength, his great source of happiness, was his love of living by *tariki* alone. Not only did he "consider the lilies of the field," he *behaved* like one. He loved nothing better than to take absolutely no thought for the morrow, then to sit back and grin when the Good Lord's grace took care of him anyhow. His athletic life, his religious life, his love life were all an undifferentiated series of heart-over-head impulses, one blind leap of faith after another. Blind leaping was his joy, it was what he'd always lived for. And his shoulder injury had suddenly made his life a marathon of the head and the will.

He didn't complain. It must have been terribly hard for him, but he never griped at all. What he did do, though, was start warning us. Every time a family member asked how he was doing, he'd say "Great," but then add that he didn't know how much longer he could keep it up. Everett and I always greeted these doubts with a barrage of Vietnam horror stories—which Irwin always listened to with a wonderful non se-quitur of a smile. But in time I realized what this smile meant: he didn't *care* how long he kept it up. He had no fear of failure, or of the draft. He adored Other Power, and trusted it to care for him even if he did end up in 'Nam. He even gave Everett an apoplectic fit once by remarking that "a guy like me just might be needed over there"!

Fortunately, as far as the draft was concerned, Irwin would have his church behind him. A number of Adventist boys—our old buddy Augie Mosk among them—had dropped or fallen out of college and gotten themselves inducted. And say what you will about the church of my childhood, it stood by its kids when the Armed Forces came for them. Every young man I knew who'd applied for Conscientious Objector status through the SDAs had received it. And though they ended up working minimum-wage "philanthropic" jobs for two years, minimum wage was more than the Army paid its 'Nam grunts. Augie spent two years fixing busted toys for Goodwill. Another guy we knew supervised an assembly line of retarded people who put cellophane wrappers on eight-track stereo tapes. And though they both complained of boredom, there was no boot-camp brainwashing, no shooting, no Napalm or Vietcong. So if worse came to worst, I figured there was still no way Irwin would end up in 'Nam.

And worse did come to worst. Irwin managed to keep his dual career as a scholar/drudge going from '67 clear through the end of '69. But shortly after Christmas he sent a little postcard that said nothing but

DEAR FAMILY: REMEMBER THIS WELL: HER NAME IS LINDA!

And somehow we recognized at once the ominousness of this message. He added nothing, elucidated nothing, and refused to speak when Mama and I phoned and Bet and Everett wrote to ask if he was in love. But in January 1970, when his mysterious Linda apparently left town for a few weeks to try to chase down some long-lost relative or other, Irwin suffered a total *tariki* takeover . . .

Without consulting anyone he dropped out of school and moved into the attic of a big shambles of a farmhouse outside Eugene—a place collectively run by a bunch of woolly-brained, Jesus-praising "Crippies" (Everett's term for Christian hippies). They called their little spread the Ark, after Noah's, though it was landlocked, which was lucky, since they never could get their roof or toilet to stop leaking. The name Ark didn't seem to do their animals much good either: the milk cow died from eating nails left lying in the bottom of the cedar feed trough they'd built her; six of the nine goats were wiped out in a single day when they were fed yew-tree trimmings; the chicken coop was raided by weasels just as often as the weasels could manage to get hungry; and after the cats all died of distemper and leukemia the cat-chasing dog, Apostle, got bored and took to chasing cars, as if he couldn't wait to be the next entry in the Ark's animal graveyard, which was already as big as the vegetable garden, and as edible, too, since the surviving three goats had eaten all the vegetables.

But Irwin, once *tariki* took him over, considered the Ark the next-best thing to heaven. And after spending his last tuition check on a little Sears stereo, a bluegrass and gospel record collection (Linda's favorites), a diamond engagement ring and a bunch of roofing and plumbing materials, he set about burying animals, plugging leaks and living like a field lily as he awaited his Linda's return—and his draft board's decree.

5. Mecca

The love of those things that are outside Christianity keeps me outside the Church.
   —Simone Weil

One Saturday morning in 1969, our twelve-year-old sister Winifred far surpassed any church going insurrections her notorious brothers had ever taken part in when she not only prayed audibly to Allah and lectured on the Prophet, but bowed to Mecca on the Sabbath School floor. Her teacher, Mrs. Babcock, responded by hospitalizing Freddy with cartilage damage to her right ear. The reason for the blow up was not entirely clear from Freddy's hysterical report, but after Mama and Bet drove over to discuss the matter with the Babcocks it became far less clear. Mrs. Babcock and Freddy agreed that the latter had called the former a "hair shirt," a "stupid fat whale" and a "porkbrained sow," that she had done so because Mrs. Babcock had lifted her off the floor by her ear, and that Freddy's purpose on the floor had been to pray in the traditional Islamic manner. But all this was the grand finale. What they couldn't agree on was everything that led up to it.

By her own report, Mrs. Babcock had been endeavoring to instruct her "Early Teens" on the "very real danger of cults and false religions." But according to Winifred—who, thanks to her correspondence with Peter, probably knew more about Hinduism, Buddhism and Islam than the entire Northwest Adventist clergy, let alone their wives—the "old cow was spraying manure all over the room and calling it Christianity." Freddy said (in words very different from these) that she was just sitting there as usual, trying to bear Mrs. Babcock's fatuous espousals with Gandhian patience, that she held up all right when Mrs. B. lumped Krishna, Buddha, Brigham Young, Karl Marx and the Pope together under the heading "Antichrists," and that she even managed to bite her tongue while the entire Hindu, Buddhist and Islamic worlds were scraped up in the same shovel as Satanists, Moonies, Darwinists, Homosexuals "and of course Catholics," then tossed onto a dungheap labeled "Cults." But when Mrs. Babcock tried to add spice to her lecture by adding that "certain ex-members of this very church have fallen under Satan's power," when she winced piously at a poster of a big brown-haired idiotically grinning Caucasian football-player-type guy who was supposed to be Jesus, then betrayed her own husband's confidences by looking straight at Winifred and huffing, "Some members of this very *class* have fallen under the influence of certain lost souls who have given their lives over to false Christs and Satanic cults!", Freddy's radiator blew.

For a while no one knew it had blown, because Mrs. Babcock had said, "Let us close our lesson with a few heartfelt moments of prayer." But these heartfelt moments usually began with a brief silence, followed by an extemporaneous chat between Mrs. Babcock and the Lord during which the former did all the latter's thinking and talking for Him. On this day, however, the silence was pierced by a high, quavering, angry voice, singing: *Bismi'Lahi'r-Rahmani'r-Rahim* . . .

With great reluctance, Mrs. Babcock later admitted to Mama, Bet and the Elder that the voice had been Freddy's. The reason for her reluctance was that the instant she heard it she'd gestured for silence and said, "Children! The Holy Spirit! Our Winifred has returned to us, and she's speaking in tongues!"

At which point the singing stopped, and Freddy laughed and said, "I am not! I was singing, 'In the Name of God, the Compassionate, the Merciful.' "

Too flustered to be angry, Mrs. Babcock said, "It sounded very . . . pretty."

"Thank you," Freddy replied. "It's Arabic. My brother Peter taught it to me. But Muhammad sang it first, and he got it straight from God." And before Mrs. B. could recover, Freddy turned to the other kids and continued: "Muhammad was the Christ of the Muslims. And he was wonderful! He liked to ride camels and eat dates off of palm trees, and to make jokes, even at church. And when he'd bow down to pray he had this little granddaughter he let ride on his back."

When some of the kids appeared to enjoy this information, Mrs. Babcock gathered enough of herself together to shout that there would be no more talk of "Antichrists" in her church. Both parties agreed that Freddy then shouted back, "Muhammad's no Antichrist and this isn't your church!" But there was vehement disagreement on whether she added: "you big shit!" When, at the discussion, Beatrice told the Babcocks that she and Freddy never used the word "shit" because it was one of the words their brothers beat to death, one of the words they disparagingly called "Camas Boy Talk," Mrs. Babcock had snapped, "They're *both* lying!" And, in that instant, Mama lost all sympathy for her and began to quietly defend her daughters, though she had to defy the Elder (and more or less accuse Mrs. B. of calling *herself* a big shit) to do it.

The mechanism of Mama's sudden loss of sympathy fascinates me. Had the Babcocks told her that all six of her kids were now irredeemable cult-worshippers who'd end up writhing eternally in hell, I know she wouldn't have batted an eye. Yet to hear her daughters accused of a simple lie was intolerable. "Ungodliness" in one's offspring is, after all, a lofty-sounding but essentially incomprehensible condition that leads one to reflect upon the terrible powers of Satan and the still greater powers of God. Whereas bald-faced lying is a tacky little crime that implies one has simply blown it as a parent.

Be that as it may, the rest of the Sabbath School episode had been straightforward crime and punishment. Mrs. Babcock had yelled "Silence!" Freddy had replied, "Okay. Just tell me which way's east. I wanna bow to Mecca." And when Mrs. Babcock did not divulge the requested information, Freddy dropped to the floor and started to pray in a direction she later realized was southwest—which she felt might explain why Allah didn't protect her when Mrs. Babcock pounced, grabbed her ear, and yanked her so violently to her feet that she required minor surgery at Vancouver General Hospital later that day.

When Papa and I joined Mama and the twins at the hospital and Papa set eyes on the bandaged ear, he turned his scariest kind of quiet, then said, "Sweetheart. I'm sorry I didn't speak up sooner, but listen. Unless you want to, you never have to go to that damned church, or any other, again."

Turning at once to Mama, whose face showed no surprise, Freddy said, "I love you, Mama. And I love God too. But I really don't like your church much. I'm sorry, but that's just how I feel."

I thought this an amazingly diplomatic speech under the circumstances. I think Mama did too. I think she might have taken it well, if she'd had a chance. (She had already called up, fought, and defeated the Elder on the subject of who was going to pay the hospital bill.) But before she could respond to Freddy's statement, Papa snapped, "Don't worry about your mother, honey. She makes her *own* choices. Those Babcock idiots are just plain vicious."

And just like that, Mama was on fire. "To save a family like this one," she said, "you'd just about *have* to be."

Papa blew his stack. "Goddammit, Laura! Use the brain God gave you! When some old rhino roughs your daughter up, it doesn't save *any*body!"

Mama said nothing more. She was afraid the noise would hurt Freddy's ear. But our dinner, back home a few hours later, consisted of boiled eggplant, burnt turbot and a bowl of half-raw baked potatoes. And after saying his usual grace, Papa looked at it, took just one bite, then slid his plate away. Smiling at Mama, he calmly, almost genially said, "The hell with this food, Laura. The hell with this cook-for-revenge strategy. Vengeance is the Lord's, not yours. I will not be punished for that Babcock woman's tiny brain and bad temper. And neither will my children."

With that he stood, marched down the hall to their bedroom, and dumbfounded us all by raiding the little blue ceramic jewelry box where Mama kept her Sabbath tithes and offerings. "You're all invited out for hamburgers," he said when he returned.

Freddy and I grinned, and stood up to leave. Mama and Bet frowned, and stayed put. "Papa," Bet said. "That money is God's. Not yours."

"Then God's buying," Papa said.

Freddy and I laughed. Bet said, "It's not funny."

"Bet honey," Papa said. "This money is your mother's till she puts it in the offering plate. And then it becomes Babcock's, not God's. If God needed money, He'd make his own. And if He wanted ours, He'd just *take* it."

Freddy and I were laughing again, but Bet ignored us. "I'll always go to church with you, Mama," she said. "And so will Irwin."

It was an odd moment, a moment that needed to be dealt with delicately. Bet meant only to show her love and loyalty, but we were breaking into factions again, we were forming armies against our will. And Papa, this time, just couldn't seem to care. "I suppose this is some sort of crisis," he sighed. "And I suppose we should talk about it for hours. But sometimes a guy just wants to go eat a goddamned hamburger. For me, this is one of those times." And he started for the door.

Freddy and I looked from Bet, to the dismal food she'd begun mouthing, to Mama, who sat crimson-faced, staring at nothing. Then we looked at each other. And both felt ashamed. But her ear still hurt, and I was hungry: we went with Papa.

6. Everett's Finger Does the Walking

The cost of a thing is the amount of what I will call life which is required to be exchanged for it, immediately, or in the long run.
  —Henry David Thoreau

Telephones are, without question, useful devices. But they are also, it seems to me, the verbal equivalent of houses without toilets. Telephones allow minds to communicate with minds (or tongues with ears, at least) in clarity or turmoil, in semisomnolence or drunkenness, in lust, joy, hysteria, stupefaction or any other state that fails to render a human physically incapable of holding up a quarter-pound chunk of perforated plastic—which is most every state there is. That telephones can connect us in seconds to any creature on earth foolhardy enough to lift its own chunk of plastic is wonderful. But it's also terrible, given what a lot of people think and feel about each other. That's why, until they're equipped with some sort of flush or filter or waste-disposal system for the billions of words that ought not to be spoken, I'll not trust the things.

In 1969—thanks to the old dial-a-prayer projects that resulted in the manifestations of G. Q. Durham and Doc Franken—Everett had an idolatrous faith in telephones. In 1969 he also still hated Elder Babcock as much as he hated anybody, but his antiwar struggles had dispersed his hate over such a wide area that the Elder seldom entered his mind anymore. When Freddy wrote and told Everett what Mrs. Babcock had done to her ear, though, the Babcocks reentered his mind in a hurry. In fact he walked straight to his phone in a rabid-dog stagger, dialed directory assistance, then the Babcocks' number, heard the Elder lift his quarter-pound chunk of plastic, and just that fast was engaged in a malediction match with the only man I know of leather-lunged and tenacious enough to rage as long and loudly as Everett himself.

What Everett later recalled was not so much the verbal blows struck as the odd rhythm of the striking. He'd expected the two of them to blaze away simultaneously, like riot cops and students at a militant demonstration, but instead their fury had fallen into a pattern: one of them would suck down a lungful of air, blaze away for as long as it lasted, then pause to catch his breath while the other poured out a lungful of abuse. It was almost mannerly, Everett said, "like an old Napoleonic duel."

But when he got around to telling me what they'd actually said, I saw nothing duel-like about it. It reminded me more of a fight I'd once seen between two hoods at my high school—two notorious street-fighting toughs who hated each other so much, but were so equally matched, that in the end they hadn't the wit or energy to avoid a single punch: they just stood there, propped up by sheer kinetic hatred, taking gentlemanly, almost golferlike swings from the heels as they smashed each other's faces into featureless pulp. Babcock's initial thesis had been that "Everett Chance" and "Satan's Minion" were virtually synonymous terms. Everett had countered by shouting that Adventism was just a quirky little nineteenth-century cult started by a barnstorming peabrain and a puritanical plagiarist, and that it had survived into this century only because of the segregated school system and financial empire built by money-sucking leeches like Babcock himself. The Elder then averred that Everett was possessed and unnatural, that he had sex with himself constantly and probably with animals and his brothers as well, and that his pimples, manners, beliefs, depraved writings and speech all proved this. Everett told the Elder that he underestimated himself terribly, and that thanks to his last visit to our house we brothers had repented, baptized each other in the upstairs tub, and enjoyed several hours of Christian group sex afterward. Babcock cried out that on the day Everett and all his brothers tumbled down into the Lake of Unquenchable Fire, he would praise and thank his Just Lord and Savior and weep copious tears of joy. "Better an eternity in that lake than a night in bed with your sow of a wife," quoth Everett. "How about your sisters, boy?" Babcock shot back. "Have you laid your lascivious hands on *them* yet?" And so on and so forth. Obviously, the AT&T conversation-flushing phone-toilet was what the situation required.

Everett and I had a telephone falling-out of our own when he bragged to me about getting in the last word. He said he'd shouted at Babcock that the kind of preacher who threatens others with hell is no different than any moron leather-jacketed greaser who shoves his middle finger in people's faces and tells them "Fuck you!"—and Babcock, instead of answering, had hung up on him.

Then I said to Everett, "I think you're right. Babcock *is* that kind of preacher. So why are you trying to be the moron greaser?"

And Everett hung up on me!

7. A Triple A Kind of Guy

As I remember, the bases were loaded.
  —Garry Maddox, ex-Phillies outfielder,
    trying to recollect his first grand slam homer

Papa Toe Chance—stuck though he was in a rickety marriage and the statistical prison of mid-inning relief—managed by the end of two and two-thirds seasons to make himself indispensable to the Tugs, to win four ballgames, and to save God-knows-how-many. No statistician kept track of saves till the Rolaids antacid company came up with a "relief" award as a publicity gimmick in 1969 (I'm not making this up). Papa guesses he saved around ten. John Hultz thought it was more like forty. But Papa thinks Johnny was confusing what he calls "turnarounds"—games that were won because the Tugs relaxed and played better ball after Papa's appearance—with legitimate saves. Be that as it may, over the course of the same two and two-thirds seasons he also lost four games (nice balance), hit five home runs (we were definitely counting those) and two triples (which he beat out on nine toes). And he maintained a 3.10 ERA in one of the worst pitcher's ballparks on the face of the earth.

But as Everett said, numbers, for all their vaunted accuracy, are amazingly inaccurate little doodads. They look nice in the books, but the flesh-and-blood actions they stand for are almost impossible to remember. That's why, silly as they can be, I prefer to remember the old words, the phrases, the names. I like to recall how, for a few years back at the dawn of the Hippie Era, the name Papa Toe could be heard in jock taverns all over the Portland-Vancouver area, and in dugouts all up and down the West Coast. I like remembering how his best pitch had been dubbed the Kamikaze in a backyard hedge hideout, but the nickname had caught on and traveled all up and down the same coast. And I like to recall how, at the height of this manageable little notoriety, Papa laughed as he and I were driving home to Camas late one summer night, and said, "You know what's so funny about this Papa Toe stuff, Kade? Nothing's changed! My shed's a little bigger now, and I'm free of the mill. But I'm still just tryin' to keep my head on straight. I'm still just throwin' those what-did-we-call-'ems? Psalmballs? Prayerballs? Harelipped prayers?"

By September 1967, the Pirate management got curious about all the glowing tales their ex-Tugs kept telling about this Papa Toe character, so they decided to fly him up to Pittsburgh for a few innings of what was, unquestionably, "stupid relief." The adventure allowed Papa to prove almost nothing to them but his physical existence—yet they flew him up *again* in 1969. In '67 the Pirates finished in sixth place; in '69 they finished third. Both years they made no bones about having zero interest in Papa's potential as a pitcher, only the mildest interest in his potential as a pitching coach or scout, but a fair amount of interest in trotting him around in front of journalists and publicists as some sort distinguished-looking mill-gimped "human-interest story."

Embarrassing as this was, it enabled Papa to throw nine bona fide innings of Big-Time Baseball (three during the first visit, six during the second) that he would never have been able to throw otherwise. True, he gave up twelve hits and six runs. But he got a fluke end-of-the-bat single off Bob Gibson. And hit Hank Aaron in the thigh with a stage-frightened Kamikaze. And got young Davey Johnson to ground into a double play. And he didn't lose. Or win. Which I think fit his entire knight-errant's legend just about perfectly. He had a slight case of jet lag the first time he pitched, but he didn't really think that was why he got shelled. "After all these years," he confessed in a postcard afterward, "I think I've finally just become a Triple A kind of guy."

8. The Fiddler on the Roof

In comparison to what I've suffered from myself, the humiliation and suffering inflicted on me by others vanishes into insignificance.
  —Heimito von Doderer

It started out as a typical march for Everett: the same old eight or ten thousand concerned campus clucks and city liberals; the same two or three hundred hard-core rads; the same Seattle city police escort service; even the same pathetic narc in the middle of the action, decked out like a Hollywood Haight Streeter, wheezing "Bodacious shit!" over and over as he passed out free reefers so they could break your head and bust you for possession later on if need be. Their destination was typical too, though Everett had a larger than usual role in creating it: they were heading to Pier 2, right in downtown Seattle, for a "nonviolent confrontation" ("i.e. impotent show of disgruntlement," said Everett) with a brand-new nuclear submarine which some highly paid panel of Pentagon damage-control experts had dubbed the *Liberty*. According to a less than substantive article Everett had written for the underground *Callipygian Quarterly*, this sub had cost "exactly what J. Edgar Hoover said CBS would have to pay him to suck Abbie Hoffman's dick on prime-time TV." But nobody seemed to mind the price tag. The sub sat at the pier for weeks, bland and matter-of-fact as a double-parked taxi, and attracting about as much attention. But then Everett happened to read a Seattle *Times* interview in which the sub's somewhat confused commander gloated that his vessel packed "the range and nuclear firepower to take out every major city on the west coast of North America." That was all it took: the next day Everett's "Give Chance a Peace" column dubbed the commander "Admiral Wrongway Peachfuzz," thirty thousand students had a good chuckle, the alternative press and peace organizations jumped on it, and the march was planned. Yelling "Go home!" to an inanimate albatross that was already almost home (it had been manufactured in nearby Bremerton) didn't sound very interesting at all. But marching off to tell Admiral Wrongway Peachfuzz to get his fucking continents straight sounded like good fun.

So off they'd gone, uptown to down, and all too soon the march had become the usual tedious battle between two radically opposed musical sensibilities—Crooners versus Chanters: "If I Had a Hammer" or "Amazing Grace" whenever things bogged down in an intersection; "Hey! Hey! LBJ!" or "One Two Three Four!" whenever their twenty thousand feet started laying down a groove. Everett didn't mind the chanting much, but about the third time the sweet sound tried to save a wretch like him he decided to obliterate his awareness by resorting to one of his tried-and-truest peace-march diversions: by speeding up to the front of the parade column, then slowing down and weaving from one side of the street to the other, it was possible within the space of a few miles and minutes to scrutinize the bottoms of literally *thousands* of women. A couple of thousand ifs, ands and butts into this exercise and he'd reached a nirvana of lust that had him bellowing "Amazing Grace" like it was his all-time favorite song. But was it excessive discharge or merely excessive ogling that Ezra Pound said would lead to imbecility? Everett used to remember, but by the time they'd reached the pier his maneuvers had him weaving like a drunk. Fearing he might muff his speech, he started struggling, like some hopeless old smoker with emphysema, to break his habit. But just as the crowd spread out round the boardwalk and pier to surround the infamous submarine, just as the portable p.a. was fired up and the first speaker began to let Admiral Peachfuzz have it, Everett nearly collided with a female lower story in frayed jeans that fit like pantyhose, raised his eyes to a second story swathed in a lavender BONG THE PENTACONG! T-shirt (one of his own slogans!), reached an incredibly profuse head of shimmering reddish-brown hair, and involuntarily told himself: *If the face and front match the rest, I'm gonna propose on the spot!*

Easing up beside her, he consciously reminded himself to swallow his drool, cranked up the aphrodisiacal eye magic, cleared his throat, waited for her eyes and lips to bequeath him his first inspired line. And she turned to him.

And loudly snorted.

Shit O. Deer. It was the Natasha wench. The one who'd told him off at Gurtzner's lecture. And her face, even smirking, *surpassed* the rest of her.

"How's the Seattle One-Seventh?" she asked.

"Huh?" quoth the urbane Everett, thinking, *How does she know I was Adventist?*

"The Chicago Seven. The Seattle One-Seventh. A joke for a joker. Get it?"

"Oh. Huh. Fine." Where was his brain? And his magic tongue? What had she done with them? How had she done it?

"It was a mean greeting, though," she said, smiling wryly but radiantly.

"If I'm going to improve your manners, I'd better start with my own. So let me take it back. 'How are you, Everett,' I should have said. And let me also admit that I usually read your column, and even enjoy it—when you pick the right targets."

She paused. And he could not think of a single word to say. "Hey, come on!" she said. "You look like you don't believe me."

He didn't, but not at all in the sense she meant.

"Want some two-cent reviews to prove it?"

He was in luck! She'd asked a question he could answer by nodding!

"The Wrongway Peachfuzz thing: brilliant. The piece on politicians and women, '21 World Liters Equals 5 U.S. Gals': weird and a little chauvinistic, but I have to admit I laughed. The behind-the-scenes portrait of the Cajun band, 'Awesome Possum': *very* funny. The Jimmy Stewart meets Jimmy Joyce meets Jimi Hendrix filibuster-on-a-page, 'Smoking Pots in Washingpan': even weirder. Pot and the pen don't mix, pal. At least not for you. Let's see . . . The character assassination of Charismatics: a complete non sequitur for a columnist like you. Who the hell raised you? Cotton Mather? And the piece on stuffy old tenured faculty, with the—what were those bourbons called? 'Old Stepdad'? 'Empty Times'? That one *really* pissed me off. Because it was great. It was right up there with Peachfuzz and Possum. And then you trashed it with the veiled attack on Dr. Gurtzner. Pathetic, Everett! Really petty. No more of those, okay? You should have listened to me the first time."

He was completely overwhelmed, mentally and visually. Was it Pound who said that excessive Natasha could lead to imbecility? "Huh," Everett told her. "Hmm. Okay. Thanks."

She cocked her head, leaned toward him, looked deep into his eyes— and the sun flared red in her auburn hair! her irises were a filigree of coppery greens and blues! the flares and filigree surpassed the face that surpassed the body that surpassed the bottom that surpassed the five thousand bottoms he'd just peace-marched past! Then she said, "Are you stoned, Everett?"

"Me?" He blushed. "Oh, *no*."

She laughed. "What's with the face? And the giant 'oh, no'? You think I care? A big ol' hippie like you? I should think you'd be ashamed to be seen straight."

"Huh." He managed a shrug. "Well, I'm not. I mean, I'm not stoned, I mean. I just, uh, have to speak in a bit."

"Ah!" She laughed. "Well, good luck!"

"Huh. I mean, thanks." *Where was his brain!*

She laughed again. "So even the Big Bad Rad gets a little stage fright, huh?"

"Huh?"

"I already said that."

"Huh."

"Hey, listen. Just . . . never mind. I'll talk to you later. Go give 'em hell. Sorry I broke your concentration. And be funny, okay?"

"Huh. Hey. Thanks. Okay, thanks."

Shit O. Deer.

"There's an old Yiddish saying that I used to find funny. It went, 'If the rich could hire others to die for them, the poor could make a good living.' "

The crowd roared—ten thousand people throwing back their heads and howling because of something Everett had said. That was power! That was euphoria! And he'd stolen the line from the dad in *Fiddler on the Roof.*

"That's right," he continued without cracking a smile—because he saw Natasha hadn't cracked a smile. "It's a funny saying to a healthy mind. It's a joke. And I grew up in a home where it was considered tasteless, if not a deadly sin, to have to explain a joke. But I feel a need to explain this one."

Some stoned-out dork back in the crowd let out a hysterical shriek of laughter. "The reason the saying was considered funny is that dead men can't spend money. Everybody knew that, back in the old days."

But now the entire crowd was yukking it up again! Ten thousand people chuckling at a joke that wasn't there! Except Natasha. Who was putting on sunglasses. And *now* look at her face. Impenetrable blankness. Look at those damned mirror shades. World's sexiest grasshopper. Look at that body! Shit O. Deer. "But the incredible thing about this joke . . ." *Go slower. Maybe they'll catch on.* ". . . the incredible thing about it, and the reason I've committed the sin of explaining it, is that the Americans in power just don't get it anymore. In the name of our country, a lot of Yanks have been asking their own sons to leave our country, to go to Vietnam, and to die a death they neither understand nor choose. In other words, to become the new Yiddish poor."

A few no-hope yo-yos chuckled, but most of the crowd seemed somewhat moved now. Whew. Apparently no one wondered why he was giving a Vietnam rap at an antisubmarine rally. The truth was, he'd been so sure of his Wrongway Peachfuzz material that he'd decided to wing it. But when he'd faced the crowd, when he'd received the glowing intro, when the palpable wind of the cheering blew through him, creating the power surge that always set his magic tongue in motion, he made the fatal blunder of smiling at Natasha . . . and all he had left after she smiled back were cotton mouth and the opening line from some antiwar talk he'd given God-knows-where. Maybe clear back in high school. And it wasn't even funny!

"Should any male student in this crowd choose to exercise his freedom by leaving school tomorrow, should he become ill, or troubled, or distracted by, say, falling in love . . ." *(oh good! very subtle, Everett!)* ". . . should he even be flunked by some grumpy ol' European Intellectual History professor . . ." *(she's flipping me the bird!)* ". . . he, uh, he . . ." (Shit O. Deer) ". . . excuse me, he will lose his deferment and become eligible for a draft created not by any democratic process, but by the decree of Americans so powerful, so imperial, that they can force the disenfranchised, the nonintellectual and the unlucky to kill and be killed in what is, for them, just a profitable military and political experiment."

Okay. Pretty decent recovery. He gave them the three-second pause, let the groundswell of anger build, collected his shredded wits, and even managed to generate some power as he asked, "How can they get away with this? In the land of the so-called free, how can our leaders get away with this Czar-like betrayal of their very own sons?"

Then she yawned. Devastation! One lousy yawn and he found himself thinking, "How do *I* get away with *this?*" He tried to fight back. He tried to summon his arrogance: *I made 'em cry with this speech once! I can still make it work!* He summoned his Sabbath School roots: *No Delilah for this Samson, thank you!* But when she yawned yet again, he nearly yawned himself as he said to the crowd, "I'll tell you how. They use the old Yiddish punchline. They *pay* us for it. Except listen. The Yiddish joke said that if the rich could hire others to die for them, the poor could make a *good* living. But for going to Vietnam, our American Czars pay us something like thirty-seven cents an hour! They can't even get the damned joke right!"

The crowd whistled and laughed and revived him enough so that, by keeping his eyes as far from Natasha as he could without turning his back on his audience, he thought he *might* be able to finish. Taking a deep breath, he tried to look solemn instead of spaced, and said, "The old Yiddish joke has become the life story of one and a half million American boys so far. And the death story of forty-seven thousand of them." There were murmurs. There was anger. There was even a moan. Fantastic. He gave them the full four-second pause. Then: "To my mind, a joke that kills forty-seven thousand of us is a joke no longer. For dirt wages, the rich and powerful *are* hiring the poor to die for them. *We* are the poor. So I ask you. At the very least, isn't it time we told our Czars to find a new fucking joke to tell us?"

The crowd went wild. All right! It hadn't gone badly after all.

But where was his brain-melting nemesis? Ah. Of course. Standing by a phone pole reading a bunch of rain-shredded year-old rock-concert posters.

"I'd heard it," she said, once he'd fought his way through the thank-you!s and far-out!s and way-to-go-man!s to stand like a mute little lapdog at her side. "Twice before, actually."

"Huh. I mean, sorry."

"No no. Don't apologize. I understand. You media-hype types have got to repeat yourselves now and then."

The poetry of her jeans! The Dow Jones Industrial Average of her sunglasses! The well-meant, emasculating, malevolent benevolence of her words! By the time he'd exhausted himself listening to and looking at her, he was honestly speaking every word he could think of when he said, yet again: "Huh."

"I'm whipped, Everett. What say we bag this Boston Tea Party and go for some real tea? Or if it's Lipton, some coffee?"

The sunsets in her eyes! the sun-flares in her hair! he, Everett? him with them? "Coffee?" he said.

"Coffee."

"I mean, sure."

"You need a rest, Everett."

"Huh."

"Huh."

They'd spent the rest of the day together. And Everett had discovered that her original name had been Laurel Lee, that she was from Knoxville, Tennessee, that her parents had divorced when she was thirteen, that she'd read *War and Peace* during the custody battle, that she'd changed her name to Natasha after her mother moved them to Phoenix, Arizona, and that Laurel Lee of Tennessee was every bit as appealing but no easier to impress than Natasha of Czarist Russia. For his part, Everett continued to say "huh" and "whew" a lot. He also managed to murmur that the march and speech had fried him. But he wasn't fried. He was far worse off than that. He was imploded. The stand-up-firebrand-playboy-super-star, the man who'd wanted Woman, had been reduced to a pile of mute brown dust by the intensity of his need for this one inimitable woman—and he sensed that the sooner he showed his need, the sooner she would reject him.

Hoping he'd sensed wrong, he finally couldn't resist venturing, while walking her home, to place a single finger in a belt loop on the side of the eudaemoniacal jeans. *Instant havoc!* She spun away in a cloud of speech and beauty that stirred the dust he'd become till the very air of the city turned brown. "I like you, Everett," she said as he peered through the sediment. "And I find you ridiculous. I might even like having sex with you, and finding that ridiculous. But I'm a dinosaur, Everett. Because I believe in romance. Understand? And if we started a romance off with a Peachfuzz march, a used speech, a coffee and a fuck, where on earth could it go from there?"

When Everett spared her the "huh" and said nothing, she gave him back his own rhetorical "I'll tell you where" and added: "Back to your imaginary revolution. And on to your next . . . girlfriend or groupie or whatever you call your rotation of female admirers. Which just ain't my style. So I'll see you around. Okay?"

That pretty well did it. Nothing left on the sidewalk beside her but a mute, half-blind, Everett-shaped pile of dry rot awaiting a dustpan. Which is why he didn't even see the lips coming as they reached right in through the brownness and bequeathed him a kiss which, for all its fleet-ingness and all his experience, he swears was his very first.

9. Cat versus Wallace Stevens

Okay, you guys. Pair up in threes.
  —Yogi Berra

In December 1969, after a brief visit home from Harvard, Peter hitch-hiked up to Seattle to catch a plane back to Boston, and also to spend an afternoon and night with Everett, whom he hadn't seen in nearly two years. They met, at Everett's suggestion, in a U-district sandwich and beer joint—a small, smoky place decorated with neon-lit posters of Vin-cent van Gogh's most lysergic-looking paintings, hence its teeth-grind-ingly groovy name, Van GoGo's. Definitely a foreign country for the non-drinking, nonsmoking, vegetarian Peter. But, contrary to Everett's expectation, Pete didn't grow faint or nauseous upon entering. Like a regular guy in a beer ad (except for the ponytail and East Indian clothes), he smiled with delight as he clapped Everett on the shoulder, said how great it was to see him, and seemed to mean it. And though he couldn't quite bring himself to order a Bud, he did spring for a pitcher of imported draft for them both.

But the old roommates had barely sucked the foam from their beers when a woman took the stool on Everett's opposite side, ordered an Olympia (never a good sign), took a sip, then seemed to say to the beer, "You look just like Cat Stevens!"

Hearing her speak, both my brothers looked at her. Peter's impression was that she was some soused suburban housewife drinking her way home from a party, where she'd worn her teenaged daughter's tackiest clothes for a joke. But Everett's reaction was quite different. Though he clearly saw the colorless, predatory eyes, the lime-green hip-hugger bellbottoms, the broad white plastic belt, and the literal bells (the kind Santa's helpers sew on Christmas stockings) round the flared cuffs, none of this prevented him from remarking to his own beer, "You look like somebody who wouldn't like Cat Stevens."

Thinking this was mere friendliness, thinking that Everett was becoming less superficial about the appearance of others, Peter tried to think good thoughts as well as he watched the woman turn to Everett, note that his ponytail was thick and clean, that the ear on her side sported a small gold ring, and that the brown beard swirled down into the black chest hair in the open shirt. But he couldn't help cringing as she moaned, again into her Oly, "I just *adore* Cat Stevens!"

"What say we move to a table?" Pete whispered to Everett.

"What for?" Everett asked.

"Exactly like him!" the woman repeated.

"To chat about matters of life, death and baseball," Peter said. "And to give this nice lady and her beer some privacy so they can chat too."

"What if she doesn't want privacy?" Everett said.

" 'On the Road to Find Out,' " she said. "That's my absolute favorite!"

"Let's just go," Peter whispered.

But Everett ignored him, and began to study the woman more closely.

Wondering what he could possibly be thinking now (deep people are often mystified by hopelessly shallow situations), Peter tried to study her too. But it wasn't easy for him. Though his vegetarianism and Buddhism didn't prevent him from noticing that her breasts were rather extensive, what really struck him was her abdomen. It was a pale, distended, sad-looking thing, completely exposed by her hideous pants and short, frilled blouse. Pete's feeling was that, no matter whether babies, groceries, or beers from previous pit stops had brought it to its present pass, it was an abdomen that had seen years of hard use and now deserved a dignified life of privacy. But no sooner had he thought this than Everett looked the woman in the face and, with a tough little shrug, told her, "I prefer Mick Jagger."

And her eyes began running up and down him like a pair of mice exploring a two-pound block of cheese.

Pete finally began to catch on: the R-rated brotherly chat for which he'd detoured through Seattle was in danger of being preempted by Everett's conflicting role in an eventually to be X-rated performance with the Sad Abdomen Lady! He could hardly believe it. He felt ashamed to even think it. But Everett was clearly onstage now: he'd come entirely to his surface; everything he did or didn't do was intended to convey messages to the woman. His manner was no longer aloof: it was a performance that said, *Isn't my manner aloof?* His hair, beard and earring were no longer whimsical hippie paraphernalia: they were calculated image-implements designed to say: *I like the Stones. I'm dangerous. What do you think of me?* What was worse, it was all working. "Mick Jagger *scares* me!" the woman half gasped. "But I just *love* Cat Stevens."

Everett swiveled round to face her now. The eyes were definitely not bright, the hair a lank blond, the clothes impossible. On the other hand, the hips and thighs were trimmer and the legs not as short as the belly led one to expect. And the breasts, truth to tell, were really *quite* large. "Don't get excited," he said, "but I *am* Cat Stevens."

Hearing this, the woman skooched her legs around each other, jingled her bells, leaned toward Everett till their shoulders touched, and laughed and squirmed the sorts of laughs and squirms that Jehovah may have witnessed on the day He created misogyny. The Cosmos kept its balance, though, because Everett was meanwhile leering the sort of testicular leer that Kali may well have had in mind when She inspired Man to create asbestos, carcinogenic beer and the trenches of World War I. Somewhere along in here Peter finally did begin to feel nauseous. But, again contrary to Everett's theories about him, this nausea was not self-centered or self-preserving: it was entirely on his brother's behalf. "What is *wrong?*" Peter was thinking. "What's happened to Everett?" Because to be doing what he was doing, it seemed obvious to Peter that Everett must despise himself. The irony was that Everett was trying to love himself—and it was coming to the same thing.

At any rate, Pete wanted to help him. And the only way he could think to do this was to break the claim these two strangers were making on each other. He had no idea how to go about it. He felt stupid and half sick as he spoke. But he loved his brother. So in his dorkiest, most over-stated attempt at a G. Q. Durham accent, he drawled, "Don't get yerself all excited 'bout this either, ma'am, but I'm Cat's younger brother, Dog!"

Maybe it was the word "ma'am" that got her. Too close to reality. Whatever it was, the woman, or old girl, or female bellbottomed person turned and looked at Peter so coldly that a big part of him wanted to just pour his beer on her head and walk away. But then he noticed Everett giving him the same cold look! It was a shock. It sent a jolt of despair through him. But it also made him mad enough to keep on fighting. "You've caught me out!" he said in a stuffy New England accent. "Most astute of you, *ma'am*. The truth is, I'm Cat's older brother, Wallace. I sell insurance mostly, but write the occasional poem. Do you know my work at all?"

This separated them a little: Everett's poetic pretensions compelled him to smile faintly, while Bellbottom-Person just lit a Salem, then eyed Peter's face as though, in a moment, she might need a place to stub it out. *Okay*, Peter thought. *Stick with Stevens. Divide and conquer them with verse.* And fortifying himself with a glug of beer, he turned to Bellbottom-Person and said, "Let me refresh your memory." Then he shut his eyes, and slowly, pompously recited:

> One must have a mind of beer to regard the cigarettes and sad
> faces of the tavern-dwellers crusted with pain, and have been
> lonely a long time to behold the hirsute youth, shagged o'er with
> self-sycophancy, and still believe you want him . . .

This did seem to divide them, but not in the way Peter had hoped. It confused the wiggles clean out of Bellbottom-Person. But Everett spun around to give him a look that said there'd be blood spilt if he didn't back off.

Peter considered it. Out of anger, but also out of regard for his deluded brother, Peter the Hindu/Buddhist/Pacifist seriously considered punching his lights out and dragging him out the door. But when he noticed the woman eyeing them, thrilled to think that she'd been the cause, in less than one Oly, of both poetry and potential violence, he sighed, turned away, and refilled his glass.

Getting back to what she apparently considered the point, Bellbottom-

Person showed her canyonesque cleavage to Everett and said, "Why, silly boy, did you think I wouldn't like Cat Stevens?"

"The truth is," Everett told her, "I could tell you loved Cat Stevens the instant you sat down. I just wanted us to have an argument. That way we'd have a little history."

"Your strange!" she gushed. (She meant "You're," but Peter felt absolutely certain that she was one of those people who spell it "Your.")

"It worked." Everett shrugged.

"Your sweet," she cooed.

"I know," said he.

That did it for Pete. He jumped off his stool and gasped, "Gimme your car keys. Gimme your address. I gotta get outta here."

"What kind of car do you drive?" the woman asked Everett, somehow ignoring all of Peter's outburst but the word "car."

"A big ol' Pontiac battle cruiser," Everett growled, duplicating her feat.

"I think maybe *your* the big ol' Pontiac battle cruiser!" she giggled.

"The keys!" Peter wheezed. *"Now."*

Everett spun on him a second time. "Lay off!"

Then, with a wriggling and giggling and tinkling of bells, Bellbottom-Person said, "I can, uh, give you a lift, Cat. I drive a li'l ol' '68 Firebird!"

For a moment Pete kicked himself for bringing up the fatal subject of cars. But when Everett flashed his perfect teeth at her and replied, "I think maybe *you're* the li'l ol' '68 Firebird!" Peter realized he could have said, "The oracle demands your exhausted crustaceans!" or "Fire off the Number Eight flea coffin!" and the results would have been exactly the same. Then he realized something else: he had just seen enough of his big brother to last for years. And Peter has always been quick to act on an understanding: saying nothing, he headed straight for the door.

"Need these?" Everett smirked, jingling his keys.

Pete kept walking.

"Takin' a taxi?"

Peter never slowed or turned.

"I didn't give you my address!"

The windowless door opened. Everett squinted. Peter's silhouette was black, the day bright white. Then the door closed, he was gone, the silhouette remained long enough to turn from green to red, then it too vanished. "If you ask me," Bellbottom-Person declared, "your brother Wallace is a real jerk!"

"Who asked you?" Everett muttered, feeling as shabby, suddenly, as he really was. For the instant Peter vanished he not only missed him, but realized that he was using the woman to punish Peter for trading baseball in for Buddhism, and to punish Natasha for not buying into his revolution, and to punish Mama for her Puritanism and Babcock for his peabrain and Camas for being Camas and on and on and on.

I'm an idiot! he thought. *I should run after him!*

But even as he thought it he settled down on his stool, turned back to the woman, and slowly refilled their glasses.

Peter made his way, by city bus and thumb, to the airport, spent the night on three molded plastic chairs, flew to Boston the next day, and didn't set eyes on Everett again for nearly four years.

Everett and Bellbottom-Person drank two more pitchers, smoked up her Salems, made a plan to drive to a nearby motel, stepped outside together—and in the rich evening light, as he strolled along with his arm around her, Everett looked down and saw a face so incurably forlorn and sad and hungry that even the breasts she now rubbed against him were no help at all.

They reached the li'l ol' Firebird. It was the same lime green as her pants.

10. The Lady Vanishes

The mind rushes on, a drunk elephant.
  —Kabir

Another Friday night, another party for Everett, and in the crowd again this evening was the incomparable Natasha, whose garb, goddammit, he aimed to vaporize and whose parts he planned to plunder just as soon as he hit on the correct technical approach. He was getting frustrated, though. He'd had to put himself rather heavily under the influence of Dr. Alcohol to protect his magic tongue from Natasha's debilitating gaze, and so far the difference between mute imbecility and drunken magniloquence had not seemed to impress her. His first assault had consisted of inserting himself in a political argument she was having with some drooling poli-sci prof, and pouring out some icebreaking innuendo which used diplomacy as a metaphor—"all hostilities must be suspended," "opposing forces must sit down face to face, in the same quiet place," "meaningful maneuvers must come from both sides," et cetera.

"Are you drunk?" she'd interrupted. And her eyes! They physically hurt him!

"No," he lied.

"Then you're an asshole," she said.

"I'm drunk!" he cried.

"Too late," she said. "I believed you the first time."

Which wasn't so unbearable. But it was her eyes that really did the damage! So beautiful, so expressive, and no mistaking their message: "*Asshole!*" they said. Damn! A few more seconds in the heat of that gaze and his nose would have spiraled up his sinuses and left a big red sphincter sitting in the middle of his face! It took him a full hour and two beers to regroup.

His second assault was made on the tail of an outburst by his old buddy Hank, a staunch SDSer ("Suckers for a Dumb Slogan," Everett called them). Hank was a doctoral student in philosophy and, once upon a time, an eloquent guy, but several years of demonstrations, knee-jerk Marxism, hash-smoking and daytime TV had pared the tree of his knowledge down into a sort of bonsai. This evening, however, Hank had dusted off an old brain lobe or two, entered a sewing circle that included Natasha, and was soon loudly proclaiming that the bloody Gandhians, Martin Luther Kingians and Catholic peace workers should stop trying to shove their nonviolence doctrine down everybody's throat. "It's time the People got pissed!" he was soon happily bellowing. "It's time some honky butt got kicked!"

It fascinated Everett to get to watch it from a distance: with a smile so beautiful that Hank didn't seem to mind, Natasha serenely informed him that he was a moron. Hank looked miffed—till he glanced at her eyes: then he accepted her assertion without protest. But since he was only a moron, not an asshole, she was polite enough to offer a little corroborating evidence; she even tried to couch it in bonsai vocabulary. "The thing is, Hank," she said, "if you kick the right honky butt, it'll turn around and make tear-gassed, riot-clubbed hamburger out of your defenseless own."

"You're saying there's a trade deficit," Hank put in.

Natasha smiled. "More like a missile gap," she said. She then went on to assert that Gandhian nonviolence and "every other deep New Testament or Buddhist or Vedantist value" was an inextricable condition of peace whether Hank liked it or not. "You just can't fight for peace," she said, "without fighting for what lies at the heart of the world's great spiritual traditions." And Everett was suddenly reminded, uncomfortably, of a certain long-lost brother of his.

"You call *hellfire* a value?" Hank roared in rebuttal.

"I call hellfire a threat," Natasha said, "and 'love thy neighbor' a value. But I believe in hell, or something close to it. I think hell is what we get right here on earth when people trade their spiritual and political values in on spiritual and political threats."

Hank seemed impressed, though it may have just been the scenery. But then Natasha committed the rookie mistake of trying to say something sincere and complicated at a party. Her little speech had to do with the tension between Christianity's belligerent, supremist dogmas and its original universal compassion, and Everett found himself reluctantly liking her general drift. But when she tried to illustrate her point by reaching into her favorite cookie jar —Russian lit—and declaring Tolstoy's late Christian novels inferior to his earlier, nonsectarian work, the buzzer went off on Hank's attention span. "I understand what you're driving at," he said. "But it's just book talk, Natasha. Student and professor talk. A campus is a flat little world, sweetie babe. And when you sail out over the edge, you really do fall off. By which I mean it's weirder and uglier than you think out there. By which I mean I speak from experience. By which I mean screw Tolstoy. You wanna find out what Christians really believe these days, just flip on your TV Sunday morning. I hate to disappoint you, Natasha, but there's no tension left between dogma and compassion out there at all. It's pure-D belligerence all the way!"

"Now wait!" Natasha interrupted. "I've got Catholic Worker friends who bend over backwards to cooperate with—"

"*Catholic Workers!*" Hank howled. "Listen, honey bunny. Catholics, outside our flat little campus, are just a pack of archaic weirdos. Their Latin, their Eucharist, their wine and bread and Pope may have wowed the Middle Ages, but that's all a lotta Satanic hooey to the TV believer of today. The blood and body have had it, toots. What the Christians want now ain't wine and bread or even Tolstoy's worst novels. What the Christians want now is—"

"Sugar!" Everett interrupted.

"Huh?" went Hank.

"C&Hianity!" Everett said.

"He's drunk," said Natasha.

"You wish," retorted Everett. "But think about it. The Crusaders, the Conquistadors, the British Navy, the U.S. Cavalry and every other form of Christian Soldier has had it. They *already* stole all the gold from all the brown people. And like Hank was saying, Neo-Christians don't want gold anyway. After a brutal day at the factory, office or bulldozer and a deadly drive home through the rat-hour rush, the evening cocktail has become to Industrial Man what vespers was to the Medieval Christian. But those who total-tee for Jesus fight the same traffic, get the same deep-fried nerves, have the same basic need. And for them that cocktail is taboo. For them the sugar rush is the only legal buzz remaining. And that's where the pure cane white folks at C&H come in."

"Told you he was drunk," Natasha said to Hank.

"You wish," Everett shot back. "But the Fundamentalists' terror of cocktails, and their resultant mass addiction to sugar, has enabled C&Hianity to quietly replace Christianity as the principal religion of the industrialized world."

"Right," Natasha sighed.

But Everett scrupulously avoided her eyes, and by now a little crowd had gathered, and Everett loved nothing—not even the sight of Natasha's blue jeans—more than he loved to play a crowd. "There's more than one kind of gold to squeeze out of a tribe of brown folks, and more than one way to squeeze it. C&Hianity's way is to buy up vast tracts of tropical rain forest, pay the native people to clear-cut, burn, bulldoze and plow their own homeland, and quickly plant that land in sugarcane so that when the natives come to their senses they'll have nothing native left to return to. They then keep a very close eye on the natives' teeth— because C&H scientists have discovered that it takes *exactly* as long for a native people to forget their traditions and become brownish but otherwise reliable White Folks as it does for their lovely white teeth to turn brown."

He got his first all-out roar of laughter. "It's a kind of litmus test," he said. "Or as the brownish White Folks say" (he made himself look toothless), "'lithmuth.'"

He got his second roar. The crowd grew bigger. His painful awareness of Natasha grew smaller. "When the teeth do start to go," he said, "the dirty work is pretty well done. C&H just fires all the workers who want a dental plan, hires a few of the cutest ones to do their TV commercials, and proudly labels the rest of their TV- and Sugar-lovin' wage slaves 'converts,' or in some translations 'employees.' And converts they are. But to C&Hianity, not Christianity."

"It's true!" giggled Melanie.

"It's fairly decent bullshit," Hank admitted.

"Bullshit?" Everett retorted. "Have you guys seen that new translation of the Bible? The one *sponsored* by C&H? I read what it called 'The Brochure of Matthew' and it blew my mind! Wanna hear a few lines?"

Natasha's solo "No!" was obliterated by the boisterous yea-sayers. So in his best Southern Baptist drawl Everett said, "I quote: *And as they were eating, Jesus took the Three Musketeers bar, and blessed it, and brake it, and gave it to the disciples, and at the top of His lungs shouted, 'TAKE! Then EAT!' Thus spake He the Two Commandments, and henceforth by C&Hians the Ten were kept no more.*"

There was laughter, and a *hallelujah!* or two.

"*Then He took out the quart Coke jug and the ten-ounce Crown Z paper chalices, and gave thanks, and poured it for them, saying, Drink ye all of it; for this is my blood of the new testament.*"

The crowd was ecstatic, or sounded like it. Everett gave them a modest little bow. But when he turned to grin at Natasha she wasn't even shooting the usual eye-bullets through his head. She was on her way to the kitchen. Dammit! This woman was starting to make him angry! She was also starting to make him desperate. *So what's to lose?* he thought. *Go with the anger!* "Very good, Natasha!" he bellowed. "The Christian woman's place is in that very room, working her slow, terrible revenge upon the Christian man!"

Natasha remained invisible. But his audience was still with him. "More!" roared Deluxe Dave.

"Yeah!" Melanie laughed. "I'm all *for* terrible revenges on men!"

"Then check out the one being worked three times a day in every Christian kitchen throughout the land," Everett growled. "Its name, as Natasha could no doubt tell you, is Christian cuisine."

"He's so *funny!*" Melanie gasped.

"He's so *ill,*" Natasha called in from the kitchen.

"You're so right!" Everett erupted. "For I was raised on food designed with a single purpose: to put the Christian Husband in his richly deserved grave so the Christian Wife can kick up her heels for a few years before she has to join him!"

Natasha reappeared with a beer and a scowl and resumed shooting her beautiful eye-bullets at him through the doorway. New life! New death! He put the spurs to his magic tongue: "*All* women are feminists. Even those who wish they weren't. Baptist women, Muslim women—liberationists all! They can't help it. It's in the blood, the glands, the DNA. Oh sure, the menfolk like to corral the ladies with patriarchal Gods, scriptures and cultures that order otherwise, and some of the ladies go, 'Whatever you say, honey! We're brood stock, we're chattel, we like it this way.' But look what these faithful little wifeys turn around and *feed* the men of the clan! These dames aren't bimbos! They're *assassins!*

They're Female Supremists! Key ingredients in the Pillsbury Patriarch-Slayer's Cookbook? Pure white sugar! Bleached white flour! Salt by the pound! Crisco by the tub! And don't forget the Wonder bread! Just one loaf and he'll wonder if he'll ever crap again!"

Ah! The sweet cacophony of laughter!

"Metastasizing meats dripping with fat! Fat dripping with amphetamines! Potatoes dripping with gravy! Hydrogenated this, saturated that! More meat! More fat! Meanwhile the Biblical Wife nibbles a stick of celery and stays in perfect shape lifting, lugging and *serving* all this tripe! And what's for dessert? Prefab cakes and cookies! Canned puddings so viscous they don't even jiggle! Du Pont chemical ice cream that changes temp but never melts! A second helping of each! Then up she jumps again, batting her lashes and saying, 'Why, look, Daddy! Your *heart's* still beating! How can *that* be? How about another cuppa coffee with a dose of this neat new nondairy liver creamer?' "

Another detonation from the delighted fans.

" 'No, thanks, honey!' wheezes the comatose Lord of the Household. 'The kids are screaming, and the Good Book says it's your job to go shut 'em up. My job is to read the paper, and after a while go try 'n' take me a humongous dump, and maybe read a little more paper in there.'

" 'How about some tea, then, hon? It only takes three seconds to brew! It's got those neat new carcinogenic dyes!'

" 'Oh well, in that case,' groans the Patriarch.

"And so it goes. Christian cuisine is not a culinary art. It's the art of taxidermy practiced upon the living!"

There was applause, cheering, an outright ovation, some of it even standing.

And, once again, Natasha was nowhere to be seen.

EVERETT

Three Kinds of Farce

1. The Genre

I've never liked guilt-tripping. I've always left the concept of sin to the Catholic Church. When I was four, my mother said, "There's millions of people starving in China. Eat your dinner." I said, "Ma, name one."
—Abbie Hoffman

Once upon a time there was a quirky little literary and theatrical genre, called farce, whose sole allegiance was to pursue comic effect. Since it was a purgative, like Ex-Lax, it was farce's duty to hit below the belt. It was also its prerogative to be tasteless if necessary, to care not a fig for veracity or integrity if necessary, and to cream-pie even blind men, re-tarded people and sleeping infants if necessary. And the only thing it defined as necessary was to grovel shamelessly after its one true god, the Funny Bone.

But lo and behold, the tacky little genre proved surprisingly powerful. Because of its announced lack of "higher considerations" it could probe darker places more blithely, take more dangerous or ludicrous risks, say more vicious and hilarious things, and be forgiven more quickly and completely than any other genre. And being purely for show, it freed artists, writers and playwrights to make a Punch-and-Judy doll out of any sacred cow or person on earth, then to attack it so outrageously and mercilessly that the genuine outrage and mercilessness pent up in its audience or readers came bubbling into the open, where it could disperse in the harmless form of laughter. So it was that artists as varied as Aristophanes and Mozart, Plato and Swift, Chuang Tzu and Shakespeare, Kabir and Apuleius, all grew to admire farce, and all used it to varied and powerful effect.

2. The Megafarce

We were young. We were arrogant. We were ridiculous. There were excesses. We were brash. We were foolish. We had factional fights. But we were right.
—Abbie Hoffman

In the decade after World War II a number of very powerful American politicians also discovered farce. These politicians had such Machiavellian philosophies and rudimentary senses of humor that they didn't recognize it as a cathartic or comic genre. But they did recognize its power over people. They therefore began applying none of farce's funniness but all of its unscrupulousness to such tasks as smearing opponents to win elections, groveling shamelessly after the lowest common prejudices of the people, blacklisting dissent, whitewashing corruption and prostituting themselves to wealthy private backers who used them to de-democratize entire constituencies. And though quite a few citizens soon recognized that incredible abuses of power were taking place, there seemed to be no rational, nonfarcical way to combat them. The crowd-pleasing, pilfered genre had mated with democracy and produced a seemingly invincible bastard: government by force of farce.

Meanwhile the Pentagon had been watching. And when they saw the humorless new style of farce catapulting one Pecksniffian lump after another into political power and keeping him there, they deployed the same little genre, not as a psychological or political purgative, but as an economic one. Pouring Bolshevik scares and Red threats like Ex-Lax down everyone's throat, the military created a kind of "emergency peace" that kept Americans crapping out tax dollars and nonrenewable resources at a suicidal rate. And again, farce worked like a charm, and no one who cared about integrity or truth had any idea how to protest or resist.

So in the early 1960s our D.C. military and political farce-artists decided to combine forces, put the petal to the metal, and see what their hot little genre could *really* do: to that end they prepackaged and mailed two million reasonably innocent and increasingly unwilling American boys to Southeast Asia, ordered them to engage in an experimental farce of a war, and further ordered them not to win this war, but only to fight and possibly die in it in support of a clique of corrupt Saigon business-men. If this clique failed to stay in power, our federal farce-artists told us, the countries of the free world would topple like dominoes and our chil-dren would worship Marx and Mao instead of Baseball and God. So the two million boys simply *had* to go.

At this point it grew apparent to a great many Americans that we were no longer the audience of our D.C. farce-writers: we had become the boobs and butts of their humorless scripts. A handful of political scrib-blers like Robert McNamara, Dean Rusk, McGeorge Bundy and Lyndon Johnson were turning *millions* of Americans and Southeast Asians into throwaway characters in an international Megafarce. And *still* nobody could stop them. Strong families like mine kept fighting for a family identity, and strong characters like my brothers and sisters still struggled to come of age in nonfarcical ways. But our lives were being violated, trivialized, and in tens of thousands of cases terminated by the trite machinations of these sickeningly powerful men.

This was when the resistance finally began. Having nothing to lose and the autonomy and integrity of our lives to regain, several million upstarts like myself began fighting fire with fire by launching little farce-missiles right back at Washington, D.C. And though for a while our efforts didn't help much politically, they were immediately therapeutic literarily—be-cause as long as we defied the feds with light hearts, as long as we protested with humor, we were doing our puny but honest best to wrestle the sword of farce away from these humorless enemies of peace and art and pound it back into the purely literary plowshare that Aristophanes, Apuleius, Shakespeare and Company intended it to be. True, terms like "Pentacong" and "Richard Outhaus Nixon" and dramas like *Hats* were a far cry from Aristophanes. But they weren't that far from Swift. And subtlety didn't pierce the armor of these antiliterary oafs anyway. Only numbers pierced them—because dollars and votes both travel in num-bers. So we poured into the streets and ROTC buildings and deans' offices in hordes, fighting the Megafarce with a billion theatrical or liter-ary farces of our own.

3. The Microfarce

The Left has a marvelous ability to snatch defeat from the jaws of victory.
—Abbie Hoffman

But every performer—even the guerrilla farce-artist—needs to maintain an ability to stop performing. The respite, the inner recess, may be the only real difference between vocation and obsession. I needed, all student rabble-rousers needed to know how to stop being witty and rhetorical, how to be a plain private person who cared about other private people, and how to speak unadorned, unmanipulative sentences simply because they were true. I desperately needed a place to take off my anarchical makeup and stop posturing and gesturing. And I had no such place. What I had instead were fame and sex.

Regarding the fame:

One spring day in 1968, while walking the two miles from my house to the campus, I was recognized and greeted by name, wave, peace sign or nod exactly 207 times. I know because I counted. I counted because it made me giddy with bliss. By the time I got to class I figured I'd single-handedly be calling a halt to that troublesome little 'Nam thing any day now. Only in retrospect, only *years* later, did it occur to me that I had looked directly at every one of those 207 passersby and tried to say or do something at least mildly witty for every one of them—and not out of politeness, not out of friendliness, but only to be sure that they recognized me again next time! Talk about compulsion! Talk about a dog pissing on posts!

By 1969, thanks to years of diligent post-pissing, I was known around the U district as "the Hippie Churchill," a nickname I took as a compliment. But it was almost too perfect—because a caricature of a great orator is exactly what I'd become. Even when I tried to be serious my tours de force came off as mere parodies of "great speeches." But attempts at seriousness were rare. I didn't know how to stop a war. All I knew was how to make people with similar politics laugh. That's why more and more of my great public outcries became cartoonish farces as verbally violent toward their perceived ideological enemies as the Saturday-morning cartoons are violent to Elmer Fudd or Sylvester when they threaten the happiness of Bugs or Tweety Bird. And the odd thing was, none of my cronies seemed to recognize the cartoon element. Virtually everything that came out of my mouth in 1969 was imbued with the sketchiness and shallowness of caricature, but with the exceptions of Natasha (whose eyes I avoided), Dr. Gurtzner (whose class I dropped) and Peter and Kade (with whom I'd stopped corresponding), everybody seemed to take me for a cogent thinker, a zany but genuine new brand of American social reformer, and even "a legend in my own time."

Which brings me to the sex:

Ever since reaching legend status I'd discovered the throngs of lithe-limbed, lifelike sleepwalkers out there who prefer the safety of making love to a legend—that is, to a construct they carry around in their heads —to the hard work of living with and loving another contrary, quirky, flesh-and-blood human being. These people had only to identify themselves ("You look just like Cat Stevens!") and I would happily proceed to hot-wire them with my legendary wit, "radical chic," incendiary eloquence, brash courage, passion, whatever it took; then we'd toggle the hell out of each other, sleep till morning, and part ways before a bunch of tedious human foibles reared up and ruined our mutually legendary impressions. The whole pattern was, in two increasingly blurry words, "a farce." But it worked. So I continued with it. Till I became addicted to it. Then I carried it a step further: I began to believe in the Hippie Churchill legend myself. Except that last step was hardly a step: it was

more
like
a
cliff.

The Hippie Churchill usurped me, the God of Farce usurped the Hippie Churchill, and the whole indistinguishable jumble of us orated, berated, joked, toked, drank and fucked our way around Seattle night after night, wittily skimming over the surface of everything, wittily skewering the character of everybody, playacting constantly, moving constantly, marching, shouting, defying constantly—because the instant the jumble lost momentum and I began to sink down into myself, the instant I truly "gave Chance a peace," I had only the eyes of the nonstop farce-artist through which to see myself. And the aching, self-doubting, harrowingly unfunny stranger those eyes glimpsed in the silence sent me fleeing in panic out to the wildest toke-fest, social turmoil, tavern or female I could find.

In other words, I had done to myself almost exactly what my sworn enemies in D.C. had done: I'd trapped myself in a script. The Megafarce script reduced me to either an expendable military part or a traitor to my country, while my own script puffed me up into a hero so essential to its plot that on sunny spring strolls he was greeted as many as 207 times per two miles. But to be scripted at all is to be prepackaged, programmed, pinned to a page.

Only the unwritten can truly live a life.

So who I was, what I was, had to be unwritten.

CHAPTER THREE

Linda

That he did not finish his studies is true, but to say that he was stupid or dull would be a great injustice. He entered upon this path only because, at the time, it alone struck his imagination and seemed to offer . . . a means of escape for his soul from darkness to light . . . He was to some extent a youth of our past generation—that is, honest in nature, desiring the truth . . . believing in it, and seeking to serve it at once with all the strength of his soul, seeking for immediate action, and ready to sacrifice everything, even life itself. These young men unhappily fail to understand that the sacrifice of life is, in many cases, the easiest sacrifice of all.
—Dostoevsky, *The Brothers Karamazov*

On the afternoon of April 14, 1970—a couple of days after Papa had returned to Camas from spring training—he got a phone call from Irwin down in Eugene, asking when the Tugs' first road trip would begin. "Today," Papa told him.

"Oh God!" Irwin said. And it was nearly a sob.

"What is it?" Papa asked.

"Oh, nothing." And now he laughed. "Just . . . just a couple weird emergencies is all. I just . . . needed to talk to you . . . pretty bad . . . is all." Another sob.

"Is your car running?" Papa asked.

"Have Nash, will travel," Irwin said.

"What does it take, three and a half hours to get here?"

" 'Bout that."

"Well, start driving. We'll have supper, and talk, and I'll catch the late flight to Phoenix and join the team tomorrow."

Still another sob! And a broken "God bless you, Papa."

"Fine by me," Papa said. "See you soon."

Four hours later Irwin, the twins, Mama and I bowed our heads, and Papa reeled off his old *GiveusgratefulheartsourFatherandmakeusevermindfuloftheneedsofothersthroughChristourLordAmen*—a moment's balm. Then Irwin let fly with a "Hear! Hear!" that sounded so silly yet heartfelt that we all turned to gape at him. And seeing us staring, he let loose with a terrible abrasive laugh. He sounded like a stranger. He sounded completely self-conscious. And he sounded scared.

"Listen," Papa told him, "if this is going to be . . . if your situation is too . . . we can go talk in private, if you like."

Irwin drew a breath, and seemed to consider it. But then he shook his head. "The things I have to say, and the things I need to ask, they're for everybody. Everybody that lives here." He let out another strangled laugh.

We waited. Nothing happened.

"All right," Papa said finally. "What's the first thing?"

The awful laugh. Then: "Just that there's this girl, Mama met her— you remember Linda, Mama? I brought her to church once last fall."

Mama half smiled, then cocked her head as if she expected to round some corner in her memory and run into Linda any second now. But when her head stayed cocked it was obvious the girl wasn't showing up.

"Well, we love each other," Irwin said. "That's the main thing. And we, uh, wanna get married too."

"Why . . . that . . . that's great!" Papa said, with an understandably sprained but quickly splinted enthusiasm.

"Congratulations," Mama said, still half smiling, still with her head cocked, and nearly dripping sweat now in the effort to recall who the hell this Linda was.

"The thing is," Irwin said, "it's happening tomorrow."

"Pardon?" said Mama, still faintly smiling.

"The wedding," Irwin said. "It's tomorrow. At the Clark County court-house, at two. It's all set up."

We looked at each other—the twins, Mama, Papa and me—perhaps to see if anyone seemed to find what Irwin was saying comprehensible. It was a relief to me that no one else did either. "You can come," Irwin said, "if you want."

"How kind!" remarked Freddy.

"We might *like* that!" Bet snorted.

"The thing is," Irwin said, without a hint of a smile, "we hate spring-ing this on you like this, and Linda's really embarrassed and all, but she's uh, we uh, well . . . the thing is, we're expecting a baby."

Very quietly, with no inflection, Papa said, "Wow."

Then Freddy turned to Bet, and in the same inflectionless tone said what sounded like "Ants."

Perhaps to avoid the main topic, Mama spun on her and snapped, "What? What are you saying?"

"Bet and me," Freddy said calmly. "We're aunts . . . *Grandma.*"

Papa smiled at this, and Bet burst into mild hysterics, but Mama just re-cocked her head and resumed her mental Linda-hunt. Then Irwin said, "That's not quite all, though. I'm afraid there's bad news too."

Papa audibly gulped. Bet stopped tittering and gaped.

Peering down into his plate, Irwin mumbled, "I got my papers today."

No one spoke or reacted—perhaps because only I knew what he was saying. But my stomach was in my throat.

"I don't understand," Mama said finally. "What paper?"

Irwin started to laugh, as if she'd really cracked a good one. "Not paper!" he wheezed. "*Papers!* It's not about school, Mama. I dropped out, remember?"

"Get a grip," Papa snapped, "and explain."

"They're my draft papers." Irwin paused, blushed, fretted, sighed. "Ex-cept the bad thing is, the real humdinger, see, is that I tried for CO status, being a Christian and all. And weird things happened. And . . . well . . . I didn't get it."

"Jesus Christ!" I whispered.

"I don't understand a word you're saying!" Mama snapped, obviously hoping that as long as she remained ignorant Irwin could come to no harm.

"Conscientious Objector status," Papa told her. "But why not, Irwin? I thought it was automatic for Adventists."

Keeping his eyes on his plate, Irwin said, "So did I. But Linda's been pregnant a couple months now, and we've been real busy and all, so, well, I just sort of piled up the draft crap when it came. But the week before last Linda read enough of it and checked enough dates to see we better do something quick. So I went to the draft counselor at U of O and applied for CO status, and we started phoning up references. But Elder Anders, our Eugene pastor, was on vacation. So I picked Randy Beal, of course, and Elder Babcock and Elder Barnes. And two days ago Brother Beal called and said they did me. So now I'm afraid I've got . . . it looks like the Good Lord intends for me to head on over to—"

"Wait!" Papa interrupted. "They *did* you? What the hell does that mean?"

"It was Babcock's idea, I guess," Irwin said. "But he talked Barnes into it, and tried for Beal too, which is how Randy knew. What they did, anyhow, was tell the draft guys I left the Adventist Church years ago. They said I was some kind of drugged-up hippie dropout running around getting girls pregnant and that the whole CO thing was a lie to keep out of the Army with."

"I'm still not understanding," Mama said. "There's been a mistake, surely. Elder Babcock wouldn't do anything of the sort."

Freddy snorted. Irwin just shook his head. But Papa shouted, "They can't get away with it! You've gone to church every damned Sabbath of your life!"

"Yeah." Irwin nodded. "But when Linda and I started living together last fall, Elder Anders wasn't—"

"You *lived* together?" Mama was flabbergasted.

Irwin blushed. "We wanted to get married, Mama. But there were problems, see. Linda's young, and needed her parents' legal permission, and they—well, I'm coming to that part. Anyhow, once we were shacked up, so to speak, Elder Anders wasn't so thrilled to have us at his church anymore. So for quite a while now we've been going to Descent of the Dove, up on the McKenzie River, which is just a falling-down barn and old apple orchard pretty much, but a beautiful place to worship, and quite a few of the younger Adventist types go there. Except we worship on Sundays. Which Elder Babcock now claims is the Mark of the Beast. And—"

"The *what?*" Papa asked.

Irwin smiled. "Sorry, Papa," he said, "but I need to tell this story in order or I'll mix it all up."

Papa nodded.

"When I found out what Babcock and Barnes had done, my draft counselor and me called Elder Anders, on his vacation down in San Diego, and asked him to help us. But Anders pointed out that I had no recent church attendance record to fight Babcock with, which is true, I'm afraid, 'cause Descent of the Dove doesn't keep attendance, since we're tryin' to be more like the fowls of the air and all. Then Elder Anders asked if Linda was pregnant, and I told him yes, but that she'd finally found her mother—which is another story, don't ask yet!—and we were getting married right away. Well, pregnant was pregnant, he said, which was all Babcock had told the Army. So I couldn't fight him on that point either. And how about drugs? he asked. 'Cause he knew I'd tried peyote with Ev— uh, one time, many moons back—because it scared me so bad I wanted him to baptize me all over again, though he said I didn't need it. Anyhow, if you looked at it one way, Elder Anders said, everything Babcock and Barnes said could be called a fact. So though I wish you well, he said, I'm afraid this thing is between you and Babcock."

"Holy *shit*," I muttered.

"You shuttup!" Mama snapped.

"So I called Babcock," Irwin said. "And it was amazing. He said if I wanted a different kind of letter I should have lived a different kind of life. I told him I'd made mistakes, sure, but that our situation was tough and Linda and me were trying our best to walk with Christ every step of the way. I told him I'd always loved his church, and him too, and couldn't believe he wouldn't want to help me. But all he said was that he wasn't about to perjure himself for scum like me."

"He said no such thing!" Mama burst out.

"Those were his exact words," Irwin said. "But he did better'n that. He called Everett *terrible* things."

"Well, he told *me* what Everett said to *him!*" Mama retorted.

"I know, I know, they hate each other. But Papa and Peter, Freddy and Kade, Babcock laid into all of 'em, Mama. And he said getting Linda pregnant was proof I wasn't a Christian, and that I had the Mark of the Beast now, because of Sundays, and that my brothers and father and me were 'hell-spawn,' that we turned our back on God a long time ago, that we'll burn in the hell of blasphemers, and that that was exactly what he'd told the U.S. Army. Then he said never to call him again and slammed down the phone."

"That *bastard!*" Freddy shouted. And this time Mama didn't object.

But Papa said, "Now hold on. Slow down. They just can't do this. They can't just up and draft you because of one pompous preacher's lies."

"*Two* pompous preachers," Irwin said, then caught himself. "Sorry, Mama," he laughed. "I just mean that Elder Barnes wrote the same sort of letter."

"They can't do it," Papa repeated.

"It's *done*, Papa. That's what I'm here to tell you. I had my physical. I'm 1-A. My shoulder's okay, unfortunately. And I'm going to—"

"Laura," Papa said. "Call Babcock. We're going to see him now. All of us. He's got to retract every goddamned word! You talk to him first! And if that won't work I'll . . . This is *wrong*. It's a lie."

From the look on Mama's face it was obvious that she wasn't going anywhere. Which threw Papa into a fury. But before he could speak, Irwin said, "Listen, Papa! It's too late. Beal and me, my counselor, we tried everything. We went to the draft board, phoned a senator, Beal argued with the Elders over and over. Nancy did too. But it's over and done. I'm in the Army, Papa. Starting day after tomorrow. And I'm going to Vietnam."

"No!" Papa said.

"No," murmured Mama.

"Which brings me," Irwin said, "to a whole 'nother world of hurt."

Everything he'd said up till now was a nightmare I'd had many times myself, so even though it made me sick it didn't quite surprise me. But when I heard there was still more, I entered, we all entered, some kind of dream-zone, some realm of numbness and inertia in which we could do nothing but stare at his mouth. And the sentences it produced began to form bodies now—vague but tangible bodies that floated, naked, into the room. "I'll be in Vietnam when the baby comes," he said, and in it drifted, minuscule, helpless, wrinkled and red. "It's going to be tough," he said. "Especially on Linda. She's only seventeen, but her life's been rough." And now the body was barefoot, faceless, with pale skin and swelling belly. "Her parents will be no help," he said. "I mean, it's a hard thing to say, but they're not the kind of people who are going to understand *any* of this. At all."

At this point Mama suffered a spasm of normalcy. "Of course they will," she told him. "You and your father and I will just sit down with them, like we're sitting here with you, and we'll all have us a talk about how we can best deal with—"

"Mama," Irwin interrupted. "Two years ago Linda's dad beat her up and raped her . . ."

And now the naked body had muscle and genitals—genitals, and an erection from which we were still recoiling when Irwin said, "And her mom's a drunk. If not worse. Linda just spent all the money we had, finding her, because we needed a notarized permission slip to get married. She stays in a county home in Florida when she's not wandering the streets. And she's as crazy as the dad, at least. So. We won't be sitting down to talk."

We were all drunk now, not just Linda's lost mommy. "The dad's the main worry," said the magic mouth. "He hurt her bad. He's hurt lots of people. He's in jail for it." *Drunk as skunks.* "He's the real reason, well . . . he's the *serious* reason we've been living together. And the thing is, another real doozy is, he gets out while I'm gone." *Blitzed. Zoned. Smashed.* "And she's got nobody . . . Nobody but me . . . And the baby . . . When it comes . . . And each of you guys, I hope." *How did we get into this?* "Because I love her a lot . . ." *Ah. So that's how.* "But my Country calls, so to speak . . . And I have to—"

"Wait!" Mama burst out. Another spasm of sanity. "Wait just one minute here. Isn't there some special kind of—is 'deferment' the word?— that the Army gives in cases like—"

Irwin's laugh was nearly a shriek. "I can see it now, Mama! Front-page headlines! PENTAGON SAYS: JUST GET YOUNG GIRL PREGNANT AND THERE'S NO VIETNAM FOR YOU!"

Freddy managed a titter. Bet and Papa and I just stared. Then Irwin, in seconds, went from laughter to a gasp to a silent stream of tears. And even though Mama was still blushing, she was somehow able to reach out, take his hand, and with no sign of paralysis say, "You've got a life of work cut out for you, you and your Linda. But the important thing is you love her, and she loves you. And I'm sure that, in time, we'll grow to love her too."

"Oh, Mama!" Irwin cried. "I'm so glad you said that! Because here's the other thing. Here's the biggest thing . . ."

We all stiffened, and my parents grabbed both arms of their chairs; we were jet passengers now, coming down into the fog for an announced crash landing.

"Linda's got nowhere to go. With me gone, she's got *nowhere* . . ." He left us a pause—the kind you'd just about *have* to call "pregnant"— then finished: ". . . unless she can come here."

I don't know how she could speak, let alone move, but before I could even focus Mama had jumped to her feet, wrapped Irwin's head in her arms, and with tears in her eyes was crooning, "Irwin, Irwin, Irwin. Of *course* your Linda can stay here!" And I have never heard her, let's face it, not so lovely voice sound more soothing than when she began gabbling on about how the girls could move up into Everett and Peter's old room, how we'd fetch the Beautyrest down for Linda ("Everett and his *back!*"), and the twins' baby things were still in the attic, weren't they? and wasn't that bassinet still up in the garage rafters? "And I'll move my sewing things into our bedroom when you're on road trips, Hugh, so the sewing room can be the nursery. Then I'll just pop the sewing stuff back in our—"

"Move anything," Papa said fiercely. "Move anything of mine anywhere you want," he said. "Except my son."

Mama's lip began to quiver. Freddy started to cry. Irwin turned to face him.

"Not you," Papa said. "Not in Vietnam."

Irwin smiled. "It's the quickest way through."

"Through what? Your *life?* This goddamned vale of *tears?*"

"Hugh!" Mama gasped.

"Through this trouble," Irwin said earnestly. "Through this giant screw-up. I've messed up big-time, Papa. And the Army, like it or not, is the fastest way back to Linda, and the baby, and all of you."

"Go to jail," Papa said.

"Hugh!"

"Stay out of it, Laura! Irwin, I'm serious."

"But why, Papa?"

"You'll *survive* jail."

"Hugh!" Mama burst out.

"*You shuttup!*" he roared.

"Please don't fight!" Irwin's smile was huge, strained, pleading. "I won't die, Papa! Not with all of you praying for me!"

"This war is no fantasy," Papa said. "No Babcock hell or heaven. It's real, Irwin. And boys like you die in it every day while their families are praying otherwise."

"Don't say it, Mama!" Irwin pleaded, seeing the red rage in her eyes. "Papa!" he said. "I've thought hard about this. I know I don't always think, but listen. You get three, four, even five years in jail for refusing induction, you come out with nothing, and you make ex-con wages for life. But just two years in the Army, maybe just twelve months of that in 'Nam, and I get paid the whole time, get help with college when I get out, get a GI loan for a house just like you did. And there's a good pension for Linda and the baby if . . . in case something terrible happens."

Papa looked at Irwin, and said nothing, for a very long time. Then he turned to Mama. "I won't divorce you," he said—and the room began to spin. "It'd just be a lot of silliness at this late date." I closed my eyes: the dark in there was spinning too. "But if you ever set foot in another Babcock church service for any reason but to spit in his face, I'll never speak to you again, Laura. I swear to God."

"I'll worship where I choose!" Mama managed to say. But her voice was broken, her face white.

"Please!" Irwin begged. "This is *my* fault!"

"Let's keep it simple," Papa said. "This is Babcock's fault."

"What about Everett?" Mama gasped. "What about *drugs?* I heard that little slip!"

"Laura, I swear to God!"

"And what's so bad about a son who's willing to fight for his country? What's so wrong about Irwin wanting to—"

"What's wrong is he's a *Christian!*" Papa roared. "He's the son who let the other kids break his toys! The one who's never hurt a fly! The one who turns the other cheek. Goddammit, Laura! How could *you* of all people forget that?"

"Please!" Irwin stood up, grabbed his forehead, let go of it, sat back down. "*I* got us into this, Papa. And with all of your help, and God's, I can get us out."

"Babcock got you into this!"

"And *Everett!*" Mama shouted.

"*Stop!*" Irwin slammed the table so hard the plates leapt in the air. My parents stopped.

"There's still something I haven't told you."

Again they grabbed their chair arms. Again we stared in awe at his mouth. "Linda," it said softly. "My Linda. Her and, well, everything we pretty much own are sitting out in the car. Right here. Right now. Waiting to hear what we all decide."

My parents looked at each other then—just a glance, it was over in a flash—but I could swear that I saw in it a complete suspension of hostility, and maybe even some form of delight, before they turned back to Irwin with the same grave scowls.

"Why didn't you say so?" Papa said.

"For God's sake, Irwin," Mama chided. "Bring the poor girl home!"

CHAPTER FOUR

The Leftovers

1. Old War, New Hate

You have no more permission to fight for me. You have killed the innocent and left my enemies standing. No more . . . no more . . .
—dying words of King Duryodhana, *Mahabharata*

Three days after Linda moved in with us, two days after her marriage to many an Adventist girl's idea of the Dream Male, and just a day after that Dream left her for basic training, another mind-boggling scene took place in our house. This one was a kind of "Psalm Wars, Part Two." And, as usual, the sequel stank.

It began late at night. Mama was watching the eleven o'clock news. I was typing a paper in the kitchen. (The twins had moved upstairs, and the noise of my old Royal manual kept them awake if I worked in my room.) Papa was still on the road, so when somebody knocked hard on the front door, I joined Mama as she unlocked it.

And in burst Everett, with hair, clothes and energy flying all over the place as he announced, with repellent bravado, that he'd been at a sit-in all week and that he'd got home just three hours ago to hear the bad news from Stoner Steve (I'd been phoning his house every night for four days). "But never fear, Kade!" he cried—as if Mama wasn't there. " 'Cause we're gonna be okay, Winnie and me! I'm arranging a little tryout for us with the Dodgers. The B.C. Dodgers, that is!" Meaning, I guess, that he thought they would go to British Columbia together to dodge the draft.

Thanks to the way he was acting, I felt no sorrow at all as I said, "You're too late."

Everett popped like a party balloon, except the sound went: "*What?*"

"Irwin's already in boot."

"No! No no *no!* Stoner said *Friday.* He wrote it down twice!"

I said, "Reality never was Stoner's strong suit." But I regretted it a little as Everett turned pale and fell silent. He looked like he might even start to cry—

till Mama stepped up and pertly informed him that he was a coward and a communist-lover and that Irwin, by choosing to serve his family, his country and his God, had become a hero to us all. Nothing perks up an ideologue like the sight of the ideological enemy. In fact, they both looked grimly pleased as they squared off like a couple of gunfighters. "Don't even start!" I said. "People are asleep. And it's too late anyway. Irwin's already gone."

But they didn't hear me. They *wanted* their idiot showdown. And, as so often happens, it was innocent bystanders who ended up taking most of the bullets.

Everett drew first. It would serve Mama right, he shouted, if Irwin got blown to shit in some fucking jungle . . .

Then Linda walked, white-faced, into the room. Her nightie—a weird wedding gift from the closet-romantic in Mama—was awfully small, her eyes and breasts awfully large. "Who are *you?*" Everett blurted.

Linda managed to move her lips a little. Then she burst into tears.

Mama's turn. It would serve Everett right, she said, if he was arrested at one of his damned antigovernment drug-and-sex orgies and locked up for life. And if he so much as opened his mouth in her house again, she would call the police and have him arrested this very night.

Everett opened his mouth as far as it would go and said, "Ahhhhh." What a moron. I was no expert, but I'd begun to think he was on speed.

Mama headed for the phone: she was definitely on patriotism.

But meanwhile Freddy, on nothing but sleepiness, had staggered into the kitchen and ended up by the phone—and when she saw Mama coming she grabbed the cord and serenely ripped the phone jack clean out of the wall.

Everett laughed, and thanked her, though I don't think she was even awake. Then Mama slapped her in the face not once, but twice. Which made me *mad*. And then Everett, right in front of Linda, called Mama a "stupid fucking bitch." Which made me even madder. Grabbing Mama in a bear hug, I pulled her away from Freddy but yelled at Everett, "Say that again and I'll hurt you!" He laughed at me. Meanwhile Mama, in a frenzy, was trying to break my hold. But I'd been wrestling with Irwin for two decades. "Stop struggling," I said. And when she didn't, I just lifted her in the air and squeezed a little. *"Hoooof!"* she went, and the wind and fight went out of her. While poor Linda gawked at us. Good God.

Hard as the slaps had been, Freddy woke rather slowly. But once she felt how much it hurt she started to cry. Then Everett did it again. "You're *pathetic!"* he shouted at Mama. "You fascist fucking bitch!"

That did it. Carrying Mama over to Everett, I set her down in front of him like bait in front of a fish, let them stare at each other till they were both about to scream something awful, then jumped out and punched Everett hard, right in the mouth.

It was no Micah Barnes love tap. I floored him. I also stopped Linda's and Freddy's tears, froze Mama, and temporarily worked wonders for my own state of mind. "Sorry," I said, when I finally got him back on his feet. "But I learned that trick from you. Asshole Therapy, you used to call it. I still love you, Everett. Barely. But I hope to hell it was a complete cure."

He was still glassy-eyed, and probably couldn't understand me. But glancing from Mama's face to Linda's and Freddy's, I saw glimmerings of sanity, if not amusement, and felt a glimmering of hope . . .

Then Bet burst into the room. "I *hate* you!" she screamed at Everett. "Get out of here! *You're* the bitch! *You* are! I hate you! Get out!"

The fierce new bond between Mama and Bet had been evident to the rest of us for a while now, but this bordered on the berserk. There was something wrong with her, something I didn't understand at all. "Get out of our house!" she shrieked. *"Never* come back! *You're* the bitch! *You* are!"

Linda started crying again. Everett seemed to move from semiconsciousness straight into shock. "Cool it!" I told Bet. "I already decked him."

But she was gone. Her eyes were pure pupil—no iris at all—and her face was a thing in a nightmare. *"Get out!"* she shrieked. "I *hate* you! Bitch! Fascist bitch!" And soon as I moved to try and calm her, Mama snuck away over to Everett, doubled her little fist, and sucker-punched him with everything she had.

His reaction was eerie: he just fell down, got up again, and went on gaping at Bet, who was now shrieking, "*Good*, Mama! Good! *He's* the bitch!"

"I'm so tired of you two," I told Mama as I threw another bear hug on her.

"This is *my* fault!" Linda began sobbing.

"This is *his* fault!" Mama shouted. "It's— *Hoooof!*" I jerked her wind out.

"*He's* the bitch!" Bet shrieked. "*He* is! *He* is!"

I had to shout to be heard, but I tried to shout calmly. "She's hysterical," I told Freddy. "Try to help her. Linda, we're sorry about all this. But maybe you can help with Bet too." Then I picked Mama up again, carried her straight into the kitchen, and kicked the door shut behind us.

I kept her in the bear hug even after she'd quit struggling. It felt weird, sick, wrong as could be, but I was afraid to let her go, so there we stood, breathing hard, listening to Bet's frenzy. Not knowing what else to do, I tried polite conversation. "What do you do for hysteria anyway? Breathe in a paper bag?"

"I'm sick of this too," she murmured into my shoulder. "I'm sicker than I can say of all this." It wasn't the answer to my question, but it sounded halfway sane. So I let her go, even tried to smile at her. And she smiled back—insanely—and raked her fingernails across my face. I grabbed her again, begged her to calm down. But she was crazy now, biting, kicking, throwing her skull back against mine, so "*Hoooof!*" "*Hoooof!*" "*Hooooof!*" we went. This was an astute businesswoman, this was my boss I was crushing. "I *hate* him, *hate* him, *hate* him!" Bet kept shrieking, while Linda just sobbed, and Freddy begged Bet to stop. My face hurt like hell. I was close to vomiting. And Mama just wouldn't quit. "*Hoooof!*"

Everett came staggering, hate-blasted and blood-smeared, through the door, glanced at us blindly, and left the house without a word.

Bet stopped screaming, but started gasping uncontrollably.

Linda and Freddy, both crying themselves, tried to soothe her.

Everett's car started, died, started, roared, and tore wildly away.

Mama finally quit struggling, so I put her down, shielded my face, and jumped away from her fast. But she just stood there.

"You're not a bitch," I told her. "Nobody thinks that. Not even Everett. But you and he are nuts. You make each other crazy."

She just stood there. Her blouse had my blood on it, and was ripped at the shoulder. The lipstick Ellen G. White said never to wear was smeared down onto her chin. I'd squeezed her so hard there was snot stopping one nostril. I said, "I hope I didn't hurt you. But it's sick. You two are killing this family. You're hurting *everybody*."

She just stood there.

Papa was in Arizona with a head full of voodoo, breaking stuff and low outside corners. Peter was in Cambridge contemplating sutras, Sanskrit, bhajans and ghazals. Bet was still gasping, Linda still sobbing. "It's okay," Freddy kept lying. "It's okay, it's okay."

I wished to hell I was smarter, or better at baseball.

2. Cards

You got to know when to hold 'em, know when to fold 'em, know when to walk away, know when to run.
—Dostoevsky, *The Gambler*[*]

A few days after I punched him, Everett announced that he was going to Canada, then burned his draft card in front of a cheering campus throng that included FBI agents and a *Post-Intelligencer* photographer who immortalized the moment for Mama (the AP photo is still in the "EVERETT" box in the attic). Had he refused induction and been arrested, his punishment would have been real enough, and going to Canada meant that he'd made a choice to take a certain amount of suffering upon himself rather than to inflict it upon Vietnamese people. Yet his action seems to me to have meant far less than it might have.

The first flaw in Everett's act of self-sacrifice was that it was aimed entirely at an audience. Not only did he announce his card-burning intentions and the exact place and time in his newspaper column, he also mailed letters to Olympia and Washington, D.C., inviting the likes of Dick Nixon, Dixie Lee Ray, Melvin Laird, Scoop Jackson and J. Edgar Hoover to come watch—and announced *that* in his column too. His devil-may-care example proved contagious: twenty other young men were inspired to stand beside him and burn their draft cards while hundreds of well-wishers cheered, sang and even wept. But that brings me to the other flaw: some of those twenty others were genuine students, so their

---

[*] Just kidding. It was really Kenny Rogers' "The Gambler."

sacrifices were real. Everett's academic career, on the other hand, had long been (what else?) a farce. By avoiding professors like Dr. Gurtzner, practicing plagiarism, cheating on tests, and stuffing his schedule full of fluffy Pass/Fail courses he'd been able to tread academic water into the spring of '70. But for Everett the Legend, classrooms were just a guaranteed series of small crowds and coeds in front of which to perform.

I wouldn't say that it was meaningless when Everett burned his draft card. When the repercussions set in, suffering would add some retroactive dignity to his initial performance. I'm just saying that his card-burning would have meant far more, on the day he did it, if he hadn't already incinerated his life.

3. Attic Document, October 1970

A paper, written for Thurman Broyle's eighth-grade Social Studies class, typifying a whole series of papers that earned Bet both her first F and her first eight mandatory interviews with the school counselor:

TWO MODERN PROBLEMS & THEIR BEST POSSIBLE SOLUTIONS

Problem #1: War

What I know about war isn't much, but I do know we're in one with Russia called The Cold War where no one wins because we all die a few minutes after it starts, and another one with Vietnam which my best brother is stuck in and my sickest brother ran away to Canada to skip out on. From listening in class I also know that the way to get a D on this paper is to say the solution to the Vietnam part of this problem is to quit fighting and bring our troops home. And since good grades mean more to me than anything, even my favorite brother's life and his wife and new little baby's happiness who I can hear downstairs crying as I write this, my solution to this problem is for us to <u>fight</u> <u>fight</u> <u>fight</u> and <u>kill</u> <u>kill</u> <u>kill</u> until we <u>win</u> <u>win</u> <u>win</u>.

Problem #2: Assassinations

The big thing I've noticed about political assassinations is how my older brothers admired a politician named Lincoln and somebody shot him and one named Gandhi and somebody shot him and two named

Kennedy and somebody shot them both and one named Martin Luther King and somebody shot him too. Then I noticed how first President Johnson and now President Nixon pretty much talk gibberish and lie like rugs and all my older brothers except Irwin hate them. But nobody shoots them. So creeps survive. That's my main political theory. Satan takes care of his own is what I believe, whereas look what God did to His only Son. So my solution to this modern problem is simple. All this country has to do to stop political assassinations is keep electing gibberish-talking, lying politicians who all my brothers except Irwin hate.

4. Shoats from Underground

Thu-that, thu-that, thu-that's all, folks.
  —Porky Pig

Apparently no self-respecting Folk Hero can depart for the Life of Exile directly. The legendary thing to do is hang around till your induction papers arrive, then Defy Authority yet again by rendering yourself Incognito and going Underground. To that end, Everett partied it up in the same old U-district haunts till he was on the verge of arrest. Then, in one busy day, he shaved his prodigious beard, chopped off his hair, closeted such telltale decals as his earring and Old Glory knee patches, purchased some nondescript wash-and-wear clothes from various secondhand shops, traded his big ol' Pontiac battle cruiser in on a spent Oldsmobile 88 as nondescript as his clothes, and vanished.

But vanishing into an Underground turned out to be a bewildering disappointment to our hero. There is less to vanishing than meets the eye. A hundred percent less.

Everett's Underground, I found out months later, consisted of a series of cheap suburban Seattle motels furnished with telephones, upon which he spent several days fuming to various old cronies over the fact that with the exception of the one *Post-Intelligencer* photo, no campus, underground or city paper took any note of his departure. What was worse, Stoner Steve rented his room in the old hippie house to some squash-playing *business* major, "Give Chance a Peace" was replaced by a culinary question-and-answer column, and very few of his old friends seemed to miss him at all. "Tough luck!" they'd say—as if his intentional sacrifice had been pure accident. "But I hear B.C. is really pretty. And don't forget your fishin' pole!" they'd add—as if lifelong political exile were some nifty little vacation. The only people who expressed any real regret over his expatriation were:

1. Papa—but then Papa, in the Hippie Churchill's opinion, was just a naïvely apolitical, ball playin' gomer. And his parting gift—a fly-tying kit —was almost as offensive as the "fishin' pole" reminders of his friends.

2. Irwin—but in the same telephone conversation in which Irwin expressed sympathy, he claimed to actually be *liking* boot camp! His drill instructor was "funny," he said. "Chewed up an entire orange, peeling and all, then spat it out and made *me* eat it! I about busted a gut!" he said. So it appeared, to Everett anyhow, that the once invincibly sweet Winnie was well on his way to becoming a typical brainwashed 'Nam grunt.

3. Natasha—but the first and last time Everett phoned her from Underground she shouted, "You dolt! You peabrain! Did you stop to think what you were doing? Do you know you can never see your family again? Do you know you're a Canuck for *life* now? Did you know I happen to *like* this stupid country? Did you know I might have liked you too if you'd've just stopped being such an asshole? Do you know you should have *asked* me about this? Do you know I never want to see you again?"

"Huh," our hero replied, long after she'd blammed down the receiver.

Because of his need to remain invisible to law enforcement officials, Everett was plunged into an idle solitude which he found physically unbearable. He therefore began to take long, destinationless walks—fifteen, twenty miles a day—through all the sprawling parts of Seattle he'd considered too bourgeois to explore before. As these districts tended to be either industrial or suburban, and as his clothes and hair allowed him to blend in with the rest of humanity for the first time in years, this regimen of destinationless drifting left him feeling perfectly secure as far as FBI-avoidance was concerned. Where it did not leave him at all secure was in regard to his own identity:

Since he had no one to regale with political witticisms and no one to fume against, his two habitual energy sources—an audience and enemy resistance—had been stripped away, leaving him aimless and intellectually listless. And after three years of possessing the classic Revolutionary Hippie's high visual impact, it was terribly disorienting to find himself ensconced in a face and garb that fit right in among the off-duty Boeing workers, school kids and scuttling housewives. All the dash and glamour he'd come to think he exuded from his pores had abruptly ceased to exude. He now attracted no one, offended no one, felt like no one. Or less than no one—for in his purposeless wanderings he'd begun to feel inferior to every suburban man, woman and child he passed. These other folks carried tools, toys, purses, thermoses, wore purposeful expressions, spoke words to each other, went places for reasons. While he without his hair, earring or Old Glory patches drifted the rain-washed streets like some insignificant, diaphanous species of jellyfish. A common species at that. *Velella velella* perhaps.

But this was only life in the streets. It was when he'd return "home" to his featureless motel room that his new featurelessness grew truly aggressive, for it was here that he was forced to keep company with the disgustingly innocent-looking, bald-faced, boyish stranger who, according to the mirror anyway, was none other than himself. Could he really be this twitchy little shit who couldn't sit still in a chair, couldn't read anything longer than a magazine article without half falling to sleep, couldn't fully fall to sleep without getting drunk, couldn't do *anything* without talking to himself, justifying himself, narrating his life to himself, trying to cast himself in a thousand increasingly empty, soap-operatic, politically or sexually heroic roles? Had revolution revolutionized him so little? In his various stark motel rooms he now felt *constantly* the way he used to feel for only an hour a week—at the First Adventist Church of Washougal! Had three years of radicalism transformed his entire world into some kind of oversized *church service?!* Was he doomed, at least till his hair and beard grew back, to look, feel and behave like the kind of squirmy, whiny, pew-bound brat his mother used to call a "flibbertigibbet"?

He didn't know. He knew almost nothing about himself. And the little he did know made him want to know less. "No question about it," our hero told the boring cretin in the mirror at 2 A.M. one night. "I gotta do somethin', find somethin'. I need somethin'. Fast. What I must need, what I really really need, maybe, to get me through this thing, this tough period, if she can be trusted not to narc . . . is a woman. Yeah. That's what I need."

What Everett felt was technically only a desire, not a need. But this could have worked to his advantage, since genuine need is repugnant to the kind of robust, physically attractive, nonprofessional female co-athlete he felt the situation required. Unfortunately, when, many nights into his search, our hero spotted an exceedingly long, exceedingly cool, exceedingly red-dressed candidate in an infamous "meat market"-type bar, his mere desire leapfrogged clean over genuine need and was swallowed alive by a howling red lust.

Fortunately, the owner of this body was not repulsed by the little *Velella velella* who drifted over and began to express—with a poetic and practiced suavity rendered ridiculous by his fresh-peeled, boyish appearance—his boundless appreciation of her person. Unfortunately, she was bored.

Fortunately, the fresh-peeled boy just happened to have, out in the trunk of his Oldsmobile, an entire suitcase full of Radical Hero memorabilia, and had no qualms about lugging it into the bar in order to reveal to her who he really was, or had been, or wished he'd been, before he'd shaved and so forth. Unfortunately, the tall, lean woman loathed student radicals.

Fortunately, she was so strongly attracted to Celebrity that the sheer bulk of the pile of clippings, writings and photos by or about this baby-faced Folk Legend Gone Underground somehow convinced her to invite both the howling red lust and its owner to bivouac upon, beside, beneath and all about her spectacular body—and not only that first night, but night after night. Unfortunately, for the first time in his redundant but really rather limited experience, our hero found that the multiple nightly deaths of his howling red lusts did absolutely *nothing* to diminish the appetite of this insatiable and mysterious woman.

Her name, we can be almost certain, was not Circe. But Circe will have to do, since in his post-Circe depression Everett's opinion was that she could only have been a gift sent by a vengeful God, god or goddess, or perhaps by Circe herself, or perhaps she *was* Circe herself, come to teach him at last the meaning or unmeaning or inescapable outcome of an all-out surrender to loveless lust. What Everett was to Circe he never discovered. But what Circe was to him was "an absolutely gorgeous conquest," which several wild and increasingly kinky nights forced him to redefine as "a co-competitor in a grim erotic marathon," which an incalculable confusion of bitterly contested nights-days-or-whatever forced him to ultimately define as an indomitable, terrifying, utterly victorious demigoddess whose sole purpose in indulging him had been to reveal to him the thing he feared most: his true inner condition.

Allow me to preface this grim revelation by describing a syndrome unknown to most women, but nightmarishly familiar to a great many men: struggle though we do to "grow up," millions of us American males spend our entire adult lives involuntarily blundering into slightly re-vamped but clearly recognizable replays of the same tedious inabilities and fears, the same pedestrian self-conceptions and the same uncorrectable limitations we first experienced during our boyhood baseball careers. To fully understand the nightmarishness of these karmic recrudescences it's important to bear in mind that, unless we happen to be major leaguers at the moment, our baseball careers invariably went up in some form of flames. It's also crucial to note that there is no simple escape: those who had no boyhood baseball career often spend their manhood reliving, repressing or rationalizing this lack.

So then. Picture our virile young campus hero doing with and to the long, lean Circe what he fancied he did best. And imagine his confusion as it dawned on him that while he had grown sated and then some, she hadn't and then some. Now picture the ferocity of his determination as he sensed her dissatisfaction, summoned his infamous radical defiance, girded his loins, again mounted her beautiful body, and threw everything he had into his efforts. And then, for the eternally recurring Little League coup de grace, imagine the sick shock of recognition when he suddenly saw in these efforts not the legendary love-warrior of the U district but Coach Donny Bunnel's inadequate little second sacker, still struggling after all these years to "make up in desire what he lacked in ability," still "giving it his very best shot," still "doing some real scrapping out there," and still impressing his devastating opponent no more than he'd once impressed the North Wenatchee High varsity with his quadruple-K effort in a 15 to 2 loss. These are the unsung dangers of an early life in baseball! Yet even at this sorry pass Everett remained so terrified of the *Velella velella*-ness his life had become that he would probably have gone on "scrapping out there" indefinitely. Only a scare of epic proportions, only a Jonah's whale or a Balaam's ass could alter his course now. And that was what Circe gave him . . .

The mythical event occurred on their last night-day-or-whatever together, when—having exhausted him, fed him, besotted him with wine, exhausted him again, revived him with an unnamed drug, and exhausted him yet again, only to goad him, everywhere and with anything, fingers, breath, tongue, teeth, fury, unthinkable curses, unthinkable curves, all to no avail—Circe finally pinned him, straddled him, and held a mirror over his face. *"Look at you!"* she'd whispered. And he'd tried. But when he peered into her mirror, Everett swears to this day that what he saw peering back at him was the bristle-chinned, beady-eyed, insensate face of a spent young pig.

Or swine, in the FitzGerald translation.

Endless objections can of course be raised. What about "Circe's" point of view, for instance? What was her story? Does the wretched Everett really expect us to believe that she was more than human? Or that he was really less? And what did the swine transform *her* into, poor woman, assuming she *was* a woman? And of course she was! Wasn't she? Valid questions and confusions all. But whereas most stories interest us because of all that they are able to tell us, the tale of Everett and Circe is most interesting for what it is *not* able to tell us. After sorting through his pig-eyed, pig-minded impressions, Everett later swore not only that he couldn't remember Circe's eye or hair color but that *she had none*. Naturally. For pigs see only in black and white. All that he recalled of his grim goddess were an approximate contour and weight in pounds, some eccentric angles from which he viewed those contours and pounds, a few of her quaint nicknames for the various entanglements of their anatomies, her initially exciting but ultimately terrifying "love" cries, and above all the craving for and stamina during erotic activity which first inspired, then exhausted, then crushed, disgraced, and routed his own.

Oh. There was one modern, non-Homeric, "literary" sort of detail. A Virginia Slim cigarette—the first of that brand he'd ever seen—which she jammed into his chest after he failed to react even to the sight of the shoat in the mirror. It was the sight of it burning his flesh, the slowness of his reaction even to the smell of it and the porcine squeal that finally came flying out of him which together convinced him to leave, that very night, for Canada.

So Everett the Campus Legend became the run-of-the-mill, unromantic and now sexually humiliated type of drifter/criminal known as "a draft-dodger." And unless he wanted to become an equally run-of-the-mill American convict, he would have to remain one for the rest of his life. His leftist years were over. Their tangible fruits were these:

1. an immeasurable but undoubtedly minute contribution to the "early" (only two and a half million dead) end of the Vietnam War;

2. an immeasurable but undoubtedly huge contribution to Babcock's sabotage of Irwin's Conscientious Objector status;

3. the permanent sabotage of his own academic career;

4. an unresolved estrangement from the government he hated most (his own);

5. an unresolved estrangement from every human being and place he'd ever known or loved;

6. a brief metamorphosis into a pig;

7. the play *Hats*. All copies of which have been lost. Though thanks to Mama, one wrinkled program, a Seattle *Times* review and a rave letter Irwin wrote her describing the play all made it into the "EVERETT" box in the attic.

5. Matthew 10:36 Revisited

God created an impossible situation.
—Tom McGuane

On the first Sabbath after Everett left for Canada and the third after Irwin left for boot camp, Mama, Linda and Bet all went to church. And when they got there, Mama did not spit in Elder Babcock's face. "I'm *proud* of my son," she told Papa when she got home. "I'm proud of what Irwin's doing, proud of his choice of a wife, and I wanted all my friends, and Elder Babcock and Elder Barnes, and God Himself to know it. So I went to church. Is that all right with you?"

Papa just looked at her. And went on looking at her. Till it was obvious that his silence was his answer.

When I got home that night after a fourteen-hour day of homework, the house was completely dark, not even a porch light. I thought it was a power outage till I unlocked the door—and stepped into the wall of cigarette smoke.

I backed up onto the porch and stood there a long time, afraid of what I'd find inside. Then it occurred to the optimist in me that there could have been a party, a visit from other ballplayers, a chain-smoking overnight guest asleep on the couch maybe. So I stepped inside, tiptoed to the kitchen, snapped on the light, looked back through to the livingroom. And there sat Papa, alone in his armchair, drinking Old Crow straight out of the bottle, and chain-smoking Lucky Strikes.

For a long time we just blinked at each other, me because of emotion, he because of the light. Then, in a voice slurred and scorched beyond recognition, he said, "I'm sorry, Kade. I'm very shorry. But Laura's taken girlsh up to Marvin Janes, see. An' her Jeejus wants me drop dead, see. So this the Lord'sh work I'm doin'. See?"

He tried to laugh, but could only make a rasping sound. He avoided my eyes. And I had no plan whatever as I walked slowly toward his chair. But when I got there I felt no qualm or hesitation as I took off my glasses, held them straight out in front of me, and dropped them into his ashtray. "No," I heard myself say as Lucky butts scattered all over the floor. "No, I *don't* see, Papa. Out my left eye I can hardly see a thing. And I thought I'd completely forgiven you for that. But if it was for nothing, if I can't see for nothing, then I'm afraid I don't forgive you at all."

"Kade," he said, struggling for air or for clarity. "Kade, listen. Listen . . . Listen . . . Thish a one-night deal. Thas all this is. An' it's over. See?" He tried to pull himself up, knocked the ashtray off his chair-arm, lunged for it, and spilled his bottle.

I didn't move to right it. Neither did he.

He said, "My wife dudn't love me, Kade. Thas all this is."

We watched the whiskey pour out onto the carpet.

"Laura hates me, is all. An' my boys 'cept you are gone. An' my girls, Kade, are so scared, an' Linda. I used to love comin' home here, is all. For a while I loved this little place. So I got sad. See? Thas all this is."

BOOK FIVE

The Brothers K

EVERETT

A Definition

K (kā) *verb*, K'ed, K'ing. 1. *baseball:* to strike out.
2. to fail, to flunk, to fuck up, to fizzle, or 3. to fall
short, fall apart, fall flat, fall by the wayside, or on
deaf ears, or hard times, or into disrepute or disre-
pair, or 4. to come unglued, come to grief, come
to blows, come to nothing, or 5. go to the dogs, go
through the roof, go home in a casket, go to hell in
a hand basket, or 6. to blow your cover, blow your
chances, blow your cool, blow your stack, shoot
your wad, bitch the deal, buy the farm, bite the
dust, only 7. to recollect an oddball notion you
first heard as a crimeless and un-K'ed child but
found so nonsensically paradoxical that you had to
ignore it or defy it or betray it for decades before
you could begin to believe that it might possibly
be true, which is that 8. to lose your money, your
virginity, your teeth, health or hair, 9. to lose your
home, your innocence, your balance, your friends,
10. to lose your happiness, your hopes, your lei-
sure, your looks, and, yea, even your memories,
your vision, your mind, your way,

   11. in short (and as Jesus K. Rist once so un-
compromisingly put it) to lose your very self,

   12. for the sake of another, is

   13. sweet irony, the only way you're ever going
to save it.

CHAPTER ONE

Names of Stars

Wait for the promise of the Father.
—Acts 1:4

Camas / Sabbath / November / 1970

Freddy was out in the backyard with a tipless bamboo fly rod she'd dragged up out of the basement. Papa had promised to take her fishing this morning, so she was trying to practice casting. But no sooner would she get the fly line airborne than her wonderful new dog with the terrible new name (Suncracker) would tear after it, bounding high as a deer, till sooner or later he'd catch it, bring it to earth, and shake it as if it were an anorexic snake whose neck needed breaking, causing Freddy to burst into laughter, drop the rod, grab the dog, sing "No no no!" then cover his muzzle with little kisses, so that of course he couldn't wait to do the very same thing again.

Papa sat slumped in his chair at the kitchen table. Because of his promise he would glance up at Freddy and the dog now and then. But even while watching them he wore the immovable expression Irwin used to call "the Face," and though none of us knew exactly what this expression meant, we did know certain implications: one was that there would be no change of mood or activity for a good long while; another was that if we spoke to Papa, he'd be unlikely to hear, let alone answer.

Of course our father was a promise-keeping man. But he could be driven to break them. Last spring, for instance, when Mama went right on going to Babcock's church after Irwin left for boot camp, he broke his promise never to speak to her again after just two weeks, when it became obvious that if he didn't speak to her he would soon be forced to break the promise made on the day they married.

His reasons for breaking his promise to Freddy were not so simple. In fact, they were complex to the point of incomprehensibility. But I can hint at the nature of what can't be comprehended by simply reciting the locations of the rest of our family that day:

Irwin was in Vietnam, learning at last how not to laugh.

Mama was at church, asking God to protect Irwin by destroying his enemies—the NVA, the Vietcong and Everett.

Everett was in British Columbia, working at two part-time jobs and trying full-time to figure out how to do things such as think and act like a human again.

Peter was in Massachusetts, studying bodhisattvas, Zen patriarchs and Maharashtran poet-saints, and trying to become one or another of them himself.

Bet was with Mama, for reasons I'll come to shortly.

Linda was back in what used to be the twins' room, tending her and Irwin's newborn baby boy.

There were two letters in Papa's shirt pocket as he sat at the kitchen table that morning. Both were from the Mekong River delta. Both had been mailed to the private PO box I'd opened in Camas to keep my correspondences with Irwin and Everett secret from Linda, Mama and the twins. But I'd recently decided to share everything with Papa. That was part of his problem. The first letter was dated September 30, 1970. Here is most of it:

. . . In Saigon on the way in, when we stalled in a traffic jam and our CO got nervous and went to check it out, this little wise-ass from Jersey, Dinky O'Neil his name was, though he changed it real quick back to Rick once he found out "gooks" are called "dinks" too.

Anyhow Dinky, as we knew him then, took it into his head to hop down off our personnel carrier and strut right up to one of those Buddhist monks they've got on the streets in those California-poppy-colored robes there. And when they were face to face, just inches apart, Dinky goes, "Hey, bro'! Wuz happenin'?" So of course the monk just freezes, smiles, and looks confused. Then Dinky goes, "No dig? No comprehende? Hey, guy, not to worry! You might not believe this, but we're actually not from around here." And we all just cracked up! I mean here is this parade of giant khaki men and machines plowing like sci-fi monsters through this sea of delicate little brown people, and here is one of the monsters touching noses with this poor monk who finds us so outer spacey he never does quit smiling and never does unfreeze. Yet Dinky acts like he's got to explain the situation, like the monk just isn't going to believe we're not local yokels! Funny as hell.

But you know, as the days creep by, inch by, crawl by, I keep seeing Dinky and the monk nose to nose there. And it's quit being funny, Kade. These were two people who never should of laid eyes on each other, is my feeling now. This was a guy who should of been hustling pool and shooting craps in Trenton and a guy who should of been chanting and begging or whatever in Saigon, and never the twain should of met. I mean, we are so totally "not from around here" it's like we *are* outer space monsters. Big alien monsters of the meanest deadliest kind. And there's just no laughs in that. There's nothing at all funny about being deadly alien monsters in real life.

Linda, despite our constant coaxing, kept herself and the baby back in their tiny room all night, and most of each day. Sometimes when the baby was napping she would dart out, scarlet-faced, and scurry round the house, cleaning this, scouring that, and apologizing, forever apologizing, for being a burden, or for Irwin's absence, or for not having money or showing more gratitude or being smarter or prettier or more invisible or less apologetic till the baby started to cry and her breasts started to leak and she turned redder still, apologized once more, and disappeared. In a way she was the opposite of Everett or Mama: rather than place blame, she hoarded it. Irwin's plight, Mama's anger, Bet's new night terrors, Everett's exile, Papa's silences—they were all her doing somehow. What I liked best about her so far was that the one thing that *was* half her doing —the baby—was not on her fault list at all. He was a small but intense little armload, dark-haired like Irwin, loud-voiced like Everett, brown-eyed like Linda, olive-skinned like nobody. And Linda was unapologetically crazy about him.

His name was Nash, and the etymology was interesting: it seemed that Irwin and Linda read somewhere, or at least convinced each other that they'd read somewhere (Freddy suggests in *The Guinness Book of Hilariously Dangerous Superstitions*), that if a couple copulates in a fairly upright position with the girl on top, for instance in an automobile, the sperm can't overcome the uphill battle to the egg and conception is out of the question. They both swore they recalled the words "for instance in an automobile" and "out of the question." They said it was these words —and maybe some vague expectation of Olympic-style points for degree of difficulty—which convinced them to test the theory out, night after rainy night, in the front and only seat of Irwin's 1958 Nash Rambler.

The result? A 1970 Nash Chance.

Freddy's dog, like Irwin and Linda's son, entered our lives with a bizarre etymology. Shortly after Irwin left for boot camp last April, Freddy went with a girlfriend to help her pick out a kitty from the Humane Society's death row, and though the friend was unable to find a kitten, Freddy, without consulting either parent, brought home a half-grown, half-breed collie/cocker spaniel whose first two tricks turned out to be piddling with confusion and piddling with joy. Afraid to face the music, Freddy had tied the pup behind Papa's old pitching shed, pilfered a box of saltines from the kitchen, snuck back outside, and was issuing a chaos of commands and crackers in hopes of perfecting the dog before introducing it to her parents, when a ghastly bawling from the direction of the Fir Haven Apartments brought her crash course to a halt.

"What's with you?" Freddy asked the little nose and lips she finally spotted bulging like a hemorrhoid through a low crack in the fence.

In the Phlegm dialect the tots all seem to use at Fir Haven, the nose and lips replied that their apartment was "No Goggies Allowed."

"Tell you what," said St. Winifred, poking half of a cracker through the crack into the ghastly little cracker. "If you promise to stop crying, you can name *my* goggie."

It took a while for the words and saltine to sink in. But once they sank, the gooey mouth vanished, a little blue eyeball appeared, squinted up at the sun, peered down at the dog, glanced over at the bright red Premium Snowflake cracker box, then back popped the mouth, and *voilà*, Suncracker had a name as inept as the treeless Fir Haven Apartments.

Of course Freddy hated the name as much as any of us. She has better than average taste in such matters. But she would allow no other. As she told us at dinner that night, "What can I do? A promise is a promise."

Which brings me back to Papa's. He and John Hultz would be off to Mexico on a scouting trip early Monday. He was taking every winter road job the Tugs sent his way, largely, I think, to minimize his time around Mama. At any rate, this was his first free Saturday in months. And when his old friend Roy stopped by on Friday evening to show off a beautiful bright chinook he'd just caught in the lower Washougal, Papa promised to take Freddy fishing on Saturday "come hell or high water—since both are always possible around here." So all that evening the two of them knocked around the basement, sorting and mending old fishing gear, laughing at its wretched condition, and swapping stories about the car doors, big fish and muscle-brained brothers that had made it all that way. But judging by the bags under his eyes at breakfast this morning, he and Mama must have had a real knock-down, drag-out battle after they went to bed last night. And Papa has a way, when he and Mama are actively feuding, of behaving as though she and Fate have conspired to put a mysterious whammy on him.

This morning's whammy was typical. He and Freddy were loaded up and ready to go, I'd dragged myself outside just to wish them luck, and the sight of Freddy almost made it worthwhile: she was wearing a pair of Peter's hip boots and an old flannel jacket of Irwin's, both newly patched; her long brown hair was in two thick braids, and the broad-brimmed Amish hat that Everett used to wear around town to weird out rednecks only made her look exotic. Suncracker was in her lap, panting but not quite piddling with joy; the day was overcast but calm—perfect fishing weather; it was her first solo outing with Papa in months, and their first solo fishing trip ever. Her smile was radiant. Then Papa fired up the old '40 Ford, noticed the same puff of tail-pipe smoke we've all seen for ages, and decided this was the puff that meant he had to install a carburetor kit he's been carrying in his glove box for years. Sensing what was coming, I told him to take Irwin's Nash or my Volkswagen Bug.

Papa said, "We're already loaded. This won't take a minute."

Under whammyless circumstances he's a competent mechanic. With Freddy acting as a kind of surgeon's assistant he got the carburetor removed by the time I'd finished breakfast. Then she idly asked how the thing worked, so he held it out, started explaining, twisted it slightly to show her the insides—and four or five tiny ball bearings came bouncing like kids out of a schoolhouse, binked down through the engine, and vanished in the gravel beneath the car. Papa didn't curse: his whole art is control. But he didn't smile either when Freddy cracked, "Looks like we lost our bearings." He just released the parking brake, rolled the car back a few feet, dropped to his knees, and proceeded to spend fifteen or twenty stupid minutes crawling around in the rocks. Freddy helped. She even found a bearing. Papa didn't find a one.

Whammy.

The sane thing to do in such circumstances is buy a new kit and bearings, or spring for a rebuilt carb. Papa said no need, he had plenty of bearings in the toolshed out back. He then drifted off with a fey look in his eye, returning maybe twenty minutes later with an MJB can of gas-soaked carb parts that looked like something Columbus used in the *Santa María*. He found bearings in it, though, and when four of them seemed to match the one original he sucked up his courage, dropped them into what he hoped were the appropriate holes, spent a half hour putting the carb back together, another half hour installing it, then started the car and watched without surprise, anger, or any other expression as gasoline spurted and streamed all over the engine till it flooded, sputtered, and died.

When it started to rain just then, Freddy looked at Papa, smiled, and said, "Perfect." He said nothing back. Ensconced in the Face now, he gathered up his tools, parts and tin cans, and for the first time in our lives carried them not into the garage or toolshed or basement, but into the kitchen, where he spread some newspaper over the table and pretended to set to work. Only now it was obvious. Papa was no longer fixing a carburetor: he was setting up a greasy little Cuban missile base smack-dab in the middle of Mama's immaculate Washington, D.C. It was a flagrant act of war. And it was probably justified. But only in the context of his endless struggle with his wife. It had nothing to do with fixing cars or fishing with Freddy. He was now breaking his promise, but failing to admit it.

I went upstairs to do homework. Hours passed. The rain stopped. Freddy and the dog began their fly-casting routine right outside Papa's kitchen window. I tried to ignore the whole show. More hours passed. Papa kept puttering.

The second letter in his shirt pocket, from the same river delta, had been mailed to my secret PO box, which was no longer secret. It was my own fault. I'd used the letter to mark my place in a textbook, then left it lying around, and Bet happened to pick up the book and find the letter. It was dated October 12:

I know it makes Mama mad and Linda jealous, but this box of yours keeps me from bursting, Kade. Because what can I really tell them about what we're doing here? I mean, Linda's so scared already, and now Bet has this weird Satan thing going, and Mama's letters all sound as if some sort of Old Testament combat sergeant wrote them. And even Freddy, Kade. I love her so much, and love hearing from her. But in her letter last week she told me that no matter how bad things were here, there must be at least one good thing about it. So "look on the bright side," she says, "just long enough to tell me what that one good thing is." And Christ! What that led to! What a simple thing like that can—

well hell. I'll just tell you. When I sat down to answer her two nights ago, the one good thing I could think of was the day I leave. Then I remembered she said a good Vietnamese thing. Which made it hard. And made me mad. So I told her so. I said we aren't here to fucking *like* Vietnamese things, we're here to kill or be killed by them, and telling me to wander around looking for bright sides and good things is like telling me how to hurry up and get dead. But of course I couldn't mail it. Not to Freddy. Because one thing we *are* fighting for here, one thing I think we really are trying to defend, is the ignorance and sweetness of some of the people back home. So I threw the truth away and went back to looking for some harmless answer. And finally decided on stars. There really are good bright stars here most nights, shining just like at home, shooting out their little tracers and flares, hurting nobody. And it's light that has already shone, right? Like scientifically, what we see twinkling here at night has travelled so far it really happened ages ago, right? So even though the stars are here, they're not here. Not like we are. Which can only be a good thing, believe me. So that was my answer. "On the bright side, Freddy, 'Nam has got beautiful stars."

But then I realized I couldn't name even one. I guess I only knew the two Dippers and Morning Star and Orion's belt back home, but that was enough, just those made it the home sky. So I figured I should name a Vietnamese star. And just as I thought this I saw a buddy of mine, George Dubash, out strolling and getting loaded. So I went and asked George what he knew about these stars. And he smiled and passed me his joint so friendly I actually smoked some instead of faking as usual. Then he touched the cross round my neck Linda gave me and said, "Lesson One for Bible-thumpers, Chance." And he showed me the Southern Cross.

Well, you know how locoweed makes me. I must have really thanked the shit out of him, judging by the way he started to laugh. But Dubash was such a nice guy, and you know how I feel about crosses, and this one hung up there so calm and bright that for the first time in weeks I felt like I knew what planet I was on and like I halfway belonged on it. So after thanking him shitless I finished my letter and thanked Freddy too, for making me look on the bright side. And the very next morning, Kade, Dubash's point man got his throat cut and died soundless, his whole recon patrol walked straight into an ambush, and a stream of 51-caliber NVA bullets sawed my friend George Dubash almost in half.

It's night again as I write this. The whole sky is spread over me, moonless and starry as hell. But you know how locoweed makes me. I've looked all over for the Southern Cross, and it's either vanished or hasn't risen or I'm looking straight at it but am too stupid to know. Which makes me feel as if George Dubash died for nothing. Yet I swear by the stars I can't even fucking find that I'll *never* ask another man to point the Cross out to me, in case asking might put the Southern curse on him too. So what to tell Freddy, Kade? See why it's tough? The truth is I'm in a place without a bright side or a one best thing. I'm in a place where, honest to God, you feel you can kill your friends just by asking the names of stars.

Beatrice, as I said, was with Mama at church. Her reason for going was that Mama was the one family member who claimed she could help protect Bet from Satan, she being the one family member who still believed in him. It struck me as odd that to facilitate this protection Mama would take Bet each week to hear the very man who betrayed Irwin, bellowing out tales of Satan's most horrific and inescapable powers. But churches always have been the leading cause of the need for churches. And direct confrontation has been Mama's style as a therapist all her life. Uncle Marv tells a story about her trying, at age nine or so, to cure her little brother Truman of his terror of water by shouting "Just *relax!*" as she flung him off a dock into Lake Erie. And lately we'd all marveled at her attempts to cure Linda of her Vietnam fears by inviting her each evening to watch Walter Cronkite give the body counts on the CBS news.

So Bet was at church, seeking protection. And whatever their true source, and whatever the cure, her night terrors were no joke. She spent hours, most nights, wandering sleeplessly round the house, and when I'd stay up late to study she'd often notice my light, give a tentative knock, then drift in, plop down on Irwin's old bed, and start looking through all the motley stuffed animals and athletic awards he left jumbled together on one shelf when he took off for college. Her movements would seem serene as she'd do this, and her face would be calm enough. But her eyes were pure pupil—no iris at all. And even as I'd try to smile and look my most relaxed, I'd be bracing myself against the moment she spoke.

"I used to think," she began, on one of the worst nights, "that if Jesus came to earth with all his niceness and innocence, but almost none of his brains, so that he was too dumb to save more than one or two people, but every bit as much fun to look at and play with and be with, he would be somebody almost exactly like Irwin."

I smiled cautiously. "That's a funny idea," I said.

She smiled back, and for a moment I thought maybe she was all right. Then she said, "Our nice, dumb, innocent brother Jesus—doing recon in 'Nam. Funny idea." And the smile twisted away.

This time I made no reply.

"I'm afraid," Bet said.

"I believe you," I answered.

Then she began, in the flat, dull monotone she's cultivated since her visits to the school counselor began, to name the things she is afraid of. To name them is good, the counselor said. To share her fears is good. So we listen. But the monotone never lasts long, and Bet's midnight fears are such disjointed, unanswerable, terrible things that I can never think of a consoling reply, so instead of dispersing they begin to collect in the air between us, gathering in grotesqueness, gathering in intensity, till my own little childhood room feels as alien and threatening to me as the Mekong Delta must feel to Irwin . . .

"Late last night I looked at Papa," she told me. "Just looked at his face, in the light of the TV, while he was resting, with his eyes closed. And a lump came out. Just under his eye, just under the skin. It came out, then started moving down his cheek, so that I hoped it was a tear, I hoped he was crying. But then it opened. It opened, and looked right at me. A horrid, bloodshot little eye, Kincaid! And after it looked at me it sank back into his cheek, and Papa opened his own eyes. But he didn't look at me. Not even a glance. He just got up and walked straight out of the room."

I said nothing. I believed nothing. Yet I couldn't help but picture it. And already my room began not to be mine.

"Peter believes in reincarnation," she said. "Freddy too. I don't. But sometimes in my dreams I'm a Nazi. And I *hate* Nazis, Kincaid, *hate* them, *hate* them. But in my dreams I have this uniform, all gray and black and perfect, with two little silver swastikas, right here at the throat. And I love my swastikas. I love them so much it makes me sick, it makes me sweat. But it also makes me feel like doing every single thing that Nazis do, just to get to keep them."

Just share with her, the counselor told us. *It's good to share . . .*

"I never joined Cub Scouts," I said, embarrassed, as soon as I spoke, by the triviality of my comparison. "It seemed boring and silly to me. But when I was nine or ten I started borrowing Irwin's old Cub Scout shirt so often that he finally just gave it to me. And I remember why I liked it, I remember the feeling perfectly. It was the Bobcat pin, Bet. And the Wolf, Lion and Bear badges, the gold and silver arrows. I still remember exactly where each of them fit against my body. And they weren't even mine. So I don't know. Insignia. Arrows and swastikas. There's just something in people that loves such things. It doesn't mean we're Nazis."

It turned out all right, my little speech. It didn't sound so foolish. But I could see, long before I'd finished, that Bet had moved off into a far deeper terror. "You *like* it, you *like* it, you *like* it," she began whispering, and her eyes were pure liquid black. "That's what he'd tell her. That's what Linda's father would say, over and over, every time he raped her."

Now the air turned utterly alien. Now my room ceased to be mine. I knew that Bet was mistaken, or else lying. Linda had told me what had happened to her, and bad as it was, it had happened only once. But why was Bet saying these things?

"Do you know how he woke her?" she asked softly, almost tenderly. "With a Number 2 pencil, just like we use at school. She'd feel a tickle, and open her eyes. And there he'd be, holding the point in her ear. *One sound,* he'd say, *and I'll jam it clear in.* Then he'd climb on top of her. *You like it, you like it* . . . She was just my age when it started. And when he'd finish he'd never say a word, he'd just get up and leave. He'd even leave the pencil lying there. And do you know where he went? In to bed with her mother! In to sleep by his wife, like a regular happy couple. And her mother *knew!* Linda swears she knew!"

And I, with my Cub Scout shirt, had wanted to make it all better.

"They slept like babies," Bet told me. "Linda knew they did, because she'd sneak in to watch them afterward, because she couldn't sleep herself. Want to hear why? Do you want to know why Linda could never sleep?"

I forced myself to nod. *Good. It's good to share . . .*

"Because she'd have a dream—the same one over and over, like my little silver swastikas—where she would sleepwalk. She'd get up out of bed, walk to the drawer where her mother kept the big sewing scissors, take them down to her father's shop in the basement, break them in two with a hammer and chisel. And then she'd walk back upstairs to her parents' room, where they'd be sleeping soundly. All tired out, the dears. Then she'd lean, ever so slowly, down over them. And she'd slide half the scissors into her mother's left ear. And half into her father's right . . ." (I watched Bet's hands, the careful pantomime. She was an artist. Her hands made it real.) "And when they felt the tickle, and woke, she'd look at them so sadly, and say to them, still in her sleep, *I'm sorry, but they're broken. Mother's scissors are broken. And I have to fix them. Now.* Then she'd laugh, or shriek, and *jam* the halves back together! And her shriek would really wake her, it would wake her in real life. And every time she woke she was sure she'd see her parents there beneath her, and feel the scissor halves wriggling in her hands."

I shut my eyes and saw Linda naked, saw swastikas and Scout shirts, saw eyeballs in cheeks, scissors in ears, NVA bullets cutting George Dubash in half. There's just something in us that loves such things. It doesn't mean we're Nazis . . .

"Have you noticed?" Beatrice asked. "Have you seen the way Ma— Linda, the way she *still* looks at scissors?"

I didn't nod, didn't know, couldn't move.

"And do you see the *real* reason why she couldn't sleep?" Bet said, smiling now. "It's so pathetic, so pathetic! It's because she *loved* them! They were her parents, she had no one else. The Bible says she *had* to love them. So she'd lay awake all night to keep from killing them. Then all day at school she *would* sleepwalk, and fall asleep at her desk, and flunk everything in sight, and the kids would tease her, even her teachers would laugh. *Stupid! Hey, stupid! Pick up your pencil! Pay attention! Wake up, stupid!* So that was the life, the hell, that was what Pa— *Irwin.* That was what Irwin saved her from."

I felt I should stop her, say something, console someone, kill someone. But before words could form she was whispering, "*Satan* . . ."

Breathing as if she too had begun to drown in the inimical air, staring past me, through me, she said, "I know you don't think so, I know that, I know. And I hate the name, the idea, hate everything about it. But Linda's mother, Kincaid. Picture her listening. *You like it, you like it!* Is that a mother, or something lying in slime on the bottom of hell? And her father! Daddy. He would smile, she says, while he held the pencil in place. So feel him there, the point against your eardrum. Smiling." Bet was gasping now, and sobbing. "That's not *human*, Kincaid! It's not! That's something so evil and strong it can enter anybody, any time or place it wants, and make even good people do the most horrible things! And it never stops. It *never* stops! And God never tries to stop it. And now even Irwin might die or do some horrid, inhuman thing. So why, Kincaid? *Why?* When Irwin believes, when he really believes, how can it happen? How? Why doesn't God ever try to stop it?"

She collapsed against me then, and I put an arm around her and tried, in a stiff, nervous, sexless way, to keep her from breaking apart. But what good was that? What good am I? I made soothing sounds, tried to hold and pat her less awkwardly, tried to earn my Bobcat pin. But Bet cried herself dry, she cried till she retched. And I never did think of a single consoling thing to say—

because I believe it *is* human. I believe it's just people who do all the horrible, incomprehensible things to other people. And I didn't see how sharing this belief would ease my sister's pain or terror in the least.

At one in the afternoon I went downstairs to make lunch, noticed that Papa's tools weren't moving, peeked over his shoulder to find out why, and spotted an oily but legible page of last summer's box scores lying beneath the scattered carb parts.

So. He had taken refuge. Fine. For him. But Freddy and Suncracker were still out back with the busted fly rod. And they'd been at it so long that the dog's tongue was gigantic and his grin had gone insane. Freddy's "See, Papa? We're fishing anyhow!" smile still looked genuine enough. But when she wore it this tenaciously it began to seem like nothing more than her version of the Face. So, little as I wanted to, I invaded Papa's refuge.

"Why are you here?" I asked, quite a bit louder than necessary.

He turned, and did his patented impersonation of a man-shaped piece of plywood.

"She's been waiting for hours. And you're reading four-month-old box scores."

He looked out at her, but still said nothing.

"She'd rather go with you and I've got homework to do. But if you can't borrow my car and take her fishing, just tell me right now and I'll take her myself."

Sentences remained beyond him, but he finally managed to start squeezing out syllables. "Damn," he went. "I, hell. The thing, Kade, is, I.

Your mother and me. Laura. With me leavin' Monday we've just got to
. . . I can't just up and. *Damn*."

Assuming he was finished, which was assuming a lot, I said, "Whatever
it is, Papa, whatever you're saying, Freddy's been waiting, and smiling, an
awful long time."

"Kincaid," he said. "You know a, you have to take . . . Much as I love
her, your sister is not the only . . . Dammit, yes! You're right. Go. But
wait. Hell. Here. I'll go tell Freddy."

CHAPTER TWO

The Kwakiutl Karamazov

As soon as I arrive in America with Grushenka we will set to work on the land, in solitude, somewhere very remote, with wild bears. There must be some remote parts even there. I am told there are still Indians there, somewhere, on the edge of the horizon.
  —Dmitri to Alyosha Karamazov

Near the southwest coast of Vancouver Island, on the flood-scoured banks of the Little Nessakoola River, sits a forty-house, one-church, one-tavern town called Shyashyakook. It's not terribly isolated—only fifty miles west of the city of Victoria, three miles inland from the Strait of Juan de Fuca shipping lanes, a quarter mile south of a well-traveled highway. But when Everett arrived in the spring of 1970, Shyashyakook's salmon cannery and sawmill had been bankrupt for a decade, the forty houses had turned so rain-grayed and ramshackle that even the Beautiful British Columbia Provincial Tour Guide could find no more glowing adjective for the town than "historic," and Everett himself thought "prehistoric" was the better word. "When they say this place is in B.C.," he wrote to Natasha, "they mean the time period, not the province."

On his first walk along the estuary a couple of miles downriver from "city center" he found an eight-foot weather-grayed chunk of totem pole —the torso of Wolf or Bear maybe (though some idiot had chain-sawed a "D.D. + A.A." into its backside). And on the same walk, a few hundred paces from the totem, his boots began making odd crunching sounds, and he found himself standing on a clam shell midden as broad as an infield and several times the height of a pitcher's mound.

Both the totem-chunk and the midden had been left behind by the Kwakiutl. An unsortable blend of archaeological evidence and folk legend had it that a southerly branch, or at least twig, of this tribe had lived on the Little Nessakoola estuary for some eight thousand years—four times the life-span of Christendom; five times the span of the Islamic world; forty times the span of that constantly backfiring experiment in self-government known as "the United States." Then, one day in the early 1800s, an enterprising young tribesman paddled his canoe out into the Strait, hailed a passing ship, traded a few furs for a nice factory-made British blanket, and never lived to learn that the stuff it had been infected with was called "smallpox." Two winters later his eight-thousand-year-old village was extinct. "But look on the bright side," Everett wrote, again to Natasha. "Kwakiutl art was such a perfect expression of integration with this landscape that even the white folks felt they couldn't live without it. So a group of generous industrial chieftains from our own fine culture got together and bequeathed Shyashyakook their own two favorite Pacific Northwest totems: Old Man Caved-In Salmon Cannery and Old Man Rusted-Out Sawmill."

The estuary's eight-thousand-year Kwakiutl history remains a mystery upon which shell-heaps and vandalized totem-chunks shed little light, but the sixty-year history of the town was so depressingly predictable that the two dead industrial totems pretty well told the whole tale. For a century or so after the mass death (or, as the B.C. tour guide prefers, "disappearance") of the Indians, the townsite was just a camp for hunters and fishermen. Then in the 1920s the cannery, sawmill, church, tavern and forty houses were erected in a three-year span, business soon boomed in all forty-four structures, and for a decade or so it seemed that Shyashyakook's industrial future might be bright despite its retrograde Indian name. But since it was a tidewater town with no oceangoing fishing fleet, its cannery was totally dependent on Little Nessakoola River gill-netting. And when the watershed was clear-cut to supply the sawmill, it brought on winter floods and mudslides that flushed the river's spawning beds out into the Strait of Juan de Fuca, forcing its salmon to join the Kwakiutl in the Land of the Dead, and driving the cannery into bankruptcy. "Still plenty of trees!" gloated the town optimists—all of whom worked at the sawmill at this point. Then the Prince George Pulp and Paper Company—which owned every mature tree within a ninety-mile radius—found a more profitable market for their unprocessed logs at a modernized mill in Esquimalt, forty miles away. That was all it took. One day the mill was the town's sole source of income; the next it was what Everett called "Shyashyakook's second great neo-Kwakiutl *objet d'art.*" Industry had come. Industry had gone. It had lasted 1/267th as long as the Indian village.

Most of Shyashyakook's population, not being neo-Kwakiutl-minded, had run off in pursuit of the falling trees and schooling fish that once meant easy money in the decreasingly Great Northwest. When his congregation dwindled to eight even the priest of the Catholic church was forced to vacate. But all forty houses survived, and after the mass exodus you could buy one for peanuts. So a number of "Shyashyakooks," as they took to calling themselves, decided to try to stick it out.

It was rough going. To defy the God of Progress is often to marry the Goddess of Poverty, and a life of constant poverty and defiance can (as Circe's mirror had recently shown Everett) lead to aesthetically and socially displeasing things. The average Shyashyakook male, when Everett first arrived, poached deer and elk year-round, killed every fish, clam and crab he could catch regardless of seasonal restrictions and bag limits, stole and sold blowdown logs from provincial parks and private forests, picked, preserved, and hoarded wild fruit and mushrooms, gardened as if his life depended on it, brewed, distilled, and illegally traded some highly unpredictable beverages, cheated on his unemployment or welfare benefits, and traded goods and services with surprising scrupulousness toward his fellow Shyashyakooks but with perfect ruthlessness toward all outsiders.

But the departure of industry had brought healing changes too. For instance the quiet. You could hear the river slapping along, and the spruce trees shishing; you could follow the changes of season by sound alone—hummingbirds warring in the April willows, skeins of geese discussing pilot error high overhead in November. Another nice change: precisely because they lacked a priest, the eight Catholics were able to procure a special dispensation from the bishop in Victoria to convert a side hall of the church into a play school and kindergarten during the week, a bingo casino on Friday nights, and a dance hall whenever anybody got lonely, happy or hyperactive enough to throw a celebration. Nor, Everett soon discovered, were the priestless community's spiritual needs being neglected: not only was the Muskrat Tavern religiously attended by townsfolk of both genders, its 280-pound Scotch-Tlingit bartender, Yulie MacVee, slung around advice with an authority and accuracy that put the departed priest to shame. She couldn't legally back her homilies with the Body and Blood that supposedly make priestly badgering palatable, but a "Muskrat Burger" (which was really beef, with an illicit bit of elk or venison mixed in from time to time) cost ninety-five cents complete with lettuce, onion, pickle and fries, a draft beer cost two bits, and in the time it took him to down just one such feast, Everett once recorded the following typical MacVee counseling gems, which he mailed on to Irwin "as a homeopathic dose of sanity: take one per day as an antidote to Army Brain":

1. "Hell *no* you can't shoot Bella's ewe for eatin' your irises, Agnes! Use your wig-holder, honey. It idn't the damned sheep's fault. What if Everett here stepped out to the john and you sat down, thought his burger was yours, and downed it? 'Zat give him the right to shoot you? Here, come 'ere. Take a load off. Have a beer. And listen, Agnes. You know Jeddy Redstone? He's got a *zillion* irises in the strip there along the south side of his barn. And Bella, it so happens, has some terrible hots on Jeddy. Get the picture? Just you sigh a little, say you sure do miss that splash o' color along your fence, but hey, maybe you'll mosey on over and get some irises from Jeddy. Believe me, honey, she'll break your legs to save you the trip! You're gonna have irises sproutin' out your kwakiutl."

2. "Hell no you can't go settin' bear traps for the game warden, Roonie! Use the hat rack God gave you! You might catch somebody's kid, or worse yet, a bear! And say you did nab the warden. Say you crippled him up good. You know he only lives over in Port Renfrew and already likes it here. What's to say he wouldn't gimp on in and bore us shitless every night? But now listen, have one on me here, Roonie, and think about this. Dudn't *everybody* need a predator? Hunt and be hunted, Roon. That was the old way. Our predators keep us healthy and on our toes. So why mangle yours? You're smarter and faster, you know the woods a hundred times better. So outsmart him, outrun him, outwoods him."

3. *[in a whisper]* "For chrissake, Lulu! Wudn't that Nina's boyfriend you were mauling out in that car there? Yeah, I know he's cute. Yeah, I know they fight. Yeah, I know it's your life, but here. Simmer down.

Come 'ere. Have one on me. And listen. Between you, me and the moose on your bottle, I heard from the best source south of God that your cute new friend has got himself one *ugly*-lookin' boo-boo smack-dab on his you-know-what. I am *not* shitting you! And Nina's checked out healthy. So see why they're fighting? If he was your man, wouldn't you wonder where the hell he'd— Huh? What's that? Oh no. Oh, Lulu. You didn't! *[laughing manically now]* Oh Christ! Judas priest, Lu! Clear the aisles! Don't touch nuthin'! Go scrub your goddamn hands!"

And sin no more. Years, tourists and the wonders of industrial progress kept passing Shyashyakook by without pausing, but small good things kept happening there. A film buff began showing rent-by-mail movies in her barn every Thursday. Four families combined skills and funds and opened a combination food co-op/hardware store/post office that made the town a little, but not too much, like a town again. A couple of enterprising strangers, pretending to be Prince George Pulp and Paper employees, spent two weeks stealing the metal guts out of Old Man Rusted-Out Sawmill, trucking them to Victoria and selling them for scrap. Scrub alders and Himalayan briars knocked Old Man Caved-In Salmon Cannery to the ground, buried him under a green shroud, and raccoons turned his remains into low-cost housing. The gardens got bigger and better. The kindergarten became a full-fledged grade school. The ex-millworkers and hippies got harder and harder to tell apart. The game warden never caught Roonie, but did his job well enough that the fishing, hunting and clamming began to improve. "I didn't see it at first," Everett wrote, again to Natasha, "but this isn't a town of townspeople, really. This is a town of tribespeople. This is a bona fide bunch of modern-day hunter-gatherers with a female chief named Yulie, really and truly muddling their way from post-industrial ruin back toward a more Kwakiutl way of life. And even if you don't visit me, Natasha, even if you stay in the room the Chief rents up over the Muskrat, you ought to come check it out. Because it's a beautiful, painful, hopeful thing to see."

But I need to slow down here a minute. My problem with Shyashyakook is that I loved it so much when I finally managed a visit that I have only to picture it and about half of me tries to fly back and live there. When Everett first arrived in 1970, though, several miserable moons passed before he ever suspected he'd crash-landed in a good place. I haven't explained just where he lived, or how. More importantly, I haven't explained why he was taking such pains to describe his new home so alluringly to a young woman whose last words to him had been: "I never want to see you again!" So let me swoop back around for another pass:

On the south slope of the Little Nessakoola estuary, directly across the river from the clamshell midden, stood three somewhat ostentatious, beautifully furnished, contemporary "second homes." All three were owned by Vancouver, B.C., professional families. All three stood empty at least ten months of the year. But on the north side of a spruce grove directly behind the houses was a caretaker's cottage. This was where Everett ended up. His job—in exchange for free rent and a hundred bucks a month—was to occupy the cottage full-time, to guard the three homes from possible depredation by the Shyashyakook hunter-gatherers, and to perform a few simple maintenance tasks on the buildings, road and land.

His most demanding task turned out to be the daily tethering of an enormous, taffy-colored, petroleum-scented billy goat who was supposed to serve the same general purpose as a lawn mower, but who, unlike any mower Everett had ever operated, had a ferocious preference for the cedar shakes on the owners' houses to the grass that grew around them. After many lost tug-of-wars and several shake repair jobs, Everett re-named the goat Booger, found that didn't really help much, headed down to the Muskrat to seek liquid therapy, met Chief Yulie MacVee instead, discussed his goat problem over a free beer, told her his life story and all the rest of his problems over four more, and ended up hiring Yulie's twelve-year-old Dr. Do-Little-ish daughter, Corey, to deal with what the Chief saw as the one unnecessary difficulty in his life: the billy goat. Within weeks Everett found Corey so competent to deal with all of his caretaking tasks that he phoned his bosses in Vancouver, told how he'd befriended the chief of the Shyashyakooks, explained that his security-guard function was obviated by her stature in the community, and said he'd like to take a part-time job for the rest of the summer—eight hours a day, three days a week—vacuuming and polishing cars at a Rub-a-Dub in Victoria while Corey covered for him at home.

His bosses said fine, and the Rub-a-Dub days proved, as hoped, to be a mindless balm: Everett just did the work, prowled the city afterward till he'd filled his noise and chaos quota, drank a nightcap or two (in memory of his abandoned Seattle self) at a posh little pub called Churchill's, slept in his car the two nights, collected his pay, and drove back home to his estuary. But the other four days of his week, the Little Nessakoola days, presented the same basic *Velella velella* situation he'd first encountered in the Underground motels of Seattle—and this time a small spheroid scar in the center of his chest wouldn't let him forget that a woman's body was no surefire cure for his dreadful sense of amorphousness.

"I don't even know me," he carped in his new journal one interminable May evening. "And if I don't know me," he added, boldly going where few Campus Rads had gone before, "no wonder I don't know how not to get pissed off or restless. Because how can you control somebody you don't even know? Maybe the real me isn't pissed off or restless at all. Maybe this temperamental guy here is somebody else, somebody completely extraneous! So maybe what I need—besides a woman, which would always be nice but can possibly wait, since the pickings in town look damned slim, or damned the opposite actually, besides which Booger, speaking of 'pickings,' has a pretty okay-lookin' little ass on him (just kidding, Posterity!)—is to do some inner work, some work on *me*, whoever that is, till I at least shuck this restless son of a bitch and this pissed-off guy here, slim myself down to its Basic Everettness, and take it a day at a time from there. (Shit O. Deer! Are all journals this dumb?)"

Dumb or not, there was nothing much else to do. And one way to seek "Basic Everettness," my brother decided, was to fill in certain irresponsible gaps in his "Previous Everettness." To that end he had Stoner Steve mail all his boxes of unread text and history books up from Seattle, then challenged the mildew in his cottage to a race to see who could get through them first. But the contest, to his surprise, gave him a new appreciation of his old college professors. Without their lectures, assignments, deadlines and tests the reading never developed into anything more than guilt-motivated drudgery: mildew won by a mile.

In July he mentioned in a letter that he was "trying to get back into poetry writing." This didn't sound all that promising, since I was unaware he'd ever left it; I told him to send along a poem as soon as he'd written one he liked. I heard no more about it.

In August he hit on the idea of reading books he wanted to read instead of books he'd hated in college, and enthusiastically began toting whole carloads of books home from the Victoria Municipal Library. But back on the estuary even the most alluring prose had a way of shriveling, by the time it reached his brain, into a dry blather that nearly crushed him with boredom. Everett had become sufficiently introspective by now to get a handle on the problem: he'd become addicted, during his radical years, to such a pugnacious, litigious style of reading that his capacity for solitary literary pleasure had atrophied. He began struggling to regain it. He tried reading aloud—but it only made him lonely. He had Corey MacVee lock him in a closet with a book and water for the better part of a day—and ended up peeing on the floor. He tried to read while walking, while eating, while rowing a boat, while driving his car, and even while hanging upside down to force more blood into his brain. No use. "I have literary anorexia!" he finally scrawled in his journal. He then reached in his pocket, pulled out the same plastic cigarette lighter he and the other draft-resisters had used back in Seattle, and torched his library card.

In September the various owners of the homes came to vacation, and Everett bagged the search for Basic Everettness in order to work hard and play with their kids and be a wit and raconteur and extrovert for a while —a huge relief. Then in October, Indian Summer, the air turned so soft, the sunlight so fragile, and each day's loveliness so poignantly doomed that even self-ignorance and restlessness felt like profound states of being, and he just wandered the empty beaches and misty headlands in a state of serene confusion and awe.

But when November arrived, it brought something terribly expected with it: his first 150-inches-of-rain Juan de Fucan winter. "All summer I worked in a car wash," he wrote during the first six-day blow. "Now I live in one." The rains flooded the estuary, they washed away the fall colors, they ended his beach walks, his daily chats with Corey, his strolls through downtown Victoria. The Little Nessakoola turned big, brown and ugly and stayed that way. His Olds 88's electrical system drowned, so that he had to caulk a leaky pram, wait for incoming tides, and bail and row the three miles to town for groceries. His thoughts, his dreams, even his lust felt as though they'd begun, like his textbooks, to mildew. His old political concerns sat inside him like indigestible lumps of meat. His nonexistent concentration, nonexistent soul and nonexistent sense of vocation all made their nonexistences painfully known. "One sad sentence says it all," he told me in a letter: "Muskrat burgers are the greatest joy of my life."

Noticing his increasingly long, pale face, Chief Yulie tried to reassure him one day that the weather change was always tough on newcomers, but that in winter things got better. "You mean the rain quits?" Everett asked.

"No," she said. "But sometimes it turns to snow."

Yulie enjoyed his mighty groan, but then took pity. "Listen, Everett," she said. "I'll tell you a secret. It's not the weather that gets better. It's your ability to see."

"See what?" he muttered, glancing outside at the ceaseless greens and grays.

"Whatever needs seeing," she answered. "Maybe something in this world, maybe something in the spirit world. You'll know when you see it."

Seeing his guard go up, she added, "I'm not talking redskin hocus-pocus. Winter just happens to be the vision time here. Don't take it personal. That's just how it is."

"But I'm not *from* here," he said. "I'm a white guy from America, remember, Yulie? And white Americans don't *have* visions."

Grabbing his shirt so casually the gesture seemed playful at first, Yulie pulled him slowly but forcefully toward her face, then held him there, till the playfulness vanished and he could see and feel the full force of the anger that had come boiling up in her. "You listen to me," she said. "You're no white American. You're a white *nothing*. You got no country, no people, no work, no plan. You're *dying* for a vision, funny man. So don't go joking about it to me."

Everett was flabbergasted. She'd never attacked him before. He'd never seen her attack *anyone* like this before. And though she released him, and poured him a free beer, she wasn't finished. "By pure accident," she said, "no credit to you, you been doing one thing right. You been living alone on an estuary where, come winter, people often see the one thing in their life that most needs seeing. It's been that way forever here. Smallpox and sawmills haven't changed it. The likes and dislikes of some guy named Everett don't change it either. We don't push the spirit world around. Understand?"

Everett nodded like a good boy at Sabbath School.

"It's the Bear. We're the fleas. Understand?"

He nodded again.

"What you *can* do, though, is get horny and lonely and bitter and pitiful, decide this place and me are full of bull, and go be a funny white nobody someplace else. But I'm telling you, Everett—and I'm telling you because I like you—you been hopping around long enough. It's time you at least *tried* to meet the Bear."

Reading his face—which was straining desperately to appear neither sceptical nor condescending nor uncomprehending nor American nor white—Yulie laughed, and added, "Relax. I said no hocus-pocus, remember? All I'm really telling you is that unless you got a better idea—and we both know you don't—you ought to promise yourself to stick it out on the Little Nessakoola for one whole Kwakiutl winter, even if all you ever see's the rain."

Everett had no better idea.

So back to his cottage he trudged, where he proceeded to see just that.

"Gray rain on green water," he wrote in his journal. "Gray rain on green trees. Gray gulls grounded on gray sandflats. Gray-blue herons hunched in half-flooded sedge. Up in the green woods, the last chanterelles rot in the rain. Is this peace? Is this the stuff that we were begging the honkies to give a chance? No wonder they wouldn't listen!"

He also passed the time by writing letters:

You really should pay me a visit, Kade. There are some exciting options here, activitywise. You can stand in the trees. You can stand in the rain. You can watch the trees stand in the rain. You can watch it rain on the trees. And with two of us (true mathematical fact!), it'll be twice as great . . .

And kept trying his hand at poetry:

I think that I shall never see a car as boring as a tree . . .

Then he'd write in his journal some more:

November 9, 1970: Another day, another sou'wester. Booger looking smug as he munches another corner off a house—knows I won't go thwack him till the gale eases. Nemo the Wandering Auto Mechanic here yesterday. Says the Olds needs an alternator, battery, plugs and wires and I'm looking at 120 clams, minimum. Jeddy Redstone says bullhockey, all it needs is time in a warm watertight building, and it just so happens he's got barn space for $15 a month. Yulie says, "Everett honey. Listen. Just keep rowing your boat." And she scares me. So I do. Though more days than not I feel awfully close to sinking.

But one sodden night in mid-November, Everett awoke in the night with an incongruous new urge. Not a vision. Not an insight. Not even a cogent thought, really. Just an urge. But it was his strongest in months. In fact, it wouldn't let him sleep. So he sat up, lit a candle, grabbed his journal, and described it like this:

I know I tried books, I know I burned my library card, I know the whole idea's ridiculous. But maybe that's the point. At any rate, I have decided to read the Russian Literary Heavyweights and that's all there is to it. No library cards this time. Payment is a commitment, so I'm buying the books. But to hell with the details. To hell with thinking it all to death. I'm hitching to Victoria tomorrow! I'm buying great

Russian novels till I'm broke! I'm reading them cover to cover if it kills me! And that really is all there is to it!

Let's face it, though: when, twice in one urge, a person takes the trouble to say "that's all there is to it," there's very little chance that that's all there is to it. Everett swears to this day that the sole purpose of his Russian reading project was to obey his mysterious midnight impulse. But I don't buy it. I think his secret purpose, right from the start, was to attain some literary learning that would enable him to correspond as dramatically as possible with the unforgettable Natasha. I think he was out to wow her and woo her with honeyed Russian words. And far be it from me to find fault with that. His midnight intuition had probably revealed to him the single stratagem that might ever have worked. An epistolary romance, after all, is often a romance between two people who bear no resemblance to either person . . .

Natasha Lee's love affair with Russian literature has always been an enigma to me. Everett once told me, back in his U-district days, that he had discovered her great weakness: any man, place or circumstance that made her feel like a character in any famous nineteenth-century Russian story or novel, he claimed, caused her to suffer a near-complete suspension of common sense. I didn't believe him for a second. Russian lit was her major, and her love for the subject was obvious. But love for a subject is not the same as romantic credulousness. Having found Natasha quite hardheaded and clear-thinking myself, I figured our campus legend was just backbiting a woman who'd found him eminently resistible.

Yet Natasha herself admits that it was the passion, the humor, the indefatigability and above all the Russian flavor of Everett's Shyashy-akook letters which first led her to believe that the old Hippie Churchill might have undergone a promising personality change . . .

Of course Everett had always hated Russian novels. They were, after all, long, and his revolutionary span of attention, at least for nonnarcissistic activities, was exceedingly short. But the post-revolutionary possibility of writing long Russianistic letters to a beautiful woman overpowered his reservations about the literature since the letters could, in content if not in style, be almost entirely about himself. All he felt he needed from Tolstoy, Turgenev, Lermentov and Company were a few key characters, proper names, stylistic quirks and prose rhythms to get his correspondence off and running. To that end he began to read at a rate of about one volume per two inches of rainfall. When Natasha started writing back, he moved on to the satellite criticism and historical texts in search of obscure, gossipy details. As the winter grew colder and her letters warmer, he even got into accessories. First it was just a pound of Russian Caravan tea; then, in Victoria, he nabbed a handful of antique ink-pens —the kind you dip in a well—and a ream of parchmentlike paper upon which to scratch his increasingly high-flown prose; next it was a couple of open-necked white cotton "peasant shirts" and a pair of knee-high black rubber neo-peasant boots (leather was "too dear," as he now put it); then it was some scratchy old Russian opera recordings, which he learned to sing at the top of his lungs, without a clue as to what he was saying. By December he'd even begun, quite by accident, to gain some respect for the literature. I remember him telling me, for instance, that Tolstoy's novella *Hadzhi Murad* was the best account he'd ever read of how Vietnams happen. But he seldom wrote to me anymore. He was far too busy. He and his rubber boots had some fat tomes to wade through, and the letters to Natasha were pouring forth at a prodigious pace. Between the wry Chekhovian and dark Dostoevskian delvings into the lives of his human and animal neighbors, the broad Tolstoyan and fey Gogolian canvases of "our congenial lives of serfdom here in the forgotten village of Shyashyakook," and the occasional Pushkinesque plunges into metered verse, his letters were a one-man nineteenth-century Russian Literary Renaissance. For all their scope, length and stylistic schizophrenia, though, they left out a few fairly crucial details. The twentieth century and its contents (including Everett), for example. The fact that much of his summer's "serfdom" had taken place at an automated urban car wash, that he still spent the greatest share of his rubles on the likes of the Stones, the Doors, the Dead and the Who, and that, come evening, his entertainment of choice was to set literature aside, crank up his stereo, and, with cheap California wines and homegrown whatever, roulette his Russian brains out—these sorts of things were not considered worth mentioning.

From comparing notes with Everett himself (before he was on to me), with Chief Yulie, and with Natasha (the quotations in this account are all according to her excellent memory), I have managed to reconstruct a crucial example of the kind of liberties our Kwakiutl Karamazov allowed himself before his poetic license was, so to speak, revoked:

A few weeks before Christmas 1970, he wrote to his beautiful pen pal to tell of a "used but exquisite old samovar, nineteenth-century Russian, I believe," which he had discovered and bought "at considerable cost" at an antique store in Victoria. He'd wanted to ship it to her at once, he went on to say, but in so doing would, as a political outlaw, run some risk of being traced, arrested, and hauled off to jail. "Of course I have no qualms about sending it on anyway," he added. But he did want to ask, with Natasha's winter semester break fast approaching, whether she might have plans to visit Shyashyakook. Natasha wrote back immediately, saying that she had no plans to visit but that he shouldn't send the samovar if doing so would put him at risk. Everett's response to this was to bust the nibs off several antique ink-pens bragging about how risk meant nothing to him where her happiness was concerned, and how he would deliver the thing personally. The only question now, he told her, was whether she wanted the samovar at once or whether some traditional occasion ("the coming Yule season, perhaps?") might be preferable. So Natasha had to write back again, telling him to simmer down and just hold on to the thing, and as for the future, they would see what they would see.

Now, here are just a few of the facts that Everett neglected to mention:

1. No draft-dodgers were ever "traced" to Canada and arrested there. They couldn't be prosecuted for refusing military induction till they reentered the States: that was why they'd all gone to Canada in the first place!

2. Within days of the letter telling of the risk of shipping the samovar, Everett, without batting an eye, took a ferry clear down to Port Angeles, Washington, where he *could* have been arrested, solely to buy a new amplifier for his stereo, having blown the old one to hell listening to the Stones/Doors/Dead/Who, etc.

3. The "used but exquisite old samovar," though jumbo-sized and rather ornate, had a broken spigot, was covered with corrosion, dents and creases, had cost him $2.50 at a Nanaimo barn sale, and was originally manufactured in Aunt Poland, not Mother Russia.

4. He had actually bought it three weeks before he mentioned it to Natasha *without even knowing what it was*. His thought at the time was that an extra bucket might come in handy, and that this weird-looking gadget was bigger, sturdier and cheaper. Which explains why

5. he stopped by Redstone's barn on his way home and paid Jeddy six bits to fire up his blowtorch, burn the top off the samovar, and weld on a galvanized wire handle!

What a romantic!

The story of the Exquisite Old Samovar had an interesting conclusion, though: Everett had been using it for weeks as a feed bucket for his billy goat, Booger (who he'd told Natasha was named Chekhov!), when, one cold sunny day not long before Christmas, his literary pen pal arrived unannounced at his doorstep . . .

Everett had been so amazed to see her that he'd simply gasped, then stood in the doorway in his big rubber boots, gaping with undisguised joy. And I think Natasha was as amazed, and perhaps as pleased, for she could see at once that the old radical cool had vanished, and that his joy at seeing her was just plain joy.

But there was still one small problem:

Though her breath smelled like apples and his like mint tea, though her eyes were a filigree of coppery greens and blues and his a pair of live embers, though their hearts had already begun to fuse and their bodies, without touching, were speaking to one another with eloquence, they both continued to say not a word. Unlike the silences of their past, this one did not grow awkward. What it did do was grow so intense that they began to feel almost reverent, and humbled, and shy. So, simultaneously, they turned—still without having spoken—Everett to watch the pale winter sun, which was setting over the estuary, Natasha to study the silver bendings of the river, the ancient grove of dark spruces, the beautiful lay of the land. Then, far off in a pasture, she noticed the sun flaring dull gold upon some mud-covered wire-handled piece of debris. And so it came to pass that her first tenuous words to my brother were: "In case you haven't guessed, I loved your letters. I may even be a little drunk from them still—because that thing out in your pasture, from here anyway, looks almost like a samovar!"

Prepared as he was to give this woman his life, loyalty, heart, home, body, soul and many other precious things he did not in fact possess, it was a terrible shock to see her pointing at the one paltry, manure-spattered object he had so far actually bequeathed her. Fortunately the shock temporarily annihilated his mind—leaving him nothing with which to speak but his heart:

"Natasha," it began. "The way I felt just now when I opened the door. The way I *still* feel. The way you, the way I . . . No. I'll just embarrass you. But listen. Before the sun sets, before another minute passes, before anything can happen to screw everything up again, let me tell you a couple of really *stupid* things. Okay?"

Hearing this, it naturally occurred to Natasha that there could be another woman in his life, or in his house at that moment. Or five other women, for that matter. Or eleven. It also occurred to her that she'd been a complete fool to drive all the way up there, that everything she'd felt up until this panic was sheer delusion, and that she should jump in her car and flee at once with what dignity she still had. But Everett, meanwhile, was pointing into the pasture.

"The first stupid thing," he announced. "That *is* a samovar. I use it as a feed bucket for Boog-, uh, for my buddy, Chekhov."

He gave her a moment to take this in. She did so.

"The second stupid thing." He pointed into his own face. "I'm an idiot, Natasha. Because what I did was describe the gift I *wanted* to give you instead of the one I'd actually found. And it was inexcusable to lie like that. I don't consider what I'm about to say an excuse. But it *is* the truth, so I hope you'll listen. The reason I thought it didn't matter, the reason I thought you'd never see the samovar you're seeing right now, is that the way my life has gone, Natasha—this isn't self-pity, it's just the way it's gone—is that all the things I've really wanted, the things I've truly *longed* to have happen, have just never happened. Ever. So I never thought, I never *dreamed* I'd ever see you standing right where you're standing."

Afraid of her silence, afraid to read her face, Everett turned once again toward the sunset. It looked brown. For the second time in his life she'd turned him into a man-shaped pile of dust awaiting the broom of her rejection. "I'll go stay at the Muskrat," he mumbled into the brownness, "or sleep in my car while you're here. If you even want to stay. And I'll eat and drink whatever's inside that samovar if it'd help convince you. Because, hell, you at least ought to check out Shyashyakook, and meet Yulie, and maybe take a beach walk, and a row in the boat. Though if you want to leave now I don't, I won't, I'll fill your thermos for you, and pay your gas and hotel and ferry, 'cause of the samovar I mean, and drive you to Victoria if you're tired, where we could pick up a samovar, by the way, or clear to Seattle maybe, with my mouth shut, I promise. Or maybe you'd prefer to just—"

Once again Everett didn't see the lips slipping in through the dust cloud to bequeath him a kiss which, he swears, was only his second.

But this time it was the dust that vanished. The lips remained.

letter from Everett / Shyashyakook / January / 1971

Dear Kade,

I dreamed last night that I was watching TV—a hockey game, boring and violent as hell, bodies all over the ice, no subtlety, where's some baseball I'm thinking—when the broadcast was interrupted and a newscaster came on to say that an entire continent had just been discovered. Not an iceberg that turned out to be land. Not some upstart volcanic island down in the South Pacific. This was the sudden correction of one <u>major</u> long-term geographic oversight. This was the whole fuckin' nation waking up from its Buick ads and hockey pucks one TV evening to hear that THAR SHE BLOWS! A whole flipping continent! It blew my mind, Kade. Even my dream mind.

What sounds even stranger (though it seemed "normal" in the dream) was that the new continent was located <u>inside</u> North America —right between the United States and Canada. It had been there all along apparently, though no one had ever seen it, and somehow it had finally just appeared, had become accessible to us, right there where it had always been. Crazy as that might sound, the dream was incredibly vivid, full of TV and radio reports, pompous statements of welcome by heads of state, gorgeous aerial footage of all the new coastlines, mountains, deserts, plains and river valleys, man-on-the-street interviews showing everyone's confusion and shock and joy over the discovery. The new continent was quite modern, as it turned out, populated with people very like us—they were even English-speakers, most of them. And beautiful though it was, there was plenty of corruption and pollution and crime and havoc and so on—and I liked this, or was relieved by it, because I felt it safeguarded the place from being overrun and exploited by the ruthless likes of ourselves. The eighth continent was almost a parallel North America, really. Yet familiarity bred no contempt: the places, names of places, cities and small towns, mountain ranges and natural wonders, regional quirks and dialects and on and on were utterly fresh and new. So even though the place had problems like ours, it seemed pristine. Somehow even its problems seemed pristine. And in some haunting, thrilling way I could feel the new continent calling to me, could feel its enormous beauty and complexity drawing me into it in a way that the U.S. and Canada have never drawn me in. I felt that, problems and all, this land was crying out to be lovingly explored and compassionately lived in. And I planned on setting out to do just that, the moment I woke up.

But now listen, Kade, because here's the great part: no sooner did I think this than I <u>did</u> wake up. And as I opened my eyes and found Natasha lying up against me and a new day dawning gray and wet and glorious outside, it dawned on me that my dream was no dream at all. It was perfectly real. That continent was <u>this</u> continent. I was, I <u>am</u> suddenly living in that gigantic, glorious, wounded place! Why I, of all the unworthy oafs, have been allowed to enter is a mystery. How Tasha, or our joined love, unlocks an entire continent is another mystery. There is little about this that isn't mysterious, nothing about it that I can control, and I know we've entered no fairyland, that pain, cruelty, fear, greed, and ignorance, especially my own, are still as real as real. I also know I'm in love in the worst way, and that it's making me effusive as hell. But I'll never have a better excuse for my effusions, so look out, Kade, here comes another one: <u>I</u> <u>love</u> <u>you</u> <u>too</u>, little brother. It's tacky to say a thing that has to be felt, not just said. But from you I <u>have</u> felt it. For years now you've been amazingly patient and brotherly, therapeutic punches included, toward a version of me I hope we never meet again. It's high time I thanked you for it.

Come visit our continent soon.

Love,

Everett

CHAPTER THREE

Ace of Hearts

Suffering is above, not below.
And everyone thinks that suffering is below.
And everyone wants to rise.
  —Antonio Porchia

1. Peter and Gandhi

Peter's life, from the time he left for college, took place in a world so far removed from the rest of us that it soon bore no relation to anything the rest of us were going through. On the Chance family stage Peter was, for five years, a blank. He chose to forget us, and to be forgotten, and this choice was intelligently made. So we did little to bridge his carefully maintained distance. But in late 1970 the pattern of his life picked up a bright new thread which I feel compelled to describe simply because, though none of us yet knew it, this thread would eventually lead him back home:

Midway through his master's program, Peter won a Fulbright grant that would enable him, beginning in August 1970, to spend a full year in India. For the majority of his stay he would be traveling extensively—a lifelong dream. His aim, without going into scholarly detail, was to study, to copy (on microfilm), and in some cases to translate a number of manuscripts by or about some of the more obscure medieval Bhakti poets of the Deccan Plateau.

Having read, while still in high school, English translations of the Vedas and Puranas, the *Mahabharata* and *Ramayana*, Sankaracharya, Manu, Kabir, Mira Bai, Tulsi Das, Bhanu Das, Eknath, Nanak, Bulleh Shah, Tukaram and every other major Sikh, Sufi or Bhakti poet-saint or metaphysician he could get his hands on, Peter had come to feel that his heart and mind had, in a sense, been dwelling in the Orient all his life, and that it was only a matter of time before his body would join them. And after five years at the Harvard School of Comparative Religion, where he learned to read and write Sanskrit, Hindi and Marathi and systematically studied the works, cultures and traditions of these same saints and sages, he felt doubly certain that, spiritually, he was a displaced Indian seeking an honorable return passage to the East, that in the Fulbright he had received that passage, and that when he finally set foot in Mother India his exterior life would begin to reflect his deepest nature more powerfully and accurately than ever before.

He did not come home to Camas before leaving for India. He hadn't been home since Christmas 1969, but money was always short and the lucrative summer jobs had always seemed to be in New England. So we weren't much surprised when, even upon this milestone departure, Peter settled for sending postcards to each of us, sharing his news in various ways. He told Mama not to worry, and little else. He told Bet and Freddy he wouldn't be far off, "just straight through the planet, on the opposite side there." He told Papa that the Fulbright was a life's dream come true, that he wished it came at a happier time for our family, but that at any rate it felt, to him, like being called up to the Bigs, and he was deeply honored to be going. To me he admitted that a number of traveling scholars and professors had warned him about culture shock and that he took the warnings seriously, but since he planned to be spending much, if not most, of his adult life in India, he said he had no real choice but "to set about transcending, or at least crucifying, my Americanness as quickly and unceremoniously as possible."

It's incredible to me how blithely even intelligent people sometimes toss around terms like "transcendence" and "crucifixion." The words move us on paper. They feel noble upon the tongue. But when they cease to be sounds and begin to caress the flesh and bones, when they leave the page and get physical, there is little that even the best of us wouldn't do to escape them. (Matthew 26:39: Jesus "went a little further, and fell on his face . . .")

Peter, for the first two weeks of his Oriental *peregrinatio*, did all his traveling in the same teeming, slat-benched, open-windowed third-class train cars that his one and only political hero, Mahatma Gandhi, had once preferred. But in no time he discovered that a 6'2" blond-braided American and the dark, diminutive Gandhi simply do not experience the same India, the same Indians, or the same third-class train cars. Gandhi, for example, had not contracted dysentery by merely inhaling the smoky air, and so had not been forced to pack up all his books and bags (lest they be stolen), jump train at every village depot, find the nearest abandoned ditch or alleyway, and void his churning bowels; nor had the Mahatma's posterior shone like an enormous new baseball, inspiring crowds of Muslim and Hindu urchins to steal up and break into gales of laughter even before it began producing its abysmal sound effects; nor had Gandhi been followed back to the depot by these same gangs of kids, all shouting like town criers about "Sahib's" explosive exploits in the back alley as bystanders stared and scowled and Sahib rushed his crimson face, queasy bowels, books and bags back to the train—to find four or five Indian gentlemen serenely seated upon the unreserved bench he'd just been forced to vacate.

It was while hunching, clammy-fleshed, with the animals and Untouchables in the aisles of these third-class train cars praying for nothing more transcendent than the strength to hold his anus shut that Peter felt driven to make his first compromise with Mother India: Gandhi or no Gandhi, he would henceforth do his traveling in first-class, glassed-in, air-conditioned train cars equipped with private, flush-toileted bathrooms.

Americanness, he was discovering, is not an easy quality to crucify—at least not without crucifying the entire American.

Not long after this first modification of the Gandhian ideals he now referred to in letters as "naïve preconceptions," Peter took to purchasing expensive private sleeping compartments as well. The first time he did it he wrote in his diary that it was a one-shot deal: "I need the peace and the privacy, just this once, both to study and to ward off illness."

The second time he did it his argument had gotten fancier: "Gandhi, for the sake of his work, traveled third-class in order to better know—in his Indian bones—what the day-to-day experience of India's people is. But my bones are American, my work here is scholarly, I need to stay healthy for the sake of the work, and by the standards of this pathetically Westernized body of mine, a first-class Indian train car is *already* third-class."

But the third, fourth and fifth times he purchased sleeping berths his health was fine, he had no pressing work to do, and he had no ready arguments: he just wanted to be alone. He tried not to subject this deepening desire for cloistered travel to scrutiny, but introspection and honesty were old habits with Peter, and his inner debate soon made its way into his journal: "A scholar-monk traveling in the same style as all these well-to-do Hindu merchants may still be a scholar, but he is hardly a monk," he wrote one day. On the other hand, "I've met Westerners whose health has been broken completely by trying to become 'Indian' too fast. It takes *time* to change a body. A careful transition is justified."

Justified or not, to sleep and read one's way through a foreign country in a private, air-conditioned cubicle is to be in no foreign country at all. That he might genuinely fear, at least physically, the very land whose literature and spiritual traditions he'd adored since childhood, that such a fear might imply a never to be assimilated core of foreignness—these kinds of thoughts did not yet occur to him. By reading and working ceaselessly, by emaciating himself physically and by increasing his theoretical knowledge of India even as he decreased his firsthand experience, he was able to continue feeling that he belonged where he was. But the strain had begun to show: "I am trying to live as a contemplative," he wrote in his journal the last night he ever debated the Sleeper Compartment Issue, "and a contemplative's work is to *renounce* worlds, not immerse himself in them."

But it was not this emphatic statement that ended the debate. What ended it was rereading the statement—and hearing a distinctly derisive snicker rise from the part of his psyche that for seventeen years had shared a room with a tactlessly observant young rabble-rouser named Everett.

"I am weak!" Peter finally wrote, if only to silence the snicker.

He then slammed the diary shut, lay down on his bed, and let the train lull him into a cool but troubled sleep.

2. Loss of a Promising Continent
letter from Everett, except for the paragraph by Dostoevsky, which was cut out by Natasha and left in the center of Everett's kitchen table, then glued by Everett (with raspberry jam) to the second page of his letter to me / Shyashyakook / February / 1971

mydearkinkade
   just because ive been ingesting a few of the small dometopped protuberances that last autumn so protuberated in a nearby cow meadow type ecology system do not for evevn onem oment assume i am in any wayless capable of the most lucid kinf og
   well maybe typewritee operation isnt so easy but do not the less youmagine such techicnal dfidculties implies me the least less trustworthy of being confided in in case tasha happens to have told why or better yet where she is/   //oh yeah/: ="!. = $these deals!&% + *
cept I meant comm,a,,   ,damn it,,i mean people do trust you kade, and sometimes write or maybe phone and say swear you'll keep this secret, but if she did, kade pleaseyou've got to unswear <u>please</u>
   because she left me kade.
   my tasha
   she left mei don't even know why be my valentine two days ago she says then didn't <u>warn</u> me file a <u>complaint</u> give a <u>scowl</u> every time we made love stereo <u>orgasm</u> me babbling more and more wildly about effing <u>marriage</u> for christsake meaning every <u>word</u> with all my heart and her smiling so unbelieveable and saying and i quote <u>a love our size eventually demands that</u> THEN NOT TELLING ME A GODDAMN ANYTHING!?! just leaving me this NOTHING of a,this this FUCK, kade!just <u>look</u> at this farewell fucking nothing of a

If I run away, even with money and a passport, even to America, I will be cheered by the thought that I am not running away for pleasure, not for happiness, but to another exile as bad, perhaps, as Siberia. It is as bad, Alyosha, it is! I hate America, damn it. How will I put up with the rabble down there, though they may be better than I, every one of them. I hate America already! They may be wonderful at machinery, damn them, but they are not of my soul. I shall choke there!

scissored straight out of a 75 cent signet classic conversation between dumkopf and alleyoopa karamazov for godsake and like <u>hell</u> will she choke there she's got her whole mom's new golf ranch somewhere in the desert she never got around to telling me and probly fifty old boyfrinds and money and cars and diningclub citizenships and didn't even leave a goddam phone or clue or frowarding address or the truth or why or anything!

except I guess, now I mention it, neither have i exactlly.

told the truth that is, so her it is:

i am actually not doing so good is the truth kade. like i for starters can't believe how much less than death did us part and feel like a piece of week-old warmed-over lied-to dogshit and on top of that miss her so bad i want to die is the other worst part, because the other truth is i love her, man, big time, no lie, no way to hide from it or not feel it, and i'd have sworn she loved me too is the part that, how can you, how can I, how could she just walk off and about <u>kill</u> me like this, or try, till luckily i scored the shrooms, man, the mindnukes, the freeze-dried meadow nodules happening here instead and so started staving off the why o why o whys since i don't know, nam, oops, except wow, man, did you never notice till now how nam backwards is man, man, because of how the men in nem are backwards too, man, which is I'm afriad the sort of noodlyheaded shit i now put my whole mind dick and soul into noticing, for survival purposes, nam, having never been in this position of suckered to the point of i'd have sworn to god tasha loved me, we loved each other, i <u>know</u> she did, so if it's truth we're talking, truthfully, sick, actually, to death, man, is how i feel at the,

how many of these canyou before you
sick. god sick. my new continent gone, nam sick
is how i

hey, that you kade?

found this on the floor what is it? three days later? real letter forthcoming instant i finish non-mycological efforts to recalculate what reality is. keep me posted on Winnie no matter what happens. sorry to lay this on you. thanks, man.

shit

everett

3. Zaccheus
letter from Irwin / Mekong Delta / February / 1971

You know how rain zuzzes when it hits the water? That soothing
sound the surface makes? Well, that's what I was hearing, just that
zuzz and the drippling of leaves and trees, when it happened. But you
wouldn't believe, Kade, how little things like that, things like rain
falling into the Mekong the same calm way it falls into the rivers back
home, can stop your heart here. Because this river, remember, is warm
as piss, and the air always smells wrong and the trees and vines feel
like they're watching and hating you and ready to kill you, and that's
tiring, understand? The fear here, and the wrongness feeling, they just
wear you out. But with my poncho, see, I could block all the
wrongness out and frame in this perfect little zuzzing piece of river
surface. And soon as I did it slid me right on down by the Columbia,
in late fall maybe, all brown and wide and floody, so that my one plan
in all of life was to sit there as forever as possible.

And that's when it happens. That's when our point, Ducky Gelman,
comes slithering through the brush, grabs Sergeant Felker, eases him
all hushhush down beside me, parts vines, scopes in a tree just
downriver. And by God, there he is. Victor. I see him bare-eyed myself.
All in black. All alone. Hunched in plain sight in this big green tree
overhanging the water.

Of course without even thinking we feel it's a trap. You always feel
this, even when it can't be, since in the long run everything about
being here's a trap. Anyhow Gelman's a big duckhunter back in Real
Life, and always has these duckhunting strategies he applies to the
situation, so what he more or less says is that the Cong in the tree is a
decoy and that a thousand or so VC with 12-gauges are out there in
duckblinds praying to the Gook God for us to shoot him and give our
position away. While Felker thinks this over I scope Victor in. I can
see him perfect. He's only 150 yards off. I see the rifle in his lap, the
radio on the limb behind him, the Chinese lettering on his rubber
slipper soles. I even see his jaw working, and for a second think he's
singing. Then his hand goes to his mouth and I realize it's food. It's
eating. He's just staring at the water eating his damned Vietnamese
lunch up there. So let's go, is my feeling. Leave him his lunch and
let's scram. Then Felker whispers He's no decoy. He's recon, same as

us, watching for things moving up or down river. And with that he turns to me.

Christ, life is hard to predict, Kade. I didn't use to worry about it. God provides, I thought, so try your best and don't worry. So I never worried, back in Boot, how high scores in target-shooting would translate to a place like Nam. I just didn't see the day coming when some big scary mother like Felker would whisper like he was doing me some huge favor: Okay, Chance. Pop him good and let's scratch gravel. He can't be as lonesome as he looks.

It was true, what Felker said. Ducky's nuts from being on point, too much duckhunting and all, but the Delta really is a place where a hundred of them can jump out of anywhere anytime. And there were six of us. And this scared me right out of my head, Kade. It scared me clean out of remembering who I am. Or was. Just do it and run, I tell myself. You didn't make the world, I tell myself. Left shoulder blade, Felker whispers, and I think, Don't shake or he'll suffer; think, Sorry, Victor, but your time is up; think, Jesus forgive me—if you can believe that. Then I start squeezing. The gun is very quiet in the rain. It sounds like a toy. But the guy in the tree, our nation's enemy, Victor flips around sideways, crashes down through the branches and ends up on his back on a wide leafy limb. His rifle splashes into the river. So does whatever he was eating. Gelman and Felker disappear, which is what I should do too of course. But I just stand there. I never shot even an animal before, so it interests me. It interests me especially since he was just sitting there same as me, and could of seen and shot me first. Or we could of gone happily on not seeing each other, not shooting each other, enjoying the same zuzz as forever as possible.

Then I notice something else interesting. He isn't dead. He's hanging on to a limb with one hand, has a leg hooked over another, and neither the hand or the leg are letting go. I see blood all over his chest though the bullet entered his back, so I know it's torn clear through him. The blood's running wet and black out of him, down through the leaves, dripping off his calves and feet, off his hair, off his elbows. He can't lift himself, he has no idea where the shot came from, he's not a VC anymore, not a Commie anymore, not a dink, not a threat, not an enemy. He's just this ruined little person whose body doesn't want to die any more than mine does. So he won't let go.

From the bushes somewhere Felker tells me come the fuck on, his friends are probably coming. He's still alive, I tell him. Then deal with it and come, he says, and I hear them moving out, and know I can't find my way through ten yards' worth of this jungle alone. So can you believe it? I do what he says. I deal with it. But I'm sick and shaking this time and don't know where I hit him, and when he falls another few feet and lands on another big limb he holds on to this one too. And now, I have to tell you Kade, now I hate him. I hate him so bad for scaring me like this and not dying like this that, God damn me to hell, I shoot him again, twice more, in the back or buttocks, I don't know where, and knock him lower each time. But still he keeps landing on things, clutching at things, grabbing things. He's on the last limb above the river now, blood all down through the tree, and the limb is sinking, the current's pulling him hard, his fist is slipping down a thorn vine that must be ripping his palm to shreds, and all this time I'm scoping him, hating him, waiting for some good part of him to show so I can squeeze a round into it too. But then the current spins him, and all I see is mouth. And it's wide open, Kade, gasping for air, and full of unharmed teeth and a small pink tongue with unchewed bits of lunch still on it. And after all I've done to him, when I see this, I can't do more. So I just watch. I watch his fist run out of vine, watch the limb, flinging blood, sway back up in the tree, watch to see what he does with nothing but water and air to clutch at. But when the current takes him and his head spins under, leaving nothing but that quiet zuzz, something in me spins under too, and I think Sparkle. Because remember the time, that little dog out of the Washougal? Because how in Christ's Name, Kade, even as a soldier, can I not do for a man what I once did for a damned dog? So I drop my weapon. I drop it and start running to save the same guy I've just murdered, and for ten or twelve seconds it's the most wonderful feeling! For ten or twelve seconds I'm me again, Kade, tearing along like it's football, doing the first clear and good and hundred and ten percent right thing I've done since joining this fucking Army. But I don't make it sixty yards before I hit jungle thicker than our laurel hedge, which knocks me down, slows me to a crawl, makes me snake toward the river thinking Swim for him then! But near the edge I hit thorn-vines where the harder you fight the harder you stick, and when I finally reach water and break free enough to see, my God, he's so far downriver. And moving so fast. And I've shot him so bad, over and over and over.

So I just hang there. I just hang in the water there, watching him drift and drift, blind now, I realize, since with one hand he's still clutching at a shoreline an easy quarter mile away. And he never did drown, Kade. He never did quit clutching. And the Mekong is huge. It took him forever to disappear.

It took him so long that by the time he was gone, everything had changed. I didn't hurt anymore, didn't feel like hiding anymore, wasn't scared anymore. Because I wasn't anything anymore. Not anything I love or know or care about. Because thou shalt not kill, Kade. <u>Thou shalt not kill</u>. With all my heart I believed this. And I killed. So what am I now? And why should I live? How am I even alive? Because if this is what our lives are—if doing this to others before they do it unto us is all our lives are—we're already dead. Honest to God I feel it, Kade. I'm dead. The hell with me.

I crawled back to my rifle because it was the one thing on earth I knew where to find. Then I threw it as far as I could out into the Mekong. That left nothing. Which suited me fine. I sat back down, closed my poncho round a piece of river, started listening again to the zuzz. Then, you know me, I tried praying too, asking Christ to do things like bless and save the guy I'd killed and damn me to hell instead if need be. But then that Sabbath School song, "Zaccheus," got stuck in my head, so I bagged the prayers and started singing it instead. And when I heard the words coming out of me I saw clear as day that Christ already <u>had</u> saved him. He'd saved the Cong I killed, then jammed the song in my head to show He doesn't need shitheads like me to tell Him His business. Because remember?

> *Zaccheus was a wee little man and a wee little man was he.*
> *He climbed up in a sycamore tree for the Lord he wanted to see.*
> *And the Lord said, Zaccheus! You come down!*
> *For I'm going to your house today.*

So the rain is falling and the river is zuzzing and *Zaccheus!* I'm singing, or blubbering really, you came down, but He's going to your house today! when <u>What the fuck are you doing</u> Felker is all of a sudden wondering out of the bushes. Singing Zaccheus, I tell him. Where's your rifle? he wonders. I nod at the river. Why? he wonders. Defective, I tell him, and so am I defective, and so are you, and so are all of us and this idiot war and our country for fighting it and on and on goes my list of defectives till I sound like Everett almost, so that it's no surprise when Felker jumps out and slugs me. He was just eating his Vietnamese lunch up there, I tell him. Shuttup, he whispers, and slugs me. I killed Zaccheus, I tell him, bawling loud enough now to wake the whole Delta, so shuttup shuttup shuttup, poor Felker goes, punching me, and I'm spitting blood back in his face and don't care if we live and won't move and keep sobbing, and if he didn't pound me good I'd be there still. So I warn you, Kade, my face is a bit different. The nose mostly. But don't be a fool. Don't blame Felker. He risked the shit out of his life for me. Gelman says he's even trying to wangle me a transfer to a place besides a brig or asylum where my lack of M-16 won't stick out so bad.

But listen, Kade. Please listen. Don't you <u>ever</u> come here. Study yourself blind like Pete, lop off a toe like Papa, hightail it like Everett, go to jail, do what you have to. But don't you come here no matter what. Because it'll kill you, this place. If the Cong don't, your own heart will.

Can't sign off. Don't know what to call me. Don't scare Linda or the twins with this, okay?

4. Boiled Eggs

After Natasha had performed, by vanishing, a kind of quack bisection of Everett's heart and wittingly or unwittingly taken the happy half with her; after the winter rains kept pouring and the memory of his lovely new continent sank like a stone and the landscape sagged back into its prehistoric greens and grays and even Chekhov née Booger seemed to grow a little depressed or confused after he'd munched through the cedar shingles and clear into the two-by-fours on the corners of several vacation homes, to find that no longer would anyone come rushing out to thwack him;

after Everett had stood for six hours in the rain in Shyashyakook's vandal-savaged but only phone booth spending his once-great faith in telephones and his last dime chasing down his beloved's old boyfriends and girlfriends and registrars and priest and faculty to learn only that she'd dropped out of her master's program at Washington in order to maybe visit her mother in Arizona (address unknown) or father in New York (address unknown) or some daft draft-dodger up in Canada ("Yeah, I knew him once," said Everett);

after he'd driven to Victoria to hawk most of his clothes, all of his fishing tackle, his wristwatch, his Russian literature and accessories, his beloved stereo, his even more beloved rock-'n'-roll record collection and even the tire iron, jack and spare tire from the trunk of his car, merely to win another sodden day in the ravaged phone booth calling random people with the last name of Lee in Phoenix, Brooklyn, Knoxville, Tucson, the Bronx, Chattanooga and so on, only to ask, in a voice clogged by mucus née boogers from the terrible cold he'd caught, questions like "Is this the Lee with the niece or daughter named Laurel or Natasha? No? No obscure branch of the family tree with one small Laurel on it? You're sure? Then is this by chance a psychic Lee, or a detective Lee, or a Ouija Lee who can help find my missing Laurel? It's not. I wonder, then, if— no, ma'am, not drunk, just cold, and I—please! One last favor! Just look out your window, it's not asking much, and tell me whether you see her right now—she'd be the beautiful one, auburn-haired, green-eyed, old jeans that fit like ballet tights, with the little red thing that looks like raw hamburger pinned like a brooch to her blouse—that's half my heart, that thing. So if you *do* see her, I beg you to— hello? hello?";

after Chief Yulie and Corey finally trudged out to the phone booth, fetched him back to the Muskrat, fed him a burger 'n' chips, stood him a pitcher of draft, then another, then another, then another, and Roon and Jeddy drove him back home and dumped him in bed, Everett, or what was left of him, awoke in the meaningless gray morning to find his mind, his possessions and half his heart still irretrievably gone. But for some reason his body still seemed to be hanging uselessly but noticeably down off his neck there. So meeting the body's feeble demands, morning after morning, became his feeble new purpose in life.

This A.M. bodily maintenance project was soon dubbed "the ABCDE." His mind was so adrift that the acronym's meaning would change now and then, but generally it stood for something like "Another Brainless Clone's Diet Effort" or "Amorphous Blob Cooks Detritus for Everett." What didn't change much was the ritual itself: the ABCDE began with three boiled eggs, cooked sometimes too soft, sometimes too hard, almost never just right. Everett loathed overly soft eggs and he loathed overly hard ones, but since his A.M. mind couldn't keep track of time without its morning coffee, and since coffee gave him heartburn on an empty stomach, he had to eat the eggs before he could drink the coffee. So every morning he mistimed, miscooked, and disliked them. He'd tried fried eggs for a while. But whenever he'd burnt them (which had been almost daily) he went through hell trying to clean his cast-iron skillet afterward. With boiled eggs, if the shells didn't break (or what the heck, even if they did), the hot water for his coffee was ready just as soon as he spooned the eggs out, and the pan was as good as clean as soon as the coffee got poured out into his cup. Clever. For an Amorphous Blob.

Everett drank drip coffee only. Percolated, cowboy or instant gave him even worse heartburn than drip, adding milk didn't help, and Canadians hadn't yet discovered cappuccino and the like, so black drip it was. He also tried fixing toast to accompany the eggs now and then. Since he had no toaster he had to use his gas oven, and since he used it in the midst of his pre-coffee stupor, he usually burnt the toast to cinders. Even if he didn't burn it he seldom ate it, because he didn't like toast unless it was hot and served with coffee and he couldn't have it with coffee yet, because his eggs were still boiling in his coffee water, and by the time he got the eggs shelled and salted and peppered the toast was stone cold. But he liked to make toast anyway, if only because by operating the gas oven in the midst of his pre-coffee stupor he daily stood a very real chance of dying.

Death. By all sorts of means. This was a topic Everett contemplated long, hard and none too carefully on these dank, gray-hued late-winter mornings. Stumbling round the kitchen, not comprehending time, he would fix and consume his preposterous breakfast till the eggy coffee did its work and his literacy kicked in. Then he'd start to read whatever printed words or numbers his eyes lit upon. Not Russian novels; not books; not even magazines or newspapers. Thought, literature, informative writing of all kinds—these were for suckers. Because they all tried to give life meaning. But once your life had acquired meaning, all it really meant was that you'd doomed yourself to hurt like a twice-hammered thumb once Unmeaning came along, as it always does, and knocked the teeth, brains and stuffing out of your puny meaning. All Everett required each morning, thank you, were some random household objects with a few meaningless words printed on them to add a little fuel to his contemplations of death . . .

The 1943 tide table Scotch-taped to the side of the rusty, perennially empty napkin dispenser, for instance. "Sept. 10, 1943," it warned. "High Water: 11:34 & 11:16; Feet: 7.4 and 8.4; Low Water: 5:00 & 5:13; Feet: −0.8 and 0.8." Or the side of the corroded half-full can of Ronsonol lighter fluid under the kitchen sink. "DO NOT USE NEAR FIRE OR FLAME," it threatened. "N.Y.F.D.C. of A. No 731. ALWAYS CLOSE SPOUT AFTER USE. Wipe lighter and hands dry before igniting. If swallowed do not induce vomiting. Call physician immediately." Then he'd sip more coffee, and more, till he could picture himself floating face-down in an 8.4 high tide, or slipping on kelp, cracking his skull and drowning in a tide puddle on a −0.8 low, or immolating or poisoning or exploding himself due to some failure to "dry" or "CLOSE" or "induce" or "call" someone or something or other. And then of course up would stroll Natasha, just in time to toss the unseeable flower, or the now unreadable note that explained everything, or just the other half of his heart into the puddle or fire or gutter where he lay, and just in time to say, "I'm sorry, I really did love you" or "I'm sorry, I never did," what's the difference, really? Then out of the cottage he'd stroll, and up to the alder woodlot to weep or cut firewood, what's the difference, really?, or down the driveway to fix the flood-ruts with a shovel, or all the way to town for supplies and mail and, when it was raining, a good camouflaged cry over the beautiful letter of apology she had once again not written. Then back to his home or his homelessness, to sleep or not sleep till morning, when he'd open his eyes to the sight of the same old body, hanging sad and silly as a turkey wattle from his neck. So out would come the saucepan, in would go the water, up would leap the blue flame. And he'd boil another three eggs.

5. Herod
letter from Irwin / Mekong Delta / February / 1971

Dear Mama,

Sorry to worry you with a thing like this, but this letter's for Nash when he's old enough to wonder who I was, in case I don't come back. I'd of sent it to Linda, but didn't want to scare her. And if I don't come back I figure her life could get crazy enough she might lose this before Nash ever saw it. Whereas knowing you, you'll read it and hate it, but still take good care of it. So I thank you in advance. Okay? XOOX.

Dear Nash.

It's weird to write somebody you love but have never met a big long letter you hope they'll never read. But if you <u>are</u> reading this it means you won't be seeing me, and I'd rather write a weird letter than leave you wondering your whole life whether I ever thought about you. I'm writing to say that I think about you and your mother every day and night, and that I love you both so much that one of the hardest things in my life now is trying not to hate myself for being fool enough to come here. How I did come, what forced me to leave, is not easy to explain. But for you I want to try. And if it just sounds dumb when I'm finished, maybe your uncles and aunts can fill in some of the holes.

Once upon a time then, as far as I can understand it, there was this place, Vietnam, where a bunch of farmers, mostly Buddhists I guess, were happily and unhappily living and farming and marrying and making babies who grew up to be unhappy and happy farmers like themselves, when politicians from their cities, then from whole other countries, started fighting over whose flag should fly over their farms. The fighting became a war, and there was money and power and beliefs and revenge involved, and though I'll never understand it, one thing led to another till several different nations including the most powerful one in the world, our nation, Nash, had sent men and tanks and jets and bombers into this quiet place, and they roared and poured out over the farmers' farmland, and they blew each other and the farms and the crops and the animals and farmers, women and children included, Nash, kids no bigger than you, and just as sweet, into a million burnt and bloody pieces. Can you believe it? I hate to even tell you such a horrible story. I'm only doing it because, as I write this, it's still happening. What's worse, I'm one of that most powerful nation's men.

So why in hell's name am I here, you must wonder. Because your granddad and uncles warned me, Nash. They told me exactly what was happening here and said go to jail or Canada instead. What I thought about their warnings may sound strange to you, but it's the truth: what I thought was how much Jesus loved me. I had so much faith I just <u>knew</u> He'd protect me here, and help me help and maybe even save others, till He brought me back home safely to Linda and you. And this wasn't wrong of me, Nash, it's good to trust Jesus. But when it came to a subject like 'Nam it wasn't very imaginative of me either. The thing was, I grew up hearing over and over how Jesus loved the little children of the world, and to me the word "love" meant He must take care of them, He must watch out for them. So I simply couldn't imagine an actual place on earth, not even when I saw it in black and white in the magazine pictures Everett sent me, where the broiling bodies of Christ's little loved ones really were lying in pools of fire in their own backyards and playgrounds and gardens, and that my country was the one dropping the fire. I looked right at those pictures, but couldn't see them. To me they were trick photography or something, and by coming here I figured I'd be able to straighten out the tricks and maybe keep Mama and Everett from going at each other's throats.

Well, I was wrong, Nash. Though now that I'm here I see two very good reasons why I couldn't imagine 'Nam from back home. One reason was that a 'Nam could only mean that the leaders of my country were as crazy and cruel as King Herod. Maybe not that cruel as individuals, but running in a pack they sure were. And the other reason was that 'Nam means that I, who always felt so loved by Jesus, didn't have the slightest idea what Christ's love really is. It was this second part that scared me most, Nash. In fact it scared my mind shut. It slammed shut like a door whenever anyone warned me not to come here. Everett's warnings especially confused me, because I knew he wouldn't lie, but he was so full of anger and hate that his truths just didn't feel true. So he with his good imagination and bad temper ran away to Canada. And I with my bad imagination and good temper came here, where I have seen and smelled and touched the things I found impossible to imagine. And now, too late, I understand Everett's hate. Now I know that sure enough, Herod is alive and well and more powerful than ever, living in Moscow and Peking and Washington D.C. And what's worse, at least for me: I no longer know what Christ's love is. He's lost me. I don't know what He could possibly mean by this place, though I'm still struggling with all my heart to find out.

That pretty much says it, strange and sad as it must sound. One thing I'm sure of, Nash, and don't ever forget this. No matter how nuts this war would of made me, I'd of loved you all my life, with all my heart, when I came home.

XOOX,
Irwin (your dad)

6. The Blue Turban

One of Holy Mother India's best-kept secrets—so Peter decided several months into his Fulbright year—was the thousand and one ways she had of making Westerners look like fools. Including even Westerners determined to live like Easterners.

During Peter's three-week stay in an embarrassingly luxurious guest-house at the University of New Delhi, a servant had literally come with the house—that is, the fellow could be found round the clock, perched like some sort of home appliance in a tiny, doorless nook near the bunga-low's back entrance. Embarrassed by the man's minuscule quarters, by his servility, and by the concept of servants in general, Peter told his faculty hosts that the man's services were not needed. To Peter's surprise, his faculty friends politely but firmly insisted that he stay. So into my brother's life came an obsequious, incomprehensible little Tamil, Lakshman by name, who chose, despite Peter's repeated attempts to send him home, to remain on call twenty-four hours a day.

Lakshman's complete services, Peter soon learned, would have cost him two rupees—about 36¢—a day, and no one but Allah would have known had he allowed himself to be waited upon hand and foot. But Peter felt his relationship with Lakshman was, like all human relationships, a spiritual test, and his strategy in taking this test was to treat his servant as a perfect equal. Peter therefore insisted, to the man's obvious consternation, on picking up after himself, making his bed, hand-washing his own clothes, buying and preparing his own food, making and serving his own tea, heating his own bath water, and so on. He also visited Lakshman in his little appliance closet at every meal or teatime, to offer him a portion of whatever food or beverage he'd made for himself. This unstinting show of equality seemed to alternately agitate and depress the servant, but Peter kept at it. There were still two annoyances in their relationship, however: the first was that Lakshman insisted, no matter how many times he was corrected, upon addressing Peter as "Sahib"; the second was that whenever Peter was not asleep (and perhaps even when he was) Lakshman would emerge from his nook every half hour like a cuckoo from a clock, to come stand in the doorway of whatever room Peter occupied, and to politely inquire, in the one English sentence he had mastered, whether Sahib yet required his assistance. The latter annoyance was especially disturbing to Peter's scholarly work, both because it broke his concentration and because he'd begun to detect a veiled air of hostility: for all his apparent servility, Lakshman's relentless interruptions seemed silently to say that Peter's fandangled attempts at "brotherhood" meant nothing to him, and that on the day Peter took himself off to whatever Western hellhole he'd come from, Lakshman would go back to serving a *real* Sahib with pleasure. After two weeks of this torment Peter ran out of patience, described the situation to his faculty hosts, and for the second time requested that the servant be sent away—

and that's when he learned that Lakshman was assigned year round to the occupant of Peter's bungalow and no other, that only by serving that occupant could he earn tips, that these tips were the sole source of income for the six kids, wife and mother-in-law with whom he shared an unplumbed one-room concrete apartment, and that, thanks to Peter's fine notions of equality, Lakshman's family had been begging their meals, or going hungry, ever since he'd arrived. Of course Peter was appalled—and he deliberately lived, and tipped, like a pasha for the rest of his stay.

Another one of Mother India's little practical jokes began one day, in Hyderabad, when Peter decided the time had come to purchase a piece of cloth suitable for a turban, both to protect himself from sunstroke and to conceal his crowd-attracting blond braid. What happened this time was that he did find a suitable piece of pale blue cloth, learned to wrap it in several traditional styles, and for the better part of a month wore it constantly, gradually growing numb to the hundreds, if not thousands of incredulous stares he continued to receive anyhow. He then learned, from a blushing female Rhodes scholar at the University of Madras, that his fine blue turban was of a color and cut of cloth which Hindu women use only as underwear. Peter managed to laugh as he ripped it off his head and presented it, with a bow and a strangled thank-you, to the woman. But he also proceeded to spend more time than ever shut up in hotel rooms and libraries, immersed in his work.

The longer Peter stayed in India the more necessary he found it to shelter himself from the crowds and the heat, the overspiced food and black marketeers, the chaotic bazaars and abused landscape, the prying children, countless beggars, overabundance of life, overabundance of death. Yet the more skilled he became at sheltering himself, the more he felt as though something inside him, some kind of inner circuitry, had ceased to function. Emotionally, and at times physically, he felt disconnected from himself. Unplugged. When he'd try to look inside himself he'd see nothing particularly frightening; things were just a little fuzzy, a little vague in there. His mind was still sharp, his scholarly work was going well, and he had made several Indian friends in academic circles. What his life sometimes reminded him of, actually, were the nights he'd spent as a boy back in Camas reading forbidden books under the blankets by flashlight—except that this time it was Mama India he was hiding from.

He did finally write to a favorite adviser at Harvard and described his "unplugged" sensation—albeit in somewhat fuzzy terms. And the adviser —one Dr. Ramchandra Majumdar, a British-born Indian, but an experienced traveler in East and West—wrote back promptly, showing a touching but necessarily fuzzy concern as he ventured to guess that Peter's uneasiness might stem not from his struggles with the difficult culture but from "a temporary state of spiritual aridity." Peter was most grateful for this diagnosis. Spiritual aridity is an impressive-sounding thing by which to be made fuzzy. Before receiving Majumdar's letter he'd feared his true pathology might be something more along the lines of "scared of running around like an imbecile with women's underclothes on my head again" or "scared of catching the screaming shits again." But those were Camas thoughts, puppy thoughts, sloppy thoughts, weren't they? Dr. Majumdar knew more than he about these matters, didn't he? So, *yes,* Pete would think. *Spiritual aridity. That's what I've got.* And when, at times, he would recognize his complete lack of conviction in this diagnosis, he would immediately calm himself by thinking: *But of course. Because lack of conviction is exactly what aridity is . . .*

There are kinds of human problems which really do seem, as our tidy expressions would have it, to "come to a head" and "demand to be dealt with." But there are also problems, often just as serious, which come to nothing that we can recognize or openly deal with. Some long-lived, insidious problems simply slip us off to one side of ourselves. Some gently rob us of just enough energy or faith so that days which once took place on a horizontal plane become an endless series of uphill slogs. And some—like high water working year after year at the roots of a riverside tree—quietly undercut our trust or our hope, our sense of place, or of humor, our ability to empathize, or to feel enthused, and we don't sense impending danger, we don't feel the damage at all,

till one day, to our amazement, we find ourselves crashing to the ground.

Peter had one of these kinds of problems.

7. Day 45

March 25, 1971, posed a different sort of problem for Everett. A statistical difficulty, primarily. Natasha had lived with him, they had shared their lovely continent together, for forty-four days. And March 25 was the forty-fifth day since she'd left him. The forty-four best days of his life followed by forty-four days of sodden hell. And today the hell began to outnumber the happiness. What should he do about this? What sort of observance should he observe? If he decided to mourn, when would the mourning end? But if he decided to celebrate, it was like celebrating her absence—and he still wanted her back!

The problem troubled him enough to keep him in bed an extra ten minutes. He then muttered, "Fuck it" and began Day 45 with three boiled eggs.

. . . .

But an hour or so later, when the coffee reached his brain and he began prowling his nearly bookless bookshelves for printed material, Everett found a grease-spattered 1929-vintage cookbook called *Thoroughly Modern Menus*. Assuming it had been abandoned by a previous tenant, Everett had never given it a glance. But in rifling quickly through the yellowed pages, he first discovered the name Maggie Lee on the inside cover, and then—folded neatly inside—Natasha's handwritten recipe for lasagna.

His first reaction to this intimate relic was a mild heart attack. Then his mouth started to water. He loved lasagna. Natasha's most of all, dammit. But wait now. What about *Everett's* lasagna? True, it didn't sound promising. But he was tired of moping, tired of hurting, tired of his three-egged Anthropoidal Borborygm Cooks Dredge for Everyman breakfasts. His behavior had been so corpselike he hadn't even squandered his last paycheck yet. And it was Day 45. So he decided, by damn, to drive to the city, buy the makings for Everett's World's Best Lasagna and a decent bottle of wine, invite his memories of Natasha to dine with him that evening, toast those memories by candlelight, and then tell them, for the last time, to leave him the hell alone.

He drove the forty miles to Victoria—and Papa Dominic's Italian Deli —in an hour. And with his reborn desire for life came a reborn love of strong opinions: the discussion he got into with old Dom on "Southern Catch-all" versus classic Romagna lasagna, earthenware versus cast-iron casseroles, chuck versus neck beef versus sausage versus chorizo, crushed-canned versus strained-fresh tomatoes, oregano versus basil, nuances of marinating, simmering, baking, kinds of Parmesan, kinds of pasta dough, kinds of pasta cutters, and so on, took another two and a half hours, led to insults, and even to violence (old Dominic twice grabbed Everett's cheeks and shook them, making his gums rattle, and the second time Everett grabbed a handy bag of breadsticks and boffed Dom up side the head). But his reborn enthusiasm and strength of opinion also led to many delicious taste tests, to a few free ingredients, and to a shared snack of cappuccino and crushed breadsticks with his fine, ferociously opinionated new friend.

When he and Papa Dom finally loaded up the three bags of hotly contested makings, the jug of cheap Chablis (for cooking, Everett lied) and the bottle of fine Italian Chianti (for formal Natasha-toasting and sipping) and started to carry them out to Everett's car, they were amazed to find that it had begun to snow. Hard.

"A spring snow!" Everett said wonderingly.

"Means a somebody's heart's a broken," Papa Dom said, giving his head a rueful little shake.

Everett didn't quite drop his groceries, but he came close. "Did you *have* to say that?" he croaked.

The old man gaped. "*Your* heart? My Everett's heart's a broken?"

Everett stared at the snow, unable to speak.

"Come back inside!" cried the old man. "I'll make you lasagna myself!"

"This whole outing," Everett said, when he found his voice, "my whole purpose in life today, Dom, is to go home alone, and to make this lasagna myself."

The old man understood. They loaded the groceries into the Olds, hugged each other goodbye, and solemnly promised to eat lasagna together soon.

Everett drove the forty miles home in a near whiteout, ten miles an hour for four hours.

Shyashyakook was pretty, though, all covered with snow, and silent. And when he turned down his transformed driveway he scared up a snowshoe hare—the first he'd ever seen—then three blacktail does, whose retreating white rumps were being disappointedly scoped by the lascivious Chekhov. Everett rolled down his window to greet him: "Hey, Booger."

"*Yehhhhhhhh?*" The goat actually said this. It was his one word.

"Come on up to the house. I got some celery for you."

"*Yehhhhhhhh?*"

Parking the car and stomping into his cold kitchen, he shouted, "*Betty! Bud! Kitten!* I'm home!" It used to crack Natasha up. It was a mistake now. He made a mental note to devise himself a new greeting, kicked the snow off his shoes, unloaded his makings, rolled up his sleeves, washed his hands, then heard a horrid chewing sound on the corner of the house. "Oops. Forgot."

He propped open the window behind the stove, tossed Chekhov three celery sticks, and the goat demolished them so fast that Everett tossed him a brown paper bag for dessert. "*Yehhhhhhhh?*"

He left the window open so they could "talk." He then gathered his inadequate cooking tools, marshaled his wits, and commenced to devise a Tasha/Dominic lasagna synthesis he hoped might put them both to shame. Spreading ingredients over every flat surface in the kitchen, he chopped garlic (he didn't own a press) and yellow onions, chopped Parmesan (didn't own a grater), made his balsamella sauce—and it turned out perfectly, first try. He poured the balsamella into a plastic yogurt container, set it aside, rewashed his only cast-iron skillet, threw Chekhov another brown bag. Then he chopped celery, a carrot, some whole canned tomatoes, opened the ricotta, sliced the mozzarella, began simmering the ground neck meat (a Papa Dominic victory), started boiling olive-oiled water for the Creamette brand lasagna noodles (an ignominious Dominic defeat).

He grabbed his cracked blue MOM mug, filled it with Chablis, sipped sedately as he worked, and realized that he was enjoying himself semithoroughly. "There's something missing," he told Chekhov, handing him the last brown bag. "But there's always something missing. Having things missing, even indispensable things, is a fact of life, don't you think? And life goes on anyhow. Except for the missing parts. Which were indispensable, so of course it goes on all out of whack. But that, hell and damn, is why we prefer things like cooking and eating brown paper bags to philosophizing. Don't you think?"

Chekhov stared at the falling snow, chewed his bag, voiced no opinion.

Looking from Natasha's recipe to his own notes on Dominic's ravings, Everett combined their most irresistible thoughts on Bolognese meat sauce. And by the time the sauce was simmering and the lasagna boiling, he felt perfectly happy: he stood steeped in delicious smells that he alone had caused to burst forth in his kitchen. He was seeing Natasha, for the time being, as nothing more than one of two schools of thought on meat sauces. He was on his feet again. "I'm back!" he told Life. Then he opened the cupboard to grab the two fourteen-inch bake-and-serve lasagna pans he'd given Natasha for Christmas—and realized he hadn't seen them in forty-some days.

"Yehhhhhhhh?"

He looked out the window. The driveway had vanished, and it was still snowing hard. His Olds was half buried. The store in Port Renfrew would be closed by now. They wouldn't have lasagna pans anyhow. Even if they did, he was broke. "Damn."

He poured more Chablis into his MOM mug, took a slow sip, realized for the first time that it was not, by any stretch of the imagination or taste bud, good. He drew a breath. He started to sing:

> It ain't no use to synthesize a sauce, babe.
> Takes good tools to make good chow.
> No it ain't no use to synthesize a sauce, babe,
> Blah blah blah bow wow wow.

I bin thinkin' and wonderin'
All the way down the road
Why I once loved a Czarist
Who kissed like a toad . . .

"Damn! Don't I wish.

With two breasts fun to hold . . .

"Don't get suicidal on me, Everett. How 'bout

Who real quick turned me old . . .

"Damn. How does Bobby D. do it? Don't he just say 'Hey, no problem' and let her rip?
"Hey. No problem. Let 'er rip:

I bin wanderin' and a wonderin'
Like the snow in these woods
Why I loved the one woman
Knew I ain't got the goods.
I gave her my totem
But she wanted my scrotum . . .

"Damn. Don't think at all, hombre. It *ain't* all right."
He smelled his Bolognese meat sauce burning. He set down his wine. He stalked over to the stove, dumped everything he'd bought, chopped, sliced, and simmered into the skillet, stirred it up into an overflowing mash, dumped some mash onto a bowlful of by now gluey pasta, threw the rest of the pasta out the window into the night. He devoured his bowlful of mash. He belched. He poured another MOM mug. Then he gave in to an impulse he'd been staving off all evening:
Sitting down on the antique milking stool he'd bought Natasha for a Valentine the very day she'd vanished, he allowed himself to conjure the circumstances that had inspired the purchase: the two of them, in bed that morning, Natasha looking out the little window at the river and rain as he stared in stunned gratitude at the perfection of her back and bottom, the gray light on her white skin, the memory of sunlight that never quite left her hair. Then she'd turned to him, smiled, and said she wanted to buy a nice nanny goat for Chekhov, so that he could be as happy as the two of them.
"Damn. Oh damn. God damn."
So much for Day 45.

. . . .

And at first light the next morning, Day 46, Everett woke from heavy sleep to the sight of cobalt Steller's jays dragging beige toboggans up into a sunlit, snow-covered spruce. He rubbed and blinked his eyes, but yes, there they were, looking like crazed kids in electric-blue snowsuits dragging lasagna sleds up a blinding white hill. So he gently reached, without thinking, behind him . . .

then caught himself: too late. The moisture was already rising to his eyes, the familiar lump forming in his throat. Forty-six days of wrong don't erase a wondrous right: he had reached back to wake her, to share the little toboggans, the beautiful blue on white.

8. Ace of Hearts

From the day he shot the man in the tree, Irwin stopped telling us anything substantial about how he was making out in 'Nam. He wrote the one long letter to Nash, and he still sent Linda a letter per week full of unmentionable molasses about her soft-little-this's and sweet-sweet-that's. But to the rest of us, after the Zaccheus incident, he sent nothing but picture postcards with a "Love you!," "Miss you!" or "Pray for Peace!" scrawled across the back, and the inevitable "XOOX, Winnie" at the end.

We did discover a secondhand way of finding out about him, though. I'm not sure what inspired the mutual trust; maybe their very different but simultaneous exiles, maybe their very different but simultaneous heartbreaks. Whatever it was, Irwin kept an intimate correspondence going with Everett, right up until the end. I found this out when I sent a copy of the Zaccheus letter up to Shyashyakook, and soon received the following in return:

Dear Kade and Family,

Got the Mekong letter. No comment for now, except to say write to him, all of you, and tell him you love him. I just did. And tell him, reassure him, right away, please, that he's still a Christian. He needs to hear that badly—and from you guys, not me. It's truer than true, by the way. Why else would he shatter like this?

Before anyone writes him off as doomed, though, consider the card I got last week, which I copy here verbatim:

Ever Everett,

Major changes for Alien 2nd Class I. D. Chance. I've been yanked off long-range recon, transferred to a fire base, promoted to Specialist Fourth Class (translation: half-assed corporal) and made aide to the CO here, guy named Dudek, an okay sort for a Captain. I'm his gofer and manservant is what it amounts to. But it beats the snot out of jungle-cruising and killing people. Pray for peace, and for me too if you remember how. XOOX, Winnie

As I read it, this is great news. We can't know how secure his fire base is, but <u>anything's</u> safer than long-range recon, and as an aide he probably won't be told to do any more shooting, which, given his reaction to Zaccheus, could save him from court-martial. So I don't know. Tell Linda, Bet and Mama to spit on their Bibles and Papa on his baseballs and maybe we'll get him back in one piece.

As you see, he didn't say a word to me about "popping" anybody. Wish I'd known. I'm afraid I reacted to his promotion news with my usual off-brand repartee. "Butt-boy to a Captain now, eh?" is, as I recall, what I wrote back. Irwin's reply will relieve you, though. Received a 'Nam-velope just two days ago containing nothing but the ace of hearts from a Sumo Wrestler card deck, featuring a rear-end view of a whale-sized specimen, upon whose dimpled cheeks he wrote:

Mine's still plenty tighter than yours, Big Fella. XOOX, Winnie

Give my love to anybody who still believes in the stuff. I miss most of you—no, sorry: <u>all</u> of you—a lot.

Everett

From what Everett remembers, their correspondence must have been one of the odder exchanges going on in the world at the time: letter after intimate letter hopscotching the Pacific, half by a conscience-stricken, Bible-thumping SDA living out a Mekong Delta nightmare, half by a countryless, Natasha-less outlaw/anarchist holed up in a sodden nowhere in B.C. Whoever censored Army mail had a surprisingly light touch: Everett said that, judging by Irwin's responses, everything he sent must have shot through unscathed—and he enclosed all the most rabid anti-war editorials, nightmarish photo essays and harrowing stories of American atrocities, South Vietnamese corruption and D.C. hypocrisy he could find in his efforts to "give you and your bullet-spraying buddies a less parochial view of Uncle Sam's little overseas endeavor." What made the correspondence really interesting, though, was that Irwin *did* show Everett's offerings to his "bullet-spraying buddies," inspiring a number of them to make suggestions (which Irwin passed on, unexpurgated, to Everett) as to how repeatedly and deeply the "chickenshit motherfuckin' turncoat Canuck-suckin' know-nuthin'" (etc. etc.) draft-dodger could shove his next batch of clippings up the various manholes, ducts and portals of his person. Everett's reaction, however, was to pen genial responses to each of his verbal assailants, to thank them for their creative suggestions, and to claim to have tried and enjoyed them all. This amused most of them, won a few of them over, and an odd correspondence had developed.

Everett's side of the exchange, when it hadn't been ribald or blackly comic, had apparently been preachy and condescending in the beginning. But when a guy named Bobby Calcagno wrote a letter that called Everett's missives "inartistic," it hit him where he lived. Or wished he lived. *Artistic?* he'd thought at first. *Strange word in the mouth of a 'Nam grunt!* But Calcagno had gone on to write a letter which even Everett admitted *was* artistic. He remembers the best part as saying something like: "Most of us are in 'Nam for the same reason you're in B.C., Chance. We thought we had no choice. We were wrong, of course: we could have been there with you. And you were also wrong: you could have been here with us. But what we have in common is that we've all been kicked out of the house. And we don't like it any better than you do. So let us proceed to please shuttup about which ear we landed on, left or right, and show each other a little courtesy and compassion."

Everett was so impressed by this that he tossed his next batch of *Berkeley Barb* and *Village Voice* clippings in the trash, took a ferry clear to Vancouver, went on a little shopping binge, and mailed his new pen pals the first of several shipments of what he called "kicked-out-of-the-House Warming Presents": he sent back issues of obscure literary journals, joke books and comics, the best *New Yorker* cartoons, the quirkiest baseball stories and box scores; he sent peppermint, cinnamon and anise-flavored rolling papers, a book of exploding matches ("my contribution to the War Effort"), a few original poems, some home-tied wet flies that imitated raw rice ("for possible paddy or Delta carp fishing") and any other heartening thing he could squeeze into a manila envelope. The arrival of these enhanced letters apparently became a series of little off-color Christmases for the guys on Irwin's fire base. A couple of them even went so far as to apologize for having told Everett where to stick it, and admitted to wishing they'd dodged the draft themselves. To this, though, Everett said, "Hey, wait a minute!" And he sat down and penned a litany of the negative attributes of permanent exile in Canada. Which of course only inspired the grunts to fire back letters of the "You think *you* got problems!" sort. As a result, Everett rounded up a few other draft-dodging contestants, put up a twenty-dollar (Canadian) first prize, and appointed himself, Irwin and Bobby Calcagno the judges of what he called "THE FIRST, LAST & ONLY V.C. VERSUS B.C. HOMESICK TEARJERKER ESSAY-WRITING CONTEST."

But before a winner could be declared, neither Irwin nor Bobby Calcagno were in any shape to judge.

I am incompetent, in obvious ways, to talk about the war in Vietnam. Though I finally did lose my student deferment, I discovered at my induction physical that I was 4-F due to legal blindness in my left eye (thank you, Vera, thank you, Papa). In other words, through what is known in some circles as *tariki* and in others as idiot luck, I was not forced to choose between serving in or running from the military, and so know nothing firsthand about this war.

Nevertheless I have one 'Nam story to tell. It was pieced together from conversations with four men over a period of years. None of these men was entirely sober when we talked. Two weren't entirely sane. But all four were veterans. And all four remembered Spec 4 Irwin Chance. To these and any other 'Nam vets who might read this, I apologize for my ignorance of the intricacies of your lives. The only claim I make for what follows is that I knew my brother as well as anyone at the time these events occurred. And the only excuse I make for it is that Irwin, when the story ended, was unable to speak for himself.

CHAPTER FOUR

The Watch

Say what you want about Hitler, but he trained killers. You train kids in their early years and you can do anything you want with that child.
  —Sparky Anderson, manager of the Detroit Tigers,
    trying to explain why he prefers younger ballplayers

near My Tho, Vietnam / May / 1971

Returning from a mad dash to the radio operators' tent, having dutifully delivered Captain Dudek's message ("Tell 'em shut the fuck up about the prisoner. We have taken no prisoner. Understood?"), Spec 4 Irwin Chance finally set eyes on the little Vietcong who'd created such a stir that morning. Irwin was shirtless, hatless, painfully sleepy, but stumbling dutifully along with a pot of coffee he'd just commandeered for the Captain. The VC was wide awake but motionless, handcuffed to the bumper of a jeep. He wore a South Vietnamese infantry uniform, the shirt pocked with several neatly sewn but wrong-colored patches where bullets or shrapnel had evicted its previous tenant, the pants enormous, crotch at his knees, cuffs a pile of baggy creases—and his toes peeked out from beneath. Bare toes. He wore no shoes. Irwin smiled as he approached. Some enemy. Some disguise . . .

Then he noticed the VC's face and his smile withered. From a distance it had appeared dirty, expressionless, and not much else. Slope face. Generic dink. But as Irwin drew closer the eyes began to dominate, growing larger, more frightened and younger at every step. This was the beginning: noticing that the eyes were so young. It changed everything for Irwin. Instead of sweat streaking the dirt on the cheeks, he now saw tears; instead of the bandage on the head, he now noticed the brownish smear leaking through at the temple; instead of a captured enemy, a neutralized threat, he now felt he was seeing some kid who'd been caught playing war by bigger, stronger, far more dangerous boys.

As he set Dudek up with a second cup of coffee and finally went to work on his own, Irwin grew awake enough to wonder about the message he'd delivered. *We have taken no prisoner* . . . He'd delivered it without thinking, but now had a suspicion as to what it might mean. Thanks to the presence of politicos, photojournalists, television crews and other observers, there'd been a Washington-hatched edict, ever since Tet, banning the execution of untried prisoners: summary executions made for bad suppertime TV back home. But just three mornings before their "nonexistent" prisoner was captured, Irwin's friend Bobby Calcagno had opened the door of his half-track and a wad of plastic explosives crammed near the hinge had blown most of his face away . . .

There is a well-known GI equation (founded, I think, upon the healthy old American distrust of anyone endowed with power) which goes: "Captain = Asshole." But Captain Dudek was aware of this equation, and worked hard to defy it. He often acted upon the advice of his sergeants, which helped. He was not a West Point man, which helped. He smoked as much dope as was discreetly possible, which gave him something in common with the average GI, whether or not it helped. He also hailed from southern Louisiana and could switch at ease from bayou slang into an idiom as cadenced and eloquent as an old plantation raconteur's— which at least made his orders a pleasure to hear, however unpleasant they might be to carry out. Dudek, as captains go, was something of a crowd pleaser. And he knew that Bobby Calcagno had been a well-liked man. He also knew that there were plenty of ways of slipping past a Washington-hatched edict. And *No fuckin' prisoner*, Irwin began to realize, might be one of them.

The little VC had been carrying a canvas satchel when he was captured. While Irwin sipped his coffee and tried to relax, the Captain invited a half dozen men in to help him analyze the satchel's contents. Dudek liked an audience. Especially a stoned one. And judging by the bloodshot eyes and odors as the men filled the tent, this audience was going to be choice. The Captain placed the satchel on a card table and began removing its contents with melodramatic flourishes. He liked to make people smile while keeping a straight face himself. He liked to make Spec 4 Chance smile most of all. But watching his flourishes, studying his coy manner, Irwin felt the same creeping panic one feels at a poker game when the stakes suddenly shoot so high that to fold or to cover are equally unthinkable. Because what had convened in this tent, he now understood, was a kangaroo court: what Dudek pulled from the satchel may well decide the Cong boy's fate.

Everything inside the canvas had been wrapped in cloth to keep it from clattering, so Dudek unwrapped each item, like a gift-wrapped present, before holding it up for the men to identify. He then placed it on one of two piles, which he verbally labeled "Ours" and "Theirs." On the "Ours" pile he set an Army-issue pocketknife, a Zippo lighter, some waterproof matches and a Prince Albert tobacco tin. "Boy was settin' up a tobacco shop," he drawled, and the men all grinned. But as he opened the Prince Albert tin he suddenly hollered, *"Kablooey!"*—and the same men lurched so violently that five or six seconds passed before even the stoutest of them could grin again. The tin was empty. On the "Theirs" pile Dudek tossed a pair of Chinese pliers, an odd little hemp-handled screwdriver, a stout pair of wire cutters, and was reaching in for the next item when he did a double take, drawled, "This is *too* good," pointed back at the cloth the wire cutters had been wrapped in, then held it up: it was a pair of baby-blue Fruit of the Loom boxer shorts.

A couple of men whooped, but Dudek quieted them with a look. He then began to toy with the shorts, not in a slapstick way, but like a small-time tragedian toying with a Yorick skull. He pondered the little horn of plenty on the label, snapped and unsnapped the two buttons, turned the shorts this way and that. "Gentlemen," he finally said, unleashing his softest Southern eloquence. "Consider this artifact carefully, and then tell me, if you can: Is this war a tragedy? Is it a farce? Or is it a blend far too deadly, sad and delicate for mere mortals to separate or define?"

There was a silence, during which the Captain's rhetorical questions sailed like three seaworthy little schooners through the thick, blue-tinged air. Then Spec 4 Chance barked, "Oh, it's tragedy! Definitely just plain tragedy, sir!"

The three schooners did nothing so scenic as sink: they just popped, leaving the air full of the reek of stale pot smoke. The Captain turned to his aide and tried to wither him with a gaze. Irwin didn't even notice. He just kept staring sorrowfully at the undershorts. Dudek finally snorted. He'd made Irwin an aide because of the guileless laugh, the muscles, the forthrightness, and Sergeant Felker's opinion that of all the men in 'Nam, this one was the least likely ever to get drunk, stoned or vengeful some dark night and shoot his commanding officer in the back. But after four months of his company, Dudek was considering transferring, or at times like this murdering, his aide for these same sterling qualities.

Dispensing with melodrama, the Captain reached abruptly back into the satchel. But as he unwrapped the next item, dramatic tension was instantly restored. He drew a sharp breath, sighed it out—*Ahhhhhhh*—and made sure that every man present, especially Irwin, saw that what he held in his hand was a wad of plastic explosives: the very same stuff that had deprived Bobby Calcagno of his face.

Calcagno had remained conscious all through the forty-minute wait for the chopper, burbling with what was left of his mouth *"Kill me! God! Please kill me!"* over and over. Of course Dudek couldn't let them do it, though even Irwin had been tempted. And later they'd learned that, in a Saigon hospital, there'd been three more days of surgery, skin grafts, infections and torment before Bobby was able to die.

Irwin was one of the men who held Bobby down, and all through the wait he'd tried to think of some appropriate prayer to shout over the screaming. But all that ever came to his mind was the famous old Memory Verse: *Unto him that smiteth thee on the one cheek, offer also the other.* And Irwin was ashamed to even think it, let alone say it aloud. Because for Bobby it had no meaning. He literally hadn't another cheek to offer.

The two men who'd made the capture that morning came into the tent and made their report. PFC Swasey—a burly New Jerseyite who brought to mind a twisted Yogi Berra—said it was the smell of gas wafting out of one of the personnel carriers that had alerted him to the fact that "some kinda bole shit was comin' down." Thinking the vehicle could be booby-trapped, the men were easing toward it when they heard noises in under the hood. Figuring that nothing human could fit in an engine or make such a sound, they decided it was an animal and that the problem should be dealt with at once. So while Swasey aimed his rifle, the other man, PFC Bork, quickly lifted the hood—and there lay the little VC, blinking in the early-morning sun.

"A treacherous babe in a greasy manger," intoned the Captain.

"Dat's correct, sir," croaked PFC Swasey.

Dudek winced slightly, and began to massage his temples.

PFC Bork, a skinny blond kid from upstate Wisconsin, spoke up to say that the VC had surrendered without a fight. But Swasey turned livid at this. Jammed as he was against the engine, Swasey maintained, it was impossible for the dink to move. Yet as soon as Bork had lifted him out, "the li'l fucker started spittin' at us."

"Flummery!" said Bork—who'd lately been devouring a stack of Nero Wolfe novels. The prisoner, he maintained, had merely been sick from heat and gas fumes, and what they'd heard in under the hood was vomiting.

"Bole *shit!*" was Swasey's reply to this. True, there was barf all over the engine. But this didn't mean the prisoner didn't spit at them, or even "aim his fuckin' gook puke," for that matter. "I have personally read how these pygmies in Brazil'll take and spit actual poison right in your goddamn face," Swasey told the Captain.

"Ingenious," said Dudek, who'd begun to enjoy himself again.

"You'd think the poison'd kill the pygmy first," remarked Bork.

"Hmm," went the Captain.

"I read it in a goddamn *book!*" Swasey exploded, "which is in my goddamn *tent* this goddamn *minute!* It explains," he added more calmly, "how they build up their immunities bit by bit, till after a while they can pract'ly drink the shit."

"Remarkable!" said the Captain.

"Bosh!" said Bork.

At any rate, this spit or vomit, whether aimed or involuntary, was why PFC Swasey had proceeded to strike the Cong in the skull, twice, with the butt of his rifle, which in turn explained how the prisoner's head had come to be bandaged.

When Swasey and Bork had finished, the prisoner was brought into the tent for interrogation. But the air was so stifling and he smelled so strongly of puke and gas that the Captain ordered the guards to seat him in the open doorway and train a fan on him, to blow the smell outside. Then the radio operators were summoned to conduct the interrogation, they being the only men on the fire base who spoke any Asian languages.

The radio men proved patient and very thorough, bending like well-meaning big sisters over a recalcitrant sibling as they asked question after question. But the little VC just stared into the whirring blades of the fan. Never flinched, never changed expression, never said a word—not in Cambodian or Laotian, not in Hmong or Vietnamese; not in French, German, Italian or Spanish either, though by the time the radio operators got to these languages they were asking nothing but Berlitz-style questions—things like "What shall we do this fine evening?" "Which local restaurants would you recommend?" "Could you please direct us to the nearest enemy stronghold?" "Do you prefer Victor or Charles?" They had Dudek and his men in stitches.

Sergeant Pillard, the demolitions man, got a chuckle too when he returned from the personnel carrier and said he "felt like a boob" for having put his demo suit on to inspect it. But Pillard wasn't after laughs. Jerking a thumb back at the prisoner, he said, "How he got onto the base or why he crawled like a damned rodent up into that engine, I have no idea. But he sure didn't know what to do once he got there."

"Bole *shit!*" PFC Swasey burst out. "He sabotaged the *fuck* out of it!"

Dudek turned to Pillard, and raised an eyebrow.

The sergeant shrugged. "He cut a fuel line, an' hooked some sorta firecracker fuse to a plug wire, an' scattered matches around. But I'd call that vandalism, not sabotage. If he thought he'd kill anybody but himself with that mess, he's crazy. Which, come to think of it, could be the answer. Insanity, I mean."

Captain Dudek strolled over to the doorway, leaned down over the prisoner, looked straight into his eyes for several seconds, straightened, stepped back inside, and said to Sergeant Pillard, "He doesn't look insane to me."

"He looks like a damned *kid*, is what he looks like," the demo man muttered. And seeing the hard smile cross Dudek's face, Irwin understood what the sergeant's game had been all along: their prisoner may well be Calcagno's killer, but Pillard was determined to play up his ineptitude no matter what—because he'd seen at a glance that, whatever he'd done, whoever he'd killed, the boy was just a boy.

"Before you perjure yourself any further," the Captain said, still smiling, "take a look at this." He pointed out the plastic explosives.

The demo man looked, but didn't react.

"And maybe this too." Dudek held up the baby-blue boxer shorts.

Most of the men laughed. Pillard didn't.

"Do either of these artifacts alter your opinion?"

The demo man said nothing.

Dudek took a satisfied slurp of coffee, scowled down into his cup, then into the heat and smoke sent a single word: *"Why?"*

Every man in the tent turned to him. *Why what?* their faces all said—but no one was willing to speak for fear of sounding stupid. Or almost no one.

"Why what?" Irwin asked.

The Captain smiled: this time, for rhetorical emphasis, he'd desired his idiot aide's reaction. "Why," he repeated, "would a mere 'kid,' if our prisoner *is* a kid, go to the trouble of sneaking onto our base with these materials? I want to hear, from Sergeant Pillard or anyone else, every possible reason he could have had—barring insanity, which I find ridiculous."

Pillard remained silent. But someone else said, "Wanted to kill our butts, obviously."

There was a snicker or two, but Dudek just nodded grimly.

"Hates our fuckin' guts!" PFC Swasey chimed in. Dudek nodded again.

"He's like one a them Japs," another man added. "Them kamikazes. Didn't care *what* the fuck happens, long as he takes out a few of us with'm."

Dudek nodded again. He had his audience right where he wanted it. He was ready to close his remarks around them like a purse-seine round a school of tuna—

until Spec 4 Chance squinched his eyes shut, gripped his temples in his big right hand, and blurted with the confidence of some yokel who's just seen his Lord and Savior, "I know! I really think I know why he did all this! We killed his *dad,* I bet! Or his brothers! We killed his sisters or mother! If they were dead, he'd do this! 'Cause put yourself in *his* shoes. If you were a kid and your family was dead, if you were a kid an' we killed 'em, isn't this just what you'd do?"

The men weren't just stunned by this outburst: they were pole-axed. A few squirmed as if a priest, or maybe somebody's mother, had walked into the tent. A few tried to snicker. But none of them could meet Irwin's earnest gaze. Except Dudek. Who was furious. "What objectivity!" he cried. "What acumen! How fortunate we are to have a psychologist such as Herr Doktor Chance in our midst!"

There was a little nervous laughter, but not enough to satisfy the Captain. "Would any of the rest of you care to regale us with a theory?" he asked. "Perhaps one of our B-52s injured the prisoner's new puppy. Or maybe one of our real trucks ran over his cute little toy one."

Pretty good lines, both of them. But no one laughed. He'd lost them completely. Irwin had whisked them all away. "All I know," Sergeant Pillard sighed, looking at the boy, "is they sure don't make saboteurs like they used to."

Almost every man in the tent followed his gaze. And almost every man nodded.

"Maybe they've run out of grownups," another voice put in. "Maybe the bombings up north are finally working."

More solemn nods.

"Which reminds me, Herr Doktor," the Captain said to Irwin. "I've run out of toothpaste. So go fetch me some. *Now.* It's what you call a fool's errand. It's also an order!"

So Irwin had saluted, stepped toward the door, and started off after a tube of toothpaste—but not before he heard the Captain say to those who remained behind, "For God's sake, gentlemen, use your brains before they get blown out of your heads! Are we still at war? Are we any kind of military force at all? Are we here to fight, and to attempt to win? Or have Congress and Herr Doktor Chance decreed that we operate some kind of summer camp here, providing our big black and white bodies as targets for little VCs to practice blowing to smithereens?"

The sun hit Irwin's back, he stopped walking, and a wave washed over him—not a memory but a conjuration: *Adventist Camp Meeting, the heat of early July.* And when he looked around, there were the rows of tents, the hot dusty sunlight, even the ripe watermelons piled in the shade of a canopied truck. An old Sabbath School song started singing itself in his head: *This little light of mine, I'm gonna let it shine . . .* And over it came the same drift of voices, as if from the lake or the softball field, the same soothing hum of humans and insects, and the same untiring, inescapable drawl of the man of righteousness, the man in the pulpit, this time crying out: "These *are* plastic explosives, gentlemen! The very same that killed our Bobby, after obliterating his face! And to imprison this creature we'd have to fly him out of here, risking a Huey and every man in it. And for what?"

Irwin turned and looked at the prisoner's small, sunlit back. There. That was what. But even he could see the problem: the back was nearly too small, too slight to believe in. Dudek's voice was far more convincing as it shook the peaceful air: "We can see that he's young. We have eyes in our heads—unlike Bobby Calcagno. But what kind of soldiers leave one another's deaths unavenged? What kind of soldiers allow Washington to impose rules that leave us here to die in agony, yet forbid us the right to kill our killers? When is the last time you saw a congressman bleedin' in this war, gentlemen? When is the last time you saw Senator Love or Senator Dove out workin' the point on recon?"

Irwin's head roared with the song now: *Hide it under a bushel, no! I'm gonna let it shine!* He looked again at the boy. The little back was motionless—as still as a gas-soaked wooden Buddha. And Irwin loved Bobby so much, Dudek's sermon was so fine, and the sun's heat was so strong that even he half wished they could be saved from their dilemma by the boy's spontaneous combustion.

"If he's taken to prison," Elder Dudek intoned, "he may escape. And if he escapes, he *will* be back!" Then the long, polished pause, during which Irwin knew the Captain's gaze was crossing each listener's face, demanding and receiving full complicity. And now the sharp intake of breath, and the confident, almost glib final lines: "Next month, next year, he *will* be back. And you can bet your butts—you can bet your sweet black an' white asses." (and Irwin smiled, knowing without seeing that the Captain was again holding the blue boxer shorts aloft) "that next time he will make no mistake!"

Will the congregation rise?

Damn right they will. And hear them pray: *"Off the little fucker!"* *"He killed Bobby!"* *"Let's go!"* *"Fuck you, Senator Dove!"* *"Time's a-wastin'!"* *"Deal me in!"*

Amen.

The music left the Captain's voice. The song stopped in Irwin's head. And he was only sad—not angry, not surprised—when he heard the quick, practical orders. Dudek was a good officer, conducting his war by the only set of rules that let an army be an army. It was the rules that ordered the sham release of the prisoner, the rules that handpicked the men who would escort him to the clearing with their M-16s, and the rules that added: "Remember. We never saw him, never caught him. None of this happened. This little VC just does not exist."

Returning from the commissary, the Captain's toothpaste in hand, Irwin saw a group of grunts gathered in the shade of the tree across from the jeep. They weren't talking. They were just sitting there, most of them smoking, looking at the VC who just didn't exist. Irwin glanced at his watch. 11:55, it said. He moved into the shade and sat down among them.

The prisoner was handcuffed to the bumper again, and flanked by guards. Irwin had a bad memory for names but an excellent one for faces and, oddly, states. He knew one of the guards as New York, the other as Alabama. In other words, he didn't know them at all. But he'd expected them. Expected their bodies, anyhow: both about 6′2″, both muscular, both jet black. Dudek had the old Confederate love of ritual. In martial ceremonies—executions, for instance—he favored height and muscular builds over squat or anemic specimens; favored what he called "two salts" or "two peppers" over what he called "mix 'n' match"; favored chivalric-sounding times such as "dawn," "sunset" or "high noon" over whatever hundred hours. In toothpastes, he favored Gleem. The good old Captain. Thirty-one years young and still going strong. Still wily too. He'd ordered the big picturesque peppers to guard the VC, but when Irwin glanced down toward his tent he saw that it was four salts who would escort the prisoner to the "escape route." Never know when a pepper might up and muff it.

11:56, said Irwin's watch.

The prisoner was so short that he was able to stand straight up despite being cuffed to the bumper. For the most part he remained motionless, but every now and then he'd twist his back in a slow circle, like a dancer or on-deck hitter loosening up. He looked tired and a little ashen, but his head had been rebandaged, perhaps to lessen his suspicion, and he no longer looked queasy from the fumes.

He did seem troubled by the men in the shade, though. He'd been caught trying to kill them, after all. He kept his head lowered, like a shy kid forced to give a report to his class at school. And he kept looking, Irwin noticed, at his left wrist, so Irwin looked at it too—and was amazed to see, right there next to the handcuff, a wristwatch. An enormous one too. One of those big black jobs that nerds and scuba divers favor— fluorescent numbers; built-in compass, maybe; made in Hong Kong or Taiwan by genuine, lifelike capitalist-satellite wage slaves. Such a deal at $9.95. Then a month after you buy it you notice it's slow, go to reset it, and as the stem snaps off in your lily-white fingers you remember: *no guarantee.*

Ha. Slave's revenge.

But why was it there at all? How had the guards missed it? Couldn't it contain poison or something? No. You could tell it was innocuous some- how. You could tell it was just a watch. And it was there, Irwin realized, because of an oversight stemming from a very rudimentary human char- acteristic: no adult, even in time of war, wants to steal a toy away from a child.

So. Back to *that* question. Was he *really* just a child? Because wasn't it important? Wasn't it crucial? Because if they were actually dealing with a kid, shouldn't they be doing everything differently?

I'd sure be doing it differently, Irwin thought. I'd shoot him, all right. I'd *Gleem* his ass with this goddamned toothpaste! *WAH-HA! Take that, Mr. Tough VC War Criminal! Eat this, Mad Bomber!* (Rub it in his hair, smear both cheeks, shoot it up his nose.) *Quit blowin' up my friends, ya brat! Don't do it! You hear me?* (A squirt in each ear, glop in each armpit.) *BLEAH! Now look at you! Had enough? Gonna be good now? Say "Uncle Ho" then. Louder! Okay. That's better. Now get your commie ass outta here 'fore I kick it in!*

Yeah. That'd fix his little red wagon.

But nobody asked Irwin's advice.

The heat was horrific. New York pretended to ignore the men in the shade, but his face was one big cramp of irritation. Meanwhile Alabama stared right through them, hangin' loose, restin' easy, lookin' like: *We got heat in 'Bama too, white muthahfucks . . .*

But maybe, Irwin thought, still obsessed with his question, *he's much older than he looks. They're very small people. If he'd speak, we could tell. If he'd say even one word we'd hear whether his voice had changed, and we'd know . . .*

11:58, said his watch. And now the numbers were shaking. Now Irwin was in knots. Because he felt he was forgetting something—some kind of order, not the toothpaste but something dire, some matter of life and death. *But what?*

The men around him lurched and stared—and Irwin realized he'd nearly shouted his *But what?* Which didn't embarrass him. He'd never been embarrassed by his own or anyone else's honesty. But he did feel he should get away from the men in order to think. So he stood, stepped out into the sunlight—

and like dust to a vortex was sucked toward the jeep, and the little Vietcong.

The boy raised his head and looked straight at him.

Irwin stopped walking, and looked straight back.

The men in the shade watched him, watched them both, but Irwin didn't know it: he only knew he'd made a mistake, coming this close. Because now he could see him. Could really see the rich brown of the skin; the fragile clavicle in the V of the shirt; the delta of blue veins running down the throat; the smooth backs of the hands—hands far smaller than those of his little sisters.

Then he made an even greater mistake: he looked into the boy's eyes—
right into the liquid and the shining and the life there. And he saw a
spark of curiosity. At a time like this, the boy was curious about Irwin
Chance! He was trying to stay poker-faced, but the brown eyes flashed as
he watched the huge, bare-chested man whose face was so gentle, yet so
troubled, stepping slowly toward him. He watched as though Irwin were
an animal—an enormous, friendly bear, maybe—coming to help or even
save him, like in a children's story . . .

Realizing that he was smiling, and maybe creating false hopes, Irwin
made himself stop. But then, fearing the quick change of expression
would confuse the boy, he smiled again. The boy's face showed nothing.
He just watched. *We're going to kill him,* Irwin thought as he smiled. *He
wanted to kill us, prob'ly did kill Bobby, so we're going to shoot him. With
bullets! Good God! We're really going to do it!*

Then he made a final mistake: he began to recollect the life-and-death
matter, the forgotten command. It started to fall together when his old
nickname, "Iron Man," flicked through his mind. After nine months of
'Nam there wasn't much of this character left. But there were shards, a
jumble of fragments, and in the heat by the jeep a few fragments con-
gealed. How did it go? *Whosoever shall humble himself . . .* like? as?
Whosoever shall humble himself as this little child something something,
*whoso shall help, or maybe receive, or anyhow shall stick up for one such
child in My Name, receiveths, or sticks up for, or anyhow stands by Me.*

Yeah.

Irwin knew as he conjured it that it was a terrible injunction to be
recalling. It came from a lost world, a world whose rules could kill him
here. But he never had been a subtle fellow. Recollecting the dead-obvious line, he promptly did the dead-obvious thing: he stepped forward. As
if he'd never left the Washougal church, as if answering an Altar Call, he
walked straight toward the jeep with nothing in his head but the insane
Sabbath plan of throwing in his lot with the boy, of somehow "receiving"
him. He was perhaps six feet away when an explosion of air stopped him.
The Captain's big peppers. They'd both snapped to. And they too had a
kind of call to answer.

"Clear the fuck out!" hissed Alabama.

"He means it, fuckface," added New York, flashing a bland, terrifying
smile.

Irwin blinked at them. Obstacles! To receiveth the boy he needed a
plan, some guile, a ruse. He needed Everett, was what he needed. But no
time, no time! So let's see . . . Rank? Pull rank? Fake an order from the

Captain? Get the keys, free the boy, and run? No. Get the keys, free him, and go straight to Dudek. Yes! Straight to the Captain, onto your knees, and beg as you have never begged before. *Now make it work . . .*

He cleared his throat, stepped up to the guards, and in his best imitation of Dudek snapped, "Excuse *me*, gentlemen! But there's been a slight change of—"

"*Get gone, muthahfuck!*" went Alabama, and spit flew with the words and landed, burning, on Irwin's chest.

"He means it, suckbrain," smiled New York.

Why? Why wasn't it working? He looked down at the spit. *His shirt.* Without his shirt they couldn't know he outranked them. Trying to regroup, he took a single backward step, taking care not to turn his face from the boy, who was watching him keenly now. *Shout!* he told himself. *Everett versus Babcock! Curse and spit right back in their faces . . .* But before he'd regained his lost step he heard murmuring in the shade behind him, heard distant footsteps, turned,

and saw Dudek and his four handpicked, armed and angry white men marching straight for them. Terror washed through him like a poison. He took another step backward. Strength gone, thoughts gone, he gawked at the boy, thinking: *Lost.* And the boy read it. He read Irwin's face, gave him a look that shot across a spectrum—*confusion, betrayal, hatred, despair.* Then the brown eyes glazed. The light fell out of them.

Struggling to hold his ground, Irwin glanced toward the Captain, recognized fury even at a distance, then looked down at himself as if to find some talisman, some magic weapon, with which to combat the fury when it arrived. In his right hand was a tube of toothpaste. On his left wrist was a watch. Gleem, said the toothpaste. 12:01, said the watch.

Lost.

Pray then, he thought. But for what? Divine intervention? Enemy attack? Rapture? The boy's soul? Had this kid heard of Jesus during his ten or twelve years of life in a hell zone? And if not, was it Irwin's Christian duty to tell about Him now?

"Show's startin', fucknose," New York said with the same terrible smile.

Then Alabama stepped right up to him, stabbed his bare chest with one finger, and shoved as he snarled, "*Fuck off!*" And as Irwin fell another step back the words bore into him, all the way in and down, where they echoed and howled and set fire to every rote-learned, impotent Sabbath School truth he'd ever learned about prayer or souls or the mechanics of salvation. *Help this boy!* his heart cried. *Help him now, or fuck off!* But everything inside him except his heart wanted to run for its life. And his heart was breaking.

Alabama and New York snapped to attention. Men appeared, standing in doorways, peering out from shaded walls, saying nothing, just wanting to watch. Camp Meeting again. Camp Meeting before a baptism. Even the song was back: *I'm gonna let it shine . . .*

Straining a little at the handcuffs now, the Cong boy peered down the road in the direction opposite the approaching men, way down beyond the snarls of concertina wire enclosing the base. The road was empty, except for a couple of little birds, yet for ten, maybe fifteen seconds the boy craned his neck and peered. Then, without warning, his mouth fell open as though his jaw had been broken. His tongue shone pink. His thin chest began to heave. The chain rattled and scraped against the bumper. Blood beaded, then dripped from his writhing wrists. Strange, strangled sobs began to rise from deep down his throat. The same sounds began to rise from Irwin. And hearing this, sensing this one man's useless compassion, the boy looked straight into his eyes and uttered, in a language no one understood, some sentence, some final plea—

and yes, his voice was high and piping. Yes, it was a child's voice, not even about to change.

Weeping now, but still trying to smile, Irwin said, *"Good Christ! Give him courage."*

Then Dudek stood before him, red-eyed, red-faced, and so beside himself with fury that he could barely whisper, *"Go!"*

"But I, this Gleem!" Irwin gasped. "I can, he, let me take him, Captain! 'Cause I . . . for Bobby! Let me mess him up good with this tube of—"

"GO!" the Captain roared.

Out of pride—out of some ineradicable pride that must be rooted in the body alone, in the purely structural integrity of tissue and bones perhaps, for even the lowest of men, convicted child molesters, say, or mass murderers, will use it to hold their heads high when thrust on display in front of other humans—out of this unkillable kind of pride Irwin was able to take a few slow, almost leisurely paces away from the jeep, the watching men, Dudek's fury and the boy. But the Sabbath School song had sprung up in his head again, *This little light of mine . . .* And Irwin's Sabbath School God was the sort who saw everything. So where was there to go? Wanting distance, wanting oblivion, wanting some nonmilitary greenness or blackness to swallow him whole, he took aim at a blur of fire-stunted weeds and low vines at the farthest corner of the base. But the farther he moved from the jeep, the harder his insides strained back toward it. All the secretions of fear swirled through his brain, screaming *forget! run! save me! go!* But the back of his skull had thinned away into a paperlike membrane that took in every sound back around the boy, and when Dudek's voice, puffed with righteousness, slammed against the membrane, shame flooded Irwin's fear, turned him nauseous, and his heart and footsteps began to detonate in time to the music, left, right, systole, diastole, *Hide it under a bushel, no!*

You can't fool a good song.

The blood left Irwin's face, left his mind, left him shambling along like some boot-mangled insect. His good green target spun out of sight, changing into a khaki tent wall which he clutched, trying to right himself. Then even the khaki spurned him, bursting into some warm, impossible abomination that gushed like pus between his fingers and oozed down the back of his hand. He fell with a groan, hit the tent, then the ground, gaped again at his hand. And it really *was* oozing—

toothpaste.

He had crushed the Captain's Gleem.

Lying in the dust there with his toothpaste, Irwin had finally rolled onto his belly and peered back toward the jeep. And what he'd seen at first, back through the watery heat waves, was about what he had expected and feared:

the four salts—two with rifles, two with shovels—all of them motionless, gazing with something like hunger and something like lust at the captive;

the Captain, also motionless, and stern and martial-looking for a while; but then wincing, then wiping at sweat, then cursing outright and rubbing his boiled temples as New York fumbled interminably through a foreign ring of keys;

Alabama, not quite snorting, not even quite smirking at Dudek, but clearly thinking, *Hot out here, ain't it, white muthahfuck;*

nothing but cigarette smoke moving through the crowd in under the tree . . .

But then New York found the right key, freed the boy's wrists, and the salts moved in close, pausing to listen to Dudek's last few instructions before leading him away—and during this lull Irwin realized that he had been looking, all along, at something unexpected: *the prisoner too was motionless.* Abandoned though he was, minuscule though he was, he stood steady as the heat now, facing the crowd, the salts and the Captain with a look almost regal for the purity of its hatred. It was then that Irwin remembered his own blurted words: *Christ, give him courage.* And it was then that the boy calmly reached, with a tiny brown thumb and forefinger, to his bleeding left wrist—

where he began, with just seconds to live, to wind his enormous watch.

The great biblical descents of grace—the kind of church-advertised descents that Irwin as a boy had so blithely admired—had all shared certain characteristics. For example they were always invoked by faith-filled prayer, by an honest cry from the heart, or by a great and selfless love; they could always be depended upon to alter even the most dire course of events—with flagrant disregard for the laws of science—in order to bring about the spiritual and physical salvation of their protagonists; and they were always comprehensible enough to allow a witness, or the recipient of grace himself, to compose a pious and grateful story about the wondrous descent afterward.

The winding of the watch marked the end of Irwin's blind love for that kind of story. Not that he doubted that he was seeing his prayer answered: his faith, despite everything, was still firmly in place. But all that his glimpse of Other Power engendered was shame for not having prayed a better prayer; all that the boy's unspeakable courage made him feel was an even greater, even more hopeless love; and after the salts led the boy away and the men under the tree, the Captain, the entire fire base grew still and listened for the shots, all that this great love did was make Irwin start to weep and gibber like an insane man. Or maybe he *was* an insane man. Hunched in the dust, crazed fingers fumbling, he was a filth-covered, sobbing ruin of a man trying to clean, to reshape, to reload a mashed tube of paste when the salts squeezed their triggers. Irwin's head snapped back. His mouth flew open. Blood ran from his nostrils and spattered the ground. And the body the bullets were striking, the life that was ending, was a quarter mile away. "*Christ!*" he kept gasping. "*Good Christ.*"

CHAPTER FIVE

Our Mistake

Dying is easy. Comedy is hard.
  —last words of Edmund Kean, actor

1. Dudek's Sabbath School Lesson

Irwin vaguely knew—when he woke in the darkness—that he had crossed some kind of line. The same crushing pain that made it impossible to remember made it impossible to forget that he had, in some kind of battle frenzy, destroyed the life he'd been leading, so that he would never have to go back to it again. But in the throes of his rage, everything had felt like a dream. From the time he'd heard the salts' rifles he'd seen nothing with any clarity—till he woke in this blackness.

He was lying on something cool but terribly hard—sheet metal, he guessed finally. And his entire skull felt broken. But when he tried to cradle it, something stopped his wrists. Handcuffs. He was cuffed to a steel floor. He stretched out a leg, found a bulge in the metal, explored it with his foot: a wheel well. A vehicle. He realized he must be locked in the empty water truck Dudek sometimes used for a brig. And the reason his head felt like it was splitting was that it must really be split. Bandaged too, it seemed. Just like the boy's.

The boy. The thought of him brought it all back at once. It had not been a dream. He'd done it. He really *had* marched down to the Captain's tent, the crushed Gleem tube on his shoulder like a rifle. And he had taken his tiny rifle and shot and shot poor Dudek, point-blank and right in the mouth, till fragments of teeth, shreds of lip and metallic ribbons of tube floated in the red-and-white foam. *Take!* he'd sung, ramming it in. *Eat!* he'd sung. *Let it shine, let it shine,* till something slammed his skull. *Crazy muthahfuck!* But he'd pulled Dudek down with him, still singing, still shoving, till the fireworks, the explosion, caved his mind completely in—

leaving him this metal bed, these handcuffs, this utter blackness.

Good, good and good.

So I am not, he told himself, *a captain's aide anymore. Nor his manservant or maidservant, nor his ox or ass, nor any other thing that is a captain's. Hell, I'm not even a soldier now, probably. And it'll be jail or worse, and Mama so sad, and Everett so proud, and fuck off, both of you! Let it shine!*

He started to laugh, but a blaze of pain shot straight from his forehead down his throat and left him moaning. Yet he still risked a smile. A little harsh, a little iffy his performance seemed now. But how strange and right it felt as Dudek squealed and gurgled and rolled his eyes. The joy that Samson must have known! Helpless as a child, the Captain seemed, his teeth snapping off like chalk. And the eloquence, the sermon, the Army logic that had been the boy's true killer had issued from that mouth. Shoot him with bullets, the mouth said, when Irwin wanted to shoot him with toothpaste. He doesn't exist, it said. So the closest thing to justice had been to show the mouth and everyone it commanded that the boy *had* existed, and that Gleem too can teach lessons that won't soon be forgotten.

2. Buttercups

On Friday, May 25, Everett spent the evening working on a letter to Natasha. He'd spent a few evenings this way, actually: his letter was on page 208. The Russianistic references, antique ink-pens, parchment paper, peasant shirts and all of that good stuff had fallen by the wayside, however. His pen of choice these days was a 19¢ Bic, his parchment a Big Chief 500 tablet, and though it's risky to ascribe pure motives even to a saint, let alone to Everett, I think it's safe to say in this case that he was not out to show off, to disingenuously woo, or to in any way deceive his lost love with the massive letter—because this letter wasn't going anywhere: he had no address to which to mail it.

We never know, with regard to the inner life, who or when lightning is going to strike. Often we don't even know when we ourselves are the one so stricken. On the morning of May 25, Everett didn't even believe in "an inner life." But that did not prevent him from having one. And this was his best attempt to describe it, that evening, to a woman he believed would never see his description:

I was hiking a south-sloping headland on the Strait this morning, trudging along in a funk the beautiful but long-lost cause of which chivalry demands that I not name, when the sun burst out of the fog, and so did I, I guess, because all of a sudden I found myself standing so funkless that I felt naked in a huge marshy meadow just blazing with early summer buttercups. A sunlit lake of brilliant yellow, Natasha. With me gasping, nearly drowning in the middle of it. And I'd scarcely noticed the coming of spring.

The word "stunning" may describe this meadow. But not "stunning" the adjective: this yellow hit like a fist. This was Stunning the Noun. And in Its presence (odd as this may sound) Everett the Noun vanished.

Want proof that I vanished? Probably not, knowing you. But being the skeptical sort, I do. So let me mull this event over a little:

You and I didn't make it close enough to Spring for you to learn this about me, but I've never liked to pick flowers. Blossoming is a sexual activity, and anything engaged in sex ought, it seems to me, to be left alone. Yet in the lake of buttercups, the instant after I vanished, what remained in my place dropped Stunned to its knees and began, regardless of my opinion, to pick buttercups as fast as it could work its fingers.

Looking back on it now, I suspect this was an act of pure gratitude not on my part, but on the part of the entire headland. My part, I think, was just to stumble into some sort of primordial Gratitude Zone. I'm making this up as I go along, but doesn't it seem obvious that when a wild headland feels the sun after six months of rain, colorlessness, cold and whatever it calls its winter loneliness (only the old spruce trees can pronounce this word right, and it takes them all six winter moons to do it), it, the headland, goes on a growing and blooming and mating and sprouting spree? And at the height of this spree isn't it possible that all that burgeoning life and energy could pile up in certain places, just the way dead leaves and melancholy pile up in places in the Fall, forming little springtime ecstasy zones—places you might call "over-joyed"? And having survived the same rain, cold and six-moon-spruce-tree-word-for-loneliness, couldn't my bones and blood have become sufficiently entwined in the whole process that when I stumbled into the Buttercup Zone, kapoof! I vanished in it, and was able to think and feel nothing but the headland's rapturous involvement in sunlight and groundwater and warming soil and rising sap and photosynthesis and blinding color and life, life, life? That's sure how it felt, Tasha. And knowing my taste in these matters, it seems even now that it could only have been a piece of the headland itself, not an Everett, that dropped to its knees and began, without thinking or qualm, to admire itself by harvesting a few of its own beautiful blossoms.

Was that a proof? Sure doesn't look like one to me. Yet when the headland let me go today I had its small, ecstatic, bright-yellow answer to Winter in my hand. And as I write these lines that answer is standing in a red and white Campbell's Chicken Noodle Soup can (I'm eating the can's previous tenants) in the center of the bright red kitchen table. And I wish I was poet enough to show you how they take the red table-top and the two blue candles and the grease-pearled bowl of industrial broth and even the label of the can ("SOUP IS GOOD FOOD!" it cries) and turn it all into a still life, a work of art, a thing of beauty. But boy am I not that poet.

I feel myself on the verge of getting silly now—probably to hide from another bad habit of mine: loneliness. But I promised when I sat down tonight to try my very best to show you two simple things without voicing my silliness, or my loneliness. One was this bouquet of buttercups. The other was the moment I vanished, and allowed them to harvest themselves.

Here they are, Natasha.

Goodnight.

3. Testimony

Irwin was not court-martialed for his attack on Captain Dudek. What the Army chose instead was to give him a battery of psychiatric tests and a sanity hearing.

Ten days after this hearing, a pale green nine-by-twelve envelope arrived at our house in Camas, addressed to "Mrs. Irwin D. Chance." It had come from the Colonel James Loffler Mental Health Center—a military-run mental institution in Mira Loma, California, east of Los Angeles. There were two documents inside. The first was a three-page letter from the head of Loffler Center, an Army major and doctor of psychiatry named Richard Keys. It told, briefly and technically, of the attack on Dudek, of the damage to his lips, tongue, gums, teeth and hands, of the two concussions and "slight" skull fracture Irwin had received from Dudek's rescuers, of the eyewitness accounts, expert psychiatric testimony and other evidence given at the hearing, and of Irwin's permanent release from active duty on psychiatric grounds. It said that Irwin had been flown shortly after his hearing from Saigon to Los Angeles and Mira Loma, where he'd been diagnosed as psychotic and violent and confined in the appropriate ward. It did not once mention the Vietcong boy. It did say that by the time we received the letter, Irwin would have been given "EST"—a term that baffled us till Major Keys began to elaborate on its benefits. Then it terrified us: EST, we realized, was electroshock therapy. Major Keys added that Irwin's chances for "the fastest and most complete recovery possible" would be "enhanced by a simple, carefully controlled environment." For that reason, he said, "the presence of any visitors, especially his loved ones, would add little but agitation and confusion at this delicate juncture."

The second document in the envelope was a stenographer's transcript of the account Irwin gave, at his sanity hearing, of his attack on Dudek. Major Keys had included it, he told Linda, "to help give you and your family at least a partial picture of your husband's unfortunate condition." But it did better than that. It painted us a near-complete picture—of a man declared insane for simply being himself.

Here is the transcript:

I know I hurt Captain Dudek and I like Captain Dudek. But the thing is, Linda. Nash has your ears she wrote me. So think. An ear. So small! I never met my son yet, but picture him. Picture his ears, like I did on that Cong boy. Because don't they, ears, work because of tiny little bones? Doesn't nothing but the wiggles our voice makes on air vibrate them? So imagine! The perfect delicateness! Or delicacy the word is. Of such bones. And my son has your ears she said. Linda. Then here this little Cong boy was, see? With one ear, my son I never met, all bloody where that guard, that idiot New Jersey hit him, never thinking, good God, what we must have done to make him want to kill Bobby or us or anybody else on earth. I mean how many little kids you know want to kill? And if they do, why? Who did what to them first? So what we did to his father, or to the mother who carried and bored him, or birth [laughs], you know, gave birth, I'm bad at words. But what happened to her, who he loved and who loved him. That's what I was feeling. And now paint her white or black or some American color. Make her my mother, or yours. Then make her dead. And now make him your own little brother, out there trying to kill her killers. Now it's different, isn't it? Now he's courageous, isn't he, and you love him, don't you, because.

Ha [laughs]. Okay. I see you don't want to. They're the enemy, I know, we're here to kill them, I know, and if I wasn't raised like I was or didn't have a baby or hadn't seen him so close maybe I could have kept him an enemy too. But after they shot him and I lay there knowing it was a child, a brave little brother, it was my own baby's ears we'd just shot, how can love ever operate in the Army is what I started feeling. Because isn't that the real problem here? It sure is <u>my</u> problem. 'Cause I'm a Christian. Or was. And Christ's love doesn't work, is what we feel in the Army. That kind of shit gets you killed here, it's an eye for an eye here, if Christ's love was real this whole war couldn't be happening. That's what we feel. But after he was gone and I'd so barely tried to stop them, how would I know, is what I started feeling. Because how can Christ's love operate anywhere, ever, if some fool doesn't just start to operate it? Some do, you know. Operate it I mean. Like here! This guy right here! Take a bow, Sergeant Felker! Okay don't. But he saved my life, this big fella. He doesn't even like me [laughs], but he crawled back to a place that could've got him killed just to save me. And that's love, see? Right here in the United States Army.

Except usually, I started thinking, right before the toothpaste thing, these thoughts were, usually it comes too late. Army love I mean. <u>Retroactive!</u> That's the word! Ha. These sedatives aren't so bad.

Retroactive love. That's the kind the Armed Forces has. The one kind that never does anybody any real good. Because Bobby Calcagno, let's get him into it here, let's admit he's the reason for every bit of this. But I loved Bobby too, and knew him better than most of you, maybe. And a little enemy boy, killing him out of love for Bobby, do you think that helped anything? Do you think Bobby wanted that? He would've hated it. Hated it! Retroactive! That's all it was. But that's how we're programmed, that's the button Captain Dudek pushed. So stuff the goddamned programming, was what I started feeling. Smash the goddamned armor the Army stuffed your heart in! Because an eye for an eye is smart, see, but love is dumb, lovers are fools. And I should've been fool enough for that boy, like Sergeant Felker was for me, to operate a little love by that jeep [*laughs, begins to cry*]. Don't you see? While his brown eyes, his ears, those tiny bones were still wriggling I should have been fool enough to beg them, or fight them, or scare them some way. I could've rammed that jeep with my head! I could've ate dirt! I could've stripped naked, shredded my face, anything, anything! till they saw you can't take a child, not ours, not theirs, you just can't take a child and treat him like a, like [*cries*]. I'm sorry. I'm sorry. But you do see, don't you? I had to hold on to him. My way, my truth, my life [*laughs, cries*]. That's all that little boy was. So too late, out of love for what I'd let die, retroactive as hell again, see, I took everything the Army turned me into and jammed it back into the mouth, Dudek's mouth, that said the boy doesn't exist, shoot him.

You don't understand [*laughs*]. I can see that. It's just too simple, is maybe the trouble. Just Irwin again, I wanted to be. Just this fool who loved kids. But I'm the moron who joined you. So do what you have to. Let it shine [*laughs*].

And hey. Thanks for listening.

4. My Brother's Keeper

For the first time in years, our ragged Camas household shared a passion: we all longed to disobey Major Keys's advice and visit Mira Loma as soon as possible. But Southern California was a long way off, and there were serious obstacles for all of us:

Linda had Nash to take care of, she didn't yet drive, and the news about Irwin seemed to render her almost catatonic with fear. Her reaction was so extreme that it struck me as cowardly at first, or at least annoyingly pathetic. Then Mama quietly reminded me that, sometime this coming summer, Linda's dad was due out of prison.

The twins were in their last week of school before eighth-grade graduation, they were indispensable part-time employees of Mama's, and they were also very busy, since Linda had come unglued, taking care of Nash.

Mama's housecleaning and dessert-making businesses were thriving, in fact our household economy would have collapsed without them; but they were also so dependent upon her arcane knowledge, energy and hands-on expertise that they would disintegrate if she didn't take a few days to train a proxy.

Unfortunately for my own longing to visit Irwin, I was that proxy. On top of that, I was trying to gear up for finals and write three different term papers. And on top and under and around and through that, I had fallen in love.

Her name was, and still is, Amy. And she was not a chapter in my life: she was, and still is, the central figure in an enormous subsequent volume. So suffice it to say in this volume that she was the person who gave me the courage to see that in order to love and serve one's land and people, in order not to betray the very things that patriots claim to hold dear, one must sometimes defy what is called "one's country." I never took my finals, never wrote the term papers, never went back to college though I knew it would cost me my deferment. And Amy and I had made meager preparations—as I awaited my induction papers—to join Everett in British Columbia, if it came to that. But, as I mentioned already, at my induction physical late that summer, my left eye kept me in the country of my choice.

Papa, on the day we phoned to read him the contents of the pale green envelope, was in Phoenix, Arizona, with the Portland Tugs. Phoenix was only an eight- or nine-hour drive from Mira Loma, but Papa was in the middle of a three-city Southwest road trip, and his baseball situation, after six amazingly stable seasons, had become tenuous again. What happened was that his friend and manager, Johnny Hultz, had jumped to the Seattle Pilots in 1969, then moved with the entire Seattle team to Milwaukee in '70, where he became the expansion Brewers' first hitting coach. The Tugs had been through three managers since. The third was a semifamous ex-Pirate infielder who as of this writing is still busy fucking up the mood of a major league team. We'll call him Howie Bowen. The Tugs were off to a fast start anyhow, thanks partly to luck and partly to Bowen's heavy but unacknowledged reliance on the advice of the team's pitching coach, stupid-situation reliever and philosopher king, Papa Toe

Chance. But the good start only seemed to intensify Bowen's toxic personality. His response to Papa's request for permission to leave the team long enough to visit Irwin, for instance, was to shout, "What are wives for, Chance? We need you here, dammit!"

Papa didn't argue. He just quietly informed his manager that he'd rejoin the Tugs in Tucson the following night, and that if Bowen didn't like it he could fine him. "I was *kidding*," Bowen lied, slapping Papa on the shoulder. "Mellow out, Papa T." He then proved his goodwill by autographing a baseball for Papa to take to Irwin. Papa was polite. He waited till he was outside Bowen's office before he rifled it into a trash can.

Papa rented a car, drove straight through the night to Mira Loma, and reached Loffler Center on Thursday, May 24, just as a pair of military police were unlocking the chain-link front gates. And he was surprised, as he crossed the sterilized-looking grounds, by the rush of gratitude he felt: just knowing that Irwin was back on North American soil had him trembling with something close to joy.

But the instant he walked into the white cinder-block building he seemed to leave U.S. soil and enter some kind of Kafka plot. The faceless, bloodless, self-perpetuating malevolence of institutions was almost unknown to Papa. He hadn't read Kafka, and lifelong poverty had spared him any intricate dealings with the IRS. So it was a disoriented amazement he felt, more than fear or anger, when he was forced to spend four solid hours sitting in a lobby before he was even able to meet with Major Keys. This disorientation deepened into a swooning sensation when he was informed—after an interminable Keys monologue that told him a lot about types of battle fatigue but nothing about Irwin's actual condition —that visiting hours were over for the day, that a visit was "inadvisable in any case," but that if he still insisted on seeing Irwin he could return at ten the next morning. The time had already come, Papa realized, to fight. Yet the swooning sensation was so strong that he felt himself smiling and couldn't make himself stop, even as he explained his desperate need to rejoin his ballclub that night.

Major Keys said he sympathized but his hands were tied. Visiting hours were from 10 A.M. to noon, and exceptions were "strictly against regulations."

"You're telling me," Papa said, still smiling, "that you actually have a regulation against exceptions to regulations?"

Major Keys, smiling back, said that this was correct.

"What's your job then, Major?" Papa asked. "Sounds like the whole place is on automatic pilot to me."

Keys's laugh was like Morse code: one long, a few shorts. Then, without smiling, he said, "I enforce the regulations."

"Who might I talk to," Papa asked, "about a regulation that would allow me to make an exception to the no-exception regulation?"

"There is no such regulation," said the Major.

"Well, who has the power to make up a new regulation?"

"The psychiatric staff of the United States Pentagon," said Keys.

"Tell you what, Major," Papa sighed. "Rather than bother those busy fellas, why don't you and I just sign whatever needs signing and I'll take my son off your hands here and now?"

Keys let out another long and a few shorts, then erased every trace of goodwill from his face. "You'll see why in the morning, Mr. Chance. And now I've got work to do." And with that he shot out of his chair, out of his office, and disappeared into the labyrinth of immaculate hallways.

So Papa had no choice but to deal with Howie Bowen again, asking if he could meet the team in Albuquerque tomorrow instead of Tucson today. "If a fine's fine with you," quoth Bowen, "that's fine with me." Papa just shook his head and hung up the phone. He then called us in Camas, gave us an irritable update, ate a fast-food dinner, checked into a motel, and spent another near-sleepless night.

But at ten the next morning Major Keys informed him that Irwin was "finally resting after a very rough episode" and that it would be hard on him if Papa disturbed that rest. Braced this time for the onslaught of institutional nonsense, Papa told the Major that he was going to have to inflict that hardship.

"As you wish," said Keys. And he summoned a nurse, who led Papa through a series of steel doors and tube-lit hallways, then paused by a reinforced indoor window looking in on a large, glaringly white, sunlit room. Seeing, in bolted-down chairs, the slack or contorted forms of eight or nine of the most broken-looking men he'd ever laid eyes on, Papa was impatient when the nurse unlocked the door and stepped inside. He thought she was tending to some irrelevant duty en route to Irwin's room, wasting more of his time. Even when she turned to him and nodded, he didn't understand for a moment. Then he panicked. The young man nearest the window. The one slumped so far forward that only his chest strap kept him from falling out of his chair. The one whose shaved and battered skull he'd glanced at and then away from, thinking, *Poor bastard, worst of the lot . . .*

Irwin.

The scabs and fracture lines showing through the shaved hair—from the rifle butts of Dudek's rescuers. The twisted, unrecognizable nose—smashed by Sergeant Felker's "Army love." Papa rushed into the room, knelt beside him, stroked his hands, half sobbed his name. Irwin's expression didn't change. His lips were slack. His lap was damp with drool. His eyes sometimes sloshed, sometimes jittered in their sockets. And he didn't know Papa from the nurse, the other patients, the walls of the room.

All that kept Papa from weeping was his rage. He held Irwin a while, told him he'd be back as soon as could, hugged him goodbye, then told the nurse, "Take me, right now, to Major Keys."

She seemed to attempt it: she took him straight to Keys's office. But the Major wasn't in it. So Papa ended up back out in the same empty lobby, where for two more hours his fury just kept making the rounds of his own bloodstream. He was then told, by one of the secretaries he kept unmercifully pestering, that Major Keys had gone home for the weekend.

Papa's first stop after leaving the asylum was a 7-Eleven, where his first purchase was a quart of Colt 45 malt liquor and his second a carton of Lucky Strikes. Toss an old ballplayer into a Kafka nightmare and the least he'll do is try to poison it back around into something recognizably American.

His second stop was the 7-Eleven's phone booth, in which he lit a cigarette, opened the malt liquor, and attempted some one-man long-range recon by calling LA and Pasadena and San Fernando and Riverside and San Bernardino and San Diego directory assistance, trying to find the residence or phone number of a Major or Richard or Dick or Rich Keys. When that failed, he sat down in the car with his Colt 45 and took stock of the situation: if he stayed in Mira Loma till Monday he'd miss the Tugs and have to fly back to Portland at his own expense—and Bowen really would fine him, if he hadn't already; he was almost out of cash, had never owned a credit card, and if he wrote checks for another day's motel and car, they'd bounce; there was little chance, on Monday, that he'd learn anything from Keys; anything he did learn would probably be no help; he really had no choice but to rejoin the Tugs. Yet to leave Irwin limp and drooling like that felt like leaving him to die.

5. Monosodium Glutamate

On Saturday, May 26, Everett was awakened early in his caretaker's cottage by a banging at his door. When he opened it, Chief Yulie's daughter, Corey, stood holding a Western Union telegram from Papa, sent care of the Muskrat. Everett thanked her, shut the door, tore the envelope open. The telegram said:

CALL ME COLLECT ASAP IN ALBUQUERQUE AT 505–787–6501 OR BACK IN CAMAS IF I LEFT STOP IRWIN'S LIFE IN TERRIBLE DANGER STOP LOVE PAPA

Everett jumped into his clothes, drove through dense morning fog to Shyashyakook's one and only and unlucky phone booth, reached Papa at his Albuquerque motel just as the Tugs were climbing on the bus, and heard a terribly rushed version of what had happened to Irwin. Everett's overwhelming first reaction was relief. "Even a loony bin," he told Papa, "is a step up from 'Nam. He's alive, and physically whole, and sooner or later the sons of bitches'll have to let him go." But in a voice ravaged by sleeplessness and smoke, Papa said, "What they let out of that asylum may be alive, but it won't be Irwin." And Everett grew frightened—so frightened that he reacted angrily, demanding that Papa explain.

"I've got no time," Papa said. But the tone of his voice explained everything. "Listen, Everett. If you think of anything at all, legal or not, that might get Irwin out of that place, call us in Camas and we'll discuss it. And *please*. Think hard. And think fast."

With that, Papa signed off.

And Everett found he couldn't think at all.

He drove back home, boiled his three morning eggs, made some sulfurous coffee, sat down to drink it—

and found himself staring at the buttercups. But in the bleak morning gray the sight of them was suddenly troubling. They were still a lovely color, still a clutch of blossoms blithely opening to daylight, still a reminder of his little epiphany on the headland the day before. But their very blitheness now disturbed him. They seemed to have no idea what had happened to them. They seemed to feel, thanks to the greasy water in their soup can and the gray light pouring through the window, that they still stood wild in their south-sloping meadow, and still had green bodies and hidden roots. His eyes lurched around for some more soothing morning cud. He tried the Campbell's label. It said "OFFICIAL

SOUP OF THE WINTER OLYMPICS." It said. "INSPECTED FOR WHOLESOMENESS." It said lots of things he'd never noticed. "EXPOSITION UNIVERSELLE INTERNATIONALE 1900," for instance. Or "SIMPLE SUGARS (GRAMS) 1, COMPLEX CARBOHYDRATES (GRAMS) 7." He noticed gold ink on the label as well as the obvious black, red and white. He noticed the way the O in the word SOUP listed off to one side, like the can drunk. Then, by accident, he glanced too high, and noticed that his buttercups had also begun to list. They were no longer standing the way he'd stood them, no longer engaged in the glorious basking that overwhelmed him on the headland. They were leaning toward the light now, *craning* toward it. He'd been dead wrong about the blitheness. The buttercups now seemed to know—to understand with that purely physical knowledge that all living things possess—that something was wrong. Their craning was like a cry: they were calling out with all the body language they possessed for a life or a place they had no minds with which to remember.

Confused by the intensity of his feelings, Everett tried to defy them: he gave the can a half twist, spinning the blossoms away from the window, then stepped outside and went about his morning chores. Hoping to clear his head and come up with a fabulous rescue plan for Irwin, he worked like a dog and left his thoughts to compost. But a few hours later, having moved a cord of wood, fixed a fence, and fitted a new handle in an ax that deer, or Booger, had gnawed for salt, he passed by the kitchen window, took a glance, and saw that the buttercups were again craning toward the light. Then he made an association he regretted at once: he realized they reminded him of Irwin.

Drifting back into the cottage, he sat down at the table, gave the flowers another half twist away from the window, and this time cupped his bare hands over them, blocking their "view" of the gray light. Bracing his elbows, ignoring the pain that gathered in his shoulders, he remained there, motionless, with his hands cupped low over the blossoms. It took time. It took a long, long time. But, ever so slowly, the buttercups swung round till their thin necks again craned and their blind faces followed the course of the sun.

So, he thought, unsure whether to hope or to weep with despair. *Yearning can pierce a hand.*

"MONOSODIUM GLUTAMATE," said the soup can.

6. Imagination Time

The sedatives, Major Keys told both my parents over the phone on Monday morning, were being administered primarily because without them Irwin would "rave." And if the Loffler staff tried to quell his raving, he would become violent.

Mama asked for a description of the raving. With the help of a file, Keys gave her a direct quote. "Jesus loves the little children," he recited without a hint of modulation or emotion. "All the children of the world. Black and yellow, brown and white, they are precious in his sight, pouring out their blood so red, till they're dead, they're dead, they're dead . . ."

Papa, wielding a pencil and paper, asked the Major what sedatives he was giving Irwin, and what dosages. His charts weren't available, Keys said, because they were in use. "The electroshock, then," Papa asked. "How much? How many times?"

Keys: "I'm afraid that's on the charts."

"Who recommends or prescribes it or whatever the word is? Who approves the electroshock?" Papa asked.

"I do," said Keys.

"And you don't know how many treatments you've given him?"

"Maybe three," said the Major. "But I can't swear to it. I have a great many patients, Mr. Chance."

"Three in two weeks," Mama said. "Is that normal? Isn't that a lot?"

"It's a little unusual," Keys admitted. "And I could be wrong. But Vietnam vets are an unusual class of patient, Mr. and Mrs. Chance. And your son, I'm sorry to tell you, is an exceptionally stubborn case."

"How so?" Mama asked.

"Part of the problem is his robustness, his great physical strength."

"That's a problem, as you see it," Mama said.

"Coupled with his religious indoctrination, yes. Your son indulges in sociopathic behaviors, but believes them justified. His attack on Captain Dudek, for instance. He feels he did it for Jesus. Add physical strength to that kind of delusion and you have a very dangerous young man on your hands."

Mama's voice began to tremble. "Did you know, Major, that everything that boy has done in his life he has tried to do for Jesus?"

"Including acts of insubordination, psychotic attacks, attempted murder?"

"Our son Irwin," Papa said, quietly but vehemently, "is the least violent human I have ever met. Bar none. That's what got him into this."

"You're entitled to your opinion, Mr. Chance. But in view of the facts, and the accepted definition of the word 'violent,' I don't know what you're talking about."

"What he's talking about," Mama said, "and what you Army people keep conveniently forgetting, is that young boy Captain Dudek ordered shot. Because that's what set Irwin off. He couldn't bear it. Because antiviolent—that's what he really is. Loving, is what he is. And you can't just shock and drug that out of him, you can't kill the Christian in him and call that a cure!"

"Calm yourself, Mrs. Chance," said the Major. "We're trying to help your son. And we're not killing anything. What we're actually—"

"Matthew eighteen, six!" Mama shouted into the receiver. "Mark nine, forty-two! Luke seventeen, two! 'But whoso shall offend one of these little ones which believe in me, it were better for him that a millstone were hanged about his neck, and that he were drowned in the depth of the sea!' That, Major Keys, is what brought on our son's attack!"

"Please," said the Major. "Please calm yourself and try to listen, Mrs. Chance. I'm very sorry to say this, I'm sorry if it shocks you both. But it is my belief—based on the testimony of every rational witness at your son's hearing—that this 'boy' Irwin keeps referring to simply does not, and never did, exist."

Linda and the twins were watching Mama when Keys said these words. They say that she turned gray instantly and sat down on the bed. And for the rest of the call she never spoke a word. I was in the kitchen with Papa, and had no idea what Keys was saying. All I knew was that one moment Papa was standing at the sink staring angrily out the window, and the next he had sunk down in a catcher's squat. But he didn't look like a catcher. He looked like a man who'd been kicked in the stomach. Very quietly, very cautiously, he said, "Let me ask this, Major. How would Irwin need to behave, what is it you're waiting to see, in order for him to be released, or at least transferred to a facility closer to his home?"

"Well." Keys gave it some thought. "We'd have to see a complete cessation of the singing episodes, the religious delusions and the violent mood swings. And of course the physical attacks on our staff—those must be months behind him."

"Months!" Papa cried.

"We can't release a man who attacks nurses and orderlies, Mr. Chance."

"Attacks," Papa said, shaking his head. "It's so hard, for us who know him, to believe, Major. You're saying that Irwin sometimes just stands up, undrugged and unprovoked, attacks people, and then sings, or somehow conveys, that he's doing it all for Jesus?"

"We're not careless enough to allow him to hurt people, Mr. Chance. But you've read what he did to Captain Dudek. And he still lashes out. You and your family, for your own safety, had better start to accept the fact that your son's condition makes him dangerous."

"This violence," Papa said, and now I could see him fighting panic. "May I ask if he's already drugged when it happens? Or if he's just refusing the sedatives? Because in the first case, couldn't the drugs themselves cause the behavior? And in the second, he hates pills, Irwin does." Papa heard his voice rising, heard his anger and fatherliness and frustration all spilling out. But he couldn't stop himself. "Chewable vitamins, baby aspirin even. He spits 'em, hates 'em, can't handle 'em at all. That's *normal* for Irwin, Major. And the songs. They're juvenile, I know, and the lyrics are silly, some of them. But he's sung them since childhood, and not just at church. In bed at night, at work, in the hallways at school, football practice—the other players used to gripe to the coach. He *always* sings. Always prays too. This kid is *loud*, Major Keys. And he wears his heart on his sleeve. It's an embarrassment at times, we know, but he really does love his cockeyed Jesus. It's what's inside him, you see. So it's important, *crucial* even, isn't it, that you and your staff not try to just wipe that away?"

When Papa finally fell silent, the Major said nothing. He just hung on the line, breathing, until my parents fully grasped the fact that their intimate understanding, their years of experience, their whole history with and love for their son meant absolutely nothing to him. "We understand 'normal,'" Keys said at last. "And I can see that you're a doting mother and father. That's commendable, in its place. And it may prove helpful, after his release. But your son, I must remind you, is psychotic. And it's the psychosis we're working to eliminate, not his virtues, whatever you imagine those to be. It's been very instructive, this chat. Most helpful. I'm grateful to you both. But now, once again, I'm afraid I'm out of time."

"But can we come down and see him?" Papa asked. And now he looked and nearly sounded like a pathetic, pleading child. "Can we come down tomorrow? The whole family, I mean?"

"During visiting hours, I suppose. If you think it serves a purpose. But it's a very long drive, Mr. Chance. And you'd have to visit him one at a time."

"But it'd be worth it, we wouldn't mind the drive at all, if there was any way you could just— Listen, Major. Please. Couldn't you ease up on the drugs enough so we could talk with him? Because he's probably confused. And all together we could explain, or try, what he has to stop doing, how he needs to behave, to get out of there. Because Irwin really is, how would you say it, on sort of a different program. But he's not dumb. And he's not mean. So if you'd just let him out of the haze, I think maybe he'd—"

"Frankly, Mr. Chance," the Major interrupted, "my best advice to you is to be patient. I warned Irwin's wife that it's far too early for the kind of visit you're describing. I also warned that the sight of Irwin might upset you at this stage. But we're making progress, believe me. We are *helping* your son. And right now you can help him too, Mr. and Mrs. Chance, by trusting us. We're very experienced in these matters. So give us time. Show a little faith. Is that too much to ask?"

Papa managed, by sinking again into a squat, to lie that it wasn't.

Mama couldn't make herself say anything at all.

So it was Imagination Time at the Chances', and Try to Sleep and Not See This, I Dare You, Time. It was Close Your Eyes and Watch Irwin on the Gurney Time, rolling down the white corridors, strapped down, preferably unsedated ("Better that they feel it," a nurse had confided to Papa), singing some one of his favorite songs, "Down in My Heart," say, or "Yes, Jesus Loves Me." Too scared to ad-lib, just the straight Sabbath stuff now. But it was this singing, Keys assured us, that lay at the heart of his "dyscrasia"—a fine term, dyscrasia, pettifogging, mist-enshrouded, immune to puncture by any sort of point, *verbum sapienti sat est*, eh, Major?, one magic word, *dyscrasia*, and Keys's ignorance became science, Irwin's singing became raving, his faith became violence, his memory became delusion, the joy joy joy down in his heart became his disgrace, and his mind could be raped and emptied with moral exaltation. "Trust us, Mr. and Mrs. Chance." It was dyscrasia that brought the Cong Boy Phantasm to life, dyscrasia that cost noble Dudek his teeth, dyscrasia that fired off every time the sedatives ran down, forcing another nurse with a syringe, or better, two orderlies with a terribly snug but stylish jacket to come running—Snowmen, Irwin called them, when an unintended lapse in medication once allowed him a moment's speech. So back in Camas, on the Deccan Plateau, by the Juan de Fuca Strait, in the back bedrooms, classrooms, dugouts and train cars of our lives, we the lifelong admirers and teasers and cultivators and sharers of his dyscrasia heard him constantly—singing as they rolled him into the place he called the Snow Room; singing as he smelled, through all the layers of antiseptic, the stench of terror that burst through the pores of the myriad mad who lay in that room before him; singing as they doubled the straps on his wrists and ankles (Keys: "his robustness a problem"), the Snowmen laughing at the futile little lyrics, *Jesus loves me, this I know* as the conductive salve was rubbed into his temples, *For the Bible tells me so* as the electrodes were taped to the salve, *Little ones to Him belong* as they slid the thing like a Little League batter's helmet onto his head, *They are weak but He is strong* as they jammed the soft plastic mouthpiece straight into the singing—"Spit this out" (the fierce Snowman named Denny) "and your lunch'll be the sausage your teeth make of your tongue"—impossible to make words now, so trying to hum through the mouthpiece, to hold fast to a chorus or melody, to a Name, or to naked love alone, when the explosion came. Then the unbearable lull, the insane-making wait, any man or woman, any poet-saint or bodhisattva on earth a gibbering lunatic now, knowing as they waited that their plastic-clogged humming could not possibly be enough; knowing that no mind, in mid-explosion, can hold to even the simplest thought; knowing they'd be blasted away, erased, pure white again; and not knowing whether a rebuildable rubble, a few shards of selfhood, would remain when, from the wreckage, the body next arose.

We all had decent imaginations. We knew about how it would go. Because Zaccheus kept clutching as he drifted down the Mekong, because the boy kept winding his watch, because of the mathematical theories of Christ and Coach Basham ("seventy times seven," "a hundred and ten percent"), we knew how hard Irwin would try when it hit: *Yes, Jesus loves me, yes, Jeeeuuach! Aeeucch! Aeeucch!* But we also knew there could be no remnant of his mind in the body that slammed up and down on the table, no remnant of song in the voice going *ungh! ungh! ungh!*, no similarity between the delicate blend of muscle, affection, nonsense and faith we called Irwin and the thing the orderlies rolled, still jerking and flopping like a fish with no river, back down the long white halls.

We knew this, were scalded by it. We saw and heard it night and day. And still we couldn't help him.

7. Tony Baldanos' Sneak Photo

Tony Baldanos—the Portland Tugs' backup catcher—was a passionate amateur photographer. He was no lowbrow Kodachrome shutterbug either. Though economic considerations reduced him, during baseball season, to cheap color film and Fotomat slides, his photographic aspiration was to one day create classic black-and-white landscapes in the Edward Weston, Ansel Adams tradition. His motivation was sound too: as a third-year second-string catcher, Tony knew he might soon be needing a second-string career. But, as is often the case with Two-Art Artists, his baseball and his photography were terribly at odds.

Ballplayers need sleep, second-stringers especially so. But on the average baseball day Tony didn't even get to play. He therefore convinced himself that there was no harm in working on a photographic series he called "Motel Dawns." The series was not ambitious. It only required him to rise with the muezzins each morning, to wake up just enough to step outside with his camera, and to take an eastward-facing color photo of whatever neon-lit motel and city the Tugs happened to be ensconced in—with the hopefully beautiful or incongruous or artfully depressing or somehow interesting urban dawn dawning in the background. He would then, according to plan, jump back into bed and catch up on his baseball rest. The crimp in the plan, though, was that the artistic process got Tony so excited that he couldn't get back to sleep. So when—eight or twelve or sixteen hours later—Manager Howie Bowen would decide to pinch-hit or play him (never with any warning, never with any warm-up, and usually terribly late in a late-night game), Tony would be half sick with the need for sleep. As a result, he would play ball about like Ansel Adams. And so would think afterward: *I've had it as a ballplayer!* And so would reach, as he crawled into bed that night, for his camera (to be sure his backup career was loaded), then for his alarm clock, which he'd set once again for dawn.

This artistic struggle is why—on May 29, at 4:55 A.M.—Tony Baldanos was half dressed, out of bed, and looking out the third-floor window of the Whitetail Motor Lodge in Spokane, Washington, when he spotted what he considered a photo opportunity. What he saw didn't fit into his "Motel Dawns" series, but Tony dug out his camera and took the shot anyway. It turned out so nicely that the first print he ever had made of it —a now badly faded color 8 × 10—sits on my desk as I write these words.

Tony presented it to me because that day, May 29, happened to be my twentieth birthday. But enlarged and framed prints of the same photo now hang on walls in the homes of my mother, my Uncle Truman, my Uncle Marv and Aunt Mary Jane, every one of my brothers and sisters, and in the homes of several ex-Tugs, all with the same little inscription hiding, handwritten, on the back:

"Art heals. —Tony Baldanos, 1971."

The first thing most people notice in the photo is the bright purple and pink of the sky over the black, pine-covered ridge in the distance. Maybe the next thing most eyes are drawn to is the same pink and purple reflected in the Spokane River, which eddies from the upper right corner of the photo, down through black silhouettes of junipers in the foreground, and on out of the frame. Fishermen like to point out the swirls on the pink river surface, and usually surmise that they're trout rises. But those who know the river there (Uncle Truman, for instance) say they're most likely squawfish. Freddy—a gung ho birdwatcher—once said that the white patch in the largest juniper could be a small hawk or prairie falcon, or at the very least a magpie. Bet, though, thinks it's trash— maybe Styrofoam, blown over from the freeway on the other side of the motor lodge.

Be that as it may, about the last thing anyone notices is the thing that caught Tony's eye in the first place: the man on the big riverside boulder in the foreground. He's wearing a plaid flannel shirt, brown leather belt, baggy tan trousers, but you can't really see the colors: everything but his head is in silhouette. As Tony opened the shutter, though, the first rays of morning sun were striking his hair, turning it a vivid, almost flaming silver. And at the very same moment the man was exhaling smoke, which the same ray of dawn sunlight turned a lovely pale pink.

On the rock beside him stands a large Styrofoam coffee cup. ("Another falcon!" Bet likes to tell Freddy.) Beside the cup is a morning paper, folded open to what Tony sensibly assumes is an account of the previous night's doubleheader, which the Tugs and the Spokane Indians had split. The man on the rock had pitched five outs in the losing game, and had given up two runs on a single. But he'd inherited loaded bases. The story of his life. The story of all our lives.

It had been a wet spring—lots of rain cancellations: there would be another game against the Indians clear down in Portland that night, and a second doubleheader the very next day. The silver-haired man would almost certainly see action, and so would (like Tony Baldanos, who is now a successful but somewhat bored commercial photographer, but a near-legendary Babe Ruth baseball coach) very much need the sleep he was missing. He also did not need the cigarette. Yet it's the cigarette, more than anything except maybe the hair, that makes the photograph so striking in terms of color, and so haunting to those of us who know the man.

Whatever his needs, he had been sitting on the boulder since well before dawn, wearing the expression Irwin used to call "the Face" on his face. And his thoughts—though the face in the photo betrays nothing— were almost certainly so tormented that he couldn't have cared less how he himself was feeling. And yet that torment was misplaced. The man was making the same blunder, there on his rock by the river, that our entire family was making that day. We could all feel, we all knew in our bones or blood that something we loved, or someone, was rapidly dying.

Our mistake?

We thought that someone was Irwin.

CHAPTER SIX

The White Train

When I lived at Naples, there stood, at the door of my palace, a female mendicant to whom I used to pitch coins before mounting the coach. One day, suddenly perplexed at the fact that she never gave me any signal of thanks, I looked at her fixedly. It was then I saw that what I had taken for a mendicant was rather a wooden box, painted green, filled with red earth and some half-rotted banana peels.
—Max Jacob

Well into his year's research on the internationally known poet-saints of medieval Maharashtra, Peter discovered a subtradition he'd never previously heard of. Most of the poets involved were low-caste. Some were illiterate, their work collected only recently in Indian books of songs. But among them were several whose verse and apparent spiritual attainment had been of a very high order. In the missive that followed his "unplugged" letter to Dr. Ramchandra Majumdar back at Harvard, Peter described some of these poets, and explained a few of the difficulties in studying them (scattered and bowdlerized manuscripts, archaic and idiosyncratic dialects, reliable scholarship nonexistent, lives lost in folk legend). But he also shared his excitement over the apparent blending of Sufistic and Vedantic imagery he'd found in some of the verse, and included a few rough translations in his letter, including this, by a sixteenth-century seamstress, Anjana by name:

> *You hide your heart from the Dark Lord's arrows*
> *Then beg to be the post that pierces His ear.*
> *You dodge the dagger that would spill your blood*
> *Then ask to be the pen in His hand.*
> *"Bring the wine of love!" sing the hired* qawalis
> *While in your vineyard grapes rot on the vine.*
> *"Grind me to dust!" they wail, as you*
> *Bathe, then carefully dress for dinner.*
> *Singers sell yearning like courtesans their favors.*
> *Is this rented noise your refuge, O king?*
> *Anjana says: Empty prayers are the smile on the face*
> *Of the assassin. Arrows still yearn in the*
> *Quiver. The ink still yearns in the pen.*
> *The dust lies at your doorstep.*
> *The Dark Lord listens.*

In another prompt and heartening reply, Dr. Majumdar predicted that this "wondrous subtradition" would soon lead Peter not only to a second full-year grant but to the publication of a book of "much more than merely scholarly appeal." "But we have nothing at all on these poets here," the doctor added, "so be sure to lay the groundwork for a complete proposal before you return."

Peter therefore set to work on a second, simultaneous, full-scale research project. Fourteen-hour workdays became routine. Physical exercise and plain human intercourse became almost nonexistent. He also chose, so far as travel and research plans would allow, to become nocturnal, sleeping through the heat of the days and working all evening and night. As a result, he encountered the Indian crowds, chaos and squalor hardly at all, the tension inside him eased dramatically, and he decided that he had finally found his niche, that this hard, cerebral work was his calling, that the troubling inner conflict with India had resolved itself at last.

All winter and spring he lived and worked this way. He meditated twice a day, lived his waking life in libraries, traveled when he had to; he grew pale and quiet, emaciated himself on a diet of fruit, nuts and endless cups of chai, worked his brain hard, collapsed from exhaustion each dawn, slept like a rock. He seldom hurt, seldom laughed, never cried or shouted. He never answered our letters. He didn't remember his dreams. The Dark Lord listens.

Secunderabad / India / late May / 1971

Even on a long train journey, from Madras across the peninsula to Nasik, Peter kept to his owl-like schedule, working through the night in his private berth, falling to sleep in his bunk at dawn. But sometime after a brief, accidental wake-up in Hyderabad (luggage banging against his door as the train crept out of the city), Peter fell into a dream in which he was dying of some kind of fever—cholera or typhoid ("I theenk most poseebly both," a disconcertingly happy Hindu doctor kept telling him). And the dream grew so protracted and painful that he finally woke himself with his own groans—

to find that his sheets really *were* drenched with sweat, that he could hardly breathe, that his body was burning up.

Tearing open his window shade, he groped for a catch, lock or lever. But in first-class air-conditioned cars the windows don't open. He fell out of bed, pulled on his pants, flung open the door of his berth, and found himself gaping into the bloody—or no, just betel-stained—mouth of a tiny South Indian porter who began screaming, over and over, a sentence that sounded like *"Sahib yabbetahgabbetah!"*

Peter's first thought was that the man was trying to quarantine him. Then he realized that the porter too was sweat-drenched and short of breath, that the train was not moving, that it was the air inside the car, not his body, that was burning up. He asked, in Hindi, what had happened.

"Sahib yabbetahgabbetah!" came the reply.

He tried English, then what he hoped was Urdu.

"Yabbetahgabbetah! Yabbetahgabbetah!"

Moving the porter aside, he started down the corridor, saw that the entire car had been vacated, found an open window in a bathroom, stuck his head out, and saw that both the men's and the women's first-class cars were not only empty but sitting alone on a side track. He realized what must have happened: while he'd been sleeping the air-conditioning had failed, the stifling cars had been uncoupled, and the passengers had been moved to replacement cars.

Stepping back into the corridor, he saw the little porter staggering off in the other direction with his luggage, his drenched pillow and his forty-pound book bag all stacked on his head, now shouting, with beautifully rolled r's, "Trainsport, yes! Trainsport! Yes yes!" Hoping he meant transfer, Peter followed.

The man led him down the stairs on the opposite side of his car, through a teeming station crowd in what turned out to be the city of Secunderabad, and over to a bona fide train—or at least to a row of cars sitting on the main track, connected to an engine. And sure enough, in the windows of the very last car Peter was relieved to recognize the hot, disgruntled faces of some of his first-class co-travelers.

Then he recognized something else: every car in the train, his included, was one of the trusty open-air third-class jobs that Gandhi had cherished. Like Americanness, raw India is not so easy to escape.

The porter placed Peter's belongings upon the only vacant seat left in the car. He then moved up so close to Peter that it became impossible to move, and remained there, rigid as a statue. Peter was baffled—till he remembered his home-appliance servant, Lakshman. He then reached in his pocket, gave life to the porter-statue with a limp rupee, and watched it join its palms, bow, and disappear.

Digging his emergency purified-water bottle out of his suitcase, Peter drained it dry against his own better judgment, grabbed a couple of texts and a dictionary out of his book bag, stashed the rest of his gear in the chickenshit-spattered luggage rack, settled as comfortably as he could onto the impossibly uncomfortable bench, looked out the jail-like bars of the window, thought of bleacher seats, thought of church pews, thought of the three hundred circuitous miles and eight or ten stops between himself and his destination, and sighed out the single, quintessentially American word: "Shit."

"My sentiments exactly," said the man on the bench across from him.

Peter was surprised. The man's complexion and clothes, the small-boned body and diffident manner, the undersized wire-rimmed glasses and little Nehru cap all said India. But the accent was plainly East Coast Yankee—maybe Long Island. The man gave Peter an exhausted smile. "Was it Chesterton or Kipling who said that an adventure is just a misfortune correctly understood?"

Peter smiled back—a little too eagerly, perhaps, but the prospect of traveling with a man who could quote even Occidental literature beat the prospect of a man who could quote nothing. He said, "Was it Dickens or

Trollope who said that train travel isn't travel at all, it's being shipped off to a place like a parcel?"

Long Island rubbed his stiff neck and sighed. "If only we *were* parcels! But was it Johnson or Jonson, Sam or Ben, who said that the miserable are sacred?"

Peter smiled. "Neither, I suspect. And you know it, I further suspect. But wasn't it Socrates who said that becoming literate was a good way to forget who said everything?"

"No no no," Long Island countered. "The way to forget everything, Socrates said, is train travel."

Peter laughed, and began fishing through his head for another quotation. But before he'd come up with one an Indian boy of eleven or twelve burst into the car and began to emit a dreadful singsong sort of sales pitch. Or Peter assumed it was a pitch, since the kid was hawking wooden snakes. What it sounded like was a dirt bike with no muffler. The kid had a sales demo too: it consisted of squeezing a sample snake's scissorlike handles, causing it to extend in a lifelike strike right into a potential customer's face. Nor were these the only distractions the boy had to offer: his lips were crimson, his cheeks covered with rouge, his eyes and lashes black with something like mascara; he wore bangles on his wrists, brass bells round his ankles, and his hips were writhing like a stoned hula dancer's. "Mother of God," sighed Long Island. "Here comes our next adventure."

Peter shook his head. "I can't understand a word he's saying. Which by our definition makes him a misfortune, not an adventure, for me."

"So you don't speak these infernal languages either," his new friend said.

Peter shrugged. "I read Hindi and Marathi, but Indians speak both so fast I don't grasp one word in five. I carry a quote unquote Practical Urdu handbook, but usually can't tell when I'm hearing it, so I hardly know when to refer to it. I read and write Sanskrit, which is exactly as useful here as Latin is in, say, New Jersey. Ich spreche Deutsch. My name's Chance, by the way. Peter Chance."

"Dessinger," said Long Island, and the two Americans shook hands. But Dessinger was growing too irritated to talk. The snake boy was manipulatively, aggressively loud. "Is he some kind of transvestite or what?"

"I think he might be a Hijara," Peter said. "Which is nearly the same thing. I've never seen one, but they're an outcaste tribe of males who dress and behave like women. Or in this case, like a nasty parody of women. Good musicians, I read somewhere, but this kid shoots that theory too. Wealthy Hindus pay them to make merry at weddings and mourn at funerals. I heard they traveled in groups to protect themselves from persecution, but again, our young friend here seems—"

His discourse ended when the sample snake darted almost into his mouth. Peter smiled wanly and shook his head no.

The boy extended the snake into Dessinger's face. Dessinger ignored it. The boy chanted louder, writhed his hips faster, sent the snake striking forward again and again. Then it hit Dessinger's glasses. In a flash he ripped it from the boy's grasp, tore it to pieces, and flung the splinters against the boy's chest. "Piss off, *faggot!*" he snarled, pointing down the aisle.

The boy stared at him without surprise, then fluttered his lids and flounced away. "Sorry," Dessinger said to Peter. "Fell back on my old subway instincts there. I've been two days on the rails, and I'm just too tired for that kinda shit."

"I know the feeling," Peter said. But he was lying. The violence of the man's reaction had shocked him.

"How far are you going?" Dessinger asked.

"Clear to Nasik," Peter murmured, trying to withdraw.

"Going to sleep soon?"

"I haven't slept on a third-class train car yet. I'm going to try to get a little work done." He tapped the books on the bench beside him.

"Would you mind waking me in Jalna, then? I'm getting off at Aurang-abad, but I hear it's a little crazy there these days, so I want plenty of time to wake up."

"No problem," Peter said.

Dessinger covered his head with a shirt, curled up on the bench, and almost instantly fell asleep. Peter opened one of his books, eyed the words for a while, but felt too claustrophobic to lose himself in them. The air was like a cross between a sauna and a latrine. He slid over next to the window. There was no breeze. Just as he began to grow frantic, the train jolted violently and began to roll. He wiped his face, and tried to steady his breathing. Dessinger didn't stir.

Nizamabad / same journey

On the blazing hot concrete of the Nizamabad station platform, a woman with no legs and a grotesquely hunched back was dragging herself along on a board with wheels, like an auto mechanic's dolly. A girl of four or five accompanied her. They were begging, in tandem, from the cars on Peter's train, dumping the coins they collected into a brass pot nailed to the front of the dolly. The girl was pitiably cute in her dirty rags—a perfect UNICEF ad for the back pages of some American fashion magazine. But the woman was something else again . . .

Her only piece of clothing was a kind of loincloth. Her hump was naked, and had been exposed to the sun till it was as cracked and crosshatched as the mud in a dry riverbed. The backs of her hands were gnarled, the knuckles worn fuzzy as old warts from pulling herself along the streets. Her face was concealed by her dusty gray hair, but when those she passed on the platform dropped coins into her pot she would blindly place her palms together, above her hair, in thanks. As she neared the train a shower of coins began to tinkle all around her, sometimes hitting her hump, once striking her head with an audible thud. She didn't seem to mind. With the patience of a sea turtle on sand she dragged her dolly along, gathering what money she could reach while the little girl chased down the rest.

As she pulled up beside the car in front of Peter's she stopped, raised herself up by her arms, and quickly scanned the passengers' faces, as if trying to assess the potential for pity and rupees. Peter still couldn't quite see her face, but he saw her breasts now: they looked like car-killed carcasses scorched on a desert road. *Yet it's calculated,* he thought with fascination and horror. *The hump, the dead breasts—they're her tools, like a ball and glove are Papa's. She exposes them just so. It's her art, a kind of dancing almost* . . . But no sooner had he thought this than the old woman turned toward his car, picked out his pale face at once, lowered herself, and began scuttling toward him with astounding speed.

Peter's hair stood up. He drew back from the window and sank low in his seat. He felt like stalked prey. But when he heard her roll up outside he grew ashamed, and forced himself to look:

She was waiting, right at the edge of the platform. And the instant he appeared she raised herself with a soft, surprisingly feminine grunt of effort into an almost vertical position—and he saw that the hair was gray with dust, not age, that the skin of her face was unlined and youthful, the eyes deep brown, the lashes long, the gaze alert, clear, even sexually attractive. Unable to stop himself, Peter let his eyes rove over the sun-cracked hump, the dead breasts, the wild hair, back to the eyes. And she smiled as he did this—a smile terrible for its intelligence, its beauty, its complete awareness of the ruin in which it lived. Then she touched her forehead with a root-wad hand, and in a voice like a little girl's said, *"Prem se bhiksha dijiye?"*

"Lover, give alms"? "Give with love"? Peter should have known what it meant, but he was mesmerized: he began blindly groping in his pockets, his eyes locked to hers—and he found himself wondering what her legs might be like if she had legs, what her breasts might be like had they not been crushed for years against the board, what she might still be like down beneath the cloth, whether the little girl might possibly be hers . . .

Then he realized that she was reading his thoughts. He felt it almost physically—felt her reach right behind his face and eyes and clutch not the language but the essence of his feelings. And though she continued to smile, her gaze now bound him, as if in ropes. Then it burst into flames. She seared him with flirtatiousness, then with malevolence; she demanded and received his pity, then scoffed him for its meaningless-ness, reveled in his horror, exulted in his helplessness and shame. *"Nange se Khuda bhi darta hai!"* she cried in her girlish yet furious yet trium-phant voice. Then the train lurched, and began to roll.

"Wait!" Peter gasped, as if that might stop it, and he turned his change pocket inside out, picked up eight or ten rupees, wadded them into a ball, jammed his arms out the window slats and threw them as hard as he could back toward her. "I'm sorry!" he shouted. "I'm so sorry!" But the breeze blew the ball to pieces, stopped the crumpled rupees far short of her reach, whisked them down the platform as the little girl chased them, then tumbled them off the edge, where they were sucked up close to the wheels of the train. The little girl scrambled down off the platform. The legless woman shrieked. Peter felt the world and every-thing in it turn to lead . . .

But the girl was still running when a man in a ripped brown T-shirt jumped down off the train and deftly scooped the rupees up. The little girl ran to him, smiled, held out her hand. The man looked down at her, smiled back—then clutched the rupees and fled, running right alongside the train, right beside Peter, before veering off and disappearing in a maze of mud-and-mat hovels. And all the while the woman kept shriek-ing, not at the thief, but at Peter:

"Nange se Khuda bhi darta hai! Nange se Khuda bhi darta hai!"

Nizamabad to Parbhani to Jalna / same journey

From Nizamabad all the way to Nanded, Peter dug through his lexicons and scribbled phonetic possibilities on a page, trying to work out the exact spelling and meaning of the phrase *Nange se Khuda bhi darta hai.* He had just concluded that it could only mean "Even God is afraid of the naked" when the train lurched once again, rolled out of Nanded station, and two Indian men walked into his car.

Or not "walked" exactly: one staggered, drunk out of his head, while the other sauntered, giving each passenger a wry, affable smile as they warily eyed his crocked compadre. The drunkard was wearing the red turban of the Sikhs and a red-handled kirpan dagger. A band of scarlet gauze squeezed his beard into a thin, greasy rope. A half-empty fifth of booze was jammed in the sash round his waist. His eyes were as red as the turban. The saunterer, on the other hand, was clear-eyed and clean-shaven, steady on his feet, and wearing the kind of clothes you'd expect to see on a Palm Springs golf nut—double-knit slacks, polyester shirt, pointy white shoes. The two men could not have been more different in mood or style. Yet Peter guessed at a glance that they were brothers, and that each had a great deal to do with the way the other looked and acted.

Every passenger in the car had a bench seat to himself. The two Sikhs were destined to upset that equation. Given the kind of day he'd been having, it did not surprise Peter at all when the drunken Sikh took one look at the sleeping Dessinger, wordlessly flung his feet off the bench, plopped down, and glared at Peter as if he dared him to do something about it. Dessinger stirred slightly, took a discreet peek at the man who'd disturbed him, and wisely decided to pretend to fall back to sleep. Meanwhile the clean-shaven Sikh nodded graciously when Peter made room on his bench, sat down beside him, squinted past him out the window, and said, "I like t'ride out alone over the wide Dakota prairie. I like m'bacon cut thick, m'whiskey straight, an' m'coffee black."

Peter acknowledged these assertions with an involuntary giggle, then set aside the lexicons and dove deep into his A. S. Barnes critical edition of Tulsi Das's *Kavitavali.*

"Book learnin's fine for some," the clean-shaven Sikh said. "But me, I like t'slip off m'boots after a long day's ride, warm m'feet by a little chip fire, rest m'head on m'saddle, an' watch those bits o' busted star come fallin' down outta the night sky."

Peter looked up long enough to give the speaker a cautious smile.

"I am Gobindh Singh," the cowboy-and-Indian said. "An' this is my strawberry stallion, Old Pal." He rolled his eyes at his besotted brother.

"I'm Peter Chance," Peter said, and he and Gobindh shook hands. But when he offered his hand to Old Pal, the red-eyed Sikh only sneered at it. Peter's adrenal glands slammed into action.

"Ropin' an' ridin', ropin' an' ridin'," sighed Gobindh Singh. "That's all there is t'this life, m'friend."

Peter said nothing. The greasy Sikh kept sneering.

"Got m'friends, Doc an' Miss Nellie, over in town," Gobindh said. "But they don't really understand me. Got m'hoss here. But Old Pal, he don't say much. Got the brandin' in spring, the roundup come fall, an' the billion stars blisterin' that black prairie sky at night. But in the end you look back, you see your life strung out behind you, an' it's plain as the color o' the Dakotas in December. Ropin' an' ridin', Pete. That's all it was. Just ropin' and ridin'."

Noticing that Old Pal had either dozed off or passed out, Peter risked a nod.

"There's got to be more, is what I tell the stars at night," said Gobindh Singh. "But them stars, they don't never answer."

Peter shook his head sadly.

Then Gobindh also noticed that his brother was asleep, and his manner changed completely. Leaning eagerly forward, he pointed at his brown arms and face and said, "You know, my skin wasn't really this color! It was a childhood disease! I was very light-skinned as a boy—as light as you, nearly." He pointed out the window at some women carrying water. "Look at those black-skinned sluts! I looked nothing like *that*, I can tell you!"

Old Pal lurched upright, saw his brother's distress, glared at Peter as if he were the cause, and literally began to growl. Gobindh shook his head sadly, reached over and slid the bottle from Old Pal's sash, took a long pull, then turned to Peter. "I don't reckon a fine gent like yourself'd take relief from a bottle that's been lipped by the likes of me. But if ya care t'cure what ails ya—" He held it out.

Peter knew better than to hesitate: he grabbed the bottle, nodded thanks, and drank as if he craved it. It was some kind of rotgut whiskey—the first hard liquor he'd tasted since he was sixteen or so; he managed to stave off a coughing fit, but it burned him and left him gasping. When he could see again, both Sikhs were smiling, though for warmth and coldness the two smiles could not have been less alike. "You got any sisters?" Gobindh Singh asked.

"Two," Peter said without thinking. Then Old Pal began to leer, and he realized he'd fallen already into another trap.

"Out in Nevada, I reckon," Gobindh said. "Or maybe up Wyomin' way."

"Washington State," Peter said. "But they're just little girls."

"I marry!" shouted Pal, pounding his chest with both fists. "You bring, I marry! No dowry! Just marry! Then live with in America!"

Gobindh smirked. "You think he'd let his sisters marry a black-faced pig like you, Kalsa Singh?"

Again the red-eyed Sikh glared at Peter as if he'd spoken the offending words. And again Gobindh Singh just smiled obliviously. "But listen, friend," he said. "Do speak to the little ladies about our life here on the wide plateaus and prairies. Tell 'em how you found us sittin' proud in the saddle. Tell 'em how we—"

"You bring!" Kalsa Singh roared, slamming his chest. "You bring, I marry!"

Dessinger was no longer playing possum: he was watching the Sikh the way a cornered mouse watches the cat. But thanks to his sleepless night and empty stomach, one swig of whiskey had given Peter a new lease on life. "Listen," he lied. "Skin color isn't important where I come from. In America, all people are equal. Every color, every sex. Which means not only that you're equal to me, but that women are equal to both of us. So marriages are never arranged. And not even a king can marry a little girl. It's the law. In America, girls grow up into women, then marry whoever they choose. So you're welcome to my sisters, Kalsa and Gobindh Singh —if you win their hearts when the time comes. But that's between you, them and the gods. I've got no part in it."

Gobindh was nodding thoughtfully at all this. Kalsa was looking more pissed off than ever. Peter decided a second puff on the peace pipe might be in order: "Gimme another swig o' that shit you got there, Gobindh," he drawled.

Gobindh Singh smiled, and did so.

When the train reached Parbhani, Kalsa and Gobindh Singh rode off over the Dakota prairie to rope some more whiskey. Dessinger was hugely relieved when the train left before they'd returned. Peter, to his own surprise, was a little disappointed: he'd had no idea how swiftly the miles could pass with the help of a little cognitive dissonance, fear and booze.

Dessinger had also left the train in Parbhani—to find a latrine, Peter assumed. But he'd returned very soon in the company of a stranger who really snapped the suspenders on Peter's disbelief: the guy was an easy 6′4″ and wore cowboy boots, a Western shirt and a black string tie with a silver buffalo clasp. He struck Peter the instant he saw him not as a flesh-and-blood human but as some sort of mock-mythical being that had sprung into the world straight out of Gobindh Singh's cattle-punchin' third eye. As the newcomer heaved two enormous suitcases up into the luggage rack, he bellowed, "Theodore Bartholomew Waites," then spun around, shook Peter's hand in bone-crunching Western fashion, and added, "But you damn better call me T Bar."

The dissonance was back. Despite a lifelong aversion to the nicking of names, Peter heard himself say, "Call me Pete, T Bar."

"I been ridin' two cars ahead since the air-conditioners blew," Waites told him. "But Dessinger here says the natives are a bit restless up the line, and that maybe us Yanks ought to stick together for a stretch. So here I am."

"Here he is," said Dessinger, looking up at Waites, then smiling hugely at Peter.

For reasons he didn't fully understand, Peter was enormously relieved to learn that boots, tie and handshake notwithstanding, T Bar knew nothing about "ropin' an' ridin'." Though he made his home in Livingston, Montana, he confessed that he'd lived all but the last year of his life in various suburbs of LA. "What was my line, you ask?" he said, though no one had asked him. He then answered himself, saying that he'd been in the import business "ever since God invented hippies," mostly incense "for head shops and guru-hounds" but also bangles, curios, a little jewelry. But his mainstay, the incense, would crap out soon, he predicted. "No offense, Pete," he said, eyeing his ponytail, "but this hippie shit's about dead in the water. Did you know the same chemical giant that makes glow-in-the-dark Frisbees for acidheads makes napalm for the Pentagon? Did you know Bob Dylan left the lyric sheet off his last mumbly record so you gotta buy the four ninety-five songbook from CBS to grasp the antimaterialistic lyrics? An' what *is* a hippie anyway? Just a dope-smokin' college brat, usually. And wait'll the war's over, the brats finish college, and daddy says, 'Kiss my ass and like it or kiss your inheritance bye-bye.' Man, we're gonna see barbers in hair up to their armpits! We're gonna see bra and Bible sales rise from the dead! We're gonna see peacemongers and acid-retreads stormin' Madison Av and Wall Street sellin' brain, body and soul to the biggest corporate buyers they can find.

We're gonna see—" And T Bar went on with a list of mostly accurate predictions. But Peter was hardly listening anymore. Waites had begun to irritate him for his style alone—because the style had begun to remind him of Everett.

Dessinger also appeared to be having trouble following the big neo-Montanan. But he seemed not so much irritated as distracted, perhaps even anxious. It made Peter want to hear more about the "restless natives" up the line. But Waites's torrential monologue made a change of topic impossible. After going into excruciating detail about the killing he'd made selling his import business, and the little gem of a cattle ranch and the downtown Bozeman sporting-goods store he'd purchased with the pelf, Waites said, "Why sportin' goods, you ask?" though again no one had asked him. He then jumped to his feet, pulled down one of his two suitcases, unlocked it, flung it open—and Dessinger's bewilderment seemed to verge on horror when all they saw inside were countless plastic bags full of exotic feathers, animal fur, tails of deer, hackles of hens, elk hide, spools of gaudy thread, vises, clamps, tinsel, scissors and literally hundreds of little cardboard boxes, each with a different-sized fishhook Scotch-taped to its top.

"Fly-tying equipment," Peter said, if only to dispel Dessinger's confusion.

Waites grinned like a gambler who's just laid down a royal flush. "You heard it first from T Bar, gents. Fly-fishing is on the brink of becoming to ex-hipsters what golf has been to the World War Two-ers. 'Cause think about it. It's cheaper, it's outdoorsier, it's less exclusive, it's less bourgeois. It's got the magic of the sand wedge, the yo-yo and the Frisbee rolled into one. It's pretty well useless, which makes it pretty well incorruptible. And—"

"I get it," Peter interrupted, because he suddenly did. "You're going to hire Indians to tie flies for zilch, then undercut the American market."

"You may dress funny, Pete," Waites replied, "but don't let 'em tell ya you're stupid. The best American outlets sell trout flies at four bits wholesale an' a buck retail, which barely covers their buns once they pay their tiers a shit wage. But if the import biz has taught me anything, it's that this continent is *crawlin'* with sweet little Hindu ladies who'll work handcrafted miracles for you for a rupee a day and fuckin' praise the great god Ramadamadiddle for the golden opportunity!"

When Peter greeted his exultant hoot with silence, Waites tried to squeeze his brow into an earnest scowl. "I'll pay one and a half rupees, Pete—a decent wage by their standards." But T Bar's brow was like

Teflon: earnestness just wouldn't stick. "The story gets better," he said. "In Hyderabad, where I just came from, and in Nasik, where I'm headin', a big Taiwanese sportin'-goods outfit beat me to the punch. Kodiak Outdoors. You've heard of 'em. They had a half a hundred women in each city tyin' flies for a penny apiece. Trouble was, even at ten for a buck the flies wouldn't sell in the States, so last summer Kodiak axed the whole operation. But ol' T Bar, see, just took a big batch o' their flies, had some Montana fly-fishin' experts fish 'em and dissect 'em, and found out the craftsmanship was fine. Only trouble was the cut-rate Indian materials. They looked gaudy, the dries wouldn't float, and they all fell to hell when a trout smacked 'em. So see where they left me?" He let out another hoot. "Kodiak trained a hundred expert fly-tiers for me, then flew the flippin' coop! All's I gotta do is waltz into Nasik same as I just did Hyderabad, win their unemployed hearts back with the half-rupee raise, hand 'em the same topflight materials the Montana fly shops use, hire the meanest to be my supervisor, jet back home, and start settin' the American fly market on its ear!"

"Hhhnn," said Peter, gulping down a violent yawn. (Dessinger had long since curled up against the window and pretended to be asleep.) But T Bar was his own best audience:

"What we got in a nutshell, Pete, is a horde o' hip-booted crazies on one side o' the world who'll pay a buck for a clump o' feathers, a horde of quick-fingered Hindu crazies on the opposite side who'll crank 'em out for squat, an' a tall, dark, not-bad-lookin' lion o' commerce name o' T Bar about to knot the two together like a mail-order man and wife. It's the Global Village concept, is all it is, really."

"Ahnmmnn," said Peter. They were coming in waves now.

"Free enterprise to the rescue o' two fine sets o' people."

"Mhmmnn."

"Beautiful, idn't it?"

"Yeahnnmmm. 'Scuse me. It's beautiful."

Jalna to Aurangabad / same journey

Dessinger left the train again in Jalna, again returned promptly, again brought company, and again they were Westerners—this time a pair of pack-toting hippies. Introducing the female as Akasha and the male as Kwester (he'd had to spell both names for the disbelieving T Bar), Dessinger had deposited them on the vacant seats across the aisle from Peter and Waites, grabbed one of two canvas satchels lying in his luggage rack, and vanished again, presumably to another car, since the train was soon rolling and he'd left his other satchel behind.

It continued to be a bizarre day for accents: though born and raised in Athens, Georgia, Kwester had been on the road so long and had sent so many nonprescription medicaments coursing through his brain that a few nonessentials such as his Southern accent and inductive reasoning had gotten Cloroxed out, making every sentence he spoke sound sort of like a Doobie Brothers lyric. Akasha, on the other hand, was a broad-beamed, enormous-breasted, decidedly down-to-earth-looking German woman who picked up and set down English as if each word was a brick, yet almost every word she spoke was in direct defiance of her broadness and down-to-earthness. Her first utterance, for example, was: "My name means Light." (To which Waites had testily replied, "Well, mine means T Bar!" Having obviously not begun the crucial migration from hippieness toward trout flies, Kwester and Akasha had thrown Waites's entrepreneurial soul into a sudden Dark Night.)

Spotting Peter's braid, Kwester, who was also braided, took it as a sure sign of joint membership in a vague but intimate International Brotherhood and became the third straight passenger to open fire at Pete with an intimate chunk of his biography. The story he chose to relate concerned a tragic first meeting between himself and Akasha in Istanbul years before, where they'd both failed to perceive (admittedly because of the low price and high quality of the local hashish) that they were made for each other. "I see the problem," Waites remarked, ogling Akasha's chest. "Prob'ly thought you'd get busted."

Kwester didn't get it. He was too busy staring into Akasha's eyes as he told how they'd just met again in Benares, discovered that they'd independently sworn off drugs, discovered that they were "twin souls," discovered love, discovered that Kwester had "scored a Master," discovered that Akasha had been "sussing out the same Dude," and so had become spiritual pilgrims, "on our way to 'Nagar, man," to visit Kwester's Master's "samadhi."

"What's a nogger?" Waites asked, still eyeing Akasha's bosoms.

"Nickname for Ahmednagar," Peter said. "A Maharashtran city."

"What's a smoddy?" he asked.

"Samadhi," Peter corrected. "A saint's tomb."

"Not a Saint!" Akasha proclaimed, in bricks. "This Is the Tomb of God Incarnate!"

"Always did figure that sucker was dead," muttered Waites.

"He Heard That!" Akasha warned.

"God never really comes and never really goes," Kwester explained. "He uses human forms like suits of clothes, and He can change His suit at will."

Giving Kwester's dust- and mango- and pee-stained cotton pants a disgusted glance, Waites said, "So can I. What's holdin' you up?"

Realizing at last that he was being insulted, Kwester made his hands into mudras and commenced to look cosmic. Akasha, on the other hand, looked about ready to drop a whole hod of English bricks on Waites's head, when Dessinger suddenly returned, looking worried. "In half an hour we'll be in Aurangabad," he said. "Have any of you heard the news from there recently?"

"How can you hear news when the common tongue is Yuggedy-yug-gedy?" Waites wanted to know. "It's bad enough tryin' to figure out which fuckin' *town* you're in. Like here . . . There we go!" He was pointing at a sign out the window. It said:

ꙇꙮꙏ꙳ꙅꙮꙇꙅ꙳ꙇꙇ:

"And ask an Indian," he ranted, "even an English-speakin' Indian, and you get the cerebral-palsy head wag and the 'Ah cha.' 'Is this Samadhi-nogger?' 'Ah cha.' 'Is it Paris?' 'Ah cha.' 'Is it Topeka, Kansas?' "

"Can I have the floor a minute?" Dessinger cut in.

"Ah cha," said Waites.

"I *get* the news. In English, from this." Dessinger opened the satchel on his shoulder and let them glimpse a complicated-looking little radio with a telescoping antenna. "I didn't want to ruin everybody's journey. But it's time you all knew that there is serious racial tension in Auranga-bad. *Anti-Western* tension."

Dessinger looked enviable, suddenly, in his Indian spectacles, complex-ion and clothes. "Large crowds have been roving the streets there," he said. "And one of the places they've been frequenting is the train station. There's been no rioting or looting. But it's not that kind of tension. I hate to say it to this group, but the whole mess started three days ago when some long-haired, overdosing Westerner killed a Muslim boy. A very young Muslim boy. Unfortunately the man was only seen, not caught, and the description was vague. 'Hippie' was about it. And I'm afraid the crowds in the streets are Muslim vigilantes."

Bursting with sudden altruism, T Bar leapt to his feet, banged his head hard on the luggage rack, but ignored it completely to suggest that Kwester, Akasha and Peter, for their own safety, should detrain at the next stop and detour the city.

"There is no next stop," Dessinger said.

"Why the fuck didn't you *tell* us!" Waites blored. "But wait wait wait wait! Calm down, ever'body! Okay, I got it. Just get your gear together, say when, an' ol' T Bar'll pull the emergency cord for ya!"

Dessinger shook his head. "To be found wandering alone this close to the city would be the most suspicious behavior possible," he said.

"Well shit!" Waites nearly squeaked. "Is there someplace to hide 'em on the train?"

"To be caught hiding would raise the same suspicions," said Dessinger.

"Hey, man," Kwester interjected. "Me an' Akasha are gettin' off at Aurangabad, we're walkin' to the bus station, we're goin' to 'Nagar, an' that's all there is to it. The Dude in the Tomb will protect us, or not, as He sees fit."

"Fine!" T Bar blurted. "Just fine! But do me one small favor first."

"What's that?"

"Get the hell outta this car!"

"Easy, Man! We're All Brothers," averred Akasha, bosoms and all.

"We're one," Kwester added, nodding solemnly.

"Listen, asshole!" snapped Waites. "You and me are *two*. One, two! Got it?"

Kwester stared at him pityingly. Peter felt sick. "Don't give me that look, Pete," Waites pleaded, his voice shaking now. "If they were clubbing cowboys up the line, I'd have the decency to leave you alone, or at least take my damn boots, shirt an' tie off. But hey! There we go! I got thirty little pairs o' fly-tyin' scissors here! How 'bout a quick haircut, Kwes and Pete?"

Kwester looked horrified. Peter considered it. Then Dessinger said, "A fresh, sloppy haircut would raise the same kind of suspicions as hiding."

"Well fuck a fucking duck, what do we *do*?" T Bar yelled.

"We calm down, to begin with," Dessinger said. "If Kwester just cleans up a bit, we should all be safe and sound as is. If there's an ugly crowd at the station, Grayson has promised to be there."

"Who the hell is Grayson?" Waites wanted to know.

Dessinger responded with a peculiar tale. Robert Louis Grayson was an expatriated Englishman who had lived in Aurangabad since early boyhood, during the final days of the Raj. He had converted to Islam more than a decade ago, and according to rumor had also been initiated into a

very secretive Sufi order. He now lived in the Muslim sector of Aurangabad, where he was held in an esteem that verged on reverence. He had
three wives and many children, made his living as some kind of counsel
to a local member of the Indian Parliament, knew virtually every Muslim
in the city, and most of the important Hindus, Sikhs and Parsis as well.
And he considered it a point of honor, whenever racial or religious ten-
sions in his hometown threatened to get out of control, to intercede
between factions. According to Dessinger, he was fearless in such situations, and invaluable: he had probably saved hundreds of lives over the
past decade. But his modesty was such that he thought nothing of it.

"I work for Grayson, by the way," Dessinger added, smiling at the
group's obvious surprise and delight. "Please," he said, looking straight at
Waites. "Try not to be tense with each other. Remember, they're looking
for a maniac who murdered a little boy. What child killer would be part
of a relaxed group of friends?"

Aurangabad / same journey

By the time the train reached the outskirts of the troubled city, Akasha
had vanished behind a sleeping bag and reemerged in a spectacularly ill-
fitting pink sari, Kwester had donned an oversized but clean white shirt
and pair of pants of Peter's, Peter had changed into his dress shirt and tie
and stuffed his braid down his collar, Waites had nailed a smile to his
face with several stiff swigs of Teacher's scotch, and the whole group was
positively vibrating with Relaxed-Group-of-Friends-type behaviors. Their
preparations were no exercise in paranoia either: as the train rolled into
the station they immediately spotted easily a hundred very unhappy-
looking Indian men milling around a tall, gaunt fellow in an elegant off-
white suit. "There!" Dessinger cried the instant he saw him. "Thank
God! It's Grayson."

Curious as he was about this mythical-sounding figure, the first thing
Peter noticed was that the vigilantes weren't on the station platform.
They were gathered on a plaza on the opposite side of the train, across an
empty second track, where the comings and goings of passengers weren't
even visible. Dessinger noticed this too, and his response was dramatic: "I
hope I'm wrong," he said, "but this looks more than a little like a trap.
Please stay here!" And before the train stopped rolling he jumped into
the crowd on the platform, circled around behind their car, crossed the
tracks, and shouldered his way in through the Muslim men, who paid

him little heed. Their reason for ignoring him was troubling, however: most of them were searching the windows of the train—and many had already pointed out, and begun muttering about, Kwester, Akasha, Peter and Waites. "Jesus *God!*" T Bar groaned.

Grayson was a tall, pallid man, slender to the verge of emaciation, with a slightly bent, possibly broken nose, dark hair combed straight back, and an easy dignity that reminded Peter slightly of Papa. The elegant white suit struck Peter as an odd touch for a man of the people. But Indians in general and Muslims in particular did seem to have a high regard for outward signs of suzerainty, and the suit made Grayson stand out like a prince. He greeted Dessinger with a perfunctory embrace, and they began speaking directly into each other's ears, probably to avoid being overheard. But after the shock of being pointed out by the mob wore off a little, Peter began to feel that the vigilantes were not as dangerous as they'd at first seemed. They were plainly on edge, and plainly interested in Peter's group. But most of them looked more puzzled or concerned than angry. They also seemed to be tremendously interested in the radio Grayson was holding—which looked, by the way, identical to the one Dessinger had in his satchel. Peter couldn't figure it out.

The two men talked for a distressingly long time, then embraced again, and Dessinger started back toward the train, turning frequently to be sure he was not being followed. When he rejoined the Westerners, Peter was surprised to see that he was breathless, and dripping with nervous sweat. "It's worse than we feared," he said. "Grayson's got this group in hand, as you can see. But they're just one wing of a much larger mob, sent in to watch the back side of the station. And the word on the group out front is that they're out for Western blood. *Any* Western blood. The Koran, I'm afraid, *can* be misread as an eye-for-an-eye sort of scripture."

"That's it!" Waites said, reaching for his suitcases. "If you all won't clear away from me, I'm clearin' the hell away from *you!*"

Dessinger grabbed his arm. "Given their mood, you're no safer than anyone else. We're gonna get through this, Waites. But we've *got* to stick together. Now listen. What Grayson wants you all to do is get off the train and greet him. And—this is crucial—he wants you to act as though you know him. He's described you to the men out there as eccentric academics, and dear personal friends. His greeting will ensure your safety with this bunch till the train departs, believe me. And should the bigger group burst into the station while you're out there, Grayson will lead you out the back and hide you. But hopefully they'll stay out front. I'll stay here to watch for them, keep an eye on your things, and so forth. So go to it. And remember to smile!"

Struggling to erase the fear from their faces, Waites and Peter set out to do as they'd been told. But Kwester and Akasha, after whispering together, began donning their backpacks. "What are you doing?" Dessinger asked.

"Just headin' to 'Nagar," Kwester said, hoisting his pack.

Waites was incredulous. "You wanna get us all killed?" he roared.

"Smile!" Dessinger reminded him, grinning hugely himself. "Kwester, Akasha, listen to me. I know it feels unreal, but this is a genuine life-and-death situation. Grayson can protect you, but only if you help. This charade has *got* to be convincing. And academics don't travel around India in dirty old backpacks."

Grinning back just as hugely, Kwester said, "What you're doin' is cool. And we'll join in, to help Pete and T Bar. But Akasha and me're *already* protected—by my Master. I got nothing to add or subtract."

Still smiling, Dessinger said, "You'll die in the streets."

"He'd better," Waites fumed. " 'Cause if I ever catch him I'll kill him myself!"

But Peter said nothing. He'd begun to admire Kwester's mindless faith: it reminded him a little of Irwin. And Akasha was a bizarre, anger-dispelling sight altogether as she climbed down onto the station platform in her filthy fluorescent-orange backpack and clashingly clean pink sari. "For God's sake get *ahead* of her!" Dessinger told the three men. "They're Muslims, remember! And don't forget you're Robert's dear old friends!"

Foisting great grins up onto their faces, the three men barged obediently past Akasha, circled the train car, and the instant Grayson saw them he threw his arms up in delight. As the Westerners drew closer, the mob confused and frightened Peter by literally backing away from them, as if they were lepers or something. But except for that the charade seemed to go well enough. T Bar and Kwester both did excellent imitations of a warm reunion with Grayson, embracing him repeatedly, beaming idiotically into his eyes. In Akasha's case the Islamic onlookers and the prodigious pink prow made embrace more problematic: Grayson settled for a courtly handshake. But when Peter's turn came he marveled at the perfect believability of Grayson's performance—his body rock-steady as they hugged, his eyes filled with what really seemed to be delight. "Very good," he murmured. "That's fine. But I'm afraid we're not out of it yet. Let's keep it muzzy with affection."

Peter nodded and kept smiling, though to his eye the crowd still appeared more confused or worried than angry. Another thing that made no sense: a lot of the restless muttering was definitely in Marathi, and Peter twice thought he heard reference to some sort of cricket team or test match—unlikely topics for a bunch of bloody-minded vigilantes. But before he could begin to sort his conflicting impressions the situation changed with terrifying speed:

Another train—a small one, just six cars and an engine—came clattering into the station on the second track, blocking the Westerners' route back to their own. And just as the train stopped rolling, Grayson's radio squawked in his hand, some sort of news commentator began chattering, and at the first burst of verbiage the vigilantes turned as one man to listen and their anxiety seemed to increase tenfold. Peter didn't understand it at all. When the broadcast ended, Grayson shook his head at the crowd, spoke several more sentences to them, and Peter recognized, but couldn't decipher, fluent Urdu. But whatever Grayson said this time obviously distressed rather than calmed the crowd. In fact, most of them were now glaring furiously, right at T Bar. "What did you *tell* them?" Waites gasped.

"Silence!" Grayson snapped, stepping up close to the Westerners—

and the bottom fell out: though he still managed a forced smile and the blade was not yet open, he was palming a switchblade. "I'm sorry," he whispered. "I didn't expect this. But the mood here is lethal. We've *got* to get out. Kwester, Akasha. Me too, I'm afraid. This is the White Train. Wait till it gathers speed, then board the last car!"

"My luggage!" Waites protested.

"They think Dessinger's one of them. It's safe with him. We'll meet him just down the line in Khuldabad. Now get ready."

But Kwester was shaking his head. "This kill-a-hippie shit is bullshit. We're goin' to 'Nagar, man. I got nothin' to add or subtract." And with that he and Akasha took each other by the hand, turned to the crowd of vigilantes, walked straight into them—and the Muslims parted like the Red Sea. Peter felt he should stop them, should dash into the crowd and drag the two idiots back out by their hair, if he had to. But before he could make himself move, the Red Sea closed. The little express train began rolling. Kwester and Akasha disappeared round a corner. "Don't turn your backs," Grayson murmured. "Watch out for knives, and for thrown rocks."

The train rolled faster. The last car approached. One of the Muslims shouted something at them. Grayson shouted something back. The Indians let out a rumble, and began to advance. "Holy *fuck!*" piped Waites.

"Now!" Grayson shouted. "The White Train!"

The three of them ran for it, leaping onto the steps of the last car. But before Peter climbed inside he leaned back and looked one last time at the receding crowd. And every last one of them was wearing the same incomprehensible expression: a look more of sadness, or even grief, than anger.

The train gathered speed.

Peter climbed up into the car—yet another third-class job—and found Grayson sitting beside a burly, disagreeable-looking Indian who, despite the blistering heat, was wearing a hideous black-and-white-plaid polyester sport coat. Peter plunked down beside T Bar, who sat on the bench facing them. "Look at my damned hands!" Waites gasped.

It seemed to impress him that they were shaking. But what impressed Peter was that his own were not. To him, the crowd never *had* felt truly threatening. What felt far more threatening to him was his own confusion now: he was wobbly with it, physically off balance with it, though he was sitting still. Because he'd heard Marathi. He'd heard a man refer to cricket. He could have spoken directly to that man. He'd spent his *life* studying the scriptures and languages of these people. And there he'd stood beside T Bar, the Aspiring Sweatshop Entrepreneur, as mute as if the crowd were words in a book . . .

Grayson asked the burly Indian a question in Urdu. The man smiled—which made his face even more disagreeable—but answered the question, and several more, at length. Grayson turned to Peter and Waites. "Our first stop will be a place called Dadagaon," he said, "which is not on the way to Khuldabad at all. My apologies. Apparently we switched tracks as we were leaving Aurangabad station. But this gentleman assures me that his taxi is parked at Dadagaon station, and that, for a hundred and fifty rupees (I haggled him down from three hundred) he can ferry all three of us over to Khuldabad well before Dessinger and your luggage arrive."

T Bar looked as though he'd received a sudden faith healing. "Fantastic!" he cackled.

"Yes. *You're* in luck," Grayson said without enthusiasm. "But now, if you'll excuse me, I'm going to borrow the engineer's wireless and ask the Aurangabad police to try and help Kwester and Akasha. Though the police too are Muslim. And they may well be beyond help."

Waites tried to work a furrow of concern into his Teflon forehead. "I tried to stop 'em," he groused. "I *told* 'em they were nuts . . ."

But Grayson was already gone, the burly Indian obviously spoke no

English, and Peter had his head down between his knees, as if trying not to faint or throw up.

Dadagaon to gully / new journey

Dadagaon, it turned out, was hardly a town, let alone a city. With a single paved exception the streets weren't even streets: they were bullock-cart-rutted dirt lanes between tiny mud-colored houses. The train station was a whitewashed building about the size of a baseball dugout, with yet another Wild West device—a hitching post—out front. There was no one and nothing inside the doorless building. But there was a single black four-door sedan parked at the hitching post. "Are we lucky or what?" T Bar marveled.

Peter had begun to suspect the answer to that might be "what." But he was too queasy to do anything but float along on the current.

Grayson took the front seat, Peter and Waites the back, and the burly Indian pulled onto the single paved strand and barreled out of town in seconds. "This is more like it!" Waites crowed, sticking his head out into the breeze. But they hadn't gone more than three or four miles when the driver turned down a dirt side road. "Shortcut," Grayson said quickly. "We discussed the route."

They drove past a few abandoned huts, dozens of drought-smitten fields and one skinny boy herding a few skinnier goats. Then the driver turned down a dusty, rock-strewn gully. "What the hell?" T Bar grunted.

"It's all right," Grayson said. "We discussed it."

But moments after he reassured them the driver parked in the shade of a solitary neem tree, shut off the engine, and reached in his jacket. "Not *car* trouble!" Waites groaned.

"No," Grayson said, turning round to face them. "This is rather a different sort of trouble."

The burly Indian drew his hand out of his jacket. He was holding a revolver. Waites was so confused, and so incurably racist, that he yelled "Watch out!" at Grayson. But Peter—to the amazement of everyone, Grayson especially—let out a burst of what sounded like genuine, de-lighted laughter.

"*Bas!*" snapped the Indian.

"He means shuttup," Grayson told Peter. "But have I missed some-thing?"

"It's just—" Peter began. "It's just the mind! Good God, the *mind!* It's such an unbelievably good liar!"

"All right, okay, I get it," T Bar cut in. "This is you guys' idea of a joke. But let me tell ya, I'm not findin' this butthead's cap gun a bit funny. An' if he doesn't get it outta my face fast, I'm gonna break his fuckin'—"

"Natu!" Grayson barked, pointing at a grapefruit-sized rock outside the car. A split second later the gun roared, the rock spat dust and bounced several feet, their ears were ringing, the barrel was right back in T Bar's face, and the driver was wearing a grin as hideous as his jacket. Waites turned pale—a considerable feat in the Deccan heat.

"This is Natu, gentlemen," Grayson said. "He speaks no English. He has no sense of humor. And his gun is going to stay where it is. So for your own sakes, behave. The loss of the hippies has put us in a foul mood."

"You mean they're *already* dead?" T Bar gasped.

Grayson smiled. "For our purposes, yes."

Waites's brain was whirring almost audibly. It didn't help. "*Your* purposes! You, you mean *you're* the vigilantes?"

Grayson started to laugh. But again, so did Peter. It stopped Grayson cold. "Is this hysteria? Or do you actually purport to be enjoying yourself?"

Peter understood that he was making the man angry, that their danger was real. But he couldn't help himself. Some kind of light had broken out inside him. "Such a liar!" he repeated. "It's wonderful, really. How it throws you in a pit and makes you think it's a beautiful palace. How it twists even love for truth into pettiness and worry and fear. How it—"

"I can't take this!" T Bar gasped, clawing at his string tie, then clutching at his throat. "Stuff like this, I get asthma! An' my medicine's in my suitcase, my suitcase is gettin' away, wonderful liar, beautiful palace, I don't get *any* of this. So somebody! Please! Just *tell* me!"

Grayson turned to Peter. "Perhaps he'd take it best," he said wryly, "if *you* described the basic situation."

Peter gave it a try. "The good news, T Bar," he began, speaking with great earnestness, but also with a sense of wonder that made every word virtually incomprehensible to Waites, "is that there was no Muslim boy killed in Aurangabad, there were no race riots, those weren't vigilantes at the station, Kwester and Akasha are safely on their way to 'Nagar, and Dessinger and Grayson, or whatever their names may be, are two of the greatest impromptu actors we'll ever live to see."

Waites just kept wheezing and gawking, but Grayson was clearly flattered by this beginning. "We do enjoy our work," he remarked, studying T Bar's panic as if it was a canvas he'd just painted. Which in a sense it was.

"The other news," Peter continued, "and it's also good, if you can just accept it for the blessing it is, is that we *needed* this to happen. Because face it, T Bar. It never could've worked if we weren't such nincompoops. It *didn't* work on Kwester and Akasha. But you and I have been stumbling around India with bags over our heads. Yours had penny-apiece trout flies sticking in it, and mine had medieval poetry scribbled all over it, but neither had eye or air holes. And when you're stumbling around that stupidly, when you're suffocating like that, T Bar, then the greatest thing that can happen is to have the damn bag ripped away. And that's just what's happening! That's exactly what Grayson and Dessinger are doing for us!"

Grayson was smiling broadly now, but T Bar just kept wheezing.

"Forget your trout flies a minute," Peter told him, "and think about some of the *bait* we swallowed today. Like about this guy." He nodded at Grayson. "Think about the exact kind of fear that Dessinger slipped into us. Then think of the portrait he drew of this British convert to Islam. This mysterious Sufi. This sage counsel to the Indian Parliament, beloved by all Aurangabadians, with his three loving wives and herd of happy offspring!"

Grayson began to laugh. So did Peter. T Bar gaped at them as if they'd both sprouted moose antlers. "How handy for us that he happened to break up race riots for a hobby!" Peter cried. "Prob'ly spends his weekends leading groups of autistic kids up Mount Everest too, don't you s'pose? And as we roll into the strife-torn station, praise Allah, there he is—the white man in the white suit in the *brown* crowd! 'Just his greeting will save you!' Dessinger tells us. So we leave everything. We dump everything we own for the great white life-giving hug!"

Grayson was roaring now—and Waites was hyperventilating.

"But now here's the great part, T Bar," Peter said, "and the part that Grayson and Dessinger maybe never planned on. Since we left everything behind, *including* our damned head bags, the whole stupid situation really *is* life-giving! Or could be. This moment is a *knife*, T Bar. But you've got to take a deep breath, calm yourself, and grab it by the handle, not the blade. Because if you look at it one way, yes, Dessinger probably *is* plowing through our suitcases even as we speak. But if none of this had happened, just think what we'd—"

It took Waites maybe three seconds to fully comprehend the phrase "plowing through our suitcases." He then grabbed it firmly—by the blade —and started roaring with rage. But it took Natu no seconds at all to comprehend the roar, grab his revolver by the barrel, and thwack T Bar hard in the forehead.

Peter caught him as he slumped sideways in the seat.

Waites was out cold.

Customer appreciation being rare in his line of work, Grayson had no objection—while Waites lay unconscious—to sharing a few trade secrets with Peter. He refused to say whether Dessinger had anything to do with the breakdown of the first-class air-conditioners way back in Secunderabad. But he took obvious pleasure in explaining how he'd created and worked the mob of "Muslim vigilantes" at Aurangabad station. "There is no sports fanatic," his discourse began, "quite like an Indian cricket fanatic . . ."

Strolling through the station a half hour or so before Peter and T Bar's train arrived, Grayson had simply mentioned to a few idle Aurangabadsmen that he'd caught a broadcast on his radio (which was really a long-range walkie-talkie) saying that the All-India cricket team had just been in a serious bus crash on the way to their test match with Australia. "A little cruel," Grayson admitted. "But within minutes it gave me my frantic throng." He'd kept his throng's interest up by grinding static into his ear and pretending to hear bits of reports as to which players had been injured, how seriously, and so forth. He then led his captive mob across the two sets of tracks so that the "White Train" would later separate the Westerners from their own. When the "static trick" got old and some of them began to talk about telephoning the *Times* of India, Grayson told them that the Westerners he'd come to meet, being cricket fanatics themselves, would be certain to have a world-band radio, and the most up-to-date news of the All-India team's condition. This was why the "vigilantes" had scanned the train for white faces the instant it rolled into the station. As for the language barrier, Grayson guessed that there had probably been more Marathi than Urdu speakers in the crowd, so Peter's Marathi had presented "an interesting technical problem." In fact, Dessinger, during one of their early communiqués on the walkie-talkies, had wanted to cull Peter from the group. But Grayson hit on the idea of telling his sports-loving mob that one Westerner—the blond-braided one, and the real cricket expert, unfortunately—would speak only to whites, and that if they crowded him he might not speak at all. This stroke served two crucial purposes: first, it convinced the mob to let

Grayson alone address the Westerners; and second, it created some genuine antipathy toward the person most likely to see through the con—i.e., Peter.

After the second train's arrival and the surprise radio broadcast (which had really been Dessinger spouting gibberish into his walkie-talkie not thirty yards away), Grayson had whipped his poor cricket-lovers into an even greater frenzy by saying that the radio report said nothing new, but that T Bar was an Australian journalist, that he had a wire service bulletin right in his pocket listing the Indian players' injuries, but that he was so absurdly nationalistic that he refused to share the information with his country's opponent. Even then the poor Indians managed to contain their ire. But when Akasha and Kwester suddenly left the group and the "White Train" began to roll out of the station, one frustrated fan finally shouted out a demand to hear the bulletin. "Then step forward," Grayson had shouted back, "and I'll read it to you myself!" Only then did the "mob" advance. And that was when Grayson turned to Peter and Waites in apparent desperation and cried, "Now! The White Train!"

The things people lug through life are seldom as valuable to others as they are to those who lug them. For this reason Grayson and Dessinger were not thieves, strictly speaking: they were luggage-nappers. Their preferred game, in other words, was to separate travelers from their possessions, then return everything in perfect condition—for "a modest price."

The ransom negotiations began with a beep from the walkie-talkie: Dessinger calling. And to judge by the background noise, or lack of it, he was no longer on a train or anywhere near the noisy station. The first step was to itemize the take and guess its value to each "client"—and T Bar Waites, needless to say, looked to be an ideal customer. In addition to his "Global Village" fly-tying gear and much-missed asthma medicine he'd been toting two more pairs of deluxe cowboy boots, two new suits, a pile of Indian curios and jewelry, his Bombay/Kuwait/Paris/New York/Chicago/Bozeman return plane ticket, two fifths of Teacher's scotch, a Rolex watch, his passport, and twelve hundred bucks in Barclay's traveler's checks. But when Grayson tried to soothe him by saying that he could have everything back within two hours by simply signing over the traveler's checks, then wiring the States for another thousand dollars, Waites surprised Grayson and Peter both by snapping, "Go fuck yourself."

Grayson remained calm, for the moment. But a ruthlessness came into his eyes that frightened Peter even more than the conscienceless grin of Natu—especially since Waites didn't see it. "Come, come," Grayson said. "No tantrums. Your position is hopeless. We'll cash your Barclay's checks on the black market days before you can cancel them. We'll scalp your plane ticket. You'll have to return to the States, repurchase all that lovely equipment, and fly all the way back again. You'll lose weeks of time, spend far more than the thousand we're asking, and—"

"Fuck you, fuck Dessinger, and fuck Butt-weasel here too!" T Bar blored.

Grayson made no reply. He just grew still, turned cold, and stared at Waites so long that even Waites himself came to see that there was no reason now why he should be allowed to leave the gully alive. At last, Grayson murmured. "Have it your way. Take off your clothes."

"I'll pay you the thousand!" T Bar blurted.

"Natu!"

"Okay okay!" Waites began struggling with his boots.

"Faster. Every stitch. Socks and undershorts too."

Waites did exactly as he was told.

"Now get out of the car on Natu's side."

T Bar stepped out into the sunlight. His skin looked blindingly white against the red rocks and dust. "Please," he said, to no one in particular.

"Sit on the ground, facing the tree. Fold your hands on top of your head."

"Please," he kept whispering. "Please . . ."

Grayson spoke a long sentence in Urdu. Natu laughed. Then, to Waites, Grayson said, "If Natu hears your voice again he's going to shoot you in the left buttock. If he sees your face, he'll shoot you in the right. Do you understand?"

Without turning, almost without breathing, T Bar nodded.

Grayson beeped Dessinger on the walkie-talkie. "Peter's turn," he said.

"Hmm," Dessinger began. "Looks like we robbed a monk. We got some Hindu-lookin' threads, worn sandals, white Jockey shorts, bare-bones shaving kit. Got our passport, our travel diary, mail from the Fulbright Foundation, Harvard, University of New Delhi, Washington State. We got our Buddha statue, and our genuine leaf from the Bo Tree—so says the cellophane wrapper. And of course the shitload of books—dictionaries, lexicons, Indian poetry, mostly. And two typewritten manuscripts by the monk himself. Oh. Here's his wallet. Empty. His cash must be on him."

Without being asked Peter emptied his pockets and handed the contents—a money clip with rupees, $120 in traveler's checks, and change—

over to Grayson. He pocketed them without a glance. "Describe the manuscripts," he told Dessinger.

"One, titled *Maharashtran Poet-Saints*, looks finished. The other, untitled, looks rough. Both full of translated verse, commentary, footnotes. The second one full of handwritten additions and corrections."

"A sentence from the finished one," said Grayson.

" 'It should hardly be necessary to point out that, despite the parallels cited above, our three Vaishnava poets considered worship of the *nirguna* paramount to—' "

"That'll do," Grayson interrupted.

Peter nearly laughed.

"Original manuscripts, I'd wager," Grayson said, watching Peter closely. "Both one of a kind."

"*Poet-Saints* isn't. But the other one is."

Grayson reached in his pockets, produced a pink pack of bidis, lit one up. "I'll be frank," he sighed. "When negotiations break down, my clients become Natu's. And in his tradition, the dacoit tradition, the aftermath of robbery is death."

Though he was careful not to speak or turn, T Bar began to wheeze again.

Grayson's bidi had gone out. Smiling at Waites' heaving back, he paused to relight it. "Dessinger and I are not dacoits," he said at last. "So in cases like T Bar's, we compromise with Natu. 'Be sure we're not followed,' we tell him. Then turn him loose. He administers an excellent beating. Sometimes it's difficult to make him stop."

To judge by his gasping, Waites was not much relieved by this upgraded ticket.

"I admire scholarship," Grayson said to Peter. "And there is no reason whatever for you to join this T Bar gowk. So come with us now, wire the States for five hundred dollars, and this entire episode can become a colorful little tale to share over drinks one day with tenured colleagues."

Though it frightened him badly, Peter said, "I just can't do that."

Grayson turned to ice. "Don't try to bluff me, my young Harvard scholar. Those manuscripts are your *life*."

"They were," Peter said, struggling to steady his voice. "But thanks to you and Dessinger, that life is over."

"Why is that?"

"If I didn't speak Marathi, if I hadn't studied Islam for years, if those poor men at the station had been anything but brokenhearted sports fans, if the train had been any color but white, then maybe I'd want my manuscripts back. But I became a scholar because I wanted *truth* in my life. And if I buy those manuscripts back, my life becomes a lie."

"Your choice here," Grayson said coldly, "is not philosophical. It's physical. You deal with me now. Or you strip down, join Waites—and deal with Natu."

T Bar began to sob on top of his asthma. Natu grinned his lizard grin. "What'll it be?" Grayson murmured.

Peter took a slow, dry swallow of almost nothing but fear—
and began to remove his clothes.

CHAPTER SEVEN

Moon People

It's good to be sensitive in life, but it stinks for baseball.
—Frank Viola, pitcher, New York Mets

1. Lellow

The Pittsburgh Pirates won the National League East in '70. They would win the World Series in '71, and four division championships over the next five years. They had great players, decent coaching, fanatical fans, and they were in the process of making a whole lot of money, so naturally it gave the young Portland Tugs a charge to say they played for the top farm club of this mighty baseball machine. It took a seasoned old pro like Papa to recognize just how vicarious this charge was. Minor league teams are like coal-mining country: the only honor a big league city can regularly be depended upon to pay them is to plunder them. You've got to pretty much love New York and kiss off Kentucky to admire the way big league baseball operates. And Papa, like his mentor G. Q. Durham, was a lifelong baseball Kentuckian.

But on May 29, 1971, one nonvicarious contributor to the Pirates'
success had managed to trickle his way down to Portland for a visit. His
name was Dr. David Hockenberry, or, as he preferred, "plain Doctor
Dave," and he was one of the first men in history to call himself a "sports
psychologist"—a discipline which, in those days, was being invented by
its practitioners as they went along. But a lot of respectable artists operate in this manner. "Plain Doctor Dave's" work with the Pirates was said
by the players themselves to have been instrumental in creating the
"great family feeling" that was now leading the team on to success. So as
the team bus rolled down along the Columbia River heading home from
Spokane, and Papa drowsed by a window, trying not to think of Irwin,
Tug skipper Howie Bowen herded his starting lineup into the front few
seats, announced that Doctor Dave of the Pirates was about to generate
some great family feeling among them, and added that they'd damn well
better not make a joke out of it or he'd fine their butts good. That said,
Bowen parked his own butt on the dash to the right of the driver and
proceeded to scrutinize his starters for taxable signs of levity. "Okay,"
was Doctor Dave's reaction to this. "I want you guys to relax while I load
my rifle, stick the barrel down your throats, and ask you a few playful
family questions."

While some of the players chuckled at this, and Bowen looked confused, Papa opened one eye and peeked out at Hockenberry, wondering
whether he might be about to witness a fellow baseball Kentuckian in
action. "I'm teasing," the psychologist told Coach Bowen. "But we *are*
about to play a game the Bucs call Round Table. And it really does have
one rule, Howie. No manager or coaches within earshot."

The glower deepened. "You're makin' that up," Bowen growled.

Doctor Dave looked surprised. "You're a manager yourself, Howie. You
must've heard why the Pirates fired Grammas and rehired Danny
Murtaugh last year."

Bowen was not at all happy to have to admit that he hadn't.

"Well," said Doctor Dave. "We'd been rained out in Frisco, and had
some hours to kill before the plane to LA. So down in the locker room
the starters and me got deep into a game of Round Table. And they were
just laying their hearts on the table, Howie—honesty like you wouldn't
believe, several men in tears, one unashamedly sucking his thumb—when
Willie Stargell stepped out to take a leak. And there was Coach Grammas
hiding amongst the urinals, spying on us!"

Bowen snorted in disbelief.

"I know," said Doctor Dave. "I didn't think Grammas'd try a wormy stunt like that either."

That wasn't what Bowen's snort had meant. But he was bewildered enough by now to shake his head and trudge muttering off down the aisle.

"Howie wants 'family feeling,' " Doctor Dave said the instant he was out of earshot. "He's ready to play Dad—if it'll win him some games. But you guys must know that though some of you will leave here to move up, others of you will be moving sideways, or down, or just plain out. And who decides which way you move?" He jerked a thumb toward the back of the bus. "Ol' Dad. Now imagine a family with a father who occasionally declares to one of his sons, 'You're cut!' or 'You're traded!' and ships the little guy off forever on the next bus or plane. Imagine it good. Because *that*, me would-be Buckos, is the only kind of dad Howie or Danny Murtaugh or any other manager will ever be to you. So let me share a Big League Baseball Psychology Secret with you: *screw dads!* Ballplayers should be like brothers to each other, and that's it. That's all the family feeling we're gonna shoot for. If that seems harsh, if you wanna feel as if you're working with Dad, Mom or Sis, you better find yourself a different job."

Seeing the majority of the men staring incredulously, and the rest looking a little glum, Doctor Dave added, "Hey. Don't you worry. Playing ball with loyal brothers is a very fine thing. Didn't it give you a brotherly rush of feeling, for instance, when I lied my head off to Howie just now to get his dadly ass outta here?"

Hearing the men roar and wondering what brought it on, Coach Bowen leaned into the aisle to glare up at them. "Family feeling!" Doctor Dave called out, giving him a thumbs-up sign. "It's already working— Dad!" The men roared again.

Round Table turned out to be nothing but a verbal pepper game, with Doctor Dave firing random questions and the Tugs all answering in turn. The only rule was that the players had to answer quickly, and the only purpose, according to Dave, was to allow the players to prove to one another that they had interesting minds. But this last assertion was greeted with visible skepticism by some of the men, and Round Table was slow to get rolling. If Hockenberry hadn't been a master at putting people at ease it could have gotten downright grim. As it was, the game soon reminded Papa of something that Bet and Freddy might have enjoyed during their Famous Science days. "What I'd like to know first—and names will slow us down, so permit me to point" (Dave pulled a silver ballpoint from his pocket)—"is where we're going, where this bus is headed. Your answer can be as simple or as complicated as you like, long as it's quick." The ballpoint pointed.

Hector Harris, the shortstop and leadoff hitter, didn't hesitate, but didn't exactly scintillate either. "We're headed for Portland, Oregon," he said.

Doctor Dave's ballpoint moved. "Same question."

Jim McGeorge, the second baseman, shrugged. "I'd say ol' Hector hit the nail smack on the head."

"Keystone cooperation," said Dave. "That's good. But now bunt back some other answer, no matter how nuts. Where are we headed?"

McGeorge glanced out at the Columbia, shrugged again, and said, "Downriver."

Ty Daniels, the starting pitcher: "Due west."

Gil Jarrel, the cowboy first baseman: "Down that long lonesome highway."

B. G. Anderson, the hippie left fielder: "T'find my baby on the magic bus."

Dwight "No Last Name" Darrel, the center fielder and resident sci-fi buff: "We are heading toward a geometrical configuration of inorganic material called a stadium, with its foundation sunk in an immense globular unit called earth, and its roof sticking up into a more nebulous substance called sky."

"New question," said Doctor Dave. "What the hell's Darrel talkin' about? Like what does he mean, for starters, by a 'globular unit called earth'?"

His pen pointed. Jaime Ramos, the Costa Rican rookie third baseman, looked panic-stricken. "Doort?" he piped. Jaime and English weren't on real close terms.

Gil Jarrel snickered. Dave's pen jumped. The starting catcher, Wilson "No First Name" Walker, said, "Our planet, Dave. The man meant our planet."

"Yes," said Doctor Dave. "Planet Doort. Now quick. Gil. What is *suelo?*"

Gil Jarrel: "Heck if I know."

"*Basura?*"

Gil: "Dunno."

"How 'bout *tierra?*"

Gil: "Beats me."

Doctor Dave: "Jaime?"

Ramos gave Gil an apologetic look, as if the intricacies of his language were all his fault, then explained, "*Suelo* ees thay soil doort. *Basura* ees feelth, or doort. *Tierra*, she ees thay planet Doort."

"Hey, Gil," said Jim McGeorge. "What is *tequila?*"

"What is a *señorita*, hombre?" Ty Daniels chimed in.

"What is *beisbol*, Gil?" McGeorge asked.

"I get the point, assholes," Jarrel muttered.

"So where would you say our fine planet is located?" asked Doctor Dave.

The right fielder, Jimmy Sims, gave it some thought, then answered, "Space."

"Astute," Dave said. "And where do you suppose this 'space' is located?"

No First Name Walker: "Everywhere. Nowhere. Fuck if I know."

"Help him out, Jaime," said Doctor Dave. "Where is space?"

The third baseman sucked his cheeks, bugged his eyes, then pointed at the sky.

Doctor Dave smiled, then pointed his pen at Gil Jarrel.

"Hey, Ramos," Gil said. "How do you say 'nail'?"

"*Clavo.*"

"How 'bout 'head'?"

"*Cabeza*," Jaime said.

"Well," said Gil. "I'd say our man Ramos hit the ol' *clavo* smack on the *cabeza*."

Jaime smiled. The men laughed. Doctor Dave said, "So what *is* space, anyhow?" And his ballpoint started bouncing.

Jim McGeorge: "What I don't know about space'd pretty well fill it."

Jimmy Sims: "Space? Hard to say what space is, Dave. But don't you worry. They's plenty of it."

Ty Daniels: "Space is space, Dave. It fills the universe."

No Last Name Darrel: "But space is empty, Ty."

Ty Daniels: "Hey, man. If you've got everything there is floatin' in you, I'd say you're *full*, not empty."

Doctor Dave: "New question. Who's right?" His pen pointed.

B. G. Anderson: "I'd say they both are. I'd say space is the full emptiness that keeps all the stars and planets and other pieces of universe from getting hideously mangled together into an unthinkably thick glob."

"I'm gettin' a fuckin' headache," groaned No First Name Walker.

"New question, then," said Dave. "World's easiest. Name one of the somethings that float in the nothing called space."

Jim McGeorge shrugged. "Planet Doort."

Dave nodded. "Name another." The pen pointed.

Jaime Ramos, still a little stage-frightened, piped, "*El sol?*"

"Damn betcha," said Doctor Dave. "And how would you describe the relationship between planet Doort and *el sol?*"

Gil Jarrel: "Warmly."

Jim McGeorge: "Distant."

No Last Name Darrel: "Essential."

"Warm, distant, essential. Which is it?" asked Doctor Dave. The pen pointed.

"Boaf," said Jimmy Sims. "Sun's like a woman, Dave. Too close she'll burn ya. 'Thout her you die."

"That was poetry, Jimmy," B.G. sighed.

"Wudn't exactly math, though," said Ty. "One 'n' one 'n' one makes boaf?"

Jimmy shrugged. "Woman do that to a man's math."

"Which is why he invented polygamy," said Doctor Dave. "But what else? What else goes on around the sun?"

No Last Name Darrel: "Planets, Dave. Our particular planet, Doort, shares space with eight others, just like a ball team. And they all circle the sun, same as us."

"So tell me more about the eight." The pen pointed.

Hector Harris: "We're the only one with life, except for bugs or lichen or something, on Mars, I think."

No First Name Walker: "Venus. Thas a planet. An' Saturn got rings."

Jim McGeorge: "There's one named Pluto, and one named Goofy."

Ty Daniels: "How important planets are to us isn't clear, exactly. Like there's people, called astrologers, who think planets are so powerful they control the whole way we act and feel. And there's normal folks who say things like 'There's the Evening Star,' not worrying about how it's really a planet. But then the astrologers turn around and say it's their planets that allows 'em not to worry."

Doctor Dave turned back to Jaime and pointed at the sky. "Anything else worth mentionin' up there?"

Ramos, with his four-hundred-word English vocabulary, was looking almost scholarly now. "*La luna,*" he said, giving his head a jaunty wiggle. "Thay moon."

Papa had been sitting quiet, eyes closed, basking in the friendly pointlessness of the game. But at the words *Thay moon* he heard a high, piping echo: *Thay moon is lellow . . .* And saw Irwin. His face at age one and a half or so. Beaming up at him. One fat little finger pointing. And just that fast Papa was struggling not to sob.

"So what do we know about the moon?" asked Doctor Dave.

"Got a lost golf ball on it," said Ty. "And an American flag."

"An' pro'ly a bag or two o' astronaut shit," said No Last Name Walker.

"So they best be watchin' out," said Jimmy Sims, "where they be takin' the next giant step for mankind."

The men roared. Dave's pen pointed. "It's round like a world, the ol' moon is," said Gil Jarrel. "But it's lots different than Earth. Like it's cold. Whereas we've got fire inside. And it's got no water. We do. And no air, I don't think. Does it?"

The pen pointed. "Nope," said No Last Name Darrel. "No air, no water. Doesn't spin on its axis either. Moon keeps its same face towards us all the time. Which is why, until that space capsule with the camera orbited, nobody knew what the back side even looked like. And it was better that way, didn't you think? Didn't you love, as a kid, to look up at the moon and wonder what might be hiding on the dark side?"

Lellow . . . Papa couldn't get a grip, couldn't shake the little voice— or the shaved head, the scars, the jittering eyes.

"You can still wonder plenty," B. G. Anderson said.

"Naw." No Last Name shook his head. "The astronauts wrecked it, for me."

"I knew an old guy," B.G. said, "a damn strange, damn smart fella too, who told me the moon is really a dead world. I don't know how he knew it, or even *if* he knew, really. But that's what he said. And the way he said it, I believed him."

"Thay moon," said Jaime Ramos, "she's fool tonight."

"Theeeeere's a dead world on the rise," sang Ty.

"There could be," B.G. insisted. "There really could be. And if it *is* a dead world, then there's still plenty to wonder about. Like maybe we all came, human beings I mean, from the moon. Like maybe it was *our* world once, in ancient times, and it was dying. So maybe we rode it here —you know, drifted here through space. Or even propelled it here, maybe, like if we were advanced then, and lost or forgot the advancements later. So maybe the first man and woman on Earth, or first non-cave-type man and woman, were just two people from that dying world who found some way to get down to this one. And once they got here, and got settled, maybe they would look back up, knowing that all the rest of their people were still there. Maybe they'd have to hold each other when it rose, all orange and full and close. Maybe that's where our romantic notions about the moon first came from. Two people holding each other to keep their hearts from breaking, because everybody they knew was dying in the cold rocks and dust piles a quarter million miles away . . ."

The sheer joy on Irwin's face as he'd pointed. As if he was the first one ever to see it. And his first impulse? Share. *Thay moon . . .*

"And tonight," B.G. was saying, "while we play ball here on Earth, there it'll be—the cold, empty world we came from. No sign of the people, nothing left of 'em now. But still shining down. And still trying to maybe tell us, *Enjoy it down there. Live like you mean it. 'Cause once upon a time, this was a world too.*"

Whether from awe or mere politeness, the players were silent for a bit. Then Jimmy Sims said, "Shit, man. You tryin' t'give us nightmares."

"*By the light,*" crooned Gil Jarrel, "*of the silvery dead world . . .*"

"If it's so dead," said Ty Daniels, "how's it do the stuff it do?"

"Except for shine," Heck Harris asked, "what *does* it do?"

"Makes ee woomawn half thee baby," said the scholarly Jaime Ramos.

"Makes ee ocean half thee tides," said Ty.

"Makes ee hoot owls hoot an' ee coyotes howl," said Jim McGeorge.

"Makes me horny," said Jimmy Sims.

"That's 'cause you're one o' them escaped moon people," said Heck.

"Don't take no moon," said No First Name Walker, "t'make *me* horny."

"That's 'cause you're a mooncalf," said Heck.

"Full o' moonshine," said Jim McGeorge.

"Who gonna moon *you* in a minute," No First Name said.

"Moon Darrel," Gil suggested. "He *likes* the dark side."

"Up *your* dark side," said No Last Name.

Jimmy Sims grabbed Doctor Dave's ballpoint and pointed it at the doc himself.

"Moonbeam," said Doctor Dave. "Moonbow. Moonblind."

"Moon-unit Zappa," said B.G. "John Blue Moon Odom. Reverend Moon."

Lellow, said Irwin. The tiny finger, delighted eyes. Of course he'd meant pink. In those days he thought that "dreen" was "boo" too. But when Papa had looked up to where the little finger pointed, there it had been in the boo-black sky—the cold dead world we maybe came from.

2. Letter to Natasha, pp. 210 & 211

The same situation that had Papa hearing echoes from early fatherhood had thrown Everett into a different sort of regression. For several days he'd been stalking the deer trails, logging roads, beaches, hills and headlands of Greater Shyashyakook with his old revolutionary blood boiling, wracking his brains for some fiendishly clever Free Irwin Plan. The problem so far was that while Everett hadn't come up with even the rough outline of a rescue operation, his old Hippie Churchill persona had come up with several. Irwin's plight, it had told Everett right off the bat, was all Washington D.C.'s doing, and D.C. had no fucking scruples whatsofuckingever: it was therefore fair and necessary that Everett "get real" about the enemy he was dealing with—and jettison his own scruples. This deft little cerebration made things exciting for a while. It freed him up to contemplate false identities, bureaucratic trickery, political bribes and blackmail schemes; it allowed him to think long and hard about bomb threats or actual bombings, kidnap threats or actual kidnappings, exchanges of hostages, guarantees of diplomatic immunity, FBI-proof getaway plans. With the help of an eggs-reefer-and-beer breakfast after an almost sleepless night it finally even vouchsafed him the vision of an army of pissed-off hippies in BONG THE PENTACONG! T-shirts mounting a full-scale, heavily armed, FREE WINNIE NOW! asylum invasion led by Che Chance himself. By the time he'd imagined all that, though, Everett was so exhausted that he had to sleep away the entire afternoon.

And later the same evening, as the full moon Jaime Ramos had predicted was sure enough rising over the Little Nessakoola, Everett sat down on an old spruce stump on the ridge behind his cottage, took a deep breath of clear night air, and realized in the time it took to exhale that not one of his schemes took the actual Irwin, the actual Linda and Nash, the rest of the family, gross reality or even the actual Everett into account. Another breath, another exhalation, and he realized that he'd just wasted two days in an insurrectionist dither—while Irwin remained in hell.

He didn't feel he had time for remorse. He settled for slapping himself —just once, but hard—in the face. He then walked back to his cottage, brewed up a cup of cowboy coffee, grabbed his Bic and Big Chief 500 tablet, sat down by the buttercups at the red kitchen table, and wrote—

on two more pages of his unmailable letter to Natasha—the following
description of what now struck him as the crux of his problem:

Remember in sex education class, back in high school, reading about
the ovum? Remember how it's got this soft protective wall around it
which hundreds of sperm reach at about the same time, and then they
all bombard it, trying to fight their way through? And then remember
how just one sperm finally breaks through the wall, and the instant it
does the ovum undergoes a drastic chemical change that seals out all
the others? Well, it's kind of a transvestite metaphor I'm making,
Tasha, in that it's my heart that's playing the ovum and you who I'm
casting as that first sperm. But the whole idea of a walled-off center or
an irreversible transformation—that's what I'm getting at. That's what
I think has happened.

Because you're in my center, Tasha. You've invaded my heart and I
can't get you out. So no one else can come in. But you're gone. You
vanished. So I have no center.

Not very romantic, this sperm and egg imagery. But what can I say?
My situation here ain't so romantic either. It's not even sad and bluesy
anymore. It's just a fucking disaster, frankly. Because, another thing it's
time I told you: you've created hurt. Real pain, real hurt. Maybe your
love was just a veiled wish to crush me from the start. And maybe I
deserved it. But the part of this I hate, and the part I think you'd hate
too, is that it's not just me you're hurting anymore.

Remember, when it was really rainy and boring, how I used to tell
you Irwin Stories? Remember how hard we'd laugh? Remember the
time you told me I better never introduce you, because you were
afraid you'd love him more than me? And remember my answer—that
if you did we'd be even, because I loved him more than anybody else
on earth? Well, the morning after I wrote you last—the morning after
I picked these poor severed buttercup heads and thought life was so
wonderful and maybe it is, too, but that only makes it worse—I got a
message from my father saying that Irwin is in a terrible trap. Dying,
maybe. Or worse. So naturally I've been busting my brains, spiking my
smarts, I've been a fucking factory of inauspicious ideas up here, trying
to invent an escape for him. But that, I'm afraid, is where you slip
back into the picture. Because what good are brains, Tasha, and how is
one thought any better than another, if you haven't got a sixth sense,
a heart, a center, to sort them out with?

I need my center back. The part you invaded and transformed and closed off and disappeared with, Natasha or Laurel or whoever you are. I need it back fast. Someone I love, someone you'd love too, is dying for me to find it. So please. Right *now*. Feel this. Feel me calling. I know you can't reverse what's irreversible or make it all better or any other sort of fairytale shit. All I need is to hear what happened to us. Just enough to undo the chemical damage. Just enough to get my godforsaken center back.

When he'd finished writing these words Everett went out on his porch and sat down on the steps to listen. He heard a ferry's horn in the Strait, miles off in the distance; heard an owl on the ridge—a great horned, maybe; heard, down on the moonlit tideflat, a killdeer cry, just once. He did not hear, feel, intuit, or expect even the faintest message from Natasha. And when the night breeze eased into the spruces, when he heard the big trees begin to pronounce the nine-hour-long word that meant Warm Full-Mooned Spring Night, even another instant of waiting was suddenly unthinkable.

He charged back into the cottage and stuffed his wallet and car keys in his pockets. He shoved his 211-page letter into a manila envelope, wrote "Laurel Lee" on it, slapped on a few stamps. He went to his bookless bookshelves, grabbed her abandoned cookbook, *Thoroughly Modern Menus*, and copied her deceased grandmother's 1932 Knoxville, Tennessee, address from the inside cover onto the manila envelope.

He was careful to add no return address.

One hour and thirty-nine miles later his three-month-long letter was irretrievably locked inside a downtown Victoria mailbox, and Everett was parking his foot on the rail at Churchill's Pub and calmly telling his friend the barkeep, "Evenin', Nelson. I'd like to get fucked up. Then I'd like to ask your advice."

"We'll see what we can do," said Nelson.

3. Worthlessness

Though we had very little time to spend together, things were going awfully well between Amy and me. So well that I would sometimes forget Irwin, the draft, the war, my family; so well that the whole suffering world would vanish for hours at a time; so well, in other words, that to the world, and to my family and friends, I had become almost worthless when Amy was available.

I worried about this worthlessness. Even agonized over it, when I could find the time. But I finally concluded that it is an inalienable right of lovers everywhere to become temporarily worthless to the world. It may even be their duty. Because when the love of two people produces things that the world deems valuable, the opportunists of the world find and exploit that value—and then God help love and lovers. Look at Irwin. Putting Linda's needs before his own, as any good romantic would, he had stopped being a student, opened himself up to the draft, and so been left with a brutal choice (as that great deck-stacking opportunist, the U.S. Government, knew he would) between exile, prison or Vietnam. Again thinking of Linda, he chose the only option that provided pay, public honor, cheap loans and widow's pensions. In other words, because Irwin loved his wife, Uncle Sam was able to purchase, for a pittance, another big strong lower-middle-class body to hurl at the gooks.

After watching what this purchase had cost Irwin and Linda, Amy and I chose a different path. Love, we figured, may be the best thing that ever happens between two people. And that the best thing is of no worldly worth struck us as a beautiful paradox—and an endangered one. We therefore began fighting to defend the worthlessness of lovers everywhere in the only way we knew how: by vowing to remain as inseparable from each other, and as utterly useless to all opportunists, as the rest of our responsibilities would allow.

4. War Prayer

Watching Papa Toe pitch through the years—the body language, the easy grace, the pure focus, time after time—any fan who didn't know him would have sworn that there was nothing more important to this man than the game he was playing. Of course, his family knew better. Most ballplayers' family members know better. But the good players are all like Papa: their faces tell you nothing. And professional baseball is beautiful to watch largely because of this.

A pro contract is a kind of vow: a man agrees, in signing it, that he will perform as though his personal life, his family, his non-baseball hopes and needs do not exist. He is paid to aspire to purity. For the duration of every game he has not only to behave but really to *feel* that the ballpark is the entire world: his body is his instrument, so any lack of this feeling will soon be reflected in his play. Everett has poked fun at the analogy, but the purity of commitment really isn't much different than that of the Hinayana monks whom Peter so admired, they with their one robe, one bowl, one icon; ballplayers with their uniforms, their bats, their gloves.

But purity has a brutal side. Sometimes a strikeout means that the slugger's girlfriend just ran off with the UPS driver. Sometimes a muffed ground ball means that the shortstop's baby daughter has a pain in her head that won't go away. And handicapping is for amateur golfers, not ballplayers. Pitchers don't ease off on the cleanup hitter because of the lumps just discovered in his wife's breast. Baseball is not life. It is a fiction, a metaphor. And a ballplayer is a man who agrees to uphold that metaphor as though lives were at stake.

Perhaps they are. I cherish a theory I once heard propounded by G. Q. Durham that professional baseball is inherently antiwar. The most over-looked cause of war, his theory runs, is that it's so damned interesting. It takes hard effort, skill, love and a little luck to make times of peace consistently interesting. About all it takes to make war interesting is a life. The appeal of trying to kill others without being killed yourself, according to Gale, is that it brings suspense, terror, honor, disgrace, rage, tragedy, treachery and occasionally even heroism within range of guys who, in times of peace, might lead lives of unmitigated blandness. But baseball, he says, is one activity that is able to generate suspense and excitement on a national scale, just like war. And baseball can only be played in peace. Hence G.Q.'s thesis that pro ballplayers—little as some of them may want to hear it—are basically just a bunch of unusually well-coordinated guys working hard and artfully to prevent wars, by making peace more interesting.

A nice little irony in his theory: even warlike ballplayers fight for peace by making it more interesting. Consider this interview:

Reporter: Tell us how things were in your day.
Ty Cobb: There's nothing to tell. It's all there in the record book.
Reporter: Who helped you the most when you were a young player?
Ty Cobb: Nobody.
Reporter: What do you think you'd hit if you were playing today?
Ty Cobb: About .320.
Reporter: Why so low?
Ty Cobb: You have to remember, I'm sixty-two years old.

Here was a man who upheld the metaphor so long and ferociously that he never did reenter any sort of outside world: till the day he died, Cobb defined himself purely in terms of a baseball world—a world in which war never has and never shall exist.

On May 29, 1971, in the ninth inning of a home game against Spokane, Papa Toe Chance did the exact opposite. For just one pitch, he played ball not for the sake of his team or his art but for the sake of someone in the outside world. And though his team forgave him for it instantly, though even Howie Bowen forgave him for it eventually, Papa, like Cobb, was a purist. For himself he had shattered the metaphor. And he never threw another pitch.

There comes a point in any game of patience—I used to reach it in chess on about the tenth move—when the longing for a spontaneous action, even a suicidal action, feels infinitely preferable to more agonized, self-controlled thought. Papa reached this "tenth move" point against the third Spokane Indian he faced. But the batter, the whole Spokane team, was irrelevant: the man against whom Papa was really making his suicide move was Major Keys.

Ty Daniels had thrown eight innings of five-hit ball at the Indians, and the Tugs had a 2 to 1 lead, when Howie Bowen sent Papa to the bullpen to warm up. Papa didn't argue. He knew his pitching staff was shot from all the makeup games and doubleheaders. And though he too was shot, he was the stupid-situation reliever.

He had nothing on the ball as Tony Baldanos warmed him up. He'd have to rely on speed if he couldn't conjure his junk, and at his age that reliance had begun to feel rash. So he was audibly muttering at Ty to hold it together—when the Indians' cleanup hitter, Joey Arguelles, drilled a double that bounced into the bullpen and nearly rolled up to Papa's feet. "Looks like I'm about to be deployed," he told Tony.

Sure enough, five pitches later, four of them balls, Arguelles was on second, the winning run was on first, Daniels was headed for the shower, and Bowen was waving for Papa.

All his life, both as a starter and as a reliever, Papa had used the walk to the mound as a time to dig down inside. It was during the walk that his body became his instrument and the upcoming pitches his only possible means of expression; it was during the walk that he'd enter the metaphor, and grow ruthless. And, even on this night, the walk was as effective as a thousand others before it: by the time he reached the edge of the infield, the entire world was once again just this diamond.

But as he passed third base, Jaime Ramos grinned, gave him a thumbs-up, and pointed back over his shoulder. "Thay moon," he said, "she's *good* for junk!"

And Papa turned inside out: thay moon became a dead lellow world, the sky a boo-black void, the diamond a tiny false haven lying unprotected beneath them, and Howie Bowen—handing him the ball, saying, "Zap 'em, Pop"—was just some bizarre biomorphic irrelevancy. Bowen trudged smugly back to the dugout. Papa stepped tentatively onto the mound. And for the first time in his life it was a pile of dirt no different than any other dirt on earth, and baseball was just a game.

No First Name Walker jogged out to double-check their signs. Papa met him partway, nodded at every word he said, stepped back onto his little dirt pile, and remembered nothing. *Mooncalf. Moon-unit. Moonblind.* He knew his shattered focus was a kind of betrayal. He knew that ballplayers from the game's beginning had been forced to clear their minds of crises as bad as, perhaps worse than his. But if the same crisis that was merely breaking his focus was obliterating Irwin's mind and life at that moment, hadn't this diamond, this profession, this calling become nothing but an escape from the intolerable suffering of his son?

He threw his warm-ups in a state of siege. Don Prelt, the sixth hitter in the Indians' lineup, stepped to the plate. The Tug infield moved in for the bunt. Papa went into the stretch, checked the two runners, shook off a sign he hoped meant fastball, threw a sinker. Prelt tried to bunt and fouled it straight down onto the plate.

Strike one. But Papa was still hearing echoes, Keys's voice this time: *Trust me . . .* Wilson Walker signed sinker again. Papa shook it off, unleashed his rage, threw a half-crazed fastball, and when Prelt tried to bunt again the pitch hopped, and he fouled it back into the ump's chest protector.

Strike two, yes. But it was Irwin putting the stuff on his throws. And now it was time to waste a pitch, if the game was still baseball. But Papa felt that Irwin was out of time. He ignored Wilson's low outside target, blew in another crazed fastball. Prelt swung from the heels. And missed by half a foot.

One out. One moon. Two tiers of fans, roaring. And two Irwins—one in Papa's arms, beaming up at the moon; one in a white room, drooling on the backs of his useless hands. Wiznewski, the Indians' hulking first baseman, stood at the plate. Again the infield moved in for the bunt. But the intuition of the Spokane manager was firing on no cylinders this night: he had Wiznewski swing away, and the first pitch was grounded hard—straight at Jaime Ramos, who forced Arguelles at third, then nearly ended the game with a long throw to first. Wiznewski beat it by an inch.

Two outs. The runners still stuck on first and second. The Tug junkies fired up and chanting now: *Papa Toe! Papa Toe!* And I've never stopped wishing that Ramos had gotten just a little more on that throw. Because Papa may have still looked like a pitcher. But his inner struggle was over. And baseball had lost.

A pinch hitter named Warren Berman came to the plate—a hunched-up, jittery little utility man who looked like a foregone conclusion, an out waiting to happen. The Indians, after all, were as used up as the Tugs. But Papa hardly glanced at him. Or at the runners. Or at Wilson Walker's signal. Though his face revealed nothing, Papa was staring at a rectangle of night sky showing at the end of an exit tunnel halfway up through the first tier of fans. And he was thinking only of Irwin. No more stupid relief. Real relief. That's what he wanted now. Divine intervention, I guess, was what he longed to invoke. How to send a heartfelt message from his little pile of dirt to God—a difficult pitching problem for even a Cy Young Award winner. Was He so far away that it required an enormous gesture? Or so close it would take something incredibly subtle? Papa didn't know. He was just an old junk pitcher. He would, then and there, have given his life for Irwin. But no one was asking him for it. So all he could think to do was give what he possessed at the moment—

and all that he possessed was his art. Looking to the body as his instrument, to the pitch as the one means of expression, and to the sports-page boxscores as the fossil record of that expression, Papa thought of a gesture both flagrant and subtle which, whatever God might make of it, he could at least share with his son . . .

An *Oregonian* sportswriter named Deke Gant—the same man who'd written the "Baseball Lazarus" story about Papa six years before—devoted an entire column to what happened next. The headline at the top of the column read:

TUG RELIEF LEGEND
HURLS WORST PITCH EVER

and the column, like its headline, got pretty melodramatic. But from any perspective but Papa's I'm afraid his last pitch *was* melodramatic. So here is Gant's account:

. . . and Chance was clearly on the verge of yet another textbook relief performance when, in the words of his catcher, Wilson Walker, "Papa T blew a head gasket."

He went into his stretch with no sign of agitation. He checked the runners. He then kicked his leg unusually high, let out a roar that sent poor Berman diving for cover, and unleashed a pitch—one would have to call it a high fastball—that flew clear up over the backstop, high over the box seats, and straight out the exit tunnel midway up the lower deck!

Chance just stood watching his throw till it disappeared. So did everyone else. I've never seen or heard the stadium so still. Even the base runners forgot to run. The general feeling, I think, was that the game must be suspended, because one needs a baseball to play baseball and Chance had obviously just thrown it away. Plate ump Ed Van Twardzik broke the silence with one of the great understatements of all time. "Ball One," he called out. A lone fan way out in the center-field bleachers then brought down the house by shouting, "Aw, get some glasses!"

Chance left the mound, the game, and apparently the Tug team without a word. He was charged with a wild pitch. The runners advanced to second and third. The scheduled starter for tomorrow night's doubleheader, Billy Drews, then retired the side with a pop foul.

In a post-game interview, winning pitcher Ty Daniels said that some kind of personal crisis must have triggered the incident. Right fielder Jimmy Sims said no, it was the full moon. Whatever it was, it wasn't an accident. The ball traveled easily 170 feet and climbed another 60 before flying out the exit. Outfielders Dwight Darrel and B. G. Anderson said they went to the mound after the game and tried throwing at the same exit, out of a stretch, and that it took Darrel three tries and Anderson nine before they hit it. Tug manager Howie Bowen called Chance's throw "the most harebrained stunt I've seen in all my years in baseball." Bowen added that his player/coach would definitely be fined, and

that he could be suspended for life if his
action is found to have resulted from any
kind of wager. But when asked what sort
of disciplinary action he thought was appropriate, young Ty Daniels said, "Suspension? Fine? Get off it. Papa Toe's the soul
of this team. He's who we all take our
troubles to. And it seems pretty obvious
he's in trouble right now himself. So we
just want him better. Then we want him
back."

Chance was unavailable for comment.

A Portland Tugs envelope arrived at the asylum in Mira Loma two days
after Papa's last pitch. Inside were three pieces of Tugs stationery. Pasted
to the first page was a stat—an iota of pure logos carefully cut out of the
Oregonian box scores. The clipping was tiny. All it said was: "WP –
H. Chance." Pasted to the second page was Deke Gant's column, the bulk of
which I've just quoted. The third page was a note, hastily written in
pencil. It said:

Irwin:

I'll be pulling into your area about the same time as this package.
And though you may not see me, I'll be staying close, and doing all I
can to get you home, from now till the day you *are* home. Meanwhile,
here's the skinny on a pitch I threw in your honor last night. It was
stupid of course. There will be consequences of course. But like you I
believe there is a time for crazy gestures. This WP stands for "War
Prayer." God bless you, and God bless your tube of Gleem. See you
soon.

Love, Papa

p.s. to Major Keys.

I know you'll intercept this, and I doubt you'll show it to him. But
I'll be there soon enough, with plenty more copies. You've got two
crazies on your hands now, Major. And more where we two came from.

5. Levelhead versus Rebelhead

Everett had never learned, during their Rub-a-Dub era conversations the
previous summer, whether Nelson was the Churchill's Pub bartender's
first name or his last. But he did learn that Nelson told some bad jokes

and some good stories, that he was an ex-American and a draft-dodger, that he poured double whiskeys for the price of singles once he learned Everett was the same, and that, if a customer really forced his hand, he could shell out some damned levelheaded advice. For general purposes Everett considered Chief Yulie the last word in Bartender Wisdom. But when Yulie got serious her advice got sort of pre-Columbian and unsettling. Everett felt unsettled enough already. And advice was only his backup reason for coming to Churchill's. His primary reason was to get plowed.

"So tell me this, Nelson," he said, two or three blended whiskeys into the predictable topic. "Is there a chance in hell that an artful and loquacious draft-dodger, if he showed up in person, could convince a U.S. Army shrink that his lunatic brother is really just a misfiled, goofball Christian?"

Nelson shook his head, as he'd been shaking it all evening. "Get this through your head, Everett. Even a *respectable* citizen couldn't help your brother. And you and me are felons down there. Anything you do in the States will be a futile gesture. And prison will be your reward."

"Yeah yeah. Okay. But so I go to prison. So what, Nelson? Because how important is my freedom at this point? I'm a civilization of one up here, dammit. Hippies, Yippies, 'Nam, the Bomb, B-ball, Baseball—what the hell's he raving about? they wonder in Shyashyakook. Milk a goat, grow an artichoke, catch a halibut, they tell me. But my *brother*, Nelson! How can I not lift even a futile finger for the sake of my idiot brother?"

"Because when you're through lifting it he'll still be in the asylum, and *you'll* be somewhere even worse. Why should *that* appease your conscience? You're going to hate what's happening to Irwin in Canada *or* America. The difference is, here you can hate it in front of a bar. Down there you'll hate it behind 'em."

Everett sighed, and felt heartsick. "You're too damned reasonable, Nelson. And so's this damned Canuck whiskey. Gimme somethin' irrational! Somethin' American! Somethin' downright *Confederate* even. Got any Rebel Yell?"

Nelson started pouring. Everett did some serious Rebel drinking. And they did a lot more vehement discussing. But after the bar had closed, the other customers had left, and Nelson had poured a half pot of coffee down Everett hoping to keep him on the road, the bartender delivered a forceful summary of all his arguments, plus a few twists Everett hadn't thought of. Among them:

1. "If you want prison for the fun of it, why don't you go beat the living shit out of that Babcock asshole?"

2. "When you dropped in last Christmas, you and Natasha weren't too subtle about being in love. And when you dropped in a couple months ago, you weren't too subtle about being heartbroken and still hoping to find her. If that's all over and done, fine—and sorry I mentioned it. But if there's a chance she'll come looking for you, and if that's something you want, you better think hard before leaving here. Because there's no chance she'll come looking for you in prison."

3. "When Irwin gets out of the asylum could be the time when he *really* needs you. And if you're doing three to five, you sure as hell won't be around to help."

4. "You warned your brother not to enlist. He did it anyway. Why punish yourself because he wouldn't listen? We all took a gamble, Everett. He bet Uncle Sam had a heart. We bet the opposite. It's a shame, but he lost."

That said, Nelson flicked on his cigarette lighter, grabbed the tab Everett had been running, and torched it "just like a draft card." "This one's on Mother Canada," he added, squeezing Everett's shoulder. "And don't forget this talk. Don't get crazy on me, Everett. We can make a life in this country. I want to see you back here soon."

Everett shook the barkeep's hand and with genuine warmth said, "I won't forget, Nelson. I won't get crazy. And *thank* you! Very much."

But not a minute later, standing alone in the parking lot beneath the stars and moon, it seemed unthinkable that he had nothing more germane to do for Irwin than drive back to Shyashyakook and sleep off a drunk.

6. Distance Between Studs

At about 9 A.M. on May 30, Elder Babcock laid aside a hot pen and the climax of a sermon, slipped on his suit coat and frown before answering the front doorbell, swung the door wide open hoping to cow some tedious church member into shame for the interruption, and immediately regretted it when he saw a tall, leathery-faced stranger standing on his new I FOUND IT doormat, smoking a filterless cigarette. "Yes," the Elder said. "May I help you?"

"Is the missus home?" the man asked.

"No," Babcock said. And immediately regretted this too.

"Are you Denzel Babcock?"

"I am."

"May I come in?" the man asked, stepping his cigarette out on the mat.

Babcock was a big, burly man, and no coward. But this stranger, physically, was a specimen. And the look on his face, the body language . . . "Do I know you, sir?"

"The name is Chance," Papa said. "Hugh Chance. I'm Laura's husband. Irwin's father."

Babcock's scowl deepened, but he extended his hand. "So," he said, and they briefly shook. "We meet at last. But why, I wonder? Nothing wrong with Laura or Bet, I hope?"

This kind of division was automatic and unconscious with Babcock: nothing wrong with the two "saved," tithe-paying church members, he hoped, but why waste breath on the rest? Papa closed the division: "There's something wrong with all of us," he said. "It's Irwin."

"Ah. Yes. Laura has told me all about the, uh, the breakdown. And now he's taken a turn for the worse, has he?"

"We don't see it as a breakdown," Papa said. "And if things were any worse, I think he'd be dead."

Babcock sighed, led Papa to a chair in his livingroom, took a far larger wing chair himself, and gave his Ministerial Sympathy Dial a twist. "Most unfortunate. And so hard on the family, I'm sure. As it happens, I'm giving the guest sermon for the *Bread of Life* radio program this Sabbath. Many thousands of listeners. And if you like, Brother Chance, I'll mention Irwin and your family in our prayers."

"That wasn't what I had in mind," Papa said.

Babcock switched off the dial. "What do you have in mind?"

"I'd like you to write a letter to a fella named Keys, the head of the mental hospital where Irwin is staying."

The Elder looked tentative now. "Your wife mentioned him to me. A difficult man, it seems. But competent in his field, I should think."

"I don't know about his field," Papa said. "But you and I both know Irwin doesn't belong in his asylum."

Babcock forced a smile. "Mental health is not my profession, Brother Chance. And though I'm flattered that you've called on me in a crisis, I doubt that my opinion, pro or con, would mean much to this Keys fellow."

"No flattery intended," Papa said evenly. "And I'm sure Keys is no more interested in your opinion than I am. But I still want you to write a letter."

The smile was long gone as Babcock asked, "What sort of letter?"

Papa got right to it. "One that retracts all the lies you wrote last year about Irwin not being a genuine Christian or a Conscientious Objector."

All pretexts of civility and concern vanished as Babcock said, "I am *not* a liar, Brother Chance. And I'm afraid I can't help you. So now"—he started to his feet—"I'd like you to get out of my—"

But before he'd finished the sentence or even quite straightened up from his chair, Papa was standing so close to him that he had to lean slightly backwards. "Like I said," Papa told him. "I'm not interested in your opinion. I'm here for a letter. I won't be leaving without it."

Babcock forced another smile. "Are you *threatening* me, Brother Chance?"

"Not at all, Brother Babcock. But I am promising you, before God Almighty, that if you don't write a letter saying that you lied about Irwin to get at the brothers you hate, I'm going to do to your head and face what your lies have done to Irwin's."

It seemed that Papa, three hundred miles to the south of Churchill's Pub, had been listening to some of Nelson the barkeep's advice.

Babcock was defiant. "You can't bully *me!*" he huffed.

The next thing he knew he was splayed back over his chair, garroted by his tie, listening to Papa whisper, *"Then you're a brave man, aren't you?"*

"It's going to be a pleasure," Babcock gritted, "to see you thrown in jail for this!"

Papa spun him around, kicked the chair away, banged his forehead against the wall hard enough to stun him, then held him there, hung him there, by the back of his collar and pants. "I throw things for a living, Babcock. I'll do the throwing here. You've taken the only son I have who trusted you and damned him half to death with your lies. Now you're going to *un*damn him. Or I'm going to put your skull through this wall. It's your choice. But your time is up."

Babcock's situation reminded me of Peter's easy use, in his early letter from India, of the words "transcendence" and "crucifixion": it's one thing to say "You can't bully *me*" to a man who has threatened you verbally; it's something else again to say it when you're staring straight at a wall of sheetrock, trying like hell to remember just how far apart the carpenters placed the studs.

"It's possible," the Elder said, "that I've misjudged one of your sons."

7. Sinking Moon, Sinking People

Everett was driving home in the wee hours, using another car's taillights to help track the road, watching for deer's eyes in the salmonberry, staying alert by chewing a whole pack of Wrigley's in time to any rock-'n'-roll-like static he could find on the radio, doing forty or so through the curves along the lower Little Nessakoola, when the car in front of him slammed on its brakes—"*Jesus!*"—fishtailed, released its brakes, sped on. Everett slowed, suspecting already what had happened . . .

And sure enough, there they were: a pair of eyes, bright green in the headlights, right in the center of his lane. "And look what it is! God damn it. An otter."

The curve where it lay was sharp, banked and blind, so he pulled his rusty Olds to the shoulder, then backed up alongside. Rolling down his window, he peered out. But the moon was casting shadows there. Couldn't see how bad it was hurt. No flashlight in the glove box, no flares, not even a book of matches. "What else is new, Mr. Equipped?" He backed up further, cocked the car as best he could. The headlights mostly lit the brush across the road, but he could make the otter out now —decent head movement; eyes plenty alert, watching him as he closed the car door. But a rivulet of blood running down the banked asphalt. And the rest of the long body inert, just lying there. "I'll get a rock," he sighed, "and get you outta this."

He started looking. But to his surprise, he couldn't find one. Nothing along the shoulder but fine gravel and blackberry shoots. Nothing in the car but an old coat and used spark plugs. Nothing in the trunk either: hocked his jack, spare and tire iron to pay for fruitcake phone calls. It went against his usual dark religion, but Everett decided to hope there was a reason for this. "Maybe you're not so bad off," he told the otter. He fetched the old coat from his car. "Maybe we'll wrap you in this," he said, easing toward it, "take you home, patch the holes, fix you up with a skateboard, roll you around for company. My pet Porta-Otter. Get ya a little surfboard too. Troll you behind the boat. And a ski for snow. You might like this new life. I'm Everett, by the way. How ya doin'?"

But when he came close the claws on the one good paw started scrabbling at the pavement, trying to run. And when he knelt down beside the dark form he saw shattered bone and a loop of intestine; saw two little rows of distended nipples, one row crushed, oozing milk with the blood.

A female. A little mother. Eyes still fully alive, fur still wet with river water. But beyond any help Everett had to offer. "Busted, aren't ya?" he whispered. "Ruined, aren't ya?"

The otter quit scrabbling, but still watched him. And her gaze made him feel nervous. Nervous and inadequate. "Shouldn't drive a car," he muttered, "without a good song to chant over road kills."

He looked out at the river. He looked up at the moon. He couldn't think of a thing. "Ought to put 'em in the damned driver's manual." He sat down beside the otter anyway, thinking the least he could do was talk softly to it. "Remember footpaths?" he asked. "Remember the people who rode horses, or rivers, to go visit each other, and worshipped Raven and Bear and Killer Whale? Well, those people are gone, you otters have got to know that, and we've got these mumbo-jumbo gods now, with names like Progress and Luxury and GNP, that make us crazy, make us killers, when we travel. What's really nuts is that a lot of us are sorry about making this a shit world for you. We'd love to stop our damned gods. But we can't figure out how. Not yet. So . . ."

His voice drifted off. He felt like a fool. This otter didn't need his politics. She needed to die. So it was his inner ineptitude that Everett was feeling, and his lack of a good death song, when, faster than seemed possible, a dead-earnest log truck came barreling around the curve . . .

No time to even stand: he somersaulted to the road's shoulder. The air horn sounded, the jake brakes fired off, he turned to watch the worthless miracle of fourteen wheels straddling the dying otter. But in the glare of headlights just before the wheels arrived he also glimpsed something impossible: a nightmare thing: a pulsing red thing, yards from the crushed body, but moving. Crawling. Coming toward him. *My God! Some organ? Her heart, trying to return home to the river?*

The tail wind blinded him. The truck was gone. Dark and silence returned. But he could *still* make out the shape. Could even faintly hear it, dragging itself across the dry asphalt, inexorable, coming for him. Everett's flesh writhed, his breath stopped. The heart-thing reached the edge of the shadows. It crept out into the moonlight—

and he saw a crayfish. A half-grown crawdad. Alive and well. But as confused as Everett himself by the kind of night it was having.

Too scared to laugh, he picked it up by the back and congratulated it. It had just broken the world's record, he told it, for quantity of terror inflicted upon a hominid by a crustacean. In answer the crawdad strained backward with both claws, trying to inflict a little something more on his fingers. "Cool it," Everett said. "Don't you know a personal lord and savior when you feel one?"

He ferried it down the highway to an opening in the briars. He said, "Remember there's a god, and its name is Everett," gave it a toss, watched the moonlit splash.

He then climbed back in his car, rolled down his window, took careful aim with his left front tire, sighed, "Save the cold-blooded, kill the warm-hearted. That's politics." Then he finished what the first car and the log truck had left undone.

He didn't look back. If he'd left anything moving, he didn't want to know. This too was politics.

But a few minutes later he was rolling along the road as it followed the Strait-bound Nessakoola. Window down, transmission in neutral, he was gliding along, exhausted, under stars and sinking moon, driving at swimming speed, otter speed, watching the same moon-silvered riffles and silent glides she'd navigated moments before. And when he pictured again the way she'd watched him—one small, rounded ear up, listening to his babble, the other ear down, listening to the world beneath the asphalt, crushed and alive, two worlds at once—it touched something in him, unlocked something, and he felt himself fall through a kind of false bottom, felt he was driving now, down, into a vast, dark pool. A pool of sorrows, it seemed at first. And not just his own, not just crushed otters and lost Tashas. The stuff of small and large losses, and of recent and ancient ones—poxed Kwakiutl and napalmed Asians, leveled cities and leveled minds, lost tribes and understandings, broken bridges between worlds—it was all somehow suspended here. Immense sadness on all sides, yet immense depth—there was room down here for all of it. And in his exhaustion he didn't panic, didn't try to escape, didn't close his mind around any one hurt. He just kept easing the Olds down through it all, watching the road and the river, the small sorrows and huge ones, Irwin thrashing on a gurney, Natasha laughing in a cloudburst, the one good paw scrabbling at the road. No matter how much he saw, more kept coming. Sorrows were endless: he'd always known this. But so, he discovered as he kept sinking and sinking, was the spaciousness of this great black pool.

I dreamt my way, as a boy, into a similar pool once. Knelt beside it in some kind of kingdom, saw perfection in it, minuscule and dressed as me. We'd touched fingers for an instant, that perfection and I. Then fear, and a dream train conductor, scared me shut. But Everett was older, and sadder. He was emptier. And I think he was braver too. Because he reached a point where he could no longer see to even glide. But he just pulled the car over. And kept sinking.

8. Pidgin Kwakiutl

"Yulie! Wake up! C'mon, hurry! It's Everett! I know it's early, but I've gotta— Oh. Hiya, Corey. Where's your big mama?"

"Where do you think?" snapped Corey MacVee, sticking only her miffed face out the door of their digs behind the Muskrat. "It's five-thirty. She worked till two. And don't call her big, you idiot."

"Okay. *Huge*, then. Go wake her up!"

Corey tried not to laugh, but something in Everett's mood overwhelmed her. "She'll kill me," she objected.

"No choice," he said.

"Why not?"

" 'Cause I love you guys. And I'm here to tell you goodbye."

Corey's face fell. "You're not!"

"Car's packed," he said, pointing. And it was.

"You can't!"

"No choice," he repeated, touching her chin with his finger.

Two minutes later Yulie stood in the doorway in an immense red bedspread and, as far as Everett could tell, nothing else. Her face was swollen with sleep. Her eyes were slits. She hadn't lost any weight lately. She looked more chief than ever. "This better be good," she rasped, scowling at the dawn.

"Listen!" Everett cried. "This is *way* better'n good! 'Cause remember the Bear, Yulie? The one you said we're fleas on? The no-hocus-pocus-no-skookumchuck-no-bullshit thing you told me to stick the winter out watching for?"

With extreme caution, Yulie nodded.

"Well, I just *met* the big bastard!" he roared. "But here! How it happened. This is so great! The car in front of me hits an otter, see, a mother no less. Shit. So I stop to mercy-kill her, I'm talking to her, it's dumb, my words, she's not impressed but I'm tryin', see, when a log truck comes and damned near kills me! But in the lights, my *God*, this thing from hell is crawling, her heart on the road, oh fuck, I think, they've had it with humans, they've sent the fiend-thing!" He stopped to cackle. Corey and Yulie just gaped. "But it's a crawdad. She was takin' it to her whelps, see?

So I pick it up and save it. Back in the river. Splash. Except I can't help the otter except to kill her, and can't help her whelps. And something about this knocks me in too. Sploosh. But not in the river, Yulie, not *that* drop of spit. This was the bottomless well! This was down the Bear's gullet, clear through the earth and out the other side! And Spirit World? Inner World? Underworld? Disney World? Blah blah blah, man! 'Cause this was, *damn!*, so oceanic who knows *what* the heck it was! But after the Bear—let's still call it the Bear, you and me, 'cause they're beautiful, bears are, and words! *hah!*, huh? So after the Bear craps me out and I'm staggerin' around like some two-legged shit-covered thimbleberry seed, what I all of a sudden for no reason know is *exactly* what to do about my brother!" He laughed again, triumphantly. "Can you believe it?"

Yulie and Corey still just gaped.

"But hey!" he cried. "You're the chief! You tell *me* what I figured, Yulie! I mean otter crushed, whelps starvin', then *gulp!* Whoa, Trigger! *Down I go!* Aiieeeee! How fucking obvious can you *get?*"

Seeing that he was finished, at least for the moment, mother and daughter MacVee turned to each other. "Tlingit?" Corey asked.

"Pidgin Kwakiutl maybe," said Yulie.

"Crawdadman talk-talk any English?" Corey asked, with gestures.

But Everett was just a quivering mass of totemic insights. "That's it, Corey! I *am* Crawdadman!" He slammed his chest with his fist. "The thing *did* possess me! And if I want to keep my crushed brother from becoming the dead otter and Linda and Nash from becoming her abandoned whelps, I've got to try—I know it's nuts, but I've at least got to *try* —to tell the other otters, who of course will be wanting to shell my ass and eat it, to get off their flaccid butts and—"

"Hey!" Yulie cut in. "You call this *English?* If you're leaving us, Crawdadhead, if you really gotta plan to help your brother, then come in, calm down, have a cuppa coffee, and tell us your damn plan."

Everett went in. He had the coffee. He told them his damn plan. And when he'd finished, Yulie's eyes were shining even as she scowled and said, "You know it might not work."

Everett laughed. "Do I ever! But it's the one thing on earth I can see to try."

Yulie grabbed him by the shirt then—just the way she had the time she'd called him a white nothing. But this time, as she held him there at arm's length, it was her hardness and toughness that vanished. And the hint of wryness that never quite left the corners of her mouth or eyes suddenly *did* leave. Immense warmth welled up in its place. Everett felt his eyes brimming before she even began to speak. "I always liked you," she said finally. "But I never trusted you. And if you'd left last winter, like I swore to Corey you would, I'd have shrugged. It wouldn't have hurt a bit. But leavin' *this* way, damn you, Everett . . ."

She never finished the sentence. She just hugged him hard, long and close. And he was surprised, though only for an instant, to find that being mashed in the arms of this eighth-of-a-ton woman was a little like sinking, all over again, down into the fathomless black pool.

"I'll write," he managed to say.

9. New Life

On May 29, 1971, two men were limping down a road in the Deccan Plateau of India. A red sun was sinking in the smoky sky behind them. A full orange moon was rising in the smoky sky before them. The fields by the road were barren, the huts uninhabited, the landscape a moonscape thanks to ten years of drought. Both men were exhausted, their bare feet bruised and bleeding. Both were silent, their lips cracked from thirst. They were also stark naked—and as white as the supposed name of the train that brought them to this pass.

Cresting a little hillock, peering in under the moonrise, they saw the faintly lit huts of the village called Dadagaon huddled beneath a blue cloud of cooking smoke. They knew already that the village had no electricity or running water, no police, hotels or taxis, no telephone or even telegraph with which to wire for help or money. Their only hope was to place themselves at the mercy of people whose lives—except for the occasional passing car or train—hadn't changed in three thousand years. And though this prospect filled one of the Americans with terror, the other looked down at the huts, then straight ahead at the moon, and whispered, *"Thank you! Thank you!"*

They made their way down to Dadagaon and picked out a hut like any other: dung-floored, mud-walled, about the size of a UPS truck. They stepped up to the open door, and waited to be discovered. A small child saw them, and let out a terrified scream. There was a stir inside. And when T Bar Waites suddenly found himself standing, double love-handles and all, before the stunned, rail-thin mother of a drought-stricken family whose annual income couldn't have purchased one of his missing boots, he lost his voice, dropped his gaze, covered his privates, and stared down at the ground. But Peter—drawing on all the strength inside him, and all the misdirected love he'd ever felt for things Indian, things simple, and things true—just joined his palms together, gave her a slight bow and a still slighter smile, and said, without panic or shame or pleading, "Ma. *Prem se bhiksha dijiye.*"*

And so began a new life.

* "Mother. What you give with love, we accept."

CHAPTER EIGHT

God's House

It's a question of being so pitiful that God takes pity on us, looks down and says, "He's done for. Let's give him a few good words."
—Walker Percy

First Adventist Church of Washougal / June 1, 1971

Brother Beal rose up from his chair, a tall, striking, athletic figure of a man. But as he stepped toward the microphoned podium, his Lord, or some such invisible Prankster, seemed to grab a hidden valve in his backside and start letting all his air out. By the time Beal reached the mike his arms had shrunk to half their previous length and hung bent before his chest like a kangaroo rat's, his head had sunk down between his shoulders like a stone thrown into mud, and a crevasse of piety so deep it looked like a tomahawk wound was fixed between his eyebrows. In a voice that carried the way flat beer tastes, he begged the congregation to please rise, and to turn, if they possibly could, to Number 108 in their hymnals. The organ plunged into the introduction like a man in hip boots trying to work his way upstream against a stiff current. Laura Chance found Number 108, held half of her hymnal out to her daughter—and Bet glanced at it, snorted, and let it drop: the hymn was "Shall We Gather at the River" —Irwin's favorite.

Mama had phoned Brother Beal a few days before and requested it, partly to give herself courage for what she planned to do once the hymn was sung, but also to surprise Bet—she hoped pleasantly. And now Bet slouched, sneering.

Mama considered a reprimand, but only reflexively. Bet had been morose or fey or hysterical ever since Irwin left a year ago for boot camp. But since Papa's phone call from the Mira Loma asylum just two nights ago— since she had snuck onto the extension just in time to hear him say to Mama that Babcock's letter of retraction hadn't helped, that he'd tried everything, that he'd lost hope and felt like he was losing his mind, that the drugs were relentless, that there'd been more electroshock, that Keys had blamed Papa for making it necessary and had banned further visits, that it couldn't have been worse if the Vietcong had Irwin, that the last time he saw him he looked (and here Papa burst into a wracked, hacking cough) as though he was being tortured, and slowly, surely killed—Bet had been worse than fey. She'd been spiteful, impossible, vicious . . . But here. Here were the words. And for Irwin's sake, Mama felt she must mean every one of them:

> Shall we gather at the river
> where bright angel feet have trod
> with its crystal tide forever
> flowing by the throne of God?

She noticed for the first time that the hymn began not as a statement, but as a question. Shall we? Or shall we not?

> Yes, we'll gather at the river
> The beautiful, the beautiful, the river . . .

The right answer. But the world was so full of wrong ones. ("The Mekong is huge. It took him forever to disappear . . ." "Christ's love gets you killed here . . ." "Herod is alive and well . . ." "I killed Zaccheus . . .")

But her thoughts were everywhere.

> Ere we reach the shining river
> lay we every burden down . . .

Yes. She must gather herself fast. Because her moment was coming—the moment she'd lain awake all night planning for, praying about, dreading: the little silence, right after the hymn, when the congregation settled back in their pews, the guest preacher (could it possibly be that odd little Oriental man?) shuffled his sermon notes, and the ushers moved into place with the offering plates. Because today, when Brother Beal said *Let us kneel*, every man, woman and child in the place would gradually see that Laura Chance had remained standing. All night she lay picturing it—the murmurings, the mystification (*Look! Poor Laura's flipped!*). Never in her life had she spoken up during a church service. But today, once everyone had noticed her standing, she would speak the words she'd rehearsed a hundred times: *I would like to ask, as a very special favor, that every person here today offer a prayer for my family, and most especially for my son Irwin, who, he . . .*

How did I— Then what?

Because this is a very difficult time for us. Him. And it would mean so much. So please. We need your prayers. Especially Irwin. We all do . . .

Amen? Thank you? Whichever seemed best.

Yes. Only then could she kneel. All night long she felt that God was asking this of her. And all night long she'd answered, *Yes, Lord! I will.* She'd even mentioned it to Bet on the way to church, hoping to surprise her, maybe bring her out of her sulk. Bet's response had been to stare at her, then snort, and roll her eyes.

But where had the verses gone? Could it be ending already? She gripped the hymnal harder, tried to steel herself.

> *Yes, we'll gather at the river*
> *the beautiful, the beautiful, the river*

But her body. What was wrong with it? She felt her tongue dry and thicken, felt cold sweat sliding, almost slithering, down her ribs, felt her skin go clammy and her mind go blank as the joyless voices roared,

> *Gather with the saints at the river*
> *that flows by the throne of God.*

With terrible speed the congregation took their seats; Bet too—and Mama felt the sideways leer, sideways spite, *never should have told her.* Then there was only Sister Harg, still fumbling with her aluminum walker, and Mama insanely hoping she'd get entangled in it somehow, just to stave off the—

Now

Only Laura Chance standing. Standing, yes, Lord, but also panting like an animal in labor as the first few faces turned. She saw Beal moving like a man underwater, *the beautiful the beautiful the,* laying aside his hymnal, swimming over to the mike, then lowering it, sinking with it, down into the river, down to his knees, where she too longed to go. She heard the words *Let us kneel,* saw the congregation move as one body: *down,*

and her jaw fell open as though it had been broken, she gasped once, loudly, and the wave of nausea and humiliation broke so hard against her that she collapsed back into the pew, nearly bounced down onto her knees, and sank deep, with the rest of the congregation, deep into the river . . .

Irwin was sitting at a table in a big white room.

On the table were colors—eight plastic bottles of bright paints.

In the chair across the table was the volunteer girl.

She opened all eight bottles. She smiled. Paint your life, she said. Paint whatever you feel, said the nice brown-eyed girl in the blue dress and white smock. Someone you love, some place you'd like to be. Anything you like, Irwin. Anything nice.

"Yerrrr shurrr?" he slurred. He didn't mean to speak this way. The shots. They'd made him a ventriloquist—a tiny ventriloquist, lost in the torso of his own gigantic puppet, struggling to reach up and operate the huge, flopping lips.

But she smiled as she nodded, touched by his effort, or his blue eyes, some remnant of his looks. And it was her. It was the girl in blue he liked. Except for her smock. She must be new, must not know. So he wanted to help her—to simply touch, with color, the dead white of the smock. But could he really?

Anything you like . . .

Okay. Ever so gently, please don't be frightened, ever so slowly, Jesus loves us, he reached across the table, a speck of bright green on the tip of his brush. But the instant it touched her he saw that she was weak, that already she felt only her aloneness, saw only his size, remembered only the warnings—*smashed teeth! phantom boys!* Her white smock became a fuse, his brush a flaming green match. He watched her explode, watched her mind turn white:

Don't! she said viciously.

"Sorrrreee . . ." Dropping the brush, pulling back as fast as the drugs would let him. But now the slowness made her think he was mocking her, toying with her. And already she was fleeing, locking him in, doing something terrible, "Nooo . . ." But she was gone.

Anything you like, Irwin. Anything nice . . .

He once saved a dog. Nice. Show her. Show her anyway.

He painted the bridge, and the floating house. He painted Sparkle. But there was still no water in his river when he heard Snowmen in the hall. Fighting his fear, trying to use his panic, he painted in an awkward frenzy, clear off the paper, clear off the tabletop. And he got some of the swirling, some of the power, but his river was still too small, too wrong, more a dirt path or road when he ran out of brown.

"*Owwwwww!*" Snowmen pounding the window, grinning at his river through the wired glass.

Show her anyway. More brown!

He tried black and yellow, got gray mud, tried red and blue, got purple, mixed it with the gray, got more gray, spilled it, saw the mess, knew she'd never understand, thought *Christ*, thought *Christmas*, thought *Nice*, took the green, started afresh, forced his flopping lips to sing, *O Grissssmuh treee . . . O Grissssmuh . . .*

"*Owwwwww!* Real purty, Irwin!"

But still he began to decorate it—the lovely ornaments, gifts piled beneath, little star at the top, red blood on the branches, bobbing head in the river, hand that never stops groping, never stops, never stops, *not nice!* But how could he fix it? It happened. And they were coming now, banging the door open:

"Gee, Irwin. Can we watch?"

He painted a box, gave it wheels. "The jeep!" he said loudly, hoping she was still out in the hall, still listening somewhere.

"And what a nice tree growing through it! *Owwwwwwwww!*"

Show her. He painted the legs, the little torso, tiny wrists, black band of the watch . . .

"You've been naughty again, Irwin. Scaring little girls. And now it's time to take your medicine." The Snowmen started for him.

"*The boy!*" he shouted, shoving the Mike one away. "Let me show her!" Painting the neck, the thin shoulders. But there was no head or eyes, there was no life when the Denny one, the savage one, grabbed him from behind, wrenched his arm up behind his back, laughed at his scream as the injured shoulder tore, shoved his head down on the table, "Look, Mike. Paint by number!," his face dragging through the river, "You're the art now, buddy!," his eyes, his lips, erasing the little boy.

"*Owwwwwwww!*"

"He wasn't afraid," he groaned, still hoping she was listening. "Not afraid!" he gasped. "And neither should we be!" But they were white, head to toe—clothes, skin and minds white—Mike and Denny, Snowmen in hell, taking him to hell too, lashing him to the gurney now, meat now, Jesus wants meat for a sunbeam. Sing it anyway: "God is my father, Jesus is my brother and the blessed Holy Spir— *Aggh!*"

"Is my mom!" Mike roared.

The white laughter. Out the door, *no*, down the hall, *no* . . . But there. There she was. So pale, so frightened. And crying now. So did she care for him a little? *Tell it.*

"Life is green. Death is white. I only wanted to show you."

Eyes darting away. *But tell it.*

"This is dying, and dying scares me. So I made you afraid. It was my fault."

"Awww. The poor little fella. *Owwwwwwww!*"

Couldn't see her now. *But tell it.*

"God loves us, but kills us anyway. I forgive Him. I forgive you. Forgive me too. It's all we can do."

No answer but the Snowmen: "Fergive me, Denny!" "Oh I do, Mike!" The long stark corridors, white tubes of light. "Fergive us, Irwin!" "Fer sure, man! It's all you can fuckin' do!" *Tell it anyway.*

"I do forgive you, Mike. I do, Denny. Forgive me too."

So *this is it,* she thought as the wide wooden boat bobbed before her: *the river.*

But someone kept jostling her: *"Mama? Mama?"*

Till a reflex snapped: *"What?"*

"Are you all right?" Bet's voice.

The reflex: "Yes." But she had to look for several seconds before she realized the bobbing boat was an offering plate. *Have I denied my son?* Then she realized that every person in the pew was staring at her, waiting for her to pass the plate.

She tore open her purse, dropped in ten dollars instead of the usual one, bowed her head, and began trying to breathe, to pray, to think. But when Bet took the plate she eyed it coolly, *removed* the ten, stuffed it back in her mother's purse, and through the insufferable new sneer whispered, "Insult God with your cowardice, Mama, but not with your bribes. It's embarrassing."

Slap her! hissed the reflex. But this was church. And the sickness inside her said, *It's true.*

Up at the podium Brother Beal had set his flat dead voice to droning: "And the Pathfinders raised over forty dollars at the big spring car wash last Sunday. Hearty congratulations, kids." And Hugh's broken voice, their son, her son: *if the Vietcong had him* . . . "The offering in your envelopes today goes to our fine new TV ministry, and the loose offering will go to the Game Room fund. Heartfelt thanks" *tortured* . . . "lovely flower arrangements this week the generous gift of Mrs. Beckenhurst, in memory of her husband, Rex. What a treat for us all. Elder Babcock sends his blessings" *slowly, surely* . . . "giving the guest sermon on the *Bread of Life* program for radio KIND, in Vancouver. But he promised to join us for the potluck dinner out at Deer Creek Park" *killed* . . . "golden opportunity to taste my famous potato salad" *my son* . . . "and what a day for it! So please, do come."

But why? When Irwin's need was so great, why did it feel so wrong to ask for a shared prayer? Having never challenged the way they worshipped here, she'd never experienced the limitations. But the instant she stood up, alone and desperate, it seemed dreadfully obvious that some antiseptic, ill-tempered god of propriety had built a transparent wall between the congregation and their own lives, and that what they now worshipped was that wall. There was no one to be angry with, no one to blame: it had simply been decided before any of them were born that a hymn, a sermon and a ritualized prayer must meet their spiritual needs. "Well, I'll not have it!" Mama whispered aloud. "This is Irwin's church, these are his people. Who is going to pray for him if we—"

Shhhhhh! People turning. *Please shush!* Behind her too, and the seasickness, the humiliation washed through her again. Then Bet leaned hard against her shoulder. "Get serious!" she hissed. "This place put Irwin where he is. 'Believe and you're saved,' they told him since Cradle Roll, so now he's believing himself to *death*. And who's gonna save him? Beal? Babcock? God? You? *Stuff* your prayers, Mama. They're an insult to Irwin's faith."

"When we get outside," Mama, or the reflex, whispered, "I'm going to *slap your face!*"

"Sure you are!" Bet retorted. "Slapping people's easy. A *thousand* times easier than speaking up for your son. It's so easy I might slap you back!"

Shhhhhh! Before and behind them.

"Please!" The woman in the pew behind them placed a well-meaning hand on each of their shoulders. But the words she spoke were too perfect: "If you two have a problem, this is *not* the place to try and solve it."

They turned, still fuming, to the front of the church. The guest preacher, an Elder Kim Joon, was being introduced by Brother Beal. "And though he's a convert from our Korean Mission," Beal was saying as the little man grinned like a shy Eskimo out of Babcock's ostentatious igloo of a chair, "Elder Joon has caught on to our ways very quickly. He finished fifth in his class at Loma Linda University. He recently completed the four-year seminary in just three years. But I'll embarrass him if I keep bragging him up like this. Elder Joon will be preaching today on the thirty-fourth and thirty-fifth chapters of Isaiah, which, by the way, are a couple of real beauties for all you nature-lovers out there."

There wasn't a stir from a nature-lover anywhere. Which left Beal no choice but to slouch back to his chair and sit down. Then Elder Joon stood, beamed his diffident Inuit smile, took a step or two forward—

and out of the darkness to the left of the altar a clown or crazy man, some disturbed-looking young man in a laughably huge suit, rushed straight to the pulpit, and every kid in the place started giggling. It seemed like a skit, some harebrained college kid out to lampoon a preacher. But when Elder Joon saw him he plopped back in his chair and began to pray in audible Korean. And Mama and Bet turned white.

The man was trembling violently. He had a choppy, do-it-yourself-looking haircut, and his jaws and throat were covered with shaving nicks, with bits of blood-spotted Kleenex making tiny Japanese flags of each cut. What looked like a pair of black rubber boots poked out from beneath the cuffs of his huge trousers. When he grabbed the microphone in both shaking hands it let out a feedback squawk, causing a woman in the front pew to do the same. The kids all roared again. But the ushers and several other men were on their feet. Then a deep voice murmured, "Could be on drugs."

"Could be armed," said another.

And hearing this, even the children fell silent.

But then Brother Beal stood, held a palm up to the ushers, and said, "Wait! I think I— Yes, I *know* this man." And with that he turned and said, "Brother Chance! Everett! What on earth . . . *Listen!* You just can't *do* this!"

"I'm very sorry to alarm you," Everett said, not to Beal, but into the microphone. "Sorry about the suit too. Couldn't find my old one, so I had to borrow my dad's." He picked one of the flags off his cheek. "Sorry about these too. I was trying to get spruced up, but it sorta backfired. The razor was Papa's too. I know what to get *him* next Christmas."

There was a single hesitant chuckle somewhere, and Everett tried to smile toward it. But the ushers had formed a huddle to decide how to handle him, and Elder Groth, back in one of the throne-chairs, had snuck out an exit, probably to call the police, and Elder Joon was still babbling in Korean. The smile just couldn't make it. "I'm sorry if I scared you," he repeated, shaking with terror himself. "But I'm not on drugs, or armed, or anything else. I was baptized here, actually. And the reason I came back today is that this good man"—he nodded sideways at Beal—"and Sister Harg there, and many others among you, used to tell my family and me that this place—this very building—was God's House."

Just this opening seemed to exhaust him. His shivering had become almost convulsive. But his first burst of courage had trapped him: no choice now but to speak. He tried to swallow, made an odd, squeaking sound, got another giggle from a few kids. " 'Scuse me," he said. "But if it's true, about God's House I mean, then I've . . . Surprising as it sounds, I've . . . I came here to talk about—"

He stopped cold. The ushers had broken their huddle and begun walking slowly toward him, and when Beal caught their eyes he nodded, and eased over behind Everett's back. Predictable as their plan was, it was a contingency he hadn't considered. And he had no answer to it. He hadn't even begun to speak his piece, and he was going to be dragged off like a fool. He was going to prison for nothing . . .

But when the ushers reached the steps below the podium and Beal seemed about to lunge, somebody stood up back in the pews and shouted, "Leave him alone, Randy!"

Beal froze, and began to literally sway with indecision.

Bet was near tears, and trembling like a Pentecostal. But in a broken voice she managed to say, "It's just my stupid brother. It's just Everett. And he's not gonna hurt anybody. Something terrible's happening to our family. Okay? And he prob'ly just wants to tell you about it. Okay? So let him."

Everett turned to Beal and tried, but again failed, to smile. "It's just Bet's stupid brother," he said.

"Make it quick," Beal said. Then he returned to his seat.

The ushers remained where they were. But Bet did too. And Elder Joon had stopped praying and started to listen.

Everett couldn't look at Bet. He knew his gratitude would unravel him completely. "Where was I?" he muttered.

"In God's House!" growled old Sister Harg.

At last, he managed to smile. "Thank you, Sister."

She gave him a grim nod.

"My problem," he began, "when I attended God's House here, was that I never really believed the Owner was at home. I guess it's no big secret that Peter, Kade and Freddy never felt it either, though they all loved, and still love, God. But I drove a long way last night and today just to remind you that one of my brothers, no matter what *I* tried to tell him, never in his life doubted that God could be found in this very place. I'm talking about Irwin. Who most of you know. And if you really know him, I'll bet you miss him too."

He glanced at the congregation, hoping to see a nod or two. But apart from the fact that Bet remained standing, there was not a sign among the three or four hundred faces present that Irwin was remembered at all. It rattled him. It stripped him of his momentum. Desperate for corroboration, he turned to Beal. "Who has the consecutive Memory Verse record here these days, Brother?"

Beal was not pleased to play Ed McMahon to this maniac's Johnny Carson, but he was too decent a man to lie. "Your brother," he mumbled.

"How 'bout the consecutive attendance record?"

"Irwin's still got that one too."

Given his own beliefs, it seemed more than a little inconsistent that Everett would beam with big-brotherly pride. But that's what he did. "That's our Winnie," he said. "Not being the pious type myself, I admit it drove me nuts growing up with the guy. Watching him miss, by choice, every single ballgame my father ever pitched on Sabbath. Watching him give his hard-earned berry-picking money to the polio and Jerry Lewis jars at the grocery store. Watching him refuse to play varsity football due to the Friday-night games—and he was the star of his team—till Elder Kent there, who loves football, convinced him that Jesus would allow an athlete's Sabbath to begin at midnight Friday if that athlete read his Bible till midnight the following day. Think about that. All through high school, with half the girls in his class dying to date him, Irwin spent his Saturday nights with Amos, Nehemiah and Job instead! You've *got* to remember a guy like that!"

For the second time he scanned the audience. For the second time, it was a mistake. Except for Elder Kent (who looked embarrassed and angry) and old Sister Harg (who looked unusually grim) he saw no signs of stirred memories, no warmth, nothing but incomprehension, offended piety, growing impatience, even hate. He'd expected a tough audience, he'd expected some antipathy. But his complete failure to touch anyone derailed him. He looked at the silly gold-glassed windows in the back of the balcony. He looked at the silly gold-carpeted floor. *God's House. What the hell was I thinking?* "I drove here," he said, drifting now, "because I thought I could— I thought you should know, mostly, how Irwin hasn't changed. But he's in a . . . we've got troubles, Irwin does. And I, uh. We . . ."

He lost his thought completely.

But back in her pew, Mama saw him lose it. Having just collided with the same invisible wall, she'd even expected it. And knowing what his effort was going to cost him, knowing he'd chosen prison whether he managed to help Irwin or not, she was amazed and moved by his courage, amazed that he'd come even this close to punching a hole in the immaculate wall. So. Though she heard no voice, saw no light, felt none of the things that a life of biblical fantasies had led her to hope she might feel, Mama suddenly knew in her bones what the situation demanded. Grabbing her purse (she didn't intend this detail, just added it without thinking), she stood up next to Bet. But then she turned her back to the pulpit, lifted her skirt a little, and stepped clear up onto the bench of her pew. As she turned round to face the pulpit, the wave of terror swashed through her and she began to sway. But Bet grabbed her knees, steadied her, held on with both hands. Then Mama looked—eye to eye across the top of the congregation—at Everett. And in a voice that quavered with conviction as well as fear, she said, "That's my oldest. That's Everett. And he's not an Adventist anymore, or even a Christian maybe. But he came here to tell you something I tried to tell but couldn't. So he's brave, I know that much. And he loves his brother. I know that now too. My family is a good family. We're not a bunch of crazies. But Irwin, what's happening to Irwin, it's making us all— Well, *look* at us . . ."

The congregation looked. They saw one of the most steadfast, innocuous members of their church wobbling, white-faced, on a pew; saw her rubber-booted, clown-suited son standing at Babcock's pulpit with a smile on his face and grateful tears running down his cheeks; saw her beautiful teenaged daughter, also in tears, holding her mother in place on a pew by gripping her stockinged knees. It grew apparent, even from the far side of the immaculate wall, that for the Chance family this was not your run-of-the-mill Sabbath. "All I ask," Mama said, "is for you to listen. And, Everett. Just do your best. Speak your heart. And know that I'm very, very happy that you're here."

Bet took Mama's hand then, helped her down off the pew, and the two of them stood there, arms linked, waiting. "I'm happy too!" Everett croaked. "But 'scuse me." He wiped his wet face on Papa's good suit sleeve, taking out a few more Japanese flags. Then he straightened up, cleared his throat, and started over:

"The reason my heart, all our hearts, are hurtin' so bad," he began, "is that the numbskulled heart of our family, the one who always managed to love *all* of us, no matter what we thought or said or believed, is in terrible trouble. And the reason I came here, to Irwin's God's House, is that his trouble started here. I'm not trying to place blame by saying that. This whole situation is a compliment to the staying power of what gets taught here, really. Irwin, after he left here, kept on keeping your faith right up till the day he was unfairly drafted. And every letter we got from him, even from 'Nam, was a Christian letter—the letter of a man who couldn't begin to reconcile *Thou shalt not kill* or *Love thy neighbor* with the duties of a soldier. He's still yours, Winnie is. That's the crux of all I'm saying. He still loves this place, still believes every blame thing he ever learned here, and still tells me I'm nuts when I try to tamper with those beliefs."

"Amen!" said an old voice—not Sister Harg's this time. And there was a little quiet laughter.

"I deserve that," Everett admitted. "And Irwin deserves a better person than me to tell you what's happened to him. But Mama and Bet aren't standing over there for nothing. So trust *them*, not me, when I say that it's the faith you all cherish that has trapped Irwin in his trouble. It's complicated, his situation, but the gist of it is this: When an Army captain in 'Nam ordered a young Vietnamese boy shot, Irwin attacked him, the officer, afterward. It's a messy story. I won't hide that. For instance, the boy may have, probably did, kill a GI with a booby trap. But he was also, clearly, just a boy. And his death caused a transformation in Irwin, or a reversion, really: U.S. soldier to Christian soldier. Irwin chose his captain for an enemy target. He chose a tube of toothpaste as his only weapon. And I guess his mission was successful enough to do some damage to his captain's teeth. In return Irwin received two concussions and a skull fracture from a rifle butt. Which seems like punishment enough, to me. But when he kept singing and praying in the brig afterward, the Army decided they wanted more than punishment. They wanted him silenced. They felt his faith, *your* faith, was recriminatory. Which of course it is. *Do good to those who hate you.* So they decided to erase it."

Everett paused to collect his thoughts, but he was no longer troubled by the blank stares of the congregation. Mama and Bet were all the audience he needed. He said, "When you hold all the cards, erasing faith is easier than you might think. All you have to do is erase the mind it inhabits. It was child's play for the Army to line up a few of their own psychiatric experts and have Irwin declared insane. Which brings us to the part that's making my family frantic. Irwin was sent, more than two weeks ago, to a military asylum in Southern California, where, as I speak, he is being erased. The Army calls the massive doses of sedatives and repeated electroshock treatments 'therapy.' But it is the songs you sing here, the scriptures you read here, it's his belief in *this* House and its God that they are out to destroy."

Feeling his voice rising and his tongue loosening, Everett stopped, drew a breath, and reminded himself: *no profanity.* "It may be hard for you to believe," he said, "that red-blooded U.S. Army doctors consider your faith a form of madness. But I tell you, Winnie— he's trying to hold himself together by singing little Sabbath School ditties down there, and saying Memory Verses and prayers, right through these terrible sedatives. And they answer those songs and verses by drugging him senseless if he's lucky. Or if he's not, by strapping him down, taping electrodes to his temples, and knocking the living— Well . . . electroshock, what it does to a mind that doesn't need it, would not make for good church talk. But Mama's son. Bet's brother. They're blasting him to pieces down there."

There were some stirrings in the pews now, there was a little emotion brewing. "What the Army wants is simple," Everett said, and his voice had a touch of the old street-corner soap-box power now. "All Irwin has to do to be considered 'cured' is agree that to practice, in the Army or in an asylum, what Seventh Day Adventists preach, is mental illness. But those of you who know Irwin know he'll *never* do this. The therapy is not going to stop until your consecutive Memory Verse and attendance champ can't even remember Christ's name. That's why I'm standing here. That's why Mama and Bet are standing there. That's why we're beside ourselves. And we're not just asking for your kind thoughts and prayers today either. Some of you are probably doing what you can in that way already. But I'm here to tell you that Irwin needs God's *answer*, that he is *dying* down there, that if he's ever going to make it back to those two ladies, or to his wife, or his little baby, he needs the help of his people *now*."

Everett saw the faces stiffen, saw that by making a demand he was losing them. It panicked and angered him. He tried to ram his notion through. "You know, you folks have your *own* doctors and shrinks. There's a med school in Loma Linda, very close to where Irwin's staying. And if some of you contacted those people by phone, or better, drove down and did it in person, I'll bet you could arrange for a *Christian* examination, by doctors who could see Irwin's faith for what it is. Doctors who could see about having him trans—"

He stopped himself abruptly, not because of the congregation's continued stiffness, but because something inside him suddenly demanded a complete change of course. "No," he murmured. "No, I'm sorry. I have no right to give orders, or to ask you to give up your time. I have no right to ask anyone but me to sacrifice anything. And this time tomorrow I'll be in jail. So I can't even sacrifice me. You've been kind to bear with me. I'm truly grateful. And I have just one brief thing to add. Then I'll be gone."

He drew a breath. "Unlike Irwin, or Bet, or Mama, I don't even believe in God. It's a little odd, for that reason, that I'd have strong feelings about His House. But I do. I feel—because I love Irwin very much—that it's crucial for me to at least *try* to address the One whose House Irwin believes this to be. Since I don't believe in Him, I'm not sure my words qualify as prayer. But I feel I must say directly to You—Irwin's dear God —that if somebody in this House doesn't hear our family's cry, if somebody isn't moved, not by me, but by You, to sacrifice some time and thought and energy for Irwin's sake, then his mind, his love for You, his belief in this House, are going to be destroyed. It's that simple, I think. Which puts the ball in Your court. Not a hopeful place to leave it, to my mind. But it's right where Irwin would want it. And for the first time in my life, I hope it's Irwin, not me, who's right about this place."

With an inaudible thank-you, and a nod to Bet and Mama, Everett walked out the same way he'd come in. The ushers didn't move. No one tried to stop him.

But in the silence after he'd left, Mama spoke up a second time. Emotion made her voice and face unrecognizable—she couldn't help that. But she met any eye that dared look at hers as she said, "I don't understand every crazy idea that passes through my kids' heads. And that boy, Everett, has got crazier ideas than all the rest put together. But he—" Her voice broke, and she gasped for breath. "I'm telling you. Every *word!*" She was trembling so hard now that Bet took hold of her arm. "Every word he— I never heard a truer sermon in my *life*. God help Irwin! And God help *us*, this church, figure out the way to help. But I've got— I'm going now. Because my other boy. My crazy. To thank him, before he's gone."

With that, Mama and Bet stepped arm in arm into the aisle, and marched straight out the back of the church. And as they moved past the pews the most evident emotion their passage inspired was relief. Thank God *that's* over, most of the faces plainly said, and the temporarily displaced piety and propriety rushed in behind them in a viscous tide. But before the congregation was quite submerged in that tide, Sister Harg, way up in the front pew, suddenly let loose with a great rumbling nineteenth-century *"Amen!"* And when no one moved, no one spoke, no one responded to it, she pulled herself up on her walker, turned round to the congregation, and defiantly growled *"Amen!"* again.

Mama and Bet were long gone now. It was time to get back to the program. But then Elder Kim Joon—the program itself—nodded thoughtfully in his big borrowed chair, and repeated the same word: "Amen."

Then Nancy Beal said it, with real gusto. And then the Brother, ol' Randy, sort of squeaked it. And after that a bunch of kids—mostly just teenagers whose hormones had been spiked by the unexpected show— but a few adults too, chimed in. It wasn't what you'd call a mass revival. It was a pretty anemic little outburst, to tell the truth. But a grain of mustard seed is an anemic-looking little specimen too.

"Today's other sermon," said Elder Joon when it was over, "is from the Book of Isaiah."

the old Camas house / same Sabbath

As they drove up over the crest of the Clark Street hill, Mama and Bet were relieved to see Everett's mud-splattered rustbucket Olds 88 parked at the curb in front of our house. No police yet. They could tell him goodbye . . .

But no matter how much we may admire each other's occasional acts of heroism, our basic characters remain as definite and unchanging as our eye color, our facial structures, the shapes of our bones: as she neared the driveway Mama couldn't help but notice that the butt end of Everett's car appeared to be virtually Band-Aided together with bumperstickers. She took care to ignore them at first, knowing they were certain to contain material corrosive to her resurrected love. But bumperstickers are to devout mothers almost what naked breasts are to prodigal sons. Who can resist a look? She read,

NO MATTER WHERE YOU GO,
THERE YOU ARE

and was relieved that she didn't get it. She read,

U.S. OUT OF NORTH AMERICA!

and thought, *Well, that one is Hugh's mother's fault.* But then she read,

HONK IF YOU LOVE GEESES!

and

LOVE THINE ENEMIES, DO GOOD TO THOSE WHO HATE YOU:
VOTE REPUBLICAN!

and

AMERICAN INDIANS HAD BAD IMMIGRATION LAWS

and

REALITY IS FOR PEOPLE WHO CAN'T HANDLE DRUGS

and Everett's sacrifice for Irwin already seemed like something she must have dreamed. Then she read,

IN TIMES LIKE THESE, EVERYBODY NEEDS SOMETHING TO BELIEVE IN
I believe I'll have another beer

and a small but wonderful thing happened. Turning to Bet, Mama began to laugh a kind of dry, openhearted laughter that had eluded her for years. "Your big brother," she said, suddenly relishing the obvious, "is an incorrigible idiot!"

But Bet didn't join in the laughter. She just pointed—and Mama turned, and saw two men coming out the front door, each with a hand round one of her incorrigible idiot's biceps. Enormous men, with enormous hands. He looked like a child in their grip.

When Mama saw their suits her first thought was: "Adventists," and she wondered why on earth they were handling him in this rude manner. But when she noticed the look on Everett's face—anger, sullenness, defiance, though in his father's huge suit he looked incredibly helpless—she realized they had to be government authorities of some kind. "Sorry, Mama!" he called out as she and Bet got out of their car. "About Papa's suit, I mean. I came to say hi, and to turn myself in. But these guys, they're FBI, were hiding inside. And they won't let me change."

Mama couldn't speak.

An unmarked black Buick with tinted windows came gliding up to the curb behind Everett's inflammatory Olds, and a third agent—the best dressed and biggest of the group—climbed out. The other two leaned Everett against the sleek car, hands flat on the roof, and began to search him. Meanwhile Freddy, Linda, Nash and I stepped out of the house to watch. Then Mama turned, and looked at us. And something in the sight of us there—something about seeing the morose remnant of her family gathered on the cracked concrete porch of the crummy but only home she'd ever owned, watching two feds prod and slap at her husband's shabby but only suit and at Everett's smallish but only body—threw her into a state. I recognized it at once by the body language: it was the same sense of violation, the same domestic outrage she had so often unleashed upon Everett. And what a twist, what a joy, to see it aimed, for Everett's sake, at three employees of the FBI.

Crossing her arms and narrowing her eyes, she scrutinized the three agents, quickly and correctly ascertained that in their protozoan world the biggest specimen was the most important, lowered her head, and started marching grimly toward him. When she drew close he reached in his suit, produced his ID, and flashed it. But Mama ignored it. Or didn't ignore it exactly. But she uncrossed her arms, stepped right in past it as if past a left jab, glared right up into his eyes, and—in the same baton/scepter/cattle prod voice that had created six pretty decent childhoods out of what would have otherwise been an endless round of teasing, lunacy, pugilism and pataphysics—said, "Would you mind telling me just what you're trying to accomplish here?"

The big fed gazed down at her, looking like some zoo-worn rhino or elephant who was sick of humanity but stuck with it, so thank God his eyes were small and his hide and skull both about six inches thick.

"Just tell me," Mama demanded, "in your own miserable words, what it is you think you're doing here!"

The agent was not what I'd call cowed. But something in him found her sufficiently annoying to speak. "Your son is under arrest, ma'am," he said. "For draft evasion. We read him his rights in the house."

Mama snorted in his face. "You walk *right* into my house when I'm not even home. You *arrest* my son, who only came back here to help his brother. And then you don't even have the decency to let him change out of my husband's only good suit of clothes!"

The agent reached in his pocket, pulled out a pack of Clove gum, and eyed her with some dim form of wonder. "We arrest criminals in the clothes they're wearing, ma'am," he said, smirking slightly. "That's the way the job works."

"Then get a *real* job!" Mama retorted. "My boys are good boys! Every darned one of them! Do you hear me?"

The big fed glanced at his partners, shrugged his shoulders, and smirked again. But he'd quit trying to meet Mama's eyes. And though he still held a stick of Clove between his thumb and finger, he hadn't yet remembered to put it in his mouth.

"Do you *hear* me, you big lug? Are you listening to me? Who do you think you are anyway? We had a *family* here once. A tax-paying, God-fearing family. This was a *home* once, dammit! And it still could be, if know-it-alls and hotshots like you would just leave my boys alone! So why *won't* you? Huh? Why don't you? Why can't you just let my sons live their lives?"

Linda and Bet were in tears now, and Everett and Freddy were sending Mama two of the most radiant smiles I've ever seen smiled. But the big fed was hanging tough. He looked kind of like a mailman now, eyeing Mama as if she were some rowdy, yapping little yard dog. He still wasn't much disturbed by her: he was far too large and well programmed for that. But his hide had gone from rhino to mailman thickness in just moments, and you could see his mailmanness kind of squirming around in there, wondering whether, when he turned his back to leave, this irate little yard dog of a woman might not dart forward and chomp him on the back of the leg. "Get a hold of yourself, ma'am," he said finally. "You can speak your piece at your son's trial. You can write the President."

Mama fired off another snort, but the agent had had enough. He darted around his big government car, climbed on in—and he never did remember to start chewing his stick of Clove. The other agents shoved Everett into the back, piled in themselves, the doors slammed shut, and that was that. We couldn't see a thing through the car's tinted windows.

But we could still see Mama, standing alone at the curb as the car pulled away, still trembling with domestic outrage, but also waving on the off chance that she could be seen. And we could hear her in the sudden quiet, murmuring, "Son. Everett. My son."

BOOK SIX
Blue Box

CHAPTER ONE

We Support Our Troops

No discuss, just try.
—Kaka Baria

1. Those Who Could

We received just three phone calls from curious churchgoers on the afternoon of Everett's sermon. But in all three cases Mama handled the calls, and in all three cases she really filled her listener's ear, pounding home the fact that Everett's return had been made at the cost of a prison sentence, that every word he spoke was true, that Irwin's disastrous circumstances began with Elder Babcock's betrayal, and that Babcock himself—after what she called "a little discussion with Papa"—had agreed to write a letter to Major Keys at the Mira Loma asylum, admitting as much. She added that if Irwin's old church mates were not interested enough in him to ask what they could do on his behalf, she would not be attending the First Adventist Church of Washougal again. Not much of a threat on the greater scale of things, maybe. But pretty strong talk from a petite little tithe-paying church lady. And it made an impression. It must have. Because on Sunday—after church and small-town gossip had had time to work their unreliable magic—we received fifteen or sixteen more calls. And these included a few tangible offers of modest economic help and so many offers of vague personal help that Mama scheduled an equally vague "What To Do About Irwin Meeting" for seven o'clock, in our livingroom, that same evening.

That our feelings had finally boiled out into the open had me in a state of euphoria all day. Our love for Irwin was no longer just a futile gnawing in our minds and chests. It was careening around the real world. It had lifted a pitch clean out of a stadium and a mother up onto a pew; it had inspired a church-hating agnostic to steal a pulpit, preach, and pray; it had hung an elder in the air by the back of his pants, had tried its flagrant and subtle best to get God's attention, had even made the sports page. Our love for Irwin had become an incarnate force, and all that remained to be done—so it seemed in my euphoria—was figure out how to bring that force to bear upon the Colonel James Loffler Mental Health Center.

Euphoria, however, is a fragile companion: my sweetheart, Amy, put the first big hematoma in mine when she phoned shortly before seven to say that her boss refused to give her the night off (she was working two jobs that summer to keep her college career afloat) but that she was sending us her "prayers and best wishes" anyway. It wasn't till I'd thanked her, hung up, and conveyed her message to my family that the hematoma was inflicted: that was when Bet told me that prayers and best wishes were the two very things Everett had promised would do Irwin no good at all.

Then those who *could* get the night off began to arrive. An old church mate and dessert-making employee of Mama's, Dolores McKibben, joined us first. A sweet lady, seventy-five years old, astigmatism so severe that friends had given up trying to straighten her crooked wig and lipstick. Sister Ethel Harg and her walker clattered in next. Eighty-three years old. Loved to tease "kids" like Dolores. ("Astigmatism, hah! Have I told you what happened last Christmas to my colostomy bag?") Sister Harg was escorted by that dynamic orator, Brother Beal, and by my preadolescent heartthrob, Nancy (massively pregnant for the third time). By the time the little Korean pastor, Elder Kim Joon, ducked in, kowtowing and glad-handing even Freddy's dog, the five feet two inches of him looked like a veritable loose cannon compared to the rest of the group. We waited another half hour for our forces to swell. No such swelling occurred. Nancy Beal finally remarked that we could increase our ranks by one if we'd just wait a week or so for her to hatch. "But by then you might lose *me*," Sister Harg pointed out with a desiccated chuckle.

"Not to mention Irwin," Bet said, with no chuckle at all.

My brother's rescue committee had arrived. So much for euphoria.

Mama and Linda started things off with cookies, milk and coffee.

Those with appetites, teeth and functioning colostomy bags ate and drank them.

Everyone then began tsk-tsk-tsking at Irwin's plight and marveling at Everett's heroism, tsk-tsk, marvel-marvel, over and over, till it grew obvious that we were an army with no weapons, no leader, no plan of attack and no notion of where or how to acquire them. Dolores McKibben asked about Babcock's letter of retraction—a hot topic for those interested in church scuttlebutt. But none of us had seen the letter. Mama said that Papa had described it over the phone as "brief but extremely sincere." But sincere or not, it hadn't helped. She then told how Papa had broken down on the phone, saying that it couldn't have been worse if the Vietcong had Irwin. And the only thing that had changed since that call, she added, was that Papa and Major Keys had "had words," that the Major had banned *all* visitors for Irwin, and that he'd promised to have Papa arrested if he so much as set foot on hospital grounds.

At this point in our gathering even the tsk-tsking stopped and we fell into a silence so long and boggy that Brother Beal finally took it as a cue. "Maybe the best thing we can do under these terribly trying circumstances," he said in his worst Sabbath School wheedle, "is get down on our knees together, right here and now, and all send our dear Irwin one *heck* of a big, heartfelt prayer . . ."

I am not normally the public-speaking type. In groups larger than two I'm seldom even the speaking type. But when Beal's suggestion met with murmurs of approval, something jolted me to my feet, and before I could think I was shouting, "Forget it! No *way!* We have to *act!* Now!"

I came to at that point and turned scarlet-faced, confused and cottonmouthed—my usual forensics tactics. But my heart remained full enough to enable me to explain. I said, "Papa and Everett aren't kidding. Irwin isn't just dying down there. He's being killed. We can't lose sight of that. Because when someone you love is being killed, you don't just sit home and pray. You steal time from your life and money from your till and try your damnedest to go *save* them. The very least we can do, the least *I* can do anyhow, is join Papa outside those locked gates in Mira Loma. And if the gates won't open, if it still seems hopeless once I'm there, *that* will be the time for the heartfelt prayers."

There was a brief silence, during which I saw that, at the very least, I had offended Mama, both the Beals and Sister Harg. But then Elder Joon, of all people, burst out, "Yes! Yes yes *yes*, Kincaid! And maybe on our journey, or once we are there, the Lord will show us the best way to help!"

The stares that most of our group gave him were more stunned or miffed than grateful. But his outburst set off a remarkable chain reaction. First Mama said, "Does this mean you're coming with us, Elder Joon?"

Then I asked Mama, "Does that mean *you're* coming with *me*?"

"Why, of course!" Elder Joon told Mama.

"What do *you* think?" Mama snapped at me.

"The crooks at Motor Vehicles stole my license when I took their damn volunteer test," growled Sister Harg. "But I've got a good car if one of you will drive it. And I'm coming too, whether you want my old bones or not."

"We want your old bones very much," Mama said. "But we won't be needing your car. I've got the transportation taken care of."

This was a neat trick, since I'd just conceived of the journey a few seconds before.

"Count us in," said Nancy Beal. "Me and this one, that is," she added, patting her huge belly. "Randy'll have to stay here and watch the kids."

Turning pale with terror, Brother Beal, with real passion, blurted, "I'm coming! I'll use some sick leave! My mom can watch the kids!"

Nancy burst out laughing, but shrugged and said fine.

"It'd take ten of me to make one of you, Laura," Dolores McKibben put in. "But what I'd like to do, if you want it done, is take your calls while you're gone, maybe handle your mail, and just do what I can to keep your businesses operating."

When Mama grew teary-eyed at this offer, and Sister Harg let loose with one of her museum-piece *Amens*, I had a sudden vision of the whole godly clump of us sitting outside a chain-link-and-barbwire-fenced compound in the California heat, watching Irwin and the other bideeps drool on themselves while we crooned "Bringing in the Sheaves" and fired off Big Heartfelt Prayers. Trouble was, I had no better plan. And there was this too: though the prospect of our journey gave me no hope whatever, it filled me at once with a surge of completely unfounded joy.

· · · · ·

What Elder Joon, the Beals, and the Sisters Harg and McKibben all failed to realize was just how quickly Mama changes from PFC to Field Commander once a course of action has been set. Ethel Harg's *Amen* was still ringing in our ears when Mama jumped up, marched into the kitchen, grabbed a notepad, pen and telephone, and turned her attention to logistical matters—where her true genius soon shone. Her first move was to enlist Uncle Marv and Aunt Mary Jane as allies and their gas-guzzling Nomad RV as a combination hotel/personnel carrier. Her second move was to return to the livingroom, thank everybody for coming, adjourn the meeting, and send everyone but Dolores McKibben home to pack. "We'll leave the minute you're all back," she announced, leaving no room for discussion or objection. "It's a long drive, and past time we got there. We can sleep in shifts on the road."

It fascinated me to see how, when faced with Mama in Command Mode, even the formidable likes of Ethel Harg and Nancy Beal just nodded and followed orders.

Her third move was to call up her mystery brother, Truman. And the instant he answered we overheard this lopsided exchange: "Truman? Laura here. Listen. Make some coffee. Eat a meal. Sober up. Close your shop. And have your camper, your automotive tools and your ugly mug on my doorstep in six hours' time. It's a matter of life and death."

When Truman asked whose, she answered, "Yours, if you're late. But drive safely. You can sleep when you get here. And one more thing, just to show you I'm serious. I'll have all the cold beer you want waiting here in the icebox. Yes, you heard me. Yes, I swear it on my Bible. No, this is not one of Marvin's pranks. Now shuttup and come on. Bye-bye." Click.

This was the first time we'd heard it so much as hinted that Uncle Truman was a drinker. At last we knew why we never saw him. And an even greater surprise: never before had Mama offered anyone on earth a beer. We all understood that she had just swallowed her deepest, most visceral prejudice to recruit a competent mechanic for our caravan. She was playing for keeps now—same as the U.S. Army.

"Kincaid," she said the instant the phone hit the cradle. "Would you change the oil in the Dodge, please? There's a filter under the spare in the wayback. Check the tires while you're at it. Then run down and buy some beer. Whatever's cheapest. But lots of it."

I was tempted to salute before starting out the door. I was also tempted to hug her. But at the rate she was moving, either would have seemed like a waste of time.

"Okay," I heard her muttering as I headed out the door. "We got our transportation. Got our accommodations. Bet, could you gather up the decent sleeping bags, and plenty of kitchen and bath towels? Freddy, would you mind watching Nash? Linda honey. There'll be thirteen people, and maybe three, four meals. Start thinking about food. Dolores. I can't tell you how much I appreciate this. Come on in by my desk and we'll talk business . . ."

2. Relativity

With the prisons full and the war beginning to wind down, most draft-dodgers at the time of Everett's sentencing were getting eighteen months. Everett got three years. According to his court-appointed lawyer, the arrest record from his radical days may have been the judge's excuse for the harsh sentence, but the real reason for it was the fact that the judge—one Saul Gosman—was a University of Washington alum who used to read Everett's "Give Chance a Peace" column in the school paper.

"Looking on the bright side," Everett wrote in his first letter home, "what a thrill for any writer to be so vividly remembered. And what a thrill for any reader to get to whack actual fractions off a hated writer's life! True, it's my life being whacked. But think how happy I made Judge Gosman. 'You think *you* write a mean sentence,' he was in effect telling me. 'Try this one on for size.' "

There was a strained quality to this good cheer. Everett was frightened, and the comic tone was bravado. But once the gavel fell, what choice did he have? It takes toughness to endure punishment—and he was trying, without losing his sense of humor, to make himself tough.

His sentence was to be served at the Wahkiakum County Work Camp outside Kashelweet, Washington, a minimum-security facility in the gloomy heart of the Coast Range. "Early parole is rare," he wrote, "which is good, since I won't have to betray my true nature trying to earn time off for good behavior." He then went into a description of the camp, and of his fellow inmates—and as he warmed up to his topic I was happy to hear him sounding more and more like himself:

A penitentiary this is not. That was the first pleasant surprise. No guard towers, no searchlights, no electric or barbwire or any other sort of fence. Nothing but a cinderblock wall around us, and this wall, I kid you not, is three feet tall. They take the term "minimum security" very seriously here! But since we're nine miles up a gravel road from Hwy 101 and twenty from a logging town whose inmates are meaner than the camp's, there's really nowhere to go but into the hills. And the guards almost seem to encourage escape attempts, since then they get to play army with their expensive bloodhounds & dirt-bikes & four-wheel drives & radios & guns & shit.

The camp's population is three hundred—all men, guards included. At first it reminded me of an Adventist Summer Camp, but lately I've seen that it's really more like a hippie health-food restaurant, i.e., it's cooperative, and the food sucks. Prisoners do the laundry, the cooking, maintain the buildings, fix the roads—we're nearly self-sufficient. If, as I keep suggesting, they'd just fire the warden and guards and put us on the honor system we could even be cost-efficient. We live in eight block "dorms," three dozen or so men to a single wide-open room, with latrines at one end, which we keep incredibly clean, but the vents are so small the main dorm smell is still piss smell. (Pray they never serve asparagus!) Our bunks line the walls, and we've got footlockers for private property—books, smokes, shaving kit, writing utensils, <u>mail</u> <u>from</u> <u>loved</u> <u>ones</u> <u>hint</u> <u>hint</u>. All mail in and out except letters to and from lawyers or Senators is stamped with my prison number, and supposedly censored. But I've heard the censors are so lazy that if you write sloppily and longwindedly (two gifts God gave me at birth) you can say most anything. Even stuff like "Meet me with the machine guns at the front gate at noon tomorrow." (If you could read that last sentence you'll know the rumors were true.)

We rise at 6:30 for a choice of cold cereal or oat glue in the mess hall, are on the job by 8, and work till 5 like the rest of America. Only big difference is the six or eight head-counts a day and the lack of hair on the heads being counted. (They gave us pig-shaves. Not a real happening look for me.) I chose a tree-planting crew for the fresh air, physical labor, chance to see the outside world. What a bonehead! The only world we see is clearcuts. We get ready-made sack lunches and a half hour to eat them—which is half an hour too long for this cuisine. Then it's back to the camp for showers and "dinner," which is one of six or seven versions of instant spuds and hamburger unless there's a newspaper reporter coming. Then we get steak.

Another culinary problem: the thieving. The con cooks get butter, for instance, but steal it for bartering and use lard in our bread. Fresh fruit and vegetables arrive by the truckload but never reach our plates. (I figure the guards cut a deal with a retail grocer somewhere.) Cons and guards both steal the good stuff, everybody knows who hoards what, and if you want something bad enough you can pay some free-enterprising son of a bitch through the nose. But I'm not that American. I live on cold cereal mostly, which tastes just like it did back home, and you can take it to the "dorm" and eat alone if you want—like me and this box of Shredded Wheat are doing this instant.

Not that I haven't made friends. Like the camp itself, the inmates aren't as scary as I'd feared. The breakdown, according to our sagacious prison officials, is:

30% "Serious Criminals"—which you'd think would mean drug-dealers, manslaughterers, grand larcenists, embezzlers, counterfeiters, etc., but mostly turns out to mean a bunch of poor yo-yos being lavishly punished for possession of minuscule amounts of pot.

30% "Mexicans"—not criminals at all, these poor pedros, but the second or third time they cross the border without papers Uncle Sam hands 'em an all-expenses-paid trip to this vacation haven.

40% "Draft-dodgers"—over 120 men in this camp alone—who our scholarly prison officials further categorize as follows:

1. "Jehovah's Witnesses"—more commonly known (thanks to me) as "T.I.'s" (stands for Theologically Impaired). And it's a rip that Uncle Sam won't give 'em C.O. status, since they spend every waking hour trying to infect the rest of us with their Impairment.

2. "Activists"—among whom I find myself lumped thanks to my various sittings-in, peace-disturbings, FBI record, SDA membership and so on . . . (Ha! Gotcha, didn't I!? SD<u>A</u> membership? Students for a Democratic Advent?)

3. "Pacifists"—by far the most likable, least selfish, most reliable men in the camp. And it breaks my heart to think how beautifully Irwin would have fit among these militantly soft-hearted clowns. But that's water under the bridge, ain't it.

4. "Hippies" is what the prison staff calls the fourth group. But what they really mean, I think, is "Guys Who Failed To Report For Induction When Reality And Unreality Got So Indistinguishable They No Longer Knew Which One To Report For It In." Or "GWFTRFIWRAUGSITNLKWOTRFII's," for short.

"Like I told my judge," one named Moonfish explained to me the other day, "judge I said, <u>truly,</u> to like <u>punish</u> a person, like with prison and shit, for failing to carry out black-and-white-type instructional material printed on two-dimensional-type surfaces such as induction papers is foolish in the <u>extreme,</u> man, scientifically speaking, since with relativity happening, like with energy equalling mass and shit, the Following-2-D-Directions-Back-Out-Into-A-3-D-World Situation has gotten totally out of control. What I'm driving at your honor, in story form, is how you yourself, to cite one razor-sharp-minded example, could park your actual two-tone Ford LTD well within the white or possibly yellow lines of an actual supermarket parking space, step inside for some shopping, tote your brown bags of products back out to said space, and find an alpaca standing there, same two tones as the LTD, man, but ready to spit in your face if you stick in the key, which could brown you off so bad you say screw the car and drive the grocks home in the alpaca anyhow, figuring (righteously, I would say) that the two-tones means the beast is, molecularly speaking, yours. Except that when you like <u>canter</u> in the driveway—and here we reach the scientific heart of the matter—even with E equalling MC, let alone squared, there could be a fuckin' thunderegg in the middle of your lawn where the split-level used to be. Or a small lake full of duckweed. Or just sand, and a fuckin' yucca plant. That's all I'm saying. But looking again at the old where-and-what-is-my-draft-board-type questions in light of events such as these, we see the truly answerous answers are not so easy to locate. So think hard, is my good word to you, your judgeship, before jailing up your fellow man for one of these 2-D hey-what's-induction? type errors."

Moonfish got three years too, by the way. But enough Wahkiakum.

The good news is, we're allowed two visitors from 1 to 3 p.m. on the first and third Sundays of every month. The bad news is, which two of you? I'll leave that to you, as long as <u>somebody</u> shows up! Meanwhile my needs are simple: I only want to hear <u>everything,</u> from <u>everyone.</u> Especially about Irwin. Write soon! Write tons!

Love, Everett

3. Presence

At 4:50 A.M. on June 3, 1971, the "We Want Winnie Caravan" (Linda had spontaneously named us during the Adventist contingent's parting round of Heartfelt Prayers) eased into the empty streets of Camas. I was sitting at the dinnertable of my aunt and uncle's thirty-two-foot Nomad as we departed, the top of which table was a four-color Formica highway map of the United States. When I lay my arm on this map with my elbow on Camas, I could touch LA with my fingertips: Irwin was an arm's length away. Outside a late-spring rain was falling, and the Crown Z mill, as we left it in our wake, was doing its best to turn the gray dawn grayer. We had no planned stops and no plan of action. When we'd telephoned Papa to tell him we were coming he'd had no words of encouragement or advice. But after so many weeks of helpless fear and waiting, the mere act of setting forth—the physical sensation of being thirteen humans moving as fast as we could toward a place where we hoped to accomplish one clear and simple good—was almost more than I could handle. If I'd had a board I could have surfed the waves of affection I kept feeling for my fellow travelers. Almost anything set me off. The way Aunt Mary Jane looked up at the wheel of the Nomad in her blue cowgirl boots, amber-lensed aviator glasses and a red baseball cap that said "Totally Electric" above the bill. The trucker-esque snoring, in the curtained-off bed in back, of old Sister Harg. The dovelike cooing of baby Nash as Linda lay nursing him in one of the bunks. The silhouettes, in the Dodge wagon up in front of us, of Elder Joon and Freddy's dog Suncracker, sitting side by side like a placid old married couple. The unshaved faces, in the ratty GMC pickup a few car lengths behind, of Brother Beal and Uncle Truman, sipping from their coffee mugs and chatting equably, though even as I watched Truman was refilling his own mug with his fourth or fifth beer. The way Uncle Marv was staggering round the Nomad's bucking cabin, stowing loose gear and food in closets and cupboards. The way Mama was staggering around right behind him, restowing everything in a more sensible place. The perfectly deadpan expression Marv kept when he noticed this, started singing the bluegrass tune "Pig in a Pen," and began stowing stuff in the stupidest, most out-of-the-way places possible. The equally deadpan expression Mama wore as she began humming "Nearer My God to Thee" and banging her kid brother into walls and closets with her hip . . .

We were headed for an insane asylum in California. We looked more as if we'd escaped from one. But in the pouring gray rain, I felt clarity. With the war still raging, I felt peace. With Papa in despair, Everett in prison and Irwin in the asylum, I felt release. I didn't understand my feelings, didn't even desire them, really, but they kept filling me so full that my eyes began to well. Which embarrassed me. So I finally stood up, darted into the tiny bathroom, locked the door.

"Why didn't you do that at home?" I heard Mama mutter outside. And even this! Even this filled me with elation. The tires began to drone against the metal grid of the Interstate Bridge. Uncle Marv started singing in tune with the drone. Little Nash kept cooing. Out the little win-

dow, green girders flashing. On the window curtains, green-headed mal-
lards facing north, flying south. The gray Columbia straight down below
us. Everything in question, nothing resolved—yet an overwhelming sense
of resolution. I didn't understand any of it, didn't know what I was
saying, but I found myself suddenly whispering to my brother, a thousand miles to the south, "You know this feeling, don't you?"

Something inside me turned fierce. "How you laugh that way. Why
you love us all. This is what you live by, isn't it?"

I heard Mama, humming still, knock Marvin right into the bathroom
door. Heard the tires' drone become a shishing as we hit the asphalt on
the Oregon side. Sister Harg kept snoring. Baby Nash kept cooing. Pain
and sorrow never end. Nothing we do is enough. It's always been this
way. "But joy," I whispered to Irwin. "This joy. It's boundless too, and
endless. So hold on. This isn't theirs to knock out of you. It's not yours to
lose. It's not mine either. But it's making the trip. It's coming. So please.
Just hold on."

4. Myshkin

The solo journey mentioned in the following letter—from Arizona to
Shyashyakook, B.C.—took place on the same days, and for one of the
same reasons, as our caravan journey to Mira Loma: somebody was trying
their desperate best, without really knowing how, to help Irwin. So here is
her letter:

Dear Everett,

I have so much to tell you and want to say it all so fast that it's too
big, too scary, there's nowhere to begin. But it was your letter—all 211
pages of it—that got me this far. So I'll try to start there. It caught up
with me four days ago. I don't know where on earth you found
Grandma Maggie's address (she's been dead twenty-two years), but the
daughter of the family who bought her old house in Knoxville, one
Bitsy Buchanan, was on high school rally squad with my mom, still
sends Xmas cards, funeral notices and so on. So she just mailed it. Or
read it and mailed it. (Her note to my mom began, "What in heaven's
name is going on between your poor daughter and this odd young
man?") (The underlines are all Bitsy's.)

Anyway, it made me feel a thousand ways, your letter did: surprised
me (especially with its ongoing gentleness); melted my heart; quelled a

hundred fears; raised a hundred more; made me feel like a worm; reminded me over and over how much I love you (even when I can't stand you). But then I reached the last two pages—the ones about Irwin—and they scared me so badly I drove the fourteen hundred miles here in two days (have I even remembered to tell you I'm in Shyashyakook?) in hopes, as you said, of "undoing the chemical damage" and giving you your center back.

But I reached the Nessakoola cottage at six yesterday morning, didn't recognize the car outside, knocked and knocked on "our" door anyway. And when Yulie McVee finally opened it wearing nothing but a big red bedspread, guess what I thought? Don't laugh. She may be forty and she may be huge, but we both know she's also hugely appealing. While I was thinking what I was thinking, though, Yulie looked me in the eye, read my mind perfectly (how does she <u>do</u> that, anyway?), then started laughing so hard she had to sit down on the steps and squeeze her legs together to keep from peeing the bedspread. "That's the nicest compliment I've had in years!" she finally told me. "And I <u>do</u> love him. But like a <u>brother</u>, honey. Only reason I'm here is that Corey landed his caretaking job."

She stood up to hug me hello then. But soon as her arms were around me she backed off, grabbed me by the shoulders, and said, "Natasha! Sweetheart! Look at you!" Which brings me to my main topic. And to my reason for running away. And to all the pain I've caused you. The subject is so complicated it's going to take pages to really describe it. But we can jump a long way toward the middle in just two words:

I'm pregnant.

Seven months pregnant, at this point.

Which puts conception back in January.

Guess who the father is?

I'd give all the money I have ($73, at the moment) to see your face right now. And I'd give everything I own (<u>including</u> my Russian-lit collection!) to know that the first thing my news did was make you smile. But I know, Yulie's made it clear, that I've hurt you terribly. And though I doubt I can explain how I came to do it, let alone inspire you to forgive me, I beg you to let me try.

We have, at the minimum, a six-part problem. On my own I'd have said "an overwhelming problem" and given up right there. But Yulie and Corey think there's hope for us still, and are trying to help me think clearly. Like when I sat down to write, and I guess did nothing

but a lot of sighing, Corey told me, "If the subject's too big or weird
to think through, draw a map. Make the parts of the subject into
rivers and mountain ranges and deserts and towns. If it's still too big,
add a whole 'nother province. That's what I do with my papers at
school. It works."

"Where'd you learn such a trick?" I asked her.

"Everett," she said. Wouldn't you know it. But here goes:

Our Problem, Part 1: One of the first things I ever said to you was
that I'm old-fashioned where romance is concerned. "A dinosaur" I
think I called myself. Being a dinosaur, I made a huge exception to my
own laws of survival when I started living with you. But I didn't start
living with you because I'd changed. I did it because I couldn't help it.
There's a big difference. I never really thought we were living "in sin."
(I'm not that Paleolithic.) But we were living with dangerously little
definition by my standards, which standards are based, by the way, on
my belief that romance isn't just romance, that it naturally leads to
love-making, which naturally leads to babies, who are naturally helpless
creatures in a naturally beautiful but lethal world, so they naturally
need as many pieces of the ancient Father-Mother-Shaman-Tribe-
Home-Hearth Paradigm as we are able to gracefully give them.

Our Problem, Part 2: Here's where I imagine you wanting to grab
me and say: "But the emphasis should be on gracefully. No romance
need lead to babies if the parents aren't ready. Not if they'd be driven
into poverty or misery. Not in the age of birth control, family
planning, safe abortions." Remember the column you wrote at U Dub
called "The Other Bomb"? The one about population explosion? One
of the unfunniest, most powerful diatribes I've ever seen on the
subject. I didn't even know you yet, but it haunted me for days. The
topic has always haunted me, Everett. Because no matter how
devastating the arguments against untimely infants get, they've never
made a real difference to something inside of me. What is that
something?

Our Problem, Part 3: I wish I knew. But here's a possible clue. I am
(as I kept trying to emphasize and you kept trying to deemphasize) an
ex-Catholic. But my reasons for ex-ness don't fit the typical Western
Woman's Agenda. If the Roman Church would merely reunite with
the Eastern Church, reinstate the Latin liturgy, trade purgatory for
reincarnation, saint Meister Eckhart, stop damning people for stuff like
condom-use (though a lot of good the damned things did us!), allow
women and married people to be priests, bishops and popes (or better

yet dispense with the bishops and popes), I'd be back at Mass in a minute. Of course they won't. Hence my ex-ness. But did you notice the popular woman's complaint my list left out? I don't know why I'm this way. I half-wish I wasn't. But you can pick this girl up, shake her well, and pour and pour and pour and one result you will never see (unless I'm raped) is an abortion. I don't think it's murder, I don't think it's criminal, I don't tell friends not to get them, I don't even think my aversion is rationally defensible. But for this dinosaur, this lifetime, nobody but me, nobody's business but mine, that aversion is an absolute.

Which brings us back to last January. Do you see what was coming? At the time when I loved and needed you most, I felt positive that my news was going to bring all your "Other Bomb" arguments crashing down upon my indefensible absolute. And if by some miracle my absolute had held up, I imagined you, me and a colicky infant living in poverty in Shyashyakook—and I was afraid you'd grow to hate me. And if my absolute had fallen and I'd agreed to abort, I was afraid I'd grow to hate you.

Our Problem, Part 4: My body. Remember telling me that you'd thought it was impossible but that my breasts had somehow become even more beautiful to you? Imbecile! Bigger is the word you were looking for! And remember teasing me, right before I left, about always locking the bathroom and turning the faucet on full-blast to cover my sound-effects? "Methane denial" you called it. And when I burst into tears you couldn't help saying "Touchy touchy!" before you apologized. And I don't blame you. I was touchy. But it was morning sickness, not "methane," that I was trying to cover up. And I don't know why, Everett, but those two little words, "touchy touchy," felt like all my worst fears beginning to come true.

Then the bleeding started. Not a lot of it. But it didn't take much to scare me with the nearest decent doctors forty miles away and our joint income your $100 a month. As soon as I saw blood I was all through thinking. Terror took over. Terror of trapping you, terror of losing you, terror of losing the baby, our love, my life, my soul. So when you went to Victoria that day (to get me a Valentine present, I know, my poor sweet, I know!), I cried as I packed, cried as I tried again and again to write to you, cried when I gave up and cut out Dmitri's America speech, cried clear to the ferry, stopped crying and threw up all the way to Port Angeles, then started crying again. Because I knew I was wrong. No matter what else was happening to me, I knew I was running away from love. But I'd come find you again, I told myself, just as soon as I knew things were okay inside me, soon as I'd honored my absolute.

I drove to Lake Havasu City, Arizona—my mom and stepdad's new home. And yes, it's a "planned community," yes, you'd hate it, it's no dream of mine either. But my mom used to make a point, every time I came home from college, of saying at least once—in front of as many guests as possible—that if I ever got pregnant and wasn't sure what to do about it, "Just come home and I'll help you with everything except your decision."

"You're embarrassing me!" I'd always whine.

"Yes," she'd say. "But only so you won't be embarrassed if the situation does arise."

"Well," I told her, patting my tummy when she answered the door last February, "The Situation is arising." And—Lake Havasu planned community and all—she just hugged me, and has kept her word. She was even right about the guest test: I'm not embarrassed. I've seen doctors too, baby and I are healthy, and I know already it's a boy. I'm keeping him too, Everett. I'm not going through this to give him away. Myshkin Lee, his name will be. After my absolute. (Do you know the prince in The Idiot?) And I know the naming should have been shared. I know that all of this should have been shared. But when I got so scared and ran, I lost all claim on you. That's the reason I haven't consulted you. Myshkin is not ammunition for a shotgun marriage. He's not some kind of bait I'm using to try and win you back. He's just someone I've chosen to love and live with and care for from now on. Except,

Our Problem, Part 5: Though I have no claim on you, I have no right to exclude you from loving or caring for or living with Myshkin, either. You are as much his parent as I am, if you choose to be. I don't want to complicate the issue, but I still have feelings for you too. Tons of them, to be honest. I just don't want you to take part in anything you don't believe in. Things like fatherhood are either in you, or they're not. My only reason for driving back up here was to tell you how sorry I am about running away, and about hurting you, and about your brother. Except,

Our Problem, Part 6: You're gone. And probably in prison by now, Yulie says, for trying to help Irwin. I started blubbering when she told me, for all sorts of reasons. But Yulie just looked me in the eye that scary way she does, and said, "Cry if you have to, honey. But listen.

The way you left him feeling, the kind of winter you put him through, you're lucky he's even <u>alive</u>. 'Cause no matter what he wrote in some damn paper once, that boy loved you with everything he had. And it was you, sweetheart, not him, who broke the trust between you."

Not till that moment did I see how inexcusable my leaving really was. Given the love between us, I <u>had</u> to share my absolute. If you couldn't honor it, we could have fought, and then I could have left. But the sickness I felt the instant Yulie said "prison," the sickness I feel this instant knowing you may be in a place where I can't see you, can't touch you, can't reach you no matter how great the need—to think I've <u>already</u> put you through this sickness, for <u>months</u>! I can hardly believe I've done this. I've poisoned our love. I've poisoned your life. I feel so wrong now that it seems like pure selfishness to ask you to forgive me. (Yet I'm asking.) I feel so wrong that it feels like sheer divisiveness to say I love you more than ever. (But I do.) Yulie says you promised to write her as soon as you could, and she promises to phone me the instant your letter arrives. So I'm heading back to Arizona. I'd love to drive down via Camas in case there's news of you there. But my condition is pretty showy and I don't want to cause a stir. So I'll wait for Yulie's call.

She and Corey have been wonderful. They send their love. So do the two of me. Until I hear from you, I don't know what more to say.

Tasha

5. A Man from Spokane

In a rest area by the upper Rogue River, beside three madrone-shaded picnic tables right next to the water, our Mira Loma-bound caravan bivouacked for its first major meal of the journey. Uncle Truman was sleeping off a six-pack in his camper, and after a long stint of driving I was relaxing at the Nomad's highway-map dinnertable. But the prospect of a fresh-cooked meal had thrown everyone else into motion. Elder Joon was down by the river with Nash on his knee, handing him rocks, which Nash would first try to eat, then would toss in the river. Suncracker was sticking his whole head under, fetching the rocks back. Uncle Marv was out under the madrones, loading up his big barbecue and loudly accusing Mama of having tidied his charcoal starter into nonexistence. Bet, Freddy and Randy Beal were marching around like soldier ants at Mama's orders, cleaning and preparing the three tables, toting foodstuffs, beverages, lawn chairs, picnic supplies—and hiding the charcoal starter (Beal's touch) right under Marv's butt when he knelt down to blow on the kindling. "If he farts I'm a widow," remarked Aunt Mary Jane, who was jammed in the Nomad's galley with Mama, Nancy Beal and Linda, slapping out hamburger patties while the other three worked at a potato salad and a fruit salad and green salad and dressing.

The only other member of our tribe who wasn't busy was Ethel Harg. She was sitting across the map from me with her big, spotted, lizardy-looking forearms smooshed out over most of the eastern seaboard, and her face, which was usually just grim, was uncharacteristically glum. I had a fair idea what was bothering her too: dumb jokes and utensils flying in all directions, men and womenfolk making themselves useful—and her too rickety to join in the fray. For a pioneer-stock Old Testament woman like her, it must have been torture. I felt sorry for her—sorry enough that I decided to try to divert her with a little conversation, though I'd never dared talk with her outside Sabbath School in my life. While I was fishing around for my opening line, though, she idly opened a drawer next to the oven beside her—and this drawer turned out to be jammed full of typical RV detritus, all stowed in strict accord with my uncle's Pig-in-a-Pen philosophy: fishermen's hootchies and five-year-old gas receipts; grease-stained playing cards and the bean-stained wool sock Marv used for a pot holder; a petrified Elmer's Glue bottle, a pair of Donald Duck sunglasses, a map of Phoenix, a half-eaten Mars bar . . .

And one glance at this chaos and the Sister's customary grimness was restored.

Upending the drawer on the Atlantic, she began piling useful stuff across the Midwest, questionable stuff in the Deep South and garbage in a brown paper bag standing south of the Mexican border. Hoping the symbolism was unintentional, I glanced outside, where Marvin was now accusing Mama of having thrown away the mesquite chips she already had soaking in a bucket of water (she says they give off more flavor wet). When I turned back, Sister Harg was reading, with grim but obvious interest, the inside cover of a plain white matchbook. Since there were no matches inside, I expected to see the book deported soon. Instead the Sister slipped it surreptitiously into the pocket of her sweater, cleared off the entire Midwest with one sweep of her arm, emptied her Mexican trash bag out where all the good stuff used to be, and reinspected every scrap of paper or cardboard in the heap. For some reason this procedure caused her to rescue the lid of a used snoose can and the top of an old

Post Toasties box. She then turned to me, and with the same unreadably grim expression growled, "Kincaid."

Involuntarily, as if we were still in Sabbath School, I piped, "Yes, Sister Harg?"

"Would you care to know the secret of your aunt and uncle's happy marriage?"

This was not the sort of question I'd expected. "Sure," I said doubtfully.

"Verse," she growled.

This was not the sort of answer I'd expected either.

"Original verse," she added.

The surprises were getting bigger. "Verse that one of them writes, you mean?" I said carefully.

"Both of 'em, actually. Tag-team verse, I'd call it."

My face made it obvious that the concept needed explaining. Sister Harg met this need by simply handing me the matchbook. The inside cover contained five lines of writing. The first two were in the neat block lettering of my Uncle Marvin, the last three in Aunt Mary Jane's unruly scrawl. And Sister Harg watched, with unadulterated grimness, as I read them. They said:

> A MAN FROM SPOKANE FELT SO AMOROUS
> HIS PLAIN JANE OF A WIFE LOOKED QUITE GLAMOROUS
> *If he wasn't so rude*
> *She'd have been in the mood.*
> *As it was she said, "Shuttup and scram fer us."*

I wasn't too surprised by the limerick. I knew my aunt and uncle pretty well. But I also thought I knew the Sister. Because of what I thought I knew, she had to wriggle, hack, and titter all by herself for a solid ten seconds before I dared crack a smile—and even then I only did it because the wriggling got me worrying about her colostomy bag. Then she handed me the Post Toasties flap. Again it was two lines by the ever-hopeful Marvin, followed by three in brutal response. These went:

> THERE WAS A YOUNG HUSBAND SO HANDSOME
> THAT HIS WIFE MARY JANE ONE DAY PANTSED'M
> *And said, "Hold still my dear*
> *While I make you a steer.*
> *I'm plumb sick of you acting so glandsome."*

"Shush!" went the Sister, peeking back at my aunt. But she was the one making all the racket. Fifty-some years spent teaching Sabbath School, this woman, and there she sat, happy as an anthropologist who, in some boringly Christianized jungle, stumbles onto the lair of a good old yoni-worshipping pagan.

I said, "You'd think he'd learn to let *her* write the first two lines."

Sister Harg shook her head vehemently. "Him writing the first two, her the last three," she growled. "That's the secret of the marriage right there."

The various chefs and salads started out of the galley. Sister Harg quickly palmed her pilfered poems, gave Linda, Nancy, Mama, Mary Jane and their culinary efforts each a stern nod, watched them parade out the door, then gave me a heinously happy smirk and handed me the snoose lid. The writing this time went in circles to accommodate the lid's shape. But the results were the same:

A YOUNG MAN FROM SPOKANE WAS SO HANDSOME
THAT HIS WIFE FOUND HIM WILDLY ENTRANCIN'
So she captured some ants
Dumped 'em straight down his pants
And cried, "Honey, I do love your dancin'!"

"Come and get it!" shouted Aunt Mary Jane.
"Don't he wish," growled Sister Harg.

6. Tea Leaves
letter from the Wahkiakum County Work Camp to the Lake Havasu City planned community

Myshkin! It's a beautiful name, Tasha, I love him already. And I understand your fears, I forgive your fleeing, and I feel your love too, I see it pouring from your letter. And I want nothing on earth so much as to accept it. But I have to refuse it long enough to say to you first: three years. Thirty-six moons, Natasha. Picture Myshkin on a trike. That's how long I'm going to be here. And it surprises me, I didn't expect this of myself, but being trapped here, I find that I too have an absolute: I have to know whether you're going to be able to wait for me.

Not that I'm asking you to wait. Given my past, there's sure as hell no moral grounds for my asking. And it was my conscience that put me here. I don't expect you to share my punishment—and to get Myshkin through his first three years alone <u>would</u> be sharing it. All I'm saying, I guess, is that I know how beautiful you are, and how desirable, and I care too much about your happiness to ask you to just hand your middle twenties over to an incarcerated pen pal. Waiting for me (to borrow a line from your letter) is either in you, or it's not. It can't be forced. But this place makes me vulnerable to you, and crazy for you, in ways I can't describe or control. I mean, I'm trying to resist you this very moment, I'm trying to sound guarded and dispassionate here! But your letter tore me so far open so fast that I can hardly keep from scrawling I love you I love you I love you till I run out of ink. And it's <u>terrifying,</u> being this open in a place like this. That's what I'm saying. Because if I anchor my heart on you again, and fall madly in love with Myshkin too, and if you then vanish, I just couldn't bear it. Not here. If it didn't just kill me, I know it would turn me into a scalded, twisted something we wouldn't want to know. So consult your heart, Tasha. That's what I'm asking. Read <u>all</u> the tea leaves before you write back to me. Remember my temper, my big mouth, all our differences, "touchy touchy." Remember I'll be an ex-con once I'm out of here, making ex-con money for life. Remember the beautiful parts too, if your heart seems to want to. But don't "feel sorry for me," or try to make up for last winter. Don't "be nice," I beg you. Say "I can" if you can wait for me—and know that I'm overjoyed to be Myshkin's father. But say "I can't" if you can't. If it's ever going to come, let the end come <u>now</u>. And then, for both our sakes, and Myshkin's, never write to me again.

Love,
Everett

7. "No Comment"

I'd been driving the Dodge wagon for hours, alone with Suncracker, trying to fight off sleepiness with some cowboy radio station that sounded as though it was designed to tranquilize cows. Fortunately, the effects showed: when our little caravan pulled into Yreka for gas, Elder Joon stepped out of the Nomad with a fresh cup of coffee for me, took one look at my face, and said, "The coffee is perhaps mine? And the sleeping bag is yours?"

I could only moo my agreement.

So Joon took over the driving, Freddy joined us and rode shotgun, and I climbed in back with Suncracker. I didn't lie down right away, though. We had set out across that overgrazed but beautiful high plateau approaching Mount Shasta, and I wanted to let the landscape sort of lull me off to sleep. But as I eavesdropped on Joon and Freddy's bantering, I was surprised to find myself growing less and less sleepy . . .

When he'd first joined us, Kim Joon struck me as a negligible addition to our would-be rescue operation. But the farther we traveled, the clearer it became that he was bright, witty, tirelessly helpful and *eccentric.* Yet he was an Adventist Elder. It didn't add up. My face must have shown it didn't too, because all of a sudden I saw him stop himself in mid-sentence, start grinning at me in the rearview mirror, and cry, "Ah ha! Joon surprises Kincaid? He even likes Joon a little? Yes? Thank you! We like Kincaid too. And maybe we understand his mind. In the view of intelligent American college students, Adventist preachers have the brains of fish. Correct?"

"Not at all," I protested.

"Don't lie to an Elder!" he blustered in a passable impersonation of Babcock. "Let us guess what Kincaid thinks of Joon. Just for fun."

I just blushed at this suggestion, but he fired away. "Kincaid believes Joon is a Korean War orphan whose life was saved by missionaries. He was brought to this country as a child, advertised on television by the philanthropist actor Danny Kaye, adopted by Adventist fanatics, and sent to schools and seminaries where dogmas and Bible verses were stenciled on the inside of his head and a Mongol-eyed Smile-face was stenciled on the outside. Joon now considered himself ready to go forth and preach the Gospel! Oops. We failed to mention that Joon's favorite Americans are Sammy Davis, Jr., President Nixon and whoever invented McDonald's hamburgers."

Freddy had been laughing throughout this recitation. I tried to chuckle along too. But I was a bit strangled by the fact that this was *very* close to what I actually thought. Joon read my face and laughed. "Don't worry," he said. "We understand your mind. Joon's speech *is* somewhat wooden. English did not come easily. Joon was an engineering student before Christ entered his life. Oh! Oh no! We see Kincaid's jaw clench when Joon says Christ entered his life. So sorry! Joon would say something different, something more clever, if something different or clever was what he felt to happen . . ." (I was blushing again.) "But once it happened," he continued, "once Christ became . . . Joon's companion?— may we put it this way?—that companionship began both to simplify and to complicate Joon's life. He sometimes felt his companion strongly. (May we say this, O jaw muscles of Kincaid?) But he could never fully express, in life, the wonderful things this companionship allowed him to feel. Joon's clearest inner guidance seems always to be negative. Is it this way for you? Back in Korea, for example, Joon felt strongly that he should stop studying engineering. So he did stop. And so was left with no calling. So, with very great faith, Joon began to pray for a new career . . ." (He started to laugh.) "In what you might call 'missionary position,' Joon prayed for days and days. He damaged his knees. He wept with longing. 'Lord! Show me the way!' he cried until his voice left him." (He laughed harder.) "And do you know what finally happened? *Nothing!* Joon grew exhausted, fell asleep, and the Lord showed him nothing!"

He threw back his head and roared. An Adventist Elder who found God's failure to answer his prayers a scream. I was really starting to like this guy.

"Since God would not speak to Joon," he said, "Joon decided, when he woke up, to speak to God. 'My goodness! My freedom is very great!' he said. 'No comment,' said God."

He laughed again. So did Freddy and I.

"Not knowing what else to do, Joon accepted his only other opportunity at the time, which was to come to this strange country and attend what Kincaid feels is a school for fools." He winked at me in the mirror.

"And was it?" Freddy asked.

Joon thought it over. "It's good to know the Bible," he said, "and good to know people who want to serve God. But the seminary has filled Joon with doubt."

"About what?" I asked.

He laughed. "Everything! Everything under the sun! Except his companion. But Him we do not see under the sun, do we?"

I told him that never in my life had I heard an Adventist Elder mention, let alone laugh at, his unanswered prayers and his doubts.

"Yes!" he cried. "That is a doubt the seminary gave me. Even the apostles doubted. Yet American Elders do not. Joon does not understand. He did not understand his teachers or fellow seminarians either. The first Christians he met as a boy in Korea were Adventist missionaries, very simple people. They had no power, and wanted no power. They told us Bible stories, it is true. But they gave us food and shelter and medicine first, and teased us and told jokes and played with us and loved us. So we *begged* them for the stories." He laughed again. "This was what Joon thought Christianity meant! Food and medicine for the body, and stories for the heart if you begged for them. Then he came here, found a country full of people begging *not* to hear the stories, went to seminary, and found out why. No food. No medicine. No doing unto others. Just a bunch of men learning how to bellow the stories at others whether they wanted to hear them or not!"

"An Elder who makes sense!" Freddy sighed.

Joon shrugged. "To be simple again—who cares if it makes sense. To unlearn what he has learned. To live like old Angus McCready, the first missionary he met as a sick and hungry boy on the streets of Seoul. That is what Joon wants." He smiled back at me in the mirror. "Ha! Kincaid was right! Joon *is* an orphan! And now he longs to do for a stranger named Irwin what Old Man McCready once did for a stranger named Joon. But this is a strange country. Your brother has a strange problem. We'll be there tomorrow. Have you got big ideas about how to help?"

"The only big idea I've got," Freddy gushed, "is I'm glad you're here!"

I finally realized, at this point, that Freddy had formed a tremendous crush on our companion. And when the Elder gushed, "Joon is glad too! He likes this family so much!" I was afraid things might start to get gloppy there in the old Dodge. But then he surprised us both—and miffed one of us—by adding, "Joon liked your brother Everett especially! He frightened me so bad, then spoke so beautifully! He is very smart, isn't he! And such a preacher! He is funny too, Joon bets!"

"And bossy and foulmouthed and bigheaded and impossible," Freddy said, turning several shades of green.

"And in prison," I added, "because he loves his brother."

"We understand his mind," said Kim Joon.

8. Anchor

Dear Everett,

I'm huge. So is my love for you. So will Myshkin's be.

I can wait. I <u>will</u> wait. Make that your anchor.

In thirty-six moons we'll buy him his first trike together.

Another thing: I'd been agonizing about graduate school—whether to go at all, which ones to apply to. Your sentence makes it easy: I'll be going back to U Dub. An advanced degree can be my Wahkiakum. And my apologies to your family, but you'd better warn them right now that Myshkin and I are going to dominate your list of bi-monthly visitors. Meanwhile let's wear out the postman.

More tomorrow.

All my love,

Natasha

9. The Personnel, the Equipment, the Expertise

Stopping for nothing but meals, gas, two strategic phone calls and one six-hour sleep, the "We Want Winnie Caravan" made it to Mira Loma by sunset, June 4, met up with Papa at the Red Desert Motor Inn, where he'd been staying, and learned that he was now known to all asylum guards and employees as "that goddamned ballplayer." But except for the new nickname, he'd gotten nowhere. And he was chain-smoking, coughing incessantly, and looking alarmingly ill. "Deathly ill" was the term Aunt Mary Jane greeted him with. And Sister Harg, who'd never met him, told him that he should go see a doctor at once. Papa eyed each of these estimable women for a moment. Then he lit another smoke. "I'm gonna wait a bit on that, thanks," he said.

"You shouldn't," Harg growled.

"You think so now, ma'am," Papa answered. "And I appreciate it. But you haven't yet seen my son."

That was the end of that.

The strategic phone calls I mentioned had been back to Camas, where a group of volunteers—friends and Sabbath School students of Randy and Nancy Beal's, mostly—had printed up and gone door to door with a petition composed over the telephone by Elder Joon, Nancy and me. It was intended for all 840 members of the Washougal church; the gist of it was that, to the best of the signer's knowledge, Irwin Chance had always been a devout Adventist, and had always struck them as theologically unwilling and psychologically unable to go to war. Perhaps fifty people who saw the petition had admitted to remembering Irwin. Twenty-one had been willing to sign it. Dolores McKibben had then mailed it to Papa's motel, where it was waiting when we arrived. So while the rest of the Camas delegation recuperated in the motel room, RV and camper the first morning, Mama, Papa, Elder Joon, Linda, baby Nash and I drove the petition over to the asylum, and made our first attempt to visit Major Keys.

．　．　．　．

To lay eyes on the Colonel James Loffler Mental Health Center was to recognize at once our insignificance, our motleyness, the fragility of our hopes, the vastness of our task. The immaculate white cinder-block walls and obedient green lawn; the immaculate white orderlies and obedient WACs; the unarguable gate and fences, the guards, the labyrinthine floor plan; the stunted palms, standing at attention, giving no shade. Babcock's idea of heaven—that's what it looked like. And Irwin had died and gone there. How could the flawed and mortal likes of us hope to bring him back home to Earth?

To my surprise (though not to Papa's), all. of us except Papa were allowed through the front gates and into the building immediately. And the first thing Major Keys did upon greeting us in the lobby was send an orderly back out to fetch Papa. He then invited us all into his office.

To my further surprise (though again not to Papa's), Keys seemed perfectly cordial. He offered us chairs, ordered a WAC secretary to serve Coke and coffee, had genuine-looking smiles for everyone but Papa and, for some reason, Elder Joon. He even read through our little petition with what seemed like interest and concern. He then said that he appreciated, and deeply regretted, our distress, and agreed that a tragic mistake had been made by Elder Babcock, and compounded by Irwin when he chose to train for combat. But our petition, like the letter from Babcock, changed nothing. Regrettable as the situation was, he told us, Irwin's mind had come unraveled in Vietnam. He had become both psychotic and dangerous, he was not the young man we thought we knew, but trained professionals who dealt with his kind of problems daily were offering their expert help.

"We're doing our very best," he concluded with a smile so warm that Linda readily returned it. "We have the personnel, the equipment and the expertise, and we're going to bring this young man around, believe me. Our progress may seem a little slow to some of you, but I'm confident we'll have him back in one piece and home to that beautiful baby within the year."

Though she began to blink back tears at the word "year," Linda kept returning the Major's smile. And Papa looked utterly used up. But Mama stood abruptly, looked Keys in the eye, and said, "That year may start to seem slow to you too, Major. Because we won't be leaving here without him."

"Is that so?" he said with a forced little Morse code chuckle.

But Mama had already spun on her heels and stormed out of his office.

"It is very much so," said Elder Joon as the rest of us got to our feet. "Mr. Chance has described his son's condition to us most thoroughly. Based on that description, we regret to say that we do not place much faith in your equipment, your personnel or your expertise. It is not our wish to cause you embarrassment, or to make trouble. But unless you begin taking steps to turn the patient over to his family, we will be back in greater numbers to express our displeasure."

Major Keys chuckled again. But this time it was derisive. "Sometimes we just have to choose between greater and lesser embarrassments," he said. "And let me tell you. Releasing a dangerous patient into the care of his unsuspecting wife and infant because a few disgruntled family members and some little Oriental fella demanded it . . ." He shook his head. "*That* would be about the greatest embarrassment I can imagine."

"Then we will see you again tomorrow," said Elder Joon.

"No," Keys told him. "That you won't. Since you've taken this adversarial tone, I'm afraid you'll all be outside the gate with Mr. Chance here. But if you like, I can wave."

"You do that," a somewhat revived Papa told him. And we all started for the door.

"Pardon me, Mrs. Chance," the Major called after Linda.

She turned.

"I know these people mean well," he said in a voice that sounded soothing even to me. "But try not to let them upset you." He gave her a reassuring wink. "Your husband has been down some pretty rough road. But we *do* care. We're on your side. And we'll get him back to you just as soon as we safely can."

Linda smiled through her tears, but said nothing.

10. Namaste

We were gathered in the asylum parking lot in the shade of the RV and camper, trying to come up with some sort of rescue plan. But the San Bernardino Mountains had vanished in the smog, the smog itself was so hot you could see it writhing, and a plan, like the mountains, was nowhere in sight. Nash was in my lap, chewing on a used spark plug—and he'd been fussing so long and loudly before I'd handed it to him that not even Mama cared about the grease on his lips. Randy Beal and Freddy were over by the chain-link fence, playing catch with a little blue rubber football. Truman was sitting on the steps of his camper, quietly downing his evening short-case. Suncracker was chained to the camper, sitting on Truman's foot, whining and watching the football. A few yards away, but through the fence, a couple of broken 'Nam vets were doing the same.

"I say signboards!" Aunt Mary Jane was saying. "I say we make like a buncha damn hippies, picket the place till they stick us on TV, and see how the Major likes the attention."

"It's the *Lord* who's going to help us, not the TV," growled Sister Harg.

"And where they'd prob'ly stick us," said Nancy Beal, "is in jail."

"Even if they didn't," Mama said, "think of Irwin. Who knows what they'll do to him if we antagonize them?"

"All the more reason to smoke 'em out fast!" said Uncle Marv.

"Perhaps we should just walk over to the gate and start singing," Elder Joon suggested. "It seems to be Irwin's singing that the Major finds intolerable. To hear the same songs from us might convince him of Irwin's sanity."

"Or our *in*sanity," muttered Bet.

"He's already convinced of that," Papa said.

"Then what have we got to lose?" asked Aunt Mary Jane. "Why not hit 'em from all sides? Prayers, songs, protest marches, Bible readings! Let's be the skunks at their tidy little lawn party! Pester 'em half to death with what we believe! Show 'em we're crazy! Just like Irwin!"

"There's somethin' to that," Sister Harg agreed.

"Well *I* think we might try being *nice* first," Linda said, her voice and face trembling. "I think Major Keys really *is* trying to help. And if you'd all just stop trying to make him mad, maybe I could go in and see Irwin."

"*You* sure roll over and play dead in a hurry," Bet muttered.

"Mind your tongue!" Mama snapped.

"We haven't even *started* makin' him mad!" Bet retorted.

"Linda has a right to her opinion."

"Didn't she hear what Papa told us? We don't need *in.* Irwin needs *out!*"

"But I want to see him!" Linda cried. "I'm his *wife*! I want to see Irwin! And thanks to you, *your* attitude, they won't let me!"

For the fourth or fifth time that afternoon, she burst into tears. So for the fourth or fifth time, so did Nash. That did it for me. I handed the baby, spark plug and all, to Mama, climbed into the Nomad, shut the door behind me, squeezed into the bathroom, and shut that door too. I then downed four aspirins and stuffed cotton in my ears, but heard Papa clear as a bell anyway, murmuring, "I feel ashamed. I feel stupid and ashamed that I can't think of some workable plan."

"Signs!" hollered Uncle Marv.

"Will you shuttup!" Mama told him.

"It's okay," Nancy Beal cooed, probably at Linda.

"Nice catch!" cried Randy Beal, probably to Freddy.

"What do you think you're *doing?*" barked Ethel Harg, probably at Randy for playing catch.

"We share your shame," said Elder Joon, probably to Papa.

Nash and Linda kept crying. The dog and the broken 'Nam vets kept whining. On the other side of the RV, Uncle Truman belched.

"I'm too pissed to pray!" I hissed, probably at God. "Just *do* something!"

Then I remembered Joon's story, back by Mount Shasta. "No comment," said God. Back by Shasta, it seemed funny.

I stepped out to the road-map dinnertable, sat down, covered my ears with my hands, and began staring at the traffic on Van Buren Boulevard. Time and a lot of cars passed. Marv and Mama kept arguing. The aspirins didn't help my headache, but they began to eat at my stomach, which sort of distracted me from my head. I noticed a little Nash Rambler sitting at the traffic light a couple hundred yards up Van Buren. It was exactly like Irwin's—the car baby Nash was named for. The driver was pale, blond crewcut, sunglasses—no resemblance at all. But I could still picture Irwin in it, looking as if he owned the world. That little car, and Linda . . . He'd wanted so little. I felt too angry to cry, but I began to quietly curse. As the little Nash came toward me I noticed it even had Washington plates. It wasn't until the driver turned into the asylum parking lot, putted slowly up into the parking space right next to my window, placed his palms together, and bowed at me that I realized the car *was* Irwin's. Without hesitation or thought, I placed my palms together and bowed back—an exotic reaction for a hopelessly American American like me. The driver broke out in a grin, and took off his sunglasses. He had two very black eyes.

I didn't care. It was still Peter.

"Thank you," I murmured. Probably to God.

The general reaction to Peter's sudden arrival was what you might call biblical: even the non-Adventists seemed to consider it the semimiraculous return of some sort of Prodigal Son. Linda, who'd never met him, was all eyelashes and blushes. Freddy was in bliss. Mama was in prayer. Truman loved his short hair, Marv his shiners, Elder Joon his Oriental bow of greeting. The one exception to the overall mood was Papa. After a brief greeting hug he moved back out of the hubbub, lit his zillionth cigarette, and began to watch Peter very closely and, it seemed to me, morosely. He didn't ask a single question. Not even about the black eyes.

Peter's own reaction to the enthusiastic welcome was just embarrassment at first: he kept saying, "Never mind me" and "Yes, Dolores told me the situation" and "I don't deserve this" and "I've been an idiot" and "I'll tell you that later." But when the questions and exclamations just kept coming—"Why the short hair?" "My God you're skinny!" "What happened to India?" "Thank God you're here!" "Who did what to your face?"—he finally grew almost angry.

"Forget me!" he said sharply. "It's a long story. We're here to help Irwin, right? So let's get back to it. Would somebody fill me in on your rescue plan?"

For the first time since we'd arrived, I thought I saw Papa smile. It faded fast when Uncle Marv blurted, "We were about to start making signs," Mama snapped, "Like heck we were!" and the argument was off and running. But Papa didn't wait for it to resolve. He just stomped out his cigarette, stepped into the center of the circle, grabbed Peter by the arm, nodded toward the Dodge, and in the two of them climbed.

"What are you doing?" Marv asked.

Papa started the car, backed it out, pulled up beside us. "Kincaid. Bet. Mary Jane. Elder Joon," he said. "Get in."

The request was so unexpected, and the selection process so incomprehensible, that we obeyed without thinking.

"We'll be back," Papa said as he whisked us away.

His first question, as we started down Van Buren, was to Elder Joon. "Kim," he said irritably. "You know this country. Where the hell's a mountain? We need *out* of this used-up air."

"How big a mountain?" Joon asked.

"The biggest we can get to fast."

"Mount Baldy has snow in winter. It has a trout pond. The road goes to the top."

"Perfect. Which way?"

"Take a right on Euclid. Just follow it north. It isn't far."

Papa nodded, then lit another cigarette. "I asked you four along," he said a puff or two later, "because this is a thinking expedition and you're all smart. I'd have asked Freddy, but she's got a crush on Kim that might put a crimp in her thinking. I'd have asked Laura, but she's so scared I think she'd rather just pray. I'd have asked Nancy Beal and Ethel Harg, they're bright ladies. But they need a rest. So I asked you."

He turned to Peter. "The truth," he said, "if you haven't guessed it, is that we *have* no plan. Or no plan that isn't idiotic. We don't know *what* the hell we're doing here, Peter. And if that doesn't change soon, we're finished. We can't keep these good folks together for no reason. We've got to make some kind of move, fast."

He said nothing for a quarter mile or so. Neither did the rest of us.

"What I have to say now might worry some of you. But it's time I came out with it. I don't know what's wrong with me—maybe it's just fear, like with Laura—but I haven't had a good clear idea in my head ever since I got here. If it's up to me to get Irwin out, I'm afraid the fight's over. I'll never leave him. After what I've seen, I could never live with that. But I can't save him either. So I want you all to know that I step back. That I'm not in charge. I'll answer questions if you've got them. I'll ask you to stop if I hear you wandering. I'd like Peter to lead us, or at least keep us organized. But whatever it is that needs to happen, I can't find it in me. So I leave the finding up to you."

Given my own feelings, I expected silence after this announcement; maybe some awe, or sadness; a little trepidation. What happened instead was that Elder Joon burst out: "Wait! Stop! Papa! Joon is so stupid!"

Mary Jane and Bet started to giggle. The Elder calling Papa "Papa"—I guess that's what got them. But Joon didn't care:

"Your other son, Everett! Don't you remember? He had an idea during his sermon, and started to boss us all around with it, but then had a deep feeling and let the idea drop. Nevertheless it was a good idea, don't you think?"

"No one but me even goes to church," Bet told him.

"Forgive me!" Joon cried—an interesting reaction, coming from an Elder. Then he scowled and said, "A shrink. This means a psychologist?"

"Or psychiatrist," said Peter.

"Well, just before Everett prayed, for his brother, to the God he cannot believe in—most unusual, most interesting, this prayer. But before he spoke it, Everett suggested that Adventist shrinks and doctors should try to gain permission to examine Irwin. Being professionals, he thought perhaps permission would be granted. Yet being Christians, he felt they would understand Irwin's mind. Joon does not know where such an exam would lead. But might it not lead to something?"

When the Elder saw the way we were looking at him he started clapping his hands like a little kid. "He did it again, didn't he! Elder Everett did it again!"

"Stop at a store when you see one, Papa," Peter said, issuing his first order. "I need pen and paper. Then I've got about a hundred questions to ask you."

It was probably more like five hundred. By the time we reached Mount Baldy his questions had fascinated, then dumbfounded, then irritated and exhausted us. At first he'd drilled us about sensible-seeming things: Did we have Irwin's Vietnam letters? His sanity trial testimony? How much did we know about his attack on Captain Dudek? Could we get records of his treatment at the asylum? Could we get his mail? What did we know about Major Keys—his personality, his clout, his superiors, his rules and regs?

But as the cross-examination went on, his questions seemed to grow decreasingly purposeful: How many buddies did Elder Joon still have around Loma Linda University? How many could he round up on short notice? Could Bet cry on cue? Could Mary Jane? What did Joon know about the Elders on the board of the Southern California Adventist Conference? Had he met them? Did he like any of them? Did any of us know how to operate a TV camera? Did Joon know where could we rent or borrow one? Could Sister Harg perform, "you know, act—like an actress"? Could Uncle Marv? Could Mama? Could every member of our group convincingly pretend to believe a useful lie?

He'd filled most of a spiral notebook with our answers and guesses when Aunt Mary Jane spotted the U-Catch trout pond that Elder Joon had predicted. "Pull in there, Hugh," she groused. "Pete's got some questions for the trout."

We laughed. But Papa really did stop. And he and I had a beer and watched Elder Joon, Bet and Mary Jane catch our Camas contingent a fresh trout dinner. But Peter just strolled off to the furthest picnic table from the pond, and went right on scribbling furiously in a second, smaller notebook—

so when we finally climbed back in the Dodge, I naturally asked what was in it.

Pete just shrugged, and said, "A rough prospectus."

Papa's face fell. "You're doing *school* work? Here? Now?"

Peter laughed. "It needs fine-tuning from all of you, and lots of help from al-Khizr. It'll take at least two days of coaching, and two more to play it out. But here. Listen. Tell me what you think."

With that, he opened his little notebook and began to lay out a rescue plan. It was astoundingly meticulous, given the amount of time he'd had to concoct it. It had an alternative B, an alternative C, and emergency ploys and backup schemes. It had weaknesses too, and took unavoidable risks. It was going to require a symphonic effort by all of us, some deft conducting by Peter, a couple of daring impromptu solos by Elder Joon and an RV-load of luck. But when Peter finally closed his notebook and said, with surprising shyness, "Well?", Elder Joon laughed—and threw his arms, not around Peter, but around Papa. "Where do these sons of yours keep coming from?" he cried.

Papa blushed at the hug, and coughed a little. But he was smiling at Peter. "You've gotten sneaky as an old spitballer," he said. "What happened?"

Peter shrugged. "I met these characters in India, Grayson and Dessinger, who were spitballers of sorts. I guess they rubbed off a little."

"A scheme this schemey ought to have a name," Mary Jane said.

"How about Operation Squeeze Play?' Bet suggested.

"Perfect," Papa said.

11. Hicks

Peter was in the Nomad, talking strategy with Elder Joon. He'd been describing Operation Squeeze all morning to groups of three and four of us, and had spent a quarter hour talking fine points alone with me. But Joon's role the next day was going to be so central to our hopes that the two of them had been talking for over an hour.

The rest of us were sitting on the strip of lawn between the street and the cyclone fence, just staring at the asylum and waiting for tomorrow. The sun was getting hot, but things weren't as smoggy as the day before. There were four or five quiet conversations going, and for quite a while I'd been basking in all of them, and staring up at the sky, when I noticed Papa telling Sister Harg about the customized greeting cards that Bet and Freddy used to make. My family knew these card stories backwards and forwards, but something about the old pitcher telling them to the old Sabbath School teacher made me want to eavesdrop anyway. Then I noticed the other conversations were all dying off too. By the time Papa reached the punchline of Bet's famous Christmas card, "Joy to the Wordl! The Savior Resigns!", he got a roar of laughter from everybody but the person he was telling the story to. "You find that funny, do you?" Harg growled. But she was wearing the grimace she used for a smile.

"I got a one-of-a-kind card from Miss Winifred once," Mary Jane remarked.

Freddy flopped down on the grass and covered her head with her arms.

"She was seven or eight at the time, and couldn't have had too many big worries. Because the thing that troubled her most, she decided one day, was how unfair it is that some holidays get tons of attention, while others get none at all. It was one of those problems that was gonna take a lot of solving. But Freddy got a start on it—one March, or April, or whenever the heck it is—by sending Marv and me our first-ever Palm Sunday card."

"Oh God!" Marvin groaned, remembering the card at once.

"It was a picture of Our Lord," Mary Jane said, "in what must have been Hawaii. Wearing a pair of gold swimming trunks" (she started wheezing and whacking the ground) "and a grin so big it wrapped clear around His face . . ."

"Whoa Jesus!" groaned Marv.

"He was just lying beneath this palm tree—'cause that's what Sunday it was, you know . . ." (Now she started pounding on Marvin.) "With a big pile of coconuts, in case He got hungry. And the carefullest little red crayon holes in his hands and feet . . ."

"Oh God!"

"And the caption! The caption!" (Mary Jane lost it completely now, and had to sort of squeak the rest into Marvin's shoulder.) "The caption said, 'After Everything He Did for Us, Jesus Gets a Well-Deserved Tan.' "

We howled.

Except for Bet. Who said, "Well, look who's comin'."

Major Keys had stepped out of the building and was marching toward us across the lawn. But it's odd what a difference a little strategy can make: yesterday Keys's approach would have filled us with panic. Today, according to our schedule, it wasn't yet time to deal with him. So he suddenly didn't matter. "Irwin made a batch o' cards too once," Marvin said, "when he was visitin' us on the farm. I can't think how old he was, but his front teeth were missin'. Christmas cards, they were, the usual Jesus and Mary and shepherds and cows. Except there was one we just couldn't figure out. 'Merry Christmas,' it says across the top of the page. But the picture below is just this crayon drawing of a bloated-up, brown-bearded fat guy in a blue shirt and green trousers."

"That was us!" Nancy Beal blurted. "I mean he sent that one to Randy and me! We never figured it out either!"

Marvin held up a hand. "Then listen! 'Who the hell's this guy?' I ast 'm. 'Geth!' Irwin yells back. 'This poor schnook's got somethin' to do with Christmas?' 'Yeth!' he yells. 'Santa in his youth?' I ast. 'NO!' 'Joseph on vacation, dressed for golf?' 'NO!' 'Give us a clue then, dang ya,' Mary Jane says. 'He's from "Silent Night!" ' Irwin yells. Well, that left me outta the race. Janey's the expert there. So she mumbles her way through every blasted verse, but doesn't turn up a word about any overweight schnooks in blue shirts and green britches. 'We give up,' we finally tell'm. 'Dummies!' Irwin yells. 'It's Round John Virgin!' "

There was another roar of laughter—till we noticed that Major Keys had joined right in. "Who invited *him?*" Uncle Truman muttered.

"Mind your manners," Mama said. But I sided with Truman. It irks me to see people enjoying the very things they're destroying.

"I'm sorry to interrupt," Keys said. "But seeing you out here—and noticing a pregnancy, and a senior citizen, and the baby and all—I wasn't sure you were familiar with our Southern California heat. You know, sunstroke is not uncommon here."

"We appreciate your concern," Mama said.

"One other thing." The Major was wincing now, as if it physically pained him to inconvenience us in any way. "I'm afraid the grounds-keepers are about to turn on the sprinkler system. Not to force you back into the parking lot, you understand. We just need to keep things spruced."

"If you were familiar with our Southern California heat," Nancy Beal said, "you might water after dark so as not to scorch your grass."

"Please mind your manners, Nancy," Mama said.

"It's how I treat my own lawn," she muttered.

"Your group's health and comfort in this heat, ma'am," the Major told her. "That was my concern."

"You *should* be concerned," Sister Harg growled. "She's nine months pregnant, I'm eighty-three years old, driving down here wore us out, and it *is* hot. We're not sleeping nights either. But we were Irwin's Sabbath School teachers, Major. We believe what we taught him. He believes what he learned. And knowing what you're doing to him for holding to that belief, we couldn't leave here if stayin' killed us."

"I doubt that staying is going to kill you, ma'am," Keys replied. "But in a moment I'm afraid it's going to get you wet."

He'd begun to make me furious, but my fury was feeling impotent, when an odd thing happened. Apropos of nothing, Uncle Marv said, "There was a fine major named Keys, who thought love for the Lord was disease . . ."

I was so surprised that my mind went blank—and Mary Jane just spun around and glared at Marvin in disgust. But Sister Harg, hardly missing a beat, growled, "Till a bunch of dumb hicks from the Washington sticks came and brought the big lug to his knees."

"*Amen*," said Papa. And there was a fresh roar of laughter. And this time the Major didn't join in. Papa looked around in the grass, located a sprinkler head, scooted right over next to it, and lit a fresh cigarette. Nancy Beal found another head and aimed her big round belly at it. The Brother set his little blue football on one, and got ready to try to catch it. Harg and Mama didn't move. Neither did the rest of us. It was pure childishness. But childishness seemed appropriate to an army drafted by love for a guy like Irwin.

"You're holding us captive, Major," said Sister Harg. "You've got something that belongs to us. We can't leave without it."

"Believe as you choose, ma'am," he said. "But don't blame me for the consequences."

He spun on his heel, and marched back the way he came. But he was looking less and less the smug autocrat, and more and more a thrall to regulations that had utterly failed to take the likes of us into account.

"Mighty quick with the ol' limerick there, Ethel," Mary Jane remarked when he'd gone.

Sister Harg shrugged, and glared innocently off across the lawn.

"I think we got ourselves a little security leak," Marvin said, grinning.

The Sister managed to keep glaring, but her mouth had begun to twitch wildly—when the sprinklers came on, and saved her.

12. Allies

The following morning we gathered our troops and transportation early, donned our best duds (which wasn't saying much), drove to the headquarters of the Southern California Seventh Day Adventist Conference down in Anaheim, made a rickety but memorable mass entry into their lobby, and listened with utter earnestness ("as if you're sitting in church, but liking it" was the stage direction Peter had given us) while our spokesman, Elder Joon, told a gaping secretary, then a stunned Elder, and finally one Dr. Bryce Brumfeld, president of the Conference, that he was himself an ordained Elder from Loma Linda University, that we'd come to them with a life-and-death crisis, that we believed no one but the Conference could help us, that time was of the essence, and that we would like to describe our difficulty to as many distinguished churchmen and Elders as could conveniently be convened.

It was not your ordinary business greeting. We were soon jammed, again en masse, into Dr. Brumfeld's office, where we attracted four glowering Elders, a couple of deacons, and one nervous secretary. Elder Joon tried to be quick but hard-hitting in outlining Irwin's situation. Puffing himself up like a rooster, he painted for the Elders, in their own pompous vernacular, a picture of a war which virtually all of America's conscientious congressmen, clergymen and churches now publicly opposed, then portrayed Irwin as a young man who, "thanks to the admitted confusion of an esteemed but tragically mistaken clergyman" (Babcock), had been sent "directly from his wedding to this fine Adventist girl" (Linda blushed beautifully, right on cue) "straight into that un-Christian chaos in Vietnam." At this point Peter handed each Elder and deacon a xeroxed copy of Babcock's letter of retraction. He then had Bet illustrate the result of Babcock's mistake by reading a few passages from Irwin's "Zaccheus" letter. With that, Elder Joon moved on to the present crisis. He briefly described the capture and execution of the Vietcong boy. He described Irwin's toothpaste attack on Captain Dudek. He scrupulously avoided mentioning that Irwin's Army peers and Captain Dudek were united in their claim that the Cong boy was a nonexistent delusion. He then handed the Elders copies of Irwin's sanity-trial testimony, pointed out that Irwin had been sedated, admitted that the testimony might have been somewhat difficult for military judges and "secular psychiatrists" to interpret, but majestically concluded that "to unbiased Christians such as yourselves, Irwin's words and actions can clearly be seen as a devout Adventist's misguided but courageous attempt to stand by his faith in an impossible situation."

Joon was proving a marvelous diplomat. I couldn't imagine a much better presentation of Irwin's case. But the situation had obviously strained the Elders' imaginations to their limits. He next tried to tell them about what "the prodigal brother, Everett," had done for Irwin's sake. "An agnostic and a draft-dodger," Joon marveled, "yet he knowingly returned home to a prison sentence just to deliver his heartfelt message to his brother's church! And I tell you, gentlemen, I've heard some wonderful sermons in my life, but I have *never* been more deeply moved!"

This was his first major blunder: all but one of the men Joon was addressing were preachers who thought rather highly of their own sermons. And to think they'd been outdone by an agnostic! You could see the Elders closing up like anemones. You could feel our scruffiness begin to grate against their conservatism. But then I heard sniffling, turned—and saw that Bet and Freddy, then Mama and Linda, and finally even Brother Beal were all in tears at the thought of what Everett had done. (What had happened was that Peter, seeing Joon's crisis, had given a secret *"Cry now!"* signal to the twins. But when they'd started to sniffle, the other three had spontaneously joined them—and the twins were so moved that their forced tears became real!)

Though Randy Beal got some odd glances, the Elders seemed to grow receptive again. Then Joon threw down our only real trump card: he described the symptoms of Irwin's so-called insanity. Told them, for instance, how up until the electroshock and sedatives stripped him of his ability to speak, he had recited Memory Verses and sung Sabbath songs day and night, and had begged Christ for forgiveness constantly. "The sole response to this behavior by the asylum staff? *Up the dosage!"*

Some of the Elders—Brumfeld in particular—had begun to look a little riled. But then one of them, the most wizened and sly-looking, said, "Sometimes insane people feel they *are* Christ. How do we know this young man isn't one of *those?"*

Elder Joon was about to say something to reassure this old earwig, but Mama blazed up first. "He was begging the Lord for help and forgiveness! That's called *prayer,* Elder!"

I didn't blame Mama, but that could have been the ballgame right there: you don't go telling a roomful of Adventist patriarchs what prayer is. But Dr. Brumfeld and Elder Earwig were apparently on the outs—because Brumfeld immediately defused the situation by smirking at Earwig, then asking exactly what it was we wanted of them.

So Joon filled them in on Operation Squeeze. And—bless their self-righteous souls—all the Elders but Earwig seemed mildly intrigued. If I'd been Sister Harg I think I might've put the spurs to 'em with one of those gnarly *Amens* of hers. But when Brumfeld mused aloud that they might in fact be in a position to help, Linda dashed forward and gave him a hug and a kiss on the cheek. (Peter's stage directions again: the guy was shameless!) But Randy Beal's eyes welled when she did it. And old Brumfeld looked pretty stoked himself.

The Elders got down to business. Phone calls were made, and medical experts enlisted; times were set, and rendezvous points established. Hands were solemnly shaken, and gratitude copiously expressed.

. . . .

We drove back to the Red Desert Motor Inn, spent the rest of the day preparing for what we hoped would be a final showdown, then tried our best to sleep. But at 1 A.M., fed up with tossing and turning, I stepped outside, snuck up alongside Truman's camper, heard my uncle snoring, just as I'd hoped, then nearly stepped on Papa, who was sitting alone on the camper's bottom step. He'd snuck out for the same reason as me, though: soon as he saw me he slipped inside, stole three more of Truman's beers to go with the one he'd already been drinking, and we strolled round to the little dead lawn on the far side of the motel to drink them.

The night was clear—or clear for LA. Not many stars, but lots of airplanes and crickets. We were just pouring the beer down, hardly saying a word, when Papa stirred and said, "What we really need, you know, is a song."

I didn't know it, actually. I'd been leaning more toward a third beer myself. And when Papa started singing, "I Gave My Love a Cherry"—my childhood favorite—it embarrassed me. It felt a little sentimental, a little forced. It wasn't like him to act like this. But after just a few bars he started to cough. Which sort of left things hanging.

So I sang it. Soft as I could. But twice—that was our tradition. It was the first time I'd ever sung to anyone but Nash, or Bet and Freddy when they were little. It felt odd the first time through—as if I was the father and Papa the kid. But by the second time I was pretty well used to it. And when we went in afterward, we both fell right to sleep.

13. Squeeze

I don't know what Major Keys thought, the next morning, as we stepped once again across the asylum parking lot. All I know is that at some point he must have looked out, seen us, and realized in an instant that the game between us had changed. It wasn't the glowering trio of three-piece-suited, Bible-toting patriarchs who changed things: self-important as they appeared, they were obviously just disgruntled churchmen. The two earnest-looking professional men weren't a worry either. Though one of them *was* carrying a medical bag, there was no regulation or reason that forced Keys to let him in. No, it was just the frizzy-headed young woman and the hippie fellow who changed things. She with the notebook, in which she was busily scribbling. He with the two cameras hanging backwards from his neck and the long-lensed Nikon busily in hand. And over by the palm trees, the big bald guy: yes, that *was* a TV camera on his shoulder. And yes, it was rolling as we marched up to the MP-guarded gates . . .

A frightening invention, mass media. The alchemical equivalent of a military uniform, in a way. Slip a uniform on a young man, whoever he may be, and his values, his judgment, even his relationship with his own inner world instantly change—*must* instantly change. But train a media camera or journalist's pen upon a united group of men, women and children, whoever they may be, and they too don a sort of uniform. We could feel it as we approached the asylum: the cameras were casting us in an entirely new light. On a TV screen or in a photo essay the same hick-town homeliness that made us laughable to Keys became our most po-tent weapon. THE BIBLE VERSUS THE PENTAGON! headlines could roar. We were no longer people: we were images. The tearful wife, infant at her breast (CAPTION: *"I only want to see my husband!"*). The grimly pious mother and appropriately haggard ballplayer father (CAPTION: *"They drug him because he prays!"*). The defiant old Sabbath School marm, growling out a hymn as she dragged her tweaked carcass along behind a walker (CAPTION: *"Hallelujah!"*). How we looked to Keys no longer mat-tered. In the eye of the camera we were a walking, talking Norman Rock-well painting. Or worse. The climax of one of those abysmally happy old Frank Capra flicks, maybe. And Keys surely saw at a glance that he hadn't a snowman's chance in hell of landing the Gary Cooper or Jimmy Stewart role . . .

When we arrived at the gates, we didn't ask or try to enter. We just gathered in a big circle, started singing Sabbath School songs, let the cameras flash and roll, and waited for Keys to come to us.

He came promptly. But it impressed me that his stride was unhurried, and that he came alone. He could have dragged a bunch of WACs and orderlies and MPs along for moral support. He obviously felt he didn't need them. A big part of me tended to agree with him—though I quickly told that part to shut up.

Peter had the cameramen hold their fire. Then Elder Joon spent a solid minute making introductions. He began with the journalists, saying nothing but their names, letting the Major imagine whatever readership or viewers or levels of fame he chose. There was no other way to play it, really, since "Dewey Dvorakowski, free-lance photographer," was really Dewey Dvorakowski, Kim Joon's college roommate, "Sheila Crantz, free-

lance religious writer," was really Sheila Crantz, Dewey's bartender girlfriend, and "Ivan Gunnarson of KGOM-TV" was really Bud Heitz, Elder
Joon's old landlord—wearing a terminally hip black jumpsuit that Mary
Jane had scored in a Riverside thrift shop, and wielding our big rented-
and-disguised portable TV camera with such authority you would have
sworn we'd been able to afford film for it too.

But Dr. Hunsberger, a Loma Linda med school M.D., and Dr. Kruk, an
Adventist psychiatrist, were the genuine articles. So in their case, and in
the case of the Elders, Joon made their standing in the medical community and the Southern California Conference abundantly clear.

"So what can I do for you all?" Keys asked with his usual convincing
cordiality. "Is there some question I can answer? Maybe some worries I
can quell?"

Dr. Brumfeld stepped forward. "What you can do for us today," he
said in his habitually rhetorical tone, "is release an upstanding young
churchman into our own very competent professional care."

The Major responded to his demand by doing something every Adventist kid has learned not to do around Elders by the age of five or so: he
chuckled.

"Does it amuse you, Major Keys," Brumfeld said slowly, "that we consider our medical people competent?"

"Not at all," the Major replied, still smiling. "But despite the opinion
of one disgruntled family, I consider myself and my staff competent as
well."

Speaking slowly, letting it build as it flowed, Dr. Brumfeld said, "To
take advantage of a military trial that I have studied in depth, and am
tempted to call criminal for its failure to take Brother Chance's lifelong
religious background into account" (he paused, both to glower and to
breathe), "to then incarcerate, electrocute, and drug our young brother
right out of his Christian devotion, and then to call *that* a kind of healing
—this is *not* what we consider competence."

The low growl of Sister Harg: "*Amen.*"

But Keys was still smiling. "May I remind you, Dr. Brumfeld, that it
was two members of your own clergy who caused Irwin Chance to be
loosed upon the Army in the first place?"

"Like you," Brumfeld replied, "we are human, and sometimes make
mistakes. Unlike you, we are trying to correct ours."

It was a good comeback. Good enough to force Keys to get tough.
"The admission of a blunder by one of your own clergy may explain how
a misfit like Chance ended up in Vietnam," he said. "But the Army is not

responsible for that blunder. Nor does it make Chance any less dangerous at present. I understand the family's feelings. I sympathize. But no psychiatric hospital, least of all mine, is in the habit of loosing violent patients upon the public at their relatives' request."

"With your kind permission," Brumfeld coolly replied, "the gentlemen before you"—he indicated the psychiatrist and the doctor—"would like to make their own assessment of Brother Chance's condition."

"Then they can step inside and make an appointment," said Keys. "I have no objection. Early next week should be fine. And I'll be happy to facilitate their examination in every way I can."

"What's wrong with today?" Dr. Brumfeld asked. "What's wrong with now?"

"I'm afraid Private Chance is under somewhat heavy sedation."

"May we ask why?" asked Brumfeld.

Major Keys sighed. "This is not the kind of thing we normally bandy about in public. But since you all seem to have come here to second-guess me, perhaps I'd better tell you. Private Chance violently attacked a young woman volunteer during an art class less than a week ago."

"Says who!" Uncle Marvin burst out.

But it was an unexpected and nasty accusation. Dr. Brumfeld backed way off on this one. Then the psychiatrist, Dr. Kruk, spoke up. "The sanest person on earth could be chronically confused, if not violent, after misdiagnosis and weeks of inappropriate therapy."

"Again," the Major said, "I am being groundlessly second-guessed. I see no reason to even respond. But I will tell you, Doctor, that a very fine officer is still suffering the effects of Private Chance's psychotic attack. And though a toothpaste tube may seem an amusing weapon, if you'll step into my office I'll show you Captain Dudek's medical report. I doubt you'll find much humor in that."

The doctors and Elders began to hem and haw. Our momentum—if we'd had any—was gone. Elder Joon turned to Peter, who gave him a nod. There was only one way to make any sense of Irwin's actions: it was time to speak of the Cong boy.

"In our scriptures," Joon said, stepping forward, "Jesus says that it is better for a man to be cast into the sea and drowned than to harm a child. Irwin has worshipped these scriptures all his life. The execution of the Vietcong boy referred to in Irwin's testimony was a transgression of these scriptures, and of the Army's own laws. Irwin's attack on his captain was a reaction to this transgression. And while we too find his attack regrettable, we find his *remorse* understandable, even commendable.

There simply *is* a difference between Christians and Army men, Major. To eradicate Irwin's remorse over the death of that boy, we believe you would have to demolish his faith completely."

Keys smiled from one end of this speech to the other. And not smugly. He was smiling sympathetically. But he replied not to Joon or to my family, but to the doctors and Elders alone. "An unfortunate subject, this Cong boy," he said. "Has anyone yet told you gentlemen, has the Chance family even mentioned to you, that at Irwin's sanity hearing it was determined that this boy did not exist? Delusions like this are rather common. And I'm afraid it's only *one* of Private Chance's many symptoms."

This was the moment we'd feared—but also the moment we'd planned for. The Elders and doctors had turned to gape at us in injured amazement—and Brumfeld looked well on his way to outrage. But before any of them could speak, Nancy Beal pointed right at Keys and shouted, "Even soldiers have laws, Major! And even soldiers break them. Yet *you* seem to expect them to jump up and *admit* to it! Every criminal who ever lived would love to declare his accuser insane!"

"And as for delusions," Bet angrily put in, "it's you and the Army who keep pretending my brother's Christianity is a delusion!"

"In fifty-nine years of Sabbath School teaching," growled Ethel Harg, "I've never met a more honest boy than Irwin Chance. That's *fifty-nine* years. Not fifty-eight, or sixty. That boy does *not tell lies.*"

"And every man who testified at Irwin's trial," Papa said, not giving Keys a second to speak or think, "has had to remain in a combat zone, under the command of Captain Dudek, living—or trying to live—with the consequences of their testimony. Think about it, Major. You'd have to have a death wish to betray your company or your commander under those circumstances!"

"Our son is being railroaded!" Mama cried. "You know it and we know it! Dudek wants to shut him up forever—and you're doing his dirty work. That's why you won't let these doctors check him. That's why you're keeping him drugged. And that's why we're not leaving till you give him back to us!"

We had one round of ammo left. It was in Papa's shirt pocket. It was a very recent letter, from a soldier on Irwin's fire base. And though this soldier begged us not to use his name, in case of retaliation against him, he corroborated Irwin's story about the death of the Cong boy. No one knew of this letter except Papa, Peter and me, and we were praying we wouldn't have to use it. The reason we were praying was that the three of us had forged it just two nights ago . . .

But the Elders and doctors had all turned angrily back to Keys. And for the first time since we'd met him, the Major looked stunned. His great trump card had been trumped.

"If you'll allow it, Major," Dr. Kruk said acidly, "Dr. Hunsberger and I would be happy to wait in the patient's room till the sedatives wear off. Clear into the night, if necessary. If nothing else, it'll give us some idea of the dosages he's having to fight."

"Chance's ward is restricted," Keys said. But you could see his face go rigid as the content of his speech became banal.

"Screw this!" said Uncle Marv. "I'm phonin' back that lady from the LA *Times!*"

It wasn't a bad threat—but the Elders turned as one body, and scowled. Adventist men "know," they "beget," they "sire." But they never screw anything. Not even enemies, or wives. Mary Jane shut Marvo up in a hurry.

Elder Joon meanwhile correctly assessed the Major's rigidity to be disguised panic. So rather than taunt him, Joon began to offer him a way out. "Despite our intense feelings on this issue," he said, "we of the Adventist Church hold our Armed Forces in deep respect. We are not here to accuse Irwin's captain, or to create scandal. We simply feel that you don't understand Irwin quite as well as we do. So we want to be the ones to care for him."

Keys said nothing. But he'd begun to look a little like one of his own patients.

Feeling left out now that things were going so well, Dr. Brumfeld puffed himself up, pointed out the various "journalists," and said, "We are, as you can see, fully prepared to take this matter to the American public. And we are losing patience, Major. For us this is not a simple matter of mental sickness or health. It is a matter of *eternal* life or death!"

While most of the Adventists nodded vigorously, the Major—and Freddy and I—rolled our eyes. (Funny how fuzzy the lines can be between friends and enemies.) But before Brumfeld could beat the stuffing out of any more dead horses, Elder Joon started crooning like some sort of Rest Home Brochure: "Surely Irwin is of little use to the military in his present condition. And in one of our own psychiatric facilities, under vigilant and cautious care, he could enjoy the healing presence of his friends and family. All we want, Major, is to take this troublesome patient off your very busy hands. Of course we would take full responsibility for him. And his discharge may be qualified in any way the Army sees fit. But

Brother Irwin's sojourn here has gone on far too long. A decision must be reached immediately, Major. Otherwise we shall feel forced, this very day, to go public with our cause."

Within an hour of Joon's ultimatum the doctors Kruk and Hunsberger were allowed in to inspect the patient. They were gone maybe twenty minutes. They returned in a pale fury. But whatever they told Keys on their way out worked. Red tape was slashed. Conditions and guarantees were made and met (for instance, Irwin's discharge had to be "dishonorable"). And later that same evening—after the Elders, doctors and mock journalists had all been thanked and sent home—Major Keys led a nurse, and a loaded wheelchair, out of the asylum . . .

"I want you all to listen," Papa said as they made their slow approach. "The day is ours. And I'll never be able to thank you all enough. Yet I've already got another favor to ask."

There were smiles at this. But Papa's face, despite his obvious exhaustion, was an eerie blend of bitterness, love and pride. "I want you to know that damage has been done," he said, "and that it's severe. Irwin is not going to recognize *any* of us, I promise you. And you may barely recognize him."

Papa's fury had been audible at first. But as the wheelchair rolled closer, his voice grew more controlled. "It's going to be a long, slow recovery," he said, "and Irwin may never be quite the same. But let's not let this man Keys see how that makes us feel. Cry later. That's the favor I ask. Let's show this man our strength."

We tried our best. But when we finally encircled Irwin, there were problems. I had known, for instance, that the nose would be smashed and the forehead dented. But his eyes were jittering in their sockets in a way I'd only seen on cartoons. And I'd expected the drool-soaked straitjacket, and even the lolling, swollen tongue. But to see Nash gazing at his father for the very first time. And Linda's huge, expectant smile, slowly fading. To see old Sis Harg and the Beals praying for instant miracles that were obviously not about to occur. And Uncle Marv, who took one fleeting look at his favorite nephew, then walked quickly away, shoulders shuddering, to hide himself before he started to weep . . . It all filled me with something I'd never felt before. A terrible kind of burning. When I looked at Major Keys—saying his glib farewells to my parents, giving them advice, even now—I truly and deeply wanted to kill him. And I believe I could have done it, with nothing but my hands. But all of a sudden, out of nowhere, Peter had an arm around me. "Let it go, Kade," he was whispering very gently, though his arm was nearly crushing me. "Open your fists," he said, "and let go of the coals."

So we loaded Irwin into the Nomad still straitjacketed—Keys's final inane stipulation—but freed him as soon as the door and blinds were closed. And mile after mile, as we drove north out of LA and I studied Irwin's new face, I kept having to reopen my fists, and to let go of more burning coals.

But even broken, Irwin seemed to have a way of creating hope. Maybe two hundred miles down the road, Freddy noticed that his eyes had stopped jiggling. And a hundred miles further he moved, all on his own, across the bed in the back. He still seemed to recognize no one, and all he'd done was crawl to the far side of the bed, pull a pillow over his head, and stay there. But whenever Linda left him, to tend to Nash or to eat or rest, Mama or Papa would take turns crawling across the same bed, just to lie there beside him. And every time he saw them there, Uncle Marv would turn to a window and smile—though his shoulders would again begin to shudder.

CHAPTER TWO

Broken Boat

Nothing ends without breaking, because everything is endless.
—Antonio Porchia

In the dream world I entered as we drove home from Mira Loma, we all had canoes and were paddling across a lake. Or not canoes exactly. These were smaller, more fragile vessels—like skin kayaks or umiaks, but open-topped. They sat so low in the water that we had to paddle very calmly to keep from swamping. And the lake was vast: no land in sight. We had to paddle so calmly that it did not seem wise to talk. But we were gliding along in a shifting V, like geese, fifteen silhouettes, each to his own vessel. Even Nash, minuscule and stalwart, paddled his own tiny craft.

The night sky was indigo. Stars hung down around us all the way to the horizon. The lake surface was so still that it reflected every star till our bows and wakes would seem to knock them from the sky. We carried nothing but our paddles, not even food. Like salmon on their upriver journey, we didn't seem to need it. When we were thirsty we'd dip a careful handful of water from the lake. It tasted wonderful, so icy cold. And arcing off our sterns were the frail ropes we'd made—of our own saliva, it seemed in the dream, as if we were spiders, or nest-weaving birds —fifteen shining threads leading back to the prow of the cumbersome raft on which Irwin lay. And fragile though they were, together the threads were holding. Wounded though he was, Irwin's life was still in him, and in a silent, steadfast V we were towing him home when,

quietly but inarguably,

Papa's little vessel sprang a leak . . .

Just a small, steady stream, about the diameter of a pencil.

It sounded almost pleasant, gurgling upward like a tiny forest spring.

But we all stopped paddling, and no one spoke. There was no need to speak. The thin skin hulls. The icy, shoreless waters. The beautiful stars, clear down to the horizon. We all knew at once that he was going down.

We encircled him in silence. We listened to the gurgling. We wondered how the water felt, so cold around his feet. But we didn't ask. And he didn't say. He didn't speak, didn't struggle, didn't try to stop or even slow the flow. He just laid his paddle across his gunnel, rested his hands on it, sat still, waited. So we sat still and waited with him . . .

The gurgling grew quieter, then stopped altogether as the water rose higher in his boat. Any moment now it would rush in over the sides, there'd be a swirl, perhaps a brief struggle. Then we would never see him again. Yet we sat so still that our wakes disappeared completely: the reflected stars crept clear in to the walls of our boats: up became no different than down, water no different than sky, stars lay deep below us, hung above us, surrounded us. And there was suddenly no question, in that great sphere of stillness, that everything, even Papa's disappearance, was going to be all right. Someone—I couldn't see who, but the voice was far from musical—even began to risk her balance and life by chanting a little death song.

I opened my eyes . . .

It was Mama.

She was sitting on the bed in the back of the old Nomad with Irwin's head in her lap, stroking his hair and softly singing. I couldn't make out the words, but the tune was that of some old hymn of which he'd been fond. Trying to jog his poor, blasted memory already.

But then I turned toward the fold-down bunk across from me, where

Papa lay sleeping, and saw, in the early-morning light, the blackness that had for days been gathering beneath his eyes. And though it felt like a betrayal of the calm and beauty of the dream, and of all that our courageous little band had just accomplished, grief and fear like water gushed up inside me.

CHAPTER THREE

Dream
Come True

The game is not over until the sixth inning is over.
—Lee Ming Chen

–I–

The leak in Papa's boat was cancer. First in his left lung, and a surgery to remove it was scheduled. But while we awaited the date the doctors ran more tests, and found it in his liver. Then in his lymphatic system. And our lives became my dream: no need to speak. The thin skin hulls. Shoreless waters. We all knew at once that he was going down . . .

We listened to the doctors' estimates of how much time he might still have. We learned the names and side effects of the painkillers and useless therapies. We wondered how it felt, running wild through his body. But we didn't ask. And Papa didn't say. He didn't complain, didn't struggle, didn't try to stop or even slow the flow. One astonishingly simple phone call to the Tug front office and he was finished with the game that had been his life. He then began to sit with his death, for most of each day and evening, in his old armchair in the livingroom. Not moving much. Not saying much. Just trying to accept—the hardest work of his life. So, when we could, we would sit there with him, trying to do the same.

–II–

"Write soon, write much," Everett told us in his first letter home from Wahkiakum. Little did he know what he was asking.

Papa insisted that he be the first to share the news. He kept his letter brief, and pulled no punches. He said that we had managed to save Irwin, "thanks to you, and the good people who answered your wake-up call." He said that Irwin had stayed in an Adventist mental hospital for a week, but that he was already back home with us, and physically healthy, though "still in pretty rough shape." He then wrote:

There's no easy way to say this, so I'll just let fly. I have cancer. Three kinds. All serious. Inoperable. The doctors tell me I'm dying, and it feels that way to me too. I hate having to tell you this when you're already on the ropes, but it's going to take all our strength and all our love to come to terms with it in the time we have left. So there you have it.

If it's all right with you, Laura and I would like to be your first two visitors, come July. We're very proud of you. More later.

Love, Papa

Mama added a note in the same envelope. Hers said:

So much has happened since your beautiful sermon that I'm afraid you may to have to wait for a Better World to receive the thanks you deserve. I want your father to be at peace, but find so little peace in myself right now that I fear I'll fail him. I'm afraid for your brother Irwin, and for his wife. I'm afraid for your sister Bet. I'm afraid for you.

Peter's home. He's staying with Kade and Amy, and working terribly long days here for me. I don't know what happened to him in India, but something did. He refuses to let me pay him, he's always smiling, he never reads, he eats like a horse. He's been a help in a hundred ways. I don't think we'd have gotten Irwin home without him.

I love my sons. I'm so sorry to send you this news.

Your mother

Peter's letter to Everett began like this:

I feel as though we're all headed in slow motion for a car wreck, knowing already that we're all going to be injured, and that one of us is going to be killed. I see no way out of this. And I'm not looking for easy consolations. But we're all so distracted by what's happened these past few days that I'm afraid we're going to forget to tell you about the past few weeks. I hope Papa finds time and strength to tell you himself, but I want to say right now that for me it feels as though if we <u>are</u> at the end of Papa's life, it's been a pretty great life, and a pretty great ending. That doesn't lessen the loss, I know. But maybe it makes the hurt more worthwhile. Let me try to tell you what I mean . . .

I don't know where he found time or focus, but Peter went on to write an incredibly detailed letter, telling Everett all about Papa's last pitch, about his encounter with Elder Babcock, about his futile but courageous one-man assault on Major Keys and the Loffler Center and about the oddities, the wonders, the outright joys of the Mira Loma rescue operation. It was a tremendous letter. Freddy and I were too screwed up with grief and confusion to add much, but we tacked on postscripts, just telling Everett that we loved him and missed him and would come see him soon as we could.

Then came a letter about which the rest of us knew nothing. Taking a page out of my book, Bet opened a PO box over in Washougal and started a secret correspondence with Everett. This is how it began:

Dear Everett,
You said you wanted to hear everything, so I'm going to tell you. Papa is dying, and that's all anyone can think about. But it's not all I think about. There's other things happening here, things as bad, maybe worse. Like with Irwin. He lives in the back bedroom, mine and Freddy's old room, alone. Linda and Nash stay upstairs now. We all take care of him, Mama the most, and he's not quite as helpless, physically, as he was at first. Like he goes to the bathroom on his own now, and he'll eat if you make him, and can usually keep it down. But so what? That's what no one but me will tell you. Because he never speaks to anyone, or even looks at anyone. His face never changes. He never wants to leave the house, or even his bed. To take him on walks Peter and Kade have to lift him and drag him. And once he's outside it's awful. Because he walks like Frankenstein. Even looks like him,

with the scar on his forehead. And when people, even old friends and neighbors, see him on the street, they look away. When strangers see him they honk and yell things. "Hey, Retard!" Or Roy. Remember Papa's old friend? When he saw Irwin he just held his hand a while, then started crying and walked away. Kincaid thinks we should let Irwin be, let him sit in his room till he's ready to act different. Mama and Peter think the walks and contact with people might help. Papa doesn't know. He sits with Irwin for an hour or so each evening, but I think he only does it because he himself is so sick. Or not sick. <u>Dying</u>. I keep forgetting. It doesn't feel real. Nothing does. Because his dying, Papa's dying, should be the worst thing we have to face. But it's not. The worst thing is, there's already been a death. Irwin's. He's dead inside, Everett, I swear. They killed him in Mira Loma, then let us save an empty body, and nobody here wants that, everybody fights it, if I told them what I'm telling you they'd think I was some kind of monster. But Linda is so afraid of what he's become, and fights it so hard, she scares me. She's out of control, Everett. We all are. But her way scares me. Like with Nash. She thinks Irwin likes Nash, that he's better around the baby, so she makes Irwin lie on his back on their bedroom floor. If Peter or Kade or somebody aren't here to help she just shoves Irwin out of bed, knocks him on the floor. And then she puts Nash on him, and leaves. Of course Nash loves it. He crawls around on Irwin like he's a jungle gym, hits him with toys, gouges at his mouth and eyes, chews on him, makes him bleed. It's sick. If Irwin could feel, Nash would be making him scream. I think Linda is using the baby to punish him, punish Irwin, for being dead. Sometimes I even think she hopes Irwin will go nuts and kill the baby.

Or listen to this: I can't sleep at night, you've probably heard. I'm sick in the head, you've probably heard. And I walk around when it's bad. No, that's a lie. I <u>sneak</u> around, Everett, and listen at doors. I've been doing it for years. I can't stand myself for doing it, I hate myself, but I said I'd tell you everything. The way people acted, nothing ever made sense, Mama especially, and I wanted to understand. So I started sneaking. And our little family! These people we think we know! Like Linda, when Nash is sleeping, I shouldn't say this, I hate myself for knowing it, but she goes in with Irwin. She takes off her clothes. Then she takes off Irwin's clothes. And she does things. Whispers to him, like lovers do, or just cries and cries, while she rubs him, everywhere. Rubs him and slaps him. "Wake up, wake up, come out of this! You can hear me, liar! You hear, you fucker! Look at me. You feel this.

Look at your penis. You couldn't do this if you were so dead! Wake up, you lying bastard!" And he doesn't know her from Nash, Everett. He doesn't know any of us. But she keeps doing things, everywhere, rides him, bites him, makes horrible sounds. Hits him. Hits him <u>hard</u>, then pleads with him. Does sick things to him, then cries on him. And he never speaks, never moves unless she moves him, stares at nothing, doesn't make a sound. She treats him like her toy. Like some life-sized sicko doll you order in the back of a dirty magazine. She's crazy, Everett. I really think she's ill. And it's my fault for listening, I'm sick too, sicker than her. But I'm starting to hate her for it. I shouldn't. I shouldn't even know. But I can't sleep knowing they're down there, and she's doing this. So I listen. But no. I'm lying again. I don't listen, Everett. I'm a worm. I'm scum. Because I have a way, if I want, if she forgets one simple thing, and she often does, where I can watch. I hate me. I hate her. But I watch. There. I've told you. And if you tell anyone, I swear to God, I'll kill myself. You know I mean it. But write to me, Everett. I can't stand this, I can't stand it. Papa's dying. Irwin's alive but dead. Linda's sick. I'm sicker. Tell me something. Help me.

Bet

–III–

For the last four months of his life the major projects of Papa's days were to dress himself, to totter out to his armchair, to read the sports page and mail, to make no mistakes in calculating his occasional need for and distance from the bathroom, and—with his secretary Freddy's help—to answer all the mail before it was time to totter back to bed. A simple enough regimen; arduous, because of the disease; yet manageable day after day in a way that led us to hope modest hopes. There was no mention among us of miracle words like "cure" or even "remission." The one of us who might have openly prayed for such things was inert now, and mute. But Papa's condition did enable us to find some solace in previously meager-sounding terms such as "no change" or "stable."

To my surprise, the worst threat to this stability did not seem to be the cancer. We all knew that our father was a much-loved man, and expected that he would receive visitors. What I didn't expect was how much I'd come to dread these near-daily invasions by friends, relatives and ballplayers, ballplayers, ballplayers, most of whom could find no way to express their love for Papa but to display their grief in advance—and so demand, however inadvertently, that he console them by displaying in return his great but dying strength. These were often people I loved, and always people I would normally have been glad to meet. It was their right to come, and Papa's right to show them whatever face he chose. But since his choice was strength, strength, strength, even when I knew he had none, and since it was we, not the visitors, who watched him pay the price for his strength later, it became all I could do not to resent, or even despise, these good people. Which made me ashamed. So I took to avoiding them.

Papa faced each day in some slight variation on the same old clothes— plaid shirt, brown leather belt, baggy tan trousers. And he approached his daily dressing ritual and trip to the chair with the same one-pointed solemnity with which he'd so recently approached every trip from the bullpen to the mound. The only variable was time: some mornings it took him just minutes to dress; some mornings it took close to an hour. In either case, he made no comment.

He ate almost nothing, though Mama, Linda and Bet kept an array of foods on a tray beside him all day. There were times when he enjoyed and even requested our company, but his usual preference, when he didn't have visitors, was to study the box scores, or just to sit quiet, watching the maple leaves wave out the window.

It took courage for newcomers to look at him. The usual desperation therapies soon caused his hair to fall out. His legs and arms became sticks. His skin grew nearly transparent, his face hollow and ascetic as an ancient elk's, the eyes huge, dark, and either beautiful or terrifying, depending on who was looking. To me he seemed to grow suddenly ageless more than suddenly aged. The cancer didn't add years, really. It just subtracted most of his body, making the life in him shine through the increasingly diaphanous skin as a kind of warmth and glow. When he was resting or sleeping in his chair and the light in him would wane, that could be troubling. He looked more an artifact than a person at such times—a disturbingly stylized sculpture of the man he'd been. And the sculptor's name was obvious. Death is a redundant (and in my opinion, pedestrian) artist, the bare skull and bones its one aesthetic idea—and we all saw its predictable hand at work on our father. But right up till the end, when Papa grew animated by love or family, by baseball or old friends, or even by sorrow, anger, or grief, he remained beautiful to look at. And this beauty (fuck you, death, and fuck your boring artwork) was not just "spiritual." It was also *physical*.

·   ·   ·   ·

Except for the Saturday ballgames he'd grown so intolerant of TV that we now kept it in Linda's room, where she could maintain her addiction to soap operas, and Mama hers to the eleven o'clock news.

And speaking of addiction: even with the cancer all through him, we'd sometimes walk into the livingroom and find Papa sitting with a Lucky Strike smoldering in his hand. He wasn't fool enough to try to inhale them, but he still loved to light and hold and study them—and it was a shock, after all that had happened, to find him sitting that way. It was Freddy who finally sucked up the courage to tell him just how it made us feel: she said she'd just as soon walk in and find him chatting with his murderer—*after* the guy had pumped him full of bullets.

But Papa just looked at her calmly, sent one of his diaphanous smiles drifting through the smoke, and said, "Love thine enemies, my girl."

–IV–
letter from Wahkiakum to Bet's Washougal PO box / July / 1971

Dear Bet,

Thank you for writing, and for being so honest. I'm so glad you're opening up with me, and it's going to help, it's going to help. But listen. It's horrible, it's a nightmare, what's happened to Irwin, and of course I don't want anyone hurting him, or him hurting Nash. But I don't want you being hurt either. And what you're doing, this spying stuff, is hurting you. For godsake don't kick yourself, you're not sick at all. I've done things as strange, we all do strange things. But it's a kind of stealing, what you're doing. Your eyes are ripping off something that belongs to someone else—a mystery called "to have and to hold," and "in sickness and in health"; a mystery called "one flesh." And to steal from the mysteries of others like this is a needless betrayal of someone I love very much: namely, Beatrice Chance. That, I think, is why you feel sick. You feel the betrayal.

I don't mean to embarrass you, but can I make a guess about certain other feelings? I would guess their bodies are beautiful when you watch—I'm sure they are, actually. So maybe you get off on watching, feel aroused yourself? I just want to say that those are normal feelings, Bet, healthy sexual feelings, there's nothing sick about them, or about you. So don't revel in some imaginary darkness, don't puff it all up into something deeply and majestically wrong. All that's wrong is that you're stealing from <u>their</u> mystery to ignite your own. All that's wrong is that there's no need to steal. I'm no sort of example, but based on my mistakes I can promise you: just show a little faith (like I didn't), be a little patient (like I wasn't), and when the time comes, your very own beautiful mystery will ignite itself.

But there's another side to this. Knowing you, your good heart, I know you also must watch them out of concern that Irwin not be hurt. The trouble with that, though, Bet, is that he <u>is</u> hurt. It already happened. He and Linda might recover, or they might not, we just don't know. But your love and concern can't help them here. If he's so numb he can watch Nash beat him bloody with toys, if that's true, then who knows what might thaw him? All I know is I'd rather have him raped by his wife than by the fucking U.S. government.

One thing you're way way wrong about. He is <u>not</u> <u>dead</u>. He's alive, so is Linda, and it's her right to try anything she can think of, anything she feels, to bring him back to his senses. For all we know, she's right. If he can be aroused, maybe he's not as broken as he looks. More mystery, Bet. And all we can do is let it solve, or not solve, itself. So let their hidden struggle remain hidden. Okay? Give them back some of the dignity the war and asylum have stolen. I know how small that damned house is, how sounds rip right through it, how hard it must be not to see and hear too much. But buy ear-plugs. Play the harmonica. Sleep in the basement. Whatever it takes. Anyone strong enough to save her stupid big brother's dignity by standing up in front of a whole damned church and shouting "Leave him alone!" is strong enough to give some dignity to another brother and his wife.

One last thing, Bet. I want you to know that I'm asking these favors for two reasons. One is because I love you, but the other is because I <u>need</u> you. The truth is, it's very hard being stuck in this place, at this time. Almost impossible. We're losing our papa together, you and me, and to be unable to even see it happening hurts like hell. For this hurt to be bearable, I need for <u>you</u> to be all right. I need that desperately. If you can get through this in one piece for me, maybe I can do the same for you. Okay? Can we make that our secret pact?

Write soon, and tell whatever needs telling. It's <u>great</u> to have you to share with again. Come see me soon too. Don't feel shamed or shy. I'm just sorry you've had to go through all this.

　　Love,
　　Everett

–V–

One day in September, out of the blue, Peter's scholarly books, manuscripts, lexicons, dictionaries and Indian journal all arrived in a small wooden crate from Bombay, with the following missive taped to the front cover of the journal:

Peter Chance:
I find myself thinking of you with surprising regularity, probably, I now realize, because my work will never again be so appreciated by a client. I continue to feel badly that I allowed Natu to give you the same treatment he gave Waites. I hope he did you no permanent damage, and that your new career, whatever it may be, is a satisfaction.

You may be interested to learn that I too have undergone a major change, though only of technique, not of vocation. When I discovered that the far too clever Dessinger had long made a habit of lying about the contents of our pilfered luggage, I gave him and Natu both the sack and went solo. Of course I can't say much about my new work, but I dare hope you'll be pleased to learn that the growing herds of Western guru-seekers and ashram-hoppers are the vein of ore I now mine, that the nature of the hoax places neither "pirateer" nor "piratee" at any physical risk, that I confine myself to devotees of gurus whom I consider to be shams, and that my first few ventures have been such smashing economic successes that I expect I'll be able to perpetrate far fewer crimes. Of course there are still difficulties. Where there is industry there is pollution, no? But enough about me.

As you see, I have enclosed the impedimenta of your previous incarnation as a Pundit. Not to tempt you into relapse, you understand. I merely admired your self-abnegating honesty—and by dint of the same honesty, these things belong to you. I managed, despite considerable curiosity, to give your journal only the fleetest of glances, but to my alarm that glance alit upon a passage from one of the very gurus whose followers I have declined to plunder. (That's an unexpected difficulty of my new line of work: in becoming expert at spotting the shams, a couple of the non-shams have begun to look remarkably attractive to me! What a disaster to my career <u>that</u> could turn out to be!) At any rate, the passage goes:

"Sinner" and "saint" are waves of differing size and magnitude on the surface of the same sea. Each is a natural outcome of forces in the universe; each is governed by time and causation. Nobody is utterly lost, and nobody need despair . . .

This being the sort of thing that catches your eye, it's little wonder I liked you. Which brings me to a parting thought: should you ever seek an Exciting Career Change, I suspect we'd work very well together. I can be found now and again (in various guises, but almost invariably sipping a lime rickey) by the pool at the Raj in Bombay, and near the fountain in the courtyard of the Hotel Matali in Benares.

Cordially,

"Robert Louis Grayson"

–VI–
fragment of a letter from Wahkiakum to Lake Havasu City, Arizona / August / 1971

Papa's going fast now, Tasha, his visit was so short, and if things go as we fear I'll never see him again. That this is asked of me, that drinking this down has become part of my "debt to society"—it's making me crazy, Tasha, probably for life, I better warn you. Yet at the same time something inside me (is it just my craziness?) keeps wanting to thank God. And not derisively. I keep getting these mind-stopping impulses, several times a day lately, to kneel, or no, to fall flat on my face actually, and to thank God, if there is One, with all my heart. Can you believe it? Why, Tasha? Why thankfulness, and why now? Is it just because it's clear to me now that the economy of the psyche, the inner checks and balances, our inner workings are so tricky, so impossibly fragile, we're so easily crushed, that I can't believe any longer that it's me alone, or even me and you alone, or even me and you and luck alone, that's keeping me alive? I feel now that we could die or be killed or be driven mad by grief or disaster at any moment. Even the strongest of us. Or be killed on the inside without even being touched. Yet my reaction to this, Tasha, has suddenly ceased to be anger and begun to be gratitude. And I don't even know why. Slogging my way along these clear-cuts, gashing the goddamned ground open, jamming in little corporate trees six feet apart, hell's idea of a forest, Papa pulling me down, down, Irwin too, poor ruined thing,

and these good men here with me, the gentlest men I've met, most of them, slaving here because they refused to hate or kill, Patriotism's idea of a convict, everything upside down, what else is new, my whole mind groaning nothing to live for, let it die, let it die—
yet right in the heart of me: gratitude.

Why?

Is it just because I'm not dying and am not quite mad and don't feel quite crushed inside? Why does my whole heart, every beat, round the clock, answer my mind's constant groaning with: but wait, but wait, but wait . . . ?

Of course I want to shout "Because of you, Tasha!" Because your letters, your love, our baby. My God how I want the whole mess I'll one day make of that! Yet knowing me, my weaknesses, my tedious anger, this tedious darkness, I know I could lose my hold even on you and find some way of flaming out here, and going down, if it weren't for . . . you.

Not you, Tasha.

I mean this other you. I refuse to resort to Uppercase here. But you hear me. And I feel you. I mean you, the who or whatever you are, being or nonbeing, that somehow comes to us and somehow consoles us. I don't know your name. I don't understand you. I don't know how to address you. I don't like people who think they do. But it's you alone, I begin to feel, who sends me this woman's love and our baby, and this new hope and stupid gratitude, even as my father goes down and my stupid brother lies broken. So:

O thing that consoles.

How clumsily I thank you.

–VII–

During the last few weeks, Papa grew so weak that he was finally unable to dress himself. Then one day—distracted by a long-winded guest and an unexpected phone call—he failed for the first time to make it to the bathroom. It was Mama who found him after the visitor left, just sitting in his problem, alone in his chair. And when she'd tried to help him, he spoke to her so harshly that she fled the room in tears, not because of what he'd said, but because she feared his anger might kill him on the spot.

There was no one home at the time but Irwin, so in desperation Mama got him out of bed, led him by the hand into the livingroom, told him "Papa needs you!" then left the house to walk, quietly sobbing, around the neighborhood. Twenty or so minutes later she returned to see whether anything had changed, but Papa was still just sitting in the armchair, and Irwin was just sitting in a straight-backed chair a few feet away.

Then she noticed that Papa's clothes had been changed.

And the instant she noticed, Papa started beaming.

He had just two words to say about what had transpired. They were: "He's hired." Irwin, as always, had no words at all. But from that day forward he was the only person whose intimate touch Papa would allow. They became inseparable. Even at night: Mama took to sleeping in my old room, and Irwin took Mama's place in the twin bed at Papa's side.

They were an unsettling pair: the huge, physically vital but vacant-eyed son; the skeletal, lake-eyed father. Irwin's robotic expression never changed no matter what the two of them were doing or how sick Papa got. But in Papa's opinion this made him the perfect attendant, both emotionally and physically: emotionally because the rest of us were devastated by each new stage of his disintegration; physically because, even as a skeleton, Papa's frame was sizable, his bones heavy, and from a bathtub or bed it was a backbreaking lift.

It feels odd, given the overall circumstances, to say that I cherish my memories of those last few weeks. But I certainly do. There were anecdotes I could tell of odd exchanges with visitors, of funny lines (all Papa's) at Irwin's expense, and of moments of such poignancy that we'd grow tired of it in mid-moment and begin, with tears still in our eyes, to make dumb jokes. But my favorite memory of all is simply of the way Papa would look at Irwin whenever they undertook a journey to a different room, a meal, a trip to the bathroom, a change of clothing after failure to reach the bathroom, or any of the other oppressive tasks that Papa had taken to calling simply "Further Adventures." It looked at such times as though all the life left in Papa moved entirely up into his eyes and the useless, riddled body became Irwin's problem, and his alone. No matter how distasteful the proceedings, Papa's eyes expressed no self-consciousness, no irritation, no embarrassment or despair; for as long as it took Irwin to tend what needed tending, he relinquished himself so completely that he seemed momentarily free of pain, free of the prison his body had become, free to hunch like two elves in his own eye sockets the way Nash would sometimes do, sending Irwin beam after beam of such unstinting affection that I half expected Irwin to thaw and heal and let out the old loon-laugh any second.

Irwin never did laugh, or smile, or even react. Not even when Papa, safely returned to his armchair, would solemnly thank him. He'd just hunker back down on his straight-backed chair and proceed to gape vacantly at the floor or out the window till Papa summoned him again. But there was still something wonderful about their togetherness. It felt as though two pieces of human wreckage had combined to form a whole human presence, as though they somehow restored to each other what had been stripped away.

There was just one drawback to their togetherness: it made us all grow so attached to the "Further Adventures" era that when things finally came to their inevitable close, we felt little better prepared than if Papa had been in perfect health.

–VIII–

On a rainy afternoon in late October, I'd gone fishing on the Washougal with results for a change. I'd hooked and landed a mint-bright twenty-nine-pound salmon—my first chinook ever, a tremendously strong fish too, it seemed to me. And as I beached and killed it I remember feeling that the river had sensed our need, that it was going to be a great blessing to carry these twenty-nine pounds of strength home and share them with Irwin and Papa.

Obeying a whim, I drove to the opposite side of the block from our house, parked at the laundromat, grabbed my fish, and snuck into the backyard through the old laurel-hedge spy-hole. Circling round the far side of the tool and pitching sheds, I then ducked down into the basement, thinking I would clean the chinook in the utility sink, lay it out on an old sports section (open, of course, to the box scores), carry it upstairs in garnished glory, and make a grand and healing presentation to Papa and Irwin both.

But when I unlocked and opened the basement door the naked bulb over the sink was already shining, and water was already running full blast into the sink. My first thought was that some comedian in the family had seen my fish and me coming and deliberately bushwhacked my surprise by turning on the tap in advance. Then I looked in the sink, saw the spread from Papa's bed—and it was stained with blood.

It was strange, what my mind decided to make of this: I didn't think of

Papa at all. Instead I looked down at my fish, wondered how on earth its blood had preceded it into the sink, looked back at the bedspread, and thought, *I'd better wash that out fast or Mama's gonna be pissed.*

Then I heard the door at the top of the stairs open. Irwin stepped through. And he had the sheets from our parents' room in one hand, Papa's blue flannel shirt in the other—and there was blood on these too. There was also blood on Irwin's shirt. There was even blood on his chin. Yet his face wore no more expression than usual. He just looked at me blankly, then said, "He's dead, Kade. Help me."

My mind was gone.

I heard him say, "One big cough. No warning. Didn't even seem to hurt. But so much blood. I tried to clear it, tried mouth-to-mouth. But he was gone."

I moved toward him, peering at the stained chin, at the shirt in his hands. But I felt no grief. Instead I found myself clinging to some simple confusion. Our father was dead—yes, apparently. That was his blood, and his shirt, yes yes. But some small oddity was blocking my feelings—and knowing what my feelings were about to become, I hoped never to remove the blockage.

In a voice as robotic as his face, I heard Irwin say, "Everyone's out, but they're coming home soon. Nash and Linda. Mama and the twins. They're just shopping. I need to change him. So please. Help."

I heard him say, "When Grandawma died, Bet and Freddy, remember? They cleaned her up so great. So it's our turn. See?"

I heard him say, "Help me, Kade. Now. He's dead."

Then, not to my joy, but to my sorrow, I had it: the voice itself. Irwin was speaking. He was making sense. And our papa was dead.

I started up the stairs. He started down. But when we met in the middle I could see he wanted to move right on past me, so I blocked his path. I needed to hug him. I tried to. But I couldn't lift one arm. I looked at it. It was holding a huge salmon. I let it go; watched it flup, flup, flup down the stairs; heard, in the quick downward slapping, the exact opposite of all its silver body and spirit had been designed to do. "He's dead, Kade," the voice repeated, "and it's a mess up there. Come on."

I started to sob, threw my arms around my brother, and hugged him and all that he held, hard against me. He stood with his arms down, stiff as wood or stone.

"Help me," he repeated. "Now."

–IX–

Mama came home first. And saw what had happened. Then she just crawled right onto the newly made bed, and took the clean, freshly clothed body into her arms. I started to gasp, covered my mouth with my forearm, and moved as fast as I could out into the backyard.

Irwin joined me after a while. We could still sort of see her through the window, and hear faint sounds. But I tried not to look or listen. I noticed that Irwin had on clean clothes, and that his face was washed, perhaps even freshly shaved. There was a load in the wash, and another tumbling in the dryer. He'd even managed somehow to clean my salmon. Seeing the way he was eyeing me, I realized finally that he had come out not to console me, or to seek consolation from me, but to inspect me for bloodstains. "Did everything look normal?" he asked in his dull, wooden way.

I just gawked at him without speaking—as if I was him now, and he was me. I'd no idea what "normal" meant.

When Mama finally called us in and I saw the tears still streaming, I began to cry again too. Then I rediscovered what "normal" meant: Mama took one look at me, scowled—and instantly stopped crying. I couldn't stop even then, but I also nearly burst out laughing. Contrariness as deep as hers has *got* to be some kind of virtue.

She had Irwin cover Papa with the unfinished afghan that Linda had been making for him. "His face too," she said evenly. Then she had me call the fire department, as Papa had made her promise to do. ("Cheaper than ambulances," he'd said, "and it's smoke inhalation that's killed me.")

While we waited for them to arrive, Mama asked me to recite the Lord's Prayer, with some challenge in her request—the old Adventist versus Rebel tension, I suppose. To show her I didn't mind I waited for the *Amens*, then threw in the Twenty-third Psalm. It may have been a mistake: when I heard myself declare that goodness and mercy would surely follow us all the days of our lives, the silence that followed—the genuine dead silence—was unbearable to me. Not knowing what to do, hoping Mama wouldn't object to a little more Bible, I spontaneously recited a single verse from the Twenty-fourth Psalm—a verse I'd memorized way back in early Sabbath School because it reminded me a little of

Papa on his pitcher's mound. I said, "Who shall ascend into the hill of the Lord? or who shall stand in his holy place?"

For some reason, Mama began to weep again when she heard this. But for me there was something soothing in the words—something right about honoring the end of a life not with a statement, but with a question. So I said it again. "Who shall ascend into the hill of the Lord? or who shall stand in his holy place?"

Mama wept harder. And on the second recitation Irwin turned to watch me, and I saw—for the first time since he'd come home—a hint of an expression on his face. Anger was what it looked like, actually. But it was definitely an expression. So I said it again: "Who shall ascend into the hill of the Lord? or who shall stand in his holy place?"

His face visibly darkened. Mama kept weeping. I began again: "Who shall ascend into the hill of the Lord?"

But before I could finish Irwin cut me off with a gesture, pointed at Papa's body, and said, "Him! Papa. That's who. So shuttup!"

And for some reason now, at the sound of his voice, the look on his face, I felt joy despite my sorrow.

CHAPTER FOUR

The Wake

The room is sparsely furnished:
A chair, a table, and a father.
—Carolyn Kizer

Camas / October / 1971

They'd talked about all of this, Papa and Mama had. Of course it hadn't been easy. But near the end certain unpleasant possibilities had begun to bother Papa, and he'd wanted them off his mind. So. No preachers, no churches, no caskets, he'd told her. No long rows of cars with their headlights on. No funeral parlor, no hired speakers, no baritone soloist, no hymns. "A wake, Laura," he'd said. "Not a mope. Just a remembering. Right here at home. If Elder Joon or Randy Beal come, make sure it's as civilians. I want *everybody* free to talk. I want good food and drink for friends and family. And if any ballplayers come—and they're all invited— I want 'em to feel at home. So serve beer."

Mama had looked mildly offended, but not very surprised, by all of this. But then the plot had thickened:

"I want to be cremated," he'd said—knowing full well that Mama, like any good Adventist, believed that death is sleep, and that the literal, physical body will be resurrected on Judgment Day. "This body's had it," he'd said when her face changed color. "It's been good to me. But I don't want it back."

Her reaction was wonderful in a way: she got spitting mad. What *did* he want? she'd asked. What *would* His Majesty allow? Could we sing the national anthem, or maybe "Take Me Out to the Ballgame"? Or were those songs, heaven forbid, too much like hymns? Could we hold hands while we drank our beer and tossed his ashes in the garbage? Or was hand-holding too sanctimonious for him?

His reply had not been quite what she'd expected. He'd just reached for her hand, and held it hard, as he said, "God, I'm gonna *miss* watchin' you do that."

Mama had sat down on the arm of his chair then, and Papa kept hold of her hand as he tried to explain. "One reason I want cremation," he'd said, "is that it's cheap, and money will be short. Another reason is that ashes keep—so you can include Everett in whatever you finally decide to do. And one other reason, or not a reason, really. Just a thought . . ." She felt his strength suddenly leave him. "This isn't a request, Laura. Or even a hope. I mean, who knows what the future might bring? But one other thing about ashes keeping, see, is that if you wanted to . . . and if, in the end, you were still, well . . . single . . . then maybe I, they, you see . . . could be buried with you."

Mama had said nothing. She'd just slid off the chair arm, and down into his lap and arms. . . . . . .

So there I stood in our diningroom—three days after his little sports-page obituary—staring at red roses, white candles, the polished wood of the table. Glancing now and then at the wonderful faces lined all the way around the room. And though none of the ballplayers among us yet seemed to be feeling anywhere near "at home," Mama had kept her end of the bargain: every one of them was religiously holding a flat, warm, forgotten glass of beer.

He'd left it to Mama to select his container, and she'd chosen—of all things—the same blue ceramic jewelry box in which she used to keep her Sabbath tithes and offerings. It gave me a turn to see it, full of powdered Papa on our dinnertable there. But once my intestines swung back around, it began to feel about perfect. Because what *is* an offering, really? What can human beings actually give to God? What can they give to each other even? And what sorts of receptacles can contain these gifts? Work camps and insane asylums, Indian trains and church pews, bullpens and little blue boxes . . . Who belongs in what? When do they belong there? Who truly gives what to whom? These were questions we were all struggling to answer not in words, but with our lives. And all her life Laura Chance had placed ten percent of all she'd earned in this same blue box before offering it—in the full faith that it would be accepted— to her Lord. So now, just as faithfully, she'd placed a hundred percent of her husband in the same box. That was her answer to the questions. And I'm hard put to think of another that would do greater honor to her husband, her Lord or her little blue box.

Staring hard at the candles, the shyest man among us had sucked up the courage to speak first. "I'm no ninety-pound weakling," Uncle Truman said. "But the first time we shook, that fella and me," he pointed at the blue box, "he about crushed my hand to ribbons. He was that strong."

With that, Truman blushed red as the roses and dipped to his beer like a shy toddler to its mother's neck. And I never heard him speak again all day.

Bet half surprised me with an old Memory Verse: "Unless a grain of wheat fall into the ground and die, it abideth alone; but if it die, it bringeth forth much fruit."

This seemed to create some emotion among the Adventists, but things still felt a little abstract to me. Then Freddy came out with this:

"Something Papa once told me, which he learned as a kid from his dad, Everett Senior. It's been on my mind all week. 'Cause most of you know that Papa, he lost—" Her voice faltered. "He lost his dad too when he was about my age. Anyhow . . ." She drew a huge breath. "A hitting tip, this supposedly was. And Papa warned me it was nonsense. Except the thing is, he said, when you lose your dad young, even his non- sense—" Her voice stopped again. "Even his nonsense starts to make sense, and maybe even to help you. That's what he told me. So here's some of Papa's nonsense, for my brothers and sister and me."

Another big breath.

"He said there are two ways for a hitter to get the pitch he wants. The simplest way is not to want *any* pitch in particular. But the best way, he said—which sounds almost the same, but is really very different—is to want the very pitch you're gonna get. Including the one you can handle.

But also the one that's gonna strike you out looking. And even the one that's maybe gonna bounce off your head."

The general reaction to this speech was incomprehension, though toward the end some listeners began to shoot Freddy sympathetic glances: *Oh dear*, their faces said. *The girl is babbling. Crazy with grief, the poor thing.* But Peter, Natasha and G. Q. Durham all nodded when she'd finished. In fact, Gale looked moved to the verge of tears. But then he'd looked that way all day.

Uncle Marv spoke up next. "But Smokey Chance, as I liked to call'm," he said, "never bounced a pitch off a head in his life, except by accident."

"If you call stickin' your noggin in front of a fastball on purpose an accident," Aunt Mary Jane put in.

"Using the bean," Marv said. "Using the bean to get Laura and Hugh together. That's what I call it."

There were baffled smiles from those who didn't know the old family story, and patient sighs from those who did. The smell of roses was overwhelming.

"He hurt people on purpose, though," Johnny Hultz said. "Hurt our feelings, that is. First time I faced him up in Tacoma I poked a wrong-field double, and was cocky enough to think it wasn't pure luck. So the next ten or twelve or, let's be honest, thirty times I faced him, he popped and grounded and fanned me silly. And talk about the pitch that gets you looking! Papa T threw third strikes that left you standin' there like a fencepost by the side of the road."

Tony Baldanos—now an ex-Tug and aspiring photographer—said, "Best pitcher I ever caught. Best pitching coach I ever watched work. Best coach or baseball mind, period. Present company included." He gave his ex-manager, John Hultz, a pointed little smile.

"But even Hugh," said Papa's friend Roy, "couldn't teach me how to fly-fish."

"He taught me," Freddy said, giving Roy a poke.

"Me too," I said.

"Some people are just unteachable," said Coach Hultz, smiling back at Tony.

G. Q. Durham tried for the day's only soliloquy, but it just didn't pan out.

"My job with the Cornshuckers, down in Oklahoma," he began, "was to analyze junk, and if possible use it. 'No offense,' I says to Hugh Chance, first time we met, 'but that's why you're here. White Sox say you're junk, Senators say it, and I wouldn't wonder but what you're thinkin' *I'm junk* yourself. But I say bullroar, Hubert! I say ballplayers are the car, not the engine. And when the engine stops runnin', you don't junk the car. You fix it. That's why you're here.' "

There were smiles over this beginning, from those who didn't know Gale. He was waving his beer around, foaming and overflowing it. But I'd seen at once that he wasn't trying to be funny. He was furious. Furious with grief. " 'Hubert,' I told him, that very first time, 'you *reek*. Bum arm, diaper stench, bad attitude and all, you reek so bad of baseball I don't see how you walk down a street on legs. Seems to me you ought to *roll . . .*' "

Then the tears did start rolling, and Gale's face and speech fell to pieces as he added, "But what I never, I wish I . . . I never had a son o' my own, you know. An' you were the—he was my . . . if there was one thing on this earth I never wanted, it was to outlive my Hubert!"

With that he fell against Irwin and began to sob like a distraught child. And Irwin, with his wooden face, just stood there, stiffly holding him. Then Peter said, "I'd like to offer a little prayer."

Heads bowed fast, if only to escape the sight of poor Gale.

"I wouldn't dare imitate a certain style," Peter began, staring at the blue box. "The loss of what's inimitable—that's what we're here to mourn. But . . . but here's the prayer part now, and this is a quote. Give us grateful hearts . . . our Father . . ." His voice broke on the last two words, as did most everyone's self-control, till we were pretty much all trying to hold each other together. "Give us grateful hearts," he croaked. "And make us ever mindful of the needs of others. Through Christ, Papa's and Mama's Lord, amen. And through love for each other, amen. And through our sufferings, if that's what it takes, and our romances, our good housekeeping and our ballplaying, our friendships and our enemyships. Whatever works best, our Father. Make us mindful through that. It's time to eat now. That's where you'd end this prayer, Papa, so that's where I'll end it too. There's nothing much left to say but the obvious anyhow. Which is we loved you. And always will. Amen."

"Amen!" sobbed Gale.

"Amen," Irwin murmured, still expressionless, but still stiffly holding him.

Amen.

CHAPTER FIVE
Woodstoves

"Do not be so anxious after doing something," said Krishna. "Sorrow follows happiness, then happiness follows sorrow. One man thinks that it is men who slay each other; another that it is Time, or Fate. This is the language of the world. The truth is—"

"The truth is," Yudishthira shouted, "that like a straw mat concealing a deep pit, your dharma is too often a mask for deceit. You may be God incarnate, but in a hundred years I could not exhaust the tale of your felonies if I spoke day and night!"

"Be calm," Krishna said. "The wind is not stained by the dust it blows away."

"I am calm!" roared Yudishthira.

—Mahabharata

–I–

In November 1971, Peter moved into a dive of a boardinghouse right in downtown Camas, then applied, and was accepted, for a graveyard-shift job at the Crown Zellerbach papermill. "What'll you be doing?" Mama asked when he first mentioned the job.

"Loading car-sized rolls of paper onto train cars with a giant forklift," he said.

"You could be injured, even killed," she told him.

"So could the guys who've been working there for years," he replied.

"They're used to machinery. You're used to books."

Peter shrugged. "That's why I took the job."

"Listen to me," Mama said firmly. "I think I see what you're up to. But you're not your father, and you're not his replacement. You've helped us through a terrible time, and I'll always be grateful. But you've got your own beliefs, Peter. And your college, I hope, to finish. You've got your own life to live. So if you took that job for me, or the twins, or Irwin, you can just go quit right now."

"I listened, Mama," Peter said, smiling. "Now it's your turn, okay?"

She scowled, but kept quiet.

"You're right about books. They're what I know. And I probably will go back and finish my degree sometime. But when I was growing up here, I didn't just skip out on church. I skipped having a hometown. I skipped the woods when they were standing, and swimming in Lackamas Lake. I skipped the Wind and the Washougal. I tried to skip the tedious things too—like dirty dishes, and the weeds in the flower beds. I still can't fix a toaster. Can't tune a car. I was sincere in all of this. I really believed that traveling light was the fastest way to truth, and that plugs, points and toasters were for those without spiritual longing, those with nothing better to do. But the things I skipped kept getting bigger, till somehow it even made sense to me to skip having brothers and sisters, and Papa and you. 'One-pointedness' is what I called it. And I was sincere even in that. But last spring, in India, I found out very suddenly that every single thing I'd skipped had left a blank place inside me. Not a sharpened point, or an emptiness. Just a dull, amorphous area that couldn't see or feel. By seeking a dharma that began where Camas ended, I had packed up and moved to a nowhere. Which left me pretty well useless. So that's why I'm driving the forklift, Mama. Not to replace anybody. Just to fill in some blanks. To begin to be from a somewhere. Is that okay with you?"

Mama didn't nod or smile. It was just too soon. When any of us said or did anything she thought Papa would especially like, those became the very things that sent her reeling. But she did manage to murmur, "It's very much okay with me."

–II–

Myshkin E. Lee was born in Lake Havasu City, Arizona, on November 30, 1971, and within a week (so his ecstatic father informed us) became a prodigy in both literature and art.

The claim was not entirely groundless. Within a week of his birth Myshkin really did begin to communicate directly with his incarcerated pop—via finger-paintings. The way he did it, though, was by hanging half asleep in a cloth sling while Natasha dabbled his limp limbs in dabs of paint she'd scattered across a big sheet of butcher paper. The tiny hand-, foot- and dimpled knee-prints thus created were just the literature Everett longed to read, however. So when he began to perceive—and to lecture his fellow cons upon—the "obvious deliberation" and "idiosyncratic flair" his son poured into his "work," even the most irascible of them finally learned to nod at the paintings and say fine, what the hell, okay, Everett, the kid's a bleeding prodigy.

In a p.s. to one such "letter," Natasha spontaneously added a life-sized full-on blue-and-green finger-paint print of her belly and breasts, just to show Everett what birth and lactation had done to her, shape- and size-wise. According to one reliable eyewitness—Moonfish, by name—the erotic dream and nocturnal emission this work of art inspired in my brother blasted a hole through the cinderblock above his cot, and five lonely Mexicans made a clean escape back home to their señoritas.

–III–

Though he'd recovered his speech, his health and a slightly thicker version of his old physique, Irwin's old spark and sparkle just weren't coming back. He never went anywhere unless we coaxed him. He never instigated a conversation, and when we tried to, he usually gave monosyllabic replies. He remained unemployed, possibly unemployable, and for two months after Papa's death just sat around the house. Then, in January 1972—without a word to anyone but Peter (from whom he borrowed the tuition money)—he suddenly signed up for two different welding classes at the local community college.

"That's good!" Mama and Linda both told him. "Welders make good money."

Irwin didn't agree, disagree, or try to explain. He just began, entirely on his own, to study woodstoves.

For weeks he did nothing but read up on the things—every single evening, far into the night. Linda didn't seem to find this obsessiveness much preferable to the nothingness that preceded it. I felt relieved just to know he *could* read.

After a few weeks of this study he began to leave the house at dawn and spend entire days loitering around a couple of small Portland wood-stove manufacturers. He also started scrounging—again with funds bor-rowed from Peter—for secondhand welding tools, reject sheet metal and a lot of inscrutable, clunky-looking equipment. Back home in the eve-nings he still ignored his family completely. But he no longer just sat there: he doodled on a sketch pad now, hour after hour, drawing a lot of strange-looking diagrams and stove designs.

His welding classes still had several weeks to go when—again consult-ing no one—he cleared off Papa's old workbench in the back of the garage, assembled his inadequate welding tools and materials, and began trying to piece together his first crude stove. I was living with Amy in a cabin up the Columbia, and still found it almost impossible to visit the vacuum Papa had left back home, so Irwin's progress, or lack of it, went unremarked by me. Mama and the twins didn't pay much attention ei-ther, except to say over and over that they hoped he didn't blow himself up. Peter's thought on the stoves was that, practical or not, anything that helped reacquaint him with gross reality was to the good. As for Linda, she'd gotten pregnant again (a huge surprise to everyone but Bet and Everett), and the prospect of providing for two kids and a stove-obsessed automaton had sent her scrambling back to school for a general equivalency diploma, with hopes of a realtor's license somewhere down the line. Her situation also began to put an edge on her previously rather spongy personality. When Irwin failed to even respond to her request that he watch Nash during her school hours, for instance, she began to just stick Nash in a stroller, roll him wordlessly into the garage, and let his screams bring Irwin out of his work stupor. The funny thing was, once Irwin fitted Nash with a little pair of industrial earplugs and handed him a few tools to pound on his stroller with, he'd sit there babbling and banging and watching his dad for hours.

When Irwin's first finished stove broke a seam during a midnight test fire, dumped its coals, and burned a bear-sized hole in the back wall of the garage, I figured that might be the end of the new hobby. But the very next day—again consulting no one, and showing no concern for the ruin he'd left in the garage—Irwin nailed a fourth wall onto Papa's old pitching shed, poured a rough concrete floor, built some crude shelves and a worktable, again set up his crummy equipment, and proceeded to spend longer days than ever, banging and clanging away at God knew just what. "Maybe his own crematorium," Linda grumped.

–IV–

Peter hadn't worked long at the mill before he and Papa's old friend Roy had become buddies. In fact, when Roy learned of another machinist who didn't want to work graveyard, he took the shift just so he and Peter could get better acquainted. Pete was living so close to the mill that he walked to work alone each midnight. But every morning, a little after eight, he and Roy would come driving up the Clark Street hill in the same old Travelall Papa used to ride to work in, and Mama would feed them breakfast, Roy would do a bit of handymanning around the house, Pete would drop off a book for Bet or Freddy, a toy or treat for Nash, or most of his paycheck for Mama. Then he and Roy would step out to Papa's backyard shed.

Peter's sole interest in visiting the shed was, of course, to see how Irwin was faring—and the monosyllabic, humorless workaholic he'd find there invariably left him depressed. Roy's interest, on the other hand, seemed to be entirely in the woodstoves—and what Roy found, just as invariably, seemed to delight him. "Buck up," he'd always tell Peter afterward. "Irwin's comin' along great!"

Peter saw no point in calling Roy on this wishful thinking, but there was no question in his own mind that improvements in Irwin's welding or riveting techniques were no proof of corresponding improvements in his psyche. After a few weeks, though, he couldn't help but notice that the only person Irwin was ever truly attentive to—and even animated with— was Roy. And that's when Peter realized that Roy was onto something: the stove work and the workman *were* somehow inseparable. Struggling though he was to return to life, Irwin was still living in a lonely, pared-down, almost subterranean place. "Stove Land," Peter began to call it. And the reason Irwin grew animated when Roy came to visit was that Roy was the only person who really did visit: none of the rest of us pored over the joins and seams of his stoves with him; none of us really climbed clear down beside him to share the dull concerns of the gloomy chamber that was all the world he could manage so far. We simply demanded—

with increasing impatience—that he somehow "snap out of it" and come all the way back to our world.

Seeing this, Peter realized something else: since Papa had died, the rest of us had at least been able to share our grief. But Irwin—who'd been almost a part of Papa's body at the end—was living in a place where one speaks of nothing but one's work. He was doing his best down there. He was working every day till he dropped. But ever since Papa had left him, he'd been utterly alone with his unspeakable feelings.

So. Ill equipped though he was for such a place, Peter began trying to follow Roy all the way down into Stove Land too.

–V–
letter from Wahkiakum / March / 1972

Dear Mama,

A few weeks after Papa died, that little shaman, Freddy, swiped a snapshot from one of your old photo albums, stuck it in an envelope, and sent it to me without adding a word. I couldn't imagine what she was up to. I mean, it wasn't a photo of Papa or anything. But something about it did begin to fascinate me. I finally stuck it on the wall by my cot here, in a place where the all-night floodlights hit, so I could study it whenever I liked. And I've ended up liking a lot. In fact my feelings soon went way past liking. One night the little photo opened like a door, and I walked on in, and stayed. It's become so much a part of me now that I no longer need to see it. It constantly pulls at my feelings like the moon pulls tides. And believe it or not, after that introduction, it's a snapshot of you and me, Mama. You'll know the one. Me sitting like a pudgy little buddha in the center of your lap in those washed-out bonegray bleachers down in Oklahoma, late spring or summer of '52 . . .

Not a pretty world, the one we're perched in: the grandstands couldn't be less grand, and they're empty but for us; the edge of the infield looks like a big hot terracotta tile; the light, the entire sky is starkest white. But the starkness forces the eye to the two faces. And the thing they most remind me of (again, believe it or not) is a medieval icon. Oklahoma Madonna and Child, you could call it. Both faces flushed, both very serious, and both, above all, rapt. That's where the icon quality comes in. And the reason for our raptness is, of course, not in the photo, but out on the ballfield, making graceful but ominous preparations, as the shutter opens and closes, to pour a five-and-a-quarter-ounce one-hundred-and-eight-stitched projectile past the bat of some far less gifted athlete.

It's a beautiful photo, Mama. Even though it's just us. And though I'd forgotten what a looker you were, it's not so much a physical or artistic beauty. It's a unity. What's wonderful here is that though one face is male and just four years old, and the other female and about the age I am today, they are the same face: we are the identically dark-eyed, identically short, identically intense admirers of the same unseen hero. And strange as it may sound, it consoles me every day, this little snapshot does—and not so much for its depiction of what we have been as for its suggestion of what we still are. The bleachers empty, but for us. The world around us a little stark, a little harsh. Both of us looking toward him, harder than ever now, day and night. So even the raptness. It's all come true. I'm not saying this because I like it, or to make "meaning" of our loss. I'm just saying that he is no less wonderful to us, that this unites us, and that our feelings about him will never change.

Trouble is, unless we do something about it, maybe neither will our feelings about each other. I don't want to stir up old wasp's nests, especially not now, but life does go on. And knowing us—our tempers, our industrial-strength opinions, our hands-on love for family—I imagine we're bound to collide again one day. I just want to say, before we do, that I'd love to find a way to collide more gently. There'll be no burying the hatchet for us, I don't think. You and I, to start fresh, would have to bury a couple of battle-cruisers. I doubt that's even possible. But mightn't it be possible to just climb out of the damned things and let 'em drift away?

It may have been his dumbest mistake, but Papa loved us both. What do you say, Mama? Wouldn't it be good to keep a few of his classic mistakes going?

Love,
Everett

–VI–

In the spring of '72, Irwin and Linda—or Linda alone, really—tried to honor Papa by bequeathing his name to their second baby. Poor kid. Even I was enough of a prophet to warn them that every TV-addicted brat on the block would nick the name to "Baby Hughie" after that moronic diapered duck on the cartoons.

Be that as it may, one day in the midst of that first baseball-less spring, Uncle Truman drove down from Walla Walla—ostensibly to meet "Baby Hughie," and to see how Mama was making out on her own. But when Truman—the lifelong body-shop man—heard the clanging of sheet metal out back in the shed, he didn't even go to the house. He just grabbed a six-pack from his camper and stepped straight down into Stove Land. And except for meals—which he and Irwin would both wolf in near silence—Truman stayed in Stove Land for the rest of his two-day stay.

Peter tried his best to cover for them, but Mama and Linda were, of course, offended. Men from small, dark worlds like Stove Land almost always offend women, because there is no gender or domesticity down there. Women and children are welcome in Stove Land, but for the same reason that men are welcome: to work on the stoves.

The following weekend Truman was back again—with his camper so full of new tools and welding equipment from his Walla Walla body shop that he had bottomed out the shocks. "Merry Christmas," he mumbled to Irwin, though it was April. And this time Truman stayed a full week: he had awarded himself a vacation (his first in years) for the "fun" of working fourteen-hour days with Irwin, and instructing him in the use of all the tools.

Their first job had been to rebuild—with Roy's weekend and after-hours help—the burnt wall of the garage, and to build new shelves and workbenches along every inside wall. "How nice!" Mama had told them as they were finishing up. And away she went to the store for dinner-makings, to reward them. While she was gone, though, they pulled a Christopher Columbus on her by hauling all of her and Papa's old stuff down into the basement without her permission, and claiming the re-vamped garage for Stove Land.

When Mama drove home to the sight of Papa-relics in motion, she got very upset—understandably. But before stepping out of the car to give the three stove-freaks a blazing piece of her mind, she waited for her tears to stop. And while she was waiting she heard Irwin suddenly call out to his cohorts in a tone of voice she hadn't heard since before Vietnam. The nicknames he used were pre-'Nam too. "True" and "Royo," he called them. That did it. Mama jumped out of the car—

and told them that since they'd already stolen her garage and turned her basement upside-down, they might as well haul the old refrigerator up out of the basement and use it in the garage, too. "It's noisy," she said, "but that'll hardly bother the likes of you. Fill it with beer to feed Truman."

Stove Land had won another heart.

Irwin's next three trial stoves all burned cordwood without burning down buildings. But every time Linda asked how much he was going to charge for them, he'd mumble that he was still "just practicin'." His fourth stove, however, was a refined little number with baffles to increase the efficiency and a glass panel in the door, all pieced together so tightly that when you spun the vents shut it killed the fire in seconds. Irwin still didn't think much of it—which naturally miffed his destitute and neglected wife. But it burned so efficiently that Mama—as a show of faith, and a marital Band-Aid too, hopefully—had Roy and Irwin install it in her livingroom.

Shortly after this installation, Roy's interest in stoves became more than a hobby: with Irwin's permission he sank a couple thousand of his hard-earned Crown Z dollars into equipment and sheet metal, then began spending three or four hours each morning after his mill-stint, working at Irwin's side. The first stove the two of them built together was a slightly larger, more aesthetically-pleasing version of the one in Mama's livingroom. And Peter—who'd been studying stoves and the stove business hard, if only to master Irwin's new dialect—took one look at it and applied for a patent.

Irwin didn't seem to care what the patent application was: he just scribbled his name where Pete pointed. He did the same with the papers that incorporated Roy, Irwin and Peter himself into a business. Roy named the fledgling operation after Papa's favorite fishing stream: Wind River Woodstoves, they called it.

–VII–
letter from Peter to the Wahkiakum Work Camp / March / 1972

Dear Everett,

I am writing, at Mama's request, to spare her the effort of repeating a story she finds almost impossible to tell. She managed to share it with Freddy, Bet, Kincaid, Irwin, Linda and me a couple of nights ago. She then swore us never to repeat it again, except to you in this letter, and asked us all—you included—never to question her about it, ever. The only reason she has shared it at all is Papa. All their married life, she said, he kept a promise to keep this thing secret. But during our teens—and all our terrible fighting with Mama—he repeatedly asked her for permission to break his promise. He felt that our sharing this thing would have stopped the fighting. But Mama, understandably, didn't want to be understood on the basis of this secret. All she ever wanted was for it to disappear. So the secret was kept.

Late last summer, though, when he learned that he was dying, Papa pointed out to Mama that once he was gone he would no longer be obligated to keep the secret. He then told her that if she wouldn't tell us what happened herself, he would write a letter to you, and put it in a safe deposit box to be opened some time after he died. Mama still disagreed vehemently, but she didn't feel that Papa had the strength to argue. So she promised to tell the secret herself.

She kept her promise just two nights ago. She began by saying that she has only told this thing twice: once to Papa, in an abandoned barn outside Walla Walla, shortly after they fell in love; then to Linda, just last year. But no sooner did Mama say this than there was an interruption—poor Bet, sobbing and apologizing, suddenly, to everybody in sight, especially Linda. It seems that on the day Mama told the story to Linda, Bet happened to hear them talking in the kitchen, then began to realize what was being said. And it just mesmerized her. She couldn't move. She listened clear to the end, then dragged herself out of the house. And she has kept this thing to herself ever since. Her only lapse was to tell some of the story to Kade once, when she was half-crazy with insomnia and fear, and to make Linda its supposed victim, rather than Mama.

There is no easy way to broach a subject like this, so I'll just put it out there, much as Mama did. "I was sexually molested by my father." That's how she began. It started in Cleveland, in January, 1941. They lived in an old rowhouse, right under the steel mill's smokestacks. Mama was eleven years old, Marvin nine, Truman six. There was no window in her room, she said, and the roar of the mill covered sounds like the door opening, or the floor creaking. So what woke her the first time was his hands, "one on my body," she told us, "and one on my throat." When she realized what he was doing she tried to die, she said, or faint—to get out of her body somehow. But the smell of him —the stale beer and sweat and tobacco—kept her conscious the way smelling salts do. When it was over her father left the room, went to bed with Beryl, and the next morning both parents acted as if nothing had happened. So Mama tried to do the same.

The next time it started she was sound asleep, and shrieked when he first touched her. So the following time what woke her was a pencil. Just the point of it, touching her eardrum. "Be still," he told her. "You're upsetting your mother."

Sooner or later, Mama said to us, we were going to ask ourselves, as she had, how it could have happened more than once. She was afraid to kill herself—that was one reason, she said. Children love their parents. That was another. And she went to the police the second time, and told them what had happened. But they called up Beryl, who just came down to the station and told the cops that her daughter was a liar. Then they went back home, and the old man beat Beryl up, threw Mama in her room, and raped her again. ("Hurt me" is the way Mama always put it.)

She ran away after that, and the parish priest she ran to said he'd help her. He then loaded her in his car, drove her straight back to her father and mother, had a chat with them, shook both their hands, and left. And soon as he was gone the old man told Mama that if she told anyone else, or tried to run away again, he'd kill her brothers.

Mama begged her mother to take them away after that, but Beryl was ill by then. When the old man came home that night, she just told him, in a weird little singsong voice, all about Mama's wish. He turned to Mama then, said, "I warned you," went to the boys' room, picked Truman up, carried him back out, and threw him into a wall. Mama screamed. Beryl just sat in a chair and watched. And seeing this —seeing her mother just sit there—Mama suddenly felt that her only duty was to survive. If she didn't survive, no one would save her brothers. If she didn't survive they couldn't run away, grow up together, come back some day, and kill her father. He began to hit her hard, over and over. But Mama said that "everything went quiet." It was as if she'd entered a silent room inside herself, and shut her body out. And there in the quiet, she could see exactly what she had to do to survive. Before he hit her again, she pulled up her skirt, and looked at him. Knowing what would happen. And sure enough, he stopped beating her and carried her back into her room. It was at this time, she said, that the dreams started. A recurring nightmare, especially, of sleepwalking, then waking to find herself in the act of killing both her parents with the halves of a broken pair of scissors. The dreams made sleep impossible. Which made school impossible. (Think, Everett. She was a <u>fifth</u> grader while all this was going on!)

She started taking her brothers to different churches around the city after that, looking—very cautiously now—for someone who might be willing to help them. But at home she stayed alive, and kept him from hurting her mother and brothers, by doing what he wanted. And five months went by this way. She said this to us twice, Everett. "<u>Five months</u>."

She finally found the help they needed—and it was Adventists who gave it. We know that part of the story: we often made fun of it in our teens. They moved to Walla Walla within days, in secret of course. And for weeks Beryl had to be guarded round the clock to keep her from writing or phoning the old man and telling him where they'd gone. Remember the way Marvin talked about this when we were kids? Outsmarting the Old Drunk and Crazy Mom? It sounded like some wonderful adventure! I envied him when he'd talk about it! And it occurs to me now that for Marvin it <u>was</u> just an adventure, and that this innocence of his is just one of the gifts that Mama ransomed with her five months.

The old man was killed the following winter in a head-on car wreck. Driving drunk, of course—they've told us that part of the legend, too. What Mama didn't tell, until two nights ago, was how long and hard she prayed for it. Her father's death, she said, is one of the pillars of her faith in prayer.

That's pretty much it, Everett. Except to say how right Papa was. Huge, incomprehensible things have been happening nonstop inside all of us these past two days. What Freddy calls "the eureka feelings" just keep coming. Our entire relationship with Mama is being unmade. I don't know how it will be for you, but my old desire to "improve" her just embarrasses me: I look at her now and see the very mother I've always longed for. All the old battles with her keep replaying themselves, and at the climax of each, just as the pain is being inflicted, I see the true source of the hurt, and am suddenly on Mama's side instead of my own! I love her so much, and feel so protective and proud, that even her theology makes sense to me now. Where was her love for the God of mercy and forgiveness, I always used to wonder. But now I think of that glowering, overpowering, judgmental Old Testament God of hers and cry "More Power to You!" —because <u>He's</u> the One who's gonna make Mama's old man pay!

We'll be years sorting this out. And we'll have to be careful to keep our word never to mention it to Mama herself. But I'm nearly leaving out the best part . . .

When she finished speaking, and saw how she'd devastated us, Mama was apologetic for a moment. Then she began, in the manner of someone telling her kids a soothing bedtime story (which is just what she was doing), to tell us what it was like to lay eyes on Papa for the first time. With all that bitter background in place, she told us how it felt to watch him pitch; then to meet him over Marvin's beaned brain at the hospital; to smell the stale tobacco on his clothes and hands; to fall head over heels in love anyway. And my God, Everett. Her eyes as she spoke! Her voice! You could feel, with every word, that there is something Papa's love gave her, something their love healed and saved, that is <u>still</u> healed, and still saved. It was right there in the room with us, this love between them. And when we went our ways that night, it stayed with each of us. It's with you right now, isn't it? It's our real inheritance, isn't it? We're rich, aren't we?

It's Freddy and my turn to see you this month. We can't wait.

Love,

Pete

–VIII–

One morning in August, that first summer of the woodstoves, the manager of the Fir Haven Apartments stepped into the garage while Irwin, Roy and Peter were all working and handed them a petition—signed by every resident of his building and by most of our Clark Street neighbors —stating that if the construction of stoves continued in our residentially zoned neighborhood, they, the undersigned, would be forced to turn the matter over to the authorities. Roy just acted embarrassed, and Peter smiled at the petition and started to say something. But before he got a word out, Irwin picked up an acetylene tank, let out a roar, and sent it flying through the side window of the garage. The apartment manager ran for his life. Then Irwin sat down on the garage floor, and for the first time in over a year, started to weep.

That very night Peter quit his job at the Crown Z mill, packed camping gear, sleeping bags and his distraught brother into Roy's borrowed Travellall, and they departed in the wee hours for Livingston, Montana. Five days later they returned home with a matching pair of hangovers, a large collection of trout flies (though neither of them fly-fished), and a ten-thousand-dollar cashier's check from Wind River Woodstoves' second investor—a fast-rising sporting-goods magnate by the name of T Bar Waites. A week or so after their return, Pete, Roy and Irwin made a down payment on a defunct gas station and garage in a commercial part of Camas, then hired Truman and me—offering us a good wage (which Truman refused but I accepted)—to spend a couple of weeks helping them turn the place into a poor man's woodstove production plant. And no sooner had we set to work than Peter took off again, this time to Seattle, to try to set up some kind of marketing and distribution plan for their stoves.

Irwin became a stove-making machine. He worked impossibly hard. Eighty-, even ninety-hour weeks. His muscles grew huge again. His arms, hands and chest became covered with small cuts and burn scars. He also remained so emotionally drab, and so absent to his wife and kids, that it frightened me. But to my worries he kept saying, "We can only do what we can do." And to Linda he kept saying, "This won't be forever. If you can stand the wait, I don't think you'll be sorry." "I *hate* this!" she told him. "I hate your stoves!" But she waited.

And in the fall of 1972, Wind River Woodstoves started selling. The business made no profit the first year because every penny got channeled right back into equipment. But Irwin and Peter both had salaries now, and the stoves sold with ease.

Another milestone of that winter: after twenty-five years, Roy quit the Crown Z mill and went to work full-time for Wind River. It was a huge decision for him. It meant the loss of a retirement pension, the temporary loss of health insurance and every other benefit, and a sizable cut in pay. His old friends at the mill assured him that he'd lost his mind. His wife and grown kids waffled some, but tended to side with his mill friends. But the Washougal had been Roy's home river since boyhood, he loved fishing more than anything, and for twenty-five years he'd watched the effluents pour from his place of employment into that river. "I'm getting too old to live like a hypocrite," he said. "Wind River Woodstoves don't kill fish."

–IX–

Our greatest fears, like our greatest hopes, often come to nothing: though Linda's father was released from the Oregon State Penitentiary in August 1971, none of us ever heard a word of him again.

–X–

In August 1974, when Irwin, Amy, myself and the recently paroled Everett were unloading a car and U-Haul trailer full of Natasha and Myshkin's stuff at their new apartment in Seattle, I thought for a moment that we were going to hear the loon laugh again. What happened was that Irwin, on two successive trips to the car, had conked his head hard on the trunk lid, and the second time he'd done it Everett had unthinkingly snapped, "Enter the third dimension, willya!" All Irwin did was straighten up, still rubbing his head, and look from Everett (who didn't even notice) to Amy, Natasha and me (who were all smiling). He didn't make a sound, and finally only smiled back. But even Tasha and Amy, who'd never heard him laugh, could tell by the look in his eyes that he'd come close.

He held out for seven more months. Then, in March 1975, while Natasha was cramming for oral exams back in Seattle, Everett and Myshkin drove down to spend a few days checking out both the new Wind River Woodstoves warehouse and the abused and bankrupt Skamania County farm that Irwin and Linda had bought with a bundle of stove proceeds. What happened this time was that Everett volunteered to babysit Hughie, Nash and Myshkin so that Amy and I could take Irwin and Linda —who'd both become chronic workaholics since buying the farm—out for a night on the town. The four of us ended up trying dinner and a movie, and Linda had dutifully mumbled, "This is fun" once or twice. But it wasn't exactly a smashing evening. Even enjoying oneself takes practice. When we started home, though, and got to speculating about how Uncle Everett was faring with three wild boys, Irwin and Linda began to enjoy themselves very much. So much that when Irwin reached the farm he turned out the headlights, glided down the last hundred yards of driveway, and the four of us crept up to the house and peeked in the window . . .

We were more than a little surprised to see Everett in an easy chair, serenely reading a book while Myshkin, Nash, Hughie, and their dog, Hoover, sat round the kitchen table, deeply—and silently—engrossed in some kind of game. When we stepped in the door, though, Everett leapt out of his chair, cried, "Okay, boys! Game's over!"—and when I first glimpsed, then smelled, the jiggling abomination he was trying to clear from the table, the picture we'd seen through the window began to make more sense.

"All right," Linda said, trying out her fierce new scowl. "What's going on?"

"We broke a window with the football," said Nash.

"And Daddy got a headache," said Myshkin.

"You're out of aspirin," Everett said.

"Hughie spilled my milk," Nash added.

"Me too!" Hughie shouted.

"Then he let Hoover in," Nash continued.

"An' Hoover got manure on the carpet," Myshkin said.

"I did it!" Hughie roared.

"Uncle Everett cried," Nash said.

"You're out of whiskey," said Everett.

"So we started playin' Attaboy," Myshkin continued.

"It was *gross*," Nash added.

"It was quiet," Everett sighed.

"It was FUN!" Hughie shouted.

"We recommend it," Everett said.

"How do you play?" Irwin asked.

"Sit down," Everett said. "I'll show you."

Irwin, Linda, Amy and I took the four chairs round the kitchen table.

"You need a dinner plate, a tablespoon, a can opener and a twelve-ounce can of wet dog food," Everett began. "Hoover's brand was Attaboy, so that's what we named the game."

The boys just grinned, and nodded vehement agreement.

"To begin, you set the plate in the center of the table, open both ends of the dog food can, stand the can on the plate, and demand silence. Silence is crucial. Bribe them if you have to. Because next you lift the can away from the food very very slowly—and you want them to hear the sucking sound. And smell the odor. And watch that gooey yellow stuff run off to one side of the plate."

The boys kept nodding.

"Now it's time to tell about dog-food factories you have visited. Explain how no part of the dead horse, however old, sick or infected, goes to waste. Mention particular body parts—such as ground-up horse noses. Mention the rats that sometimes fall in the grinder."

Still nothing but happy nods from the boys: *Yep! That's what we did . . .*

"If your brand was well chosen," Everett continued, "the brown cylinder on the plate should have sagged to one side by now, like the stovepipe hat of the cat in *The Cat in the Hat.* If your lecture was effective, the players should be doing the same. You then take the tablespoon (teaspoons are too small, mixing spoons too overwhelming), scoop a heaping mound of sagging cat hat, set it on the plate, and say to the sagging kids: 'The next person to make a peep—and I mean any sound at all, even breathing; out any orifice: anuses, navels, ears—is going to eat the contents of this spoon.' Let 'em think about that a second. Then add: 'If anyone else makes a peep while the first peeper is eating, he will have to eat *two* spoonfuls. And if that strikes the third person funny, he'll have to eat *three.*' You then take them into the kitchen and show them the nineteen other Attaboy cans in the cupboard. And the full case in the closet. Tell 'em it's not that far to the store, either."

Wide-eyed and pleased with all of it, the boys kept nodding.

"You then sit down in your easy chair with a thickish novel, or your knitting, or your double margarita, and say, 'Ready? Set? Begin!' "

That was when it started. At first Irwin only jiggled (rather like the Attaboy) and shot air rapidly in and out his nostrils. But when the rest of us started laughing, the dam inside him finally burst. Loon sounds filled and overflowed the room. And though Nash, Myshkin and Amy were soon looking more than a little appalled, little Hughie—after a five- or six-second study of his father—began to let out the very same sounds in a higher octave, and to flap his arms while he did it, like a nestling who's just realized he's got wings. When this brought on a whole new wave from Irwin, the neophytes plugged their ears and Hoover ran for cover. But Irwin and Hughie stood face to face, howling till they were too tired to stand.

And Hughie laughs that same way to this day.

And Irwin has added the arm-flaps.

–XI–

There's not much more that I can say without slipping into the beginnings of stories that belong to other people.

I still run the warehouse and do the billing at Wind River Woodstoves, and I married Amy and had kids too. Make that kids three. There's one beginning. But I bequeath that story to my children—who look unlikely to write or tell it at this point, though they may one day turn it into a truly strange Nintendo game.

Bet and Freddy went to college—Washington State, both of them. Bet dropped out twice, both times "for love," and went some exciting places —Rome, London, Bali—but both times crash-landed back at Mama's and went gratefully back to school. Freddy went straight through and became a veterinarian—and will curse me when she reads this, for making her very interesting life sound boring.

Everett ended up getting an M.F.A. at Washington, and Natasha a Ph.D. in Russian lit. Natasha teaches at Seattle University now, and Everett scrounges an income by free-lancing his kamikaze prose, by teaching writing workshops in prisons, community colleges and upscale retirement centers, and now and then by landing an actual one-or-two-semester position at a regular college—where he usually gets stuck teaching English comp, but saves wear and tear on his sanity by basing his courses entirely on Delmar (the basalt chunk) Hergert's impeccable old ninth-grade grammar classes.

To Everett's delight and Natasha's mostly mock dismay, Myshkin now insists that everyone call him Mike.

Peter finished his master's at Harvard and published the academic book on Maharashtran poet-saints. But he's kept a part-time interest in the stoves, which remain his bread and butter. His latest passion—and the work he shares with the woman he now lives with (Marta is her name)—is teaching people, urban teenagers mostly, how to go into wilderness areas and achieve some kind of inner direction. "Vision quest" seems to be the going buzzword for such procedures. But Peter plays down the "vision" side of things. His experience of the inner life, he tells the kids, is more like a blind man learning to get around a dark but beautiful city with one of those long, sensitive canes. Going into wilderness alone is simply a way of getting your cane.

Irwin and Linda kept working fifteen-hour days till the woodstove business was thriving and they'd completely resurrected their farm. Then the Boat People and other refugees started pouring in from Southeast Asia—and Irwin came out of Stove Land completely, and told Linda the secret dream he'd been working toward for years. I think their marriage might have ended if she hadn't been willing to share it. And without her, Irwin's dream could not have come true. But she *did* share it.

In November 1977, they drove down to San Francisco, fought their way through the last snarl of red tape, and adopted two Laotian orphans, for whom they'd been negotiating for months. They'd had names waiting for months too—and with Baby Hughie as the cautionary example, Linda and Irwin had nicked these names themselves. The four-year-old boy, Yao Tha, would be called by his initials, Y.T. And the two-year-old girl—formally Laura II, after Mama—would be called simply Two.

"What kind of name is *that?*" Laura One had snapped when she first heard it.

"*Your* name," Irwin responded.

"My name is Laura," Mama huffed. "And one of me's enough."

"That's why we're going to call her Two," said Irwin.

Which threw the conversation back to Square One:

"What kind of name is *that?*"

"A strange name, because the world's a strange place," Irwin said.

Which appeased Mama not at all. But then Linda, with great sincerity, added, "I think Two makes a *lovely* girl's name, Laura."

And Mama—having spent nearly a decade telling Linda to stand up and speak her mind—was hog-tied. "She'll be *your* child," she muttered. "Call her what you like."

They did. And Mama hadn't seen anything yet. Everett III, alias Little Everett (a Cambodian boy who became an instant hit with his 5'8" uncle by automatically shunting him into the Big Everett category), followed in 1978. Then came Mi Tu—a Vietnamese girl whose name Linda found so adorable that she left it unnicked. That gave them a Nash, a Baby Hughie, a Laura Two, a Y.T., an Everett Three and a Me Too. So by the time 1979 rolled around and they adopted a three-year-old Vietnamese boy, Hung Yi, it was Mama herself who suggested, since they first met him on the winter solstice, that they name him simply Winter.

With seven kids of four nationalities, twenty-some cattle, a dozen or so sheep, a hundred laying hens, five guinea hens, five guinea pigs, a turkey, three bass and bluegill ponds, Hoover the dog, feral cats, skunks, packrats and a booming woodstove business to drive him mad, Irwin regained all the sanity he'd ever wanted, and way more of a laugh than all his kids except Hughie could want.

As for Mama, she sold the Camas home six years after Papa died, and moved into a house-trailer on Irwin and Linda's farm, where she mostly orchestrates, but occasionally contributes to the chaos. "The eighth kid," she sometimes calls herself.

"Ma," Irwin tells her whenever she makes trouble for him. "*Prem se bhiksha dijiye.*"

CHAPTER SIX

Winter

I want the magnificent American dream: a wife, a dog, a house, a bathroom.
—Laotian refugee

Skamania County, Washington / February / 1980

Irwin is in his easy chair, reading last October's *Organic Gardening*. Winter is lying across his lap. Later Irwin will rise to his feet and the lap will divide into parts—green-and-purple rugby shirt, brown leather belt, faded blue jeans—but for now the lap is one thing: a ground, a region, an earth. Winter's head rests on one wide, cushioned arm of the chair, his bare brown feet on the other. The rest of him rests on his papa.

Winter can't see into the magazine or read the words on the cover. But he can see the cover photo. The straw-hatted gardener has a salt-and-pepper beard and a bright red shirt, and looks incredibly happy considering he's just standing there holding a turnip. But Winter's father's face is serious. And the hands that grip the magazine are blue-veined, huge, work-scarred, powerful.

Winter asks no questions. He stays quiet. He hears his father's slow, even breathing. He feels his pulse.